John Irving was born in Exeter, New Hampshire, in 1942, and he once admitted that he was a 'grim' child. Although he excelled in English at school and knew by the time he graduated that he wanted to write novels, it was not until he met a young Southern novelist named John Yount, at the University of New Hampshire, that he received encouragement. 'It was so simple,' he remembers. 'Yount was the first person to point out that anything I did except writing was going to be vaguely unsatisfying.'

In 1963, Irving enrolled at the Institute of European Studies in Vienna, and he later worked as a university lecturer. His first novel, *Setting Free the Bears*, about a plot to release all the animals from the Vienna Zoo, was followed by *The Water-Method Man*, an hilarious tale of a man with a complaint more serious than Portnoy's, and *The 158-Pound Marriage*, which exposes the complications of spouse-swapping. Irving achieved international recognition with *The World According to Garp*, which he hoped would 'cause a few smiles among the tough-minded and break a few softer hearts'.

The Hotel New Hampshire is a startlingly original family saga, and *The Cider House Rules* is the story of Doctor Wilbur Larch – saint, obstetrician, founder of an orphanage, ether addict and abortionist – and of his favourite orphan, Homer Wells, who is never adopted. *A Prayer for Owen Meany* features the most unforgettable character he has yet created. John Irving's latest novel is *A Son of the Circus*.

John Irving has a life-long passion for wrestling, and he plays a wrestling referee in the film of *The World According to Garp*. He now writes full-time, has three children and lives in Vermont and Toronto.

A SON OF THE CIRCUS

John Irving

BLACK SWAN

A SON OF THE CIRCUS
A BLACK SWAN BOOK : 0 552 99605 X

Originally published in Great Britain by Bloomsbury Publishing Ltd

PRINTING HISTORY
Bloomsbury edition published 1994
Black Swan edition published 1995

Set in 11/12pt Linotype Melior by
County Typesetters, Margate, Kent.

Black Swan Books are published by Transworld Publishers Ltd,
61–63 Uxbridge Road, Ealing, London W5 5SA,
in Australia by Transworld Publishers (Australia) Pty Ltd,
15–25 Helles Avenue, Moorebank, NSW 2170
and in New Zealand by Transworld Publishers (NZ) Ltd,
3 William Pickering Drive, Albany, Auckland.

Reproduced, printed and bound in Great Britain by
Cox & Wyman Ltd, Reading, Berks.

AUTHOR'S NOTES

This novel isn't about India. I don't know India. I was there only once, for less than a month. When I was there, I was struck by the country's foreignness; it remains obdurately foreign to me. But long before I went to India, I began to imagine a man who has been born there and has moved away; I imagined a character who keeps coming back again and again. He's compelled to keep returning; yet, with each return trip, his sense of India's foreignness only deepens. India remains unyieldingly foreign, even to him.

My Indian friends said, 'Make him an Indian – definitely an Indian but *not* an Indian.' They told me that everywhere he goes – including where he lives, outside India – should also strike him as foreign; the point is, he's always the foreigner. 'You just have to get the details right,' they said.

I went to India at the request of Martin Bell and his wife, Mary Ellen Mark. Martin and Mary Ellen asked me to write a screenplay for them, about the child performers in an Indian circus. I've been working on that screenplay and this novel, simultaneously, for more than four years; as of this writing, I'm revising the screenplay, which is also titled *A Son of the Circus*, although it isn't the same story as the novel. Probably I'll continue to rewrite the screenplay until the film is produced – *if* the film is produced. Martin and Mary Ellen took me to India; in a sense, they began *A Son of the Circus*.

I also owe a great deal to those Indian friends who were with me in Bombay in January of 1990 – I'm thinking of Ananda Jaisingh, particularly – and to those members of the Great Royal Circus who gave me so much of their time when I was living with the circus in Junagadh. Most of all, I'm

7

indebted to four Indian friends who've read and reread the manuscript; their efforts to overcome my ignorance and a multitude of errors made my writing possible. I want to acknowledge them by name; their importance to *A Son of the Circus* is immeasurable.

My thanks to Dayanita Singh in New Delhi; to Farrokh Chothia in Bombay; to Dr Abraham Verghese in El Paso, Texas; and to Rita Mathur in Toronto. I would also like to thank my friend Michael Ondaatje, who introduced me to Rohinton Mistry – it was Rohinton who introduced me to Rita. And my friend James Salter has been extremely tolerant and good-humored in allowing me to make mischievous use of several passages from his elegant novel *A Sport and a Pastime*. Thanks, Jim.

As always, I have other writers to thank: my friend Peter Matthiessen, who read the earliest draft and wisely suggested surgery; my friends David Calicchio, Craig Nova, Gail Godwin and Ron Hansen (not to mention his twin brother, Rob) also suffered through earlier drafts. And I'm indebted to Ved Mehta for his advice, through correspondence.

As usual, I have more than one doctor to thank, too. For his careful reading of the penultimate draft, my thanks to Dr Martin Schwartz in Toronto. In addition, I'm grateful to Dr Sherwin Nuland in Hamden, Connecticut, and to Dr Burton Berson in New York; they provided me with the clinical studies of achondroplasia. (Since this novel was completed, the gene for achondroplasia was found; the chief research biologist at the University of California at Irvine, Dr John J. Wasmuth, wrote to me that he wished he had read *A Son of the Circus* before he wrote the article describing identification of the gene for achondroplastic dwarfism – 'because I would have plagiarized some of your statements.' I can only guess that my main character, the fictional Dr Daruwalla, would have been pleased.)

The generosity of June Callwood, and of John Flannery – the director of nursing at Casey House in Toronto – is also much appreciated. And over the four years I've been writing *A Son of the Circus*, the work of three assistants has been outstanding: Heather Cochran, Alison Rivers and Allan Reeder. But there's only one reader who's read, or heard aloud, every draft of this story: my wife, Janet. For, literally, the thousands of pages she's endured – not to mention her

8

tolerance of enforced travel – I thank her, with all my love.

Lastly, I want to express my affection for my editor, Harvey Ginsberg, who officially retired before I handed him the 1,094-page manuscript; retired or not, Harvey edited me.

I repeat: I don't 'know' India, and *A Son of the Circus* isn't 'about' India. It is, however, a novel set in India – a story about an Indian (but *not* an Indian), for whom India will always remain an unknown and unknowable country. If I've managed to get the details right, my Indian friends deserve the credit.

—J. I.

For Salman

CONTENTS

1. THE CROW ON THE CEILING FAN

2. THE UPSETTING NEWS

3. THE REAL POLICEMAN

4. THE OLD DAYS

5. THE VERMIN

6. THE FIRST ONE OUT

7. DR DARUWALLA HIDES IN HIS BEDROOM

8. TOO MANY MESSAGES

9. SECOND HONEYMOON

10. CROSSED PATHS

11. THE DILDO

12. THE RATS

13. NOT A DREAM

14. TWENTY YEARS

15. DHAR'S TWIN

20. THE BRIBE

21. ESCAPING MAHARASHTRA

22. THE TEMPTATION OF DR DARUWALLA

23. LEAVING THE CHILDREN

24. THE DEVIL HERSELF

25. JUBILEE DAY

26. GOOD-BYE, BOMBAY

27. EPILOGUE

A SON OF
THE CIRCUS

1. THE CROW
ON THE CEILING FAN

Blood from Dwarfs

Usually, the dwarfs kept bringing him back – back to
the circus *and* back to India. The doctor was familiar
with the feeling of leaving Bombay 'for the last time';
almost every time he left India, he vowed that he'd
never come back. Then the years would pass – as a
rule, not more than four or five – and once again he'd
be taking the long flight from Toronto. That he was
born in Bombay was *not* the reason; at least this
was what the doctor claimed. Both his mother and
father were dead; his sister lived in London, his
brother in Zürich. The doctor's wife was Austrian, and
their children and grandchildren lived in England
and in Canada; none of them wanted to live in India –
they rarely visited the country – nor had a single one of
them been born there. But the doctor was fated to go
back to Bombay; he would keep returning again and
again – if not forever, at least for as long as there were
dwarfs in the circus.

Achondroplastic dwarfs comprise the majority of
circus clowns in India; they are the so-called circus
midgets, but they're not midgets – they're dwarfs.
Achondroplasia is the most common type of short-
limbed dwarfism. An achondroplastic dwarf can be
born of normal parents, but the dwarf's children have
a 50 percent chance of being dwarfs. This type of
dwarfism is most often the result of a rare genetic
event, a spontaneous mutation, which then becomes
a dominant characteristic in the dwarf's children.
No one has discovered a genetic marker for this

characteristic – and none of the best minds in genetics are bothering to search for such a marker.

Quite possibly, only Dr Farrokh Daruwalla had the far-fetched idea of finding a genetic marker for this type of dwarfism. By the passion of such a wishful discovery, the doctor was driven to gather samples of dwarf blood. The whimsy of his idea was plain: his dwarf-blood project was of no orthopedic interest, and he was an orthopedic surgeon; genetics was only one of his hobbies. Yet, although Farrokh's visits to Bombay were infrequent and the duration of his stay was always short, no one in India had ever drawn blood from so many dwarfs; no one had bled as many dwarfs as Dr Daruwalla had bled. In those Indian circuses that passed through Bombay, or in such circuses as frequented the smaller towns in Gujarat and Maharashtra, it was with affection that Farrokh was called 'the vampire.'

This is not to suggest that a physician in Dr Daruwalla's field in India wouldn't stumble across a fair number of dwarfs; they suffer from chronic orthopedic problems – aching knees and ankles, not to mention low back pain. Their symptoms are progressive, according to their age and weight; as dwarfs grow older and heavier, their pain gradually radiates into the buttocks, posterior thighs and calves.

At the Hospital for Sick Children in Toronto, Dr Daruwalla saw very few dwarfs; however, at the Hospital for Crippled Children in Bombay – where, from time to time, upon his return visits, Farrokh enjoyed the title of Honorary Consultant Surgeon – the doctor examined many dwarf patients. But these dwarfs, although they would provide Dr Daruwalla with their family histories, would not readily give him their blood. It would have been unethical of him to draw the dwarfs' blood against their will; the majority of orthopedic ailments afflicting achondroplastic dwarfs don't necessitate testing their blood. Therefore, it was only fair that Farrokh would explain the scientific nature of his research project and that he would *ask* these dwarfs for their blood. Almost always, the dwarfs said no.

A case in point was Dr Daruwalla's closest dwarf acquaintance in Bombay; in the vernacular of friendship, Farrokh and Vinod went back a long way, for the dwarf was the doctor's most visceral connection to the circus – Vinod was the first dwarf whom Dr Daruwalla had asked for blood. They had met in the examining room of the doctor's office at the Hospital for Crippled Children; their conversation coincided with the religious holiday of Diwali, which had brought the Great Blue Nile Circus to Bombay for an engagement at Cross Maidan. A dwarf clown (Vinod) and his normal wife (Deepa) had brought their dwarf son (Shivaji) to the hospital to have the child's ears examined. Vinod had never imagined that the Hospital for Crippled Children concerned itself with *ears* – ears weren't a common area of orthopedic complaint – but the dwarf correctly assumed that all dwarfs were cripples.

Yet the doctor could never persuade Vinod to believe in the genetic reasons for either his or his son's dwarfism. That Vinod came from normal parents and was nonetheless a dwarf was not in Vinod's view the result of a mutation. The dwarf believed his mother's story: that, the morning after she conceived, she looked out the window and the first living thing she saw was a dwarf. That Vinod's wife, Deepa, was a normal woman – 'almost beautiful,' by Vinod's description – didn't prevent Vinod's son, Shivaji, from being a dwarf. However, in Vinod's view, this was *not* the result of a dominant gene, but rather the misfortune of Deepa forgetting what Vinod had told her. The morning after Deepa conceived, the first living thing she looked at was Vinod, and *that* was why Shivaji was also a dwarf. Vinod had told Deepa not to look at him in the morning, but she forgot.

That Deepa was 'almost beautiful' (or at least a

21

normal woman), and yet she was married to a dwarf – this was the result of her having no dowry. She'd been sold to the Great Blue Nile Circus by her mother. And since Deepa was still very much a novice trapeze artist, she earned almost no money at all. 'Only a dwarf would be marrying her,' Vinod said.

As for their child, Shivaji, recurrent and chronic middle-ear infections are common among the achondroplastic dwarfs until the age of 8 or 10; if untreated, such infections often lead to significant hearing loss. Vinod himself was half deaf. But it simply wasn't possible for Farrokh to educate Vinod on this matter, or on other matters pertaining to the genetics of his and Shivaji's type of dwarfism; his so-called trident hands, for example – the stubby fingers were characteristically splayed. Dr Daruwalla also noted the dwarf's short, broad feet and the flexed position of his elbows, which could never be fully extended; the doctor tried to make Vinod admit that, like his son's, his fingertips reached only to his hips, his abdomen protruded and – even lying on his back – the dwarf exhibited the typical forward curvature of the spine. This lumbar lordosis and a tilted pelvis explain why all dwarfs waddle.

'Dwarfs are just naturally waddling,' Vinod replied. He was religiously stubborn and utterly unwilling to part with as much as a single Vacutainer of his blood. There he sat on the examining table, shaking his head at Dr Daruwalla's theories of dwarfism.

Vinod's head, like the heads of all achondroplastic dwarfs, was exceedingly large. His face failed to convey a visible intelligence, unless a bulging forehead could be attributed to brain power; the midface, again typical of achondroplasia, was recessed. The cheeks and the bridge of the nose were flattened, although the tip of the nose was fleshy and upturned; the jaw protruded to such a degree that Vinod's chin was prominent; and while his thrusting head did not communicate the greatest common sense, Vinod's overall manner proclaimed a personality of great determination. His aggressive appearance was further enhanced by a trait common among achondroplastic dwarfs: because their tubular bones are shortened, their muscle mass is concentrated, creating an impression of considerable strength. In Vinod's case, a life of tumbling and other acrobatics had given him especially well delineated shoulder muscles; his forearms and his biceps bulged. He was a veteran circus clown, but he looked like a miniature thug. Farrokh was a little afraid of him.

'And just what are you wanting with my blood?' the dwarf clown asked the doctor.

'I'm looking for that secret thing which made you a dwarf,' Dr Daruwalla replied.

'Being a dwarf is no secret!' Vinod argued.

'I'm looking for something in your blood that, if I find it, will help other people not to give birth to dwarfs,' the doctor explained.

'Why are you wanting to put an end to dwarfs?' the dwarf asked.

'It doesn't hurt to give blood,' Dr Daruwalla reasoned. 'The needle doesn't hurt.'

'All needles are hurting,' Vinod said.

'So you're afraid of needles?' Farrokh asked the dwarf.

'I am just needing my blood right now,' Vinod answered.

The almost-beautiful Deepa wouldn't permit the doctor to prick her dwarf child with a needle, either, although both Deepa and Vinod suggested that the Great Blue Nile Circus, which was in Bombay for another week, was full of other dwarfs who might give Dr Daruwalla *their* blood. Vinod said he'd be happy to introduce the doctor to the Blue Nile's clowns. Furthermore, Vinod advised the doctor to bribe the clowns with alcohol and tobacco, and it was at Vinod's prompting that Farrokh revised his stated reason for wanting the dwarfs' blood. 'Tell them you are using

23

their blood to give strength to a dying dwarf,' Vinod suggested.

This was the way the dwarf-blood project began. It had been 15 years ago when Dr Daruwalla drove to the circus grounds at Cross Maidan. He brought his needles, his plastic needle holders, his glass vials (or Vacutainers). To bribe the dwarfs, he brought two cases of Kingfisher lager and two cartons of Marlboro cigarettes; according to Vinod, the latter were popular among his fellow clowns because of the dwarfs' high regard for the Marlboro Man. As it turned out, Farrokh should have left the beer at home. In the stillness of the early-evening heat, the Great Blue Nile's clowns drank too many Kingfishers; two dwarfs fainted while the doctor was drawing their blood, which provided further evidence for Vinod that he should retain every drop of his own.

Even poor Deepa guzzled a Kingfisher; shortly before her performance, she complained of a slight dizziness, which was exacerbated when she hung by her knees from the high trapeze. Deepa then tried swinging in a sitting position, but the heat had risen to the top of the tent and the dwarf's wife felt that her head was trapped in the hottest possible air. She felt only a little better when she gripped the bar in both hands and swung herself with more and more force; hers was the simplest exchange for an aerialist to master, but she still hadn't learned how to let the catcher grab her wrists before she tried to grab his. Deepa simply would release the bar when her body was parallel to the ground; then she'd throw back her head so that her shoulders dropped below the level of her feet, and the catcher would catch hold of her by her ankles. Ideally, when the catcher caught her, Deepa's head was approximately 50 feet above the safety net, but the dwarf's wife was a beginner and she let go of the trapeze before her body was fully extended. The catcher had to lunge for her; he was able to grab only one of her feet, and he caught her at an unfortunate

24

angle. Deepa screamed so loudly when her hip was dislocated that the catcher thought the best thing he could do for her was to drop her into the safety net, which he did. Dr Daruwalla had never seen a more awkward fall.

A small, dark girl from rural Maharashtra, Deepa might have been 18 but she looked 16 to the doctor; her dwarf son, Shivaji, was not quite two. Her mother had sold her to the Great Blue Nile when Deepa was 11 or 12 – at an age when her mother might also have been tempted to sell her to a brothel. Deepa knew she was lucky to have been sold to a circus. She was so thin that the Blue Nile had at first tried to train her as a contortionist – a so-called boneless girl, a plastic lady. But as Deepa grew older, she became too inflexible to be 'boneless.' Even Vinod was of the opinion that Deepa was too old when she began her training as a flyer; most trapeze artists learn to fly when they're children.

The dwarf's wife was, if not almost beautiful, at least pretty from a certain distance; her forehead was pockmarked and she bore the stigmata of rickets ... frontal bossing, rachitic rosary. (It's called a 'rosary' because at every junction of rib and cartilage there's a marblelike protuberance, like a bead.) Deepa was so small-breasted that her chest was nearly as flat as a boy's; however, her hips were womanly, and it was partly the way the safety net sagged with her weight that made her appear to be lying facedown in the net while her pelvis was tilted *up* – toward the empty, swinging trapeze.

From the way she'd fallen and was lying in the safety net, Farrokh felt almost certain that the problem was Deepa's hip, not her neck or back. But until someone could keep her from flopping around in the net, the doctor didn't dare go to her. Vinod had instantly crawled into the net. Now Farrokh told him to clamp Deepa's head between his knees and hold her shoulders with his hands. Only when the dwarf securely held

25

her – only when Deepa couldn't move her neck or her back, or even rotate her shoulders – did Dr Daruwalla dare to enter the net.

In the time it had taken Vinod to crawl into the net with her, and all the time that the dwarf held his wife's head tightly between his knees – while Dr Daruwalla crawled into the sagging net and made his slow, awkward way toward them – the net never stopped swaying and the empty trapeze that dangled above them moved out of rhythm with the net.

Farrokh had never been in a safety net before. He was a nonathlete who was (even 15 years ago) noticeably plump, and his climb into the trapeze artists' net was a monumental struggle, aided only by his gratitude for his first samples of dwarf blood. As Dr Daruwalla proceeded on all fours across the dipping, swaying net to where poor Deepa lay in her dwarf husband's clutches, the doctor most resembled a fat, tentative mouse traversing a vast spiderweb.

Farrokh's unreasonable fear of being pitched out of the net at least distracted him from the murmuring of the circus audience; they were impatient for the rescue process to hurry up. That the loudspeaker had introduced him to the restless crowd did nothing to prepare Dr Daruwalla for the arduousness of his adventure. 'Here is coming the doctor!' the ringmaster had declared over the loudspeaker, in a melodramatic effort to hold the crowd. But what a long time it took the doctor to reach the fallen flyer! Furthermore, Farrokh's weight caused the net to dip nearer the ground; he was like an ungainly lover approaching his prey in a soft bed that sags in the middle.

Then, suddenly, the net sagged so steeply that Dr Daruwalla was thrown off balance; clumsily, he fell forward. The plump physician thrust his fingers through the holes in the net; since he'd already removed his sandals before climbing into the net, he tried to insert his toes (like claws) through the holes in the net, too. But in spite of this effort to slow his own

26

momentum, which was now of a pace to at last be of interest to the bored audience, gravity prevailed. Dr Daruwalla pitched headfirst into the sequined belly of Deepa's tight singlet.

Deepa's neck and back were undamaged – the doctor had correctly diagnosed her injury from his view of her fall. Her hip was dislocated; it hurt her when Farrokh fell upon her abdomen. The doctor's forehead was scratched by the pink and fire-engine-red sequins that formed a star over Deepa's pelvis, and the bridge of Dr Daruwalla's nose ground to a sharp halt against her pubis.

Under vastly different circumstances, their collision might have been sexually thrilling, but not to a woman with a dislocated hip (and with her head clamped tightly between a dwarf's knees). For Dr Daruwalla – the fallen flyer's pain and her screams notwithstanding – this encounter with Deepa's pubic bone would be recorded as his single extramarital experience. Farrokh would never forget it.

Here he'd been called out of the audience to aid a dwarf's wife in distress. And then, in full view of the unimpressed crowd, the doctor had ended up with his face jammed into the injured woman's crotch. Was it any wonder he couldn't forget her, or the mixed sensations that she'd caused him?

Even today, so many years later, Farrokh felt flushed with embarrassment and titillation, for his memory of the trapeze artist's taut belly still excited him. Where his cheek had come to rest against her inner thigh, Farrokh could still feel how her tights were soaked with sweat. All the time he heard Deepa screaming in pain (as the doctor clumsily struggled to move his weight off her), he also heard the cartilage in his nose cracking, for Deepa's pubis was as hard as an ankle or an elbow. And when Dr Daruwalla breathed in her dangerous aroma, he thought he'd at last identified the smell of sex, which struck him as an earthy com-mingling of death and flowers.

It was there, in the swaying safety net, that Vinod first accused him. 'All this is happening because you are wanting blood from dwarfs,' the dwarf said.

The Doctor Dwells on
Lady Duckworth's Breasts

In 15 years, the Indian customs authorities had detained Dr Daruwalla only twice; both times, the disposable hypodermic needles – about a hundred of them – had caught their attention. It had been necessary for the doctor to explain the difference between syringes, which are used to give injections, and Vacutainers, which are used to draw blood; in the Vacutainer system, neither the glass vials nor the plastic needle holders are equipped with plungers. The doctor wasn't carrying syringes, for putting drugs in; he was carrying Vacutainers, for taking blood out.

'Whose blood is being taken out?' the customs man had asked.

Even the answer to that question had been easier to explain than the problem that currently presented itself to the doctor.

The current problem was, Dr Daruwalla had upsetting news for the famous actor with the unlikely name of Inspector Dhar. Not sure of the degree to which Dhar would be distressed, the doctor was impelled by cowardice; he planned to give the movie star the bad news in a public place. Inspector Dhar's poise in public was renowned; Farrokh felt he could rely on the actor to keep his composure. Not everyone in Bombay would have thought of a private club as a public place, but Dr Daruwalla believed that the choice was both private and public enough for the crisis at hand.

That morning, when Dr Daruwalla had arrived at the Duckworth Sports Club, he had thought it was unremarkable to see a vulture high in the sky above the golf course; he didn't consider the bird of death as an omen

28

attached to the unwelcome news he carried. The club was in Mahalaxmi, not far from Malabar Hill; everyone in Bombay knew why vultures were attracted to Malabar Hill. When a corpse was placed in the Towers of Silence, the vultures – from as far as 30 miles outside Bombay – could scent the ripening remains.

Farrokh was familiar with Doongarwadi. The so-called Towers of Silence are seven huge cairns on Malabar Hill where the Parsis lay out the naked cadavers of their dead to be picked clean by the carrion eaters. As a Parsi, Dr Daruwalla was descended from Persian Zoroastrians who had come to India in the seventh and eighth centuries to escape Muslim persecution. Farrokh's father, however, was such a virulent, acerbic atheist that the doctor had never been a practicing Zoroastrian. And Farrokh's conversion to Christianity would doubtless have killed his godless father, except that his father was already dead; the doctor didn't convert until he was almost 40.

Because Dr Daruwalla was a Christian, his own mortal body would never be exposed in the Towers of Silence; but despite his father's inflammatory atheism, Farrokh respected the habits of his fellow Parsis and practicing Zoroastrians – and he *expected* to see vultures flying to and from Ridge Road. Nor was the doctor surprised that the particular vulture above the Duckworth golf course appeared in no hurry to arrive at the Towers of Silence; the area was entangled with vines, and not even other Parsis, unless they were dead, were welcome at the burial wells.

In general, Dr Daruwalla wished the vultures well. The limestone cairns contributed to the swift decomposition of even the larger bones, and those parts of Parsis that stayed intact were washed away in the monsoon season. In regard to disposing of the dead, in the doctor's opinion, the Parsis had found an admirable solution.

As for the living, Dr Daruwalla had this morning, as on most mornings, been up early. His first surgeries at the Hospital for Crippled Children, where he continued to enjoy the title of Honorary Consultant Surgeon, included one operation for clubfoot and another for wryneck; the latter is an infrequent operation nowadays, and it was not the sort of surgery that reflected Farrokh's main interest in practicing orthopedics, albeit intermittently, in Bombay. Dr Daruwalla was interested in bone and joint infections. In India, such infections typically follow a motor-vehicle accident and a compound fracture; the fracture is exposed to the air because the skin is broken, and five weeks after the injury, pus is bubbling from a sinus (a puckered opening) in the wound. These infections are chronic because the bone is dead, and dead bone behaves like a foreign body. Dead bone is called sequestrum; in Bombay, Farrokh's fellow orthopedists liked to call him 'Dead Bone' Daruwalla – those who knew him best called him 'Dwarf Blood' Daruwalla, too. Teasing aside, infected bones and joints were not another hobby – they were Farrokh's field.

In Canada, it often seemed to the doctor that his orthopedic practice involved almost as many sports injuries as birth defects or spasmodic contractions. In Toronto, Dr Daruwalla still specialized in orthopedics for children, but he felt more essentially needed – hence more exhilarated – in Bombay. In India, it was common to see orthopedic patients with little handkerchiefs tied around their legs; the handkerchiefs covered sinus tracts, which drained small amounts of pus – for years. In Bombay, there was also more willingness among patients *and* surgeons to accept amputations and the quick fitting of a simple prosthesis; such solutions were unacceptable in Toronto, where Dr Daruwalla was known for a new technique in microvascular surgery.

In India, without removal of the dead bone, there was no cure; often there was too much dead bone to remove – to take it out would compromise the ability of the limb to bear weight. But in Canada, with the aid of prolonged intravenous antibiotics, Farrokh could combine dead-bone removal with a plastic procedure – a muscle and its blood supply are brought into the infected area. Dr Daruwalla couldn't duplicate such procedures in Bombay, unless he limited his practice to very rich people in hospitals like Jaslok. At the Hospital for Crippled Children, the doctor resorted to the quick restoration of a limb's function; this often amounted to an amputation and a prosthesis in place of a cure. To Dr Daruwalla, a sinus tract draining pus wasn't the worst thing; in India, he let the pus drain.

And in keeping with the enthusiasm characteristic of converts to Christianity – the doctor was a confirmed Anglican who was both suspicious and in awe of Catholics – Dr Daruwalla was also exhilarated by the Christmas season, which in Bombay isn't as garishly festooned with commercial enterprise as it has become in Christian countries. This particular Christmas was cautiously joyous for the doctor; he'd attended a Catholic Mass on Christmas Eve *and* an Anglican service on Christmas Day. He was a holiday churchgoer, if hardly a regular one; yet his double churchgoing was an inexplicable overdose – Farrokh's wife was worried about him.

The doctor's wife was Viennese, the former Julia Zilk – no relation to the city mayor of that name. The former *Fräulein* Zilk came from an aristocratic and imperious family of Roman Catholics. During the Daruwalla family's short, infrequent visits to Bombay, the Daruwalla children had attended Jesuit schools; however, this wasn't because the children were brought up as Catholics – it was only the result of Farrokh maintaining 'family connections' with these schools, which were otherwise difficult to get into. The Daruwalla children were confirmed Anglicans; they'd received Anglican schooling in Toronto.

But despite Farrokh's preference for a Protestant faith, he'd been pleased to entertain his few Jesuit acquaintances on Boxing Day; they were much livelier

31

conversationalists than the Anglicans he knew in Bombay. Christmas itself was a glad tiding, surely; it was a season that produced in the doctor an effusion of goodwill. In the spirit of Christmas, Farrokh could almost forget that the effects of his 20-year-old conversion to Christianity were weakening.

And Dr Daruwalla didn't give a second thought to the vulture high above the golf course at the Duckworth Club. The only cloud on the doctor's horizon was how to tell Inspector Dhar the upsetting news. These were not glad tidings for Dhar. But until this unforeseen bad news, it hadn't been that bad a week.

It was the week between Christmas and New Year's. The weather in Bombay was uncommonly cool and dry. The active membership of the Duckworth Sports Club had reached 6,000; considering that there was a 22-year waiting list for new members, this number had been rather gradually achieved. That morning, there was a meeting of the Membership Committee, of which the distinguished Dr Daruwalla was guest chairman, to determine whether member number 6,000 should receive any special notification of his extraordinary status. The suggestions ranged from a plaque in the snooker room (where there were sizable gaps among the trophies), to a small reception in the Ladies' Garden (where the usual bloom of the bougainvillea was diminished by an undiagnosed blight), to a simple typewritten memo thumbtacked alongside the list of Temporarily Elected Members.

Farrokh had often objected to the title of this list, which was posted in a locked glass case in the foyer of the Duckworth Club. He complained that 'temporarily elected' meant merely nominated – they weren't elected at all – but this term had been the accepted usage since the club had been founded 130 years ago. A spider crouched beside the short column of names; it had crouched there for so long, it was presumed dead – or perhaps the spider was also seeking permanent membership. This was Dr Daruwalla's joke, but the joke was old; it was rumored to have been repeated by all 6,000 members.

It was midmorning, and the committeemen were drinking Thums Up cola and Gold Spot orange soda in the card room when Dr Daruwalla suggested that the matter be dropped.

'Stopped?' said Mr Dua, who was deaf in one ear from a tennis injury, never to be forgotten; his doubles partner had double-faulted and flung his racquet. Since he was only 'temporarily elected' at the time, this shocking display of bad temper had put an end to the partner's quest for permanent membership.

'I move,' Dr Daruwalla now shouted, 'that member number six thousand *not* be notified!' The motion was quickly seconded and passed; not even so much as a typewritten memo would announce the event. Dr Sorabjee, Farrokh's colleague at the Hospital for Crippled Children, said facetiously that the decision was among the wisest ever made by the Membership Committee. In truth, Dr Daruwalla thought, no one wanted to risk disturbing the spider.

In the card room, the committeemen sat in silence, satisfied with the conclusion of their business; the ceiling fans only slightly ruffled the trim decks of cards that stood perfectly in place at the appropriate tables, which were topped with tightly stretched green felt. A waiter, removing an empty Thums Up bottle from the table where the committeemen sat, paused to straighten one errant deck of cards before leaving the room, although only the top two cards of the deck had been edged out of alignment by the nearest ceiling fan.

That was when Mr Bannerjee walked into the card room, looking for his golfing opponent, Mr Lal. Old Mr Lal was late for their regular nine holes, and Mr Bannerjee told the committee the amusing results of their competition together the day before. Mr Lal had lost a one-stroke lead in a spectacular blunder on the ninth hole: he'd chipped a shot entirely over the green and into a profusion of the blighted bougainvillea, where he'd hacked away in misery and in vain.

Rather than return to the clubhouse, Mr Lal had shaken Mr Bannerjee's hand and marched in a fury to the bougainvillea; there Mr Bannerjee had left him. Mr Lal was intent on practicing how to escape from this trap should he ever blunder into it again. Petals were flying when Mr Bannerjee parted from his friend; that evening, the gardener (the head mali, no less) was dismayed to observe the damage to the vines and to the flowers. But old Mr Lal was among the more venerable of the Duckworth's members – if he insisted on learning how to escape the bougainvillea, no one would be so bold as to prevent him. And now Mr Lal was late. Dr Daruwalla suggested to Mr Bannerjee that quite possibly his opponent was still practicing, and that he should search for him in the ruined bougainvillea.

Thus the committee meeting disbanded in characteristic and desultory laughter. Mr Bannerjee went seeking Mr Lal in the men's dressing room; Dr Sorabjee went off to the hospital for office calls; Mr Dua, whose deafness somehow suited his retirement from the percussiveness of the tire business, wandered into the snooker room to have a crack at some innocent balls, which he would barely hear. Others stayed where they were, turning to the ready decks of cards, or else they found comfort in the cool leather chairs in the reading room, where they ordered Kingfisher lagers or London Diet beers. It was getting on toward late morning, but it was generally thought to be too early for gin and tonics or adding a shot of rum to the Thums Up colas.

In the men's dressing room and the clubhouse bar, the younger members and actual athletes were returning from their sets of tennis or their badminton or their squash. For the most part, they were tea drinkers at this time of the morning. Those returning from the golf course heartily complained about the mess of flower petals that by now had drifted over the ninth green.

34

(These golfers wrongly assumed that the bougainvillea blight had taken a new and nasty turn.) Mr Bannerjee told his story several more times; each time, the efforts of Mr Lal to defeat the bougainvillea were described in more reckless and damaging terms. A generous good humor pervaded the clubhouse and the dressing room. Mr Bannerjee didn't seem to mind that it was now too late in the morning to play golf.

The unexpected cool weather could not change the habits of the Duckworthians; they were used to playing their golf and tennis before 11:00 in the morning or after 4:00 in the afternoon. During the midday hours, the members drank or lunched or simply sat under the ceiling fans or in the deep shade of the Ladies' Garden, which was never exclusively used by (or especially full of) ladies – not nowadays. Yet the garden's name was unchanged from purdah times, when the seclusion of women from the sight of men or strangers was practiced by some Muslims and Hindus. Farrokh found this odd, for the founding members of the Duckworth Sports Club were the British, who were still welcome there and even comprised a small proportion of the membership. To Dr Daruwalla's knowledge, the British had never practiced purdah. The Duckworth's founders had intended the club for any and all citizens of Bombay, provided that they'd distinguished themself in community leadership. As Farrokh and the other members of the Membership Committee would attest, the definition of 'community leadership' could be argued for the length of the monsoon, and beyond.

By tradition, the chairman of the Duckworth Club was the governor of Maharashtra; yet Lord Duckworth himself, for whom the club was named, had never been governor. Lord D. (as he was called) had long sought the office, but the eccentricities of his wife were too notorious. Lady Duckworth was afflicted with exhibitionism in general – and with the astonishing wild habit of exposing her breasts in particular. Although this affliction endeared both Lord *and* Lady

35

Duckworth to many members of the club, it was a gesture thought lacking in gubernatorial merit.

Dr Daruwalla stood in the penetrating cool of the empty dance hall, viewing – as he often did – the splendid and abundant trophies and the spellbinding old photographs of Members Past. Farrokh enjoyed such controlled sightings of his father, and of his grandfather, and of the countless avuncular gentlemen among his father's and grandfather's friends. He imagined that he could remember every man who'd ever laid a hand on his shoulder or touched the top of his head. Dr Daruwalla's familiarity with these photographs belied the fact that the doctor himself had spent very few of his 59 years in India. When he was visiting Bombay, Dr Daruwalla was sensitive to anyone or anything that reminded him of how little he knew or understood the country of his birthplace. The more time he spent in the haven of the Duckworth Club, the more the doctor could sustain the illusion that he was comfortable being in India.

At home, in Toronto, where he'd spent most of his adult life, the doctor enjoyed the reputation – especially among Indians who'd never been to India, or who'd never gone back – of being a genuine 'old India hand'; he was even considered quite brave. After all, it was every few years that Farrokh returned to his native land under what were presumed to be primitive conditions – practicing medicine in a country of such claustrophobic overpopulation. And where were the amenities that could live up to a Canadian standard of comfort?

Weren't there water shortages and bread strikes, and the rationing of oil or rice, not to mention food adulteration and those gas cylinders that always ran out of gas in the midst of a dinner party? And one often heard about the shoddy construction of buildings, the falling plaster and so on. But only rarely did Dr Daruwalla return to India during the monsoon months, which were the most 'primitive' in Bombay. Furthermore, to his fellow Torontonians, Farrokh tended to down-play the fact that he never stayed in India for long.

In Toronto, the doctor spoke of his childhood (as a Bombayite) as if it had been both more colorful and more authentically Indian than it truly had been. Educated by the Jesuits, Dr Daruwalla had attended St Ignatius School in Mazagaon; for recreation, he'd enjoyed the privileges of organized sports and dances at the Duckworth Club. When he reached university age, he was sent to Austria; even his eight years in Vienna, where he completed medical school, were tame and controlled – he'd lived the whole time with his elder brother.

But in the Duckworth's dance hall, in the sacred presence of those portraits of Members Past, Dr Daruwalla could momentarily imagine that he truly came from somewhere, and that he belonged some-where. Increasingly, as he approached 60, the doctor acknowledged (only to himself) that in Toronto he often *acted* far more Indian than he was; he could instantly acquire a Hindi accent, or drop it, depending on the company he kept. Only a fellow Parsi would know that English had been his veritable mother tongue, and that the doctor would have learned his Hindi in school. During Farrokh's visits to India, he was similarly ashamed of himself for how completely European or North American he pretended to be. In Bombay, his Hindi accent disappeared; one had only to hear the doctor's English to be convinced that he'd been totally assimilated in Canada. In truth, it was only when he was surrounded by the old photographs in the dance hall of the Duckworth Club that Dr Daru-walla felt at home.

Of Lady Duckworth, Dr Daruwalla had only heard her story. In each of her stunning photographs, her breasts were properly if not modestly covered. Yes, a highly elevated and sizable bosom could be detected in her pictures, even when Lady Duckworth was well advanced in years; and yes, her habit of exposing herself supposedly increased as she grew older – her breasts were reported to be well formed (and well worth revealing) into her seventies.

She'd been 75 when she revealed herself in the club's circular driveway to a horde of young people arriving for the Sons and Daughters of Members' Ball. This incident resulted in a multivehicle collision that was reputed to bear responsibility for the enlargement of the speed bumps, which were implanted the entire length of the access road. In Farrokh's opinion, the Duckworth Club was permanently fixed at the speed indicated by those signs posted at both ends of the drive: DEAD SLOW. But this, for the most part, contented him; the admonition to go dead slow didn't strike Dr Daruwalla as an imposition, although the doctor did regret not being alive for at least one glimpse of Lady Duckworth's long-ago breasts. The club couldn't have been dead slow in her day.

As he had sighed aloud in the empty dance hall perhaps a hundred times. Dr Daruwalla sighed again and softly said to himself, 'Those were the good old days.' But it was only a joke; he didn't really mean it. Those 'good old days' were as unknowable to him as Canada – his cold, adopted country – or as the India he only pretended to be comfortable in. Furthermore, Farrokh never spoke or sighed loudly enough to be heard by anyone else.

In the vast cool hall, he listened: he could hear the waiters and the busboys in the dining room, setting the tables for lunch; he could hear the clicks and thumps of the snooker balls and the flat, authoritative snap of a card turned faceup on a table. And although it was now past 11:00, two die-hards were still playing tennis; by the soft, slowly paced *pops* of the ball, Dr Daruwalla concluded that it wasn't a very spirited match.

It was unmistakably the head gardener's truck that sped along the access road, hitting each of the speed bumps with abandon; there followed the resounding clatter of hoes and rakes and spades, and then an abstract cursing – the head mali was a moron.

There was a photograph that Farrokh was particularly fond of, and he looked intently at it; then he closed his eyes so that he might see the picture better. In Lord Duckworth's expression there was much charity and tolerance and patience; yet there was something stupefied in his faraway gaze, as if he'd only recently recognized and accepted his own futility. Although Lord Duckworth was broad-shouldered and had a deep chest and he firmly held a sword, there was also a kind of gentle idiot's resignation at the turned-down corners of his eyes and the drooping ends of his mustache. He was perpetually *almost* the governor of Maharashtra, but never the governor. And the hand that he placed around Lady Duckworth's girlish waist was clearly a hand that touched her without weight, that held her without strength – if it held her at all.

Lord D. committed suicide on New Year's Eve, precisely at the turn of the century. For many more years Lady Duckworth would reveal her breasts, but it was agreed that, as a widow, although she exposed herself more often, she did so halfheartedly. Cynics said that had she lived, and continued to show India her gifts, Lady D. might have thwarted Independence.

In the photograph that so appealed to Dr Daruwalla, Lady Duckworth's chin was tilted down, her eyes mischievously gazing up, as if she'd just been caught peering into her own thrilling cleavage and had instantly looked away. Her bosom was a broad, strong shelf supporting her pretty face. Even fully clothed, there was something unrestrained about the woman; her arms hung straight down at her sides, but her fingers were spread wide apart – with her palms presented to the camera, as if for crucifixion – and a wild strand of her allegedly blond hair, which was otherwise held high off her graceful neck, was childishly twisted and coiled like a snake around one of the world's perfect little ears.

39

In future years, her hair turned from blond to gray without losing its thick body or its deep luster; her breasts, despite being so often and so long exposed, never sagged. Dr Daruwalla was a happily married man; however, he would have admitted – even to his dear wife – that he was in love with Lady Duckworth, for he'd fallen in love with her photographs *and* with her story when he was a child.

But it could have a lugubrious effect on the doctor – if he spent too much time in the dance hall, reviewing the photographs of Members Past. Most of the Members Past were deceased; as the circus people said of their dead, they had fallen without a net. (Of the living, the expression was reversed. Whenever Dr Daruwalla inquired after Vinod's health – the doctor never failed to ask about the dwarf's wife, too – Vinod would always reply, 'We are still falling in the net.')

Of Lady Duckworth – at least, from her photographs – Farrokh would say that her breasts were still falling in the net; possibly they were immortal.

Mr Lal Has Missed the Net

And then, suddenly, a small and seemingly unimportant incident distracted Dr Daruwalla from his entrancement with Lady Duckworth's bosom. The doctor would need to be in touch with his subconsious to remember this, for it was only a slight disturbance from the dining room that drew his attention. A crow, with something shiny seized in its beak, had swept in from the open veranda and had landed rakishly on the broad, oar-shaped blade of one of the ceiling fans. The bird precariously tilted the fan, but it continued to ride the blade around and around, shitting in a consistently circular form – on the floor, on a portion of one tablecloth and on a salad plate, just missing a fork. A waiter flapped a napkin and the crow took flight again, raucously cawing as it escaped through the veranda and rose above the golf course that stood shimmering in the noon sun. Whatever had been in its beak was gone, perhaps swallowed. First the waiters and busboys rushed to change the befouled tablecloth and place setting, although it was still early for lunch; then a sweeper was summoned to mop the floor.

Owing to his early-morning surgeries, Dr Daruwalla lunched earlier than most Duckworthians. Farrokh's appointment for lunch with Inspector Dhar was at half past noon. The doctor strolled into the Ladies' Garden, where he located a break in the dense bower that afforded him a view of the expanse of sky above the golf course; there he seated himself in a rose-colored wicker chair. His little pot belly seemed to get his attention, especially when he sat down; Farrokh ordered a London Diet beer, although he wanted a Kingfisher lager.

To Dr Daruwalla's surprise, he saw a vulture (possibly the same vulture) above the golf course again; the bird was lower in the sky, as if it was *not* en route to or from the Towers of Silence but as if it was descending. Knowing how ferociously the Parsis defended their burial rites, it amused Farrokh to imagine that they might be offended by any distraction caused to any vulture. Perhaps a horse had dropped dead on the Mahalaxmi race course; maybe a dog had been killed in Tardeo or a body had washed ashore at Haji Ali's Tomb. Whatever the reason, here was one vulture that was not performing the sacred chore at the Towers of Silence.

Dr Daruwalla looked at his watch. He expected his luncheon companion at any moment; he sipped his London Diet beer, trying to pretend it was a Kingfisher lager – he was imagining that he was slim again. (Farrokh had never been slim.) While he watched the vulture carve its descending spirals, another vulture joined it, and then another; this gave him an unexpected chill. Farrokh quite forgot to prepare himself for the news he had to deliver to Inspector Dhar – not

41

that there was any good way to do it. The doctor grew so entranced by the birds that he didn't notice the typically smooth, eerily graceful arrival of his handsome younger friend.

Putting his hand on Dr Daruwalla's shoulder, Dhar said, 'Someone's dead out there, Farrokh – who is it?' This caused a new waiter – the same waiter who'd driven the crow off the ceiling fan – to mishandle a soup tureen and a ladle. The waiter had recognized Inspector Dhar; what shocked him was to hear the movie star speak English without a trace of a Hindi accent. The resounding clatter seemed to herald Mr Bannerjee's sudden arrival in the Ladies' Garden, where he seized both Dr Daruwalla and Inspector Dhar by an arm.

'The vultures are landing on the ninth green!' he cried. 'I think it's poor Mr Lal! He must have *died* in the bougainvillea!'

Dr Daruwalla whisped in Inspector Dhar's ear. The younger man's expression never changed as Farrokh said, 'This is *your* line of work, Inspector.' Typical of the doctor, this was a joke; yet without hesitation Inspector Dhar led them across the fairways. They could see a dozen of the leathery birds flapping and hopping in their ungainly fashion, dirtying the ninth green; their long necks rose above and then probed into the bougainvillea, their hooked beaks brightly spattered with gore.

Mr Bannerjee wouldn't step on the green, and the smell of putrefaction that clung to the vultures took Dr Daruwalla by surprise; he stopped, overcome, near the flag at the ninth hole. But Inspector Dhar parted the stinking birds as he kicked his way, straight ahead, into the bougainvillea. The vultures rose all around him. My God, thought Farrokh, he looks like he's a *real* police inspector – he's just an actor, but he doesn't know it!

The waiter who'd saved the ceiling fan from the crow, and had wrestled with the soup tureen and ladle with less success, also followed the excited Duck-worthians a short distance onto the golf course, but he turned back to the dining room when he saw Inspector Dhar scatter the vultures. The waiter was among that multitude of fans who had seen every Inspector Dhar movie (he'd seen two or three of them a half-dozen times); therefore, he could safely be characterized as a young man who was enthralled by cheap violence and criminal bloodshed, not to mention enamored of Bombay's most lurid element – the city's sleaziest underscum, which was so lavishly depicted in all the Inspector Dhar movies. But when the waiter saw the flock of vultures that the famous actor had put to flight, the reality of an actual corpse in the vicinity of the ninth green greatly upset him. He retreated to the club, where his presence had been missed by the eld-erly disapproving steward, Mr Sethna, who owed his job to Farrokh's late father.

'Inspector Dhar has found a *real* body this time!' the waiter said to the old steward.

Mr Sethna said, 'Your station today is in the Ladies' Garden. Kindly remain at your station!'

Old Mr Sethna disapproved of Inspector Dhar movies. He was exceptionally disapproving in general, a quality regarded as enhancing to his position as steward at the Duckworth Club, where he routinely behaved as if he were empowered with the authority of the club secretary. Mr Sethna had ruled the dining room and the Ladies' Garden with his disapproving frowns longer than Inspector Dhar had been a member – although Mr Sethna hadn't always been steward for the Duckworthians. He'd previously been steward at the Ripon Club, a club that only Pasis join, and a club unsullied by sports of any kind; the Ripon Club existed for the purpose of good food and good con-versation, period. Dr Daruwalla was also a member there. The Ripon *and* the Duckworth suited Farrokh's diverse nature: as a Parsi *and* a Christian, a Bombayite *and* a Torontonian, an orthopedic surgeon *and* a

43

dwarf-blood collector, Dr Daruwalla could never have been satisfied by just one club.

As for Mr Sethna, who was descended from a not-so-old-money family of Parsis, the Ripon Club had suited him better than the Duckworth; however, circumstances that had brought out his highly disapproving nature had led to his dismissal there. His 'highly disapproving nature' had already led Mr Sethna to lose his not-so-old money, and the steward's money had been exceedingly difficult to lose. It was money from the Raj, British money, but Mr Sethna had so disapproved of it that he'd most cunningly and deliberately pissed it all away. He'd endured more than a normal lifetime at the Mahalaxmi race course; and all he'd retained from his betting years was a memory of the tattoo of the horses' hooves, which he expertly drummed on his silver serving tray with his long fingers.

Mr Sethna was distantly related to the Guzdars, an old-money family of Parsis who'd kept their money; they'd been shipbuilders for the British Navy. Alas, it happened that a young Ripon Club member had offended Mr Sethna's extended-family sensibilities; the stern steward had overheard compromising mention of the virtue of a Guzdar young lady – a cousin, many times removed. Because of the vulgar wit that amused these younger, nonreligious Parsis, there'd also been compromising mention of the cosmic intertwinement between Spenta Mainyu (the Zoroastrian spirit of good) and Angra Mainyu (the spirit of evil). In the case of Mr Sethna's Guzdar cousin, the spirit of *sex* was said to be winning her favors.

The young dandy who was doing this verbal damage wore a wig, a vanity of which Mr Sethna also disapproved. Therefore, Mr Sethna poured hot tea on top of the gentleman's head, causing him to leap to his feet and literally snatch himself bald in the presence of his surprised luncheon companions.

Mr Sethna's actions, although considered most honorable among many old-money and new-money Parsis, were judged as unsuitable behavior for a steward; 'violent aggression with hot tea' were the stated grounds for Mr Sethna's dismissal. But the steward received the highest recommendation imaginable from Dr Daruwalla's father; it was on the strength of the elder Daruwalla's praise that Mr Sethna was instantly hired at the Duckworth Club. Farrokh's father viewed the tea episode as an act of heroism: the impugned Guzdar young lady was above reproach; Mr Sethna had been correct in defending the mistreated girl's virtue. The steward was such a fanatical Zoroastrian that Farrokh's fiercely opinionated father had described Mr Sethna as a Parsi who carried all of Persia on his shoulders.

To everyone who'd suffered his disapproving frowns in the Duckworth Club dining room or in the Ladies' Garden, old Mr Sethna looked like a steward who would gladly pour hot tea on *anyone's* head. He was tall and exceedingly lean, as if he generally disapproved of eating, and he had a hooked, disdainful nose, as if he also disapproved of how everything smelled. And the old steward was so fair-skinned – most Parsis are fairer-skinned than most Indians – that Mr Sethna was presumed to be racially disapproving, too.

At present, Mr Sethna looked disapprovingly at the commotion that engulfed the golf course. His lips were thin and tightly closed, and he had the narrow, jutting, tufted chin of a goat. He disapproved of sports, and most avowedly disliked the mixing of sporting activities with the more dignified pursuits of dining and sharp debate.

The golf course was in riot: half-dressed men came running from the locker room – as if their sporting attire (when they were fully clothed) weren't distasteful enough. As a Parsi, Mr Sethna had a high regard for justice; he thought there was something immoral about a death, which was so enduringly serious, occurring on a golf course, which was so disturbingly trivial. As a true believer whose naked body would one day lie in the Towers of Silence, the old steward found the presence of so many vultures profoundly moving; he preferred, therefore, to ignore them and to concentrate his attention and his scorn on the human turmoil. The moronic head mali had been summoned; he stupidly drove his rattling truck across the golf course, gouging up the grass that the assistant malis had recently groomed with the roller.

Mr Sethna couldn't see Inspector Dhar, who was deep in the bougainvillea, but he had no doubt that the crude movie star was in the thick of this crisis; the steward sighed in disapproval at the very idea of Inspector Dhar.

Then there came a high-pitched ringing of a fork against a water glass – a vulgar means by which to summon a waiter. Mr Sethna turned to the offending table and realized that *he*, not the waiter, was being summoned by the second Mrs Dogar. She was called the beautiful Mrs Dogar to her face and the second Mrs Dogar behind her back. Mr Sethna didn't find her especially beautiful, and he most adamantly disapproved of second marriages.

Furthermore, it was generally admitted among the members of the club that Mrs Dogar's beauty was coarse in nature and had faded over time. No amount of *Mr* Dogar's money could improve his new wife's garish tastes. No degree of physical fitness, which the second Mrs Dogar was reputed to worship to excess, could conceal from even the most casual observer that she was at least 42. To Mr Sethna's critical eye, she was already pushing (if not past) 50; he also thought she was much too tall. And there was many a golf-loving Duckworthian who took offense at her outspoken, insensitive opinion that golf was insufficient exercise for anyone in pursuit of good health.

This day, Mrs Dogar was lunching alone – a habit of which Mr Sethna also disapproved. At a proper club, the steward believed, women wouldn't be allowed to eat alone.

The marriage was still new enough that Mr Dogar often joined his wife for lunch; the marriage was also old enough that Mr Dogar felt free to cancel these luncheon dates, should some matter of more important business intervene. And lately he'd taken to canceling at the last minute, which left his wife no time to make plans of her own. Mr Sethna had observed that being left alone made the new Mrs Dogar restless and cross.

On the other hand, the steward had also observed a certain tension between the newlyweds when they dined together; Mrs Dogar was inclined to speak sharply to her husband, who was considerably older than she was. Mr Sethna supposed this was a penalty to be expected, for he especially disapproved of men who married younger women. But the steward thought it best to put himself at the aggressive wife's disposal lest she shatter her water glass with another blow from her fork; the fork itself looked surprisingly small in her large, sinewy hand.

'My dear Mr Sethna,' said the second Mrs Dogar.

Mr Sethna answered: 'How may I be of service to the beautiful Mrs Dogar?'

'You may tell me what all the fuss is about,' Mrs Dogar replied.

Mr Sethna spoke as deliberately as he would pour hot tea. 'It is most assuredly nothing to upset yourself about,' the old Parsi said. 'It is merely a dead golfer.'

2. THE UPSETTING NEWS

Still Tingling

Thirty years ago, there were more than 50 circuses of
some merit in India; today there aren't more than 15
that are any good. Many of them are named the Great
This or the Great That. Among Dr Daruwalla's favorites were the Great Bombay, the Jumbo, the Great
Golden, the Gemini, the Great Rayman, the Famous,
the Great Oriental and the Raj Kamal; of them all,
Farrokh felt most fond of the Great Royal Circus.
Before Independence, it was called simply the Royal;
in 1947 it became the 'Great.' It began as a two-pole
tent; in '47 the Great Royal added two more poles. But
it was the owner who'd made such a positive impression on Farrokh. Because Pratap Walawalkar was
such a well-traveled man, he seemed the most sophisticated of the circus owners to Dr Daruwalla; or else
Farrokh's fondness for Pratap Walawalkar was simply
because the Great Royal's owner never teased the
doctor about his interest in dwarf blood.

In the 1960's, the Great Royal traveled everywhere.
Business was bad in Egypt, best in Iran; business was
good in Beirut and Singapore, Pratap Walawalkar said
– and of all the countries where the circus traveled,
Bali was the most beautiful. Travel was too expensive
now. With a half-dozen elephants and two dozen big
cats, not to mention a dozen horses and almost a dozen
chimpanzees, the Great Royal rarely traveled outside
the states of Maharashtra and Gujarat. With uncounted
cockatoos and parrots, and dozens of dogs (not to
mention 150 people, including almost a dozen dwarfs),
the Great Royal never left India.

This was the real history of a real circus, but Dr

Daruwalla had committed these details to that quality of memory which most of us reserve for our childhoods. Farrokh's childhood had failed to make much of an impression on him; he vastly preferred the history and the memorabilia he'd absorbed as a behind-the-scenes observer of the circus. He remembered Pratap Walawalkar saying in an offhand manner: 'Ethiopian lions have brown manes, but they're just like other lions – they won't listen to you if you don't call them by their right names.' Farrokh had retained this morsel of information as if it were part of a beloved bedtime story.

In the early mornings, en route to his surgeries (even in Canada), the doctor often recalled the big basins steaming over the gas rings in the cook's tent. In one pot was the water for tea, but in two of the basins the cook was heating milk; the first milk that came to a boil wasn't for tea – it was to make oatmeal for the chimpanzees. As for tea, the chimps didn't like it hot; they liked their tea tepid. Farrokh also remembered the extra flatbread; it was for the elephants – they enjoyed roti. And the tigers took vitamins, which turned their milk pink. As an orthopedic surgeon, Dr Daruwalla could make no medical use of these cherished details; nevertheless, he'd breathed them in as if they were his own background.

Dr Daruwalla's wife wore wonderful jewelry, some of which had belonged to his mother; none of it was at all memorable to the doctor, who (however) could describe in the most exact detail a tiger-claw necklace that belonged to Pratap Singh, the ringmaster and wild-animal trainer for the Great Royal Circus – a man much admired by Farrokh. Pratap Singh had once shared his remedy for dizziness with the doctor: a potion of red chili and burned human hair. For asthma, the ringmaster recommended a clove soaked in tiger urine; you allow the clove to dry, then you grind it up and inhale the powder. Moreover, the animal trainer warned the doctor, you should never swallow a tiger's whiskers; swallowing tiger whiskers will kill you.

Had Farrokh read of these remedies in some crackpot's column in *The Times of India*, he'd have written a scathing letter for publication in the Opinion section. In the name of real medicine, Dr Daruwalla would have denounced such 'holistic folly,' which was his phrase of choice whenever he addressed the issue of so-called unscientific or magical thinking. But the source of the human-hair-and-red-chili recipe, as well as of the tiger-urine cure (not to mention the tiger-whiskers warning), was the great Pratap Singh. In Dr Daruwalla's view, the ringmaster and wild-animal trainer was undeniably a man who knew his business.

This kind of lore, and blood from dwarfs, enhanced Farrokh's abiding feeling that, as a result of flopping around in a safety net and falling on a poor dwarf's wife, he had become an adopted son of the circus. For Farrokh, the honor of clumsily coming to Deepa's rescue was lasting. Whenever *any* circus was performing in Bombay, Dr Daruwalla could be found in a front-row seat; he could also be detected mingling with the acrobats and the animal trainers – most of all, he enjoyed observing the practice sessions and the tent life. These intimate views from the wing of the main tent, these close-ups of the troupe tents and the cages – they were the privileges that made Farrokh feel he'd been adopted. At times, he wished he were a *real* son of the circus; instead, Farrokh supposed, he was merely a guest of honor. Nevertheless, this wasn't a fleeting honor – not to him.

Ironically, Dr Daruwalla's children and grandchildren were unimpressed by the Indian circuses. These two generations had been born and raised in London or Toronto; they'd not only seen bigger and fancier circuses – they'd seen cleaner. The doctor was disappointed that his children and grandchildren were so dirt-obsessed; they considered the tent life of the acrobats and the animal trainers to be shabby, even 'underprivileged.' Although the dirt floors of the tents were swept several times daily, Dr Daruwalla's children and grandchildren believed that the tents were filthy.

To the doctor, however, the circus was an orderly, well-kept oasis surrounded by a world of disease and chaos. His children and grandchildren saw the dwarf clowns as merely grotesque; in the circus, they existed solely to be laughed at. But Farrokh felt that the dwarf clowns were appreciated – maybe even loved, not to mention gainfully employed. The doctor's children and grandchildren thought that the risks taken by the child performers were especially 'harsh'; yet Farrokh felt that these acrobatic children were the lucky ones – they'd been rescued.

Dr Daruwalla knew that the majority of these child acrobats were (like Deepa) sold to the circus by their parents, who'd been unable to support them; others were orphans – they'd been truly adopted. If they hadn't been performing in the circus, where they were well fed and protected, they'd have been begging. They would be the street children you saw doing handstands and other stunts for a few rupees in Bombay, or in the smaller towns throughout Gujarat and Maharashtra, where even the Great Royal Circus more frequently performed – these days, fewer circuses came to Bombay. During Diwali and the winter holidays, there were still two or three circuses performing in or around the city, but TV and the videocassette recorder had hurt the circus business; too many people rented movies and stayed at home.

To hear the Daruwalla children and grandchildren discuss it, the child acrobats who were sold to the circus were long-suffering child laborers in a high-risk profession; their hardworking, no-escape existence was tantamount to slavery. Untrained children were paid nothing for six months; thereafter, they started with a salary of 3 rupees a day – only 90 rupees a month, less than 4 dollars! But Dr Daruwalla argued that safe food and a safe place to sleep were better than nothing; what these children were given was a chance.

Circus people boiled their water and their milk. They bought and cooked their own food; they dug and cleaned their own latrines. And a well-trained acrobat was often paid 500 or 600 rupees a month, even if it was only 25 dollars. Granted, although the Great Royal took good care of its children, Farrokh couldn't say with certainty that the child performers were as well treated in *all* the Indian circuses; the performances in several of these circuses were so abject – not to mention unskilled and careless – that the doctor surmised that the tent life in such places was shabbier, too.

Life was surely shabby in the Great Blue Nile; indeed, among the Great This and Great That circuses of India, the Great Blue Nile was the shabbiest – or at least the least great. Deepa would agree. A former child contortionist, the dwarf's wife, reincarnated as a trapeze artist, was lacking both in polish and in common sense; it wasn't merely the beer that had made her let go of the bar too soon.

Deepa's injuries were complicated but not severe; in addition to the dislocation of her hip joint, she'd suffered a tear in the transverse ligament. Not only would Dr Daruwalla brand Deepa's hip with a memorable scar, but, in prepping the area, he would be confronted by the irrefutable blackness of Deepa's pubic hair; this would be a dark reminder of the disturbing contact between her pubis and the bridge of his nose.

Farrokh's nose was still tingling when he helped Deepa be admitted to the hospital; out of guilt, he'd left the circus grounds with her. But the admitting process had barely begun when the doctor was summoned by one of the hospital secretaries; there'd been a phone call for him while he was en route from the Blue Nile.

'Do you know any clowns?' the secretary asked him.

'Well, as a matter of fact, yes,' Farrokh admitted.

'*Dwarf* clowns?' asked the secretary.

'Yes – several! I just met them,' the doctor added. Farrokh was too ashamed to admit that he'd also just bled them.

'Apparently, one of them has been injured at that circus at Cross Maidan,' the secretary said.

'Not Vinod!' Dr Daruwalla exclaimed.

'Yes, that's him,' she said. 'That's why they want you back at the circus.'

'What happened to Vinod?' Dr Daruwalla asked the somewhat disdainful secretary; she was one of many medical secretaries who embraced sarcasm.

'I couldn't ascertain the clown's condition from a phone message,' she replied. 'The description was hysterical. I gather he was trampled by elephants or shot from a cannon, or both. And now that this dwarf lies dying, he is declaring *you* to be his doctor.'

And so to the circus grounds at Cross Maidan did Dr Daruwalla go. All the way back to the deeply flawed performance of the Great Blue Nile, the doctor's nose tingled.

For 15 years, merely remembering the dwarf's wife would activate Farrokh's nose. And now, the fact that Mr Lal had fallen without a net (for the body on the golf course was indeed dead) – even this evidence of death reminded Dr Daruwalla that Deepa had survived her fall *and* her unwelcome and painful contact with the clumsy doctor.

The Famous Twin

Upon Inspector Dhar's intrusion, the vultures had risen but they'd not departed. Dr Daruwalla knew that the carrion eaters still floated overhead because their putrescence lingered in the air and their shadows drifted back and forth across the ninth green and the bougainvillea, where Dhar – a mere movie-star detective – knelt beside poor Mr Lal.

'Don't touch the body!' Dr Daruwalla said.

'I know,' the veteran actor replied coldly.

Oh, he's not in a good mood, Farrokh thought; it would be unwise to tell him the upsetting news now. The doctor doubted that Dhar's mood would *ever* be good enough to make him magnanimous upon receiving such news – and who could blame him? An overwhelming sense of unfairness lay at the heart of it, for Dhar was an identical twin who'd been separated from his brother at birth. Although Dhar had been told the story of his birth, Dhar's twin knew nothing of the story; Dhar's twin didn't even know he was a twin. And now Dhar's twin was coming to Bombay.

Dr Daruwalla had always believed that nothing good could come from such deception. Although Dhar had accepted the willful arbitrariness of the situation, a certain aloofness had been the cost; he was a man who, as far as Farrokh knew, withheld affection and resolutely withstood any display of affection from others. Who could blame him? the doctor thought. Dhar had accepted the existence of a mother and father and identical twin brother he'd never seen; Dhar had abided by that tiresome adage, which is still popularly evoked – to let sleeping dogs lie. But now: this most upsetting news was surely in that category of another tiresome adage which is still popularly evoked – this was the last straw.

In Dr Daruwalla's opinion, Dhar's mother had always been too selfish for motherhood; and 40 years after the accident of conception, the woman was demonstrating her selfishness again. That she'd arbitrarily decided to take one twin and abandon the other was sufficient selfishness for a normal lifetime; that she'd chosen to protect herself from her husband's potentially harsh opinion of her by keeping from him the fact that there'd *ever been* a twin was selfishness of a heightened, even of a monstrous, kind; and that she'd so sheltered the twin whom she'd kept from any knowledge of his identical brother was yet again as selfish as it was deeply insensitive to the feelings of the twin she'd left behind . . . the twin who knew everything.

Well, the doctor thought, Dhar knew everything except that his twin was coming to Bombay and that his mother had begged Dr Daruwalla to be sure that the twins didn't meet!

In such circumstances Dr Daruwalla felt briefly grateful for the distraction of old Mr Lal's apparent heart attack. Except when eating, Farrokh embraced procrastination as one greets an unexpected virtue. The belch of exhaust from the head gardener's truck blew a wave of flower petals from the wrecked bougainvillea over Dr Daruwalla's feet; he stared in surprise at his light-brown toes in his dark-brown sandals, which were almost buried in the vivid pink petals.

That was when the head mali, who'd left the truck running, sidled over to the ninth green and stood smirking beside Dr Daruwalla. The mali was clearly more excited by the sight of Inspector Dhar in action than he appeared to be disturbed by the death of poor Mr Lal. With a nod toward the scene unfolding in the bougainvillea, the gardener whispered to Farrokh, 'It looks like a movie!' This observation quickly returned Dr Daruwalla to the crisis at hand, namely the impossibility of shielding Dhar's twin from the existence of his famous brother, who, even in a city of movie stars, was indubitably the most recognizable star in Bombay.

Even if the famous actor agreed to keep himself in hiding, his identical twin brother would constantly be mistaken for Inspector Dhar. Dr Daruwalla admired the mental toughness of the Jesuits, but the twin – who was what the Jesuits call a scholastic (in training to be a priest) – would have to be more than mentally tough in order to endure a recurring mistaken identity of this magnitude. And from what Farrokh had been told of Dhar's twin, self-confidence was not high on the man's listed features. After all, who is almost 40 and only 'in training' to be a priest? the doctor wondered. Given Bombay's feelings for Dhar, Dhar's Jesuit twin might be killed! Despite his conversion to Christianity, Dr Daruwalla had little faith in the powers of a presumably naïve American missionary to survive – or even comprehend – the depth of resentment that Bombay harbored for Inspector Dhar.

For example, it was common in Bombay to deface all the advertisements for all the Inspector Dhar movies. Only on the higher-placed hoardings – those larger-than-life billboards that were everywhere in the city – was the giant likeness of Inspector Dhar's cruel, handsome face spared the abundant filth that was flung at it from street level. But even above human reach, the familiar face of the detested antihero couldn't escape creative defilement from Bombay's most expressive birds. The crows and the fork-tailed kites appeared to be drawn, as to a target, to the dark, piercing eyes – and to that sneer which the famous actor had perfected. All over town, Dhar's movie-poster face was spotted with bird shit. But even his many detractors admitted that Inspector Dhar achieved a kind of perfection with his sneer. It was the look of a lover who was leaving you, while thoroughly relishing your misery. All of Bombay felt the sting of it.

The rest of the world, even most of the rest of India, didn't suffer the sneer with which Inspector Dhar constantly looked down upon Bombay. The box-office success of the Inspector Dhar movies was inexplicably limited to Maharashtra and stood in violent contradiction to how unanimously Dhar himself was loathed; not only the character, but also the actor who brought him to life, was one of those luminaries in popular culture whom the public loves to hate. As for the actor who took responsibility for the role, he appeared to so enjoy the passionate hostility he inspired that he undertook no other roles; he used no other name – he had *become* Inspector Dhar. It was even the name on his passport.

It was the name on his *Indian* passport, which was a fake. India doesn't permit dual citizenship. Dr Daruwalla knew that Dhar had a Swiss passport, which was genuine; he was a Swiss citizen. In truth, the crafty actor had a Swiss *life*, for which he would always be grateful to Farrokh. The success of the Inspector Dhar movies was based, at least in part, on how closely Dhar had guarded his privacy, and how well hidden he'd kept his past. No amount of public scrutiny, which was considerable, could unearth more biographical information on the mystery man than he permitted – and, like his movies, Dhar's autobiography was highly far-fetched and contrived, wholly lacking in credible detail. That Inspector Dhar had invented himself, and that he appeared to have got away with his preposterous and unexaminable fiction, was surely a contributing reason for the virulence with which he was despised.

But the fury of the film press only fed Dhar's stardom. Since he refused to give these gossip journalists the facts, they wrote completely fabricated stories about him; Dhar being Dhar, this suited him perfectly – lies merely served to heighten his mystery and the general hysteria he inspired. Inspector Dhar movies were so popular, Dhar must have had fans, probably a multitude of admirers; but the film audience swore that they despised him. Dhar's indifference to his audience was also a reason to hate him. The actor himself suggested that even his fans were largely motivated to watch his films because they longed to see him fail; their faithful attendance, even if they hoped to witness a flop, assured Dhar of one hit after another. In the Bombay cinema, demigods were common; hero worship was the norm. What was uncommon was that Inspector Dhar was loathed but that he was nonetheless a star.

As for twins separated at birth, the irony was that this is an extremely popular theme with Hindi screenwriters. Such a separation frequently happens at the hospital – or during a storm, or in a railway accident. Typically, one twin takes a virtuous path while the other wallows in evil. Usually, there is some key that links them – maybe a torn two-rupee note (each twin keeps a half). And often, at the moment they are about to kill each other, the telltale half of the two-rupee note flutters out from one twin's pocket. Thus reunited, the twins vent their always-justifiable anger on a *real* villain, an inconceivable scoundrel (conveniently introduced to the audience at an earlier stage in the preposterous story).

How Bombay hated Inspector Dhar! But Dhar was a *real* twin, *truly* separated at birth, and Dhar's actual story was more unbelievable than any story concocted in the imagination of a Hindi screenwriter. Moreover, almost no one in Bombay, or in all of Maharashtra, knew Dhar's true story.

The Doctor as Closet Screenwriter

On the ninth green, with the pink petals of the bougainvillea caressing his feet, Dr Daruwalla could detect the hatred that the moronic head mali felt for Inspector Dhar. The lout still lurked at Farrokh's side, clearly relishing the irony that Dhar, who only pretended to be a police inspector, found himself playing the role in close proximity to an actual corpse. Dr Daruwalla then remembered his own first response to the awareness that poor Mr Lal had fallen prey to vultures; he recalled how he'd relished the irony, too! What had he whispered to Dhar? 'This is *your* line of work, Inspector.' Farrokh was mortified that he'd said this.

If Dr Daruwalla felt vaguely guilty that he knew very little about either his native or his adopted country, and if his self-confidence was a mild casualty of his general out-of-itness in both Bombay and Toronto, the doctor was *more* clearly and acutely agonized by anything in himself that identified him with the lowly

masses – the poor slob on the street, the mere com-
moner: in short, his fellow man. If it embarrassed him
to be a passive resident of both Canada and India,
which was a passivity born of insufficient knowledge
and experience, it shamed him hugely to catch himself
thinking like anyone else. He may have been alienated
but he was also a snob. And here, in the presence of
death itself, Dr Daruwalla was humiliated by his apparent lack of originality – namely, he discovered he
was on the same wavelength as an entirely stupid and
disagreeable gardener.

The doctor was so ashamed that he briefly turned his
attention to Mr Lal's grief-stricken golfing partner, Mr
Bannerjee, who'd approached no closer than a spot
within reach of the number-nine flag, which hung
limply from the slender pole stuck in the cup.

Then Dhar spoke quite suddenly, and with more
curiosity than surprise. 'There's quite a lot of blood by
one ear,' he said.

'I suppose the vultures were pecking at him for some
time,' Dr Daruwalla replied. He wouldn't venture any
nearer himself – after all, he was an orthopedist, not a
medical examiner.

'But it doesn't look like that,' said Inspector Dhar.

'Oh, stop playing the part of a policeman!' Farrokh
said impatiently.

Dhar gave him a stern, reproachful look, which the
doctor believed he absolutely deserved. He sheepishly
scuffed his feet in the flowers, but several bright petals
of the bougainvillea were caught between his toes. He
was embarrassed by the visible cruelty on the head
mali's eager face; he felt ashamed of himself for not
attending to the living, for quite clearly Mr Bannerjee
was suffering all alone – there was nothing the doctor
could do for Mr Lal. To poor Mr Bannerjee, Dr
Daruwalla must have seemed indifferent to the body!
And of the upsetting news that he couldn't yet bring
himself to impart to his dear younger friend, Farrokh
felt afraid.

Oh, the injustice that such unwelcome news should be *my* burden! Dr Daruwalla thought – momentarily forgetting the greater unfairness to Dhar. For hadn't the poor actor already contended with quite enough? Dhar had not only kept his sanity, which nothing less than the fierce maintenance of his privacy could ensure; he'd honored Dr Daruwalla's privacy, too, for Dhar knew that the doctor had written the screenplays for all the Inspector Dhar movies – Dhar knew that Farrokh had created the very character whom Dhar was now condemned to be.

It was supposed to be a gift, Dr Daruwalla remembered; he'd so loved the young man, as he would his own son – he'd expressly written the part *just for him.* Now, to avoid the reproachful look that Dhar gave him, Farrokh knelt down and picked the petals of bougainvillea from between his toes.

Oh, dear boy, what have I gotten you into? Dr Daruwalla thought. Although Dhar was almost 40, he was still a boy to Dr Daruwalla. The doctor had not only invented the character of the controversial police inspector, he'd not only created the movies that inspired madness throughout Maharashtra; he'd also fabricated the absurd autobiography that the famous actor attempted to pass off to the public as the story of his life. Quite understandably, the public didn't buy it. Farrokh knew that the public wouldn't have bought Dhar's true story, either.

Inspector Dhar's fictional autobiography manifested a fondness for shock value and sentiment that was remindful of his films. He claimed to have been born out of wedlock; he said his mother was an American – currently a has-been Hollywood movie star – and his father was an actual Bombay police inspector, long since retired. Forty years ago (Inspector Dhar was 39), the Hollywood mother had been shooting a film in Bombay. The police inspector responsible for the star's security had fallen in love with her; their trysting place had been the Taj Mahal Hotel. When the movie star knew she was pregnant, she struck a deal with the inspector.

At the time Dhar was born, the lifetime support of an Indian police inspector seemed no more prohibitive an expense to the Hollywood star than her habit of adding coconut oil to her bath, or so the story went. A baby, especially out of wedlock, and with an Indian father, would have compromised her career. According to Dhar, his mother had paid the police inspector to take full responsibility for the child. Enough money was involved so that the inspector could retire; he clearly passed on his intimate knowledge of police business, including the bribes, to his son. In his movies, Inspector Dhar was always above being bribed. All the *real* police inspectors in Bombay said that, if they knew who Dhar's father was, they would kill him. All the real policemen made it clear that they would enjoy killing Inspector Dhar, too.

To Dr Daruwalla's shame, it was a story full of holes, beginning with the unknown movie. More movies are made in Bombay than in Hollywood. But in 1949, no American films were made in Maharashtra – at least none that were ever released. And, suspiciously, there were no records of the policemen assigned to foreign film sets for security, although copious records exist in other years, suggesting that the accounts for 1949 were liberated from the files, doubtless by means of a bribe. But why? As for the so-called has-been Hollywood star, if she was an American in Bombay making a movie, she would have been *considered* a Hollywood star – even if she was an unknown actress, and a terrible actress, and even if the movie had never been released.

Inspector Dhar had claimed, at best, indifference regarding her identity. It was said that Dhar had never been to the United States. Although his English was reported to be perfect, even accentless, he said that he preferred to speak Hindi and that he dated only Indian women.

Dhar had confessed, at worst, a mild contempt for his mother, whoever she was. And he professed a fierce and abiding loyalty to his father, which was marked by Dhar's resolute vow to keep his father's identity secret. It was rumored that they met only in Europe!

It must be said, in Dr Daruwalla's defense, that the improbable nature of his fiction was at least based on reality. The fault rested with the unexplained gaps in the story. Inspector Dhar made his first movie in his early twenties, but where was he as a child? In Bombay, such a handsome man wouldn't have gone unnoticed as a boy, especially as a teenager; furthermore, his skin was simply too fair – only in Europe or in North America would he have been called dark-skinned. He had such dark-brown hair that it was almost black, and such charcoal-gray eyes that they were almost black, too; but if he actually had an Indian father, there wasn't a discernible trace of even a fair-skinned Indian in the son.

Everyone said that possibly the mother was a blue-eyed blonde, and all that the police inspector could contribute to the child was a racially neutralizing effect and a fervor for homicide cases. Nevertheless, all of Bombay complained that the box-office star of its Hindi movie madness *looked* to all the world like a 100 percent North American or European. There was no credible explanation for his all-white appearance, which fueled the rumor that Dhar was the child of Farrokh's brother, who'd married an Austrian; and since it was well known that Farrokh was married to this European's sister, it was also rumored that Dhar was the doctor's child.

The doctor expressed boredom for the notion, in spite of the fact that there were many living Duckworthians who could remember Dr Daruwalla's father in the company of an ephemeral, fair-skinned boy who was only an occasional summer visitor. And this suspiciously all-white boy was reputed to be the senior

Daruwalla's grandson! But the best way to answer these charges, Farrokh knew, was not to answer them beyond the bluntest denial.

It's well known that many Indians think fair skin is beautiful; in addition, Dhar was ruggedly handsome. However, it was considered perverse of Inspector Dhar that he refused to speak English in public, or spoke it with an obviously exaggerated Hindi accent. It was rumored that he spoke accentless English in private, but how would anyone know? Inspector Dhar granted only a limited number of interviews, which were restricted to questions regarding his 'art'; he insisted that his personal life was a forbidden topic. (Dhar's 'personal life' was the only topic of possible interest to anyone.) When cornered by the film press at a nightclub, at a restaurant, at a photo session in connection with the release of a new Inspector Dhar movie, the actor would apply his famous sneer. It didn't matter what question he was asked; either he answered facetiously or, regardless of the question, he would say in Hindi, or in English with his phony accent, 'I have never been to the United States. I have no interest in my mother. If I have babies, they will be Indian babies. They are the most clever.'

And Dhar could return and outlast anyone's stare; he could also manipulate the eye of any camera. Alarmingly, he possessed an increasingly bulky strength. Until he was in his mid-thirties, his muscles had been well defined, his stomach flat. Whether it was middle age, or whether Dhar had yielded to the usual bodily measurements for success among Bombay's matinee idols – or whether it was his love of weight lifting in tandem wih his professed capacity for beer – the actor's stoutness threatened to overtake his reputation as a tough guy. (In Bombay, he was perceived as a well-fed tough guy.) His critics liked to call him Beer Belly, but not to his face; after all, Dhar wasn't in bad shape for a guy who was almost 40.

As for Dr Daruwalla's screenplays, they deviated

from the usual masala mixture of the Hindi cinema. Farrokh's scripts were both corny and tawdry, but the vulgarity was decidedly Western – the hero's own nastiness was extolled as a virtue (Dhar was routinely nastier than most villains) – and the peculiar sentimentality bordered on undergraduate existentialism (Dhar was beyond loneliness in that he appeared to enjoy being alienated from everyone). There were token gestures to the Hindi cinema, which Dr Daruwalla viewed with the mocking irony of an outsider: gods frequently descended from the heavens (usually to provide Inspector Dhar with inside information), and all the villains were demonic (if ineffectual). Villainy, in general, was represented by criminals and the majority of the police force; sexual conquest was reserved for Inspector Dhar, whose heroism operated both within and above the law. As for the women who provided the sexual conquests, Dhar remained largely indifferent to them, which was suspiciously European.

There was music of the standard Hindi combination: choruses of girls oohing and aahing to the clamor of guitars, tablas, violins and vinas. And Inspector Dhar himself, despite his ingrained cynicism, would occasionally lip-sync a song. Although he lip-synced well, the lyrics are not worth repeating – he would snarl such poetry as, 'Baby, I guarantee it, you're gonna find me gratifying!' Such songs, in the Hindi cinema, are in Hindi, but this was another instance of how the Inspector Dhar films were deliberately scripted against the grain. Dhar's songs were in English, with his deplorable Hindi accent; even his theme song, which was sung by an all-girl chorus and repeated at least twice in every Inspector Dhar movie, was in English. It, too, was loathed; it was also a hit. Although he'd written it, it made Dr Daruwalla cringe to hear it.

> So you say Inspector Dhar is
> a mere mortal –

so you say, so you say!
He looks like a god to us!

So you say this is
a little rain shower –
so you say, so you say!
It looks like the monsoon to us!

If Dhar was a good lip-syncer, he also demonstrated no enthusiasm for the much-maligned art. One critic had dubbed him 'Lazy Lips.' Another critic complained that nothing energized Dhar – he lacked enthusiasm for everything. As an actor, Dhar had mass appeal – possibly because he seemed constantly depressed, as if sordidness were a magnet to him, and his eventual triumph over evil were a perpetual curse. Therefore, a certain wistfulness was ascribed to every victim whom Inspector Dhar sought to rescue or avenge; a graphic violence attended Dhar's punishment of each and every evildoer.

As for sex, satire prevailed. In place of lovemaking, old newsreel footage of a rocking train would be substituted; ejaculation was characterized by listless waves breaking on shore. Furthermore, and in compliance with the rules of censorship in India, nudity, which was *not* permitted, was replaced by wetness; there was much fondling (fully clothed) in the rain, as if Inspector Dhar solved crimes only during the monsoon season. The occasional nipple could be glimpsed, or at least imagined, under a fully soaked sari; this was more titillating than erotic.

Social relevance and ideology were similarly muted, if not altogether absent. (Both in Toronto *and* in Bombay, these latter instincts were similarly undeveloped in Dr Daruwalla.) Beyond the commonplace observation that the police were thoroughly corrupted by a system based on bribery, there was little preaching. Scenes of violent but maudlin death, followed by scenes of tearful mourning, were more important than messages intended to inspire a national conscience.

The character of Inspector Dhar was brutally vindictive; he was also utterly incorruptible – except
sexually. Women were easily and simplistically identified as good or bad; yet Dhar permitted himself the
greatest liberties with both – indeed, with all. Well,
with *almost* all. He wouldn't indulge a Western
woman, and in every Inspector Dhar movie there was
always at least one Western, ultra-white woman who
craved a sexual adventure with Inspector Dhar; that he
faithfully and cruelly spurned her was his signature,
his trademark, and the part of his films that made
Indian women and young girls adore him. Whether
this aspect of Dhar's character reflected his feelings for
his mother or gave fictional evidence of his stated
intentions to sire only Indian babies – well, who
knew? Who really knew anything about Inspector
Dhar? Hated by all men, loved by all women (who *said*
that they hated him).

Even the Indian women who'd dated him were
uniform in the zeal they demonstrated in protection of
his privacy. They would say, 'He's not at all like he is
in his movies.' (No examples were ever forthcoming.)
They would say, 'He's very old-fashioned, a real gentleman.' (No examples were ever asked for.) 'He's very
modest, really – and very quiet,' they would say.

Everyone could believe he was 'quiet'; there were
suspicions that he never spoke an unscripted line –
these were happy, mindless contradictions of the rumor
regarding his accentless English.. No one believed
anything, or else they believed everything they'd ever
heard. That he had two wives – one in Europe. That he
had a dozen children – none he would acknowledge,
all of them illegitimate. That he actually lived in Los
Angeles, in his vile mother's house!

In the face of all rumors, and in keeping with the
violent contrasts created by the extreme popularity of
his movies and the extreme animosity toward him that
was inspired by his sneer, Dhar himself remained

inscrutable. No small amount of sarcasm was detectable in his sneer; no other thick-set, middle-aged man could possibly have seemed so self-possessed.

Dhar endorsed only one charity; so totally and convincingly did he solicit the public's support of his personal crusade that he had achieved a philanthropic status as high as any among the several benefactors of Bombay. He made television commercials for the Hospital for Crippled Children. The advertisements were made at Dhar's own expense and they were devastatingly effective. (Dr Daruwalla was the author of these commercials as well.)

On the TV, Inspector Dhar faces the camera in medium close-up, wearing a loose-fitting white shirt – a collarless or mandarin-style kurta – and he holds his practiced sneer only as long as he imagines it takes to get the viewer's full attention. Then he says, 'You may love to hate me – I make a lot of money and I don't give any of it to anyone, except to these children.' There then follows a series of shots of Dhar among the crippled children at the orthopedic hospital: a deformed little girl crawls toward Inspector Dhar, who holds out his hands to her; Inspector Dhar is surrounded by staring children in wheelchairs; Inspector Dhar lifts a little boy from a swirling whirlpool bath and carries him to a clean white table, where two nurses assemble the child's leg braces for him – the boy's legs aren't as big around as his arms.

Regardless, Inspector Dhar was still hated; on occasion, he was even attacked. Local bullies wanted to see if he was as tough and practiced in the martial arts as the police inspector he portrayed; apparently, he was. He would respond to any and all verbal abuse with a queerly restrained version of his sneer. It made him appear mildly drunk. But if physically threatened, he wouldn't hesitate to retaliate in kind; once, assaulted by a man with a chair, Dhar struck back with a table. He was reputed to be as dangerous as his screen persona. He'd occasionally broken other people's bones; perhaps from his understanding of orthopedics, he'd caused serious injuries to the joints of his assailants. He was capable of real damage. But Dhar didn't pick fights, he simply won them.

His trashy films were hastily made, his publicity appearances minimal; the rumor was, he spent next to no time in Bombay. His chauffeur was an unfriendly dwarf, a former circus clown whom the film-gossip press had confidently labeled a thug. (Vinod was proud of this allegation.) And except for the plentiful number of Indian women who'd dated him, Dhar wasn't known to have any friends. His most public acquaintance – with an infrequent visitor to Bombay, an Honorary Consultant Surgeon at the Hospital for Crippled Children who was the hospital's usual spokesman for its foreign fund-raising efforts – was accepted as a longstanding relationship that had withstood invasions from the media. Dr Daruwalla – a distinguished Canadian physician and family man, and a son of the former chief of staff of Bombay's Hospital for Crippled Children (the late Dr Lowji Daruwalla) – was witheringly brief to the press. When asked about his relationship to and with Inspector Dhar, Dr Daruwalla would say, 'I'm a doctor, not a gossip.' Besides, the younger and the elder man were seen together only at the Duckworth Club. The media weren't welcome there, and among the members of the club, eavesdropping (except by the old Parsi steward) was generally deplored.

There was, however, much speculation about how Inspector Dhar could conceivably have become a member of the Duckworth Club. Movie stars weren't welcome there, either. And given the 22-year waiting list and the fact that the actor became a member when he was only 26, Dhar must have applied for membership when he was four! Or someone had applied for him. Furthermore, it had *not* been sufficiently demonstrated to many Duckworthians that Inspector Dhar had distinguished himself in 'community leadership';

some members pointed to his efforts for the Hospital for Crippled Children, but others argued that Inspector Dhar's movies were destructive to all of Bombay. Quite understandably, there was no suppressing the rumors or the complaints that circulated through the old club on this subject.

Dr Daruwalla Is Stricken with Self-doubt

There was also no suppressing the exciting news about the dead golfer in the bougainvillea near the ninth green. True to his fictional character, Inspector Dhar himself had located the body. Doubtless the press would expect Dhar to solve the crime. It didn't appear there had been a crime, although there was talk among the Duckworthians that Mr Lal's excesses on the golf course were of a criminal nature, and surely his exertions in the wrecked bougainvillea hadn't served the old gentleman well. The vultures had spoiled a clear impression, but it seemed that Mr Lal had been the victim of his own chip shot. His lifelong opponent, Mr Bannerjee, told Dr Daruwalla that he felt as if he'd murdered his friend.

'He always fell apart at the ninth hole!' Mr Bannerjee exclaimed. 'I never should have teased him about it!'

Dr Daruwalla was thinking that he'd often teased Mr Lal along similar lines; it had been irresistible to tease Mr Lal in regard to the zeal with which he played a game for which he manifested minimal talent. But now that he appeared to have died at the game, Mr Lal's enthusiasm for golf seemed less funny than before.

Farrokh found himself sensing some faint analogy between his creation of Inspector Dhar and Mr Lal's golf game, and this unwanted connection came to him as the result of a sudden, unpleasant odor. It wasn't as strong an impression as the stench of a man defecating at close quarters, but instead the smell was at once more familiar and more removed – sun-rotted garbage, perhaps, or clogged drains. Farrokh thought of potted flowers and human urine.

Far-fetched or not, the nature of the comparison between Mr Lal's lethal golf habit and Dr Daruwalla's screenwriting was simply this: the Inspector Dhar movies were judged to be of no artistic merit whatsoever, but the labors that the doctor performed to write these screenplays were intense; the nature of Inspector Dhar's character was crude to most viewers, and outrageously offensive to many, but the doctor had created Dhar out of the purest love; and Farrokh's fragile self-esteem rested as much on his sense of himself as a closet writer as it did on his established reputation as a surgeon, even if he was only a *screen*writer and, worse, even though he was perceived to be such a shameless hack – such a whore for the money – that he wouldn't even lend his name to his creations. Understandably, since the actor who played Inspector Dhar had himself become (in the public eye) the very character he portrayed, the authorship of the screenplays was ascribed to Dhar. What gave Farrokh so much pleasure was the actual writing of the screenplays themselves; yet, despite his own enjoyment of the craft, the results were ridiculed and hated.

Recently, in the light of certain death threats that Inspector Dhar had received, Dr Daruwalla had even considered retiring; the doctor had meant to sound out the actor in regard to this notion. If I stop, Farrokh wondered, what will Dhar do? If I stop, what will *I* do? he'd also wondered, for he'd long suspected that Dhar wouldn't be opposed to the idea of getting out of the business of being Dhar – especially now. To suffer the verbal abuse of *The Times of India* was one thing, death threats were something altogether different.

And now this unlikely association to Mr Lal's golf game, this unveiled reek of sun-rotted garbage, this ancient smell from a clogged drain – or had someone been peeing in the bougainvillea? These thoughts were most unwelcome. Dr Daruwalla suddenly saw himself as the poor, doomed Mr Lal; he thought he was as bad but as compulsive a writer as Mr Lal had been a golfer. For example, he'd not only written another screenplay; they'd already finished the final cut of the picture. Coincidentally, the new movie would be released shortly before or after the arrival in Bombay of Dhar's twin. Dhar himself was just hanging around – he was under contract for a very limited number of interviews and photo opportunities to publicize the new release. (This forced intimacy with the film press could never be limited enough to suit Dhar.) Also, there was every reason to believe that the new film might make as much trouble as the last. And so the time to stop is *now*, thought Dr Daruwalla, before I begin another one!

But how could he stop? It was something he loved. And how could he hope to improve? Farrokh was doing the best that he could; like poor Mr Lal, he was hopelessly returning to the ninth green. Each time, the flowers would fly but the golf ball would remain more or less unresponsive; each time, he would be knee-deep in the blighted bougainvillea, slashing wildly at the little white ball. Then, one day, the vultures would be overhead and descending.

There was just one choice: either hit the ball and *not* the flowers, or stop the game. Dr Daruwalla understood this, yet he couldn't decide – no more than he could bring himself to tell Inspector Dhar the upsetting news. After all, the doctor thought, how can I hope to be any better than my proven abilities? And how can I stop it, when 'it' is merely what I do?

It soothed him to think of the circus. Like a child who's proud to recite the names of Santa's reindeer or the Seven Dwarfs, Farrokh tested himself by remembering the names of the Great Royal's lions: Ram, Raja, Wazir, Mother, Diamond, Shanker, Crown, Max, Hondo, Highness, Lillie Mol, Leo and Tex. And then there were the cubs: Sita, Gita, Julie, Devi, Bheem and

Lucy. The lions were most dangerous between their first and second feedings of meat. The meat made their paws slippery; while they paced in their cages, in expectation of their second serving, they often slipped and fell down, or they slid sideways into the bars. After their second feeding, they calmed down and licked the grease off their paws. With lions, you could count on certain things. They were always themselves. Lions didn't try to be what they couldn't be, the way Dr Daruwalla kept trying to be a writer – the way I keep trying to be an Indian! he thought.

And in 15 years, he'd not found a genetic marker for achondroplastic dwarfism, nor had anyone encouraged him to look. But he kept trying. The doctor's dwarf-blood project wasn't dead; he wouldn't let it die – not yet.

Because an Elephant Stepped on a Seesaw

By the time Dr Daruwalla was in his late fifties, the exuberant details of the doctor's conversion to Christianity were entirely absent from his conversation; it was as if he were slowly becoming converted. But 15 years ago – as the doctor drove to the circus grounds at Cross Maidan to assess what damage had been done to the dwarf – Farrokh's faith was still new enough that he'd already imparted the miraculous particulars of his belief to Vinod. If the dwarf was truly dying, the doctor was at least slightly comforted by his memory of their religious discussion – for Vinod was a deeply religious man. In the coming years, Farrokh's faith would comfort him less deeply, and he would one day flee from *any* religious discourse with Vinod. Over time, the dwarf would strike the doctor as a giant zealot.

But while the doctor was en route to discover whatever disaster had befallen the dwarf at the Great

Blue Nile, he found it heartening to dwell on the dwarf's expressed excitement over the parallels between Vinod's version of Hinduism and Dr Daruwalla's Christianity.

'We are having a kind of Trinity, too!' the dwarf had exclaimed.

'Brahma, Shiva, Vishnu – is that what you mean?' the doctor asked.

'All creation is being in the hands of three gods,' Vinod said. 'First is Brahma, the God of Creation – there is only one temple in all of India to him! Second is Vishnu, the God of Preservation or Existence. And third is Shiva, the God of Change.'

'Change?' Farrokh asked. 'I thought Shiva was the Destroyer – the God of Destruction.'

'Why is everyone saying this?' the dwarf exclaimed. 'All creation is being cyclic – there is no finality. I am liking it better to think of Shiva as the God of Change. Sometimes death is change, too.'

'I see,' Dr Daruwalla replied. 'That's a positive way of looking at it.'

'This is our Trinity,' the dwarf went on. 'Creation, Preservation, Change.'

'I guess I don't understand the *female* forms,' Farrokh boldly admitted.

'The power of the gods is being represented by the females,' Vinod explained. 'Durga is the female form of Shiva – she is the Goddess of Death and Destruction.'

'But you just said Shiva was the God of Change,' the doctor interjected.

'His *female* form, Durga, is the Goddess of Death and Destruction,' the dwarf repeated.

'I see,' Dr Daruwalla responded; it seemed best to say so.

'Durga is looking after me – I am praying to her,' Vinod added.

'The Goddess of Death and Destruction is looking after you?' Farrokh inquired.

73

'She is always protecting me,' the dwarf insisted.

'I see,' Dr Daruwalla said; he guessed that being protected by the Goddess of Death and Destruction had a kind of karmic ring to it.

Finally, Farrokh found Vinod lying in the dirt under the bleachers; it appeared that the dwarf had fallen through the wooden planks, from perhaps the fourth or fifth row of seats. The roustabouts had cleared the crowd from only a small section of the audience area, below which Vinod lay, unmoving. But how and why the dwarf had landed there wasn't immediately clear. Was there a clown act that required audience participation?

On the far side of the ring, a desultory gathering of dwarf clowns was bravely trying to keep the crowd's attention; it was the familiar Farting Clown act – through a hole in the seat of his colorful pants, one dwarf kept 'farting' talcum powder on the other dwarfs. They didn't appear to be weakened or otherwise the worse for giving the doctor a Vacutainer of their blood, which Vinod had shamelessly entreated them to do; just as shamelessly, Dr Daruwalla had lied to them – exactly as Vinod had advised him. The dwarfs' blood would be used to give strength to a dying dwarf; Vinod had even compounded this fiction by telling his fellow clowns that he'd already been bled to the doctor's satisfaction.

This time, mercifully, the ringmaster's voice on the loudspeaker had not heralded the doctor's arrival. Since Vinod lay under the bleacher seats, most of the crowd couldn't see him. Farrokh knelt in the dirt, which was littered with the audience's leavings: greasy paper cones, soft-drink bottles, peanut shells and discarded betel-nut pieces. On the underside of the bleachers, Farrokh could see the white stripes of lime paste that streaked the wooden planks; the paan users had wiped their fingers under their seats.

'I think I am not ending up here,' Vinod whispered to the doctor. 'I think I am not dying – just changing.'

'Try not to move,' Dr Daruwalla replied. 'Just tell me where you're hurting.'

'I am not moving. I am not hurting,' the dwarf answered. 'I am just not feeling my backside.'

Quite in character for a man of faith, the dwarf lay stoically suffering with his trident hands crossed upon his chest. He complained later that no one had dared to approach him, except a vendor – a channa-walla with his tray of nuts around his neck. Vinod had told the vendor about the numbness in his backside; hence the ringmaster assumed that the dwarf had broken his neck or his back. Vinod thought that someone should at least have talked to him or listened to the story of his life; someone should have held his head or offered him water until the stretcher bearers in their dirty-white dhotis came for him.

'This is Shiva – this is being his business,' the dwarf told Dr Daruwalla. 'This is change – not death, I think. If Durga is doing this, then okay – I am dying. But I think I am merely changing.'

'Let's hope so,' Dr Daruwalla replied; he made Vinod grip his fingers. Then the doctor touched the backs of Vinod's legs.

'I am feeling you only a little,' the dwarf responded.

'I'm touching you only a little,' Farrokh explained.

'This is meaning I am not dying,' said the dwarf. 'This is merely the gods advising me.'

'What are they telling you?' the doctor asked.

'They are saying I am ready to leave the circus,' Vinod answered. 'At least *this* circus.'

Slowly, the faces from the Great Blue Nile gathered around them. The ringmaster, the boneless girls and the plastic ladies – even the lion tamer, who toyed with his whip. But the doctor wouldn't allow the stretcher bearers to move the dwarf until someone explained how Vinod had been injured. Vinod believed that only the other dwarfs could describe the accident properly; for this reason, the Farting Clown act had to be halted. By now the act had deteriorated in the usual fashion: the offending dwarf was farting talcum powder into the front-row seats. Since the front row of the audience was chiefly populated with children, the farting was considered no great offense. However, the crowd was already dispersing; the Farting Clown act was never funny for very long. The Great Blue Nile had exhausted its entire repertoire in a half-successful effort to keep the audience seated until the doctor arrived.

Now the gathering clowns confessed to the doctor that Vinod had been injured in other acts, before. Once he'd fallen off a horse; once he'd been chased and bitten by a chimpanzee. Once, when the Blue Nile had a female bear, the bear had butted Vinod into a bucket of diluted shaving lather; this was a scripted part of the act, but the bear had butted Vinod too hard – he'd had his breath knocked out, and (as a consequence) the dwarf had then inhaled and swallowed the soapy water. Vinod's fellow clowns had also seen him hurt in the Cricket-Playing Elephants act. Apparently, to the degree that Dr Daruwalla could understand the stunt at all, one elephant was the bowler and a second elephant was the batsman; it held and swung the bat with its trunk. Vinod was the cricket ball. It *hurt* to be bowled by one elephant and batted by another, even though the bat was made of rubber.

As Farrokh would learn later, the Great Royal Circus never put *their* dwarf clowns at such risk, but this was the Great Blue Nile. The terrible teeterboard accident, which was responsible for Vinod's pained position under the bleacher seats, was simply another elephant act of ill repute. The acts in an Indian circus are called 'items'; in terms of accuracy, the Elephant on a Teeterboard item wasn't as precise as the Cricket-Playing Elephants but it was a favorite with children, who were more familiar with a seesaw or a teeter-totter than with cricket.

In the Elephant on a Teeterboard item, Vinod acted the part of a crabby clown, a spoilsport who wouldn't

76

play with his fellow dwarfs on the seesaw. Whenever they balanced the teeter-totter, Vinod jumped on one end and knocked them all off. Then he sat on the teeterboard with his back to them. One by one, they crept onto the other end of the board, until Vinod was up in the air; whereupon, he turned around and slid down the board into the other dwarfs, knocking them all off again. It was thus established for the audience that Vinod was guilty of antisocial behavior. His fellow dwarfs left him sitting on one end of the seesaw, with his back to them, while they fetched an elephant.

The only part of this act that is of possible interest to grownups is the demonstration that elephants can count – at least as high as three. The dwarfs tried to coax the elephant to stamp on the raised end of the teeterboard while Vinod was sitting on the other end, but the elephant was taught to delay stamping on the teeterboard until the third time. The first two times that the elephant raised its huge foot above the teeterboard, it *didn't* stamp on the board; twice, at the last second, it flapped its ears and turned away. The idea was planted with the audience that the elephant wouldn't really do it. The third time, when the elephant stamped down on the seesaw and Vinod was propelled into the air, the crowd was properly surprised.

Vinod was supposed to be launched upward into the rolled nets that were lowered only for the trapeze performance. He would cling to the underside of this netting like a bat, screaming at his fellow dwarfs to get him down. Naturally, they couldn't reach him without the help of the elephant, of which Vinod was demonstrably afraid. Typical circus slapstick; yet it was important that the teeterboard was aimed *exactly* at the rolled-up safety nets. That fateful night his life changed, Vinod realized (as he sat on the seesaw) that the teeterboard was pointed into the audience.

This could be blamed on the Kingfisher lager; such big bottles of beer had an unsteadying effect on dwarfs. Dr Daruwalla would never again bribe dwarfs with beer. Sadly, the seesaw was pointed in the wrong direction *and* Vinod had neglected to count the number of times that the elephant had raised its foot, which the dwarf had previously managed to do without seeing the elephant; Vinod always counted the times the elephant raised its foot by the gasps of anticipation in the audience. Of course, Vinod could have turned his head and looked at the elephant to see where the beast's great foot was. But Vinod held himself accountable for certain standards: if he'd turned to look at the elephant, it would have spoiled the act completely.

As it happened, Vinod was flung into the fourth row of seats. He remembered hoping that he wouldn't land on any children, but he needn't have worried; the audience scattered before he arrived. He struck the empty wooden bleachers and fell through the space between the planks.

Created by spontaneous mutation, an achondroplastic dwarf lives in pain; his knees ache, his elbows ache – not to mention that they won't extend. His ankles ache and his back aches, too – not to mention the degenerative arthritis. Of course there are worse types of dwarfism: pseudoachondroplastic dwarfs suffer so-called windswept deformities – bowleg on one limb, knock-knee on the other. Dr Daruwalla had seen dwarfs who couldn't walk at all. Even so, given the pain that Vinod was accustomed to, the dwarf didn't mind that his backside was numb; it was possibly the best that the dwarf had felt in years – in spite of being catapulted 40 feet by an elephant and landing on his coccyx on a wooden plank.

Thus did the injured dwarf become Dr Daruwalla's patient. Vinod had suffered a slight fracture in the apex of his coccyx, and he'd bruised the tendon of his external sphincter muscle, which is attached to this apex; in short, he'd quite literally busted his ass. Vinod had also torn some of the sacrosciatic ligaments, which are attached to the narrow borders of the coccyx. The numbness of his backside, which soon abated – thence Vinod would return to the world of his routine aches and pains – was possibly the result of some pressure on one or more of the sacral nerves. His recovery would be complete, although slower than Deepa's; yet Vinod insisted he'd been permanently disabled. What he meant was he'd lost his nerve.

Future flight experiments with the clowns of the Great Blue Nile would have to be conducted without Vinod's participation – or so the dwarf claimed. If Shiva was the God of Change, and not merely the Destroyer, perhaps the change that Lord Shiva intended for Vinod was actually a career move. But the veteran clown would always be a dwarf, and Vinod struck Farrokh as lacking the qualifications for a job outside the circus.

Vinod and his wife were recovering from their respective surgeries when the Great Blue Nile completed its term of engagement in Bombay. While both Deepa and her dwarf husband were hospitalized, Dr Daruwalla and his wife took care of Shivaji; after all, someone had to look after the dwarf child – and the doctor still held himself accountable for the King-fisher. It had been some years since the Daruwallas had struggled to manage a two-year-old, and they'd never before tried to manage a *dwarf* two-year-old, but this period of convalescence proved fruitful for Vinod.

The dwarf was a compulsive list maker, and he enjoyed showing his lists to Dr Daruwalla. There was quite a long list of Vinod's acquired circus skills, and a sadly shorter list of the dwarf's other accomplishments. On the shorter list, Dr Daruwalla saw it written that the dwarf could drive a car. Farrokh felt certain that Vinod was lying; after all, hadn't Vinod proposed that very lie which the doctor had used to bleed the dwarfs of the Great Blue Nile?

'What sort of car can you drive, Vinod?' the doctor asked the recuperating dwarf. 'How can your feet reach the pedals?'

It was to another word on the short list that Vinod proudly pointed. The word was 'mechanics'; Farrokh had at first ignored it – he'd skipped straight to 'car driving.' Dr Daruwalla assumed that 'mechanics' meant fixing unicycles or other toys of the circus, but Vinod had dabbled in auto mechanics *and* in unicycles; the dwarf had actually designed and installed hand controls for a car. Naturally, this was inspired by a dwarf item for the Great Blue Nile: ten clowns climb out of one small car. But first a dwarf had to be able to drive the car; that dwarf had been Vinod. The hand controls had been complicated, Vinod confessed. ('Lots of experiments are failing,' Vinod said philosophically.) The driving, the dwarf said, had been relatively easy.

'You can drive a car,' Dr Daruwalla said, as if to himself.

'Both fast and slow!' Vinod exclaimed.

'The car must have an automatic transmission,' Farrokh reasoned.

'No clutching – just braking and speeding,' the dwarf explained.

'There are *two* hand controls?' the doctor inquired.

'Who is needing more than two?' the dwarf asked.

'So . . . when you slow down or speed up, you must have just *one* hand on the steering wheel,' Farrokh inferred.

'Who is needing both hands for steering?' Vinod replied.

'You can drive a car,' Dr Daruwalla repeated.

Somehow, this seemed harder to believe than the Elephant on a Teeterboard or the Cricket-Playing Elephants – for Farrokh could imagine no other life for Vinod. The doctor believed that the dwarf was doomed to be a clown for the Great Blue Nile forever.

'I am teaching Deepa to do car driving, too,' Vinod added.

'But Deepa doesn't need hand controls,' Farrokh observed.

The dwarf shrugged. 'At the Blue Nile, we are naturally driving the same car,' he explained.

Thus, it was there – in the dwarf's ward in the Hospital for Crippled Children – that a future hero of 'car driving' was first introduced to Dr Daruwalla. Farrokh simply couldn't imagine that, 15 years later, a veritable limousine legend would have been born in Bombay. Not that Vinod would immediately escape the circus; all legends take time. Not that Deepa, the dwarf's wife, would in the end entirely escape the circus. Not that Shivaji, the dwarf's son, would ever dream of escaping it. But all this was truly happening because Dr Farrokh Daruwalla wanted blood from dwarfs.

3. THE REAL POLICEMAN

Mrs Dogar Reminds Farrokh of Someone Else

For 15 years, Dr Daruwalla would indulge himself with his memory of Deepa in the safety net. Of course this is an exaggeration, of that kind which caused the doctor to often reflect on his surprise at Vinod becoming a veritable limousine legend in Bombay; in the heyday of the dwarf's success at car driving, Vinod could never be credited with chauffering a *limo*, much less owning a limousine company. At best, Vinod owned a half-dozen cars; none of them was a Mercedes – including the two that the dwarf drove, with hand controls.

What Vinod would briefly manage to achieve was a modest profit in the private-taxi business, or 'luxury taxis' as they're called in Bombay. Vinod's cars were never luxurious – nor could the dwarf have managed private ownership of these thoroughly secondhand vehicles without accepting a loan from Dr Daruwalla. If the dwarf was even fleetingly a legend, neither the number nor the quality of Vinod's automobiles was the reason – they were *not* limousines. The dwarf's legendary status owed its existence to Vinod's famous client, the aforementioned actor with the improbable name of Inspector Dhar. At most, Dhar lived part-time in Bombay.

And poor Vinod could never completely sever his ties to the circus. Shivaji, the dwarf's dwarf son, was now a teenager; as such, he suffered from strong and contrary opinions. Had Vinod continued to be an active clown in the Great Blue Nile, Shivaji would doubtless have rejected the circus; the contentious boy

82

would probably have chosen to drive a taxi in Bombay – purely out of hatred for the very idea of being a *comic* dwarf. But since his father had made such an effort to establish a taxi business, and since Vinod had struggled to free himself from the dangerous daily grind of the Great Blue Nile, Shivaji was determined to become a clown. Therefore, Deepa often traveled with her son; and while the Blue Nile was performing throughout Gujarat and Maharashtra, Vinod devoted himself to the car-driving business in Bombay.

For 15 years, the dwarf had been unable to teach his wife how to drive. Since her fall, Deepa had given up the trapeze, but the Blue Nile paid her to train the child contortionists; while Shivaji developed his skills as a clown, his mother put the plastic ladies through their boneless items. When the dwarf succumbed to missing his wife and son, he'd go back to the Blue Nile. There Vinod eschewed the riskier acts in the dwarf-clown repertoire, contenting himself with instructing the younger dwarfs, his own son among them. But whether clowns are shot off seesaws by elephants, or chased by chimps, or butted by bears, there's only so much for them to learn. Beyond the demanding drills, which require practice – how to dismount the collapsing unicycle, and so forth – only makeup, timing and falling can be taught. At the Great Blue Nile, it seemed to Vinod that there was mainly falling.

In his absence from Bombay, Vinod's taxi enterprise would suffer and the dwarf would feel compelled to return to the city. Since Dr Daruwalla was only periodically in India, the doctor couldn't always keep track of where Vinod was; as if trapped in a ceaseless clown item, the dwarf was constantly moving.

What was also constant was Farrokh's habit of letting his mind wander to that long-ago night when he had bashed his nose on Deepa's pubic bone. Not that this was the only circus image that the doctor's mind would wander to; those scratchy sequins on Deepa's tight singlet, not to mention the conflicting scents of

Deepa's earthy aroma – these were understandably the most vivid circus images in Farrokh's memory. And at no time did Dr Daruwalla daydream so vividly about the circus as he did when anything unpleasant was pending.

Currently, Farrokh found himself reflecting that, for 15 years, Vinod had steadfastly refused to give the doctor a single Vacutainer of blood. Dr Daruwalla had drawn the blood from almost every active dwarf clown, in almost every active circus in Gujarat and Maharashtra, but the doctor hadn't drawn a drop from Vinod. As angry as this fact made him, Farrokh preferred to reflect on it rather than to concern himself with the more pressing problem, which was suddenly at hand.

Dr Daruwalla was a coward. That Mr Lal had fallen on the golf course, without a net, was no reason not to tell Inspector Dhar the upsetting news. Quite simply, the doctor didn't dare tell Dhar.

It was characteristic of Dr Daruwalla to tell belabored jokes, especially when he'd made a disquieting self-discovery. Inspector Dhar was characteristically silent – 'characteristically,' depending on which rumors you believed. Dhar knew that Farrokh had been fond of Mr Lal, and that the doctor's strident sense of humor was most often engaged when he sought to distract himself from any unhappiness. At the Duckworth Club, Dhar spent most of lunch listening to Dr Daruwalla go on and on about this new offense to the Parsis: how the recent Parsi dead had been overlooked by the vultures attending to Mr Lal on the golf course. Farrokh found a forced humor in imagining the more fervent Zoroastrians who'd be up in arms about the interference caused to the vulture community by the dead golfer. Dr Daruwalla thought they should ask Mr Sethna if *he* was offended; throughout lunch the old steward had managed to look most offended, although the source of the particular offense appeared to be the second Mrs Dogar. It was clear that Mr Sethna disapproved of her, whatever her intentions.

She'd deliberately positioned herself at her table so that she could stare at Inspector Dhar, who never once returned her gaze. Dr Daruwalla assumed it was just another case of an immodest woman seeking Dhar's attention – in vain, the doctor knew. He wished he could prepare the second Mrs Dogar for how rejected she would soon feel from the actor's obliviousness to her. For a while, she'd even pushed her chair away from the table so that her fetching navel was beautifully framed by the bold colors of her sari; her navel was pointed at Dhar like a single and very determined eye. Although Mrs Dogar's advances appeared to go unnoticed by Inspector Dhar, Dr Daruwalla found it most difficult not to look at her.

In the doctor's view, her behavior was shameless for a married, middle-aged lady – Dr Daruwalla calculated that she was in her early fifties. Yet Farrokh found the second Mrs Dogar attractive, in a threatening kind of way. He couldn't locate exactly what it was that attracted him to the woman, whose arms were long and unflatteringly muscular, and whose lean, hard face was handsome and challenging in an almost masculine way. To be sure, her bosom was shapely (if not full) and her bottom was high and firm – especially for a woman her age – and there was no question that her long waist and aforementioned navel were enhancing contributions to the pleasurable impression she made in a sari. But she was too tall, her shoulders were too pronounced and her hands appeared absurdly large and restless; she picked up her silverware and toyed with it as if she were a bored child.

Furthermore, Farrokh had caught a glimpse of Mrs Dogar's feet – actually, just one of her feet, which was bare. She must have kicked her shoes off under her table, but all that Dr Daruwalla saw was a flash of her gnarled foot; a thin gold chain hung loosely around her surprisingly thick ankle and a wide gold ring gripped one of her clawlike toes.

Perhaps what attracted the doctor to Mrs Dogar was

how she reminded him of someone else, but he couldn't think of who it might be. A long-ago movie star, he suspected. Then, as a doctor whose patients were children, he realized that he might have known the new Mrs Dogar as a child; why this would make the woman attractive to him was yet another, exasperating unknown. Moreover, the second Mrs Dogar seemed not more than six or seven years younger than Dr Daruwalla; virtually, they'd been children together.

Dhar caught the doctor by surprise when he said, 'If you could see yourself looking at that woman, Farrokh, I think you'd be embarrassed.' When he was embarrassed, the doctor had an annoying habit of abruptly changing the subject.

'And you! You should have seen *yourself*!' Dr Daruwalla said to Inspector Dhar. 'You looked like a bloody police inspector – I mean, you looked like the real bloody thing!'

It irritated Dhar when Dr Daruwalla spoke such absurdly unnatural English; it wasn't even the English with a singsong Hindi lilt, which was also unnatural for Dr Daruwalla. This was worse; it was something wholly fake – the affected British flavor of that particularly Indian English, the inflections of which were common among young college graduates working as food-and-beverage consultants at the Taj, or as production managers for Britannia Biscuits. Dhar knew that this unsuitable accent was Farrokh's self-consciousness talking – he was so out of it in Bombay.

Quietly, but in accentless English, Inspector Dhar spoke to his excited companion. 'Which rumor about me are we encouraging today? Should I shout at you in Hindi? Or is this a good day for English as a second language?'

Dhar's sardonic tone and expression hurt Dr Daruwalla, notwithstanding that these mannerisms were trademarks of the fictional character Dr Daruwalla had created and that all of Bombay had come to loathe. Although the secret screenwriter had grown morally uncertain of his creation, this doubt was not discernible in the unreserved fondness that the doctor felt for the younger man; in public or in private, it was Dr Daruwalla's love for Dhar that showed.

The taunting quality of Dhar's remarks, not to mention the sting of Dhar's delivery, wounded Dr Daruwalla; even so, he regarded the slightly spoiled handsomeness of the actor with great tenderness. Dhar allowed his sneer to soften into a smile. With an affection that alarmed the nearest and ever-observant waiter – the same poor fellow whose daily course had coincided with the shitting crow and with the troublesome tureen and ladle – the doctor reached out and clasped the younger man's hand.

In plain English, Dr Daruwalla whispered, 'I'm really just so sorry – I mean, I feel so sorry for you, my dear boy,' he said.

'Don't,' Inspector Dhar whispered back. His smile faded and his sneer returned; he freed his hand from the elder man's grip.

Tell him now! Dr Daruwalla told himself, but he didn't dare – he didn't know where to begin.

They were sitting quietly with their tea and some sweets when the *real* policeman approached their table. They'd already been interrogated by the duty officer from the Tardeo Police Station, an Inspector Somebody – not very impressive. The inspector had arrived with a team of subinspectors and constables in two Jeeps – hardly necessary for a golfing death, Dr Daruwalla had felt. The Tardeo inspector had been unctuous but condescending to Inspector Dhar and servile to Farrokh.

'I am hoping you are excusing me, Doctor,' the duty officer had begun; his English was a strain. 'I am being most sorry I am taking *your* time, saar,' the inspector added to Inspector Dhar. Dhar responded in Hindi.

'You are not examining the body, Doctor?' the policeman asked; he persisted with his English.

'Certainly not,' Dr Daruwalla replied.

87

'You are never touching the body, saar?' the duty officer asked the famous actor.

'I are never touching it,' Dhar answered in English – in a flawless imitation of the policeman's Hindi accent.

Upon departing, the duty officer's heavy brogues had scraped a little too loudly on the stone floor of the Duckworth Club's dining room; thus had the policeman's exit drawn Mr Sethna's predictable disapproval. Doubtless the old steward had also disapproved of the condition of the duty officer's uniform; his khaki shirt was soiled by the thali the inspector must have encountered for lunch – a generous portion of dhal was slopped on his breast pocket, and a brightly colored stain (the obvious orange-yellow of turmeric) lit up the messy policeman's drab collar.

But the second policeman, who now approached their table in the Ladies' Garden, was no mere inspector; this man was of a higher rank – and of a noticeably elevated neatness. At the very least, he looked like a deputy commissioner. From Farrokh's research – for the Inspector Dhar screenplays were scrupulously researched, if not aesthetically pleasing – the screenwriter was certain that they were about to be confronted by a deputy commissioner from Crime Branch Headquarters at Crawford Market.

'All this for *golf*?' whispered Inspector Dhar, but not so loudly that the approaching detective could hear him.

Not a Wise Choice of People to Offend

As the most recent Inspector Dhar movie had pointed out, the official salary of a Bombay police inspector is only 2,500 to 3,000 rupees a month – roughly 100 dollars. In order to secure a more lucrative posting, in an area of heavy crime, an inspector would need to bribe an administrative officer. For a payment in the vicinity of 75,000 to 200,000 rupees (but generally for less than 7,000 dollars), an inspector might secure a posting that would earn him from 300,000 to 400,000 rupees a year (usually not more than 15,000 dollars). One issue posed by the new Inspector Dhar movie concerned just *how* an inspector making only 3,000 rupees a month could get his hands on the 100,000 rupees that were necessary for the bribe. In the movie, an especially hypocritical and corrupt police inspector accomplishes this by doubling as a pimp and a landlord for a eunuch-transvestite brothel on Falkland Road.

In the pinched smile of the second policeman who approached Dr Daruwalla and Inspector Dhar at their table, there could be discerned the unanimous outrage of the Bombay police force. The prostitute community was no less offended; the prostitutes had greater cause for anger. The most recent movie, *Inspector Dhar and the Cage-Girl Killer*, seemed to be responsible for putting the lowliest of Bombay's prostitutes – the so-called cage girls – in particular peril. Because of the movie, about a serial killer who murders cage girls and draws an inappropriately mirthful elephant on their naked bellies, a *real* murderer appeared to have stolen the idea. Now *real* prostitutes were being killed and decorated in this cartoonish fashion; the actual murders were unsolved. In the red-light district, on Falkland Road and Grant Road – and throughout the multitude of brothels in the many lanes of Kamathipura – the hardworking whores had expressed a *real* desire to kill Inspector Dhar.

The feeling for vengeance toward Dhar was especially strong among the eunuch-transvestite prostitutes. In the movie, a eunuch-transvestite prostitute turns out to be the serial cartoonist and killer. This was offensive to eunuch-transvestites, for by no means were all of them prostitutes – nor were they ever known to be serial killers. They are an accepted third gender in India; they are called 'hijras' – an Urdu word of masculine gender meaning 'hermaphrodite.' But hijras are not born hermaphrodites; they are emasculated – hence

89

'eunuch' is the truer word for them. They are also a cult; devotees of the Mother Goddess Bahuchara Mata, they achieve their powers – either to bless or to curse – by being neither male nor female. Traditionally, hijras earn their living by begging; they also perform songs and dances at weddings and festivals – most of all, they give their blessings at births (of male infants, especially). And hijras dress as women – hence the term 'eunuch-transvestite' comes closest to what they are.

The mannerisms of hijras are ultra-feminine but coarse; they flirt outrageously, and they display themselves with sexually overt gestures – inappropriate for women in India. Beyond their castration and their female dress, they do little to otherwise feminize themselves; most hijras eschew the use of estrogens, and some of them pluck their facial hair so indifferently, it's not uncommon to see them with several days' growth of beard. Should hijras find themselves abused or harassed, or should they encounter those Indians who've been seduced by Western values and who therefore don't believe in the hijras' 'sacred' powers to bless and curse, hijras will be so bold as to lift their dresses and rudely expose their mutilated genitals.

Dr Daruwalla, in creating his screenplay for *Inspector Dhar and the Cage-Girl Killer*, never intended to offend the hijras – there are more than 5,000 in Bombay alone. But, as a surgeon, Farrokh found their method of emasculation truly barbarous. Both castration and sex-change operations are illegal in India, but a hijra's 'operation' – they use the English word – is performed by other hijras. The patient stares at a portrait of the Mother Goddess Bahuchara Mata; he is advised to bite his own hair, for there's no anesthetic, although the patient is sedated with alcohol or opium. The surgeon (who is not a surgeon) ties a string around the penis and the testicles in order to get a clean cut – for it is with one cut that both the testicles and the penis are removed. The patient is allowed to bleed freely; it's believed that maleness is a kind of poison, purged by bleeding. No stitches are made; the large, raw area is cauterized with hot oil. As the wound begins to heal, the urethra is kept open by repeated probing. The resultant puckered scar resembles a vagina.

Hijras are no mere cross-dressers; their contempt for simple transvestites (whose male parts are intact) is profound. These fake hijras are called 'zenanas.' Every world has its hierarchy. Within the prostitute community, hijras command a higher price than real women, but it was unclear to Dr Daruwalla why this was so. There was considerable debate as to whether hijra prostitutes were homosexuals, although it was certain that many of their male customers used them in that way; and among hijra teenagers, even before their emasculation, studies indicated frequent homosexual activity. But Farrokh suspected that many Indian men favored the hijra prostitutes because the hijras were more like women than women; they were certainly bolder than any Indian woman – and with their almost-a-vagina, who knew what they could imitate?

If hijras themselves were homosexually oriented, why would they emasculate themselves? It seemed probable to the doctor that, although there were many customers in the hijra brothels who were homosexuals, not every customer went there for anal intercourse. Whatever one thought or said about hijras, they *were* a third gender – they were simply (or not so simply) another sex. What was also true was that, in Bombay, fewer and fewer hijras were able to support themselves by conferring blessings or by begging; more and more of them were becoming prostitutes.

But why had Farrokh chosen a hijra to be the serial killer and cartoonist in the most recent Inspector Dhar movie? Now that a real killer was imitating the behavior of the fictional character – the police would say only that the real killer's drawing was 'an obvious variation on the movie theme' – Dr Daruwalla had *really* gotten Inspector Dhar in trouble. This particular film had inspired something worse than hatred, for the hijra prostitutes not only approved of killing Dhar – they wanted to maim him first.

'They want to cut off your cock and balls, dear boy,' Farrokh had warned his favorite young man. 'You must be careful how you get around town!'

With a sarcasm that was consistent with his famous role, Dhar had replied in his most deadpan manner: 'You're telling me.' (It was something he said at least once in all his movies.)

In contrast to the lurid agitation caused by the most recent Inspector Dhar movie, the appearance of a real policeman among the proper Duckworthians seemed dull. Surely the hijra prostitutes hadn't murdered Mr Lal! There'd been no indication that the body had been sexually mutilated, nor was there a possibility that even a demented hijra could have mistaken the old man for Inspector Dhar. Dhar never played golf.

A Real Detective at Work

Detective Patel, as Dr Daruwalla had guessed, was a deputy commissioner of police – D.C.P. Patel, officially. The detective was from Crime Branch Headquarters at Crawford Market – *not* from the nearby Tardeo Police Station, as Farrokh had also correctly surmised – because certain evidence, discovered during the examination of Mr Lal's body, had elevated the old golfer's death to a category of interest that was special to the deputy commissioner.

What such a category of interest could be wasn't immediately clear to Dr Daruwalla or to Inspector Dhar, nor was Deputy Commissioner Patel inclined to clarify the matter promptly.

'You must forgive me, Doctor – please do excuse me,

Mr Dhar,' the detective said; he was in his forties, a pleasant-looking man whose formerly delicate, sharp-boned face had slightly given way to his jowls. His alert eyes and the deliberate cadence of the deputy commissioner's speech indicated that he was a careful man. 'Which one of you was the very first to find the body?' the detective asked.

Dr Daruwalla could rarely resist making a joke. 'I believe the very first to find the body was a vulture,' the doctor said.

'Oh, quite so!' said the deputy commissioner, smiling tolerantly. Then Detective Patel sat down, uninvited, at their table – in the chair nearer Inspector Dhar. '*After* the vultures,' the policeman said to the actor, 'I believe *you* were the next to find the body.'

'I didn't move it or even touch it,' Dhar said, anticipating the question; it was a question *he* usually asked – in his movies.

'Oh, very good, thank you,' said D.C.P. Patel, turning his attention to Dr Daruwalla. 'And *you*, most naturally, examined the body, Doctor?' he asked.

'I most naturally did *not* examine it,' Dr Daruwalla replied. 'I'm an orthopedist, not a pathologist. I merely observed that Mr Lal was dead.'

'Oh, quite so!' Patel said. 'But did you give any thought to the cause of death?'

'Golf,' said Dr Daruwalla; he'd never played the game but he detested it at a distance. Dhar smiled. 'In Mr Lal's case,' the doctor continued, 'I suppose you might say he was killed by an excessive desire to improve. He most probably had high blood pressure, too – a man his age shouldn't repeatedly lose his temper in the hot sun.'

'But our weather is really quite cool,' the deputy commissioner said.

As if he'd been thinking about it for an extended time, Inspector Dhar said, 'The body didn't smell. The vultures stank, but not the body.'

Detective Patel appeared to be surprised and favorably

93

impressed by this report, but all he said was, 'Precisely.'

Dr Daruwalla spoke with impatience: 'My dear Deputy Commissioner, why don't you begin by telling us what you know?'

'Oh, that's absolutely not our way,' the deputy commissioner cordially replied. 'Is it?' he asked Inspector Dhar.

'No, it isn't,' Dhar agreed. 'Just when do you estimate the time of death?' he asked the detective.

'Oh, what a very good question!' Patel remarked. 'We estimate this morning – not even two hours before you found the body!'

Dr Daruwalla considered this. While Mr Bannerjee had been searching the clubhouse for his opponent and old friend, Mr Lal had strolled to the ninth green and the bougainvillea beyond, once more to practice a good escape from his nemesis of the day before. Mr Lal had *not* been late for his appointed game; if anything, poor Mr Lal had been a little too early – at least, too eager.

'But there wouldn't have been vultures so soon,' Dr Daruwalla said. 'There would have been no scent.'

'Not unless there was quite a lot of blood, or an open wound . . . and in this sun,' Inspector Dhar said. He'd learned much from his movies, even though they were very bad movies; even D.C.P. Patel was beginning to appreciate that.

'Quite so,' the detective said. 'There *was* quite a lot of blood.'

'There was a lot of blood by the time we *found* him!' said Dr Daruwalla, who still didn't understand. 'Especially around his eyes and mouth – I just assumed that the vultures had begun.'

'Vultures start pecking where there's already blood, and at the naturally wet places,' said Detective Patel. His English was unusually good for a policeman, even for a deputy commissioner, Dr Daruwalla thought.

The doctor was sensitive about his Hindi; he was

aware that Dhar spoke the language more comfortably than he did. This was a slight embarrassment for Dr Daruwalla, who wrote all of Dhar's movie dialogue and his voice-over in English. The translation into Hindi was done by Dhar; those phrases that particularly appealed to him – there weren't many – the actor left in English. And here was a not-so-common policeman indulging in the one-upmanship of speaking English to the renowned *Canadian*; it was what Dr Daruwalla called 'the Canadian treatment' – when a Bombayite wouldn't even try to speak Hindi or Marathi to him. Although almost everyone spoke English at the Duckworth Club, Farrokh was thinking of something witty to say to Detective Patel in Hindi, but Dhar (in his accentless English) spoke first. Only then did the doctor realize that Dhar had not once used his showbusiness Hindi accent with the deputy commissioner.

'There was quite a lot of blood by one ear,' the actor said, as if he'd never stopped wondering about it.

'Very good – there absolutely was!' said the encouraging detective. 'Mr Lal was struck behind one ear, and also in the temple – probably after he fell.'

'Struck by *what*?' Dr Daruwalla asked.

'By *what*, we know – it was his putter!' said Detective Patel. 'By *whom*, we don't know.'

In the 130-year history of the Duckworth Sports Club – through all the perils of Independence and those many diverting occasions that could have led to violence (for example, those wild times when the inflammatory Lady Duckworth bared her breasts) – there had never been a murder! Dr Daruwalla thought of how he would phrase this news to the Membership Committee.

It was characteristic of Farrokh not to consider his esteemed late father as the actual first murder victim in the 130-year history of Duckworthians in Bombay. The chief reason for this oversight was that Farrokh tried very hard not to think about his father's murder at all, but a secondary reason was surely that the doctor didn't want his father's violent death to cloud his otherwise sunny feelings for the Duckworth Club, which has already been described as the only place (other than the circus) where Dr Daruwalla felt at home.

Besides, Dr Daruwalla's father wasn't murdered *at* the Duckworth Club. The car that he was driving exploded in Tardeo, not in Mahalaxmi, although these are neighboring districts. But it was generally admitted, even among Duckworthians, that the car bomb was probably installed while the senior Daruwalla's car was parked in the Duckworth Club parking lot. Duckworthians were quick to point out that the only other person who was killed had no relationship to the club; the poor woman wasn't even an employee. She was a construction worker, and she was said to be carrying a straw basket full of rocks on her head when the flying right-front fender of the senior Daruwalla's car decapitated her.

But this was old news. The first Duckworthian to be murdered on the actual property of the Duckworth Club was Mr Lal.

'Mr Lal,' explained Detective Patel, 'was engaged in swinging what I believe they call a "mashie," or is it a "wedgie" – what *do* they call the club you hit a chip shot with?' Neither Dr Daruwalla nor Inspector Dhar was a golfer; a mashie *or* a wedgie sounded close enough to the real and stupid thing to them. 'Well, it doesn't matter,' the detective said. 'Mr Lal was holding one club when he was struck from behind with another – his own putter! We found it and his golf bag in the bougainvillea.'

Inspector Dhar had assumed a familiar film pose, or else he was merely thinking; he lifted his face as his fingers lightly stroked his chin, which enhanced his sneer. What he said was something that Dr Daruwalla and Deputy Commissioner Patel had heard him say many times before; he said it in every movie.

'Forgive me for sounding most theoretical,' Dhar said. This favorite bit of dialogue was of that kind which Dhar preferred to deliver in English, although he'd delivered the line on more than one occasion in Hindi, too. 'It seems,' Dhar said, 'that the killer didn't care especially *who* his victim was. Mr Lal was not scheduled to meet anyone in the bougainvillea at the ninth green. It was an accident that he was there – the killer couldn't have known.'

'Very good,' said D.C.P. Patel. 'Please go on.'

'Since the killer didn't seem to care who he killed,' Inspector Dhar said, 'perhaps it was intended only that the victim be one of *us*.'

'Do you mean one of the *members*?' cried Dr Daruwalla. 'Do you mean a *Duckworthian*?'

'It's just a theory,' said Inspector Dhar. Again, this was an echo; it was something he said in every movie.

'There is some evidence to support your theory, Mr Dhar,' Detective Patel said almost casually. The deputy commissioner removed his sunglasses from the breast pocket of his crisp white shirt, which showed not a trace of evidence of his latest meal; he probed deeper into the pocket and extracted a folded square of plastic wrapping, large enough to cover a wedge of tomatoe or a slice of onion. From the plastic he unwrapped a two-rupee note that had previously been rolled into a typewriter, for typed on the serial-number side of the bill, in capital letters, was this warning: MORE MEMBERS DIE IF DHAR REMAINS A MEMBER.

'Forgive me, Mr Dhar, if I ask you the obvious,' said Detective Patel.

'Yes, I have enemies,' Dhar said, without waiting for the question. 'Yes, there are people who'd like to kill me.'

'But *everyone* would like to kill him!' cried Dr Daruwalla. Then he touched the younger man's hand. 'Sorry,' he added.

Deputy Commissioner Patel returned the two-rupee note to his pocket. As he put on his sunglasses, the detective's pencil-thin mustache suggested to Dr Daruwalla a punctiliousness in shaving that the doctor had abandoned in his twenties. Such a mustache, etched both below the nose and above the lip, requires a younger man's steady hand. At his age, the deputy commissioner must have had to prop his elbow fast against the mirror, for shaving of this kind could only be accomplished by removing the razor blade from the razor and holding the blade *just so*. A time-consuming vanity for a man in his forties, Farrokh imagined; or maybe someone else shaved the deputy commissioner – possibly a younger woman, with an untrembling hand.

'In summary,' the detective was saying to Dhar, 'I don't suppose you know who *all* your enemies are.' He didn't wait for an answer. 'I suppose we could start with *all* the prostitutes – not just the hijras – and most policemen.'

'I would start with the hijras,' Farrokh broke in; he was thinking like a screenwriter again.

'I wouldn't,' said Detective Patel. 'What do the hijras care if Dhar is or isn't a member of this club? What they want is his penis and his testicles.'

'You're telling me,' said Inspector Dhar.

'I very much doubt that the murderer is a member of this club,' said Dr Daruwalla.

'Don't rule that out,' Dhar said.

'I won't,' said Detective Patel. He gave both Dr Daruwalla and Inspector Dhar his card. 'If *you* call me,' he said to Dhar, 'you better call me at home – I wouldn't leave any messages at Crime Branch Headquarters. You know all about how we policemen can't be trusted.'

'Yes,' the actor said. 'I know.'

'Excuse me, Detective Patel,' said Dr Daruwalla. 'Where did you find the two-rupee note?'

'It was folded in Mr Lal's mouth,' the detective said.

When the deputy commissioner had departed, the two friends sat listening to the late-afternoon sounds.

They were so absorbed in their listening that they didn't notice the prolonged departure of the second Mrs Dogar. She left her table, then she stopped to look over her shoulder at the unresponsive Inspector Dhar, then she walked only a little farther before she stopped and looked again, then she looked *again*.

Watching her, Mr Sethna concluded that she was insane. Mr Sethna observed every stage of the second Mrs Dogar's most complicated exit from the Ladies' Garden and the dining room, but Inspector Dhar didn't appear to see the woman at all. It interested the old steward that Mrs Dogar had stared so exclusively at Dhar; not once had her gaze shifted to Dr Daruwalla, and never to the policeman – but then, Detective Patel had kept his back to her.

Mr Sethna also watched the deputy commissioner make a phone call from the booth in the foyer. The detective was momentarily distracted by Mrs Dogar's agitated condition; as the woman marched to the driveway and ordered the parking-lot attendant to fetch her car, the policeman appeared to make note of her attractiveness, her haste and her expression of something like rage. Perhaps the deputy commissioner was considering whether or not this woman looked like someone who'd recently clubbed an old man to death; in truth, thought Mr Sethna, the second Mrs Dogar looked as if she *wanted* to murder someone. But Detective Patel paid only passing attention to Mrs Dogar; he seemed more interested in his phone call.

The apparent topic of conversation was so domestic that it surpassed even the interest of Mr Sethna, who eavesdropped only long enough to assure himself that D.C.P. Patel was not engaged in police business. Mr Sethna was certain that the policeman was talking to his wife.

'No, sweetie,' said the detective, who then listened patiently to the receiver before he said, 'No, I would have told you, sweetie.' Then he listened again. 'Yes, of course I promise, sweetie,' he finally said. For a while, the deputy commissioner shut his eyes while he listened to the receiver; in observing him, Mr Sethna felt extremely self-satisfied that he'd never married. 'But I *haven't* dismissed your theories!' Detective Patel suddenly said into the phone. 'No, of course I'm not angry,' he added with resignation. 'I'm sorry if I *sounded* angry, sweetie.'

Not even as veteran a snoop as Mr Sethna could stand another word; he decided to permit the policeman to continue his conversation in privacy. It was only a mild surprise to Mr Sethna that D.C.P. Patel spoke English to his own wife. The old steward concluded that this was why the detective's English was above average – practice. But at what a demeaning cost! Mr Sethna returned to that part of the dining room nearest the Ladies' Garden, and to his lengthy observation of Dr Daruwalla and Inspector Dhar. They were still absorbed in the late-afternoon sounds. They weren't much fun to observe, but at least they weren't married to each other.

The tennis balls were back in action, and someone was snoring in the reading room; the busboys, making their typical clatter, had cleared every dining table but the table where the doctor and the actor sat with their cold tea. (Detective Patel had polished off all the sweets.) The sounds of the Duckworth Club spoke distinctly for themselves: the sharp shuffling of a fresh deck of cards, the crisp contact of the snooker balls, the steady sweeping out of the dance hall – it was swept at the same time every afternoon, although there were rarely dances on weeknights. There was also a ceaseless insanity to the patter and squeak of the shoes on the polished hardwood of the badminton court; compared to the frenzy of this activity, the dull whacking of the shuttlecock sounded like someone killing flies.

Dr Daruwalla believed that this wasn't a good moment to give Inspector Dhar more bad news. The murder and the unusual death threat were quite enough for one afternoon. 'Perhaps you should come home for supper,' Dr Daruwalla said to his friend.

'Yes, I'd like that, Farrokh,' Dhar said. Normally, he might have said something snide about Dr Daruwalla's use of the word 'supper.' Dhar disliked too loose a use of the word; in the actor's fussy opinion, the word should be reserved for either a light meal in the early evening or for an after-the-theater repast. In Dhar's opinion, North Americans tended to use the word as if it were interchangeable with dinner; Farrokh felt that supper *was* interchangeable with dinner.

There was something fatherly in his voice to Dhar when Dr Daruwalla adopted a critical tone. He said to the actor, 'It's quite out of character for you to sound off in such accentless English to a total stranger.'

'Policemen aren't exactly strangers to me,' Dhar said. 'They talk to each other but they never talk to the press.'

'Oh, I forgot you knew everything about police business!' Farrokh said sarcastically. But Inspector Dhar was back in character; he was good at keeping quiet. Dr Daruwalla regretted what he'd said. He'd wanted to say, Oh, dear boy, you may not be the hero of *this* story! Now he wanted to say, Dear boy, there *are* people who love you – *I* love you. You surely must know I do!

But instead, Dr Daruwalla said, 'As guest chairman of the Membership Committee, I feel I must inform the committeemen of this threat to the other members. We'll vote on it, but I feel there will be strong opinion that the other members should know.'

'Of course they should know,' said Inspector Dhar. 'And I should *not* remain a member,' he said.

It was unthinkable to Dr Daruwalla that an extortionist and a murderer could so swiftly and concretely disrupt the most cherished aspect of the character of the Duckworth Club, which (in his view) was a deep, almost remote sense of privacy, as if Duckworthians were afforded the luxury of not actually living in Bombay.

'Dear boy,' said the doctor, 'what will you do?'

Dhar's answer shouldn't have surprised Dr Daruwalla as forcefully as it did; the doctor had heard the response many times, in every Inspector Dhar movie. After all, Farrokh had *written* the response. 'What will I do?' Dhar asked himself aloud. 'Find out who it is and get them.'

'Don't speak to me in character!' Dr Daruwalla said sharply. 'You're not in a movie now!'

'I'm always in a movie,' Dhar snapped. 'I was *born* in a movie! Then I was almost immediately put into another movie, wasn't I?'

Since Dr Daruwalla and his wife thought they were the only people in Bombay who knew exactly where the younger man had come from and everything about who he was, it was the doctor's turn to keep quiet. In our hearts, Dr Daruwalla thought, there must abide some pity for those people who have always felt themselves to be separate from even their most familiar surroundings, those people who either *are* foreigners or who suffer a singular point of view that makes them *feel* as if they're foreigners – even in their native lands. In our hearts, Farrokh knew, there also abides a certain suspicion that such people *need* to feel set apart from their society. But people who initiate their loneliness are no less lonely than those who are suddenly surprised by loneliness, nor are they undeserving of our pity – Dr Daruwalla felt certain of that. However, the doctor was unsure if he'd been thinking of Dhar or of himself.

Then Farrokh realized he was alone at the table; Dhar had departed as eerily as he'd arrived. The glint of Mr Sethna's silver serving tray caught Dr Daruwalla's eye, reminding him of that shiny something which the crow had held so briefly in its beak.

The old steward reacted to Dr Daruwalla's recognition as if summoned. 'I'll have a Kingfisher, please,' the doctor said.

The late-afternoon light cast longer and longer shadows in the Ladies' Garden, and Dr Daruwalla gloomily observed that the bright pink of the bougainvillea had turned a darker shade; it seemed to him that the flowers had a blood-red hue, although this was an exaggeration – quite characteristic of the creator of Inspector Dhar. In reality, the bougainvillea was as pink (*and* as white) as before.

Later, Mr Sethna grew alarmed that the doctor hadn't touched his favorite beer.

'Is there something wrong?' the old steward asked, his long finger indicating the Kingfisher lager.

'No, no – it's not the beer!' Farrokh said; he took a swallow that gave him little comfort. 'The beer is fine,' he said.

Old Mr Sethna nodded as if he knew everything that was troubling Dr Daruwalla; Mr Sethna presumed to know such things routinely.

'I know, I know,' muttered the old Parsi. 'The old days are gone – it's not like the old days.'

Insipid truths were an area of Mr Sethna's expertise that Dr Daruwalla found most irritating. The next thing you know, Farrokh thought, the tedious old fool will tell me that I'm not my esteemed late father. Truly, the steward seemed on the verge of making another observation when an unpleasant sound came from the dining room; it reached Mr Sethna and Dr Daruwalla in the Ladies' Garden with the crass, attention-getting quality of a man cracking his knuckles.

Mr Sethna went to investigate. Without moving from his chair, Farrokh already knew what was making the sound. It was the ceiling fan, the one the crow had landed on and used as a shitting platform. Perhaps the crow had bent the blade of the fan, or else the bird had knocked a screw loose; maybe the fan was operated by ball bearings running in a groove, and one of these was out of position, or if there was a ball-and-socket joint, it needed grease. The ceiling fan appeared to catch on something; it clicked as it turned. It faltered; it almost stopped but it kept turning. With each revolution, there was a snapping sound, as if the mechanism were about to grind to a halt.

Mr Sethna stood under the fan, staring stupidly up at it. He probably doesn't remember the shitting crow, Dr Daruwalla thought. The doctor was readying himself to take charge of the situation when the unpleasant noise simply stopped. The ceiling fan turned freely, as before. Mr Sethna looked all around, as if he weren't sure how he'd arrived at this spot in the dining room. Then the steward's gaze fixed upon the Ladies' Garden, where Farrokh was still sitting. He's not the man his father was, the old Parsi thought.

4. THE OLD DAYS

The Bully

Dr Lowji Daruwalla took a personal interest in the crippling conditions affecting children. As a child, he'd developed tuberculosis of the spine. Although he recovered sufficiently to become India's most famous pioneer in orthopedic surgery, he always said it was his own experience with spinal deformity – the fatigue and the pain imposed on him – that made his commitment to the care of cripples so steadfast and long-enduring. 'A personal injustice is stronger motivation than any instinct for philanthropy,' Lowji said. He tended to speak in statements. As an adult, he would forever be recognized by the telltale gibbousness of Pott's disease. All his life, Lowji was as humpbacked as a small, upright camel.

Is it any wonder that his son Farrokh felt inferior to such a commitment? He would enter his father's field, but only as a follower; he would continue to pay his respects to India, but he'd always feel he was a mere visitor. Education and travel can be humbling; the younger Dr Daruwalla took naturally to feelings of intellectual inferiority. Possibly Farrokh too simplistically attributed his alienation to the one conviction in his life that was as paralyzing as his conversion to Christianity: that he was utterly without a sense of place, that he was a man without a country, that there was nowhere he could go where he felt he belonged – except the circus and the Duckworth Club.

But what can be said about a man who keeps his needs and his obsessions largely to himself? When a man expresses what he's afraid of, his fears and longings undergo revision in the telling and retelling –

friends and family have their own ways of altering the material – and soon the so-called fears and longings become almost comfortable with overuse. But Dr Daruwalla held his feelings inside himself. Not even his wife knew how out of it the doctor felt in Bombay – and how could she, if he wouldn't tell her? Since Julia was Viennese, however little Dr Daruwalla knew about India, he knew more than she did. And 'at home' in Toronto, Farrokh allowed Julia to be the authority; she was the boss there. This was an easy privilege for the doctor to extend to his wife because she believed that *he* was in charge in Bombay. For so many years now, he'd got away with this.

Of course his wife knew about the screenplays – but only that he wrote them, not what he truly felt about them. Farrokh was careful to speak lightly of them to Julia. He was quite good at mocking them; after all, they were a joke to everyone else – it was easy for Farrokh to convince his wife that the Inspector Dhar movies were just a joke to him. More important, Julia knew how much Dhar (the dear boy) meant to him. So what if she had no idea how much the screenplays meant to Farrokh, too? And so these things, because they were so deeply concealed, were more important to Dr Daruwalla than they should have been.

As for Farrokh's not belonging, surely the same could never be said of his father. Old Lowji liked to complain about India, and the nature of his complaints was often puerile. His medical colleagues chided him for his intrepid criticism of India; it was fortunate for his patients, they said, that his surgical procedures were more careful – and more accurate. But if Lowji was off-the-wall about his own country, at least it *was* his own country, Farrokh thought.

A founder of the Hospital for Crippled Children in Bombay and the chairman of India's first Infantile Paralysis Commission, the senior Daruwalla published monographs on polio and various bone diseases that were the best of his day. A master surgeon, he perfected procedures for the correction of deformities, such as clubfoot, spinal curvature and wryneck. A superb linguist, he read the work of Little in English, of Stromeyer in German, of Guerin and Bouvier in French. An outspoken atheist, Lowji Daruwalla nevertheless persuaded the Jesuits to establish clinics, both in Bombay and in Poona, for the study and treatment of scoliosis, paralysis due to birth injuries, and poliomyelitis. It was largely Muslim money that he secured to pay for a visiting roentgenologist at the Hospital for Crippled Children; it was wealthy Hindus he hit on for the research and treatment programs he initiated for arthritis. Lowji even wrote a sympathy letter to U.S. President Franklin D. Roosevelt, an Episcopalian, mentioning the number of Indians who suffered from the president's condition; he received a polite reply and a personal check.

Lowji made a name for himself in the short-lived movement called Disaster Medicine, especially during the demonstrations prior to Independence and the bloody rioting before and after the Partition. To this day, volunteer workers in Disaster Medicine attempt to revive the movement by quoting his much-advertised advice. 'In order of importance, look for dramatic amputations and severe extremity injuries before treating fractures or lacerations. Best to leave all head injuries to the experts, if there are any.' Any experts, he meant – there were always head injuries. (Privately, he referred to the failed movement as Riot Medicine – 'something India will always be in need of,' old Lowji said.)

He was the first in India to respond to the revolutionary change in thinking about the origin of low back pain, for which he said the credit belonged to Harvard's Joseph Seaton Barr. Admittedly, Farrokh's esteemed father was better remembered at the Duckworth Sports Club for his ice treatments of tennis elbow and his habit, when drinking, of denouncing the waiters for their deplorable posture. ('Look at me! I have a hump, and I'm still standing up straighter than you!') In reverence of the great Dr Lowji Daruwalla, rigidity of the spine was a habit ferociously maintained by the old Parsi steward Mr Sethna.

Why, then, did the younger Dr Daruwalla *not* revere his late father?

It wasn't because Farrokh was the second-born son and the youngest of Lowji's three children; he'd never felt slighted. Farrokh's elder brother, Jamshed, who'd led Farrokh to Vienna and now practiced child psychiatry in Zürich, had also led Farrokh to the idea of a European wife. But old Lowji never opposed mixed marriages – not on principle, surely, and not in the case of Jamshed's Viennese bride, whose younger sister married Farrokh. Julia became old Lowji's favorite in-law; he preferred her company even to the London otologist who married Farrokh's sister – and Lowji Daruwalla was an unabashed Anglophile. After Independence, Lowji admired and clung to whatever Englishness endured in India.

But the source of Farrokh's lack of reverence for his famous father wasn't old Lowji's 'Englishness,' either. His many years in Canada had made a moderate Anglophile out of the younger Dr Daruwalla. (Granted, Englishness in Canada is quite different from in India – not politically tainted, always socially acceptable; many Canadians like the British.)

And that old Lowji was outspoken in his loathing for Mohandas K. Gandhi did not upset Farrokh in the slightest. At dinner parties, especially with non-Indians in Toronto, the younger Daruwalla was quite pleased at the surprise he could instantly evoke by quoting his late father on the late Mahatma.

'He was a bloody charka-spinning, loin-clothed pandit!' the senior Daruwalla had complained. 'He dragged his religion into his political activism – then he turned his political activism into a religion.' And the old man was unafraid of expressing his views *in* India – and not only in the safety of the Duckworth

Club. 'Bloody Hindus ... bloody Sikhs ... bloody Muslims,' he would say. 'And bloody Parsis, too!' he would add, if the more fervent of the Zoroastrian faith pressed him for some display of Parsi loyalty. 'Bloody Catholics,' he would murmur on those rare occasions when he appeared at St Ignatius – only to attend those dreadful school plays in which his own sons took small parts.

Old Lowji declared that dharma was 'sheer complacency – nothing but a justification for nondoing.' He said that caste and the upholding of untouchability was 'nothing but the perpetual worship of shit – if you worship shit, most naturally you must declare it the duty of certain people to take the shit away!' Absurdly, Lowji presumed he was permitted to make such irreverent utterances because the evidence of his dedication to crippled children was unparalleled.

He railed that India was without an ideology. 'Religion and nationalism are our feeble substitutes for constructive ideas,' he pronounced. 'Meditation is as destructive to the individual as caste, for what is it but a way of diminishing the self? Indians follow groups instead of their own ideas: we subscribe to rituals and taboos instead of establishing goals for social change – for the improvement of our society. Move the bowels before breakfast, not after! Who cares? Make the woman wear a veil! Why bother? Meanwhile, we have no rules against filth, against chaos!'

In such a sensitive country, brashness is frankly stupid. In retrospect, the younger Dr Daruwalla realized that his father was a car bomb waiting to happen. No one – not even a doctor devoted to crippled children – can go around saying that 'karma is the bullshit that keeps India a backward country.' The idea that one's present life, however horrible, is the acceptable payment for one's life in the past may fairly be said to be a rationale for doing nothing conducive to self-improvement, but it's surely best *not* to call such a belief 'bullshit.' Even as a Parsi, and as a convert to

Christianity – and although Farrokh was never a Hindu – the younger Dr Daruwalla saw that his father's overstatements were unwise.

But if old Lowji was dead set against Hindus, he was equally offensive in speaking of Muslims – 'Everyone should send a Muslim a roast pig for Christmas!' – and his prescriptions for the Church of Rome were dire indeed. He said that every last Catholic should be driven from Goa, or, preferably, publicly executed in remembrance of the persecutions and burnings at the stake that they themselves had performed. He proposed that 'the disgusting cruelty depicted on the crucifix shouldn't be allowed in India' – he meant the mere sight of Christ on the cross, which he called 'a kind of Western pornography.' Furthermore, he declared that all Protestants were closet Calvinists – and that Calvin was a closet Hindu! Lowji meant by this that he loathed anything resembling the acceptance of human wretchedness – not to mention a belief in divine predestination, which Lowji called 'Christian dharma.' He was fond of quoting Martin Luther, who had said: 'What wrong can there be in telling a downright good lie for a good cause and for the advancement of the Christian Church?' By this Lowji meant that he believed in free will, and in so-called good works, *and* in 'no damn God at all.'

As for the car bomb, there was an old rumor at the Duckworth Club that it had been the brainchild of a Hindu-Muslim-Christian conspiracy – perhaps the first cooperative effort of its kind – but the younger Dr Daruwalla knew that even the Parsis, who were rarely violent, couldn't be ruled out as contributing assassins. Although old Lowji was a Parsi, he was as mocking of the true believers of the Zoroastrian faith as he was of *any* true believers. Somehow, only Mr Sethna had escaped his contempt, and Lowji stood alone in Mr Sethna's esteem; he was the only atheist who'd never suffered the zealous steward's undying scorn. Perhaps it was the hot-tea incident that bound them together and overcame even their religious differences.

To the end, it was the concept of dharma that Lowji could least leave alone. 'If you're born in a latrine, it's better to die in the latrine than to aspire to a better-smelling station in life! Now I ask you: Is that not nonsense?' But Farrokh felt that his father was crazy – or that, outside the field of orthopedic surgery, the old humpback simply didn't know what he was talking about. Even beggars aspired to improve, didn't they? One can imagine how the calm of the Duckworth Club was often shattered by old Lowji declaring to everyone – even the waiters with bad posture – that caste prejudice was the root of all evil in India, although most Duckworthians privately shared this view.

What Farrokh most resented about his father was how the contentious old athiest had robbed him of a religion *and* a country. More than intellectually spoiling the concept of a nation for his children, because of his unrestrained hatred of nationalism, Dr Lowji Daruwalla had driven his children away from Bombay. For the sake of their education and refinement, he'd sent his only daughter to London and his two sons to Vienna; then he had the gall to be disappointed with all three of them for not choosing to live in India.

'Immigrants are immigrants all their lives!' Lowji Daruwalla had declared. It was just another of his pronouncements, but this one had a lasting sting.

Austrian Interlude

Farrokh had arrived in Austria in July of 1947 to prepare for his undergraduate studies at the University of Vienna; hence he missed Independence. (Later he thought he'd simply not been at home when it counted; thereafter, he supposed, he was never 'at home.') What a time to be an Indian in India! Instead, young Farrokh Daruwalla was acquainting himself

111

with his favorite dessert, *Sachertorte mit Schlag*, and making himself known to the other residents of the Pension Amerling on the Prinz Eugene Strasse, which was in the Soviet sector of occupation. In those days, Vienna was divided in four. The Americans and British grabbed the choicest residential districts, and the French took the best shopping areas. The Russians were realistic: they settled themselves in the outlying working-class precincts, where all the industry was, and they crouched around the Inner City, near the embassies and government buildings.

As for the Pension Amerling, its tall windows, with the rusted-iron flower boxes and yellowing curtains, overlooked the war rubble on the Prinz Eugene Strasse and faced the chestnut trees of the Belvedere Gardens. From his third-story bedroom window, young Farrokh could see that the stone wall between the upper and the lower Belvedere Palace was pock-marked from machine-gun fire. Around the corner, on the Schwindgasse, the Russians had taken charge of the Bulgarian Embassy. There was no explanation for the round-the-clock armed guard in the foyer of the Polish Reading Room. On the Schwindgasse corner of the Argentinierstrasse, the Café Schnitzler was emptied periodically so that the Soviets could conduct a bomb search. Sixteen out of 21 districts had Communist police chiefs.

The Daruwalla brothers were certain that they were the only Parsis in the occupied city, if not the only Indians. To the Viennese, they didn't *look* especially Indian; they weren't brown enough. Farrokh wasn't as fair-skinned as Jamshed, but both brothers reflected their faraway Persian ancestry; to some Austrians, they might have looked like Iranians or Turks. To most Europeans, the Daruwalla brothers more closely resembled the immigrants from the Middle East than those from India; yet, if Farrokh and Jamshed weren't as brown as many Indians, they were browner than most Middle Easterners – browner than Israelis and

Egyptians, browner than Syrians and Libyans and the Lebanese, and so on.

In Vienna, young Farrokh's first racial mistreatment occurred when a butcher mistook him for a Hungarian Gypsy. On more than one occasion, Austria being Austria, Farrokh was jeered by drunks in a *Gasthof*; they called him a Jew, of course. And before Farrokh's arrival, Jamshed had discovered it was easier to find housing in the Russian sector; no one really wanted to live there, and so the pensions were less discriminatory. Jamshed had earlier tried to rent an apartment on the Mariahilferstrasse, but the landlady had refused him on the grounds that he would create unwelcome cooking smells.

It wasn't until he was in his fifties that Dr Daruwalla appreciated the irony: he'd been sent away from home precisely at the time India became its own country; he would spend the next eight years in a war-damaged city that was occupied by four foreign powers. When he returned to India in September of 1955, he just missed the Flag Day festivities in Vienna. In October, the city celebrated the official end of the occupation – Austria was its own country, too. Dr Daruwalla wouldn't be on hand for the historic event; once more, he'd moved just ahead of it.

As the smallest of footnotes, the Daruwalla brothers were nonetheless among the actual recorders of Viennese history. Their youthful vigor for foreign languages made them useful transcribers of the minutes for the Allied Council meetings, at which they scribbled profusely but were told to remain as silent as cobblestones. The British respresentative had vetoed their promotion to the more sought-after jobs of interpreters, the stated reason being that they were only university students. (It was racially reassuring that at least the British knew they were Indians.)

If only as flies on the wall, the Daruwalla brothers were witnesses to the many grievances expressed against the methods of occupation conducted in the old city. For example, both Farrokh and Jamshed attended the investigations of the notorious Benno Blum Gang – a cigarette-smuggling ring and the alleged black marketeers of the much-desired nylon stocking. For the privilege of operating unmolested in the Soviet sector, the Benno Blum Gang eliminated political undesirables. Naturally, the Russians denied this. But Farrokh and Jamshed were never molested by the alleged cohorts of Benno Blum, who himself was never apprehended or even identified. And the Soviets, in whose sector the two brothers lived for years, never once bothered them.

At the Allied Council meetings, young Farrokh Daruwalla's harshest treatment came from a British interpreter. Farrokh was transcribing the minutes for a reinvestigation of the Anna Hellein rape and murder case when he discovered an error in translation; he quickly pointed it out to the interpreter.

Anna Hellein was a 29-year-old Viennese social worker who was dragged off her train by a Russian guard at the Steyregg Bridge checkpoint on the United States–Soviet demarcation line; there she was raped and murdered and left on the rails, later to be decapitated by a train. A Viennese witness to all this, a local housewife, was quoted as saying that she didn't report the incident because she was sure that *Fräulein* Hellein was a giraffe.

'Excuse me, sir,' young Farrokh said to the British interpreter. 'You've made a slight error. *Fräulein* Hellein was not mistaken for a giraffe.'

'That's what the witness said, mate,' the interpreter replied. He added, 'I don't care to have my English corrected by a bloody wog.'

'It isn't your English that I'm correcting, sir,' Farrokh said. 'It's your German.'

'It's the same word in German, mate,' the British interpreter said. 'The *Hausfrau* called her a bloody *giraffe*!'

'*Nur Umgangssprache,*' Farrokh Daruwalla said. 'It's

114

merely colloquial speech; *giraffe* is Berliner slang – for a prostitute. The witness mistook *Fräulein* Hellein for a whore.'

Farrokh was almost relieved that his assailant was British and that the term 'wog' – at least the correct racial slur – was used. Doubtless it would have unnerved him to have been mistaken for a Hungarian Gypsy *twice*. And by his bold interference, young Daruwalla had saved the Allied Council from committing an embarrassing error; it was, therefore, never entered into the official minutes that a witness to *Fräulein* Hellein's rape and murder and decapitation had mistaken the victim for a giraffe. On top of everything else that the deceased had suffered, she was spared this further outrage.

But when young Farrokh Daruwalla returned to India in the fall of 1955, this episode was as much a part of history as he felt himself to be; he didn't come home a confident young man. Granted, he had not spent the entire eight years outside of India, but a brief visit in the middle of his undergraduate studies (in the summer of 1949) hardly prepared him for the confusion he would encounter six years later – when he came 'home' to an India that would forever make him feel like a foreigner.

He was used to feeling like a foreigner; Vienna had prepared him for that. And his several pleasant visits to London to see his sister were marred by his one trip to London that coincided with his father's invitation to address the Royal College of Surgeons – a great honor. It was the obsession of Indians, and of former British colonies in general, to become Fellows of the Royal College of Surgeons – old Lowji was extremely proud of his 'F,' as it was called. The 'F' would mean less to the younger Dr Daruwalla, who would also become an F.R.C.S. – of Canada. But on the occasion of Farrokh attending his father's lecture in London, old Lowji chose to pay tribute to the American founder of the British Orthopaedic Association – the celebrated Dr

Robert Bayley Osgood, one of the few Americans to captivate this British institution – and it was during Lowji's speech (which would go on to emphasize the problems of infantile paralysis in India) that young Farrokh overheard a most disparaging remark. It would keep him from ever considering a life in London.

'What monkeys they are,' said a florid orthopedist to a fellow Brit. 'They are the most presumptuous imitators. They observe us for all of five minutes, then they think they can do it, too.'

Young Farrokh sat paralyzed in a room of men fascinated by the diseases of bones and joints; he couldn't move, he couldn't speak. This wasn't a simple matter of mistaking a prostitute for a giraffe. His own medical studies had just begun; he wasn't sure if he understood what the 'it' referred to. Farrokh was so unsure of himself, he first supposed that the 'it' was something medical – some actual knowledge – but before his father's speech had ended, Farrokh understood. 'It' was only Englishness, 'it' was merely *being them*. Even in a gathering of what his father boastfully called 'fellow professionals,' the 'it' was all they'd noticed – simply what of their Englishness had been successfully or unsuccessfully copied. And for the remainder of old Lowji's exploration of infantile paralysis, young Farrokh was ashamed that he saw his ambitious father as the British saw him: a smug ape who'd succeeded in imitating *them*. It was the first time Farrokh realized how it was possible to love Englishness and yet loathe the British.

And so, before he ruled out India as a country where he could live, he'd already ruled out England. It was the summer of '49, during an at-home stay in Bombay, when young Farrokh Daruwalla suffered the experience that would (for him) rule out living in the United States, too. It was the same summer that another of his father's more embarrassing weaknesses was revealed to him. Farrokh discounted the continuous discomfort

116

of his father's spinal deformity; this was not in the category of a weakness of any kind – on the contrary, Lowji's hump was a source of inspiration. But now, in addition to Lowji's overstatements of a political and religious nature, the senior Daruwalla unveiled a taste for romantic movies. Farrokh was already familiar with his father's unbridled passion for *Waterloo Bridge;* tears sprang to his father's eyes at the mere mention of Vivien Leigh, and no concept in storytelling struck old Lowji with such tragic force as those twists of fate that could cause a woman, both good and pure, to fall to the lowly rank of prostitute.

But in the summer of '49, young Farrokh was quite unprepared to find his father so infatuated with the commonplace hysteria of a film-in-progress. To make matters worse, it was a Hollywood film – of no special distinction beyond that endless capacity for compromise which was the principal gift of the film's participants. Farrokh was appalled to witness his father's slavishness before everyone who was even marginally involved.

One shouldn't be surprised that Lowji was vulnerable to movie people, or that the presumed glamour of postwar Hollywood was magnified by its considerable distance from Bombay. These particular lowlifes who'd invaded Maharashtra for the purpose of moviemaking had sizably damaged reputations – even in Hollywood, where shame is seldom suffered for long – but how could the senior Daruwalla have known this? Like many physicians the world over, Lowji imagined that he could have been a great writer – if medicine hadn't attracted him first – and he further deluded himself that a second career opportunity lay ahead of him, perhaps in his retirement. He supposed that, with more time on his hands, it would take no great effort to write a novel – and surely less to write a screenplay. Although the latter assumption is quite true, even the effort of a screenplay would prove too great for old Lowji; it was never necessarily the power of his imagination that gave him great technique and foresight as a surgeon.

Sadly, a natural arrogance often attends the ability to heal and cure. Renowned in Bombay – even recognized abroad for his accomplishments in India – Dr Lowji Daruwalla nevertheless craved intimate contact with the so-called creative process. In the summer of 1949, with his highly principled younger son as a witness, the senior Daruwalla got what he desired.

Inexplicable Hairlessness

Often when a man of vision and character falls among the unscrupulous cowards of mediocrity, there is an intermediary, a petty villain in the guise of a matchmaker – one skilled in currying favor for small but gratifying gain. In this instance, she was a Malabar Hill lady of imposing wealth and only slightly less imposing presence; although she wouldn't have categorized herself as a maiden aunt, she played this role in the lives of her undeserving nephews – the two scoundrel sons of her impoverished brother. She'd also suffered the tragic history of having been jilted by the same man on two different wedding days, a condition that prompted Dr Lowji Daruwalla to privately refer to her as 'the Miss Havisham of Bombay – times two.'

Her name was Promila Rai, and prior to her insidious role of introducing Lowji to the movie vermin, her communications with the Daruwalla family had been merely rude. She'd once sought the senior Daruwalla's advice regarding the inexplicable hairlessness of the younger of her loathsome two nephews – an odd boy named Rahul Rai. At the time of the doctor's examination, which Lowji had at first resisted conducting on the grounds that he was an orthopedist, Rahul was only 8 or 10. The doctor found nothing 'inexplicable' about his hairlessness. The absence of body hair wasn't that unusual; the lad had bushy eyebrows and a thick head of hair. Yet Miss Promila Rai found old Lowji's analysis lacking. 'Well, after all, you're only a *joint* doctor,' she said dismissively, to the orthopedist's considerable irritation.

But now Rahul Rai was 12 or 13, and the hairlessness of his mahogany skin was more apparent. Farrokh Daruwalla, who was 19 in the summer of '49, had never liked the boy; he was an oily brat of a disquieting sexual ambiguity – possibly influenced by his elder brother, Subodh, a dancer and occasional actor in the emerging Hindi film scene. Subodh was better known for his flamboyant homosexuality than for his theatrical talents.

For Farrokh to return from Vienna to find his father on friendly terms with Promila Rai and her sexually suspect nephews – well, one can imagine. In his undergraduate years, young Farrokh had developed intellectual and literary pretensions that were easily offended by the Hollywood scum who'd ingratiated themselves with his vulnerable, albeit famous, father.

Quite simply, Promila Rai had wanted her actor-nephew Subodh to have a role in the movie; she also had wanted the prepubescent Rahul to be employed as a plaything of this court of creativity. The hairless boy's apparently unformed sexuality made him the little darling of the Californians; they found him an able interpreter and an eager errand boy. And what had the Hollywood types wanted from Promila Rai in exchange for making creative use of her nephews? They wanted access to a private club – to the Duckworth Sports Club, which was highly recommended even in their lowlife circles – and they wanted a doctor, someone to look after their ailments. In truth, it was their terror of all the *possible* ailments of India that needed looking after, for in the beginning there was nothing in the slightest that was ailing them.

It was a shock to young Farrokh to come home to this unlikely degradation of his father; his mother was mortified by his father's choice of such crude companions and by what she considered to be his father's shameless manipulation by Promila Rai. By giving this American movie rabble unlimited access to the club, old Lowji (who was chairman of the Rules Committee) had bent a sacred law of the Duckworthians. Previously, guests of members were permitted in the club only if they arrived *and remained with* a member, but the senior Daruwalla was so infatuated with his newfound friends that he'd extended special privileges to them. Moreover, the screenwriter, from whom Lowji believed he had the most to learn, was unwanted on the set; this sensitive artist and outcast had become a virtual resident of the Duckworth Club – and a constant source of bickering between Farrokh's parents.

It's often embarrassing to discover the marital cuteness that exists among couples whose social importance is esteemed. Farrokh's mother, Meher, was renowned for flirting with his father in public. Because there was nothing coarse in her overtures to her husband, Meher Daruwalla was recognized among Duckworthians as an exceptionally devoted wife; therefore, she'd attracted all the more attention at the Duckworth Club when she *stopped* flirting with Lowji. It was plain to everyone that Meher was feuding with Lowji instead. To young Farrokh's shame, the whole Duckworth Club was put on edge by this obvious tension in the venerable Daruwalla marriage.

A sizable part of Farrokh's summer agenda was to prepare his parents for the romance that was developing for their two sons with the fabulous Zilk sisters – 'the Vienna Woods girls,' as Jamshed called them. It struck Farrokh that the state of his parents' marriage might make an unfavorable climate for a discussion of romance of any kind – not to mention his parents' possible reluctance to accept the idea of their only sons marrying Viennese Roman Catholics.

It was typical of Jamshed's successful manipulation of his younger brother that Farrokh had been selected to return home for the summer in order to broach this subject. Farrokh was less intellectually challenging to Lowji; he was also the baby of the family, and therefore he appeared to be loved with the least reservation. And Farrokh's intentions to follow his father in orthopedics doubtless pleased the old man and made Farrokh a more welcome bearer of conceivably unwelcome tidings than Jamshed would have been. The latter's interest in psychiatry, which old Lowji spoke of as 'an inexact science' – he meant in comparison with orthopedic surgery – had already driven a wedge between the father and his elder son.

In any case, Farrokh saw that it would be poor timing for him to introduce the topic of the *Fräuleins* Josefine and Julia Zilk; his praise of their loveliness and virtues would have to wait. The story of their courageous widowed mother and her efforts to educate her daughters would have to wait, too. The dreadful American movie was consuming Farrokh's helpless parents. Even the young man's intellectual pursuits failed to capture his father's attention.

For example, when Farrokh admitted that he shared Jamshed's passion for Freud, his father expressed alarm that Farrokh's devotion to the more exact science of orthopedic surgery was waning. It was certainly the wrong idea to attempt to reassure his father on this point by quoting at length from Freud's 'General Remarks on Hysterical Attacks'; the concept that 'the hysterical fit is an equivalent to coitus' wasn't welcome information to old Lowji. Furthermore, Farrokh's father absolutely rejected the notion of the hysterical symptom corresponding to a form of sexual gratification. In regard to so-called multiple sexual identification – as in the case of the patient who attempted to rip off her dress with one hand (this was said to be her *man's* hand) while at the same time she desperately clutched her dress to her body (with her *woman's* hand) – old Lowji Daruwalla was outraged by the concept.

'Is this the result of a European education?' he cried.

121

'To attach any meaning whatsoever to what a woman is thinking when she takes off her clothes – this is true madness!'

The senior Daruwalla wouldn't listen to a sentence with Freud's name in it. That his father should reject Freud was further evidence to Farrokh of the tyrant's intellectual rigidity and his old-fashioned beliefs. As an intended put-down of Freud, Lowji paraphrased an aphorism of the great Canadian physician Sir William Osler. A bedside clinician extraordinaire and a gifted essayist, Osler was a favorite of Farrokh's, too. It was outrageous of Lowji to use Sir William to refute Freud; the old blunderbuss referred to the well-known Osler admonition that warns against studying medicine without textbooks – for this is akin to going to sea without a chart. Farrokh argued that this was a half-understanding of Osler and less than half an understanding of Freud, for hadn't Sir William also warned that to study medicine without studying patients was not to go to sea at all? Freud, after all, had studied patients. But Lowji was unbudgeable.

Farrokh was disgusted with his father. The young man had left home as a mere 17-year-old; at last he was a worldly and well read 19. Far from being a paragon of brilliance and nobility, old Lowji now looked like a buffoon. In a rash moment, Farrokh gave his father a book to read. It was Graham Greene's *The Power and the Glory*, a modern novel – at least it was 'modern' to Lowji. It was also a religious novel, which was (in Lowji's case) akin to holding the cape before the bull. Farrokh presented the novel to his father with the added temptation that the book had given considerable offense to the Church of Rome. This was a clever bit of baiting, and the old man was especially excited to learn that the book had been denounced by French bishops. For reasons Lowji never bothered to explain, he didn't like the French. For reasons he explained entirely too often, Lowji thought *all* religions were 'monsters.'

It was surely idealistic of young Farrokh to imagine that he could draw his fierce, old-fashioned father into his recently acquired European sensibilities – especially by as simple a device as a favorite novel. Naïvely, Farrokh hoped that a shared appreciation of Graham Greene might lead to a discussion of the enlightened Zilk sisters, who, although Roman Catholics, did not share the consternation caused the Church of Rome by *The Power and the Glory*. And this discussion might lead to the matter of who these liberal-thinking Zilk sisters might be, and so on and so forth.

But old Lowji despised the novel. He denounced it as morally contradictory – in his own words, 'a big confusion of good and evil.' In the first place, Lowji argued, the lieutenant who puts the priest to death is portrayed as a man of integrity – a man of high ideals. The priest, on the other hand, is utterly corrupted – a lecher, a drunk, an absent father to his illegitimate daughter.

'The man *should* have been put to death!' the senior Daruwalla exclaimed. 'Only not necessarily because he was a priest!'

Farrokh was bitterly disappointed by this pig-headed reaction to a novel he so loved that he'd already read it a half-dozen times. He deliberately provoked his father by telling him that his denouncement of the book was remarkably similar to the line of attack taken by the Church of Rome.

And so the summer and the monsoon of 1949 began.

Stuck in the Past

Here come the characters who comprise the movie vermin, the Hollywood scum, the film slime – the aforementioned 'unscrupulous cowards of mediocrity.' Fortunately, they are minor characters, yet so distasteful that their introduction has been delayed as long as possible. Besides, the past has already made an unwelcome intrustion into this narrative; the younger Dr Daruwalla, who's no stranger to unwanted and lengthy intrusions from the past, has all this time been sitting in the Ladies' Garden of the Duckworth Club. The past has descended upon him with such lugubrious weight that he hasn't touched his Kingfisher lager, which has grown undrinkably warm.

The doctor knows he should at least get up from the table and call his wife. Julia should be told right away about poor Mr Lal and the threat to their beloved Dhar: MORE MEMBERS DIE IF DHAR REMAINS A MEMBER. Farrokh should also forwarn her that Dhar is coming home for supper, not to mention that the doctor owes his wife some explanation regarding his cowardice; she will surely think him a coward for not telling Dhar the upsetting news – for Dr Daruwalla knows that, any day now, Dhar's twin is expected in Bombay. Yet he can't even drink his beer or rise from his chair; it's as if he were the second bludgeoned victim of the putter that cracked the skull of poor Mr Lal.

And all this time, Mr Sethna has been watching him. Mr Sethna is worried about the doctor – he's never seen him not finish a Kingfisher before. The busboys are whispering; they must change the tablecloths in the Ladies' Garden. The tablecloths for dinner, which are a saffron color, are quite different from the luncheon tablecloths, which are more of a vermillion hue. But Mr Sethna won't allow them to disturb Dr Daruwalla. He's not the man his father was, Mr Sethna knows, but Mr Sethna's loyalty to Lowji is unquestionably extended beyond the grave – not only to Lowji's children but even to that mysterious fair-skinned boy whom Mr Sethna heard Lowji call 'my grandchild' on more than one occasion.

Such is Mr Sethna's loyalty to the Daruwalla name that he won't tolerate the gossip in the kitchen. There is, for example, an elderly cook who swears that this so-called grandchild is the very same all-white actor who parades before them as Inspector Dhar. Although

124

Mr Sethna privately may believe this, he violently maintains that this couldn't be true. If the younger Dr Daruwalla claims that Dhar is neither his nephew nor his son – which he *has* claimed – this is good enough for Mr Sethna. He declares emphatically to the kitchen staff, and to all the waiters and the busboys, too: 'That boy we saw with old Lowji was someone else.'

And now a half-dozen busboys glide into the failing light in the Ladies' Garden, Mr Sethna silently directing them with his piercing eyes and with hand signals. There are only a few saucers and an ashtray, together with the vase of flowers and the warm beer, on Dr Daruwalla's table. Each busboy knows his assignment: one takes the ashtray and another removes the tablecloth, precisely following the exact second when Mr Sethna plucks up the neglected beer. There are three busboys who, between them, exchange the vermillion tablecloth for the saffron; then the same flower vase and a different ashtray are returned to the table. Dr Daruwalla doesn't notice, at first, that Mr Sethna has substituted a cold Kingfisher for the warm one.

It's only after they've departed that Dr Daruwalla appears to appreciate how the dusk has softened the brightness of both the pink and the white bougainvillea in the Ladies' Garden, and how his brimming glass of Kingfisher is freshly beaded with condensation; the glass itself is so wet and cool, it seems to draw his hand. The beer is so cold and biting, he takes a long, grateful swallow – and then another and another. He drinks until the glass is empty, but still he stays at the table in the Ladies' Garden, as if he's waiting for someone – even though he knows his wife is expecting him at home.

For a while, the doctor forgets to refill his glass; then he refills it. It's a 21-ounce bottle – entirely too much beer for dwarfs, Farrokh remembers. Then a look crosses his face, of the kind one hopes will pass quickly. But the look remains, fixed and distant, and

125

as bitter as the aftertaste of the beer. Mr Sethna recognizes this look; he knows at once that the past has reclaimed Dr Daruwalla, and by the bitterness of the doctor's expression, Mr Sethna thinks he knows *which* past. It's those *movie* people, Mr Sethna knows. They've come back again.

5. THE VERMIN

Learning the Movie Business

The director, Gordon Hathaway, would meet his end on the Santa Monica Freeway, but in the summer of '49 he was riding the fading success of a private-investigator movie. Perversely, it had inflamed his long-dormant desire to make what movie people call a 'quality' picture. This picture wouldn't be it. Although the director would manage to shoot the film, overcoming considerable adversity, the movie would never be released. Having had his fling with 'quality,' Hathaway would return with a modest vengeance, and more modest success, to the so-called P.I. genre. In the 1960's, he would make the downward move to television, where he awaited the unnoticed conclusion of his career.

Few aspects of Gordon Hathaway's personality were unique. He called all actors and actresses by their first names, including the ones he'd never met, which was the case with most of them, and he wetly kissed on both cheeks both the men and women he was saying adieu to, which included those he'd met for only the first or second time. He would marry four times, in each marriage goatishly siring children who would revile him before they were teenagers. In each account, Gordon would be unsurprisingly cast as the villain, while the four respective mothers (his ex-wives) emerged as highly compromised yet sainted. Hathaway said he'd had the misfortune to sire only daughters. Sons, he claimed, would have taken *his* side – to quote him, 'At least one out of four fuckin' times.'

As for his dress, he was a marginal eccentric; as he

127

aged – and as he more peaceably embraced a directorial career of complete compromise – he grew more outlandish in his attire, as if his clothes had become his foremost creative act. Sometimes he wore a woman's blouse, open to the waist, and he arranged his hair in a long white ponytail, which became his trademark; in his many films and TV crime dramas, there could be found no such identifying features. And all the while, he decried the 'suits' – which was his word for the producers – 'the fuckin' three-piece mentalities,' who, Hathaway said, had 'a fuckin' stranglehold on all the talent in Hollywood.'

This was an odd accusation, in that Gordon Hathaway had spent a long and modestly profitable career in close cahoots with these same 'suits.' Producers, in truth, *loved* him. But none of these details is original, or even memorable.

In Bombay, however, the first truly distinctive element of Gordon Hathaway's character was brought to light: namely, he was so frightned of the food in India – and so hysterically conscious of those diseases that, he was certain, would destroy his intestinal tract – that he ate nothing but room-service food, which he personally washed in his bathtub. The Taj Mahal Hotel was not unused to such habits among the foreign, but by this extremely selective diet Hathaway had severely constipated himself and suffered from hemorrhoids.

In addition, the hot, damp weather of Bombay had excited his chronic proneness to fungal infections. Hathaway stuck cotton balls between his toes – he had the most persistent case of athlete's foot that Dr Lowji Daruwalla had ever seen – and a fungus as unstoppable as bread mold had invaded his ears. Old Lowji believed that the director was capable of producing his own mushrooms. Gordon Hathaway's ears itched to the point of madness, and he was so deaf from both the fungus and the fungicidal ear drops – not to mention the cotton balls that he stuck in his ears – that his communication on the film set was comedic with mis-understanding.

As for the ear drops, they were a solution of gentian violet, an indelible purple dye. Therefore, the collars and shoulders of Hathaway's shirts were dotted with violet stains, for the cotton balls frequently fell out of his ears – or else Hathaway, in his frustration at being deaf, plucked out the cotton balls himself. The director was a born litterer; everywhere he went, the world was colorfully marked by his violet ear-cottons. Sometimes the purple solution streaked Hathaway's face, giving him the appearance of someone who'd been deliber-ately painted; he looked like a member of a religious cult, or of an unknown tribe. Gordon Hathaway's fingertips were similarly stained with gentian violet; he was always poking his fingers in his ears.

But Lowji was nevertheless impressed by the fabled artistic temperament of the first (and only) Hollywood director he'd ever met. The senior Daruwalla told Meher (she told Farrokh) that it was 'charming' how Hathaway had blamed his hemorrhoids and his fungus *neither* on his bathtub diet *nor* on the Bombay climate. Instead, the director faulted 'the fuckin' stress' of the compromising relationship he was compelled to con-duct with the film's philistine producer, a much defamed 'suit,' who (coincidentally) was married to Gordon's ambitious sister.

'That cunt of misery!' Gordon would often exclaim. Failing originality in all his cinematic pursuits, Gor-don Hathaway was nevertheless rumored to be the first to coin this vulgar phrase. 'Fuckin' ahead of my time' was a way he often spoke of himself; in this coarse instance, he may have been correct.

It was a great source of frustration to Meher and Farrokh to hear Lowji defend the grossness of Gordon Hathaway on grounds of the man's 'artistic tempera-ment.' It was never clear if the philistine producer's success in exerting certain pressures on Gordon was because of Gordon's desire to please the suit himself, or whether the true force of the exertion emanated from Gordon's sister – the so-called C. of M. herself. It was never clear who had whom 'by the balls,' as Gordon put it; it was unclear who 'jerked' whose 'wire,' as he otherwise put it.

As an admitted newcomer to the creative process, Lowji was undeterred by such talk; he sought to draw out of Gordon Hathaway the presumed aesthetic principles that guided the director through the frenzy with which this particular movie was being made. Even a novice could sense the hectic pace at which the film was being shot; even Lowji's untested artistic sensibilities could detect the aura of tension with which the screenplay underwent revision every evening in the dining room of the Duckworth Club.

'I trust my fuckin' instinct for storytellin', pal,' Gordon Hathaway confided to the senior Daruwalla, who was in such earnest search of a retirement career. 'That's the fuckin' key.'

How it shamed Farrokh and his poor mother: to observe, throughout dinner, that Lowji was taking notes.

As for the screenwriter, whose shared dream of a 'quality' picture was nightly and disastrously changing before his eyes, he was an alcoholic whose bar bill at the Duckworth Club theatened to exceed the Daruwalla family's resources; it was a tab that pinched even the seemingly bottomless purse of the well-heeled Promila Rai. His name was Danny Mills, and he'd started out with a story about a married couple who come to India because the wife is dying of cancer; they'd promised themselves that they would go to India 'one day.' It was originally titled, with the utmost sincerity, *One Day We'll Go to India;* then Gordon Hathaway retitled it *One Day We'll Go to India, Darling.* That small change initiated a major revision of the story, and sank Danny Mills all the deeper into his alcoholic gloom.

It was actually a step up for Danny Mills – to have begun this screenplay from scratch. It was, if only in the beginning, his original story. He'd started out as the lowliest of studio contract writers; his first job, at Universal, was for 100 dollars a week, and all he did was tamper with existing scripts. Danny Mills still had more screen credits for 'additional dialogue' than for 'co-script,' and his solo screenplay credits (there were only two) were for flops – utter bombs. At the moment, he prided himself for being an 'independent,' which is to say he was under no studio contract; however, this was because the studios thought he was unreliable, not only for his drinking but for his reputation as a loner. Danny wasn't content to be a team player, and he became especially cantankerous in the cases of those screenplays that had already engaged the creative genius of a half-dozen or more writers. Although it clearly depressed Danny to revise on demand, which he was doing as a result of the nightly whims of Gordon Hathaway, it was entirely rare for Danny to be working on a story that had at least originated with him. For this reason, Gordon Hathaway thought that Danny shouldn't complain.

It wasn't as if Danny had contributed a word to *The Big Sleep* or even *Cobra Woman,* and he'd had nothing to do with *Woman of the Year* or even *Hot Cargo*; he'd written neither *Rope* nor *Gaslight* – he hadn't added so much as a comma to *Son of Dracula*, or taken one away from *Frisco Sal* – and although for a while he'd been identified as the uncredited screenwriter for *When Strangers Marry*, this proved to be false. In Hollywood, he simply hadn't been playing in the big leagues; the general feeling was that 'additional dialogue' was the very zenith of his ability, and so he came to Bombay with more experience in fixing other people's messes than with creating his own. Doubtless it hurt Danny that Gordon Hathaway didn't refer to him as 'the writer' at all. Gordon called Danny Mills 'the fixer,' but in truth there was more that needed fixing in *One Day We'll Go to India, Darling* after Hathaway started changing it.

Danny had envisioned the movie as a love story with a twist; the 'twist' was the wife dying. In the original screenplay, the couple – in her dying days – succumb to the fakery of a snake guru; they are rescued from this charlatan and his gang of demonic snake-worshipers by a *true* guru. Instead of pretending to cure the wife, the true guru teaches her how to die with dignity. According to the philistine producer, or else to his wife – Gordon Hathaway's interfering C. of M. sister – this last part was lacking in both action and suspense.

'Despite how happy the wife is, she still fuckin' dies, doesn't she?' Gordon said.

Therefore, against the slightly better instincts of Danny Mills, Gordon Hathaway altered the story. Gordon believed that the snake guru wasn't villainous enough; hence the snake-worshipers were revised. The snake guru actually abducts the wife from the Taj and keeps her a prisoner in his harem of drugged women, while he instructs them in a method of meditation that concludes with having sex – either with the snakes or with him. This is an ashram of evil, surely. The distraught husband, in the company of a Jesuit missionary – a none-too-subtle replacement for the true guru – tracks the wife down and saves her from a fate presumed worse than her anticipated death by cancer. It is Christianity that the dying wife embraces at the end, and – no surprise! – she doesn't die after all.

Gordon Hathaway explained it to a surprised Lowji Daruwalla: 'The cancer just sort of goes away – it just fuckin' dries up and goes away. That happens sometimes, doesn't it?'

'Well, it doesn't exactly "dry up," but there are cases of remission,' the senior Dr Daruwalla answered uncertainly, while Farrokh and Meher suffered enormous embarrassment for him.

'What's that?' Gordon Hathaway asked. He knew what a remission was; he just hadn't heard the doctor because his ears were crammed full of fungus and gentian violet and cotton balls.

'Yes! Sometimes a cancer can just sort of go away!' old Lowji shouted.

'Yeah, that's what I thought – I knew that!' Gordon Hathaway said.

In his embarrassment for his father, Farrokh sought to turn the conversation toward India itself. Surely the gravity of the Partition and Independence – when a million Hindus and Muslims were killed, and 12 million became refugees – interested the foreigners a *little*.

'Listen, kid,' Gordon Hathaway said, 'when you're makin' a fuckin' movie, nothin' else interests you.' There was hearty consent to this at the dinner table; Farrokh felt that even the silence of his usually opinionated father served to rebuke him. Only Danny Mills appeared to be interested in the subject of local color; Danny also appeared to be drunk.

Although Danny Mills considered religion and politics as tedious forms of 'local color,' Danny was nevertheless disappointed that *One Day We'll Go to India, Darling* had very little to do with India. Danny had already suggested that the climate of religious violence in the days of the Partition might at least make a brief appearance in the background of the story.

'Politics is just fuckin' exposition,' Gordon Hathaway had said, dismissing the idea. 'I'd end up cutting the shit out of it later.'

In response to the present debate between the director and Farrokh, Danny Mills once more expressed his desire that the movie reflect at least a *hint* of Muslim-Hindu tensions, but Gordon Hathaway bluntly challenged Farrokh to tell him just one 'sore point' between Muslims and Hindus that wouldn't be boring on film. And since this was the year that Hindus had snuck into the Mosque of Babar with idols of their god-prince Rama, Farrokh imagined that he knew a good story. The Hindus had claimed that the site of the mosque was the birthplace of Rama, but the placing of Hindu idols in an historic mosque wasn't well received by Muslims – they hate idols of any kind. Muslims

133

don't believe in representations of God, not to mention lots of gods, while Hindus pray to idols (*and* to lots of gods) all the time. To avoid more Hindu-Muslim bloodshed, the state had locked up the Mosque of Babar. 'Perhaps they should have removed the idols of Rama first,' Farrokh explained. Muslims were enraged that these Hindu idols were occupying their mosque. Hindus not only wanted the idols to remain – they wanted to build a temple to Rama at the site.

At this point, Gordon Hathaway interrupted Farrokh's story to express anew his dislike of exposition. 'You'll never write for the movies, kid,' Gordon said. 'You wanna write for the movies, you gotta get to the point quicker than this.'

'I don't think we can use it,' said Danny Mills thoughtfully, 'but I thought it was a nice story.'

'Thank you,' Farrokh said.

Poor Meher, the oft-neglected *Mrs* Daruwalla, was sufficiently provoked to change the subject. She offered a comment on the pleasure of a sudden evening breeze. She noted the rustling of a neem tree in the Ladies' Garden. Meher would have elaborated on the merits of the neem tree, but she saw that the foreigners' interest – which was never great – had already waned.

Gordon Hathaway was holding the violet-colored cotton balls he'd taken from his ears, shaking them in the closed palm of one hand, like dice. 'What's a fuckin' *neem* tree?' he asked, as if the tree itself had annoyed him.

'They're all around town,' said Danny Mills. 'They're a tropical kind of tree, I think.'

'I'm sure you've seen them,' Farrokh said to the director.

'Listen, kid,' said Gordon Hathaway, 'when you're makin' a movie, you don't have time to look at the fuckin' trees.'

It must have hurt Meher to see by her husband's expression that Lowji had found this remark most sage. Meanwhile, Gordon Hathaway indicated that the conversation was over by turning his attention to a pretty, underage girl at an adjacent table. This left Farrokh with a view of the director's arrogant profile, and an especially alarming glimpse of the deep and permanent purple of Hathaway's inner ear. The ear was actually a rainbow of colors, from raw red to violet, as unsuitably iridescent as the face of a mandrill baboon.

Later, after the colorful director had returned to the Taj – presumably to wash more food in his bathtub before retiring to bed – Farrokh was forced to observe his father fawning over the drunken Danny Mills.

'It must be difficult to revise a screenplay under these conditions,' Lowji ventured.

'You mean at night? Over food? After I've been drinking?' Danny asked.

'I mean so spur-of-the-moment,' Lowji said. 'It would seem more prudent to shoot the story you've already written.'

'Yes, it would,' poor Danny agreed. 'But they never do it that way.'

'They like the spontaneity, I suppose,' Lowji said.

'They don't think the writing is very important,' said Danny Mills.

'They *don't*?' Lowji exclaimed.

'They never do,' Danny told him. Poor Lowji had never considered the unimportance of the writer of a movie. Even Farrokh looked with compassion on Danny Mills, who was an affectionate, sentimental man with a gentle manner and a face that women liked – until they knew him better. Then they either disliked his central weakness or exploited it. Alcohol was certainly a problem for him, but his drinking was more a symptom of his failure than a cause of it. He was always out of money and, as a consequence, he rarely finished a piece of writing and sold it from any position of strength; usually, he would sell only an idea for a piece of writing, or a piece of writing that was very much a fragment – a story barely in progress

– and as a result he lost all control of the outcome of whatever the piece of writing was.

He'd never finished a novel, although he'd begun several; when he needed money, he would put the novel aside and write a screenplay – selling the screenplay before he finished it. That was always the pattern. By the time he went back to the novel, he had enough distance from it to see how bad it was.

But Farrokh couldn't dislike Danny the way he disliked Gordon Hathaway; Farrokh could see that Danny liked Lowji, too. Danny also made an effort to protect Farrokh's father from further embarrassing himself.

'Here's the way it is,' Danny told Lowji. He swirled the melting ice in the bottom of his glass; in the kilnlike heat before the monsoon, the ice melted quickly – but never as quickly as Danny drank the gin. 'You're screwed if you sell something before you finish it,' Danny Mills told the senior Daruwalla. 'Never even *show* anybody what you're writing until you finish it. Just do the work. When you know it's good, show it to someone who's made a movie you like.'

'Like a director, you mean?' asked Lowji, who was still writing everything down.

'Definitely a director,' said Danny Mills. 'I don't mean a studio.'

'And so you show it to someone you like, a director, and *then* you get paid?' asked the senior Daruwalla.

'No,' said Danny Mills. 'You take *no* money until the whole deal is in place. The minute you take any money, you're screwed.'

'But when *do* you take the money?' Lowji asked.

'When they've signed the actors you want, when they've signed the director – *and* given him the final cut of the picture. When everyone likes the screenplay so much, you know they wouldn't dare change a word of it – and if you doubt this, demand final script approval. Then be prepared to walk away.'

'This is what you do?' Lowji asked.

'Not me,' Danny said. 'I take the money up front, as much as I can get. Then they screw me.'

'But who does it the way you suggest?' Lowji asked; he was so confused, he'd stopped writing.

'Nobody I know,' said Danny Mills. 'Everyone I know gets screwed.'

'So you didn't go to Gordon Hathaway – you didn't choose him?' Lowji asked.

'Only a studio would choose Gordon,' Danny said.

He had that uncommon smoothness of skin which appears so confounding on the faces of some alcoholics; it was as if Danny's baby-faced complexion were the direct result of the pickling process – as if the growth of his beard were as arrested as his speech. Danny looked like he needed to shave only once a week, although he was almost 35.

'I'll tell you about Gordon,' Danny said. 'It was Gordon's idea to expand the role of the snake guru in the story – Gordon's idea of the epitome of evil is an ashram with snakes. I'll tell you about Gordon,' Danny Mills went on, when neither Lowji nor Farrokh had interrupted him. 'Gordon's never *met* a guru, with or without snakes. Gordon's never *seen* an ashram, not even in California.'

'It would be easy to arrange a meeting with a guru,' Lowji said. 'It would be easy to visit an ashram.'

'I'm sure you know what Gordon would say to that idea,' said Danny Mills, but the drunken screenwriter was looking at Farrokh.

Farrokh attempted the best imitation of Gordon Hathaway that he could manage. 'I'm makin' a fuckin' movie,' Farrokh said. 'Do I got the time to meet a fuckin' guru or go to a fuckin' ashram when I'm in the middle of makin' a fuckin' movie?'

'Smart boy,' said Danny Mills. It was to old Lowji that Danny confided: 'Your son understands the movie business.'

Although Danny Mills appeared to be a destroyed man, it was hard not to like him, Farrokh thought.

137

Then he looked down in his beer and saw the two vivid violet cotton balls from Gordon Hathaway's ears. How did they end up in my beer? Farrokh wondered. He needed to use a parfait spoon to extract them, dripping, from his beer glass. He put Gordon Hathaway's soggy ear-cottons on a tea saucer, wondering how long they'd been soaking in his beer – and how much beer he'd drunk while Gordon Hathaway's ear-cottons were sponging up the beer at the bottom of his glass. Danny Mills was laughing so hard, he couldn't speak. Lowji could see what his critical son was thinking.

'Don't be ridiculous, Farrokh!' his father told him. 'Surely it was an accident.' This made Danny Mills laugh harder and harder, drawing Mr Sethna to their table – where the steward stared in disapproval at the tea saucer containing the beer-soaked, still-purple cotton balls. Farrokh's remaining beer was purple, too. Mr Sethna was thinking that it was at least fortunate that *Mrs* Daruwalla had already gone home for the evening.

Farrokh helped his father arrange Danny Mills in the back seat of the car. Danny would be sound asleep before they'd traveled the length of the driveway of the Duckworth Club, or at least by the time they'd left Mahalaxmi. The screenwriter was always asleep by that time, if he didn't go home earlier; when they dropped him at the Taj, Farrokh's father would tip one of the tall Sikh doormen, who would transport Danny to his room on a luggage cart.

This night – Farrokh in the passenger seat, his father driving, and Danny Mills asleep in the back seat – they had just entered Tardeo when his father said, 'In your nearly constant expression, you might be wise not to display such obvious distaste for these people. I know you think you're very sophisticated – and that they are vermin, beneath your contempt – but I'll tell you what is most *un*sophisticated, and that is to wear your feelings so frankly on your face.'

138

Farrokh would remember this, for he took the sting of such a rebuke very much to heart, while at the same time he sat silently seething in anger at his father, who wasn't as entirely stupid as his young son had presumed him to be. Farrokh would remember this, too, because the car was exactly at that location in Tardeo where, 20 years later, his father would be blown to smithereens.

'You should listen to these people, Farrokh,' his father was telling him. 'It isn't necessary for them to be your moral equals in order for you to learn something from them.'

Farrokh would remember the irony, too. Although this was his father's idea, Farrokh would be the one who actually learned something from the wretched foreigners; he'd be the one who took Danny's advice.

But Had He Learned Anything Worth Knowing?

Farrokh wasn't 19 now; he was 59. It was already past dusk at the Duckworth Club, but the doctor still sat slumped in his chair in the Ladies' Garden. The younger Dr Daruwalla wore an expression generally associated with failure; although he'd maintained absolute control of his Inspector Dhar screenplays – Farrokh was always granted 'final script approval' – what did it matter? Everything he'd written was crap. The irony was, he'd been very successful writing movies that were no better than *One Day We'll Go to India, Darling*.

Dr Daruwalla wondered if other screenwriters who'd written crap nevertheless dreamed, as he did, of writing a 'quality' picture. In Farrokh's case, his quality story always began in the same way; he just couldn't get past the beginning.

There was an opening shot of Victoria Terminus, the Gothic station with its stained-glass windows, its

139

friezes, its flying buttresses, its ornate dome with the watchful gargoyles – in Farrokh's opinion, it was the heart of Bombay. Inside the echoing station were a half-million commuters and the ever-arriving mi-grants; these latter travelers had brought everything with them, from their children to their chickens.

Outside the huge depot was the vast display of produce in Crawford Market, not to mention the pet stalls, where you could buy parrots or piranhas or monkeys. And among the porters and the vendors, the beggars and the newcomers and the pickpockets, the camera (somehow) would single out his hero, although he was just a child and crippled. What *other* hero would an orthopedic surgeon imagine? And with the magical simultaneity that movies can occasionally manage, the boy's face (a close-up) would let us know that *his* story had been chosen – among millions – while at that exact moment the boy's voice-over would tell us his name.

Farrokh was overly fond of the old-fashioned tech-nique of voice-over; he'd used it to excess in every Inspector Dhar movie. There's one that begins with the camera following a pretty young woman through Crawford Market. She's anxious, as if she knows she's being followed, and this causes her to topple a heaped-up pile of pineapples at a fruit stand, which makes her run; *this* causes her to slip on the rotting compost underfoot, which makes her bump into a pet stall, where a vicious cockatoo pecks her hand. That's when we see Inspector Dhar. As the young woman runs on, Dhar calmly follows her. He pauses by the stand of exotic birds only long enough to give the cockatoo a cuff with the back of his hand.

His voice-over says, 'It was the third time I'd tailed her, but she was still crazy enough to think she could shake me.'

Dhar pauses again as the pretty girl, in her haste, collides with a heaped-up pile of mangoes. Dhar is enough of a gentleman to wait for the vendor to clear a path through the fallen fruit, but the next time he catches up with the women, she's dead. A bullet hole is smack between her wide-open eyes, which Dhar politely closes for her.

His voice-over says, 'It's a pity I wasn't the only one tailing her. She had trouble shaking someone else, too.'

From his view of the younger Dr Daruwalla in the Ladies' Garden, old Mr Sethna was sure he knew the source of the hatred he saw in the doctor's eyes; the steward thought he knew the particular, long-ago vermin that the doctor was thinking of. But Mr Sethna was unfamiliar with self-doubt and self-loathing. The old Parsi would never have imagined that Dr Daruwalla was thinking about himself.

Farrokh was taking himself to task for leaving that crippled boy at Victoria Terminus, where he'd arrived; so many Bombay stories began at Victoria Terminus, but Dr Daruwalla had been unable to imagine *any* story for that abandoned child. The doctor was still wondering what could happen to the boy *after* he came to Bombay. Anything and everything could happen, Farrokh knew; instead, the screenwriter had settled for Inspector Dhar, whose tough-guy talk was as unoriginal as the rest of him.

Dr Daruwalla tried to save himself by thinking of a story with the innocence and purity of his favorite acts from the Great Royal Circus, but Farrokh couldn't imagine a story as good as even the simplest of the so-called items that he loved. He couldn't even think of a story as good as the daily routine of the circus. There were no wasted efforts in the course of the long day, which began with tea at 6:00 in the morning. The child performers and other acrobats did their strength and flexibility exercises and practiced their new items until 9:00 or 10:00, when they ate a light breakfast and cleaned their tents; in the rising heat, they sewed sequins on their costumes or they attended to other, almost motionless chores. There was no animal training

141

from midmorning on; it was too hot for the big cats, and the horses and the elephants stirred up too much dust.

Through the middle of the day, the tigers and lions lolled in their cages with their tails and paws and even their ears sticking out between the bars, as if they hoped that these extremities might attract a breeze; only their tails moved, among an orchestra of flies. The horses remained standing – it was cooler than lying down – and two boys took turns dusting the elephants with a torn cloth sack that had once held onions or potatoes. Another boy watered the floor of the main tent with a hose; in the midday heat, this didn't dampen the dust for long. The overall torpor affected even the chimpanzees, who stopped swinging from their cages; they still screamed occasionally – and they jumped up and down, as always. But if a dog so much as whined, not to mention barked, someone kicked it.

At noon, the animal trainers and the acrobats ate a big lunch; then they slept until midafternoon – their first performance always began after 3:00. The heat was still stultifying, and the motes of dust rose and sparkled like stars in the sunlight, which slanted through the vents in the main tent; in these harsh slashes of light, the dust appeared to swarm as intensely as the flies. In the breaks between their musical numbers, the band members passed a wet rag with which they wiped their brass instruments and, more often, their heads.

There was usually a sparse audience in attendance at the 3:30 performance. They were an odd mix of people too old for a full day's work and preschool children; in both cases, their alertness to the performances of the acrobats and the animals was below average, as if their limited powers of concentration were further impaired by the lingering heat and dust. Over the years, Dr Daruwalla had never sensed that the 3:30 performance itself was ever a diminished effort; the acrobats and the animal trainers, and even the animals, were as steady as they had to be. It was the audience that was a little off.

For this reason, Farrokh preferred the early-evening performance. Whole families came – young working-men and -women, and children who were old enough to pay attention – and the scant, dying sunlight seemed distant, even gentle; the dust motes weren't visible. It was the time of the evening when the flies appeared to have departed with the glare, and it was still too early for the mosquitoes. For the 6:30 performance, the place was always packed.

The first item was the Plastic Lady, a 'boneless' girl named Laxmi (the Goddess of Wealth). She was a beautiful contortionist – no sign of rickets. Laxmi was only 14, but the sharp definition of the bones in her face made her seem older. She wore a bright-orange bikini with yellow and red sequins that glittered in the strobe light; she looked like a fish with its scales reflecting a light that shone from underwater. It was dark enough in the main tent so that the changing colors of the stroboscope were effective, but enough of the late sunlight still illuminated the tent so that you could make out the faces of the children in the audience. Dr Daruwalla thought that whoever said circuses were for children was only half right; the circus was also for grownups who enjoyed seeing children so enthralled.

Why can't I do that? the doctor wondered, thinking about the simple brilliance of the boneless girl named Laxmi – thinking of the crippled boy abandoned in Victoria Terminus, where Dr Daruwalla's imagination had stalled as soon as it had begun. Instead of creating something as pure and riveting as the circus, he'd turned his mind to mayhem and murder – personified by Inspector Dhar.

What old Mr Sethna mistook in Dr Daruwalla's miserable expression was simply the doctor's deep disappointment with himself. With a sympathetic nod to the doctor, who sat forlornly in the Ladies' Garden,

143

the Parsi steward allowed himself a rare moment of
familiarity with a passing waiter.

'I'm glad *I'm* not the rat he's thinking of,' Mr Sethna
said.

Not the Curry

Of course there was more wrong with *One Day We'll
Go to India, Darling* that Danny Mills's alcoholism or
his unsubtle plagiarism of *Dark Victory*; much more
was amiss than Gordon Hathaway's crass alterations of
Danny's 'original' screenplay, or the director's attendant hemorrhoids and fungus. To make matters worse,
the actress who was playing the dying but saved wife
was that talentless beauty and denizen of the gossip
columns Veronica Rose. Her friends and colleagues
called her Vera, but she was born in Brooklyn with the
name Hermione Rosen and she was Gordon Hathaway's niece (the C. of M.'s daughter). Small world,
Farrokh would learn.

The producer, Harold Rosen, would one day find his
daughter as tiresomely tasteless as the rest of the world
judged her to be upon the merest introduction;
however, Harold was as easily bullied by his wife (the
C. of M. sister of Gordon Hathaway) as Gordon was.
Harold was operating on his wife's assumption that
Hermione Rosen, by her transformation to Veronica
Rose, would one day be a star. Vera's lack of talent and
intelligence would prove too great an obstacle for such
a goal – this in tandem with a compulsion to expose
her breasts that even Lady Duckworth would have
scorned.

But at the Duckworth Club in the summer of '49, a
rumor was in circulation that Vera was soon to have
a huge success. Concerning Hollywood, what did
Bombay know? That Vera had been cast in the role of
the dying but saved wife was all that Lowji Daruwalla
knew. It would take a while for Farrokh to find out that

Danny Mills had objected to Vera having the part –
until she seduced him and made him imagine that he
was in love with her. Then he trotted at her heels like a
dog. Danny believed it was the intense pressure of the
role that had cooled Vera's brief ardor for him – Vera
had her own room at the Taj, and she'd refused to sleep
with Danny since the commencement of principal
photography – but, in truth, she was having an
obvious affair with her leading man. It wasn't obvious
to Danny, who usually drank himself to sleep and got
up late.

As for the leading man, he was a bisexual named
Neville Eden. Neville was an uprooted Englishman
and a properly trained actor, if not exactly brimming
with natural ability, but his move to Los Angeles had
turned sour when a certain predictability in the parts
he was offered grew clear to him. He'd become too
easy to cast as any number of stereotypical Brits.
There was the Brit-twit role – the kind of instant Brit
whom more rowdy and less educated Americans
deplore – and then there was the sophisticated English
gentleman who becomes the love interest of an
impressionable American girl before she realizes
her mistake and chooses the more substantial (if
duller) American male. There was also the role of the
visiting British cousin – sometimes this was a war
buddy – who would comically display his inability to
ride a horse, or to drive a car on the right-hand side
of the road, or to successfully engage in fisticuffs in
low bars. In all these roles, Neville felt he was
supplying moronic reassurance to an audience that
equated manliness with qualities only to be found in
American men. This discovery tended to irritate him;
doubtless it also fueled what he called his 'homosexual
self.'

About *One Day We'll Go to India, Darling* Neville
was philosophic: at least it was a leading role, and the
part wasn't quite in the vein of the dimly perceived
British types he was usually asked to portray – after all,

in this story he was a happily married Englishman with a dying American wife. But even for Neville Eden the loser combination of Danny Mills, Gordon Hathaway and Veronica Rose was a trifle daunting. Neville knew from past experience that contact with a compromised script, a second-rate director and a floozy for a co-star tended to make him churlish. And Neville cared nothing for Vera, who was beginning to imagine that she was in love with him; yet he found fornicating with her altogether more inspiring, and amusing, than *acting* with her – and he was mightily bored.

He was also married, which Vera knew; it caused her great anguish, or at least virulent insomnia. Of course she did *not* know that Neville was bisexual; this revelation was often the means by which Neville broke off such passing affairs. He'd found it instantly effective – to tell whichever floozy it was that she was the first *woman* to capture his heart and his attention to such a degree, but that his homosexual self was simply stronger than both of them. That usually worked; that got rid of them, in a hurry. All but the wife.

As for Gordon Hathaway, he had his hands full; his hemorrhoids and his fungus were trifling in comparison to the certain catastrophe he was facing. Veronica Rose wanted Danny Mills to go home so she could lavish even more obvious attention on Neville Eden. Gordon Hathaway complied with Vera's request only to the degree that he forbade Danny's presence on the set. The writer's presence, Gordon claimed, 'fuckin' confused' the cast. But Gordon could hardly comply with his niece's request to send Danny home; he needed Danny every night, to revise the ever-changing script. Understandably, Danny Mills wanted to reinstate his original script, which Neville Eden had agreed was better than the picture they were making. Danny thought Neville was a good chap, though it would have destroyed him to learn that Neville was fornicating with Vera. Vera, above all, dearly desired to *sleep*, and Dr Lowji Daruwalla was alarmed by the sleeping pills she requested; yet he was such a fool for movies – he found her 'charming,' too.

His son Farrokh wasn't exactly charmed by Veronica Rose; neither was he altogether immune to her attractions. Soon a conflict of emotions engulfed the tender 19-year-old. Vera was clearly a coarse young woman, which is not without allure to 19-year-olds, especially when the woman in question is intriguingly older – Vera was 25. Furthermore, while he knew nothing of the random pleasure Vera took in exposing her breasts, Farrokh found that the actress bore a remarkable resemblance to the old photographs he so relished of Lady Duckworth.

It had been an evening in the empty dance hall when not even that depth of stone and the constant stirring of the ceiling fans could cool the stifling and humid night air, which had entered the Duckworth Club as heavily as a fog from the Arabian Sea. Even atheists, like Lowji, were praying for the monsoon rains. After dinner, Farrokh had escorted Vera from the table to the dance hall, not to dance with her but to show her Lady Duckworth's photographs.

'There is someone you resemble,' the young man told the actress. 'Please come and see.' Then he'd smiled at his mother, Meher, who didn't appear to be very happily entertained by the surly arrogance of Neville Eden, who sat to her left, or by the drunken Danny Mills, who sat to her right with his head upon his folded arms, which rested in his plate.

'Yeah!' Gordon Hathaway said to his niece. 'You oughta see the pictures of this broad, Vera. She showed her tits to everybody, too!' By this word 'too,' Farrokh should have been forewarned, but he supposed Gordon meant only that Lady Duckworth exposed herself 'in addition to' her other traits.

Veronica Rose wore a sleeveless muslin dress that clung to her back where she'd sweated against her chair; her bare upper arms caused excruciating offense to the Duckworthians, and especially to the recently acquired Parsi steward, Mr Sethna, who thought that for a woman to bare her upper arms in public was a violation of scandalous proportion – the slut might as well show her breasts, too!

When Vera saw Lady Duckworth's pictures, she was flattered; she lifted her damp blond hair off the back of her slender wet neck and she turned to young Farrokh, who felt an erotic flush at the sight of a rivulet of sweat that coursed from Vera's near armpit. 'Maybe I oughta wear my hair like hers,' Vera said; then she let her hair fall back in place. As Farrokh followed her to the dining room, he couldn't help but notice – through the drenched back of her dress – that she wore no bra.

'So how'd ya like the fuckin' exhibitionist?' her uncle asked her upon her return to the table.

Vera unbuttoned the front of her white muslin dress, showing her breasts to them all – Dr Lowji Daruwalla and Mrs Daruwalla, too. And the Lals, dining with the Bannerjees at a nearby table, certainly saw Veronica Rose's breasts very clearly. And Mr Sethna, so recently dismissed from the Ripon Club for attacking a crass member there with hot tea – Mr Sethna clutched his silver serving tray, as if he thought of striking the Hollywood wench dead with it.

'Well, whatta ya think?' Vera asked her audience. 'I don't know if she was an exhibitionist – I think she was just too fuckin' *hot*!' She added that she wanted to return to the Taj, where at least there was a sea breeze. In truth, she looked forward to feeding the rats that gathered at the water's edge beneath the Gateway of India; the rats were unafraid of people, and Vera enjoyed teasing them with expensive table scraps – the way some people enjoy feeding ducks or pigeons. Thereafter, she would go to Neville's room and straddle him until his cock was sore.

But in the morning, in addition to suffering the tribulation of her insomnia, Vera was sick; she was sick every morning for a week before she consulted Dr Lowji Daruwalla, who, even though he was an orthopedist, had no trouble ascertaining that the actress was pregnant.

'Shit,' Vera said. 'I thought it was the fuckin' curry.'

But no; it was just the fucking. Either Danny Mills or Neville Eden was the father. Vera hoped it was Neville, because he was better-looking. She also theorized that alcoholism like Danny's was genetic.

'Christ, it *must* be Neville!' said Vera Rose. 'Danny's so pickled, I think he's sterile.'

Dr Lowji Daruwalla was understandably taken aback by the crudeness of the lovely movie star, who wasn't really a movie star and who was suddenly terrified that her uncle, the director, would discover that she was pregnant and fire her from the picture. Old Lowji pointed out to Miss Rose that she had fewer than three weeks remaining on the shooting schedule; she wouldn't begin to *look* pregnant for another three months or more.

Miss Rose then became obsessed with the question of whether or not Neville Eden would leave his wife and marry her. Dr Lowji Daruwalla thought not, but he chose to soften the blow with an indirect remark.

'I believe that Mr Danny Mills would marry you,' the senior Daruwalla offered tactfully, but this truth only depressed Veronica Rose, who commenced to weep. As for weeping, it wasn't as commonplace at the Hospital for Crippled Children as one might suppose. Dr Lowji Daruwalla led the sobbing actress out of his office and through the waiting room, which was full of injured and crippled and deformed children; they all looked pityingly upon the crying fair-haired lady, imagining that she'd just received some awful news regarding a child of her own. In a sense, she had.

A Slum Is Born

At first, the news that Vera was pregnant didn't spread far. Lowji told Meher, and Meher told Farrokh. No one

149

else knew, and a special effort was made to keep this news from Lowji's South Indian secretary, a brilliant young man from Madras. His name was Ranjit and he, too, had high hopes of becoming a screenwriter. Ranjit was only a few years older than Farrokh, his spoken English was impeccable, but thus far his writing had been limited to the excellent case histories of the senior Dr Daruwalla's patients that he composed, and to his lengthy memos to Lowji concerning what recent articles he'd read in the doctor's orthopedic journals. These memos were written not to gain favor with old Lowji but as a means of giving the busy doctor some shorthand information regarding what he might like to read himself.

Although he came from a Hindu family of strictly vegetarian Brahmins, Ranjit had told Lowji – in his job interview – that he was wholly without religion and that he considered caste as 'largely a means to hold everyone down.' Lowji had hired the young man in an instant.

But that had been five years ago. Although Ranjit totally pleased the senior Daruwalla as a secretary and Lowji had made every effort to further brainwash the young man in an atheistic direction, Ranjit was finding it exceedingly difficult to attract a prospective bride – or, more important, a prospective father-in-law – by the matrimonial advertisements he regularly submitted to *The Times of India.* He wouldn't advertise that he was a Brahmin and a strict vegetarian, and although these things might not have mattered to him, they were of great concern to prospective fathers-in-law; it was usually the fathers-in-law, not the would-be brides, who responded to the advertisements – if anyone responded.

And now there was bickering between old Lowji and Ranjit because Ranjit had given in. His most recent advertisement in *The Times of India* had drawn over 100 responses; this was because he'd presented himself as someone who cared about caste and followed a strict vegetarian diet. After all, he told Lowji, he'd been made to observe these things as a child and they hadn't killed him. 'If it helps me to get married,' Ranjit said, 'sporting a fresh puja mark, so to speak, will not kill me now.'

Lowji was crushed by this traitorousness; he'd considered Ranjit like a third son, and a cohort in atheism. Furthermore, the interviews (with over 100 prospective fathers-in-law) were having a deleterious influence on Ranjit's efficiency; he was exhausted all the time, and no wonder – his mind was reeling with comparisons among 100 future wives.

But even in this state of mind, Ranjit was very attentive to the office visit of the Hollywood film goddess Veronica Rose. And since it was Ranjit's job to formally compose old Lowji's scribbles into a proper Orthopedic Report, the young man was surprised – after Vera's teary departure – to see that Lowji had scrawled no more than 'joint problem' in the sex symbol's file. It was highly unusual for the senior Daruwalla to escort any of his patients home, particularly following a mere office visit – and especially when there were other patients waiting to see him. Furthermore, old Dr Daruwalla had called his *own* home and told his wife that he was bringing Miss Rose *there*. All this for a joint problem? Ranjit thought it was most irregular.

Fortunately, the rigorous interviews that were the result of his highly successful matrimonial ads didn't allow Ranjit much time or energy for speculation on Vera's 'joint problem.' His interest was provoked no further than to ask the senior Daruwalla what *sort* of joint problem the actress was suffering; Ranjit wasn't used to typing up an incomplete Orthopedic Report.

'Well, actually,' Lowji said, 'I have referred her to another physician.'

'*Not* a joint problem then?' Ranjit inquired. All he cared about was correctly typing the report.

'Possibly gynecological,' Lowji answered warily.

'What sort of joint problem did she *think* she had?' Ranjit asked in surprise.

'Her knees,' Lowji said vaguely, with a dismissive wave of his hand. 'But I judged this to be psychosomatic.'

'The gynecological problem is psychosomatic, too?' Ranjit inquired. He foresaw difficult typing ahead.

'Possibly,' Lowji said.

'What *sort* of gynecological problem is it?' Ranjit persisted. At his age, and with his ambition to be a screenwriter, he was thinking that the problem was venereal.

'Itching,' said the senior Daruwalla – and to halt the inquisition at this juncture, he wisely added, 'Vaginal itching.' No young man, he knew, cared to contemplate this. The matter was closed. Ranjit's Orthopedic Report on Veronica Rose was the closest he would ever come to writing a screenplay (many years later, the younger Dr Daruwalla would read this report with consistent pleasure – whenever he desired to make some contact with the old days).

The patient is confused by her knees. She imagines that she has no vaginal itching, which indeed she has, while at the same time she feels some pain in her knees, which in fact she does not have. Most naturally, a gynecologist is recommended.

And *what* a gynecologist was selected for the task! Few patients would ever claim that their confidence soared when they placed themselves in the hands of the ancient, accident-prone Dr Tata. Lowji chose him because he was so senile, he was certain to be discreet; his powers of memory were too depleted for gossip. Sadly, the selection of Dr Tata was lacking in obstetrical merit.

At least Lowji had the good sense to entrust his wife with the psychological care of Veronica Rose. Meher tucked the pregnant bombshell into a guest bed in the

Daruwalla family mansion on old Ridge Road. Meher treated Vera like a little girl who'd just suffered a tonsillectomy. Although doubtless soothing, this mothering wouldn't solve Vera's problem; nor was Vera much comforted by Meher's claim that, in her own case, she hadn't really remembered the agony and the gore of childbirth. Over time, Meher told the knocked-up actress, only the positive parts of the experience stood out in her mind.

To Lowji, Meher was less optimistic. 'Here is a bizarre and thankless situation that you have gotten us into,' she informed her husband. Then the situation worsened.

The next day, Gordon Hathaway called the senior Dr Daruwalla from the slum set with the bothersome news that Veronica Rose had collapsed between takes. Actually, that was not what had happened. Vera's so-called collapse had had nothing whatsoever to do with her unwanted pregnancy; she'd simply fainted because a cow had licked her and then sneezed on her. Not that this wasn't disturbing to Vera, but the incident – like so many day-to-day occurrences in an actual slum – had been poorly observed and fervently misinterpreted by the horde of onlookers who reported the confused event.

Farrokh couldn't remember if the rudiments for a real slum existed in the area of Sophia Zuber Road in the summer of '49; he recalled only that there was both a Muslim and a Hindu population in that vicinity, for it wasn't far from where he'd attended school – at St Ignatius in Mazagaon. Probably, some kind of slum was already there. And certainly today there is a slum of good size and modest respectability on Sophia Zuber Road.

It's fair to say that Gordon Hathaway's movie set at least contributed to what now passes for acceptable housing in the slum on Sophia Zuber Road, for it was there that the slum set was hastily constructed. Naturally, among those hired as extras – to act the part of

153

the slum residents – were actual citizens of Bombay who were looking for an actual slum to move into. And once they'd moved in, they objected to these movie people, who were constantly invading their privacy. Rather quickly, it had become *their* slum.

Also, there was the matter of the latrine. An army of movie-crew coolies – thugs with entrenching tools – had dug the latrine. But one cannot create a new place to shit without expecting people to shit there. A universal code of defecation applies: if some people are shitting somewhere, others will shit there, too. This is only fair. Defecation in India is endlessly creative. Here was a new latrine; quickly it wasn't new. And one mustn't forget the intense heat before the monsoon breaks, and the ensuing floods that attend the onset of the monsoon; these factors, in addition to the sudden plenitude of human excrement, doubtless exacerbated Vera's morning sickness – not to mention her proneness to fainting on that particular day when she was both licked and sneezed on by a cow.

Gordon Hathaway and the film crew were shooting the scene where the abductors of the dying wife (Vera) are carrying her through the slum en route to the ashram of the snake guru. This is the moment when the idealistic Jesuit missionary, who just happens to be performing various labors of selflessness in the slum, sees the beautiful and unmistakably blond woman whisked along Sophia Zuber Road by a band of ruffians unsuitable for her company. There later follows the distraught husband (Neville) and a stereotypically stupid policeman who has clumsily lost the trail. This is the first meeting between the husband and the Jesuit, but it was *not* the first meeting between Neville and the arrogant Indian actor Subodh Rai, who played the missionary with inappropriately secular handsomeness and cunning.

Meanwhile, many of the new slum's residents had been forced to move out of 'their' slum in order for Gordon Hathaway to shoot this scene. Many more future residents of this new slum were crowding around, desirous to move in. Had any of these onlookers *not* been so transfixed by Veronica Rose, Neville and Subodh could have been observed flirting with each other off-camera; they were playfully pinching and tickling each other when Vera unaccountably found herself face-to-face with the cow.

Cows, Vera had heard, were holy – although not to the majority of beef-eating bystanders, who were Muslims – but Vera was so shocked to see *this* cow, first standing in her path and then approaching her, that she took rather a long time to determine what course of action she should choose. By then, the cow's moist breath was detectable in her cleavage; since she'd been abducted from the Taj (in the movie) in her nightgown, Vera's cleavage was quite considerable and exposed. The cow was garlanded with flowers; brightly colored beads were strung on thongs tied around its ears. Neither the cow nor Vera seemed to know what to make of this confrontation, although Vera was certain that she didn't want to cause some religious offense by being in the least aggressive toward the cow.

'Oh, what pretty flowers!' she remarked. 'Oh, what a *nice* cow!' she said to it. (Veronica Rose's repertoire of friendly, inoffensive responses was exceedingly small.) She didn't think she should throw her arms around the cow's neck and kiss its long, sad face; she wasn't sure if she should touch the cow at all. But the cow made the first move. It was simply on its way somewhere, and suddenly a film crew in general and a silly woman in particular stood in its way; therefore, it stepped slowly forward – it trod on Vera's bare foot. Since she'd just been abducted (in the movie), her foot was bare.

Even in great pain, Vera had such a fear of religious zealotry that she didn't dare scream in the cow's face, the wet muzzle of which was now pressed against her chest. Not only because of the humid weather but also because of her fear and pain, Vera was soaked with sweat; whether it was merely the salt on her fair skin, or her inviting fragrance – for doubtless Vera smelled vastly better than the other residents of Sophia Zuber Road – the cow at this moment licked her. Both the length and feel of the cow's tongue was a new experience for Vera, who fainted when the cow violently sneezed in her face. Then the cow bent over her and licked her chest and shoulders.

Thereafter, no one saw clearly what happened. There was demonstrable consternation for Miss Rose's welfare, and some rioting by those onlookers who were outraged by what they'd seen; the rioters themselves were uncertain of what they'd seen. Only Vera would later conclude that the rioters had rioted on behalf of a sacred cow. Neville Eden and Subodh Rai vaguely wondered if Vera had fainted in response to their observed sexual interest in each other.

By the time the Daruwallas found their way to the van, which served as Miss Rose's makeup room and a first-aid station, the Muslim owner of a bidi shop had spread the word all along Sophia Zuber Road that a blond American movie star, naked to her waist, had licked a cow and thereby caused widespread rioting among the sensitive Hindu population. Such mischief was unnecessary; riots didn't need reasons. If there was a reason for this one, it was probably that too many people wanted to move into the movie-set slum and they were impatient that they had to wait for the movie; they wanted to start living there immediately. But Vera, of course, would always imagine that everything had happened because of her and the cow.

It was into the midst of this bedlam that the Daruwalla family arrived to rescue the indelicately pregnant Miss Rose. Her state of mind hadn't been improved by the cow, but the senior Dr Daruwalla could conclude only that Vera had a bruised and swollen right foot – and that she was still pregnant. 'If Neville won't have me, I'll put the baby up for

156

adoption,' Vera said. 'But *you've* got to arrange it all here,' she told Lowji and Meher and Farrokh. She felt certain that her 'American audience' wouldn't sympathize with her for a child born out of wedlock; more to the point, her uncle wouldn't use her in another picture (if he knew); worse, Danny Mills, out of a drunk's special sentimentality, would insist on adopting the baby himself (if *he* knew). 'This has gotta be strictly between us!' Miss Rose told the helpless Daruwallas. 'Find me some fuckin' rich people who want a white baby!'

The interior of the van was a virtual sauna; the Daruwallas wondered if Vera was suffering from dehydration. Admittedly, Lowji and Meher felt unfamiliar with the moral logic of Westerners; they turned to their European-educated son for some guidance on this subject. But even to Farrokh it seemed an odd, questionable gift – to present India with *another* baby. Young Farrokh politely suggested that a baby might be more welcome for adoption in Europe or America, but Miss Rose sought secrecy at all cost – as if, morally, whatever she did in India, and whomever she left behind here, would somehow remain unrecorded, or at least never be counted against her.

'You could have an abortion,' the senior Dr Daruwalla suggested.

'Don't you *dare* mention that word to me,' said Veronica Rose. 'I'm not that kind of person – I was brought up with certain moral values!'

While the Daruwallas puzzled over Vera's 'moral values,' the van was rocked violently from side to side by a rowdy mob of men and boys. Lipstick and eyeliner rolled off the shelves of the van – and powders, and moisturizers, and rouge. A jar of sterile water crashed, and one of alcohol; Farrokh caught a falling box of gauze pads, and another of Band-Aids, as his father made his way to the sliding panel door. Veronica Rose screamed so loudly that she didn't hear what old Lowji shouted to the men outside; nor did she hear the sound of the several beatings, as various thugs among the film-crew coolies fell upon the mob with the entrenching tools they'd used to dig the not-so-new latrine. Miss Rose lay on her back, clutching the sides of her trembling cot, as small, colorful jars of this and that dropped harmlessly on her.

'Oh, I *hate* this country!' she yelled.

'It is merely a passing riot,' Meher assured her.

'I *hate* it, I *hate* it, I *hate* it!' Vera cried. 'It is the most *awful* country in the world – I simply *hate* it!'

It occurred to young Farrokh to ask the actress *why*, then, she would ever want to leave her own baby here in Bombay, but he felt he was too ignorant of the cultural differences between Miss Rose and himself to be critical. Farrokh wished to remain forever ignorant of the differences between these movie people and himself. At 19, young men are given to moral generalizations of a sweeping kind. To hold the rest of the United States responsible for the behavior of the former Hermione Rosen was a tad severe; nevertheless, Farrokh felt himself edging away from a future residence in the United States.

In short, Veronica Rose made Farrokh feel physically ill. Surely the woman should take *some* responsibility for her own pregnancy. And she'd tarnished Farrokh's sacred memory of Lady Duckworth's exhibitionism! In legend, Lady Duckworth's self-exposure had seemed elegant but not greatly tempting. In Farrokh's mind, Lady Duckworth's breasts were only a symbolic display. But, forever after, Farrokh was left with the more tangible memory of Vera's raw tits – they were such a sincerely carnal offering.

The Camphor Man

With all this trash in his past, it's little wonder that Farrokh was *still* sitting at his table in the darkening Ladies' Garden of the Duckworth Club. In the time it had taken the younger Dr Daruwalla to recall such a past, Mr Sethna had provided him with another cold Kingfisher. Farrokh hadn't touched his new beer. The faraway look in Dr Daruwalla's eyes was almost as distant as that gaze of death which the doctor had recently seen in the eyes of Mr Lal, although (it's already been said) the vultures had spoiled a clear impression.

At the Great Royal Circus, about an hour before the early-evening performance, a stooped man carrying a burning brazier would walk along the avenue of troupe tents; live coals were glowing in the brazier, and the aromatic camphor smoke drifted into the tents of the acrobats and the animal trainers. The camphor man would pause by each tent to be sure that enough smoke wafted inside. In addition to the medicinal properties attributed to camphor – it was often used as a counter-irritant for infections and in the treatment of itching – the smoke was of superstitious importance to the circus performers. They believed that inhaling camphor smoke protected them from the evil eye and the dangers of their profession – animal attacks, falling.

When Mr Sethna saw Dr Daruwalla close his eyes and throw back his head and draw a deep breath of the flowery air in the Ladies' Garden, the old Parsi steward mistook the reason. Mr Sethna wrongly assumed that Farrokh had felt an evening breeze and therefore was enjoying a sudden infusion of the scent from the surrounding bougainvillea. But Dr Daruwalla was sniffing for the camphor man, as if the doctor's memories of the past were in need of both a disinfectant and a blessing.

6. THE FIRST ONE OUT

Separated at Birth

As for Vera, young Farrokh wouldn't be a witness to
the woman's worst behavior; he would be back in
school in Vienna when Veronica Rose gave birth to
twins and elected to leave one of them in the city she
hated – she took the other one home with her. This was
a shocking decision, but Farrokh wasn't surprised;
Vera was a spur-of-the-moment sort of woman, and
Farrokh had observed the monsoon months of her
pregnancy – he knew the kind of insensitivity that she
was capable of. In Bombay, the monsoon rains begin
in mid-June and last until September. To most Bombayites, the rains are a relief from the heat, despite the
blocked drains. It was only July when the shooting of
the terrible film was finished and the movie rabble left
Bombay – alas, leaving poor Vera behind for the remainder of the monsoon and beyond.

It was for 'soul-searching' that she told them all she
was staying. Neville Eden didn't care whether she was
staying or going; he'd taken Subodh Rai to Italy – a
pasta diet, Neville told young Farrokh with relish,
improved one's stamina for the rigors of buggery.
Gordon Hathaway was attempting to edit *One Day
We'll Go to India, Darling* in Los Angeles; despite
changing its title to *The Dying Wife*, no amount or
convolution of editing could save the picture. Every
day, Gordon cursed his family for burdening him with
a niece as willful and untalented as Vera.

Danny Mills was drying out in a private sanitarium
in Laguna Beach, California; the sanitarium was
slightly ahead of its time – it favored vigorous calis-
thenics in tandem with a grapefruit-and-avocado diet.

Danny was also being sued by a limousine company, because Harold Rosen the producer was no longer paying for Danny's so-called business trips. (When Danny couldn't stand it another second in the sanitarium, he'd call a limo to drive him to L.A. and wait for him while he consumed a hearty beef-oriented dinner and two or three bottles of a good red wine; then the limo would return him to Laguna Beach, where Danny would arrive sated but with his tongue the shape and color of a raw chicken liver. Whenever he was drying out, it was red wine he craved above all else.) Danny wrote to Vera daily – staggeringly claustrophobic love letters, some of them running 20 typed pages. The gist of these letters was always the same and quite simple to understand: that Danny would 'change' if Vera would marry him.

Vera, meanwhile, had made her plans, presuming the complete cooperation of the Daruwallas. She would move into hiding, with Dr Lowji and his family, until the child was born. The prenatal care and delivery would be the responsibility of the senile friend of the senior Dr Daruwalla, the ancient and accident-prone Dr Tata. It was unusual for Dr Tata to make house calls, but he agreed, given his friendship with the Daruwallas and his understanding of the extreme sensitivity ascribed to the hypochondriac movie star. This was just as well, Meher said, because Veronica Rose would *not* have responded confidently to the peculiar sign with large lettering that was posted outside Dr Tata's office building.

DR TATA'S BEST,
MOST FAMOUS CLINIC
FOR GYNECOLOGICAL &
MATERNITY NEEDS

It was surely wise to spare Vera the knowledge that Dr Tata found it necessary to advertise his services as 'best' and 'most famous,' for Vera would doubtless conclude that Dr Tata suffered from insecurity. And so Dr Tata made frequent house calls to the esteemed Daruwalla residence on Ridge Road; because Dr Tata was far too old to drive a car safely, his arrivals and departures were usually marked by the presence of taxis in the Daruwallas' driveway – except for one time when Farrokh observed Dr Tata stumbling into the driveway from the back seat of a private car. This wouldn't have been of special interest to the young man except that the car was driven by Promila Rai; beside her in the passenger seat was her allegedly hairless nephew, Rahul – the very boy whose sexual ambiguity so discomforted Farrokh.

This loomed as a violation of that secrecy which all the Daruwallas sought for Vera and her pending child; but Promila and her unnerving nephew drove off as soon as Dr Tata was deposited in the driveway, and Dr Tata told Lowji that he was sure he'd thrown Promila 'off the trail.' He'd told her he was making a house call to see Meher. Meher was offended that a woman as loathsome to her as Promila Rai would be presuming all sorts of female plumbing problems of an intimate nature. It was long after Dr Tata had departed that Meher's irritation subsided and she thought to ask Lowji and Farrokh what Promila and Rahul Rai were doing with old Dr Tata in the first place. Lowji pondered the question as if for the first time.

'I suppose she was concluding an office visit and he asked her for a ride,' Farrokh informed his mother.

'She is a woman past childbearing years,' Meher delightedly pointed out. 'If she was concluding an office visit, it would have been for something gynecological. For such a visit, why would she take her nephew?'

Lowji said, 'Perhaps it was the *nephew's* office visit – probably it has something to do with the hairlessness business!'

'I know Promila Rai,' Meher said. 'She won't believe for one minute that Dr Tata was house-calling to see *me*.'

And then, one evening, following a function where there'd been interminable speeches at the Duckworth Club, Promila Rai approached Dr Lowji Daruwalla and said to him, 'I know all about the blond baby – I will take it.'

The senior Dr Daruwalla cautiously said, 'What baby?' Then he added, 'There's no certainty it will be blond!'

'Of course it will,' said Promila Rai. 'I know these things. At least it will be fair-skinned.'

Lowji considered that the child might indeed be fair-skinned; however, both Danny Mills and Neville Eden had very dark hair, and the doctor sincerely doubted the baby would be as blond as Veronica Rose.

Meher was opposed, on principle, to Promila Rai being an adoptive mother. In the first place, Promila was in her fifties – not only a spinster but an evil, spurned woman.

'She's a bitter, resentful witch,' Meher said. 'She'd be an *awful* mother!'

'She must have a dozen servants,' Lowji replied, but Meher accused him of forgetting how offended he'd once been by Promila Rai.

As a Malabar Hill resident, Promila had led a protest campaign against the Towers of Silence. She'd offended the entire Parsi community, even old Lowji. Promila had claimed that the vultures were certain to drop body parts in various residents' gardens, or on their terraces. Promila even alleged that she'd spotted a bit of a finger floating in her balcony birdbath. Dr Lowji Daruwalla had written an angry letter explaining to Promila that vultures didn't fly around with the fingers or toes of corpses in their beaks; vultures consumed what they wanted on the ground – anyone who knew anything about vultures knew that.

'And now you want Promila Rai to be a *mother*!' Meher exclaimed.

'It isn't that I *want* her to be a mother,' the senior Dr Daruwalla said. 'However, there isn't exactly a lineup of wealthy matrons seeking to adopt an American movie star's unwanted child!'

'Furthermore,' Meher said, 'Promila Rai is a man-hater. What if that poor baby is a boy?'

Lowji didn't dare tell Meher what Promila had already said to him. Promila was not only certain that the baby would be blond, she was also quite sure it would be a girl.

'I know these things,' Promila had told him. 'You're only a doctor – and one for joints, not babies!'

The senior Dr Daruwalla didn't suggest that Veronica Rose and Promila Rai discuss their transaction with each other; instead, he did everything he could to keep them from such a discussion – they didn't seem to have much interest in each other, anyway. It mattered to Vera only that Promila was rich, or so it appeared. It mattered most of all to Promila that Vera was healthy. Promila had a sizable fear of drugs; it was drugs, she was certain, that had poisoned her fiancé's brain and caused him to change his mind about marrying her – twice. After all, had he been drug-free and clear-headed, why wouldn't he have married her – at least once?

Lowhi could assure Promila that Vera was drug-free. Now that Neville and Danny had left Bombay and Vera wasn't trying to be an actress every day, she didn't need the sleeping pills; in fact, she slept most of the time.

Almost anyone could see where this was going; it was a pity that Lowji couldn't. His own wife thought him criminal even to consider putting a newborn baby into the hands of Promila Rai; Promila would doubt-less reject the child if it was male, or even slightly dark-haired. And then Lowji heard the worst news, from old Dr Tata – namely, that Veronica Rose wasn't a true blonde.

'I've seen where you haven't seen,' old Dr Tata told him. 'She has *black* hair, very black – maybe the blackest hair I've ever seen. Even in India!'

Farrokh felt he could imagine the conclusion to this melodrama. The child would be a boy with black hair; Promila Rai wouldn't want him, and Meher wouldn't want Promila to have him, anyway. Therefore, the Daruwallas would end up adopting Vera's baby. What Farrokh failed to imagine was that Veronica Rose wasn't entirely as artless as she'd appeared; Vera had already chosen the Daruwallas as her baby's adoptive parents. Upon the child's birth, Vera had planned to stage a breakdown; the reason she'd appeared so indifferent to discussions with Promila was that Vera had decided she'd reject *any* would-be adoptive parent – not only Promila. She'd guessed that the Daruwallas were suckers when it came to children, and she'd not guessed wrong.

What no one had imagined was that there wouldn't be just one dark-haired baby boy, there would be *two* – identical twin boys with the most gorgeous, almond-shaped faces and jet-black hair! Promila Rai wouldn't want them, and not only because they were dark-haired boys; she would claim that any woman who had twins was clearly taking drugs.

But the most unexpected turn of events would be engineered by the persistent love letters of Danny Mills to Veronica Rose, and by the death of Neville Eden – the victim of a car crash in Italy, an accident that also ended the flamboyant life of Subodh Rai. Until the news of the car crash, Vera had been illogically hoping that Neville might come back to her; now she determined that the fatal accident was divine retribution for Neville's preferring Subodh to her. She would carry this thought still further in her elder years, believing that AIDS was God's well-intentioned effort to restore a natural order to the universe; like many morons, Vera would believe the scourge was a godsent plague in judgment of homosexuals. This was remarkable thinking, really, for a woman who wasn't imaginative enough to believe in God.

It had been clear to Vera that if Neville ever would

have wanted her, he wouldn't have wanted her cluttered up with a baby. But upon Neville's abrupt departure, Vera turned her thoughts to Danny. Would Danny *still* want to marry her if she brought him home a little surprise? Vera was sure he would.

'Darling,' Vera wrote to Danny. 'I've not wanted to test how much you love me, but all this while I've been carrying *our* child.' (Her months with Lowji and Meher had markedly improved Vera's English.) Naturally, when she first saw the twins, Vera immediately pronounced them to be Neville's; in her view, they were far too pretty to be Danny's.

Danny Mills, for his odd part, hadn't considered having a child before. He was descended from weary but pleasant parents who'd had too many children before Danny had been born and who'd treated Danny with cordial indifference bordering on neglect. Danny wrote cautiously to his beloved Vera that he was thrilled she was carrying *their* child; a child was a fine idea – he hoped only that she didn't desire to start a whole family.

Twins are 'a whole family' unto themselves, as any fool knows, and thus the dilemma would sort itself out in the predictable fashion: Vera would take one home and the Daruwallas would keep the other. Simply put, Vera didn't want to overwhelm Danny's limited enthusiasm for fatherhood.

Among the host of surprises awaiting Lowji, not the least would be the advice given to him by his senile friend Dr Tata: 'When it comes to twins, put your money on the first one out.' The senior Dr Daruwalla was shocked, but being an orthopedist, not an obstetrician, he sought to comply with Dr Tata's recommendation. However, such excitement and confusion attended the birth of the twins that none of the nurses kept track of which one came out first; old Dr Tata himself couldn't remember.

In this respect was Dr Tata said to be 'accident-prone'; he blamed the unprofessionalism of the house calls for his failure to hear the two heartbeats whenever he put his stethoscope to Vera's big belly; he said that in his office, under appropriate conditions, he would surely have heard the two hearts. As it was – whether it was the music that Meher played or the constant sounds of housecleaning by the several servants – old Dr Tata simply assumed that Vera's baby had an unusually strong and active heartbeat. On more than one occasion, he said, 'Your baby has just been exercising, I think.'

'I could have told you that,' Vera always replied.

And so it wasn't until she was in labor that the monitoring of the fetal heartbeats told the tale. 'What a lucky lady!' Dr Tata told Vera Rose. 'You have not one but two!'

A Knack for Offending People

In the summer of '49, when the monsoon rains drenched Bombay, the aforementioned melodrama lay, heavy and unseen, in young Farrokh Daruwalla's future – like a fog so far out in the Indian Ocean, it hadn't yet reached the Arabian Sea. He would be back in Vienna, where he and Jamshed were continuing their lengthy and proper courtship of the Zilk sisters, when he heard the news.

'Not one but two!' And Vera took only one with her.

To Farrokh and Jamshed, their parents were already elderly. Even Lowji and Meher might have agreed that the most vigorous of their child-raising abilities were behind them; they'd do their best with the little boy, but after Jamshed married Josefine Zilk, it made sense for the younger couple to take over the responsibility. Theirs was a mixed marriage, anyway; and Zürich, where they would settle, was an international city – a dark-haired boy of strictly white parentage would easily fit in. By then he knew Hindi in addition to English; in Zürich he would learn German, although

Jamshed and Josefine would start him in an English-speaking school. After a time, the senior Daruwallas became like grandparents to the boy; from the beginning, Lowji had legally adopted him.

And after Jamshed and Josefine had children of their own – and there came that inevitable passage through adolescence, wherein the orphaned twin expressed a disgruntled alienation from them all – it was only natural that Farrokh would emerge as a kind of big brother to the boy. The 20-year difference between them made Farrokh something of another father to the child, too. By then, Farrokh was married to the former Julia Zilk, and they'd started a family of their own. Wherever he went, the adopted boy appeared to belong, but Farrokh and Julia were his favorites.

One shouldn't feel sorry for Vera's abandoned child. He was always part of a large family, even if there was something dislocating in the geographical upheavals in the young man's life – between Toronto, Zürich and Bombay – and even if, at an early age, there could be detected in him a certain detachment. And later there was in his language – in his German, in his English, in his Hindi – something decidedly odd, if not exactly a speech impediment. He spoke very slowly, as if he were composing a written sentence, complete with punctuation, in his mind's eye. If he had an accent, it was nothing traceable; it was more a matter of his enunciation, which was so very deliberate, as if he were in the habit of speaking to children, or addressing crowds.

And the issue that naturally intrigued them all, which was whether he was the offspring of Neville Eden or of Danny Mills, would not be easily decided. In the medical records of *One Day We'll Go to India, Darling* – which are, to this day, the only enduring records that the film was ever made – it was clearly noted that Neville and Danny were of the same common blood group, and the very same type that the twins would share.

Various Daruwallas argued that *their* twin was too good-looking, and too disinclined toward strong drink, to be a conceivable creation of Danny's. Furthermore, the boy showed little interest in reading, much less in writing – he didn't even keep a diary – whereas he was quite a gifted and highly disciplined young actor, even in grammar school. (This pointed the finger at the late Neville.) But, of course, the Daruwallas knew very little about the *other* twin. If one is determined to feel sorry for either of these twins, perhaps one should indulge such a feeling for the child Vera kept.

As for the little boy who was abandoned in India, his first days were marked by the necessity of giving him a name. He would be a Daruwalla, but in concession to his all-white appearance, it was agreed he should have an English first name. The family concurred that his name should be John, which was the Christian name of none other than Lord Duckworth himself; even Lowji conceded that the Duckworth Club was the source of the responsibility he bore for Veronica Rose's cast-off child. Needless to say, no one would have been so stupid as to name a boy *Duckworth* Daruwalla. *John* Daruwalla, on the other hand, had a friendly Anglo-Indian ring.

Everyone could more or less pronounce this name. Indians are familiar with the letter *J;* even German-speaking Swiss don't badly maul the name John, although they tend to Frenchify the name as 'Jean.' Daruwalla is as phonetic as most names come, although German-speaking Swiss pronounce the *W* as *V*, hence the young man was known in Zürich as Jean Daruvalla; this was close enough. His Swiss passport was issued in the name of John Daruwalla – plain but distinctive.

Not for 39 years did there awaken in Farrokh that first stirring of the creative process, which old Lowji would never experience. Now, nearly 40 years after the birth of Vera's twins, Farrokh found himself wishing that he'd never experienced the creative process, either. For it was by the interference of Farrokh's imagination that little John Daruwalla had become Inspector Dhar, the man Bombay most loved to hate – and Bombay was a city of many passionate hatreds.

Farrokh had conceived Inspector Dhar in the spirit of satire – of *quality* satire. Why were there so many easily offended people? Why had they reacted to Inspector Dhar so humorlessly? Had they no appreciation for comedy? Only now, when he was almost 60, did it occur to Farrokh that he was his father's son in this respect: he'd uncovered a natural talent for pissing people off. If Lowji had long been perceived as an assassination-in-progress, why had Farrokh been blind to this possible result in the case of Inspector Dhar? And he'd thought he was being so careful!

He'd written that first screenplay slowly and with great attention to detail. This was the surgeon in him; he hadn't learned such carefulness or authenticity from Danny Mills, and certainly not from his attendance at those three-hour spectacles in the shabby downtown cinema palaces of Bombay – those art-deco ruins where the air-conditioning was always 'undergoing repair' and the urine frequently overflowed the lavatories.

More than the movies, he'd watched the audience eating their snacks. In the 1950's and '60's, the masala recipe was working – not only in Bombay but throughout South and Southeast Asia and the Middle East, and even in the Soviet Union. There was music mixed with murder, sob stories intercut with slapstick, mayhem in tandem with the most maudlin sentimentality – and, above all, the satisfying violence that occurs whenever the forces of good confront and punish the forces of evil. There were gods, too; they helped the heroes. But Dr Daruwalla didn't believe in the usual gods; when he started writing, he'd just recently become a convert to Christianity. To that Hindi hodgepodge which was the Bombay cinema, the doctor added his tough-guy voice-over and Dhar's antiheroic sneer. Farrokh would wisely leave his newfound Christianity out of the picture.

He'd followed Danny Mills's recommendations to the letter. He selected a director he liked. Balraj Gupta was a young man with a less heavy hand than most – he had an almost self-mocking manner – and more important, he was not such a well-known director that Dr Daruwalla couldn't bully him a little. The deal was as Danny Mills had said a deal should be, including the doctor's choice of the young, unknown actor who would play Inspector Dhar. John Daruwalla was 22.

Farrokh's first effort to pass off the young man as an Anglo-Indian wasn't at all convincing to Balraj Gupta. 'He looks like some kind of European to me,' the director complained, 'but his Hindi is the real thing, I guess.' And after the success of the first Inspector Dhar movie, Balraj Gupta would never dream of interfering with the orthopedist (from Canada!) who'd given Bombay its most hated antihero.

The first movie was called *Inspector Dhar and the Hanging Mali*. This was more than 20 years after a *real* gardener had been found hanging from a neem tree on old Ridge Road in Malabar Hill, a posh part of town for anyone to be hanged in. The mali was a Muslim who'd just been dismissed from tending the gardens of several Malabar Hill residents; he'd been accused of stealing, but the charge had never been proven and there were those who claimed that the real-life gardener had been fired because of his extremist views. The mali was said to be furious about the closing of the Mosque of Babar.

Although Farrokh fictionalized the mali's story 20 years after the little-known facts of the case, *Inspector Dhar and the Hanging Mali* wasn't viewed as a period piece. For one thing, the 16th-century Babri mosque was still in dispute. The Hindus still wanted their idols to remain in the mosque in honor of the birthplace of Rama. The Muslims still wanted the idols removed.

171

In the late 1960's, very much in keeping with the language of that time, the Muslims said they wanted to 'liberate' the Mosque of Babar – whereas it was the birthplace of Rama that the Hindus said *they* wanted to liberate

In the movie, Inspector Dhar sought to keep the peace. And, of course, this was impossible. The essence of an Inspector Dhar movie was that violence could be relied upon to erupt around him. Among the earliest of the victims was Inspector Dhar's wife! Yes, he was married in the first movie, albeit briefly; the car-bomb death of his wife apparently justified his sexual licentiousness for the rest of the movie – and for all the other Inspector Dhar movies to come. And everyone was supposed to believe that this all-white Dhar was a Hindu. He's seen lighting his wife's cremation fire, he's seen wearing the traditional dhoti, with his head traditionally shaved. All during the course of the first movie, his hair is growing back. Other women rub the stubble, as if in the most profound respect for his late wife. His status as a widower gains him great sympathy and lots of women – a very Western idea, and very offensive.

To begin with, both Hindus and Muslims were offended. Widowers were offended, not to mention widows and gardeners. And from the very first Inspector Dhar movie, policemen were offended. The misfortune of the real-life hanging mali had never been explained. The crime – that is, if it *was* a crime, if the gardener hadn't hanged himself – was never solved.

In the movie, the audience is offered three versions of the hanging, each one a perfect solution. Thus the unfortunate mali is hanged three times, and each hanging offended some group. Muslims were angry that Muslim fanatics were blamed for hanging the gardener. Hindus were outraged that Hindu fundamentalists were blamed for hanging the gardener; and Sikhs were incensed that Sikh extremists were blamed for hanging the gardener, as a means of setting

Muslims and Hindus against each other. The Sikhs were also offended because every time there's a taxi in the movie, it's driven wildly and aggressively by someone who's perceived to be a crazed Sikh.

But the film was terribly *funny*! Dr Daruwalla had thought.

In the darkness of the Ladies' Garden, Farrokh reconsidered. *Inspector Dhar and the Hanging Mali* might have been terribly funny to *Canadians*, he imagined – with the notable exception of Canadian gardeners. But Canadians had never seen the film, except those former Bombayites who lived in Toronto; they'd watched all the Inspector Dhar movies on videocassettes, and even *they* were offended. Inspector Dhar himself had never found his films especially funny. And when Dr Daruwalla had questioned Balraj Gupta concerning the comic (or at least satiric) nature of the Inspector Dhar movies, the director had responded in a most offhand manner. 'They make lots of lakhs!' the director had said. 'Now *that's* funny!'

But it was no longer funny to Farrokh.

What if Mrs Dogar Was a Hijra?

In the first darkness of the evening, the Duckworthians with small children had begun to occupy the tables in the Ladies' Garden. The children enjoyed eating outdoors, but not even their enthusiastic high-pitched voices disturbed Farrokh's journey into the past. Mr Sethna disapproved of all small children – he especially disapproved of eating with them – but he nevertheless considered it his duty to oversee Dr Daruwalla's state of mind in the Ladies' Garden.

Mr Sethna had seen Dhar leave with the dwarf, but when Vinod returned to the Duckworth Club – the steward assumed that the nasty-looking midget was simply making his taxi available to Dr Daruwalla, too – the dwarf hadn't waddled in and out of the foyer, as

173

usual; Vinod had gone into the Sports Shop, where the dwarf was on friendly terms with the ball boys and the racquet stringers. Vinod had become their favorite scavenger. Mr Sethna disapproved of scavenging *and* of dwarfs; the steward thought dwarfs were disgusting. As for the ball boys and the racquet stringers, they thought Vinod was cute.

If the film press was at first being facetious when they referred to Vinod as 'Inspector Dhar's dwarf bodyguard' – they also called the dwarf 'Dhar's thug chauffeur' – Vinod took his reputation seriously. The dwarf was always well armed, and his weapons of choice were both legal and easily concealed in his taxi. Vinod collected squash-racquet handles from the racquet stringers at the Duckworth Sports Shop. When a racquet head was broken, a stringer sawed the head off and sanded down the stump until it was smooth; the remaining squash-racquet handle was of the right length and weight for a dwarf, and the wood was very hard. Vinod wanted only wooden racquet handles, which were becoming scarce. But the dwarf hoarded them; and the way he used them, he rarely broke one. He would jab or strike with only one racquet handle – he would go for the balls or the knees, or both – while he held the other handle out of reach. Invariably, the man under attack would grab hold of the offending racquet handle; thereupon Vinod would bring the other handle down on the man's wrist.

It had been an unbeatable tactic. Invite the man to grab one racquet handle, then break his wrist with the other handle. The hell with a man's head – Vinod often couldn't reach a man's head, anyway. A broken wrist usually stopped a fight; if a fool wanted to keep fighting, he would be fighting with one hand against two squash-racquet handles. If the film press had turned the dwarf into a bodyguard and a thug, Vinod didn't mind. He was genuinely protective of Inspector Dhar.

Mr Sethna disapproved of such violence, *and* of the

Sport Shop racquet stringers who happily provided Vinod with his arsenal of squash-racquet handles. The ball boys also gave the dwarf dozens of discarded tennis balls. In the car-driving business, as Vinod described it, there was a lot of 'just waiting' in his car. The former clown and acrobat liked to keep busy. By squeezing the dead tennis balls, Vinod strengthened his hands; the dwarf also claimed that this exercise relieved his arthritis, although Dr Daruwalla believed that aspirin was probably a more reliable source of relief.

It had occurred to Mr Sethna that Dr Daruwalla's longstanding relationship with Vinod was probably the reason the doctor didn't drive a car; it had been years since Farrokh had even owned a car in Bombay. The dwarf's reputation as Dhar's driver tended to obscure, for most observers, the fact that Vinod also drove for Dr Daruwalla. It spooked Mr Sethna how the doctor and the dwarf seemed so aware of each other – even as the dwarf loaded up his car with squash-racquet handles and old tennis balls, even as the doctor went on sitting in the Ladies' Garden. It was as if Farrokh always knew that Vinod was available – as if the dwarf were waiting only for him. Well, either for him or for Dhar.

It now occurred to Mr Sethna that Dr Daruwalla was intending to occupy his luncheon table through the dinner hours; perhaps the doctor was expecting dinner guests and had decided it was the simplest way to hold the table. But when the old steward inquired of Dr Daruwalla about the number of place settings, Mr Sethna was informed that the doctor was going home for 'supper.' Promptly, as if he'd been awakened from a dream, Farrokh got up to leave.

Mr Sethna observed and overheard him calling his wife from the telephone in the foyer.

'Nien, Liebchen,' said Dr Daruwalla. 'I have *not* told him – there wasn't a good moment to tell him.' Then Mr Sethna listened to Dr Daruwalla on the subject of the murder of Mr Lal. So it *is* a murder! Mr Sethna thought. Bonked by his own putter! And when he heard the part about the two-rupee note in Mr Lal's mouth, and specifically the intriguing threat that was connected to Inspector Dhar – MORE MEMBERS DIE IF DHAR REMAINS A MEMBER – Mr Sethna felt that his eavesdropping efforts had been rewarded, at least for this day.

Then something mildly remarkable happened. Dr Daruwalla hung up the phone and turned into the foyer without first looking where he was going, and who should he run smack into but the second Mrs Dogar. The doctor bumped into her so hard, Mr Sethna was excited by the possibility that the vulgar woman would be knocked down. But instead it was Farrokh who fell. More astonishing, upon the collision, Mrs Dogar was shoved backward into *Mr* Dogar – and *he* fell down, too. What a fool for marrying such a younger, stronger woman! Mr Sethna thought. Then there was the usual bowing and apologizing, and everyone assured everyone else that he or she was absolutely fine. Sometimes the absurdities of good manners, which were demonstrated in such profusion at the Duckworth Club, gave Mr Sethna gas.

Thus, finally, Farrokh escaped from the old steward's overseeing eye. But while he waited for Vinod to fetch the car, Dr Daruwalla – unobserved by Mr Sethna – touched the sore spot in his ribs, where there would surely be a bruise, and he marveled at the hardness and sturdiness of the second Mrs Dogar. It was like running into a stone wall!

It crossed the doctor's mind that Mrs Dogar was sufficiently masculine to be a hijra – not a hijra prostitute, of course, but just an *ordinary* eunuch-transvestite. In which case Mrs Dogar might not have been eyeballing Inspector Dhar for the purpose of seducing him; instead, she might have had it in her mind to *castrate* him!

Farrokh felt ashamed of himself for thinking like a

screenwriter again. How many Kingfishers have I had? he wondered; it relieved him to hold the beer accountable for his far-fetched fantasizing. In truth, he knew nothing about Mrs Dogar – where she'd come from – but hijras occupied such a marginal position in Indian society; the doctor was aware that most of them came from the lower classes. Whoever she was, the second Mrs Dogar was an upper-class woman. And *Mr* Dogar – although he was a foolish old fart, in Farrokh's opinion – was a Malabar Hill man; he came from old money, and lots of it. Nor was Mr Dogar *such* a fool that he wouldn't know the difference between a vagina and a burn scar from the famous hijra hot-oil treatment.

While he waited for Vinod, Dr Daruwalla watched the second Mrs Dogar help Mr Dogar into their car. She towered over the poor parking-lot attendant, who sheepishly opened the driver's-side door for her. Farrokh was unsurprised to see that Mrs Dogar was the driver in the family. He'd heard all about her fitness training, which he knew included weight lifting and other unfeminine pursuits. Perhaps she takes testosterone, too, the doctor imagined, for the second Mrs Dogar looked as if her sex hormones were raging – her *male* sex hormones, Dr Daruwalla speculated. He'd heard that such women sometimes develop a clitoris as large as a finger, as long as a young boy's penis!

When either too much Kingfisher *or* his run-amuck imagination caused Dr Daruwalla to speculate in this fashion, the doctor was grateful that he was merely an orthopedic surgeon. He truly didn't want to know too much about these other things. Yet Farrokh had to force himself from further contemplation, for he found that he was wondering what would be worse: that the second Mrs Dogar sought to emasculate Inspector Dhar, or that she was in amorous pursuit of the handsome actor – *and* that she possessed a clitoris of an altogether unseemly size.

Dr Daruwalla was in such a transfixed state of mind,

he didn't notice that Vinod had one-handedly wheeled into the circular driveway of the Duckworth Club and was, with his other hand, belatedly applying the brakes. The dwarf nearly ran the doctor down. At least this served to take Dr Daruwalla's mind off the second Mrs Dogar. If only for the moment, Farrokh forgot her.

Load Cycle

The better of the dwarf's two taxis – of those two that were equipped with hand controls – was in the shop. 'The carburetor is being revised,' Vinod explained. Since Dr Daruwalla had no idea how one accomplished a carburetor revision, he didn't press the dwarf for details. They departed the Duckworth Club in Vinod's decaying Ambassador, which was the off-white color of a pearl – like graying teeth, Farrokh reflected. Also, its hand control for acceleration was inclined to stick.

Nevertheless, Dr Daruwalla abruptly asked the dwarf to drive him past his father's former house on old Ridge Road, Malabar Hill; this was doubtless because Farrokh had his father and Malabar Hill on his mind. Farrokh and Jamshed had sold the house shortly after their father's murder – when Meher had decided to live out the rest of her life in the company of her children and her grandchildren, all of whom had already chosen *not* to live in India. Dr Daruwalla's mother would die in Toronto, in the doctor's guest bedroom. Meher's death, in her sleep – when it had snowed all night – was as peaceful as the bombing of old Lowji had been violent.

It wasn't the first time Farrokh had asked Vinod to drive by his old Malabar Hill home. From the moving taxi, the house was barely visible. The former Daruwalla family estate reminded the doctor of how tangential his contact with the country of his birthplace had become, for Farrokh was a foreigner on

178

Malabar Hill. Dr Daruwalla lived, like a visitor, in one of those ugly apartment buildings on Marine Drive; he had the same view of the Arabian Sea as could be found from a dozen similar places. He'd paid 60 lakhs (about 250,000 dollars) for a flat of less than 1,200 square feet, and he hardly lived there at all – he visited India so rarely. He was ashamed that, the rest of the time, he didn't rent it out. But Farrokh knew he would have been a fool to do so; the tenancy laws in Bombay favor the tenants. If Dr Daruwalla had tenants, he'd never get them out. Besides, from the Inspector Dhar movies, the doctor had made so many lakhs that he supposed he should spend some of them in Bombay. Through the marvels of a Swiss bank account and the guile of a cunning money-dealer, Dhar had been successful in getting a sizable portion of their earnings out of India. Dr Daruwalla also felt ashamed of that.

Vinod seemed to sense when Dr Daruwalla was vulnerable to charity. It was his own charitable enterprise that the dwarf was thinking of; Vinod was routinely shameless in seeking the doctor's support of his most fervent cause.

Vinod and Deepa had taken it upon themselves to rescue various urchins from the slums of Bombay; in short, they recruited street kids for the circus. They sought the more acrobatic beggars – demonstrably well coordinated children – and Vinod made every effort to steer these talented waifs toward circuses of more merit than the Great Blue Nile. Deepa was particularly devoted to saving child prostitutes, or would-be child prostitutes; rarely were these girls suitable circus material. To Dr Daruwalla's knowledge, the only circus that had stooped to adopt any of Vinod and Deepa's discoveries was the less-than-great Blue Nile.

To Farrokh's considerable discomfort, many of these girls were Mr Garg's discoveries – that is, long before Vinod and Deepa had found them. Mr Garg was the owner and manager of the Wetness Cabaret, where a kind of concealed grossness was the norm. Strip joints, not to mention sex shows, aren't permitted in Bombay – at least not to the degree of explicitness that exists in Europe and in North America. In India, there's no nudity, whereas 'wetness' – meaning wet, clinging, almost transparent clothing – is much in evidence, and sexually suggestive gestures are the mainstay of so-called exotic dancers in such seedy entertainment spots as Mr Garg's. Among such spots, even including the Bombay Eros Palace, the Wetness Cabaret was the worst; yet the dwarf and his wife insisted to Dr Daruwalla that Mr Garg was the Good Samaritan of Kamathipura. In the many lanes of brothels that were there, and throughout the red-light districts on Falkland Road and on Grant Road, the Wetness Cabaret was a haven.

It was only a haven compared to a brothel, Farrokh supposed. Whether one called Garg's girls strippers or 'exotic dancers,' most of them weren't whores. But many of them were runaways from the Kamathipura brothels, or from the brothels on Falkland Road and on Grant Road. In the brothels, the virginity of these girls had been only briefly prized – until the madam supposed they were old enough, or until there was a high enough offer. But when many of these girls ran away to Mr Garg, they were much too young for what the Wetness Cabaret offered; ironically, they were old enough for prostitution but far too young to be exotic dancers.

According to Vinod, most men who wanted to *look* at women wanted the women to look like women; apparently, these weren't the same men who wanted to have sex with underage girls – and even those men, Vinod claimed, didn't necessarily want to *look* at those young girls. Therefore, Mr Garg couldn't use them at the Wetness Cabaret, although Farrokh fantasized that Mr Garg *had* used them in some private, unmentionable way.

Dr Daruwalla's Dickensian theory was that Mr Garg was perverse *because of* his physical appearance. The man gave Farrokh the creeps. Mr Garg had made an

180

astonishingly vivid impression on Dr Daruwalla, considering that they had met only once; Vinod had
introduced them. The enterprising dwarf was also
Garg's driver.

Mr Garg was tall and of military erectness, but with
the sort of sallow complexion that Farrokh associated
with a lack of exposure to daylight. The skin on
Garg's face had an unhealthy, waxy sheen, and it was
unusually taut, like the skin of a corpse. Further enhancing Mr Garg's cadaverlike appearance was an
unnatural slackness to his mouth; his lips were always
parted, like the lips of someone who'd fallen asleep in
a seated position, and his eye sockets were dark and
bloated, as if full of stagnant blood. Worse, Mr Garg's
eyes were as yellow and opaque as a lion's – and as
unreadable, Dr Daruwalla thought. Worst of all was
the burn scar. Acid had been flung in Mr Garg's face,
which he'd managed to turn to the side; the acid had
shriveled one ear and burned a swath along his jawline
and down the side of his throat, where the raw pink
smear disappeared under the collar of his shirt. Not
even Vinod knew who'd thrown the acid, or why.

All Mr Garg's girls needed from Dr Daruwalla was
the trusted physician's assurance to the circuses that
these girls were in the pink of health. But what could
Farrokh say about the health of those girls from the
brothels? Some of them were *born* in brothels; certain
indications of congenital syphilis were easy to spot.
And nowadays, the doctor couldn't recommend them
to a circus without having them tested for AIDS; few
circuses – not even the Great Blue Nile – would take a
girl if she was HIV-positive. Most of them carried
something venereal; at the very least, the girls always
had to be de-wormed. So few of them were ever taken,
even by the Great Blue Nile.

When the girls were rejected by the circus, what
became of them? ('We are being good by trying,' Vinod
would answer.) Did Mr Garg sell them back to a
brothel, or did he wait for them to grow old enough to

be Wetness Cabaret material? It appalled Farrokh that, by the standards of Kamathipura, Mr Garg was considered a benevolent presence; yet Dr Daruwalla knew of no evidence against Mr Garg – at least nothing beyond the common knowledge that he bribed the police, who only occasionally raided the Wetness Cabaret.

The doctor had once imagined Mr Garg as a character in an Inspector Dhar movie; in a first draft of *Inspector Dhar and the Cage-Girl Killer*, Dr Daruwalla had written a cameo role for Mr Garg – he was a child molester named Acid Man. Then Farrokh had thought better of it. Mr Garg was too well known in Bombay. It might have become a legal matter, and there'd been the added risk of insulting Vinod and Deepa, which Dr Daruwalla would never do. If Garg was no Good Samaritan, the doctor nevertheless believed that the dwarf and his wife were the real thing – they were saints to these children, or they tried to be. They were, as Vinod had said, 'being good by trying.'

Vinod's off-white Ambassador was approaching Marine Drive when the doctor gave in to the dwarf's nagging. 'All right, all right – I'll examine her,' Dr Daruwalla told Vinod. 'Who is she this time, and what's her story?'

'She is being a virgin,' the dwarf explained. 'Deepa is saying that she is already an almost boneless girl – a future plastic lady!'

'Who is saying she's a virgin?' the doctor asked.

'She is saying so,' Vinod said. 'Garg is telling Deepa that the girl is running away from a brothel before anyone is touching her.'

'So *Garg* is saying she's a virgin?' Farrokh asked Vinod.

'Maybe almost a virgin – maybe close,' the dwarf replied. 'I am thinking she used to be a dwarf, too,' Vinod added. 'Or maybe she is being part-dwarf. I am almost thinking so.'

'That's not possible, Vinod,' said Dr Daruwalla.

182

As the dwarf shrugged, the Ambassador surged into a rotary; the roundabout turn caused several tennis balls to roll across Farrokh's feet, and the doctor heard the clunking of squash-racquet handles from under Vinod's elevated seat. The dwarf had explained to Dr Daruwalla that the handles of badminton racquets were too flimsy – they broke – and the handles of tennis racquets were too heavy to swing with sufficient quickness. The squash-racquet handles were just right.

Only because he already knew where it was, Farrokh could faintly make out the odd billboard that floated on the boat moored offshore in the Arabian Sea; the hoarding bobbled on the water. TIKTOK TISSUES were being advertised again tonight.

And tonight, and every night, the metal signs on the lampposts promised a good ride on APOLLO TYRES. The rush-hour traffic along Marine Drive had long ago subsided, and the doctor could tell by the lights from his own apartment that Dhar had already arrived; the balcony was lit up and Julia never sat on the balcony alone. They'd probably watched the sunset together, the doctor thought; he was aware, too, that the sun had set a long time ago. They'll both be mad at me, Farrokh decided.

The doctor told Vinod that he'd examine the 'almost boneless' girl in the morning – the almost-a-virgin, Dr Daruwalla almost said. The half-dwarf or former dwarf, the doctor imagined. Mr Garg's girl! he thought grimly.

In the stark lobby of his apartment building, Farrokh felt for a moment that he could have been anywhere in the modern world. But when the elevator door opened, he was greeted by a familiar sign, which he detested.

SERVANTS ARE NOT ALLOWED
TO USE THE LIFT
UNLESS ACCOMPANIED BY CHILDREN

The sign assaulted him with a numbing sense of

inadequacy. It was a part of the pecking order of Indian life – not only the acceptance of discrimination, which was worldwide, but the deification of it, which Lowji Daruwalla had believed was so infuriatingly Indian, even though much of it was inherited from the Raj.

Farrokh had tried to convince the Residents' Society to remove the offensive sign, but the rules about servants were inflexible. Dr Daruwalla was the only resident of the building who wasn't in favor of forcing servants to use the stairs. Also, the Residents' Society discounted Farrokh's opinion on the grounds that he was a Non-Resident Indian – 'NRI' was the doctor's official government category. If this dispute about the use of the lift was the kind of issue that old Lowji would have got himself killed over, the younger Dr Daruwalla self-deprecatingly viewed his failure with the Residents' Society as typical of his political ineffectualness and his general out-of-itness.

As he got off the elevator, he said to himself, I'm not a functioning Indian. The other day, someone at the Duckworth Club had been outraged that a political candidate in New Delhi was conducting a campaign 'strictly on the cow issue'; Dr Daruwalla had been unable to contribute an opinion because he was unsure what the cow issue *was*. He was aware of the rise of groups to protect cows, and he supposed they were a part of the Hindu-revivalist wave, like those Hindu-chauvinist holy men proclaiming themselves to be reincarnations of the gods themselves – and demanding to be worshiped as gods, too. He knew that there was *still* Hindu-Muslim rioting over the Mosque of Babar – the underlying subject of his first Inspector Dhar movie, which he'd found so funny at the time. Now thousands of bricks had been consecrated and stamped SHRI RAMA, which means 'respected Rama,' and the foundation for a temple to Rama had been laid less than 200 feet from the Babri mosque. Not even Dr Daruwalla imagined that the outcome of the 40-year feud over the Mosque of Babar would be 'funny.'

Here he was again, with his pathetic sense of *not belonging*. He knew that there were Sikh extremists, but he didn't know one personally. At the Duckworth Club, he was on the friendliest terms with Mr Bakshi – a Sikh novelist, and a great conversationalist on the subject of American movie classics – yet they'd never discussed Sikh terrorists. And Farrokh knew about the Shiv Sena and the Dalit Panthers and the Tamil Tigers, but he knew nothing *personally*. There were more than 600 million Hindus in India; there were 100 million Muslims, and millions of Sikhs and Christians, too. There were probably not even 80,000 Parsis, Farrokh thought. But in his own small part of India – in his ugly apartment building on Marine Drive – all these contentious millions were reduced in the doctor's mind to what he called the elevator issue. Concerning the stupid lift, all these warring factions concurred: they disagreed only with *him*. Make the servants climb the stairs.

Farrokh had recently read about a man who was murdered because his mustache gave 'caste offense'; apparently, the mustache was waxed to curl up – it should have drooped down. Dr Daruwalla decided: Inspector Dhar should leave India and never come back. And *I* should leave India and never come back, too! he thought. For *so what* if he helped a few crippled children in Bombay? What business did he have even imagining 'funny' movies about a country like this? He wasn't a writer. And what business did he have taking blood from dwarfs? He wasn't a geneticist, either.

Thus, with a characteristic loss of self-confidence, Dr Daruwalla entered his apartment to face the music he was certain he would hear. He'd been late in telling his beloved wife that he'd invited his beloved John Daruwalla for the evening meal, and the doctor had kept them both waiting. Also, he'd lacked the courage to tell Inspector Dhar the upsetting news.

Farrokh felt he was trapped in a circus act of his own

creation, an annoying pattern of procrastination that he couldn't break out of. He was reminded of an item in the Great Royal Circus; at first he'd found it a charming sort of madness, but now he thought it might drive him crazy if he ever saw it again. It conveyed such a meaningless but relentless insanity, and the accompanying music was so repetitious; in Dr Daruwalla's mind, the act stood for the lunatic monotony that weighed on everyone's life from time to time. The item was called Load Cycle, and it was a case of simplicity carried to idiotic extremes.

There were two bicycles, each one pedaled by a very solid, strong-looking woman. The pair followed each other around the ring. They were joined by other plump, dark-skinned women, who found a variety of means by which to mount the moving bicycles. Some of the women perched on little posts that extended from the hubs of the front and back wheels; some mounted the handlebars and wobbled precariously there – others teetered on the rear fenders. And regardless of how many women mounted the bicycles, the two strong-looking women kept pedaling. Then little girls appeared; they climbed on the shoulders and stood on the heads of the other women – including the laboring, sturdy pedalers – until two struggling *pyramids* of women were clinging to these two bicycles, which never stopped circling the ring.

The music was of a sustained madness equal to one fragment of the cancan, repeated and repeated, and all the dark-skinned women – both the fat, older women *and* the little girls – wore too much face powder, which gave them a minstrel-like aura of unreality. They also wore pale-purple tutus, and they smiled and smiled and smiled as they tottered around and around and around the ring. The last time the doctor had seen a performance of this item, he'd thought it would never end.

Perhaps there's a Load Cycle in everyone's life, thought Dr Daruwalla. As he paused at the door of his apartment, Farrokh felt he'd been enduring a Load Cycle sort of day. Dr Daruwalla could imagine the cancan music starting up again, as if he were about to be greeted by a dozen dark-skinned girls in pale-purple tutus – all of them white-faced and moving to the insane, incessant rhythm.

7. DR DARUWALLA HIDES
IN HIS BEDROOM

Now the Elephants Will Be Angry

But the past is a labyrinth. Where's the way out? In the front hall of his apartment, where there were no dark-skinned, white-faced women in tutus, the doctor was halted by the clear but distant sound of his wife's voice. It reached him all the way from the balcony, where Julia was indulging Inspector Dhar with his favorite view of Marine Drive. On occasion, Dhar slept on that balcony, either when he stayed so late that he preferred to spend the night, or else when he'd just arrived in Bombay and needed to reacquaint himself with the city's smell.

Dhar swore this was the secret to his successful, almost instant adjustment to India. He could arrive from Europe, straight from Switzerland's fresh air – tainted, in Zürich, with restaurant fumes and diesel exhaust, with burning coal and hints of sewer gas – but after just two or three days in Bombay, Dhar claimed, he was unbothered by the smog, or by the two or three million small fires for cooking food in the slums, or by the sweet rot of garbage, or even by the excremental horror of the four or five million who squatted at the curb or at the water's edge of the surrounding sea. For in a city of nine million, surely the shit of half of these was evident in the Bombay air. It took Dr Daruwalla two or three weeks to adjust to that permeating odor.

In the front hall, where the prevailing smell was of mildew, the doctor quietly removed his sandals; he deposited his briefcase and his old dark-brown doctor's bag. He noted that the umbrellas in the umbrella stand were dusty with disuse; it had been three months since the end of the monsoon rains. Even from the closed kitchen he could detect the mutton and the dhal – so that's what we're having, again, he thought – but the aroma of the evening meal couldn't distract Dr Daruwalla from the powerful nostalgia of his wife speaking German, which she always spoke whenever she and Dhar were alone.

Farrokh stood and listened to the Austrian rhythms of Julia's German – always the *ish* sound, never the *ick* – and in his mind's eye he could see her when she was 18 or 19, when he'd courted her in her mother's old yellow-walled house in Grinzing. It was a house cluttered with Biedermeier culture. There was a bust of Franz Grillparzer by the coat tree in the foyer. The work of a portraitist obsessively committed to children's innocent expressions dominated the tea room, which was crowded with more cutesiness in the form of porcelain birds and silver antelopes. Farrokh remembered the afternoon he'd made a nervous, sweeping gesture with the sugar bowl – he broke a painted-glass lamp shade.

There were two clocks in the room. One of them played a fragment of a waltz by Lanner on the half hour and a slightly longer fragment of a Strauss waltz on the hour; the second clock paid similar token acknowledgments to Beethoven and Schubert – understandably, it was set a full minute behind the other. Farrokh remembered that, while Julia and her mother cleaned up the mess he'd made of the lamp shade, first the Strauss and then the Schubert played.

Whenever he recalled their many afternoon teas together, he could visualize his wife as a teenager. She was always dressed in a fashion Lady Duckworth would have admired. Julia wore a cream-colored blouse with flounced sleeves and a high, ruffled collar. They spoke German because her mother's English wasn't as good as theirs. Nowadays, Farrokh and Julia spoke German only occasionally. It was still their love-making language, or what they spoke in the dark. It was the language in which Julia had told him, 'I find you very attractive.' After two years of courting her, he'd nevertheless felt this was forward of her; he'd been speechless. He was struggling with how to phrase the question – whether or not she was troubled by his darker color – when she'd added, 'Especially your skin. The picture of your skin against my skin is very attractive.' (*Das Bild* – 'the picture.')

When people say that German or any other language is romantic, Dr Daruwalla thought, all they really mean is that they've enjoyed a past in the language. There was even a certain intimacy in listening to Julia speak German to Dhar, whom she always called John D. This was the servants' name for him, which Julia had adopted, much as she and Dr Daruwalla had 'adopted' the servants.

They were a feeble old couple, Nalin and Swaroop – Dr Daruwalla's children and John D. had always called her Roopa – but they'd outlived Lowji and Meher, whom they'd first served. It was a form of semiretirement to work for Farrokh and Julia; they were so infrequently in Bombay. The rest of the time, Nalin and Roopa were caretakers for the flat. If Dr Daruwalla sold the apartment, where could the old couple go? He'd agreed with Julia that they would try to sell the place, but only after the old servants died. Even if Farrokh kept returning to India, he was rarely in Bombay so long that he couldn't afford to stay in a decent hotel. Once, when one of the doctor's Canadian colleagues had teased him for being so conservative about things, Julia had remarked, 'Farrokh isn't conservative – he's absolutely extravagant. He maintains an apartment in Bombay so that his parents' former servants will have a place to live!'

Just then the doctor overheard Julia say something about the Queen's Necklace, which was the local name for the string of lights along Marine Drive. This name originated when the lamplights were white; the

190

smog lights were yellow now. Julia was saying that yellow wasn't a proper color for the necklace of a queen.

What a European she is! Dr Daruwalla thought. He had the greatest affection for the way she'd managed to adapt to their life in Canada and to their sporadic visits to India without ever losing her old-world sensibility, which remained as distinctive in her voice as in her habit of 'dressing' for dinner – even in Bombay. It wasn't the content of Julia's speech that Dr Daruwalla was listening to – he wasn't eavesdropping. It was only to hear the sound of her German, her soft accent in combination with such exact phrasing. But he realized that if Julia was talking about the Queen's Necklace, she couldn't possibly have told Dhar the upsetting news; the doctor's heart sank because he realized how much he'd been hoping that his wife would have told the dear boy.

Then John D. spoke. If it soothed Farrokh to hear Julia's German, it disturbed him to hear German from Inspector Dhar. In German, the doctor could barely recognize the John D. he knew, and it disquieted Dr Daruwalla to hear how much more energetically Dhar spoke in German than he spoke in English. This emphasized to Dr Daruwalla the distance that had grown between them. But Dhar's university education had been in Zürich; he'd spent most of his life in Switzerland. And his serious (if not widely recognized) work as an actor in the theater, at the Schauspielhaus Zürich, was something that John Daruwalla took more pride in than he appeared to take in the commercial success of his role as Inspector Dhar. Why wouldn't his German be perfect?

There was also not the slightest edge of sarcasm in Dhar's voice when he spoke to Julia. Farrokh recognized a longstanding jealousy. John D. is more affectionate to Julia than he is to me, Dr Daruwalla thought. And after all I've done for him! There was a fatherly bitterness to this idea, and it shamed him.

191

He slipped quietly into the kitchen, where the racket of the apparently never-ending preparation of the evening meal kept him from hearing the actor's well-trained voice. Besides, Farrokh had at first (and falsely) assumed that Dhar was merely contributing to the conversation about the Queen's Necklace. Then Dr Daruwalla had heard the sudden mention of his own name – it was that old story about 'the time Farrokh took me to watch the elephants in the sea.' The doctor hadn't wanted to hear more, because he was afraid of the detectable tone of complaint he heard emerging in John D.'s memory. The dear boy was recalling that time he'd been frightened during the festival of Ganesh Chaturthi; it seemed that half the city had flocked to Chowpatty Beach, where they'd immersed their idols of the elephant-headed god, Ganesh. Farrokh hadn't prepared the child for the orgiastic frenzy of the crowd – not to mention the size of the elephant heads, many of which were larger than the heads of real elephants. Farrokh remembered the outing as the first and only time he'd seen John D. become hysterical. The dear boy was crying, 'They're drowning the elephants! Now the elephants will be angry!'

And to think that Farrokh had criticized old Lowji for keeping the boy so sheltered. 'If you take him only to the Duckworth Club,' Farrokh had told his father, 'what's he ever going to know about India?' What a hypocrite I've turned out to be! Dr Daruwalla thought, for he knew of no one in Bombay who'd hidden from India as successfully as he'd concealed himself at the Duckworth Club – for years.

He'd taken an eight-year-old to Chowpatty Beach to watch a mob; there were hundreds of thousands dunking their idols of the elephant-headed god in the sea. What had he thought the child would make of this? It wasn't the time to explain the British ban on 'gathering,' their infuriating anti-assembly strictures; the hysterical eight-year-old was too young to appreciate this symbolic demonstration for freedom of

192

expression. Farrokh tried to carry the crying boy against the grain of the crowd, but more and more the giant idols of Lord Ganesha were pressed against them; they were herded back to the sea. 'It's just a celebration,' he'd whispered in the child's ear. 'It's not a riot.' In his arms, Farrokh felt the little boy trembling. Thus had the doctor realized the full weight of his ignorance, not only of India but of the fragility of children.

Now he wondered if John D. was telling Julia, 'This is my first memory of Farrokh.' And I'm *still* getting the dear boy in trouble! Dr Daruwalla thought.

The doctor distracted himself by poking his nose into the big pot of dhal. Roopa had long ago added the mutton, and she reminded him that he was late by remarking how fortunate it was that mutton usually defied overcooking. 'The rice has dried out,' she added sadly.

Old Nalin, ever the optimist, tried to make Dr Daruwalla feel better. In his fragmentary English, Nalin said, 'But plenty of beer!'

Dr Daruwalla felt guilty that there was always so much beer around; the doctor's capacity for beer alarmed him, and Dhar's fondness for the brew seemed limitless. Since Nalin and Roopa did the shopping, the thought of the old couple struggling with those heavy bottles also made Dr Daruwalla feel guilty. And there was the elevator issue: because they were servants, Nalin and Roopa weren't permitted to ride in the lift. Even with all those beer bottles, the elderly servants trudged up the stairs.

'And plenty of messages!' Nalin told the doctor. The old man was very fond of the new answering machine. Julia had insisted on it because Nalin and Roopa were terrible at taking messages; they couldn't transcribe a phone number or spell anyone's name. When the machine answered, the old man was thrilled to listen to it because he was absolved of any responsibility for the messages.

Farrokh took a beer with him. The apartment seemed so small. In Toronto, the Daruwallas owned a huge house. In Bombay, the doctor had to sneak through the living room, which was also the dining room, in order to get to the bedroom and the bathroom. But Dhar and Julia were still talking on the balcony; they didn't see him. John D. was reciting the most famous part of the story; it always made Julia laugh.

'They're drowning the elephants!' John D. was crying. 'Now the elephants will be angry!' Dr Daruwalla never thought that this sounded quite right in German.

If I run a bath, Farrokh speculated, they'll hear it and know I'm home. I'll have a quick wash in the sink instead, the doctor thought. He spread out a clean white shirt on the bed. He chose an uncharacteristically loud necktie with a bright-green parrot on it; it was an old Christmas present from John D. – not a tie that the doctor would ever wear in public. Farrokh was unaware how the tie would at least enliven his navy-blue suit. These were absurd clothes for Bombay, especially when dining at home, but Julia was Julia.

After he'd washed, the doctor took a quick look at his answering machine; the message light was flickering. He didn't bother to count the number of messages. Don't listen to them now, he warned himself. Yet the spirit of procrastination was deeply ingrained in him; to join in John D. and Julia's conversation would lead to the inevitable confrontation concerning John D.'s twin. As Farrokh was deliberating, he saw the bundle of mail on his writing desk. Dhar must have gone out to the film studio and collected the fan mail, which was mostly hate mail.

It had long been their understanding that Dr Daruwalla deserved the task of opening and reading the mail. Although the letters were addressed to Inspector Dhar, the content of these letters only rarely concerned Dhar's acting or lip-syncing skills; instead, the letters were invariably about the creation of Dhar's character or about a particular script. Because it was presumed that Dhar was the author of the screenplays, and thus the creator of his own character, the author himself was the source of the letter writers' principal outrage; their attacks were leveled at the man who'd made it all up.

Before the death threats, especially before the real-life murders of actual prostitutes, Dr Daruwalla had been in no great hurry to read his mail. But the serial killings of the cage girls had become so publicly acknowledged as imitations of the movie murders that Inspector Dhar's mail had taken a turn for the worse. And in the light of Mr Lal's murder, Dr Daruwalla felt compelled to search the mail for threats of any kind. He looked at the sizable bundle of new letters and wondered if, under these circumstances, he should ask Dhar and Julia to help him read through them. As if their evening together didn't promise to be difficult enough! Maybe later, Farrokh thought – if the conversation comes around to it.

But, as he dressed, the doctor couldn't ignore the insistent flickering of the message light on his answering machine. Well, he needn't take the time to call anyone back, he thought, as he knotted his tie. Surely it wouldn't hurt to hear what these messages were about – he could just jot them down and return the calls later. And so Farrokh searched for a pad of paper and a pen, which wasn't easy to do without being heard, because the tiny bedroom was crammed full of the fragile, tinkling Victoriana he'd inherited from Lowji's mansion on Ridge Road. Although he'd taken only what he couldn't bear to auction, even his writing desk was crowded with the bric-a-brac of his childhood, not to mention the photographs of his three daughters; they were married, and therefore Dr Daruwalla's writing desk also exhibited their wedding pictures – and the pictures of his several grandchildren. Then there were his favorite photographs of John D. – downhill-skiiing at Wengen and at Klosters, cross-country skiing in Pontresina and hiking in Zermatt – and several framed playbills from the Schauspielhaus Zürich, with John Daruwalla in both supporting and leading roles. He was Jean in Strindberg's *Fräulein Julie,* he was Christopher Mahon in John Millington Synge's *Ein wahrer Held,* he was Achilles in Heinrich von Kleist's *Penthesilea,* he was Fernando in Goethe's *Stella,* he was Ivan in Chekhov's *Onkel Vanja,* he was Antonio in Shakespeare's *Der Kaufmann von Venedig* – once he'd been Bassanio. Shakespeare in German sounded so foreign to Farrokh. It depressed the doctor that he'd lost touch with the language of his romantic years.

At last he found a pen. Then he spotted a pad of paper under the silver statuette of Ganesh as a baby; the little elephant-headed god was sitting on the lap of his human mother, Parvati – a cute pose. Unfortunately, the grotesque reaction to *Inspector Dhar and the Cage-Girl Killer* had sickened Farrokh with elephants. This was unfair, for Ganesh was merely elephant-headed; the god had four human arms with human hands, and two human feet. Also, Lord Ganesha sported only one whole tusk – although sometimes the god held his broken tusk in one of his four hands.

Ganesh truly bore no resemblance to the drawing of that inappropriately mirthful elephant which, in the most recent Inspector Dhar film, was the signature of a serial killer – that unsuitable cartoon which the movie murderer drew on the bellies of slain prostitutes. That elephant was no god. Besides, *that* elephant had both tusks intact. Even so, Dr Daruwalla was off elephants – in any form. The doctor wished he'd asked Deputy Commissioner Patel about those drawings that the *real* murderer was making, for the police had said no more to the press than that the artwork of the real-life killer and serial cartoonist was 'an obvious variation on the movie theme.' What did that mean?

The question deeply disturbed Dr Daruwalla, who shuddered to recall the origin of his idea for the cartoon-drawing killer; the source of the doctor's inspiration had been nothing less than an *actual* drawing on the belly of an *actual* murder victim. Twenty years ago, Dr Daruwalla had been the examining physician at the scene of a crime that was never solved. Now the police were claiming that a killer-cartoonist had stolen the mocking elephant from a movie, but the screenwriter knew where the original idea had come from. Farrokh had stolen it from a murderer – maybe from the *same* murderer. Wouldn't the killer know that the most recent Inspector Dhar movie was imitating *him*?

I'm over my head, as usual, Dr Daruwalla decided. He also decided that he should give this information to Detective Patel – in case, somehow, the deputy commissioner didn't already know it. But how would Patel already know it? Farrokh wondered. Second-guessing himself was the doctor's second nature. At the Duckworth Club, Dr Daruwalla had been impressed by the composure of the deputy commissioner; moreover, the doctor couldn't rid himself of the impression that Detective Patel had been hiding something.

Farrokh interrupted these unwelcome thoughts as quickly as they'd come to him. Sitting next to his answering machine, he turned the volume down before he pushed the button. Still in hiding, the secret screenwriter listened to the messages.

The First-Floor Dogs

Upon hearing Ranjit's complaining voice, Dr Daruwalla instantly regretted his decision to forsake even one minute of Dhar and Julia's company for as much as one phone message. A few years older than the doctor, Ranjit had nevertheless maintained both unsuitable expectations and youthful indignation; the former involved his ongoing matrimonial advertisements, which Dr Daruwalla found inappropriate for a medical secretary in his sixties. Ranjit's 'youthful indignation' was most apparent in his responses to those women

197

who, upon meeting him, turned him down. Naturally, Ranjit hadn't all this time been conducting nonstop matrimonial advertisements, dating back to his earliest employment as old Lowji's secretary. After exhaustive interviews, Ranjit had been successfully married – and long enough before Lowji's death so that the senior Dr Daruwalla had once more enjoyed the secretary's prematrimonial industriousness.

But Ranjit's wife had recently died, and he was only a few years away from retirement. He still worked for the surgical associates at the Hospital for Crippled Children, and he always served as Farrokh's secretary whenever the Canadian was an Honorary Consultant Surgeon in Bombay. And Ranjit had decided that the time for remarrying was ripe. He thought he should do it without delay, for it made him sound younger to describe himself as a working medical secretary than to confess he was retired; just to be sure, in his more recent matrimonial advertisements, he'd attempted to capitalize on both his position *and* his pending retirement, citing that he was 'rewardingly employed' *and* 'anticipating a v. active, early retirement.'

It was things like 'v. active' that Dr Daruwalla found unseemly about Ranjit's present matrimonials, and the fact that Ranjit was a shameless liar. Because of a standard policy at *The Times of India* – the advertising brides and grooms eschewed revealing their names, preferring the confidentiality of a number – it was possible for Ranjit to publish a half-dozen ads in the same Sunday's matrimonial pages. Ranjit had discovered it was popular to claim that caste was 'no bar,' while it was also still popular to declare himself a Hindu Brahmin – 'caste-conscious and religion-minded, matching horoscopes a must.' Therefore, Ranjit advertised several versions of himself simultaneously. He told Farrokh that he was seeking the very best wife, with or without caste-consciousness or religion. Why not give himself the benefit of meeting everyone who was available?

Dr Daruwalla was embarrassed that he'd been inexorably drawn into the world of Ranjit's matrimonials. Every Sunday, Farrokh and Julia read through the marriage advertisements in *The Times of India*. It was a contest, to see which of them could identify all of Ranjit's ads. But Ranjit's phone message was not of a matrimonial nature. Once again, the aging secretary had called to complain about 'the dwarf's wife.' This was Ranjit's condemning reference to Deepa, for whom he harbored a fobidding disapproval – the kind that only Mr Sethna might have shared. Dr Daruwalla wondered if medical secretaries were universally cruel and dismissive to anyone seeking a doctor's attention. Was such hostility engendered only by a heartfelt desire to protect all doctors from wasting their time?

To be fair to Ranjit, Deepa was exceptionally aggressive in wasting Dr Daruwalla's time. She'd called to make a morning appointment for the runaway child prostitute – even before Vinod had persuaded the doctor to examine this new addition to Mr Garg's stable of street girls. Ranjit described the patient as 'someone allegedly without bones,' for Deepa had doubtless used her circus terminology ('boneless') with him. Ranjit was communicating his scorn for the vocabulary of the dwarf's wife. From Deepa's description, the child prostitute might have been made of pure plastic – 'another medical marvel, and no doubt a virgin,' Ranjit concluded his sardonic message.

The next message was an old one, from Vinod. The dwarf must have called while Farrokh was still sitting in the Ladies' Garden at the Duckworth Club. The message was really for Inspector Dhar.

'Our favorite inspector is telling me he is sleeping on your balcony tonight,' the dwarf began. 'If he is changing his mind, I am just cruising – just killing time, you know. If the inspector is wanting me, he is already knowing the doormen at the Taj and at the Oberoi – for message-leaving, I am meaning. I am having a late-night picking-up at the Wetness Cabaret,'

Vinod admitted, 'but this is being while you are sleeping. In the morning, I am picking up you, as usual. By the way, I am reading a magazine with *me* in it!' the dwarf concluded.

The only magazines that Vinod read were movie magazines, where he could occasionally glimpse himself in the celebrity snapshots opening the door of one of his Ambassadors for Inspector Dhar. There on the door would be the red circle with the *T* in it (for taxi) and the name of the dwarf's company, which was often partially obscured.

VINOD'S BLUE
NILE, LTD.

As opposed to 'great,' Farrokh presumed.

Dhar was the only movie star who rode in Vinod's cars; and the dwarf relished his occasional appearances with his 'favorite inspector' in the film-gossip magazines. Vinod was enduringly hopeful that other movie stars would follow Dhar's lead, but Dimple Kapadia and Jaya Prada and Pooja Bedi and Pooja Bhatt – not to mention Chunky Pandey and Sunny Deol, or Madhuri Dixit and Moon Moon Sen, to name only a few – had all declined to ride in the dwarf's 'luxury' taxis. Possibly they thought it would damage their reputations to be seen with Dhar's thug.

As for the 'cruising' back and forth between the Oberoi and the Taj, these were Vinod's favorite territories for moonlighting. The dwarf was recognized and well treated by the doormen because whenever Dhar was in Bombay, the actor stayed at the Oberoi *and* at the Taj. By maintaining a suite at both hotels, Dhar was assured of good service; as long as the Oberoi and the Taj knew they were in competition with each other, they outdid themselves to give Dhar the utmost privacy. The house detectives were harsh with autograph seekers or other celebrity hounds; at the reception desk of either hotel, if you didn't know the given code name, which kept changing, you were told that the movie star was not a guest.

By 'killing time,' Vinod meant he was picking up extra money. The dwarf was good at spotting hapless tourists in the lobbies of both hotels; he would offer to drive the foreigners to a good restaurant, or wherever they wanted to go. Vinod was also gifted at recognizing those tourists who'd had harrowing taxi experiences and were therefore vulnerable to the temptations of his 'luxury' service.

Dr Daruwalla understood that the dwarf could hardly have supported himself by driving only the doctor and Dhar around. Mr Garg was a more regular customer. Farrokh was also familiar with the dwarf's habit of 'message-leaving,' for Vinod had taken advantage of Inspector Dhar's celebrity status with the doormen at the Oberoi and at the Taj. It may have been awkward, but it was Vinod's only means of putting himself 'on call.' There were no cellular phones in Bombay; car phones were unknown – a decided inconvenience in the private-taxi business, which Vinod complained about periodically. There were radio pagers, or 'beepers,' but the dwarf wouldn't use them. 'I am preferring to be holding out,' Vinod maintained, by which he meant he was waiting for the day when cellular phones would upgrade his car-driving enterprise.

Therefore, if Farrokh or John D. wanted the dwarf, they left a message for him with the doormen at the Taj and the Oberoi. But there was another reason for Vinod to call. Vinod didn't like showing up at Dr Daruwalla's apartment building unannounced; there was no phone in the lobby, and Vinod refused to see himself as a 'servant' – he refused to climb the stairs. When it came to climbing stairs, his dwarfism was a handicap. Dr Daruwalla had protested, on Vinod's behalf, to the Residents' Society. At first, Farrokh had argued that the dwarf was a cripple – cripples shouldn't be forced to use the stairs. The

Residents' Society had argued that cripples shouldn't be servants. Dr Daruwalla had countered that Vinod was an independent businessman; the dwarf was nobody's servant. After all, Vinod owned a private-taxi company. A chauffeur was a servant, the Residents' Society said.

Regardless of the absurd ruling, Farrokh had told Vinod that if he ever had to come to the Daruwallas' sixth-floor flat, he was to take the restricted residents' elevator. But whenever Vinod stood in the lobby and waited for the elevator – regardless of the lateness of the hour – his presence would be detected by the first-floor dogs. The first-floor flats harbored a disproportionate number of dogs; and although the doctor was disinclined to believe Vinod's interpretation – that all dogs hated all dwarfs – he could offer no scientifically acceptable reason why all the first-floor dogs should suddenly awake and commence their frenzied barking whenever Vinod was waiting for the forbidden lift.

And so it was tediously necessary for Vinod to arrange an exact time for picking up Farrokh or John D. so that the dwarf could wait in the Ambassador at the curb – or in the nearby alley – and not enter the lobby of the apartment building at all. Besides, it sorely tested the delicate ecosystem of the apartment building to have Vinod attract the late-night, furious attention of the first-floor dogs; and Farrokh was already in hot water with the Residents' Society – his dissent to their opinion on the elevator issue had offended the building's other residents.

Since the doctor was the son of an acknowledged great man – and a famously assassinated great man, too – there was other fuel for resenting Dr Daruwalla. That he lived abroad and could still afford to have his apartment occupied by his servants – often, for years without a single visit – had certainly made him unpopular, if not openly despised.

That the dogs appeared guilty of discrimination

against dwarfs wasn't the sole reason that Dr Daruwalla disliked them. Their insane barking disturbed the doctor because of its total irrationality; *any* irrationality reminded Farrokh of everything he failed to comprehend about India.

Only that morning he'd stood on his balcony and overheard his fifth-floor neighbor, Dr Malik Abdul Aziz – a model 'Servant of the Almighty' – praying on the balcony below him. When Dhar slept on the balcony, he often commented to Farrokh on how soothing it was to wake up to the prayers of Dr Aziz.

'Praise be to Allah, Lord of Creation' – that much Dr Daruwalla had understood. And later there was something about 'the straight path.' It was a very pure prayer – Farrokh had liked it, and he'd long admired Dr Aziz for his unswerving faith – but Dr Daruwalla's thoughts had veered sharply away from religion, in the direction of politics, because he was reminded of the aggressive billboards he'd seen around the city. The messages on such hoardings were essentially hostile; they merely purported to be religious.

ISLAM IS THE ONE PATH
TO HUMANITY FOR ALL

And that wasn't as bad as those Shiv Sena slogans, which were all over Bombay. (MAHARASHTRA FOR MAHARASHTRIANS. Or, SAY IT WITH PRIDE: I'M A HINDU.)

Something evil had corrupted the purity of prayer. Something as dignified and private as Dr Aziz, with his prayer rug rolled out on his own balcony, had been compromised by proselytizing, had been distorted by politics. And if this madness had a sound, Farrokh knew, it would be the sound of irrationally barking dogs.

Inoperable

In the apartment building, Dr Daruwalla and Dr Aziz were the most consistent early risers; surgeries for both – Dr Aziz was a urologist. If he prays every morning, so should I, Farrokh thought. Politely, that morning, he had waited for the Muslim to finish. There followed the shuffling sound of Dr Aziz's slippers as he rolled up his prayer rug while Dr Daruwalla leafed through his *Book of Common Prayer*; Farrokh was looking for something appropriate, or at least familiar. He was ashamed that his ardor for Christianity seemed to be receding into the past, or had his faith entirely retreated? After all, it had been only a minor sort of miracle that had converted him; perhaps Farrokh needed another small miracle to inspire him now. He realized that most Christians were faithful without the incentive of any miracle, and this realization instantly interfered with his search for a prayer. As a Christian, too, he'd lately begun to wonder if he was a fake.

In Toronto, Farrokh was an unassimilated Canadian – *and* an Indian who avoided the Indian community. In Bombay, the doctor was constantly confronted with how little he knew India – and how unlike an Indian he thought himself to be. In truth, Dr Daruwalla was an orthopedist and a Duckworthian, and – in both cases – he was merely a member of two private clubs. Even his conversion to Christianity felt false; he was merely a holiday churchgoer, Christmas and Easter – he couldn't remember when he'd last partaken of the innermost pleasure of prayer.

Although it was quite a mouthful – and it was the whole story of what he was supposed to believe, in a nutshell – Dr Daruwalla had begun his experiment in prayer with the so-called Apostles' Creed, the standard Confession of the Faith. '"I believe in God the Father Almighty, Maker of heaven and earth . . ."' Farrokh recited breathlessly, but the capital letters were a distraction to him; he stopped.

Later, as he had stepped into the elevator, Dr Daru-walla reflected on how easily his mood for prayer had been lost. He resolved that he would compliment Dr Aziz on his highly disciplined faith at the first opportunity. But when Dr Aziz stepped into the elevator at the fifth floor, Farrokh was completely flustered. He scarcely managed to say, 'Good morning, Doctor – you're looking well!'

'Why, thank you – so are you, Doctor!' said Dr Aziz, looking somewhat sly and conspiratorial. When the elevator door closed and they were alone together, Dr Aziz said, 'Have you heard about Dr Dev?'

Farrokh wondered, *Which* Dr Dev? There was a Dr Dev who was a cardiologist, there was another Dev who was an anesthesiologist – there are a bunch of Devs, he thought. Even Dr Aziz was known in the medical community as Urology Aziz, which was the only sensible way to distinguish him from a half-dozen other Dr Azizes.

'Dr Dev?' Dr Daruwalla asked cautiously.

'Gastroenterology Dev,' said Urology Aziz.

'Oh, yes, *that* Dr Dev,' Farrokh said.

'But have you heard?' asked Dr Aziz. 'He has AIDS – he caught it from a patient. And I don't mean from sexual contact.'

'From *examining* a patient?' Dr Daruwalla said.

'From a colonoscopy, I believe,' said Dr Aziz. 'She was a prostitute.'

'From a colonoscopy ... but *how*?' Dr Daruwalla asked.

'At least forty percent of the prostitutes must be infected with the virus,' Dr Aziz said. 'Among my patients, the ones who see prostitutes test HIV-positive twenty percent of the time!'

'But from a colonoscopy. I don't understand *how*,' Farrokh insisted, but Dr Aziz was too excited to listen.

'I have patients telling *me* – a urologist – that they have cured themselves of AIDS by drinking their own urine!' Dr Aziz said.

'Ah, yes, urine therapy,' said Dr Daruwalla. 'Very popular, but—'

'But *here* is the problem!' cried Dr Aziz. He pulled a folded piece of paper from his pocket; some words were scrawled on the paper in longhand. 'Do you know what the *Kama Sutra* says?' Dr Aziz asked Farrokh. Here was a Muslim asking a Parsi (and a convert to Christianity) about a Hindu collection of aphorisms concerning sexual exploits – some would say 'love.' Dr Daruwalla thought it wise to be careful; he said nothing.

As for urine therapy, it was also wise to say nothing. Moraji Desai, the former prime minister, was a practitioner of urine therapy – and wasn't there something called the Water of Life Foundation? Best to say nothing about that, too, Farrokh concluded. Besides, Urology Aziz wanted to read something from the *Kama Sutra*. It would be best to listen.

'Among the *many* situations where adultery is allowed,' Dr Aziz said, 'just listen to *this*: "When such clandestine relations are safe and a sure method of earning money."' Dr Aziz refolded the often-folded piece of paper and returned this evidence to his pocket. 'Well, do you see?' he said.

'What do you mean?' Farrokh asked.

'Well, that's the problem – obviously!' Dr Aziz said.

Farrokh was still trying to figure out how Dr Dev had caught AIDS while performing a colonoscopy; meanwhile, Dr Aziz had concluded that AIDS among prostitutes was caused directly by the bad advice given in the *Kama Sutra*. (Farrokh doubted that most prostitutes could read.) This was another example of the first-floor dogs – they were barking again. Dr Daruwalla smiled nervously all the way to the entrance to the alley, where Urology Aziz had parked his car.

There'd been some brief confusion, because Vinod's Ambassador had momentarily blocked the alley, but Dr Aziz was soon on his way. Farrokh had waited in the alley for the dwarf to turn his car around. It was a close, narrow alley – briny-smelling, because of the proximity of the sea, and as warm and steamy as a blocked drain. The alley was a haven for the beggars who frequented the small seaside hotels along Marine Drive. Dr Daruwalla supposed that these beggars were especially interested in the Arab clientele; they were reputed to give more money. But the beggar who suddenly emerged from the alley wasn't one of these.

He was a badly limping boy who could occasionally be seen standing on his head at Chowpatty Beach. The doctor knew that this wasn't a trick of sufficient promise for Vinod and Deepa to offer the urchin a home at the circus. The boy had slept on the beach – his hair was caked with sand – and the first sunlight had driven him into the alley for a few more hours' sleep. The two automobiles, arriving and departing, had probably attracted his attention. When Vinod backed the Ambassador into the alley, the beggar blocked the doctor's way to the car. The boy stood with both arms extended, palms up; there was a veil of mucus over his eyes and a whitish paste marked the corners of his mouth.

The eyes of the orthopedic surgeon were drawn to the boy's limp. The beggar's right foot was rigidly locked in a right-angle position, as if the foot and ankle were permanently fused – a deformity called ankylosis, which was familiar to Dr Daruwalla from the common congenital condition of clubfoot. Yet both the foot and ankle were unusually flattened – a crush injury, the doctor guessed – and the boy bore his weight on his heel alone. Also, the bad foot was considerably smaller than the good one; this led the doctor to imagine that the injury had damaged the epiphyseal plates, which is the region in bones where growth takes place. It wasn't only that the boy's foot had fused with his ankle; his foot had also stopped growing. Farrokh felt certain that the boy was inoperable.

Just then, Vinod opened the driver's-side door. The beggar was wary of the dwarf, but Vinod wasn't brandishing his squash-racquet handles. The dwarf was nevertheless determined to open the rear door for Dr Daruwalla, who observed that the beggar was taller but frailer than Vinod – Vinod simply pushed the boy out of the way. Farrokh saw the beggar stumble; his mashed foot was as stiff as a hammer. Once inside the Ambassador, the doctor lowered the window only enough so that the boy could hear him.

'*Maaf karo*,' Dr Daruwalla said gently. It was what he always said to beggars: 'Forgive me.'

The boy spoke English. 'I *don't* forgive you,' he said.

Also in English, Farrokh said what was on his mind: 'What happened to your foot?'

'An elephant stepped on it,' the cripple replied.

That would explain it, the doctor thought, but he didn't believe the story; beggars were liars.

'Was it being a circus elephant?' Vinod inquired.

'It was just an elephant stepping off a train,' the boy told the dwarf. 'I was a baby, and my father left me lying on the station platform – he was in a bidi shop.'

'You were stepped on by an elephant while your father was buying cigarettes?' Farrokh asked. This certainly sounded like a tall tale, but the cripple listlessly nodded. 'So I suppose your name is Ganesh – after the elephant god,' Dr Daruwalla asked the boy. Without appearing to notice the doctor's sarcasm, the cripple nodded again.

'It was the wrong name for me,' the boy replied.

Apparently Vinod believed the beggar. 'He is being a doctor,' the dwarf said, pointing to Farrokh. 'He is fixing you, maybe,' Vinod added, pointing to the boy. But the beggar was already limping away from the car.

'You can't fix what elephants do,' Ganesh said.

The doctor didn't believe he could fix what the elephant had done, either. '*Maaf karo*,' Dr Daruwalla repeated. Neither stopping nor bothering to look back, the cripple made no further response to Farrokh's favorite expression.

Then the dwarf drove Dr Daruwalla to the hospital,

where one surgery for clubfoot and another for wryneck awaited him. Farrokh tried to distract himself by daydreaming about a back operation – a laminectomy with fusion. Then Dr Daruwalla dreamed of something more ambitious – the placement of Harrington rods for a severe vertebral infection, with vertebral collapse. But even in prepping his surgeries for the clubfoot and the wryneck, the doctor would keep thinking about how he might fix the beggar's foot.

Farrokh could cut through the fibrous tissue and the contracted, shrunken tendons – there were plastic procedures to elongate tendons – but the problem with such a crush injury was the bony fusion; Dr Daruwalla would have to saw through bone. By damaging the vascular bundles around the foot, he could compromise the blood supply; the result might be gangrene. Of course there was always amputation and the fitting of a prosthesis, but the boy would probably refuse such an operation. In fact, Farrokh knew, his own father would have refused to perform such an operation; as a surgeon, Lowji had lived by the old adage *primum non nocere* – above all, do no harm.

Forget the boy, Farrokh had thought. Thus he'd performed the clubfoot and the wryneck and, thereafter, he'd faced the Membership Committee at the Duckworth Club, where he had also lunched with Inspector Dhar, a lunch much disturbed by the death of Mr Lal and the discomfort that D.C.P. Patel had caused them. (Dr Daruwalla had had a busy day.)

And now, as he listened to the phone messages on his answering machine, Farrokh was trying to imagine the precise moment in the bougainvillea by the ninth green when Mr Lal had been struck down. Perhaps when Dr Daruwalla was in surgery; possibly before, when he'd encountered Dr Aziz on the elevator, or one of the times when he'd said '*Maaf karo*' to the crippled beggar whose English was unbelievably good.

Doubtless the boy was one of those enterprising beggars who sold himself as a guide to foreign tourists.

Cripples were the best hustlers, Farrokh knew. Many of them had maimed themselves; some of them had been purposefully injured by their parents – for being crippled improved their opportunities as beggars. These thoughts of mutilation, especially of self-inflicted wounds, led the doctor to thinking about the hijras again. Then his thoughts returned to the golf-course murder.

In retrospect, what astonished Dr Daruwalla was how anyone could have gotten close enough to Mr Lal to strike the old golfer with his own putter. For how could you sneak up on a man who was flailing away in the flowers? His body would have been twisting from side to side, and bending over to fuss with the stupid ball. And where would his golf bag have been? Not far away. How could anyone approach Mr Lal's golf bag, take out the putter and then hit Mr Lal – all when Mr Lal wasn't looking? It wouldn't work in a movie, Farrokh knew – not even in an Inspector Dhar movie.

That was when the doctor realized that Mr Lal's murderer had to have been someone Mr Lal knew, and if the murderer had been another golfer – presumably with his own bag of clubs – why would he have needed to use Mr Lal's putter? But what a nongolfer could have been doing in the vicinity of the ninth green – and still not have aroused Mr Lal's suspicions – was at least for the moment quite beyond the imaginative powers of Inspector Dhar's creator.

Farrokh wondered what sort of dogs were barking in the killer's head. Angry dogs, Dr Daruwalla supposed, for in the murderer's mind there was such a terrifying irrationality; the mind of Dr Aziz would appear reasonable in comparison. But then Farrokh's speculations on this subject were interrupted by the third phone message. The doctor's answering machine was truly relentless.

'Goodness!' cried the unidentified voice. It was a voice of such lunatic exuberance, Dr Daruwalla presumed it was no one he knew.

8. TOO MANY MESSAGES

For Once, the Jesuits Don't Know Everything

At first Farrokh failed to recognize the hysterical enthusiasm that characterized the voice of the ever-optimistic Father Cecil, who was 72 and therefore easily panicked by the challenge to speak clearly and calmly to an answering machine. Father Cecil was the senior priest at St Ignatius, an Indian Jesuit of unrelenting good cheer; as such, he stood in startling juxtaposition to the Father Rector – Father Julian – who was 68 years old and English and one of those intellectual Jesuits with a caustic disposition. Father Julian was so sarcastic that he was an instant source of renewing Dr Daruwalla's combined awe and suspicion of Catholics. But the message was from Father Cecil – therefore free of facetiousness. 'Goodness!' Father Cecil began, as if offering a general description of the world he saw all around him.

What now? thought Dr Daruwalla. Because he was among the distinguished alumni of St Ignatius School, Farrokh was frequently asked to give inspirational speeches to the students; in previous years, he'd also addressed the Young Women's Christian Association. He'd once been an almost active member of the Catholic and Anglican Community for Christian Unity and the so-called Hope Alive Committee. But such activities failed to interest him anymore. Dr Daruwalla sincerely hoped that Father Cecil wasn't calling him with a repeat request for the doctor to relate *again* the stirring experience of his conversion.

After all, despite Dr Daruwalla's past commitment to Catholic and Anglican unity, he was an Anglican; he felt uncomfortable in the presence of a certain over-zealous, albeit small, percentage of the faithful followers of St Ignatius Church. Farrokh had declined a recent invitation to speak at the Catholic Charismatic Information Centre; the suggested topic had been 'The Charismatic Renewal in India.' The doctor had replied that his own *small* experience – the entirely quiet, *little* miracle of his conversion – didn't compare to ecstatic religious experiences (speaking in tongues and spon-taneous healing, and so forth). 'But a miracle is a miracle!' Father Cecil had said. To Farrokh's surprise, Father Julian had taken the doctor's side.

'I quite agree with Dr Daruwalla,' Father Julian had said. 'His experience hardly qualifies as a miracle at all.'

Dr Daruwalla had been miffed. He was quite willing to portray his conversion experience as a low-key kind of miracle; he was always humble when relating the story. There were no marks on his body that even remotely resembled the wounds on the crucified body of Christ. His was no stigmata story. He wasn't one of those nonstop bleeders! But for the Father Rector to dismiss his experience as hardly qualifying as a miracle *at all* . . . well, this sorely vexed Dr Daruwalla. The insult fueled Farrokh's insecurities and prejudices in regard to the superior education of the Jesuits. They were not only holier than thou, they were more *knowing* than thou! But the message was about Dhar's twin, not about the doctor's conversion.

Of course! Dhar's twin was the first American missionary in the highly esteemed 125-year history of St Ignatius; neither the church nor the school had been blessed with an American missionary before. Dhar's twin was what the Jesuits call a scholastic, which Dr Daruwalla already understood to mean that he'd endured much religious and philosophic study and that he'd taken his simple vows. However, the doctor knew, Dhar's twin was still a few years away from being ordained as a priest. This was a period of soul-searching, Dr Daruwalla supposed – the final test of those simple vows.

The vows themselves gave Farrokh the shivers. Poverty, chastity, obedience – they weren't so 'simple.' It was hard to imagine the progeny of a Hollywood screenwriter like Danny Mills opting for poverty; it was harder still to conceive of the offspring of Veronica Rose choosing chastity. And regarding the tricky Jesuitical ramifications of obedience, Dr Daruwalla knew that he himself didn't know nearly enough. What he also suspected was that, should one of those crafty Jesuits try to explain 'obedience' to him, the explanation itself would be a marvel of equivocation – of oversubtle reasoning – and, in the end, Farrokh would have no clearer understanding of a vow of obedience than he'd had before. In Dr Daruwalla's estimation, the Jesuits were intellectually crafty and sly. And this was hardest of all for the doctor to imagine: that a child of Danny Mills and Veronica Rose could be intellectually crafty and sly. Even Dhar, who'd had a decent European education, was no intellectual.

But then Dr Daruwalla reminded himself that Dhar and his twin could also be the genetic creation of Neville Eden. Neville had always struck Farrokh as crafty and sly. What a puzzle! Just what was a man who was almost 40 *doing* by becoming – or trying to become – a priest? What failures had led him to this? Farrokh assumed that only blunders or disillusionments could lead a man to vows of such a radically repressive nature.

Now here was Father Cecil saying that 'young Martin' had mentioned, in a letter, that Dr Daruwalla was 'an old friend of the family.' So his name was Martin – Martin Mills. Farrokh remembered that, in *her* letter to him, Vera had already told him this. And 'young Martin' wasn't so young, Dr Daruwalla knew – except to Father Cecil, who was 72. But the gist of Father Cecil's phone message caught Dr Daruwalla by surprise.

'Do you know exactly when he's coming?' Father Cecil asked.

What does he mean – do *I* know? Farrokh thought. Why doesn't *he* know? But neither Father Julian nor Father Cecil could remember exactly when Martin Mills was arriving; they blamed Brother Gabriel for losing the American's letter.

Brother Gabriel had come to Bombay and St Ignatius after the Spanish Civil War; he'd been on the Communist side, and his first contribution to St Ignatius had been to collect the Russian and Byzantine icons for which the mission chapel and its icon-collection room were famous. Brother Gabriel was also in charge of the mail.

When Farrokh was 10 or 12 and a student at St Ignatius, Brother Gabriel would have been 26 or 28; Dr Daruwalla remembered that Brother Gabriel was at that time still struggling to learn Hindi and Marathi, and that his English was melodious, with a Spanish accent. The doctor recalled a short, sturdy man in a black cassock, exhorting an army of sweepers to raise more and more clouds of dust from the stone floors. Farrokh also remembered that Brother Gabriel was in charge of the other servants, and the garden, and the kitchen, *and* the linen room – in addition to the mail. But the icons were his passion. He was a friendly, vigorous man, neither an intellectual nor a priest, and Dr Daruwalla calculated that, today, Brother Gabriel would be around 75. No wonder he's losing letters, Farrokh thought.

So no one knew exactly when Dhar's twin would arrive! Father Cecil added that the American's teaching duties would commence almost immediately. St Ignatius didn't recognize the week between Christmas and New Year's as a holiday; only Christmas Day and New Year's Day were school vacations, an annoyance that Farrokh remembered from his own school days. The doctor guessed that the school was still sensitive to the charge made by many non-Christian parents that Christmas was overemphasized.

It was possible, Father Cecil opined, that young Martin would make contact with Dr Daruwalla before he contacted anyone at St Ignatius. Or perhaps the doctor had already heard from the American? *Already heard?* thought Dr Daruwalla, in a panic.

Here was Dhar's twin – due to arrive any day now – and Dhar still didn't know! And the naïve American would arrive at Sahar Airport at 2:00 or 3:00 in the morning; that was when all the flights from Europe and North America arrived. (Dr Daruwalla presumed that *all* Americans coming to India were 'naïve.') At that dreadfully early hour, St Ignatius would quite literally be closed – like a castle, like an army barracks, like the compound or the cloister that it was. If the priests and brothers didn't know exactly when Martin Mills was arriving, no one would leave any lights on or any doors open for him – no one would meet his plane. And so the bewildered missionary might come directly to Dr Daruwalla; he might simply show up on the doctor's doorstep at 3:00 or 4:00 in the morning. (Dr Daruwalla presumed that *all* missionaries coming to India were 'bewildered.')

Farrokh couldn't remember what he'd written to Vera. Had he given the horrid woman his home address or the address of the Hospital for Crippled Children? Fittingly, she'd written to him in care of the Duckworth Club. Of Bombay, of all of India, it was possibly only the Duckworth Club that Vera remembered. (Doubtless she'd repressed the cow.)

Damn other people's messes! Dr Daruwalla was muttering aloud. He was a surgeon; as such, he was an extremely neat and tidy man. The sheer sloppiness of human relationships appalled him, especially those relationships to which he felt he'd brought a special responsibility and care. Brother-sister, brother-brother, child-parent, parent-child. What was the matter with human beings, that they made such a shambles out of these basic relationships?

Dr Daruwalla didn't want to hide Dhar from his

twin. He didn't want to hurt Danny – with the cruel evidence of what his wife had done, and how she'd lied – but he felt he was largely protecting Vera by helping her to keep her lie intact. As for Dhar, he was so disgusted by everything he'd heard about his mother, he'd stopped being curious about her when he was in his twenties; he'd never expressed a desire to know her – not even to meet her. Admittedly, his curiosity about his father had persisted into his thirties, but Dhar had lately seemed resigned to the fact that he would never know him. Perhaps the proper word was 'hardened,' not 'resigned.'

At 39, John D. had simply grown accustomed to not knowing his mother and father. But who wouldn't want to know, or at least meet, his own twin? Why not simply introduce the fool missionary to his twin? the doctor asked himself. 'Martin, this is your brother – you'd better get used to the idea.' (Dr Daruwalla presumed that all missionaries were, in one way or another, fools.) Telling the truth to Dhar's twin would serve Vera right, Farrokh thought. It might even prevent Martin Mills from doing anything as confining as becoming a priest. It was most definitely the Anglican in Dr Daruwalla that stopped short of the very idea of chastity, which seemed utterly confining to him.

Farrokh remembered what his contentious father had had to say about chastity. Lowji had considered the subject in the light of Gandhi's experience. The Mahatma had been married at 13; he was 37 when he took a vow of sexual abstinence. 'By my calculations,' Lowji had said, 'this amounts to twenty-four years of sex. Many people don't have that many years of sex in their entire lifetime. So the Mahatma chose sexual abstinence after twenty-four years of sexual activity. He was a bloody womanizer flanked by a bunch of Mary Magdalens!'

As with all his father's pronouncements, that voice of steadfast authority rang down through the years, for old Lowji proclaimed everything in the same strident, inflammatory tones; he mocked, he defamed, he provoked, he advised. Whether he was giving good advice (usually of a medical nature) or speaking out of the most dire prejudice – or expressing the most eccentric, simplistic opinion – Lowji had the tone of voice of a self-declared expert. To everyone, and in consideration of all subjects, he used the same famous tone of voice with which he'd made a name for himself in the days of Independence and during the Partition, when he'd so authoritatively addressed the issue of Disaster Medicine. ('In order of importance, look for dramatic amputations and severe extremity injuries before treating fractures or lacerations. Best to leave all head injuries to the experts, if there are any.') It was a pity that such sensible advice was wasted on a movement that didn't last, although the present volunteers in the field still spoke of Disaster Medicine as a worthy cause.

Upon that memory, Dr Farrokh Daruwalla attempted to extricate himself from the past. He forced himself to view the melodrama of Dhar's twin as the particular crisis at hand. With refreshing and unusual clarity, the doctor decided that it should be Dhar's decision whether or not poor Martin Mills should know that he had a twin brother. Martin Mills wasn't the twin the doctor knew and loved. It should be a matter of what the doctor's beloved John D. wanted: to know his brother or not to know him. And to hell with Danny and Vera, and whatever mess they might have made of their lives – especially to hell with Vera. She would be 65, Farrokh realized, and Danny was almost 10 years older; they were both old enough to face the music like grownups.

But Dr Daruwalla's reasoning was entirely swept away by the next phone message, alongside which everything to do with Dhar and his twin assumed the lesser stature of gossip, of mere trivia.

'Patel here,' said the voice, which instantly impressed Farrokh with a moral detachment he'd never known. Anesthesiology Patel? Radiology Patel? It was a Gujarati name – there weren't all that many Patels in Bombay. And then, with a sensation of sudden coldness – almost as cold as the voice on his answering machine – Farrokh knew who it was. It was Deputy Commissioner Patel, the *real* policeman. He must be the only Gujarati on the Bombay police force, Farrokh thought, for surely the local police were mostly Maharashtrians.

'Doctor,' the detective said, 'there is quite a different subject we must discuss – *not* in Dhar's presence, please. I want to speak with you alone.' The hanging up of the phone was as abrupt as the message.

Had he not been so agitated by the call, Dr Daruwalla might have prided himself for his insight as a screenwriter, for he'd always given Inspector Dhar a similar succinctness when speaking on the telephone – especially to answering machines. But the screenwriter took no pride in the accuracy of his characterization; instead, Farrokh was overcome with curiosity regarding what the 'different subject' that Detective Patel wished to discuss *was*, not to mention why this subject couldn't be discussed in front of Dhar. At the same time, Dr Daruwalla absolutely dreaded the deputy commissioner's presumed knowledge of crime.

Was there another clue to Mr Lal's murder, or another threat to Dhar? Or was this 'different subject' the cage-girl killings – the real-life murders of those prostitutes, not the movie version?

But the doctor had no time to contemplate the mystery. With the *next* phone message, Dr Daruwalla was once more ensnared by the past.

The Same Old Scare:
a Brand-New Threat

It was an old message, one he'd been hearing for 20 years. He'd received these calls in Toronto and in

Bombay, both at his home and at his office. He'd tried having the calls traced, but without success; they were made from public phones – from post offices, hotel lobbies, airports, hospitals. And regardless of how familiar Farrokh was with the content of these calls, the hatred that inspired them never failed to engage his complete attention.

The voice, full of cruel mockery, began by quoting old Lowji's advice to the Disaster Medicine volunteers – '". . . look for dramatic amputations and severe extremity injuries,"' the voice began. And then, interrupting itself, the voice said, 'When it comes to "dramatic amputations" – your father's head was off, completely *off*! I saw it sitting on the passenger seat before the flames engulfed the car. And when it comes to "severe extremity injuries" – his hands couldn't let go of the steering wheel, even though his fingers were on fire! I saw the burned hairs on the backs of his hands, before the crowd formed and I had to slip away. And your father said it was "best to leave all head injuries to the experts" – when it comes to "head injuries," *I'm* the expert! I did it. I blew his head off. I watched him burn. And I'm telling you, he deserved it. Your whole family deserves it.'

It was the same old scare – he'd been hearing it for 20 years – but it never affected Dr Daruwalla any less. He sat shivering in his bedroom as he'd sat shivering about a hundred times before. His sister, in London, had never received these calls. Farrokh assumed that she was spared only because the caller didn't know her married name. His brother, Jamshed, had received these calls in Zürich. The calls to both brothers had been recorded on various answering machines and on several tapes made by the police. Once, in Zürich, the Daruwalla brothers and their wives had listened to one of these recordings over and over again. No one recognized the voice of the caller, but to Farrokh's and Jamshed's surprise, their wives were convinced that the caller was a woman. The brothers had always thought the voice was unmistakably a man's. As sisters, Julia and Josefine were adamant in regard to the mystical correctness of anything they agreed about. The caller was a woman – they were sure.

The dispute was still raging when John D. arrived at Jamshed and Josefine's apartment for dinner. Everyone insisted that Inspector Dhar should settle the argument. After all, an actor had a trained voice and acute powers for studying and imitating the voices of others. John D. listened to the recording only once.

'It's a man trying to sound like a woman,' he said.

Dr Daruwalla was outraged – not so much by the opinion, which the doctor found simply outlandish, but by the infuriating authority with which John D. had spoken. It was the actor speaking, the doctor was certain – the actor in his role as detective. That was where the arrogant, self-assured manner came from – from *fiction*!

Everyone had objected to Dhar's conclusion, and so the actor had rewound the tape; he'd listened to it again – actually, two more times. Then suddenly the mannerisms that Dr Daruwalla associated with Inspector Dhar vanished; it was a serious, apologetic John D. who spoke to them.

'I'm sorry – I was wrong,' John D. said. 'It's a woman trying to sound like a man.'

Because this assessment was spoken with a different kind of confidence and not at all as Inspector Dhar would have delivered the line, Dr Daruwalla said, 'Rewind it. Play it again.' This time they'd all agreed with John D. It was a woman, and she was trying to sound like a man. It was no one whose voice they'd ever heard before – they'd all agreed to that, too. Her English was almost perfect – very British. She had only a trace of a Hindi accent.

'I did it. I blew his head off. I watched him burn. And I'm telling you, he deserved it. Your whole family deserves it,' the woman had said for 20 years, probably more than 100 times. But who was she? Where did her hatred come from? And had she really done it?

Her hatred might be even stronger if she'd *not* done it. But then why take credit for doing it? the doctor wondered. How could anyone have hated Lowji *that* much? Farrokh knew that his father had said much to offend everybody, but, to Farrokh's knowledge, his father hadn't *personally* wronged anyone. It was easy, in India, to assume that the source of any violence was either political outrage or religious offense. When someone as prominent and outspoken as Lowji was blown up by a car bomb, it was automatic to label the killing an assassination. But Farrokh had to wonder if his father might have inspired a more personal anger, and if his killing hadn't been just a plain old murder.

It was hard for Farrokh to imagine anyone, especially a woman, with a private grievance against his father. Then he thought of the deeply personal loathing that Mr Lal's murderer must feel for Inspector Dhar. (MORE MEMBERS DIE IF DHAR REMAINS A MEMBER.) And it occurred to Dr Daruwalla that perhaps they were all being hasty to assume it was Dhar's movie persona that had inspired such a venomous anger. Had Dr Daruwalla's dear boy – his beloved John D. – got himself into some *private* trouble? Was this a case of a personal relationship that had soured into a murderous hatred? Dr Daruwalla felt ashamed of himself that he'd inquired so little about Dhar's personal life. He feared he'd given John D. the impression that he was indifferent to the younger man's private affairs.

Certainly, John D. was chaste when he was in Bombay; at least he *said* he was. There were the public appearances with starlets – the ever-available cinema bimbos – but such couplings were choreographed to create the desired scandal, which both parties would later deny. These weren't 'relationships' – they were 'publicity.'

The Inspector Dhar movies thrived on giving offense – in India, a risky enterprise. Yet the senselessness of murdering Mr Lal indicated a hatred more vicious than anything Dr Daruwalla could detect in the usual reactions to Dhar. As if on cue, as if prompted by the mere thought of giving or taking *offense*, the next phone message was from the director of all the Inspector Dhar movies. Balraj Gupta had been pestering Dr Daruwalla about the extremely touchy subject of *when* to release the new Inspector Dhar movie. Because of the prostitute killings and the general disfavor incurred by *Inspector Dhar and the Cage-Girl Killer,* Gupta had delayed its opening and he was increasingly impatient.

Dr Daruwalla had privately decided that he never wanted the new Inspector Dhar film to be seen, but he knew that the movie *would be* released; he couldn't stop it. Nor could he appeal to Balraj Gupta's deficient instincts for social responsibility much longer; such maladroit feelings as Gupta might have had for the real-life murdered prostitutes were short-lived.

'Gupta here!' the director said. 'Look at it this way. The new one will cause *new* offense. Whoever is killing the cage girls might give it up and kill someone else! We give the public something new to make them wild and crazy – we'll be doing the prostitutes a favor!' Balraj Gupta possessed the logic of a politician; the doctor had no doubt that the new Inspector Dhar movie would make a different group of moviegoers 'wild and crazy.'

It was called *Inspector Dhar and the Towers of Silence*; the title alone would be offensive to the entire Parsi community, because the Towers of Silence were the burial wells for the Parsi dead. There were always naked corpses of Parsis in the Towers of Silence, which was why Dr Daruwalla had first supposed that *they* were the attraction to the first vulture he'd seen above the golf course at the Duckworth Club. The Parsis were understandably protective of their Towers of Silence; as a Parsi, Dr Daruwalla knew this very well. Yet in the new Inspector Dhar movie, someone is murdering Western hippies and depositing *their*

222

bodies in the Towers of Silence. Many Indians readily took offense at European and American hippies when they were *alive*. Doongarwadi is an accepted part of Bombay culture. At the very least, the Parsis would be disgusted. And all Bombayites would reject the premise of the film as absurd. No one can get near the Towers of Silence – not even other Parsis! (Not unless they're dead.) But of course, Dr Daruwalla thought proudly, that was what was neat and tricky about the film – *how* the bodies are deposited there, and *how* the intrepid Inspector Dhar figures this out.

With resignation, Dr Daruwalla knew that he couldn't stall the release of *Inspector Dhar and the Towers of Silence* much longer; he could, however, fast-forward through Balraj Gupta's remaining arguments for releasing the film immediately. Besides, the doctor enjoyed the high-speed distortion of Balraj Gupta's voice far more than he appreciated the real thing.

While the doctor was being playful, he came to the last message on his answering machine. The caller was a woman. At first Farrokh supposed it was no one he knew. 'Is that the doctor?' she asked. It was a voice long past exhaustion, of someone who was terminally depressed. She spoke as if her mouth were too wide open, as if her lower jaw were permanently dropped. There was a deadpan, don't-give-a-damn quality to her voice, and her accent was plain and flat – North American, surely, but Dr Daruwalla (who was good at accents) guessed more specifically that she was from the American Midwest or the Canadian prairies. Omaha or Sioux City, Regina or Saskatoon.

'Is that the doctor?' she asked. 'I know who you really are, I know what you really do,' the woman went on. 'Tell the deputy commissioner – the *real* policeman. Tell him who you are. Tell him what you do.' The hang-up was a little out of control, as if she'd meant to slam the phone into its cradle but, in her restrained anger, had missed the mark.

Farrokh sat trembling in his bedroom. From the

dining room of his apartment, he could now hear Roopa laying out their supper on the glass-topped table. She would any minute announce to Dhar and Julia that the doctor was home and that their extra-ordinarily late meal was finally served. Julia would wonder why he'd snuck into the bedroom like a thief. In truth, Farrokh felt like a thief – but one unsure of what he'd stolen, and from whom.

Dr Daruwalla rewound the tape and replayed the last message. This was a brand-new threat; and because he was concentrating so hard upon the meaning of the call, the doctor almost missed the most important clue, which was the caller. Farrokh had always known that *someone* would discover him as Inspector Dhar's creator; that part of the message was not unexpected. But why was this any business of the *real* policeman? Why did someone think that Deputy Commissioner Patel should know?

'I know who you really are, I know what you really do.' But so what? the screenwriter thought. 'Tell him who you are. Tell him what you do.' But why? Farrokh wondered. Then, by accident, the doctor found himself listening repeatedly to the woman's opening line, the part he'd almost missed. 'Is that the doctor?' He played it again and again, until his hands were shaking so badly that he rewound the tape all the way into Balraj Gupta's list of reasons for releasing the new Inspector Dhar film now.

'Is that the doctor?'

Dr Daruwalla's heart had never seemed to stand so still before. It can't be *her*! he thought. But it *was* her – Farrokh was sure of it. After all these years – it *couldn't* be! But of course, he realized, if it was her, she would know; with an intelligent guess, she could have figured it out.

That was when his wife burst into the bedroom. 'Farrokh!' Julia said. 'I never knew you were home!'

But I'm not 'home,' the doctor thought; I'm in a very, very foreign country.

'*Liebchen,*' he said softly to his wife. Whenever he used the German endearment, Julia knew he was feeling tender – or else he was in trouble.

'What is it, *Liebchen*?' she asked him. He held out his hand and she went to him; she sat close enough beside him to feel that he was shivering. She put her arms around him.

'Please listen to this,' Farrokh said to her. '*Bitte.*'

The first time Julia listened, Farrokh could see by her face that she was making *his* mistake; she was concentrating too hard on the content of the message.

'Never mind what she says,' said Dr Daruwalla. 'Think about who she is.'

It was the third time before Farrokh saw Julia's expression change.

'It's *her,* isn't it?' he asked his wife.

'But this is a much older woman,' Julia said quickly.

'It's been twenty years, Julia!' Dr Daruwalla said. 'She *would be* a much older woman now! She *is* a much older woman!'

They listened together a few more times. At last Julia said, 'Yes, I think it *is* her, but what's her connection with what's happening now?'

In the cold bedroom – in his funereal navy-blue suit, which was comically offset by the bright-green parrot on his necktie – Dr Daruwalla was afraid that he knew what the connection was.

The Skywalk

The past surrounded him like faces in a crowd. Among them, there was one he knew, but whose face was it? As always, something from the Great Royal Circus offered itself as a beacon. The ringmaster, Pratap Singh, was married to a lovely woman named Sumitra – everyone called her Sumi. She was in her thirties, possibly her forties; and she not only played the role of mother to many of the child performers, she was also a

225

gifted acrobat. Sumi performed in the item called Double-Wheel Cycle, a bicycle act, with her sister-in-law Suman. Suman was Pratap's unmarried, adopted sister; she must have been in her late twenties, possibly her thirties, when Dr Daruwalla last saw her – a petite and muscular beauty, and the best acrobat in Pratap's troupe. Her name meant 'rose flower' – or was it 'scent of the rose flower,' or merely the scent of flowers in general? Farrokh had never actually known, no more than he knew the story concerning *when* Suman had been adopted, or by whom.

It didn't matter. Suman and Sumi's bicycle duet was much loved. They could ride their bicycles backward, or lie down on them and pedal them with their hands; they could ride them on one wheel, like unicycles, or pedal them while sitting on the handlebars. Perhaps it was a special softness in Farrokh that he took such pleasure from seeing two pretty women do something so graceful together. But Suman was the star, and her Skywalk item was the best act in the Great Royal Circus.

Pratap Singh had taught Suman how to 'skywalk' after he'd seen it performed on television; Farrokh supposed that the act had originated with one of the European circuses. (The ringmaster couldn't resist training everyone, not just the lions.) He'd installed a ladderlike device on the roof of the family troupe tent; the rungs of the ladder were loops of rope and the ladder was bracketed to extend horizontally across the tent roof. Suman hung upside down with her feet in the loops. She swung herself back and forth, the loops chafing the tops of her feet, which she kept rigid – at right angles to her ankles. When she'd gathered the necessary momentum, she 'walked' upside down – from one end of the ladder to the other – simply by stepping her feet in and out of the loops as she swung. When she practiced this across the roof of the family troupe tent, her head was only inches above the dirt floor. Pratap Singh stood next to her, to catch her if she fell.

But when Suman performed the Skywalk from the top of the main tent, she was 80 feet from the dirt floor and she refused to use a net. If Pratap Singh had tried to catch her – *if* Suman fell – they both would have been killed. If the ringmaster threw his body under her, trying to guess where she'd land, Pratap might break Suman's fall; then only he would be killed.

There were 18 loops in the ladder. The audience silently counted Suman's steps. But Suman never counted her steps; it was better, she said, to 'just walk.' Pratap told her it wasn't a good idea to look down. Between the top of the tent and the faraway floor, there were only the upside-down faces of the audience, staring back at her – waiting for her to fall.

That was what the past was like, thought Dr Daruwalla – all those swaying, upside-down faces. It wasn't a good idea to look at them, he knew.

9. SECOND HONEYMOON

Before His Conversion,
Farrokh Mocks the Faithful

Twenty years ago, when he was drawn to Goa by his epicurean nostalgia for pork – scarce in the rest of India, but a staple of Goan cuisine – Dr Daruwalla was converted to Christianity by the big toe of his right foot. He spoke of his religious conversion with the sincerest humility. That the doctor had recently visited the miraculously preserved mummy of St Francis Xavier was *not* the cause of his conversion; previous to his personal experience with divine intervention, Dr Daruwalla had even mocked the saint's relics, which were kept under glass in the Basilica de Bom Jesus in Old Goa.

Farrokh supposed that he'd made fun of the missionary's remains because he enjoyed teasing his wife about her religion, although Julia was never a practicing Catholic and she often expressed how it pleased her to have left the Roman trappings of her childhood in Vienna. Nevertheless, prior to their marriage, Farrokh had submitted to some tedious religious instruction from a Viennese priest. The doctor had understood that he was demonstrating a kind of theological passivity only to satisfy Julia's mother; but – again, to tease Julia – Farrokh insisted on referring to the ring-blessing ceremony as the 'ring-washing ritual,' and he pretended to be more offended by this Catholic charade than he was. In truth, he'd enjoyed telling the priest that, although he was unbaptized and had never been a practicing Zoroastrian, he nonetheless had always believed in 'something'; at the time, he'd believed in nothing at all. And he'd calmly lied to both the priest and Julia's mother – that he had no objections to his children being baptized and raised as Roman Catholics. He and Julia had privately agreed that this was a worthwhile, if not entirely innocent deception – again, to put Julia's mother at ease.

It hadn't hurt his daughters to have them baptized, Farrokh supposed. When Julia's mother was still alive, and only when she'd visited the Daruwallas and their children in Toronto, or when the Daruwallas had visited her in Vienna, it had never been too painful to attend Mass. Farrokh and Julia had told their little girls that they were making their grandmother happy. This was an acceptable, even an honorable, tradition in the history of Christian churchgoing: to go through the motions of worship as a favor to a family member who appeared to be that most intractable personage, a true believer. No one had objected to this occasional enactment of a faith that was frankly quite foreign to them all, maybe even to Julia's mother. Farrokh sometimes wondered if *she* had been going through the motions of worship only to please *them*.

It was exactly as the Daruwallas had anticipated: when Julia's mother died, the family's intermittent Catholicism more than lapsed – their churchgoing virtually stopped. In retrospect, Dr Daruwalla concluded that his daughters had been preconditioned to accept that *all* religion was nothing more than going through the motions of worship to make someone else happy. It had been to please the doctor, after his conversion, that his daughters were administered the sacrament of marriage and other rites and ceremonies according to the Anglican Church of Canada. Maybe this was why Father Julian was so dismissive of the miracle by which Farrokh had been converted to Christianity. In the Father Rector's opinion, it must have been only a minor miracle, if the experience managed merely to make Dr Daruwalla an Anglican. In other words, it hadn't been enough of a miracle to make the doctor a Roman Catholic.

It was a good time to go to Goa, Farrokh had

229

thought. 'The trip is a kind of second honeymoon for Julia,' he'd told his father.

'What kind of honeymoon is it when you take the children?' Lowji had asked; he and Meher resented that their three granddaughters weren't being left with them. Farrokh knew that the girls, who were 11, 13, and 15, would not have stood for being left behind; the reputation of the Goa beaches was far more exciting to them than the prospect of staying with their grand-parents. And the girls were determinedly committed to this vacation because John D. was going to be there. No other babysitter could command such authority over them; they were decidedly in love with their adopted elder brother.

In June of 1969, John D. was 19, and – especially to Dr Daruwalla's daughters – an extremely handsome European. Julia and Farrokh certainly admired the beautiful boy, but less for his good looks than for his tolerant disposition toward their children; not every 19-year-old boy could stomach so much giddy affec-tion from three underage girls, but John D. was patient, even charming, with them. And having been schooled in Switzerland, John D. would probably be undaunted by the freaks who overran Goa – or so Farrokh had thought. In 1969, the European and American hippes were called 'freaks' – especially in India.

'This is some second honeymoon, my dear,' old Lowji had said to Julia. 'He is taking you and the children to the dirty beaches where the freaks debauch themselves, and it is all because of his love of *pork*!'

With this blessing did the younger Daruwallas de-part for the former Portuguese enclave. Farrokh told Julia and John D. and his indifferent daughters that the churches and cathedrals of Goa was among the gaudier landmarks of Indian Christendom. Dr Daru-walla was a connoisseur of Goan architecture: monumentality and massiveness he enjoyed; excess-iveness, which was also reflected in the doctor's diet, he found thrilling.

He preferred the Cathedral of St Catherine da Se and the façade of the Franciscan Church to the unimpressive Church of the Miraculous Cross, but his overall preference for the Basilica de Bom Jesus wasn't rooted in his architectural snobbery; rather, he was wildly amused by the silliness of the pilgrims – even Hindus! – who flocked to the basilica to view the mummified remains of St Francis.

It is suspected, especially among non-Christians in India, that St Francis Xavier contributed more to the Christianization of Goa *after* his death than the Jesuit had managed – in his short stay of only a few months – while he was alive. He died and was buried on an island off the Cantonese coast; but when he suffered the further indignity of disinterment, it was discovered that he'd hardly decomposed at all. The miracle of his intact body was shipped back to Goa, where his remarkable remains drew crowds of frenzied pilgrims. Farrokh's favorite part of the story concerned a woman who, with the worshipful intensity of the most devout, bit off a toe of the splendid corpse. Xavier would lose more of himself, too: the Vatican required that his right arm be shipped to Rome, without which evidence St Francis's canonization might never have occurred.

How Dr Daruwalla loved this story! How hungrily he viewed the shriveled relic, which was richly swaddled in vestments and brandished a staff of gold; the staff itself was encrusted with emeralds. The doctor assumed that the saint was kept under glass and elevated on a gabled monument in order to discourage other pilgrims from demonstrating their devotion with more zealous biting. Chuckling to himself while remaining outwardly most respectful, Dr Daruwalla had surveyed the mausoleum with restrained glee. All around him, even on the casket, were numerous depictions of Xavier's missionary heroics; but none of the saint's adventures – not to mention the surrounding silver, or the crystal, or the alabaster, or the jasper, or even the purple marble – was as impressive to Farrokh as St Francis's gobbled toe.

'Now *that's* what I call a miracle!' the doctor would say. 'To have seen that might even have made a Christian out of *me*!'

When he was in a less playful temper, Farrokh harangued Julia with tales of the Holy Inquisition in Goa, for the missionary zeal that followed the Portuguese was marked by conversions under threat of death, confiscation of Hindu property and the burning of Hindu temples – not to mention the burning of heretics and grandly staged acts of faith. How it would have pleased old Lowji to hear his son carrying on in this irreverent fashion. As for Julia, she found it irritating that Farrokh so resembled his father in this respect. When it came to baiting anyone who was even remotely religious, Julia was superstitious and opposed.

'I don't mock your lack of belief,' the doctor's wife told him. 'Don't blame me for the Inquisition or laugh about St Francis's poor toe.'

The Doctor Is Turned On

Farrokh and Julia rarely argued with any venom, but they enjoyed teasing each other. An exaggerated, dramatic banter, which they weren't inclined to suppress in public places, made the couple appear quarrelsome to the usual eavesdroppers – hotel staff, waiters or the sad couple with nothing to say to each other at an adjacent table. In those days, in the '60's, when the Daruwallas traveled *en famille*, the girlish hysteria of their daughters added to the general rumpus. Therefore, when they undertook their outing in June of '69, the Daruwallas declined several invitations to lodge themselves in some of the better villas in Old Goa.

Because they were such a loud mob, and because Dr

232

Daruwalla enjoyed eating at all times of the day and night, they thought it wiser and more diplomatic – at least until the children were older – *not* to stay in another family's mansion, with all the breakable Portuguese pottery and the polished rosewood furniture. Instead, the Daruwallas occupied one of those beach hotels that even then had seen better days, but could neither be destroyed by the children nor offended by Dr Daruwalla's unceasing appetite. The spirited teasing between Farrokh and Julia was entirely overlooked by the ragged staff and the world-weary clientele of the Hotel Bardez, where the food was plentiful and fresh if not altogether appetizing, and where the rooms were almost clean. After all, it was the beach that mattered.

The Bardez had been recommended to Dr Daruwalla by one of the younger members of the Duckworth Club. The doctor wished he could remember exactly who had praised the hotel, and why, but only snippets of the recommendation had remained in his memory. The guests were mostly Europeans, and Farrokh had thought that this would appeal to Julia and put young John D. at ease. Julia had teased her husband regarding the concept of putting John D. 'at ease'; it was absurd, she pointed out, to imagine that the young man could be more at ease than he already was. As for the European clientele, they weren't the sort of people Julia would ever want to know; they were trashy, even by John D.'s standards. In his university days in Zürich, John D. was probably as morally relaxed as other young men – or so Dr Daruwalla supposed.

As for the Daruwalla contingent, John D. certainly stood out among them; he was as serenely composed, as ethereally calm, as the Daruwalla daughters were frenetic. The daughters were fascinated by the more unlikable European guests at the Hotel Bardez, although they clung to John D.; he was their protector whenever the young women or the young men, both in their string bikinis, would come too close. In truth, it appeared that these young women *and* young men approached the Daruwalla family solely to have a better view of John D., whose sublime beauty surpassed that of other young men in general and other 19-year-olds in particular.

Even Farrokh tended to gape at John D., although he knew from Jamshed and Josefine that only the dramatic arts interested the young man and that, especially for these thespian pursuits, he seemed inappropriately shy. But to *see* the boy, Farrokh thought, belied all the worries he'd heard expressed by his brother and sister-in-law. It was Julia who first said that John D. looked like a movie star; she said she meant by this that you were drawn to watch him even when he appeared to be doing nothing or thinking of nothing. In addition, his wife pointed out to Dr Daruwalla, John D. projected an indeterminate age. When he was closely shaven, his skin was so perfectly smooth that he seemed much younger than 19 – almost prepubescent. But when he allowed his beard to grow, even only as much as one day's stubble, he became a grown man – at least in his late twenties – and he looked savvy and cocksure and dangerous.

'This is what you mean by a movie star?' Farrokh asked his wife.

'This is what's attractive to women,' Julia said frankly. 'That boy is a man *and* a boy.'

But for the first few days of his vacation, Dr Daruwalla was too distracted to think about John D.'s potential as a movie star. Julia had made Farrokh nervous about the Duckworthian source of the recommendation for the Hotel Bardez. It was amusing to observe the European trash and the interesting Goans, but what if other *Duckworthians* were guests of the Hotel Bardez? It would be as if they'd never left Bombay, Julia said.

And so the doctor neverously examined the Hotel Bardez for stray Duckworthians, fearing that the

Sorabjees would mysteriously materialize in the café-restaurant, or the Bannerjees would float ashore from out of the Arabian Sea, or the Lals would leap out and surprise him from behind the areca palms. Meanwhile, all Farrokh wanted was the peace of mind to reflect on his growing impulse to be more creative.

Dr Daruwalla was disappointed that he was no longer the reader he'd once been. Watching movies was easier; he felt he'd been seduced by the sheer laziness of absorbing images on film. He was proud that he'd at least held himself above the masala movies – those junk films of the Bombay cinema, those Hindi hodgepodges of song and violence. But Farrokh was enthralled by any sleazy offering from Europe or America in the hard-boiled-detective genre; it was all-white, tough-guy trash that attracted him.

The doctor's taste in films was in sharp contrast to what his wife liked to read. For this particular holiday Julia had brought along the autobiography of Anthony Trollope, which Farrokh was not looking forward to hearing. Julia enjoyed reading aloud to him from passages of a book she found especially well written or amusing or moving, but Farrokh's prejudice against Dickens extended to Trollope, whose novels he'd never finished and whose autobiography he couldn't imagine even beginning. Julia generally preferred to read fiction, but Farrokh supposed that the autobiography of a novelist almost qualified as fiction – surely novelists wouldn't resist the impulse to make up their autobiographies.

And this led the doctor to daydreaming further on the matter of his underdeveloped creativity. Since he'd virtually stopped being a reader, he wondered if he shouldn't try his hand at writing. An autobiography, however, was the domain of the already famous – unless, Farrokh mused, the subject had led a thrilling life. Since the doctor was neither famous nor had he, in his opinion, led a life of much excitement, he believed that an autobiography was not for him. Nevertheless, he thought, he would glance at the Trollope – when Julia wasn't looking, and only to see if it might provide him with any inspiration. He doubted that it would.

Unfortunately, his wife's only other reading material was a novel that had caused Farrokh some alarm. When Julia wasn't looking, he'd already glanced at it, and the subject seemed to be relentlessly, obsessively sexual; in addition, the author was totally unknown to Dr Daruwalla, which intimidated him as profoundly as the novel's explicit erotica. It was one of those very skillful novels, exquisitely written in limpid prose – Farrokh knew that much – and this intimidated him, too.

Dr Daruwalla began all novels irritably and with impatience. Julia read slowly, as if she were tasting the words, but Farrokh plunged restlessly ahead, gathering a list of petty grievances against the author until he happened on *something* that persuaded him the novel was worthwhile – or until he encountered some perceived blunder or an entrenched boredom, either of which would cause him to read not one more word. Whenever Farrokh had decided against a novel, he would then berate Julia for the apparent pleasure she was taking from the book. His wife was a reader of broad interests, and she finished almost everything she started; her voraciousness intimidated Dr Daruwalla, too.

So here he was, on his second honeymoon – a term he'd used much too loosely, because he'd not so much as flirted with his wife since they'd arrived in Goa – and he was fearfully on the lookout for Duckworthians, whose dreaded appearance threatened to ruin his holiday altogether. To make matters worse, he'd found himself greatly upset – but also sexually aroused – by the novel his wife was reading. At least he *thought* she was reading it; maybe she hadn't begun. If she was reading it, she'd not read any of it aloud to him, and given the calm but intense depiction of act after sexual act, surely Julia would be too embarrassed to read such passages aloud to him. Or would it be *me* who'd be embarrassed? he wondered.

The novel was so compelling that his covert glances at it were insufficient satisfaction; he'd begun concealing it in a newspaper or a magazine and sneaking off to a hammock with it. Julia didn't appear to miss it; perhaps she was reading the Trollope.

The first image that captured Farrokh's attention was only a couple of pages into the first chapter. The narrator was riding on a train in France. 'Across from me the girl has fallen asleep. She has a narrow mouth, cast down at the corners, weighted there by the sourness of knowledge.' Immediately, Dr Daruwalla felt that this was good stuff, but he also surmised that the story would end unhappily. It had never occurred to the doctor that a stumbling block between himself and most serious literature was that he disliked unhappy endings. Farrokh had forgotten that, as a younger reader, he'd once preferred unhappy endings.

It wasn't until the fifth chapter that Dr Daruwalla became disturbed by the first-person narrator's frankly voyeuristic qualities, for these same qualities strongly brought out the doctor's own troubling voyeurism. 'When she walks, she leaves me weak. A hobbled, feminine step. Full hips. Small waist.' Faithfully, as always, Farrokh thought of Julia. 'There's a glint of white slip where her sweater parts slightly at the bosom. My eyes keep going there in quick, helpless glances.' Does Julia *like* this kind of thing? Farrokh wondered. And then, in the eighth chapter, the novel took a turn that made Dr Daruwalla miserable with envy and desire. Some second honeymoon! he thought. 'Her back is towards him. In a single move she pulls off her sweater and then, reaching behind herself in that elbow-awkward way, unfastens her brassiere. Slowly he turns her around.'

Dr Daruwalla was suspicious of the narrator, this first person who is obsessed with every detail of the sexual explorations of a young American abroad and a

French girl from the country – an 18-year-old Anne-Marie. Farrokh didn't understand that without the narrator's discomforting presence, the reader couldn't experience the envy and desire of the perpetual on-looker, which was precisely what haunted Farrokh and impelled him to read on and on. 'The next morning they do it again. Grey light, it's very early. Her breath is bad.'

That was when Dr Daruwalla knew that one of the lovers was going to die; her bad breath was an unpleasant hint of mortality. He wanted to stop reading but he couldn't. He decided that he disliked the young American – he was supported by his father, he didn't even have a job – but his heart ached for the French girl, whose innocence was being lost. The doctor didn't know that he was supposed to feel these things. The book was beyond him.

Because his medical practice was an exercise of almost pure goodness, he was ill prepared for the real world. Mostly he saw malformations and deformities and injuries to children; he tried to restore their little joints to their intended perfection. The real world had no purpose as clear as that.

I'll read just one more chapter, Dr Daruwalla thought. He'd already read nine. At the inland edge of the beach, he lay in the midday heat in a hammock under the dead-still fronds of the areca and coconut palms. The smell of coconut and fish and salt was occasionally laced with the smell of hashish, drifting along the beach. Where the beach touched the tropical-green mass of tangled vegetation, a surgarcane stall competed for a small triangle of shade with a wagon selling mango milkshakes. The melting ice had wet the sand.

The Daruwallas had commandeered a fleet of rooms – an entire floor of the Hotel Bardez – and there was a generous outdoor balcony, although the balcony was outfitted with only one sleeping hammock and young John D. had claimed it. Dr Daruwalla felt so comfortable in the beach hammock that he resolved he would persuade John D. to allow him to sleep in the balcony hammock for at least one night; after all, John D. had a bed in his own room, and Farrokh and Julia could stand to be separated overnight – by which the doctor meant that he and his wife weren't inclined to make love as often as every night, or even as often as twice a week. Some second honeymoon! Farrokh thought again. He sighed.

He should have left the tenth chapter for another time, but suddenly he was reading again; like any good novel, it kept lulling him into an almost tranquil state of awareness before it jolted him – it caught him completely by surprise. 'Then hurriedly, as an after-thought, he takes off his clothes and slips in beside her. An act which threatens us all. The town is silent around them. On the milk-white faces of the clock the hands, in unison, jerk to new positions. The trains are running on time. Along the empty streets, yellow head-lights of a car occasionally pass and bells mark the hours, the quarters, the halves. With a touch like flowers, she is gently tracing the base of his cock, driven by now all the way into her, touching his balls, and beginning to writhe slowly beneath him in a sort of obedient rebellion while in his own dream he rises a little and defines the moist rim of her cunt with his finger, and as he does, he comes like a bull. They remain close for a long time, still without talking. It is these exchanges which cement them, that is the terrible thing. These atrocities induce them towards love.'

It wasn't even the end of the chapter, but Dr Daru-walla had to stop reading. He was shocked; and he had an erection, which he concealed with the book, allow-ing it to cover his crotch like a tent. All of a sudden, in the midst of such lucid prose, of such terse elegance, there were a 'cock' and 'balls' and even a 'cunt' (with a 'moist rim') – and these acts that the lovers performed were 'atrocities.' Farrokh shut his eyes. Had Julia read *this* part? He was usually indifferent to his wife's

239

pleasure in the passages she read aloud to him; she enjoyed discussing how certain passages affected her – they rarely had *any* effect on Farrokh. Dr Daruwalla felt a surprising need to discuss the effect of *this* passage with his wife, and the thought of discussing such a thing with Julia inspired the doctor's erection; he felt his hard-on touching the astonishing book.

The Doctor Encounters a
Sex-Change-in-Progress

When he opened his eyes, the doctor wondered if he'd died and had awakened in what the Christians call hell, for standing beside his hammock and peering down at him were two Duckworthians who were no favorites of his.

'Are you reading that book, or are you just using it to put you to sleep?' asked Promila Rai. Beside her was her sole surviving nephew, that loathsome and formerly hairless boy Rahul Rai. But something was wrong with Rahul, the doctor noticed. Rahul appeared to be a woman now. At least he had a woman's breasts; certainly, he wasn't a boy.

Understandably, Dr Daruwalla was speechless.

'Are you still asleep?' Promila Rai asked him. She tilted her head so that she could read the novel's title and the author's name, while Farrokh tightly held the book in its tentlike position above his erection, which he naturally preferred *not* to reveal to Promila – or to her terrifying nephew-with-breasts.

Aggressively, Promila read the title aloud. '*A Sport and a Pastime.* I've never heard of it,' she said.

'It's very good,' Farrokh assured her.

Suspiciously, Promila read the author's name aloud. 'James Salter. Who is he?' she asked.

'Someone wonderful,' Farrokh replied.

'Well, what's it about?' Promila asked him impatiently.

240

'France,' the doctor said. 'The real France.' It was an expression he remembered from the novel.

Already Promila was bored with him, Dr Daruwalla realized. It had been some years since he'd last seen her; Farrokh's mother, Meher, had reported on the frequency of Promila's trips abroad, and the incomplete results of her cosmetic surgery. Looking up at Promila from his hammock, the doctor could recognize (under her eyes) the unnatural tightness of her latest face lift; yet she needed more tightening elsewhere. She was strikingly ugly, like a rare kind of poultry with an excess of wattles at her throat. It wasn't astonishing to Farrokh that the same man had left her at the altar twice; what astonished him was that the same man would have dared to come as close to Promila a second time – for she seemed, as old Lowji put it, 'a Miss Havisham times two' in more than one way. Not only had she been jilted twice, but she seemed twice as vindictive, and twice as dangerous, and – to judge by her ominous nephew-with-breasts – twice as covert.

'You remember Rahul,' Promila said to Farrokh, and, to be certain that she commanded the doctor's full attention, she tapped her long, veiny fingers on the spine of the book, which still concealed Farrokh's cowering erection. When he looked up at Rahul, Dr Daruwalla felt his hard-on wither.

'Yes, of course – Rahul!' the doctor said. Farrokh had heard the rumors, but he'd imagined nothing more outrageous than that Rahul had embraced his late brother's flamboyant homosexuality, possibly in homage to Subodh's memory. It had been that terrible monsoon of '49 when Neville Eden had deliberately shocked Farrokh by telling him that he was taking Subodh Rai to Italy because a pasta diet improved one's stamina for the rigors of buggery. Then they'd both died in that car crash. Dr Daruwalla supposed that young Rahul had taken it rather hard, but not *this* hard!

'Rahul has undergone a little sex change,' said

241

Promila Rai, with a vulgarity that was generally accepted as the utmost in sophistication by the out of it and the insecure.

Rahul corrected his aunt in a voice that reflected conflicting hormonal surges. 'I'm still undergoing it, Auntie,' he remarked. 'I'm not quite *complete*,' he said pointedly to Dr Daruwalla.

'I see,' the doctor replied, but he didn't see – he couldn't conceive of the changes Rahul had undergone, not to mention what was required to make Rahul 'complete.' The breasts were fairly small but firm and very nicely shaped; the lips were fuller and softer than Farrokh remembered them, and the makeup around the eyes was enhancing without tending to excess. If Rahul had been 12 or 13 in '49 – and no more than 8 or 10 when Lowji had examined him for what his aunt had called his inexplicable hairlessness – Rahul was now 32 or 33, Farrokh figured. From his back, in the hammock, the doctor's view of Rahul was cut off just below the waist, which was as slender and pliant as a young girl's.

It was clear to the doctor that estrogens were in use, and to judge these by Rahul's breasts and flawless skin, the estrogens had been a noteworthy success; the effects on Rahul's voice were at best still in progress, because the voice had both male and female resonances in rich confusion. Had Rahul been castrated? Did one dare ask? He looked more womanly than most hijras. And why would he have had his penis removed if he intended to be 'complete,' for didn't that mean a fully fashioned vagina, and wasn't this vagina surgically constructed from the penis turned inside out? I'm just an orthopedist, Dr Daruwalla thought gratefully. All the doctor asked Rahul was, 'Are you changing your name, too?'

Boldly, even flirtatiously, Rahul smiled down at Farrokh; once again, the male and the female were at war with Rahul's voice. 'Not until I'm the real thing,' Rahul answered.

'I see,' the doctor replied; he made an effort to return Rahul's smile, or at least to imply tolerance. Once more Promila startled Farrokh by drumming her fingers on the spine of his tightly held book.

'Is the whole family here?' Promila asked. She made 'the whole family' sound like a grotesque element, like an entire population that was out of control.

'Yes,' Dr Daruwalla answered.

'And that beautiful boy is here, too, I hope – I want Rahul to see him!' Promila said.

'He must be eighteen – no, nineteen,' Rahul said dreamily.

'Yes, nineteen,' the doctor said stiffly.

'Don't anyone point him out to me,' Rahul said. 'I want to see if I can pick him out of the crowd.' Upon this remark, Rahul turned from the hammock and moved away across the beach. Dr Daruwalla thought that the angle of Rahul's departure was deliberate – to give the doctor, from his hammock, the best possible view of Rahul's womanly hips. Rahul's buttocks were also shown to good advantage in a snug sarong, and the tight-fitting halter top was similarly enhancing to Rahal's breasts. Still, Farrokh critically observed, the hands were too large, the shoulders too broad, the upper arms too muscular . . . the feet were too long, the ankles too sturdy. Rahul was neither perfect nor complete.

'Isn't she delicious?' Promila whispered in the doctor's ear. She leaned over him in the hammock and Farrokh felt the heavy silver pendant, the main piece of her necklace, thump against his chest. So Rahul was already a full-fledged 'she' in Promila's mind.

'She seems so . . . womanly,' Dr Daruwalla said to the proud aunt.

'She *is* womanly!' replied Promila Rai.

'Well . . . yes,' the doctor said. He felt trapped in the hammock, with Promila suspended above him like some bird of prey – some *poultry* of prey. Promila's scent was permeating – a blend of sandalwood and embalming fluid, something oniony but also like moss. Dr Daruwalla made an effort not to gag. He felt Promila pulling the novel by James Salter away from him, but he grasped the book in both hands.

'If this is such a wonderful book,' she said doubtingly, 'I hope you'll lend it to me.'

'I think Meher's reading it next,' he said, but he didn't mean Meher, his mother; he'd meant to say Julia, his wife.

'Is Meher here, too?' Promila asked quickly.

'No – I meant Julia,' Farrokh said sheepishly. By Promila's sneer, he could tell she was judging him, as if his sexual life were so dull that he'd confused his mother with his wife – and before he was 40! Farrokh felt ashamed, but he was also angry. What had initially upset him about *A Sport and a Pastime* was now enthralling to him; he felt highly stimulated, but not in that guilty way of pornography. This was something so refined *and* erotic, he wanted to share it with Julia. Quite simply, and wonderfully, the novel had made him feel young again.

Dr Daruwalla saw Rahul and Promila as sexually aberrant beings. They'd ruined his mood; they'd overshadowed something that was sexy and sincerely written, because they were so unnatural – so perverse. Farrokh supposed he should go warn Julia that Promila Rai and her nephew-with-breasts were on the prowl. The Daruwallas might have to give their underage daughters some explanation about what wasn't quite right with Rahul. Farrokh decided he would tell John D., in any case. The doctor hadn't liked how Rahul had been so eager to pick John D. 'out of the crowd.'

Promila had doubtless impressed her nephew-with-breasts with her own opinion – that John D. was entirely too beautiful to be the child of Danny Mills. Dr Daruwalla thought that Rahul had gone looking for John D. because the would-be transsexual hoped to glimpse something of Neville Eden in the doctor's dear boy!

244

Promila had turned away from his hammock, as if she were scanning the beach for the 'delicious' Rahul; Dr Daruwalla took this occasion to stare at the back of her neck. He regretted it, for staring back at him among the discolored wrinkles was a tumorous growth with melanoid characteristics; the doctor couldn't bring himself to advise Promila that she should have a doctor look at this. It wasn't a job for an orthopedist, anyway, and Farrokh remembered how unkindly Promila had responded to Lowji's dismissal of Rahul's hairlessness. Thinking of Rahul, Dr Daruwalla wondered if his father's diagnosis might have been hasty; possibly the hairlessness had been an early signal that something sexual needed rectifying in Rahul.

He struggled to recall the unanswered question concerning Dr Tata. He remembered that day when Promila and Rahul had delivered the old fool to the Daruwalla estate: there'd been some speculation regarding what either Promila or Rahul would have been seeing Dr Tata *for*. It was unlikely that DR TATA'S BEST, MOST FAMOUS CLINIC FOR GYNECOLOGICAL & MATERNITY NEEDS could have been treating Promila, who would never have risked her precious parts to a physician reputed to be worse than ordinary. It was Lowji who'd suggested that it might have been Rahul who was Dr Tata's patient. 'Something to do with the hairlessness business,' the senior Daruwalla had said, hadn't he?

Now old Dr Tata was dead. In keeping with the more low-key times, his son, who was also an obstetrician and gynecologist, had deleted the 'best, most famous' from the clinic's name – although, as a physician, the son was reputed to be as far below ordinary as his father; within the Bombay medical community he was consistently referred to as 'Tata Two.' Nevertheless, maybe Tata Two had kept his father's records. Farrokh thought it might be interesting to know more about Rahul's hairlessness.

It amused Dr Daruwalla to imagine that Promila and Rahul had been so single-minded about getting Rahul

a sex change that they might have assumed a gynecological surgeon was the correct doctor to ask. You
don't ask the physician who's familiar with the parts
you *want*, but rather the doctor who knows and understands the parts you *have*! A urological surgeon would
be required. Dr Daruwalla presumed there would have
to be a psychiatric evaluation, too; surely no responsible physician would perform a complete sex-change
operation on demand.

Then Farrokh remembered that sex-change operations were illegal in India, although this hardly
prevented the hijras from castrating themselves; emasculation appeared to be the caste duty of the hijras.
Apparently, Rahul suffered from no such burden of
'duty'; Rahul's choice seemed to be motivated by
something else – not to be the isolated third gender of a
eunuch-transvestite, but to be 'complete.' An actual
woman – this was what Rahul wanted to be, Dr
Daruwalla imagined.

'I suppose it was young Sidhwa who recommended
the Hotel Bardez to you,' Promila coolly said to the
doctor, which forced Dr Daruwalla to remember
the unlikely source of his information. Sidhwa was a
young man whose tastes struck Farrokh as entirely too
trendy, but in the case of the Hotel Bardez, Sidhwa had
spoken with unbridled enthusiasm – and at length.

'Yes, it was Sidhwa,' the doctor replied. 'I suppose
he told you, too.'

Promila Rai peered down at Dr Daruwalla in his
hammock. There was in her expression a condescension of a cold, reptilian nature; there wasn't even a
flicker of pity in her gaze, but only that which passes
for eagerness in a lizard's eyes as it singles out a
fly.

'I told *him*.' Promila told Farrokh. 'The Bardez is *my*
hotel. I've been coming here for years.'

Oh, what a choice I've made! thought Dr Daruwalla.
But Promila was through with him, at least for the
moment. She simply wandered away, not standing on

a single ceremony that could even faintly be associated with common politeness, although she'd certainly been exposed to good manners and she could apply such etiquette in excess whenever she chose.

So that was the bad news that he had for Julia, Farrokh thought: two detestable Duckworthians had arrived at the Hotel Bardez, which turned out to be one of their personal favorites. But the good news was *A Sport and a Pastime* by James Salter, for Farrokh was 39 and it had been a long time since a book had so possessed his mind and body.

Dr Daruwalla desired his wife – as suddenly, as disturbingly, as unashamedly as he'd ever desired her – and he marveled at the power of Mr Salter's prose to do that: both to be aesthetically pleasing *and* to give him far more than a simple hard-on. The novel seemed like a heroic act of seduction; it had enlivened all of the doctor's senses.

He felt how the beach sand was cooling; at midday it had so burned underfoot that he could cross it only with his sandals on, but now he comfortably walked barefoot in the sand – it seemed an ideal temperature. He vowed to get up very early one morning so that he could also experience the sand at its coldest, but he would forget his vow. Nevertheless, these were the stirrings within him of a second honeymoon, for sure. I shall write a letter to Mr James Salter, he resolved. The rest of his life, Dr Daruwalla would regret his neglecting to write that letter, but on this day in June – in 1969, on Baga Beach in Goa – the doctor briefly felt like a new man. Farrokh was only one day away from meeting the stranger whose voice on his answering machine 20 years later still commanded the authority to fill him with dread.

'Is that him? Is that the doctor?' she would ask. When Farrokh had first heard those questions, he had no idea of the world he was about to enter.

10. CROSSING PATHS

Testing for Syphilis

At the Hotel Bardez, the front-desk staff told Dr
Daruwalla that the young woman had limped down
the beach, all the way from a hippie enclave at
Anjuna; she was checking the hotels for a doctor. 'Any
doctor?' she'd asked. They were proud of themselves
for sending her away, but they warned the doctor that
they were sure she'd be back; she wouldn't find anyone to care for her foot at Calangute Beach, and if she
made it as far as Aguada, she'd be turned away.
Because of how she looked, someone might call the
police.

Farrokh desired to uphold the Parsi reputation for
fairness and social justice; certainly he sought to help
the crippled and the maimed – a girl with a limp was at
least in a category of patients the orthopedist felt
familiar with. It wasn't as if his services were sought
for the purpose of making Rahul Rai complete. Yet
Farrokh couldn't be angry with the staff at the Hotel
Bardez. It was out of respect for Dr Daruwalla's
privacy that they'd sent the limping woman away;
they'd meant only to protect him, although doubtless they took a degree of pleasure in abusing an
apparent freak. Among the Goans, especially as the
1960's were ending, there was a felt resentment of
the European and American hippies who roamed the
beaches; the hippies weren't big spenders – some of
them even stole – and they were perceived as an
undesirable element by the wealthier Western and
Indian tourists whom the Goans wished to attract. And
so, without condemning their behavior, Dr Daruwalla
politely informed the staff at the Hotel Bardez that he

wished to examine the lame hippie should she return.

The doctor's decision seemed especially disappointing to the aged tea-server who shuffled back and forth between the Hotel Bardez and the various encampments of thatch-roofed shelters; these four-poled structures, stuck in the sand and roofed with the dried fronds of coconut palms, dotted the beach. The tea-server had several times approached Dr Daruwalla in his hammock under the palms, and it was largely out of diagnostic interest that Farrokh had observed the old man so closely. His name was Ali Ahmed; he said he was only 60 years old, although he looked 80, and he exhibited a few of the more easily recognizable and colorful physical signs of congenital syphilis. Upon his first tea service, the doctor had spotted Ali Ahmed's 'Hutchinson's teeth' – the unmistakable peg-shaped incisors. The tea-server's deafness, in addition to the characteristic clouding of the cornea, had confirmed Dr Daruwalla's diagnosis.

Farrokh was chiefly interested in positioning Ali Ahmed in such a way that the tea-server faced the morning sun. Dr Daruwalla was trying to spot a fourth symptom, a rarity in congenital syphilis – the Argyll Robertson pupil is much more common in syphilis acquired later in life – and the doctor had cleverly thought of a way to examine the old man without his knowledge.

From his hammock, where he received his tea, Farrokh faced the Arabian Sea. Inland, at his back, the morning sun was a hazy glare above the village; from that direction, wafting over the beach, there emanated an aroma of fermented coconuts. Looking into the cloudly eyes of Ali Ahmed, Farrokh asked with feigned innocence, 'What's that smell, Ali, and where's it coming from?' To be sure he'd be heard, Farrokh had to raise his voice.

The tea-server was at the time focused on handing the doctor a glass of tea; his pupils were constricted to accommodate the object nearby – namely, the tea glass. But when the doctor asked him from whence the powerful odor came, Ali Ahmed looked in the direction of the village; his pupils dilated (to accommodate the distant tops of the coconut and areca palms), but even as his face was lifted to the harsh sunlight his pupils did *not* constrict in reaction to the glare. It was the classic Argyll Robertson pupil, Dr Daruwalla decided.

Farrokh recalled his favorite professor of infectious diseases, *Herr Doktor* Fritz Meitner; Dr Meitner was fond of telling his medical students that the best way to remember the behavior of the Argyll Robertson pupil was to think of a prostitute: she accommodates, but doesn't react. It was an all-male class; they all had laughed, but Farrokh had felt uncertain of his laughter. He'd never been with a prostitute, although they were popular in both Vienna and Bombay.

'Feni,' the tea-server said, to explain the smell. But Dr Daruwalla already knew the answer, just as he knew that the pupils of some syphilitics don't respond to light.

A Literary Seduction Scene

In the village – or perhaps the source of the smell was as far away as Panjim – they were distilling coconuts for the local brew called feni; the heavy, sickly-sweet fumes of the liquor drifted over the few tourists and families on holiday at Baga Beach.

Dr Daruwalla and his family were already favorites with the staff of the small hotel, and they were passionately welcomed in the little lean-to restaurant and taverna that the Daruwallas frequented on the beachfront. The doctor was a big tipper, his wife was a classical beauty of a European tradition (as opposed to the seedy, hippie trash), his daughters were vibrantly bright and pretty – they were still of the innocent school – and the striking John D. was mesmerizing to

Indians and foreigners alike. It was only to those rare families as likable as the Daruwallas that the staff of the Hotel Bardez apologized for the smell of the feni.

In those days, in the premonsoon months of May and June, both knowledgeable foreigners and Indians avoided the Goa beaches; it was too hot. It was, however, when the Goans who lived away from Goa came home to visit their families and friends. The children were through with school. The shrimp and lobster and fish were plentiful, and the mangoes were at their peak. (Dr Daruwalla was enamored of mangoes.) In keeping with the holiday spirit and in order to placate all the Christians, the Catholic Church provided an abundance of feast days; although he wasn't yet religious, the doctor had nothing against a banquet or two.

The Catholics were no longer the majority in Goa – the migrant iron miners who'd arrived early in this century were Hindus – but Farrokh, like his father, persisted in the belief that 'the Romans' still overran the place. The Portuguese influence endured in the monumental architecture that Dr Daruwalla adored; it could distinctly be tasted in the cuisine that the doctor relished. And among the names of the boats of the Christian fishermen, 'Christ the King' was quite common. Bumper stickers, of both the comic and proselytizing variety, were a new if not widespread fad in Bombay; the doctor joked that the names of the boats of the Christian fishermen were *Goan* bumper stickers. Julia was no more amused by this than by Farrokh's constant ridicule of St Francis's violated remains.

'I don't know how anyone can justify canonization,' Dr Daruwalla reflected to John D., largely because Julia wouldn't listen to her husband but also because the young man had studied some theology in university. In Zürich, it would have been Protestant theology, Farrokh assumed. 'Just imagine it!' Farrokh lectured to the young man. 'A violent woman swallows Xavier's

251

toe, and they cut off his arm and send it to Rome!'

John D. smiled silently over his breakfast. The Daruwalla daughters smiled helplessly at John D. When he
looked at his wife, Farrokh was surprised that she was
looking straight back at him – she was smiling, too.
Clearly, she'd not been listening to a word he was
saying. The doctor blushed. Julia's smile wasn't in the
least cynical; on the contrary, his wife's expression
was so sincerely amorous, Farrokh felt certain that
she was determined to remind him of their pleasure
the night before – even in front of John D. and the
children! And judging from their night together, and
the visible randiness of his wife's thoughts on the
morning after, their holiday had become a second
honeymoon after all.

Reading in bed would never seen innocent again, the
doctor thought, although everything had begun quite
innocently. His wife had been reading the Trollope,
and Farrokh hadn't been reading at all; he'd been
trying to get up the nerve to read *A Sport and a
Pastime* in front of Julia. Instead, he lay on his back
with his fingers intertwined upon his rumbling belly –
an excess of pork, or else the dinner conversation had
upset him. Over dinner, he'd tried to explain to his
family his need to be more creative, his desire to write
something, but his daughters had paid no attention to
him and Julia had misunderstood him; she'd suggested
a medical-advice column – if not for *The Times of
India*, then for *The Globe and Mail*. John D. had
advised Farrokh to keep a diary; the young man said
he'd kept one once, and he'd enjoyed it – then a
girlfriend had stolen it and he'd gotten out of the habit.
At that point, the conversation entirely deteriorated
because the Daruwalla daughters had pestered John D.
about the number of girlfriends the young man had
had.

After all, it was the tail end of the '60's; even innocent young girls *talked* as if they were sexually
knowledgeable. It disturbed Farrokh that his daughters

were clearly asking John D. to tell them the number of young women he'd slept with. Typical of John D., and to Dr Daruwalla's great relief, the young man had skillfully and charmingly ducked the question. But the matter of the doctor's unfulfilled creativity had been dismissed or ignored.

The subject, however, hadn't eluded Julia. In bed after dinner, propped up with a stack of pillows – while Farrokh lay flat upon his back – his wife had assaulted him with the Trollope.

'Listen to this, *Liebchen*,' Julia said. '"Early in life, at the age of fifteen, I commenced the dangerous habit of keeping a journal, and this I maintained for ten years. The volumes remained in my possession, unregarded – never looked at – till 1870, when I examined them, and, with many blushes, destroyed them. They convicted me of folly, ignorance, indiscretion, idleness, extravagance, and conceit. But they had habituated me to the rapid use of pen and ink, and taught me how to express myself with facility."'

'I don't want or need to keep a *journal*,' Farrokh said abruptly. 'And I already know how to express myself *with facility*.'

'There's no need to be defensive,' Julia told him. 'I just thought you'd be interested in the subject.'

'I want to *create* something,' Dr Daruwalla announced. 'I'm not interested in recording the mundane details of my life.'

'I wasn't aware that our life was altogether mundane,' Julia said.

The doctor, realizing his error, said, 'Certainly it's not. I meant only that I prefer to try my hand at something imaginative – I want to *imagine* something.'

'Do you mean fiction?' his wife asked.

'Yes,' Farrokh said. 'Ideally, I should like to write a novel, but I don't suppose I could write a very good one.'

'Well, there are all kinds of novels,' Julia said helpfully.

Thus emboldened, Dr Daruwalla withdrew James Salter's *A Sport and a Pastime* from its hiding place, which was under the newspaper on the floor beside the bed. He brought forth the novel carefully, as if it were a potentially dangerous weapon, which it was.

'For example,' Farrokh said, 'I don't suppose I could ever write a novel as good as this one.'

Julia glanced at the Salter quickly before returning her eyes to the Trollope. 'No, I wouldn't think so,' she said.

Aha! the doctor thought. So she *has* read it! But he asked with forced indifference, 'Have you read the Salter?'

'Oh, yes,' his wife said, not taking her eyes off the Trollope. 'I brought it along to *re*read it, actually.'

It was hard for Farrokh to remain casual, but he tried. 'So you *liked* it, I presume?' he inquired.

'Oh, yes – very much,' Julia answered. After a weighty pause, she asked him, 'And you?'

'I find it rather good,' the doctor confessed. 'I suppose,' he added, 'some readers might be shocked, or offended, by certain parts.'

'Oh, yes,' Julia agreed. Then she closed the Trollope and looked at him. 'Which parts are you thinking of?'

It hadn't happened quite as he'd imagined it, but this was what he wanted. Since Julia had most of the pillows, he rolled over on his stomach and propped himself up on his elbows. He began with a somewhat cautious passage. '"He pauses at last,"' Farrokh read aloud. '"He leans over to admire her, she does not see him. Hair covers her cheek. Her skin seems very white. He kisses her side and then, without force, as one stirs a favorite mare, begins again. She comes to life with a soft, exhausted sound, like someone saved from drowning."'

Julia also rolled over on her stomach, gathering the pillows to her breasts. 'It's hard to imagine anyone being shocked or offended by *that* part,' she said.

Dr Daruwalla cleared his throat. The ceiling fan was

stirring the down on the back of Julia's neck; her thick hair had fallen forward, hiding her eyes from his view. When he held his breath, he could hear her breathing. '"She cannot be satisfied,"' he read on, while Julia buried her face in her arms. '"She will not let him alone. She removes her clothes and calls to him. Once that night and twice the next morning he complies and in the darkness between lies awake, the lights of Dijon faint on the ceiling, the boulevards still. It's a bitter night. Flats of rain are passing. Heavy drops ring in the gutter outside their window, but they are in a dove-cote, they are pigeons beneath the eaves. The rain is falling all around them. Deep in feathers, breathing softly, they lie. His sperm swims slowly inside her, oozing out between her legs."'

'Yes, that's better,' Julia said. When he looked at her, he saw she'd turned her face to look at him; the yellow, unsteady light from the kerosene lamps wasn't as ghostly pale as the moonlight he'd seen on her face on their *first* honeymoon, but even this tarnished light conveyed her willingness to trust him. Their wedding night, in the Austrian winter, was in one of those snowy Alpine towns, and their train from Vienna had arrived almost too late for them to be admitted to the *Gasthof*, despite their reservation. It must have been 2:00 in the morning by the time they'd undressed and bathed and got into the feather bed, which was as white as the mountains of snow that reflected the moonlight – it was a timeless glowing – in their window.

But on their *second* honeymoon, Dr Daruwalla came dangerously close to ruining the mood when he offered a faint criticism of the Salter. 'I'm not sure how accurate it is to suggest that sperm swim "slowly,"' he said, 'and technically, I suppose, it's *semen*, not sperm, that would be oozing out between her legs.'

'For God's sake, Farrokh,' his wife said. 'Give me the book.'

She had no difficulty locating the passage she was looking for, although the book was unmarked. Farrokh lay on his side and watched her while she read aloud to him. '"She is so wet by the time he has the pillows under her gleaming stomach that he goes right into her in one long, delicious move. They begin slowly. When he is close to coming he pulls his prick out and lets it cool. Then he starts again, guiding it with one hand, feeding it in like a line. She begins to roll her hips, to cry out. It's like ministering to a lunatic. Finally he takes it out again. As he waits, tranquil, deliberate, his eye keeps falling on lubricants – her face cream, bottles in the *armoire*. They distract him. Their presence seems frightening, like evidence. They begin once more and this time do not stop until she cries out and he feels himself come in long, trembling runs, the head of his prick touching bone, it seems."'

Julia handed the book back to him. 'Your turn,' she said then. She also lay on her side, watching him, but as he began to read to her, she shut her eyes; he saw her face on the pillow almost exactly as he'd seen it that morning in the Alps. St Anton – that was the place – and he'd awakened to the sound of the skiers' boots tramping on the hard-packed snow; it seemed that an army of skiers was marching through the town to the ski lift. Only Julia and he were *not* there to ski. They were there to *fuck*, Farrokh thought, watching his wife's sleeping face. And that was how they'd spent the week, making brief forays into the snowy paths of the town and then hurrying back to their feather bed. In the evenings, they'd had no less appetite for the hearty food than the skiers had. Watching Julia as he read to her, Farrokh remembered every day and night in St Anton.

'"He is thinking of the waiters in the casino, the audience at the cinema, the dark hotels as she lies on her stomach and with the ease of sitting down at a well-laid table, but no more than that, he introduces himself. They lie on their sides. He tries not to move. There are only the little, invisible twitches, like a nibbling of fish."'

Julia opened her eyes as Farrokh searched for another passage.

'Don't stop,' she told him.

Then Dr Daruwalla found what he was looking for – a rather short and simple part. '"Her breasts are hard,"' he read to his wife. '"Her cunt is sopping."' The doctor paused. 'I suppose there'd be some readers who'd be shocked or offended by that,' he added.

'Not me,' his wife told him. He closed the book and returned it to the newspaper on the floor. When he rolled back to Julia, she'd arranged the pillows under her hips and lay waiting for him. He touched her breasts first.

'*Your* breasts are hard,' he said to her.

'They are *not*,' she told him. 'My breasts are old and soft.'

'I like soft better,' he said.

After she kissed him, she said, 'My cunt is sopping.'

'It *isn't*!' he said instinctively, but when she took his hand and made him touch her, he realized she wasn't lying.

In the morning, the sunlight passed through the narrow slats of the blinds and stood out in horizontal bars across the bare coffee-colored wall. The newspaper on the floor was stirred by a small lizard, a gecko – only its snout protruded from between the pages – and when Dr Daruwalla reached to pick up *A Sport and a Pastime*, the gecko darted under the bed. *Sopping!* the doctor thought to himself. He opened the book quietly, thinking his wife was still asleep.

'Keep reading – aloud,' Julia murmured.

Lunch Is Followed by Depression

It was with a renewed sexual confidence that Farrokh faced the situation of the morning. Rahul Rai had struck up a conversation with John D., and although – even by the doctor's standard's – Rahul looked fetching

in 'her' bikini, the small *lump* of evidence in the
bikini's bottom half provided Dr Daruwalla with
sufficient reason to rescue John D. from a potential
confrontation. While Julia sat on the beach with the
Daruwalla daughters, the doctor and John D. strolled
in manly and confiding fashion along the water's edge.

'There's something you should know about Rahul,'
Farrokh began.

'What's her name?' John D. asked.

'*His* name is Rahul,' Farrokh explained. 'If you were
to look under *his* panties, I'm almost certain you
would find a penis and a pair of balls – rather small,
in both cases.' They continued walking along the
shoreline, with John D. appearing to pay obsessive
attention to the smooth, sand-rubbed stones and the
rounded, broken bits of shells.

Finally, John D. said, 'The breasts look real.'

'Definitely induced – hormonally induced,' Dr Daruwalla said. The doctor described how estrogens
worked . . . the development of breasts, of hips; how
the penis shrank to the size of a little boy's. The testes
were so reduced they resembled vulva. The penis was
so shrunken it resembled an enlarged clitoris. The
doctor explained as much as he knew about a *complete* sex-change operation, too.

'Far out,' John D. remarked. They discussed whether
Rahul would be more interested in men or women.
Since he *wanted* to be a woman, Dr Daruwalla deduced that Rahul was sexually interested in men. 'It's
hard to tell,' John D. suggested; indeed, when they
returned to where the Daruwalla daughters were en-
camped under a thatch-roofed shelter, there was Rahul
Rai in conversation with Julia!

Julia said later, 'I think it's young men who interest
him, although I suppose a young woman would do.'

Would *do?* Dr Daruwalla thought. Promila had
confided to Farrokh that this was a bad time for 'poor
Rahul.' Apparently, they'd not traveled from Bombay
together, but Promila had met her nephew at the

Bardez; he'd been alone in the area for more than a week. He had 'hippie friends,' Promila said – somewhere near Anjuna – but things hadn't worked out as Rahul had hoped. Farrokh didn't desire to know more, but Promila offered her speculations anyway.

'I presume that sexually confusing things must have happened,' she told Dr Daruwalla.

'Yes, I suppose,' the doctor said. Normally, all of this would have upset Farrokh greatly, but something from his sexual triumphs with Julia had carried over into the following day. Despite everything that was 'sexually confusing' about Rahul, which was sexually disturbing to Dr Daruwalla, not even the doctor's appetite was affected, although the heat was fierce.

It was unmercifully hot at midday, and there was no perceptible breeze. Along the shoreline, the fronds of the areca and coconut palms were as motionless as the grand old cashew and mango trees farther inland in the dead-still villages and towns. Not even the passing of a three-wheeled rickshaw with a damaged muffler could rouse a single dog to bark. Were it not for the heavy presence of the distilling feni, Dr Daruwalla would have guessed that the air wasn't moving at all.

But the heat didn't dampen the doctor's enthusiasm for his lunch. He started with an oyster guisado and steamed prawns in a yogurt-mustard sauce; then he tried the vindaloo fish, the gravy for which was so piquant that his upper lip felt numb and he instantly perspired. He drank an ice-cold ginger feni with his meal – actually, he had two – and for dessert he ordered the bebinca. His wife was easily satisfied with a xacuti, which she shared with the girls; it was a fiery curry made almost soothing with coconut milk, cloves and nutmeg. The daughters also tried a frozen mango dessert; Dr Daruwalla had a taste, but nothing could abate the burning sensation in his mouth. As a remedy, he ordered a cold beer. Then he criticized Julia for allowing the girls to drink so much sugarcane juice.

'In this heat, too much sugar will make them sick,' Farrokh told his wife.

'Listen to who's talking!' Julia said.

Farrokh sulked. The beer was an unfamiliar brand, which he would never remember. He would recall, however, the part of the label that said LIQUOR RUINS COUNTRY, FAMILY AND LIFE.

But as much as Dr Daruwalla was a man of unstoppable appetites, his plumpness had never been – nor would it become – displeasing to the eye. He was a fairly small man – his smallness was most apparent in the delicacy of his hands and in the neat, well-formed features of his face, which was round, boyish and friendly – and his arms and legs were thin and wiry; his bum was small, too. Even his little pot belly merely served to emphasize his smallness, his neatness, his tidiness. He liked a small, well-trimmed beard, for he also liked to shave; his throat and the sides of his face were usually clean-shaven. When he wore a mustache, it, too, was neat and small. His skin wasn't much browner than an almond shell; his hair was black – it would soon turn gray. He would never be bald; his hair was thick, with a slight wave, and he left it long on top, although he kept it cut short on the back of his neck and above his ears, which were also small and lay perfectly flat against his head. His eyes were such a dark-brown color that they looked almost black, and because his face was so small, his eyes seemed large – maybe they *were* large. If so, only his eyes reflected his appetites. And only in comparison to John D. would someone *not* have thought of Dr Daruwalla as handsome – *small*, but handsome. He was not a fat man, but a plump one – a little, pot-bellied man.

While the doctor struggled to digest his meal, it might have crossed his mind that the others had behaved more sensibly. John D., as if demonstrating the self-discipline and dietary restraint that future movie stars would be wise to imitate, eschewed eating in the midday heat. He chose this time of day to take long walks on the beach; he swam intermittently and lazily – only to cool off. From his languid attitude, it was hard to tell if he walked the beach in order to look at the assembled young women or to afford them the luxury of looking at him.

In the torpid aftermath of his lunch, Dr Daruwalla barely noticed that Rahul Rai was nowhere to be seen. Farrokh was frankly relieved that the would-be transsexual wasn't pursuing John D.; and Promila Rai had accompanied John D. for only a short distance along the water's edge, as if the young man had immediately discouraged her by declaring his intentions to walk to the next village, or to the village after that. Wearing an absurdly wide-brimmed hat – as if it weren't already too late to protect her cancerous skin – Promila had returned, alone, to the spot of shade allotted by her thatch-roofed shelter, and there she appeared to embalm herself with a variety of oils and chemicals.

Under their own array of thatch-roofed shelters, the Daruwalla daughters applied different oils and chemicals to their vastly younger and superior bodies; then they ventured among the intrepid sunbathers – mostly Europeans, and relatively few of them at this time of year. The Daruwalla girls were forbidden to follow John D. on his midday hikes; both Julia and Farrokh felt that the young man deserved this period of time to be free of them.

But the most sensibly behaved person at midday was always the doctor's wife. Julia retired to the relative cool of their second-floor rooms. There was a shaded balcony with John D.'s sleeping hammock and a cot; the balcony was a good place to read or nap.

It was clearly nap time for Dr Daruwalla, who doubted he could manage the climb to the second floor of the hotel. From the taverna, he could see the balcony attached to his rooms, and he looked longingly in that direction. He thought the hammock would be nice, and he considered that he would try sleeping there tonight; if the mosquito netting was good, he'd be very comfortable, and all night he'd hear the Arabian Sea. The longer he allowed John D. to sleep there, the more firmly the young man would presume it was *his* place to sleep. But Farrokh's renewed sexual interest in Julia gave him pause in regard to his sleeping-hammock plan; there were passages of *A Sport and a Pastime* he'd not yet discussed with his wife.

Dr Daruwalla wished he knew what else Mr James Salter had written. However, as exhilarating as this unexpected stimulation to his marriage had been, Farrokh felt slightly depressed. Mr Salter's writing was so far above anything Dr Daruwalla could hope to imagine – much less hope to achieve – and the doctor had guessed right: one of the lovers dies, strongly implying that a love of such overpowering passion never lasts. Moreover, the novel concluded in a tone of voice that was almost physically painful to Dr Daruwalla. In the end, Farrokh felt that the very life he led with Julia – the life he cherished – was being mocked. Or was it?

Of the French girl – Anne-Marie, the surviving lover – there is only this final offering: 'She is married. I suppose there are children. They walk together on Sundays, the sunlight falling upon them. They visit friends, talk, go home in the evening, deep in the life we all agree is so greatly to be desired.' Wasn't there an underlying cruelty to this? Because such a life *is* 'greatly to be desired,' isn't it? Dr Daruwalla thought. And how could anyone expect the married life to compete with the burning intensity of a love affair?

What disturbed the doctor was that the end of the novel made him feel ignorant, or at least inexperienced. And what was more humiliating, Farrokh felt certain, was that Julia could probably explain the ending to him in such a way that he'd understand it. It was all a matter of tone of voice; perhaps the author had intended irony, but not sarcasm. Mr Salter's use of language was crystalline; if something was unclear,

262

the fuzzy-headedness surely should be attributed to the reader.

But more than technical virtuosity separated Dr Daruwalla from Mr James Salter, or from any other accomplished novelist. Mr Salter and his peers wrote from a vision; they were convinced about something, and it was at least partly the passion of these writers' convictions that gave their novels such value. Dr Daruwalla was convinced only that he would like to be more creative, that he would like to make something up. There were a lot of novelists like that, and Farrokh didn't care to embarrass himself by being one of them. He concluded that a more shameless form of entertainment suited him; if he couldn't write novels, maybe he could write screenplays. After all, movies weren't as serious as novels; certainly, they weren't as long. Dr Daruwalla presumed that his lack of a 'vision' wouldn't hamper his success in the screenplay form.

But his conclusion depressed him. In the search for something to occupy his untapped creativity, the doctor had already accepted a compromise – before he'd even begun! This thought moved him to consider consoling himself with his wife's affections. But gazing again to the distant balcony didn't bring the doctor any closer to Julia, and Dr Daruwalla doubted that imbibing feni and beer was a wise prelude to an amorous adventure – especially in such abiding heat. Something Mr Salter had written appeared to shimmer over Dr Daruwalla in the midday inferno: 'The more clearly one sees this world, the more one is obliged to pretend it does not exist.' There is a growing list of things I don't know, the doctor thought.

He didn't know, for example, the name of the thick vine that had crawled upward from the ground to embrace both the second- and the third-floor balconies of the Hotel Bardez. The vine was put to active use by the small striped squirrels that scurried over it; at night, the geckos raced up and down the vine with far greater speed and agility than any squirrel. When the sun shone against this wall of the hotel, the smallest, palest-pink flowers opened up along the vine, but Dr Daruwalla didn't know that these flowers were not what attracted the finches to the vine. Finches are seed eaters, but Dr Daruwalla didn't know this, nor did the doctor know that the green parrot perching on the vine had feet with two toes pointing forward and two backward. These were the details he missed, and they contributed to the growing list of things he didn't know. This was the kind of Everyman he was – a little lost, a little misinformed (or uninformed), almost everywhere he ever was. Yet, even overfed, the doctor was undeniably attractive. Not every Everyman is attractive.

A Dirty Hippie

Dr Daruwalla grew so drowsy at the littered table, one of the Bardez servant boys suggested he move into a new hammock that was strung in the shade of the areca and coconut palms. Complaining to the boy that he feared the hammock was too near the main beach and he'd be bothered by sand fleas, the doctor nevertheless tested the hammock; Farrokh wasn't sure it would support his weight. But the hammock held. For the moment, the doctor detected no sand fleas. Therefore, he was obliged to give the boy a tip.

This boy, Punkaj, seemed employed solely for the purpose of tipping, for the messages that he delivered to the Hotel Bardez and the adjacent lean-to restaurant and taverna were usually of his own invention and wholly unnecessary. For example, Punkaj asked Dr Daruwalla if he should run to the hotel and tell 'the Mrs Doctor' that the doctor was napping in a hammock near the beach. Dr Daruwalla said no. But in a short while, Punkaj was back beside the hammock. He reported: 'The Mrs Doctor is reading what I think is a book.'

'Go away, Punkaj,' said Dr Daruwalla, but he tipped the worthless boy nonetheless. Then the doctor lay wondering if his wife was reading the Trollope or rereading the Salter.

Considering the size of his lunch, Farrokh was fortunate that he was able to sleep at all. The strenuousness of his digestive system made a sound sleep impossible, but throughout the grumbling and rumbling of his stomach – and the occasional hiccup or belch – the doctor fitfully dozed and dreamed, and woke up all of a sudden to wonder if his daughters were drowned or suffering from sunstroke or sexual attack. Then he dozed off again.

As Farrokh fell in and out of sleep, the imagined details of Rahul Rai's complete sex change appeared and disappeared in his mind's eye, drifting in and out of consciousness like the fumes from the distilling feni. This exotic aberration clashed with Farrokh's fairly ordinary ideals: his belief in the purity of his daughters, his fidelity to his wife. Only slightly less common was Dr Daruwalla's vision of John D., which was simply the doctor's desire to see the young man rise above the sordid circumstances of his birth and abandonment. And if I could only play a part in *that*, Dr Daruwalla dreamed, I might one day be as creative as Mr James Salter.

But John D.'s only visible qualities were of a fleeting and superficial nature; he was arrestingly handsome, and he was so steadfastly self-confident that his poise concealed his lack of other qualities – sadly, the doctor presumed that John D. lacked other qualities. In this belief, Farrokh was aware that he relied too heavily on his brother's estimation and his sister-in-law's confirmation, for both Jamshed and Josefine were chronically worried that the boy had no future. He was 'uninvolved' with his studies, they said. But couldn't this be an early indication of thespian detachment?

Yes, why not? John D. could be a movie star! Dr

Daruwalla decided, forgetting that this notion had originated with his wife. It suddenly seemed to the doctor that John D. was *destined* to be a movie star, or else he would be nothing. It was Farrokh's first realization that a hint of despair can start the creative juices flowing. And it must have been these juices, in combination with the more scientifically supported juices of digestion, that got the doctor's imagination going.

But, just then, a belch so alarming he failed to recognize it as his own awakened Dr Daruwalla from these imaginings; he shifted in his hammock in order to confirm that his daughters had not been violated by either the forces of nature or the hand of man. Then he fell asleep with his mouth open, the splayed fingers of one hand lolling in the sand.

Dreamlessly, the noonday passed. The beach began to cool. A slight breeze rose; it softly gave sway to the hammock where Dr Daruwalla lay digesting. Something had left a sour taste in his mouth – the doctor suspected the vindaloo fish or the beer – and he felt flatulent. Farrokh opened his eyes slightly to see if anyone was near his hammock – in which case it would be impolite for him to fart – and there was that pest Punkaj, the worthless servant boy.

'She come back,' Punkaj said.

'Go away, Punkaj,' said Dr Daruwalla.

'She looking for you – that hippie with her bad foot,' the boy said. He pronounced the word 'heepee,' so that Dr Daruwalla, in his digestive daze, still didn't understand.

'Go away, Punkaj!' the doctor repeated. Then he saw the young woman limping toward him.

'*Is that him? Is that the doctor?*' she asked Punkaj.

'You wait there! *I* ask doctor first!' the boy said to her. At a glance, she could have been 18 or 25, but she was a big-boned young woman, broad-shouldered and heavy-breasted and thick through her hips. She also had thick ankles and very strong-looking hands, and she lifted the boy off the ground – holding him by the front of his shirt – and threw him on his back in the sand.

'Go fuck yourself,' she told him. Punkaj picked himself up and ran toward the hotel. Farrokh swung his legs unsteadily out of the hammock and faced her. When he stood up, he was surprised at how much the late-afternoon breeze had cooled the sand; he was also surprised that the young woman was so much taller than he was. He quickly bent down to put on his sandals; that was when he saw she was barefoot – and that one foot was nearly twice the size of the other. While the doctor was still down on one knee, the young woman rotated her swollen foot and showed him the filthy, inflamed sole.

'I stepped on some glass,' she said slowly. 'I thought I picked it all out, but I guess not.'

He took her foot in his hand and felt her lean heavily on his shoulder for balance. There were several small lacerations, all closed and red and puckered with infection, and on the ball of her foot was a fiery swelling the size of an egg; in its center was an inch-long, oozing gash that was scabbed over.

Dr Daruwalla looked up at her, but she wasn't looking down at him; she was gazing off somewhere, and the doctor was shocked not only by her stature but by her solidity as well. She had a full, womanly figure and a peasant muscularity; her dirty, unshaven legs were ragged with golden hair, and her cut-off blue jeans were slightly torn at the crotch seam, through which poked an outrageous tuft of her golden pubic hair. She wore a black, sleeveless T-shirt with a silver skull-and-crossbones insignia, and her loose, low-slung breasts hung over Farrokh like a warning. When he stood up and looked into her face, he saw she couldn't have been older than 18. She had full, round, freckled cheeks, and her lips were badly sun-blistered. She had a child's little nose, also sunburned, and almost-white blond hair, which was matted and tangled and discolored by the suntan oil she'd used to try to protect her face.

Her eyes were startling to Dr Daruwalla, not only for their pale, ice-blue color but because they reminded him of the eyes of an animal that wasn't quite awake – not fully alert. As soon as she noticed he was looking at her, her pupils constricted and fixed hard upon him – also like an animal's. Now she was wary; all her instincts were suddenly engaged. The doctor couldn't return the intensity of her gaze; he looked away from her.

'I think I need some antibiotics,' the young woman said.

'Yes, you have an infection,' Dr Daruwalla said. 'I have to lance that swelling. There's something in there – it has to come out.' She had a pretty good infection going; the doctor had also noticed the lymphangitic streaking.

The young woman shrugged; and when she moved her shoulders only that slightly, Farrokh caught the scent of her. It wasn't just an acrid armpit odor; there was also something like the tang of urine in the way she smelled, and there was a heavy, ripe smell – faintly rotten or decayed.

'It is essential for you to be clean before I cut into you,' Dr Daruwalla said. He was staring at the young woman's hands; there appeared to be dried blood caked under her nails. Once more the young woman shrugged, and Dr Daruwalla took a step back from her.

'So . . . where do you want to do it?' she asked, looking around.

At the taverna, the bartender was watching them. In the lean-to restaurant, only one of the tables was occupied. There were three men drinking feni; even these impaired feni drinkers were watching the girl.

'There's a bathtub in our hotel,' the doctor said. 'My wife will help you.'

'I know how to take a bath,' the young woman told him.

268

Farrokh was thinking that she couldn't have walked very far on that foot. As she hobbled between the taverna and the hotel, her limp was pronounced; she leaned hard on the rail as they climbed the stairs to the rooms.

'You didn't walk all the way from Anjuna, did you?' he asked her.

'I'm from Iowa,' she answered. For a moment, Dr Daruwalla didn't understand – he was trying to think of an 'Iowa' in Goa. Then he laughed, but she didn't.

'I meant, where are you staying in Goa?' he asked her.

'I'm not staying,' she told him. 'I'm taking the ferry to Bombay – as soon as I can walk.'

'But where did you cut your foot?' he asked.

'On some glass,' she said. 'It was sort of near Anjuna.'

This conversation, and watching her climb the stairs, exhausted Dr Daruwalla. He preceded the girl into his rooms; he wanted to alert Julia that he'd found a patient on the beach, or that she'd found him.

Farrokh and Julia waited on the balcony while the young woman took a bath. They waited quite a long time, staring – with little comment – at the girl's battered canvas rucksack, which she'd left with them on the balcony. Apparently, she wasn't considering a change of clothes, or else the clothes in the rucksack were dirtier than the clothes she wore, although this was hard to imagine. Odd cloth badges were sewn to the rucksack – the insignia of the times, Dr Daruwalla supposed. He recognized the peace symbol, the pastel flowers, Bugs Bunny, a U.S. flag with the face of a pig superimposed on it, and another silver skull and crossbones. He didn't recognize the black-and-yellow cartoon bird with the menacing expression; he doubted it was a version of the American eagle. There was no way the doctor could have been familiar with Herky the Hawk, the wrathful symbol of athletic teams from the University of Iowa. Looking more closely, Farrokh read the words under the black-and-yellow bird: GO, HAWKEYES!

'She must belong to some sort of strange club,' the doctor said to his wife. In response, Julia sighed. It was the way she feigned indifference; Julia was still somewhat in shock at the sight of the huge young woman, not to mention the great clumps of blond hair the girl had grown in her armpits.

In the bathroom, the girl filled and emptied the tub twice. The first time was to shave her legs, but not her underarms – she valued the hair in her armpits as an indication of her rebellion; she thought of it and her pubic hair as her 'fur.' She used Dr Daruwalla's razor; she thought about stealing it, but then she remembered she'd left her rucksack out on the balcony. The memory distracted her; she shrugged, and put the razor back where she'd found it. As she settled into the second tub of water, she fell instantly asleep – she was so exhausted – but she woke up as soon as her mouth dipped below the water. She soaped herself, she shampooed her hair, she rinsed. Then she emptied the tub and drew a *third* bath, letting the water rise around her.

What puzzled her about the murders was that she couldn't locate in herself the slightest feeling of remorse. The murders weren't her fault – whether or not they might be judged her unwitting responsibility. She refused to feel guilty, because there was absolutely nothing she could have done to save the victims. She thought only vaguely about the fact that she hadn't tried to prevent the murders. After all, she decided, she was also a victim and, as such, a kind of eternal absolution appeared to hover over her, as detectable as the steam ascending from her bathwater.

She groaned; the water was as hot as she could stand it. She was amazed at the scum on the surface of the water. It was her third bath, but the dirt was still coming out of her.

11. THE DILDO

Behind Every Journey Is a Reason

It was her parents' fault, she decided. Her name was Nancy, she came from an Iowa pig-farming family of German descent and she'd been a good girl all through high school in a small Iowa town; then she'd gone to the university in Iowa City. Because she was so blond and bosomy, she'd been a popular candidate for the cheerleading squad, although she lacked the requisite personality and wasn't chosen; still, it was her contact with the cheerleaders that led her to meet so many football players. There was a lot of partying, which Nancy was unfamiliar with, and she'd not only slept with a boy for the first time; she'd slept with her first black person, her first Hawaiian person, and the first person she'd ever known who came from New England – he was from somewhere in Maine, or maybe it was Massachusetts.

She flunked out of the University of Iowa at the end of her first semester; when she went home to the small town she'd grown up in, she was pregnant. She thought she was still a good girl, to the degree that she submitted to her parents' recommendation without questioning it: she would have the baby, put it up for adoption and get a job. She went to work at the local hardware store, in feed-and-grain supply, while she was still carrying the child; soon she began to doubt the wisdom of her parents' recommendation – men her father's age began propositioning her, *while* she was pregnant.

She delivered the child in Texas, where the orphanage physician never let her see it – the nurses never even let her know which sex it was – and when she came home, her parents sat her down and told her that they hoped she'd learned her 'lesson'; they hoped she would 'behave.' Her mother said she prayed that some decent man in the town would be 'forgiving' enough to marry her, one day. Her father said that God had been 'lenient' with her; he implied that God was disinclined toward leniency twice.

For a while, Nancy tried to comply, but so many men of the town attempted to seduce her – they assumed she'd be easy – and so many women were worse; they assumed she was already sleeping with everyone. This punitive experience had a strange effect on her; it didn't make her revile the football players who'd contributed to her downfall – oddly, what she loathed most was her own innocence. She refused to believe she was immoral. What degraded her was to feel stupid. And with this feeling came an anger she was unfamiliar with – it felt foreign; yet this anger was as much a part of her as the fetus she'd carried for so long but had never seen.

She applied for a passport. When it came, she robbed the hardware store – feed-and-grain, especially – of every cent she could steal. She knew that her family originally came from Germany; she thought she should go there. The cheapest flight (from Chicago) was to Frankfurt; but if Iowa City had been too sophisticated for her, Nancy was unprepared for the enterprising young Germans who frequented the area of the Hauptbahnhof and the Kaiserstrasse, where almost immediately she met a tall, dark drug dealer named Dieter. He was enduringly small-time.

The first thrilling, albeit petty, crime he introduced her to involved her posing as a prostitute on those nasty side streets off the Kaiserstrasse – the ones named after the German rivers. She'd ask for so much money that only the wealthiest, stupidest tourist or businessman would follow her to a shabby room on the Elbestrasse or the Moselstrasse; Dieter would be waiting there. Nancy made the man pay her before she unlocked the door of the room; once they were inside, Dieter would pretend to surprise her – grabbing her roughly and throwing her on the bed, abusing her for her faithlessness and her dishonesty, threatening to kill her while the man who'd paid for her services invariably fled. Not one of the men ever tried to help her. Nancy enjoyed taking advantage of their lust, and there was something gratifying about their uniform cowardice. In her mind, she was repaying those men who'd made her feel so miserable in feed-and-grain supply.

It was Dieter's theory that all Germans were sexually ashamed of themselves. That was why he preferred India; it was both a spiritual and a sensual country. What he meant was that, for very little, you could buy anything there. He meant women and young girls, in addition to the bhang and the ganja, but he told her only about the quality of the hashish – what he would pay for it there, and what he would get for it back in Germany. He didn't tell her the whole plan – specifically, that her American passport and her farm-girl looks were the means by which he would get the stuff through German customs. Nancy was also the means by which he'd planned to get the Deutsche marks through Indian customs. (It was marks he took to India; it was hashish he brought back.) Dieter had made the trip with American girls before; he'd also used Canadian girls – their passports aroused even less suspicion.

With both nationalities, Dieter followed a simple procedure: he never flew on the same plane with them; he made sure they'd arrived and passed through customs before he boarded a plane for Bombay. He always told them he wanted them to recover from the jet lag in a comfortable room at the Taj, because, when he got there, they'd be doing some 'serious business'; he meant they'd be staying in less conspicuous lodgings, and he knew that the bus ride from Bombay to Goa could be disagreeable. Dieter could

273

buy what he wanted in Bombay; but, inevitably, he'd be persuaded – usually by the friend of a friend – to do his buying in Goa. The hash was more expensive there, because the European and American hippies bought up the stuff like bottled water, but the quality was more reliable. It was the quality that fetched a good price in Frankfurt.

As for the trip back to Germany, Dieter would precede the designated young woman by a day; if she were ever delayed in German customs, Dieter would take this as a sign that he shouldn't meet her. But Dieter had a system, and not one of his young women had ever been caught – at either end.

Dieter's women were outfitted with the kind of well-worn travel guides and paperback novels that suggested earnestness in the extreme. The travel guides were dog-eared and scribbled in to draw the attention of customs officials to those areas of cultural or historical importance so keenly boring that they attracted only graduate students in the field. As for the paperback novels, by Hermann Hesse or Lawrence Durrell, they were fairly standard indications of their readers' proclivities for the mystical and poetic; these latter tendencies were dismissed by customs officials as the habitual concerns of young women who'd never been motivated by money. Without a profit motive, surely drug trafficking could be of no interest to them.

However, these young women were not above suspicion as occasional drug users; their personal effects were thoroughly searched for a modest stash. Not once had a shred of evidence been found. Dieter was undeniably clever; a large amount of the stuff was always successfully secreted in a dog-proof container of unflinchingly crass but basic ingenuity.

In retrospect, poor Nancy would agree that the enslavement of sexual corruption empowered all of Dieter's other abilities. In the relative safety of the Daruwallas' bathtub at the Hotel Bardez, Nancy supposed that she'd gone along with Dieter strictly because of the sex. Her football players had been friendly oafs, and most of the time she'd been drunk on beer. With Dieter, she smoked just the right amount of hashish or marijuana – Dieter was no oaf. He had the gaunt good looks of a young man who'd recently recovered from a life-theatening illness; had he not been murdered, he doubtless would have become one of those men who progress through a number of increasingly young and naïve women, his sexual appetite growing confused with his desire to introduce the innocent to a series of successively degrading experiences. For as soon as he gave Nancy some courage in her sexual potential, he undermined what slight self-esteem she had; he made her doubt herself and hate herself in ways she'd never thought possible.

In the beginning, Dieter had simply asked her, 'What is the first sexual experience that you had some confidence in?' And when she didn't answer him – because she was thinking to herself that masturbation was the *only* sexual experience that she had *any* confidence in – he suddenly said, 'Masturbation, right?'

'Yes,' Nancy said quietly. He was very gentle with her. At first, they'd just talked about it.

'Everyone is different,' Dieter said philosophically. 'You just have to learn what your own best way is.'

Then he told her some stories to relax her. One time, as an adolescent, he'd actually stolen a pair of panties from the lingerie drawer of his best friend's mother. 'When they lost whatever scent they had, I put them back in her drawer and stole a fresh pair,' he told Nancy. 'The thing about masturbation was that I was always afraid I'd be caught. I knew a girl who could make it work only when she was standing up.'

Nancy told him, 'I have to be lying down.'

This conversation itself was more intimate than anything she'd known. It seemed so natural, how he'd led her to show him how she masturbated. She would lie rigidly on her back with her left hand clenching her left buttock; she wouldn't actually touch the spot (it never worked when she did). Instead, she'd rub herself just above the spot with three fingers of her right hand – her thumb and pinky finger spread like wings. She turned her face to the side and Dieter would lie beside her, kissing her, until she needed to turn away from him to breathe. When she finished, he entered her; at that point, she was always aroused.

One time, when she'd finished, he said, 'Roll over on your stomach. Just wait right there. I have a surprise for you.' When he came back to their bed, he snuggled beside her, kissing her again and again – deep kisses, with his tongue – while he moved one hand underneath her until he could touch her with his fingers, exactly as she'd touched herself. The first time, she never saw the dildo.

Slowly, with the other hand, he began to work the device into her; at first she pressed herself down into his fingers, as if to get away from it, but later she lifted herself up to meet the dildo. It was very big but he never hurt her with it, and when she was so excited that she had to stop kissing him – she had to scream – he took the dildo out of her and entered her himself, from behind and with the fingers of his hand still touching her and touching her. (Compared to the dildo, Dieter was a little disappointing.)

Her parents had once warned Nancy that 'experimenting with sex' could make her crazy, but the madness that Dieter had incited didn't seem to be a dangerous madness. Still, it wasn't the best reason to go to India.

A Memorable Arrival

There'd been some trouble with her visa, and she was worried if she'd had the right shots; because the names were in German, she hadn't understood all the inoculations. She was sure she was taking too many antimalarial pills, but Dieter couldn't tell her how many to take; he seemed indifferent to disease. He was more concerned that an Indian customs official would confiscate the dildo – but only if Nancy took pains to conceal it, he said. Dieter insisted that she carry it casually – with her toilet articles, in her carry-on bag. But the thing was enormous. Worse, it was of a frightening pink, mock-flesh color, and the tip, which was modeled on a circumcised penis, had a bluish tinge – like a cock left out in the cold, Nancy thought. And where the fake foreskin was rolled, there seemed to linger a residue of the lubricating jelly, which could never quite be wiped away.

Nancy put the thing in an old white athletic sock – the long kind, meant to be worn above the calf. She prayed that the Indian customs officials would ascribe to the dildo some unmentionable medicinal purpose – anything other than that most obvious purpose for which it was intended. Understandably, she wanted Dieter to take it with *him*, on *his* plane, but he pointed out to her that the customs officials would then conclude he was a homosexual; homosexuals, she should know, were routinely abused at every country's port of entry. Dieter also told Nancy that the excessive illegal Deutsche marks were traveling with him, on his plane, and that the reason he didn't want her flying with him was that he didn't want her to be incriminated if he was caught.

Soaking herself in the bathtub at the Hotel Bardez, Nancy wondered why she'd believed him; with hindsight, such errors of judgment are plain to see. Nancy reflected that it hadn't been difficult for Dieter to convince her to bring the dildo to Bombay. It hadn't been the first time that a dildo gained such easy access to India, but what a lot of trouble this particular instrument inspired.

Nancy had never been to the East; she was introduced to it at the Bombay airport, at about 2:00 in the morning. She'd not seen men so diminished, so

277

damaged and so transformed by turmoil, by din and by wasteful energy; their ceaseless motion and their aggressive curiosity reminded her of scurrying rats. And so many of them were barefoot. She tried to concentrate on the customs inspector, who was attended by two policemen; they weren't barefoot. But the policemen – a couple of constables in blue shirts and wide blue shorts – were wearing the most absurd leg warmers she'd ever seen, especially in such hot weather. And she'd never seen Nehru caps on cops before.

In Frankfurt, Dieter had arranged for Nancy to be examined – in regard to the proper size for a diaphragm – but when the doctor had discovered she'd had a baby, he'd outfitted her with an intra-uterine device instead. She hadn't wanted one. When the customs inspector was examining her toiletries and one of the overseeing policemen opened a jar of her moisturizer and scooped out a gob of the cream with his finger, which the other policeman then sniffed, Nancy was grateful that there was no diaphragm or spermicidal ointment for them to play with. The constables couldn't see or touch or smell her IUD.

But of course there was the dildo, which lay untouched in the long athletic sock while the police-men and the customs inspector pawed through the clothes in her rucksack and emptied her carry-on bag, which was really just an oversized imitation-leather purse. One of the policemen picked up the battered paperback copy of Lawrence Durrell's *Clea*, the fourth novel of the Alexandria Quartet, of which Dieter had read only the first, *Justine*. Nancy hadn't read any of them; but the novel was dog-eared where the last reader had presumably stopped reading, and it was at this marked page that the constable opened the book, his eyes quickly finding that passage which Dieter had underlined in pencil for just such an occasion. In truth, this copy of *Clea* had made the trip to India and the return trip to Germany with two of Dieter's other women, neither of whom had read the novel or even the passage Dieter had marked. He'd chosen the particular passage because it would doubtless identify the reader to any international customs authority as a harmless fool.

The policeman was so stymied by the passage that he handed the book to his fellow constable, who looked stricken, as if he'd been asked to crack an indecipherable code; he, too, passed the book on. It was the customs inspector who finally read the passage. Nancy watched the clumsy, involuntary movement of the man's lips, as if he were isolating olive pits. Gradually the words, or something like the words, emerged aloud; they frankly seemed incomprehensible to Nancy. She couldn't imagine what the customs inspector and the constables made of them.

'"The whole quarter lay drowsing in the umbrageous violet of approaching nightfall,"' the customs inspector read. '"A sky of palpitating velours which was cut into by the stark flare of a thousand electric light bulbs. It lay over Tatwig Street, that night, like a velvet rind."' The customs inspector stopped reading, looking like a man who'd just eaten something odd. One of the policemen stared angrily at the book, as if he felt compelled to confiscate it or destroy it on the spot, but the other constable was as distracted as a bored child; he picked up the dildo in the athletic sock and unsheathed the giant penis as one would unsheathe a sword. The sock drooped limply in the policeman's left hand while his right hand grasped the great cock at its root, at the rock-hard pair of makeshift balls.

Suddenly seeing what he held, the policeman quickly extended the dildo to his fellow constable, who took hold of the instrument by the rolled foreskin before he recognized the exaggerated male member, which he instantly handed to the customs inspector. Still holding *Clea* in his left hand, the customs inspector seized the dildo at the scrotum; then he dropped the

279

novel and snatched the sock from the first, gaping policeman. But the impressive penis was more difficult to sheathe than to unsheathe, and in his haste the customs inspector inserted the instrument the wrong way. Thus were the balls jammed into the heel of the sock, where they made an awkward lump – they didn't fit – and the bluish tip of the thing (the circumcised head) protruded loosely from the open end of the sock. The hole at the end of the enormous cock appeared to stare out at the constables and the customs inspector like the proverbial evil eye.

'Where you stay?' one of the policemen asked Nancy. He was furiously wiping his hand on his leg warmers – a trace of the lubricating jelly, perhaps.

'Always carry your own bag,' the other constable advised her.

'Agree to a price with the taxi-walla before you get in the car,' the first policeman said.

The customs inspector wouldn't look at her. She'd expected something worse; surely the dildo would provoke leering – at least rude or suggestive laughter, she'd thought. But she was in the land of the lingam – or so she imagined. Wasn't the phallic symbol worshipped here? Nancy thought she'd read that the penis was a symbol of Lord Shiva. Maybe what Nancy carried in her purse was as realistic (albeit exaggerated) a lingam as these men had ever seen. Maybe she'd made an unholy use of such a symbol – was that why these men wanted nothing to do with her? But the constables and the customs inspector weren't thinking of lingams or Lord Shiva; they were simply appalled at the portable penis.

Poor Nancy was left to find her own way out of the airport and into the shrill cries of the taxi-wallas. An unending lineup of taxis extended into the infernal blackness of this outlying district of Bombay; except for the oasis, which was the airport, there were no lights in Santa Cruz – there was no Sahar in 1969. It was then about 3:00 in the morning.

Nancy had to haggle with her taxi-walla over the fare into Bombay. After she arranged the prepaid trip, she still encountered some difficulty with her driver; he was a Tamil, apparently new to Bombay. He claimed to not understand Hindi or Marathi; it was in uncertain English that Nancy heard him asking the other taxi-wallas for directions to the Taj.

'Lady, you don't want to go with him,' one of the taxi-wallas told her, but she'd already paid and was sitting in the back seat of the taxi.

As they drove toward the city, the Tamil continued a lengthy debate with another Tamil driver who drove his taxi perilously close to theirs; for several miles, they drove like this – past the unlit slums in the predawn, immeasurable darkness, wherein the slum dwellers were distinguishable only by the smell of their excrement and their dead or dying fires. (What were they burning? Rubbish?) When the sidewalks on the outskirts of Bombay first appeared, still without electric light, the two Tamils raced side by side – even through the traffic circles, those wild roundabouts – their discourse progressing from an argument to a shouting match to threats, which sounded (even in Tamil) quite dire to Nancy.

The seemingly unconcerned passengers in the other Tamil's taxi were a well-dressed British couple in their forties. Nancy guessed they were also headed to the Taj, and that this coincidence lay at the heart of the dispute between the two Tamils. (Dieter had warned her of this common practice: two drivers with two separate fares, headed for the same place. Naturally, one of the drivers was attempting to persuade the other to carry both fares.)

At a traffic light, the two stopped taxis were suddenly surrounded by barking dogs – starving curs, all snapping at one another – and Nancy imagined that, if one jumped through the open window at her, she could club it with the dildo. This passing idea perhaps prepared her for what happened at the next intersection, where again the light was against them; while they waited this time, they were slowly approached by beggars instead of dogs. The shouting Tamils had attracted some of the sidewalk sleepers, whose mounded bodies under their light-colored clothing could be dimly seen to contrast with the darkened streets and buildings. First a man in a ragged, filthy dhoti stuck his arm in Nancy's window. Nancy noticed that the prim British couple – not in fear but out of sheer obstinacy – had closed their windows, despite the moist heat. Nancy thought she would suffocate if she closed hers.

Instead, she spoke sharply to her driver – to *go*! After all, the light had changed. But her Tamil and the other Tamil were too engrossed in their confrontation to obey the traffic signal. Her Tamil ignored her, and, to Nancy's further irritation, the other Tamil now coerced his British passengers into the street; he was beckoning to them that they must join Nancy in *her* cab, exactly as Dieter had foretold.

Nancy shouted at her driver, who turned to her and shrugged; she shouted out the window to the other Tamil, who shouted back at her. Nancy shouted to the British couple that they shouldn't allow themselves to be so taken advantage of; they should demand of their driver that he bring them to their prearranged, prepaid destination.

'Don't let the bastards screw you!' Nancy shouted. Then she realized that she was waving the dildo at them; to be sure, it was still in the sock and they didn't *know* it was a dildo; they could only suppose she was an hysterical young woman threatening them with a sock.

Nancy slid over in her seat. 'Please get in,' she said to the British couple, but when they opened the door, Nancy's driver protested. He even jerked the car a little forward. Nancy tapped him on his shoulder with the dildo – still in the sock. Her driver looked indifferent; his counterpart was already stuffing the British couple's

282

luggage into the trunk as the twosome squeezed into the seat beside her.

Nancy was pressed against the window when a beggar woman pushed a baby in the window and held it in front of her face; the child was foul-smelling, unmoving, expressionless – it looked half dead. Nancy raised the dildo, but what could she do? Whom should she hit? Instead, she screamed at the woman, who indignantly withdrew the baby from the taxi. Maybe it wasn't even her baby, Nancy considered; possibly it was just a baby that people used for begging. Perhaps it wasn't even a real baby.

Ahead of them, two young men were supporting a drunken or a drugged companion. They paused in crossing the road, as if they weren't sure that the taxi had stopped. But the taxi was stopped, and Nancy was incensed that her driver and the other Tamil were *still* arguing. She leaned forward and brought the dildo down across the back of her driver's neck. That was when the sock flew off. The driver turned to face her. She struck him squarely on his nose with the huge cock in her hand.

'Drive on!' she shouted at the Tamil. Suitably impressed with the giant penis, he lurched the taxi forward – through the traffic light, which had turned red again. Fortunately, no other traffic was on the street. Unfortunately, the two young men and their slumped companion were directly in the taxi's path. At first, it seemed to Nancy that all three of them were hit. Later, she distinctly remembered that two of them had run away, although she couldn't say that she'd actually seen the impact; she must have closed her eyes.

While the Englishman helped the driver put the body in the front seat of the taxi, Nancy realized that the young man who'd been hit was the one who'd appeared to be drunk or drugged. It never occurred to her that the young man might already have been dead when the car hit him. But this was the subject of the Englishman's conversation with the Tamil driver: had the boy or young man been pushed into the path of the taxi deliberately, and was he even conscious before the taxi struck him?

'He *looked* dead,' the Englishman kept saying.

'Yes, he is dying before!' the Tamil shouted. '*I* am not killing him!'

'Is he dead now?' Nancy asked quietly.

'Oh, definitely,' the Englishman replied. Like the customs inspector, he wouldn't look at her, but the Englishman's wife was staring at Nancy, who still clutched the fierce dildo in her fist. Still not looking at her, the Englishman handed her the sock. She covered the weapon and returned it to her big purse.

'Is this your first visit to India?' the Englishwoman asked her, while the crazed Tamil drove them faster and faster through the streets now more and more blessed with electric light; the colorful mounds of the sidewalk sleepers were visible all around them. 'In Bombay, half the population sleeps on the streets – but it's really quite safe here,' the Englishwoman said. Nancy's pinched expression implied to the British couple that she was a newcomer to the city and its smells. Actually, it was the lingering smell of the baby that pinched Nancy's face – how something so small could reek with such force.

The body in the front seat made its deadness known. The young man's head lolled lifelessly, his shoulders impossibly slack. Whenever the Tamil braked or cornered, the body responded as heavily as a bag of sand. Nancy was grateful that she couldn't see the young man's face, which was making a dull sound against the windshield – his face rested flush against the glass – until the Tamil cornered again and then accelerated.

Still not looking at Nancy, the Englishman said, 'Don't mind the body, dear.' It seemed unclear whether he'd spoken to Nancy or to his wife.

'It doesn't bother me,' his wife answered.

Over Marine Drive, a thick smog hung suspended, as warm as a woolen shroud; the Arabian Sea was veiled, but the Englishwoman pointed to where the sea should have been. 'Out there is the ocean,' she told Nancy, who began to gag. Overhead, on the lampposts, not even the advertisements were visible in the smog. The lights strung along Marine Drive weren't smog lights, then; they were white, not yellow.

In the careening taxi, the Englishman pointed out the window into the veil of smog. 'This is the Queen's Necklace,' he told Nancy. As the taxi raced on, he added – more to assure himself and his wife than to comfort Nancy – 'Well, we're almost there.'

'I'm going to throw up,' Nancy said.

'If you don't *think* about being sick, dear, you won't *be* sick,' the Englishwoman said.

The taxi departed Marine Drive for the narrower, winding streets; the three living passengers leaned in to the corners, and the dead boy in the front seat appeared to come alive. His head walloped the side window; he slid forward and his face glanced off the windshield, skidding him into the Tamil driver, who elbowed the body away. The young man's hands flew up to his face, as if he'd just remembered something important. Then, once again, the boy's body appeared to forget everything.

There were whistles, piercing sharp and loud: these were the sounds of the tall Sikh doormen who directed the traffic at the Taj, but Nancy was searching for some evidence of the police. Nearby, at the looming Gateway of India, Nancy thought she'd seen some sort of police activity; there were lights, the sound of hysterics, a sort of disturbance. At first, some beggar urchins were reputed to be the cause; the story was, they'd failed to beg a single rupee from a young Swedish couple who'd been photographing the Gateway of India with an ostentatious and professional use of bright-white lights and reflectors. Hence the urchins had urinated on the Gateway of India in an effort to spoil the picture, and when they'd failed to gain suitable attention from the foreigners – the Swedes allegedly found this demonstration symbolically interesting – the urchins then attempted to urinate on the photographic equipment, and that was the cause of the ruckus. But further investigation would reveal that the Swedes had paid the beggars to pee on the Gateway of India, which had little effect – the Gateway of India was already soiled. The urchins had never attempted to pee on the Swedes' photographic equipment; that would have been far too bold for them – they'd merely complained that they weren't paid enough for pissing on the Gateway of India. *That* was the true cause of the ruckus.

Meanwhile, the dead boy in the taxi had to wait. In the driveway of the Taj, the Tamil driver became hysterical; a dead man had been thrown into the path of his car – apparently, there was a dent. The British couple confided to a policeman that the Tamil had run a red light (upon being struck by a dildo). The policeman was the bewildered constable who'd finally freed himself from the crime of urination at the Gateway of India. It wasn't clear to Nancy if the British couple was blaming her for the accident, if it even had been an accident. After all, the Tamil and the Englishman agreed that the boy had looked dead before the taxi hit him. What was clear to Nancy was that the policeman didn't know what a 'dildo' was.

'A penis – a rather large one,' the Englishman explained to the constable.

'*She?*' the policeman asked, pointing to Nancy. 'She is hitting the taxi-walla with a *what*?'

'You'll have to show him, dear,' the Englishwoman told Nancy.

'I'm not showing him anything,' Nancy said.

Our Friend, the Real Policeman

It took an hour before Nancy was free to register in the hotel. A half hour later – she'd just finished soaking in

286

a hot bath – a second policeman came to her room. This one wasn't a constable – no blue shorts a yard wide, no silly leg warmers. This one wasn't another nerd in a Nehru cap; he wore an officer's cap with the Maharashtrian police insignia and a khaki shirt, long khaki pants, black shoes, a revolver. It was the duty officer from the Colaba Police Station, which has jurisdiction over the Taj. Without his jowls, but even then sporting that pencil-thin mustache – and 20 years before he would have occasion to question Dr Daruwalla and Inspector Dhar at the Duckworth Club – the young Inspector Patel gave a good first impression of himself. A future deputy commissioner could be discerned in the young policeman's composure.

Inspector Patel was aggressive but courteous, and even in his twenties he was an intimidating detective in the way that he invited a certain misunderstanding of his questions. His manner persuaded you to believe that he already knew the answers to many of the questons he asked, although he usually didn't; thus he encouraged you to tell the truth by implying that he already knew it. And his method of questioning carried the added implication that, within your answers, Inspector Patel could discern your moral character.

In her current state, Nancy was vulnerable to such an uncommonly proper and pleasant-looking young man. To sympathize with Nancy's situation: Inspector Patel did not present himself as a person whom even a brazen or a supremely self-confident young woman would *choose* to show a dildo to. Also, it was about 5:00 in the morning. There may have been some eager early risers who were heralding the sunrise that – when viewed across the water, and perfectly framed in the arch of the Gateway of India – could still summon the vainglorious days of the British Raj, but poor Nancy wasn't among them. Besides, her only windows and the small balcony didn't afford her a view of the sea. Dieter had arranged for one of the cheaper rooms.

Below her, in the gray-brown light, was the usual gathering of beggars – child performers, for the most part. Those international travelers who were still staggered by jet lag would find these early-morning urchins their first contact with India in the light of day.

Nancy sat at the foot of her bed in her bathrobe. The inspector sat in the only chair not strewn with her clothes or her bags. They could both hear the emptying of Nancy's bath. Highly visible, as Dieter had advised, were the used-looking but unused guidebook and the unread novel by Lawrence Durrell.

It was not uncommon, the inspector told her, for someone to be murdered and then shoved in front of a moving car. In this case, what was unusual was that the hoax had been so obvious.

'Not to me,' Nancy told him. She explained that she'd not seen the moment of impact; she'd thought all three of them were hit – probably because she'd shut her eyes.

The Englishwoman hadn't observed the moment of impact, either, Inspector Patel informed Nancy. 'She was looking at you instead,' the policeman explained.

'Oh, I see,' Nancy said.

The Englishman was quite sure that a body – at least an unconscious body, if not a dead one – had been pushed into the path of the oncoming car. 'But the taxi-walla doesn't know what he saw,' said Inspector Patel. 'The Tamil keeps changing his story.' When Nancy continued to stare blankly at him, the policeman added, 'The driver says he was distracted.'

'By what?' Nancy asked, although she knew by what.

'By what you hit him with,' Inspector Patel replied.

There was an uncomfortable pause while the policeman looked from chair to chair, surveying her emptied bags, the two books, her clothes. Nancy thought he must be at least five years older than she was, although he looked younger. His self-assurance made him seem

288

disarmingly grown-up; yet he didn't exhibit the cock-sure arrogance of cops. Inspector Patel didn't swagger; there was something in his controlled mannerisms that came from an absolute correctness of purpose. What struck Nancy as his pure goodness was riveting. And she thought he was a wonderful coffee-and-cream color; he had the blackest hair – and such a thin, perfectly edged mustache that Nancy wanted to touch it.

The overall nattiness of the young man stood in obvious contrast to that absence of vanity which is commonly associated with a happily married man. Here in the Taj, in the presence of such a buxom blonde in her bathrobe, Inspector Patel was obviously unmarried; he was as alert to the details of his appearance as he was to every inch of Nancy, and to the particular revelations of Nancy's room. She didn't realize he was looking for the dildo.

'May I see the thing you hit the taxi-walla with?' the inspector asked finally. God knows how the idiot Tamil had described it. Nancy went to get it from the bathroom, having decided to keep it with her toilet articles. God knows what the British couple had told the inspector. If the inspector had talked to them, they'd doubtless described her as a rude young woman brandishing an enormous cock.

Nancy gave the dildo to Inspector Patel, and again sat down at the foot of her bed. The young policeman politely handed the instrument back without looking at her.

'I'm sorry – it was necessary for me to see it,' Inspector Patel said. 'I was having some difficulty *imagining* it,' he explained.

'Both drivers were paid their fares at the airport,' Nancy told him. 'I don't like to be cheated,' she said.

'It's not the easiest country for a woman traveling alone,' the inspector said. By the quick way he glanced at her, she understood this was a question.

'Friends are meeting me,' Nancy told him. 'I'm just

waiting for them to call.' (Dieter had advised her to say this; anyone assessing her student clothing and her cheap bags would know that she couldn't afford many nights at the Taj.)

'So will you be traveling with your friends or staying in Bombay?' the inspector asked her.

Nancy recognized her advantage. As long as she held the dildo, the young policeman would find it awkward to look in her eyes.

'I'll do what they do,' she said indifferently. She held the penis in her lap; with the slightest movement of her wrist, she discovered, she could tap the circumcised head against her bare knee. But it was her bare feet that appeared to transfix Inspector Patel; perhaps it was their impossible whiteness, or else their improbable size – even bare, Nancy's feet were bigger than the inspector's little shoes.

Nancy stared at him without mercy. She enjoyed the prominent bones in his sharply featured face; it would have been impossible for her to look at his face and imagine it – even in 20 years – with jowls. She thought he had the blackest eyes and the longest eyelashes.

Still staring at Nancy's feet, Inspector Patel spoke forlornly: 'I suppose there's no known phone number or an address where I could reach you.'

Nancy felt she understood everything that attracted her to him. She'd certainly tried hard to lose her innocence in Iowa, but the football players hadn't touched it. She'd spoiled her real innocence in Germany, with Dieter, and now it was lost for good. But here was a man who was still innocent. She probably both frightened and attracted him – if he even knew it, Nancy thought.

'Do you want to see me again?' she asked him. She thought the question was ambiguous enough, but he stared at her feet – with both longing and horror, she imagined.

'But you couldn't identify the two other men, even if we found them,' said Inspector Patel.

'I could identify the other taxi driver,' Nancy said.

'We've already got him,' the inspector told her.

Nancy stood up from the bed and carried the dildo to the bathroom. When she came back, Inspector Patel was at the window, watching the beggars. She didn't want to have any advantage over him anymore. Maybe she was imagining that the inspector had fallen hopelessly in love with her and that, if she shoved him on the bed and fell on top of him, he would worship her and be her slave forever. Maybe it wasn't even *him* she wanted; possibly it was only his obvious propriety, and only because she felt she'd given away her essential goodness and would never get it back.

Then it struck her that he was no longer interested in her feet; he kept glancing at her *hands*. Even though she'd put away the dildo, he wouldn't look in her eyes.

'Do you want to see me again?' Nancy repeated. There was no ambiguity to her question now. She stood closer to him than was necessary, but he ignored the question by pointing to the child performers far below them.

'Always the same stunts — they never change,' Inspector Patel remarked. Nancy refused to look at the beggars; she continued to stare at Inspector Patel.

'You could give me your phone number,' she said. 'Then I could call you.'

'But why would you?' the inspector asked her. He kept watching the beggars. Nancy turned away from him and stretched out on the bed. She lay on her stomach with the robe gathered tightly around her. She thought about her blond hair; she thought it must look nice, spread out on the pillows, but she didn't know if Inspector Patel was looking at her. She just knew that her voice would be muffled by the pillows, and that he'd have to come closer to the bed in order to hear her.

'What if I need you?' she asked him. 'What if I get in some trouble and need the police?'

'That young man was strangled,' Inspector Patel told

291

her; by the sound of his voice, she knew he was near her.

Nancy kept her face buried in the pillows, but she reached out to the sides of the bed with her hands. She'd been thinking that she'd never learn anything about the dead boy – not even if the act of killing him had been wicked and full of hatred or merely inadvertent. Now she knew – the young man couldn't have been inadvertently strangled.

'*I* didn't strangle him,' Nancy said.

'I know that,' said Inspector Patel. When he touched her hand, she lay absolutely motionless; then his touch was gone. In a second, she heard him in the bathroom. It sounded as if he was running a bath.

'You have big hands,' he called to her. She didn't move. 'The boy was strangled by someone with small hands. Probably another boy, but maybe a woman.'

'You suspected *me*,' Nancy said; she couldn't tell if he'd heard her over the running bathwater. 'I said, you suspected *me* – until you saw my hands,' Nancy called to him.

He shut the water off. The tub couldn't be very full, Nancy thought.

'I suspect everybody,' Inspector Patel said, 'but I didn't really suspect you of strangling the boy.'

Nancy was simply too curious; she got up from the bed and went to the bathroom. Inspector Patel was sitting on the edge of the tub, watching the dildo float around and around like a toy boat.

'Just as I thought – it floats,' he said. Then he submerged it; he held it under the water for almost a full minute, never taking his eyes off it. 'No bubbles,' he said. 'It floats because it's hollow,' he told her. 'But if it came apart – if you could open it – there would be bubbles. I thought it would come apart.' He let the water out of the tub and wiped the dildo dry with a towel. 'One of your friends called while you were registering,' Inspector Patel told Nancy. 'He didn't want to speak with you – he just wanted to know if you'd checked in.' Nancy was blocking the bathroom door; the inspector paused for her to get out of his way. 'Usually, this means that someone is interested to know if you've passed safely through customs. Therefore, I thought you were bringing something in. But you weren't, were you?'

'No,' Nancy managed to say.

'Well, then, as I leave, I'll tell the hotel to give you your messages directly,' the inspector said.

'Thank you,' Nancy replied.

He'd already opened the door to the hall before he handed her his card. '*Do* call me if you get into any trouble,' he told her. She chose to stare at the card; it was better than watching him leave. There were several printed phone numbers, one circled with a ballpoint pen, and his printed name and title.

VIJAY PATEL
POLICE INSPECTOR
COLABA STATION

Nancy didn't know how far from home Vijay Patel was. When his whole family had left Gujarat for Kenya, Vijay had come to Bombay. For a Gujarati to make any headway on a Maharashtrian police force was no small accomplishment; but the Gujarati Patels in Vijay's family were merchants – they wouldn't have been impressed. Vijay was as cut off from them – they were in business in Nairobi – as Nancy was from Iowa.

After she'd read and reread the policeman's card, Nancy went out to the balcony and watched the beggars for a while. The children were enterprising performers, and there was a monotony to their stunts that was soothing. Like most foreigners, she was easily impressed by the contortionists.

Occasionally, one of the guests would throw an orange to the child performers, or a banana; some threw coins. Nancy thought it was cruel the way a crippled boy, with one leg and a padded crutch, was always beaten by the other children when he attempted to hop and stagger ahead of them to the money or the fruit. She didn't realize that the cripple's role was choreographed; he was central to the dramatic action. He was also older than the other chidren, and he was their leader; in reality, he could beat up the other children – and, on occasion, had.

But the pathos was unfamiliar to Nancy and she looked for something to throw to him; all she could find was a 10-rupee note. This was too much money to give to a beggar, but she didn't know any better. She weighted the bill down with two bobby pins and stood on the balcony with the money held above her head until she caught the crippled boy's attention.

'Hey, lady!' he called. Some of the child performers paused in their handstands and their contortions, and Nancy sailed the 10-rupee note into the air; it rose briefly in an updraft before it floated down. The children ran back and forth, trying to be in the right place to catch it. The crippled boy appeared content to let one of the other children grab the money.

'No, it's for you – for *you*!' Nancy cried to him, but he ignored her. A tall girl, one of the contortionists, caught the 10-rupee note; she was so surprised at the amount, she didn't hand it over to the crippled boy quite quickly enough, and so he struck her in the small of her back with his crutch – a blow with sufficient force to knock her to her hands and knees. Then the cripple snatched up the money and hopped away from the girl, who had begun crying.

Nancy realized that she'd disrupted the usual drama; somehow *she* was at fault. As the beggars scattered, one of the tall Sikh doormen from the Taj approached the crying girl. He carried a long wooden pole with a gleaming brass hook on one end – it was a transom pole, for opening and closing the transom windows above the tall doors – and the doorman use this pole to lift the ragged skirt of the girl's torn and filthy dress. He deftly exposed her before she could snatch the skirt of her dress between her legs and cover herself. Then he poked the girl in the chest with the brass end of the pole, and when she tried to stand, he whacked her hard in the small of her back, exactly where the cripple had hit her with his crutch. The girl cried out. Then she scurried away from the Sikh on all fours. He was skillful in pursuing her – at herding her with sharp jabs and thrusts with the pole. Finally, she got to her feet and outran him.

The Sikh had a dark, spade-shaped beard flecked with silver, and he wore a dark-red turban; he shouldered the transom pole like a rifle, and he cast a cursory glance to Nancy on her balcony. She retreated into her room; she was sure he could see under her bathrobe and straight up her crotch – he was directly below her. But the balcony itself prevented such a view. Nancy imagined things.

Obviously, there were rules, she thought. The beggars could beg, but they couldn't cry; it was too early in the morning, and crying would wake the guests who were managing to sleep. Nancy instantly ordered the most American thing she could find on the room-service menu – scrambled eggs and toast – and when they brought her tray, she saw two sealed envelopes propped between the orange juice and the tea. Her heart jumped because she hoped they were declarations of undying love from Inspector Patel. But one was the message from Dieter that the inspector had intercepted; it said simply that Dieter had called. He was glad she'd arrived safely – he'd see her soon. And the other was a printed request from the hotel management, asking her to kindly refrain from throwing things out her window.

She was ravenous, and as soon as she'd finished eating, she was sleepy. She closed the curtains against the light of day and turned up the ceiling fan as fast as it would go. For a while she lay awake, thinking of Inspector Patel. She even toyed with the idea of Dieter being caught with the money as he tried to pass through customs. Nancy was still naïve enough to imagine that the Deutsche marks were coming into the country with Dieter. It hadn't even crossed her mind that she'd already brought the money in.

The Unwitting Courier

It seemed to her that she slept for days. It was dark when she woke. She would never know if it was the predawn darkness of the next day, or the predawn of the day after that. She awoke to some sort of commotion in the hall outside her room; someone was trying to get in, but she'd double-locked the door and there was a safety chain, too. She got out of bed. There, in the hall, was Dieter; he was surly to the porter, whom he sent away without a tip. Once inside the room, but only after he'd double-locked the door and hooked the safety chain in place, he turned to her and asked her where the dildo was. This wasn't exactly gallant of him, Nancy thought, but in her sleepiness she supposed it was merely his aggressive way of being amorous. She pointed to it in the bathroom.

Then she opened her robe and let it slip off her shoulders and fall at her feet; she stood in the bathroom doorway, expecting him to kiss her, or at least look at her. Dieter held the dildo over the sink; he appeared to be heating the unnatural head of the penis with his cigarette lighter. Nancy woke up in a hurry. She picked up her bathrobe and put it back on; she stepped away from the bathroom door, but she could still observe Dieter. He was careful not to let the flame blacken the dildo, and he concentrated the heat not at the tip but at the place where the fake foreskin was rolled. It then appeared to Nancy that he was slowly melting the dildo; she realized that there was a substance, like wax, dripping into the sink. Where the fake foreskin was rolled, there emerged a thin line, circumscribing the head. When Dieter had melted the wax seal, he ran the tip of the big penis under cold water and then grasped the circumcised head with a towel. He needed quite a lot of force to unscrew the dildo, which was as hollow as Inspector Patel had observed. The wax seal had prevented any air from escaping; there'd been no bubbles underwater. Inspector Patel had been half right; he'd looked in the right place, but not in the right way – a young policeman's error.

Inside the dildo, rolled very tightly, were thousands of Deutsche marks. For the return trip to Germany, quite a lot of high-quality hashish could be packed very tightly in such a big dildo; the wax seal would prevent the dogs at German customs from smelling the Indian hemp inside.

Nancy sat at the foot of the bed while Dieter removed a roll of marks from the dildo and spread the bills out flat in his hand. Then he zipped the marks into a money belt, which was around his waist under his shirt. He left several sizable rolls of marks in the dildo, which he reassembled; he screwed the tip on tight, but he didn't bother resealing it with wax. The line where the thing unscrewed was barely visible anyway; it was partially hidden by the fake foreskin. When Dieter had finished with this, his chief concern, he undressed and filled the bathtub. It wasn't until he settled into the tub that Nancy spoke to him.

'What would have happened to me if I'd been caught?' she asked him.

'But they wouldn't have caught you, babe,' Dieter told her. He'd picked up the 'babe' from watching American movies, he said.

'Couldn't you have *told* me?' Nancy asked him.

'Then you would have been nervous,' Dieter said. 'Then they *would* have caught you.'

After his bath, he rolled a joint, which they smoked together; although Nancy thought she was being cautious, she got higher than she wanted to, and just a little disoriented. It was strong stuff; Dieter assured her

297

that it was by no means the best stuff – it was just something he'd bought en route from the airport.

'I made a little detour,' he told her. She was too stoned to ask him where he could have gone at 2:00 or 3:00 in the morning, and he didn't bother to tell her that he'd gone to a brothel in Kamathipura. He'd bought the stuff from the madam, and while he was at it he'd fucked a 13-year-old prostitute for only five rupees. He was told she was the only girl not with a customer at the time, and Dieter had fucked her standing up, in a kind of hall, because all the cots in all the cubicles were occupied – or so the madam had said.

After Dieter and Nancy smoked the joint, Dieter was able to encourage Nancy to masturbate; it seemed to her that it took a long time, and she couldn't remember him leaving the bed to get the dildo. Later, when he was asleep, she lay awake and thought for a while about the thousands of Deutsche marks that were inside the thing that had been inside her. She decided not to tell Dieter about the murdered boy or Inspector Patel. She got out of bed and made sure the card the inspector had given her was well concealed among her clothes. She didn't go back to bed; she was standing on the balcony at dawn when the first of the beggars arrived. After a while, the same child performers were perfectly in place, like figures painted by the daylight itself – even the crippled boy with his padded crutch. He waved to her. It was so early, he was careful not to call too loudly, but Nancy could hear him distinctly.

'Hey, lady!'

He made her cry. She went back inside the room and watched Dieter while he was sleeping. She thought again about the thousands of Deutsche marks; she wanted to throw them out the window to the child performers, but it frightened her to imagine what a terrible scene she might cause. She went into the bathroom and tried to unscrew the dildo to count how many marks were inside, but Dieter had screwed the thing too tightly together. This was probably deliberate, she realized; at last, she was learning.

She went through his clothes, looking for the money belt – she thought she could count how many marks were there – but she couldn't find it. She lifted the bedsheet and saw that Dieter was naked except for the money belt. It worried her that she couldn't remember falling asleep, nor could she remember Dieter getting out of bed to put the money belt on. She would have to be more careful, she thought. Nancy was beginning to appreciate the extent to which Dieter might be willing to use her; she worried that she'd developed a morbid curiosity about how far he would go.

Nancy found it calming to speculate about Inspector Patel. She indulged herself with the comforting notion that she could turn to the inspector if she needed him, if she was *really* in trouble. Although the morning was intensely bright, Nancy didn't close the curtains; in the light of day, it was easier for her to imagine that leaving Dieter was merely a matter of picking the right time. And if things get *too* bad, Nancy thought to herself, I can just pick up the phone and ask for Vijay Patel – Police Inspector, Colaba Station.

But Nancy had never been to the East. She didn't know where she was. She had no idea.

12. THE RATS

Four Baths

In Bombay, in his bedroom, where Dr Daruwalla sat shivering in Julia's embrace, the unresolved nature of the majority of the doctor's phone messages depressed him: Ranjit's peevish complaints about the dwarf's wife; Deepa's expectations regarding the potential bonelessness of a child prostitute; Vinod's fear of the first-floor dogs; Father Cecil's consternation that none of the Jesuits at St Ignatius knew exactly when Dhar's twin was arriving; and director Balraj Gupta's greedy desire to release the new Inspector Dhar movie in the midst of the murders inspired by the last Inspector Dhar movie. To be sure, there was the familiar voice of the woman who tried to sound like a man and who repeatedly relished the details of old Lowji's car bombing; this message wasn't lacking in resolution, but it was muted by excessive repetition. And Detective Patel's cool delivery of the news that he had a private matter to discuss didn't sound 'unresolved' to the doctor; although Dr Daruwalla may not have known what the message meant, the deputy commissioner seemed to have made up his mind about the matter. But all these things were only mildly depressing in comparison to Farrokh's memory of the big blonde with her bad foot.

'*Liebchen*,' Julia whispered to her husband. 'We shouldn't leave John D. alone. Think about the hippie another time.'

Both to break him from his trance and as a physical reminder of her affection for him, Julia squeezed Farrokh. She simply hugged him, more or less in the area of his lower chest, or just above his little beer belly. It surprised her how her husband winced in pain. The sharp tweak in his side – it must have been a rib – instantly reminded Dr Daruwalla of his collision with the second Mrs Dogar in the foyer of the Duckworth Club. Farrokh then told Julia the story: how the vulgar woman's body was as hard as a stone wall.

'But you said you fell down,' Julia told him. 'I would guess it was your contact with the stone floor that caused your injury.'

'No! It was that damn woman herself – her body is a rock!' Dr Daruwalla said. '*Mr* Dogar was knocked down, too! Only that crude woman was left standing.'

'Well, she's supposed to be a fitness freak,' Julia replied.

'She's a weight lifter!' Farrokh said. Then he remembered that the second Mrs Dogar had reminded him of someone – definitely a long-ago movie star, he decided. He imagined that one night he would discover who it was on the videocassette recorder; both in Bombay and in Toronto, he had so many tapes of old movies that it was hard for him to remember how he'd lived before the VCR.

Farrokh sighed and his sore rib responded with a little twinge of pain.

'Let me rub some liniment on you, *Liebchen*,' Julia said.

'Liniment is for muscles – it was my *rib* she hurt,' the doctor complained.

Although Julia still favored the theory that the stone floor was the source of her husband's pain, she humored him. 'Was it Mrs Dogar's shoulder or her elbow that hit you?' she asked.

'You're going to think it's funny,' Farrokh admitted to Julia, 'but I swear I ran right into her bosom.'

'Then it's no wonder she hurt you, *Liebchen*,' Julia replied. It was Julia's opinion that the second Mrs Dogar had no bosom to speak of.

Dr Daruwalla could sense his wife's impatience on John D.'s behalf, but less for the fact that Inspector

301

Dhar had been left alone than that the dear boy hadn't been forewarned of the pending arrival of his twin. Yet even this dilemma struck the doctor as trivial – as insubstantial as the second Mrs Dogar's bosom – in comparison to the big blonde in the bathtub at the Hotel Bardez. Twenty years couldn't lessen the impact of what had happened to Dr Daruwalla there, for it had changed him more than anything in his whole life had changed him, and the long-ago memory of it endured unfaded, although he'd never returned to Goa. All other beach resorts had been ruined for him by the unpleasant association.

Julia recognized her husband's expression. She could see how far away he was; she knew exactly *where* he was. Although she wanted to reassure John D. that the doctor would join them soon, it would have been heartless of her to leave her husband; dutifully, she remained seated beside him. Sometimes she thought she ought to tell him that it was his own curiosity that had got him into trouble. But this wasn't entirely a fair accusation; dutifully, she remained silent. Her own memory, although it didn't torture her with the same details that made the doctor miserable, was surprisingly vivid. She could still see Farrokh on the balcony of the Hotel Bardez, where he'd been as restless and bored as a little boy.

'What a long bath the hippie is taking!' the doctor had said to his wife.

'She looked like she needed a long bath, *Liebchen*,' Julia had told him. That was when Farrokh pulled the hippie's rucksack closer to him and peered into the top of it; the top wouldn't quite close.

'Don't look at her things!' Julia told him.

'It's just a book,' Farrokh said; he pulled the copy of *Clea* from the top of the rucksack. 'I was just curious to know what she was reading.'

'Put it back,' Julia said.

'I *will*!' the doctor said, but he was reading the marked passage, the same bit about the 'umbrageous violet' and the 'velvet rind' that one customs official and two policemen had already found so spellbinding. 'She has a poetic sensibility,' Dr Daruwalla said.

'I find that hard to believe,' Julia told him. 'Put it back!'

But putting the book back presented the doctor with a new difficulty: something was in the way.

'Stop groping through her things!' Julia said.

'The damn book doesn't fit,' Farrokh said. 'I'm *not* groping through her things.' An overpowering mustiness embraced him from the depths of the rucksack, a stale exhalation. The hippie's clothing felt damp. As a married man with daughters, Dr Daruwalla was particularly sensitive to an abundance of dirty underpants in *any* woman's laundry. A mangled bra clung to his wrist as he tried to extract his hand, and still the copy of *Clea* wouldn't lie flat at the top of the rucksack; something poked against the book. What the hell *is* this thing? the doctor wondered. Then Julia heard him gasp; she saw him spring away from the rucksack as if an animal had bitten his hand.

'What is it?' she cried.

'I don't know!' the doctor moaned. He staggered to the rail of the balcony, where he gripped the tangled branches of the clinging vine. Several bright-yellow finches with seeds falling from their beaks exploded from among the flowers, and a gecko sprang from the branch nearest the doctor's right hand; it wriggled into the open end of a drainpipe just as Dr Daruwalla leaned over the balcony and vomited onto the patio below. Fortunately, no one was having afternoon tea there. There was only one of the hotel's sweepers, who'd fallen asleep in a curled position in the shade of a large potted plant. The doctor's falling vomit left the sweeper undisturbed.

'*Liebchen!*' Julia cried.

'I'm all right,' Farrokh said. 'It's nothing, really – it's just . . . lunch.' Julia was staring at the hippie's rucksack as if she expected something to crawl out from under the copy of *Clea*.

303

'What was it – what did you see?' she asked Farrokh.

'I'm not sure,' he said, but Julia was thoroughly exasperated with him.

'You don't know, you're not sure, it's nothing, really – it just made you throw up!' she said. She reached for the rucksack. 'Well, if you don't tell me, I'll just see for myself.'

'No, don't!' the doctor cried.

'Then tell me,' Julia said.

'I saw a penis,' Farrokh said.

Not even Julia could think of anything to say.

'I mean, it can't be a *real* penis,' he continued. 'I don't mean that it's someone's severed penis, or anything ghastly like that.'

'What *do* you mean?' Julia asked him.

'I mean, it's a very lifelike, very graphic, very *large* male member – it's an enormous cock, with balls!' Dr Daruwalla said.

'Do you mean a dildo?' Julia asked him. Farrokh was shocked that she knew the word; he barely knew it himself. A colleague in Toronto, a fellow surgeon, kept a collection of pornographic magazines in his hospital locker, and it was only in one of these that Dr Daruwalla had ever seen a dildo; the advertisement hadn't been nearly as realistic as the terrifying thing in the hippie's rucksack.

'I think it *is* a dildo, yes,' Farrokh said.

'Let me see,' Julia said; she attempted to dodge past her husband to the rucksack.

'No, Julia! Please!' Farrokh cried.

'Well, *you* saw it – *I* want to see it,' Julia said.

'I don't think you do,' the doctor said.

'For God's sake, Farrokh,' Julia said. He sheepishly stood aside; then he glanced nervously at the bathroom door, behind which the huge hippie was *still* bathing.

'Hurry up, Julia, and don't mess up her things,' Dr Daruwalla said.

'It's not as if everything has been neatly folded – *oh*, my goodness!' Julia said.

'Well, there it is – you've seen it. Now get away!' said Dr Daruwalla, who was a little surprised that his wife had not recoiled in horror.

'Does it use batteries?' Julia asked; she was still looking at it.

'Batteries!' Farrokh cried. 'For God's sake, Julia – please get away!' The concept of such a thing being battery-powered would haunt the doctor's dreams for 20 years. The idea certainly worsened the agony of waiting for the hippie to finish her bath.

Fearing that the freakish girl had drowned, Dr Daruwalla timidly approached the bathroom door, through which he heard neither singing nor splashing; there wasn't a sign of bathtub life. But before he could knock on the door, the doctor was surprised by the uncanny powers of the bathing hippie; she seemed to sense that someone was near.

'Hello out there,' the girl said laconically. 'Would you bring me my rucksack? I forgot it.'

Dr Daruwalla fetched the rucksack; for its size, it was uncommonly heavy. Full of batteries, Farrokh supposed. He opened the bathroom door cautiously, and only partially – just enough to reach his hand with the rucksack inside the door. Steam, with a thousand, conflicting scents, engulfed him. The girl said, 'Thanks. Just drop it.' The doctor withdrew his hand and closed the door, wondering at the sound of metal as the rucksack struck the floor. Either a machete or a machine gun, Farrokh imagined; he didn't want to know.

Julia had arranged a sturdy table on the balcony and covered it with a clean white sheet. Even late in the day, there was better light for surgery outside than in the rooms. Dr Daruwalla assembled his instruments and prepared the anesthetic.

In the bathroom, Nancy managed to reach her rucksack without getting out of the bathtub; she began a search for anything marginally cleaner than what she'd been wearing. It was a matter of exchanging one kind of dirt for another, but she wanted to wear a long-sleeved cotton blouse and a bra and long pants; she also wanted to wash the dildo, and – if she was strong enough – she wanted to unscrew the thing and count how much money was left. It was repellent to her to touch the cock, but she managed to withdraw it from the rucksack by pinching one of the balls between the thumb and index finger of her right hand; then she dropped the dildo into the bath, where (of course) it floated, the balls slightly submerged, the circumcised head raised – almost in the manner of a perplexed, solitary swimmer. Its single, evil eye was on her.

As for Dr Daruwalla and his wife, their growing anxiety was in no way lessened by the unmistakable sounds of the bathtub being emptied and refilled. It was the hippie's *fourth* bath.

One can sympathize with Farrokh and Julia for their misunderstanding of the grunts and groans that Nancy made while she was struggling to unscrew the preposterous penis and determine the amount of Deutsche marks that it contained. After all, despite their rekindling of the sexual flame, the pleasure of which was partially owed to Mr James Salter, the Daruwallas were sexually tame souls. Given the size of the intimidating instrument that they'd seen in the hippie's rucksack, and the sounds of physical exertion that passed from behind the bathroom door, it's forgivable that Farrokh and Julia allowed their imaginations to run away with them. How could the Daruwallas have known that Nancy's cries and curses of frustration were simply the result of her being unable to unscrew the dildo? And despite how far the Daruwallas allowed their imaginations to run, they never could have imagined what truly had happened to Nancy.

Four baths wouldn't wash away what had happened to her.

From the moment Dieter had moved them out of the Taj, everything for Nancy had gone from bad to worse. Their new lodgings were in a small place on Marine Drive, the Sea Green Guest House, which Nancy noticed was an off-white color – or maybe, in the smog, a kind of blue-gray. Dieter said he favored the place because it was popular with an Arab clientele, and Arabs were safe. Nancy didn't notice many Arabs, but she might not have spotted all of them, she supposed. She also didn't know what Dieter meant by 'safe' – he meant only that the Arabs were indifferent to drug trafficking on such a small scale as his.

At the Sea Green Guest House, Nancy was introduced to one of the featured activities involved in buying high-quality narcotics – namely, waiting. Dieter made some phone calls; then they waited. According to Dieter, the best deals came to you indirectly. No matter how hard you tried to make a direct deal, and to make it in Bombay, you always ended up in Goa, doing your business with the friend of a friend. And you always had to wait.

This time the friend of a friend was known to frequent the brothel area of Bombay, although the word on the street was that the guy had already gone to Goa; Dieter would have to find him there. The way you found him was, you rented a cottage on a certain beach; then you waited. You could ask for him, but even so you'd never find him; he always found you. This time his name was Rahul. It was always a common name and you never knew the last name – just Rahul. In the red-light district, they called him 'Pretty.'

'That's a funny thing to call a guy,' Nancy observed.

'He's probably one of those chicks with dicks,' Dieter said. This expression was new to Nancy; she doubted that Dieter had picked it up from watching American movies.

Dieter attempted to explain the transvestite scene to Nancy, but he'd never understood that the hijras were eunuchs – that they'd truly been emasculated. He'd confused the hijras with the zenanas – the unaltered transvestites. A hijra had once exposed himself to Dieter, but Dieter had mistaken the scar for a vagina – he'd thought the hijra was a real woman. As for the zenanas, the so-called chicks with dicks, Dieter also called them 'little boys with breasts.' Dieter said that they were all fags who took estrogens to make their tits bigger, but the estrogens also made their pricks get smaller and smaller until they looked like little boys.

Dieter tended to dwell on sexual things, and he used the halfhearted hope of finding Rahul in Bombay as an excuse to take Nancy to the red-light district. She didn't want to go; but Dieter seemed destined to act out the old dictum that there is at least a kind of certainty in degradation. Debasement is specific. There is something exact about sexual corruption that Dieter probably found comforting in comparison to the vagueness of looking for Rahul.

For Nancy, the wet heat and ripe smell of Bombay were only enhanced by close proximity to the cage girls on Falkland Road. 'Aren't they amazing?' Dieter asked her. But why they were 'amazing' eluded Nancy. On the ground floor of the old wooden buildings, there were cagelike rooms with beckoning girls inside them; above these cages, the buildings rose not more than four or five stories, with more girls on the windowsills – or else a curtain was drawn across a window to indicate that a prostitute was with a customer.

Nancy and Dieter drank tea at the Olympia on Falkland Road; it was an old, mirror-lined café frequented by the street prostitutes and their pimps, several of whom Dieter seemed to know. But these contacts either couldn't or wouldn't shed any light on the whereabouts of Rahul; they wouldn't even speak of Rahul – except to say that he belonged to the transvestite scene, which they wanted no part of.

'I told you he was one of those chicks with dicks,' Dieter told Nancy. It was growing dark when they left the café, and the cage girls demonstrated a more aggressive interest in her as she and Dieter passed. Some of them lifted their skirts and made obscene gestures, some of them threw garbage at her, and sudden groups of men surrounded her on the street; Dieter, almost casually, drove them away from her. He seemed to find the attention amusing; the more vulgar the attention was, the more it amused Dieter.

Nancy had been too overwhelmed to question him, which she realized (as she sank deeper into Dr Daruwalla's bathtub) was a pattern she had finally broken. She submerged the dildo, holding it against her stomach. Because the dildo had not been resealed with wax, there were bubbles. Afraid that the Deutsche marks might get wet, Nancy stopped toying with the instrument. Instead, she thought of the entrenching tool in her rucksack; the doctor had surely heard it clank against the floor.

Dieter had bought it at an army-surplus shop in Bombay. The tool was an olive-drab color; fully extended, it was a spade with a short, two-foot handle which could be folded by means of an iron hinge, and the blade of the spade could be turned at a right angle to the handle and it resembled a foot-long hoe. If Dieter were alive, he would be the first to agree that it could also be successfully employed as a tomahawk. He'd told Nancy that the entrenching tool might be useful in Goa, both for defense against the dacoits – bandits occasionally preyed upon the hippies there – and for digging the spontaneous latrine. Nancy now smiled ruefully as she reflected on the expanded features of the tool. Certainly, she'd found it adequate for digging Dieter's grave.

When she shut her eyes and sank deeper into the tub, she could still taste the sweet, smoky tea that they served at the Olympia; she could remember its dry, bitter aftertaste, too. With her eyes shut and the warm water holding her, she could remember her changing expression in the pitted mirrors of the café. The tea had made her feel lightheaded. She was unfamiliar with the red spittle from the betel chewing that was expectorated everywhere around them, and not even the Hindi film songs and the Qawwali on the jukebox in the Olympia had prepared her for the assault of noise along Falkland Road. A drunken man followed her and pulled her hair until Dieter knocked him down and kicked him.

'The better brothels are in the rooms above the cages,' Dieter told her knowingly. A boy with a goat-skin full of water collided with her; she was sure he'd meant to step on her foot. Someone pinched her breast, but she didn't see who it was – man, woman or child.

Dieter pulled her into a bidi shop, where they also sold stationery and silver trinkets and the small pipes for smoking ganja.

'Hey, ganja-man – Mistah bhang-walla!' the proprietor greeted Dieter. He smiled happily at Nancy as he pointed to Dieter. 'He Mistah bhang-master – the very best ganja-walla!' the proprietor said appreciatively.

Nancy was fingering an unusual ballpoint pen; it was real silver, and *Made in India* was written in script lengthwise along the pen. The bottom part said *Made in*, the top part said *India;* the pen wouldn't close securely if the script wasn't perfectly aligned. She thought this was a stupid flaw. Also, when you wrote with the pen, the words were all wrong; *in Made India*, the pen said – and *in Made* was upside down. 'Very best quality,' the proprietor told her. 'Made in England!'

'It says it's made in India,' Nancy said.

'Yes – they make it in India, too!' the proprietor agreed.

'You're a shitty liar,' Dieter told him, but he bought Nancy the pen.

Nancy was thinking she'd like to go somewhere cool

and write postcards. In Iowa, wouldn't they be surprised to hear where she was? But, at the same time, she was thinking. They'll never hear from me again. Bombay both terrified and exhilarated her; it was so foreign and seemingly lawless that Nancy felt she could be anybody she wanted to be. It was the clean slate she was looking for, and in the back of her mind, with the persistence of something permanent, was that impossible goal of purity to which she'd been drawn in the person of Inspector Patel.

In the overly dramatic manner of many fallen young women, Nancy believed that only two roads remained open to her: she could keep on falling until she was indifferent to her own defilement, or else she could aspire to acts of social conscience so great and self-sacrificing that she could reclaim her innocence and redeem everything. In the world she'd descended to, there were only these choices: stay with Dieter or go to Inspector Patel. But what had *she* to give to Vijay Patel? Nancy feared it was nothing that the good policeman wanted.

Later, in the doorway of a transvestite brothel, a hijra exposed himself so boldly and suddenly that Nancy hadn't time to look away. Even Dieter was forced to admit that there was no evidence of a penis – not even a little one. As to what was there, Nancy wasn't sure. Dieter concluded that Rahul might be one of these – 'a kind of radical eunuch,' he said.

Dieter's questions about Rahul were greeted with sullenness, if not hostility. The only hijra who permitted them to come inside his cage was a fussy middle-aged transvestite who sat before a mirror in growing disappointment with his wig. In the same tiny room, a younger hijra was feeding a watery gray milk to a newborn goat by means of a baby's bottle.

On the subject of Rahul, all the younger one would say was, 'He is not being one of us.' The older one said only that Rahul was in Goa. Neither of the hijras could be drawn into a discussion of Rahul's nickname. At the

311

mere mention of 'Pretty,' the one who was feeding the goat abruptly pulled the baby bottle out of the goat's mouth; it made a *pop* and the goat bleated in surprise. The younger hijra pointed the baby bottle at Nancy and made a disparaging gesture. Nancy interpreted the bottle-pointing as an indication that she wasn't as pretty as Rahul. She was relieved that Dieter seemed disinclined to fight, although she could sense he was angry; he wasn't exactly gallant on her behalf, but at least he was angry.

Back on the street, to assure him she was philosophic about the insult of being ill compared to Rahul, Nancy said something that she hoped sounded tolerant in a live-and-let-live sort of way.

'Well, they weren't very nice,' she observed, 'but it was nice how they were taking care of the goat.'

'Don't be a fool,' Dieter told her. 'Some people fuck girls, some people fuck eunuchs in drag – others fuck goats.' This terrible thought made her anxious again; she knew she'd deceived herself if she'd believed she'd stopped falling.

In Kamathipura, there were other brothels. Outside a warren of small rooms, a fat woman in a magenta sari sat cross-legged on a rope bed supported by orange crates; either the woman or the bed swayed slightly. She was the madam for a higher class of prostitutes than one could find on Falkland Road or Grant Road. Naturally, Dieter didn't tell Nancy that this was the same brothel where he'd fucked the 13-year-old girl for only five rupees because they had to do it standing up.

It seemed to Nancy that Dieter knew the enormous madam, but she couldn't understand their conversation; two of the bolder prostitutes had come out of the brothel to stare at her close up.

A third girl, who was perhaps 12 or 13, was especially curious; she remembered Dieter from the night before. Nancy saw the blue tattoo on her upper arm, which Dieter later said was just the prostitute's name. It was impossible for Nancy to know if her body's other ornaments were of any religious significance or if they were merely decorative. Her bindi – the cosmetic dot on her forehead – was a saffron color edged with gold, and she wore a gold nose ring in her left nostril.

The girl's curiosity was a little too extreme for Nancy, who turned away – Dieter was still talking to the madam. Their conversation had grown heated; vagueness made Dieter angry, and *everyone* was vague about Rahul.

'You go to Goa,' the fat madam had advised. 'You say you looking for him. Then he find you.' But Nancy could tell that Dieter preferred to be in more control of the situation.

She also knew what would happen next. Back at the Sea Green Guest House, Dieter was very desirous; anger frequently had this effect on him. First he made Nancy masturbate; then he used the dildo rather roughly on her. She was surprised she was even remotely excited. Afterward, Dieter was still angry. While they waited for an overnight bus to Goa, Nancy was beginning to imagine how she would leave him. The country was so intimidating, it was hard to see herself leaving him if there was no one else.

On the bus, they saw a small American girl; she was being bothered by some Indian men. Nancy spoke up: 'Are you a coward, Dieter? Why don't you tell those guys to leave that girl alone? Why don't you ask that girl to sit with us?'

Nancy Gets Sick

Remembering when her relationship with Dieter took such a heralded turn, Nancy felt a renewal of self-confidence in the bathroom of the Hotel Bardez. So what if she couldn't unscrew the dildo? She would find someone with stronger hands, if not a pair of pliers. With that relaxing thought, she threw the dildo

313

across the bathroom; it struck the blue-tiled wall and bounced back toward the bathtub. Thereupon Nancy pulled the plug, the drain gurgled loudly, and Dr Daruwalla scurried away from his side of the bathroom door.

On the balcony, he told his wife, 'I think she's finally finished. I believe she threw the cock against the wall – she threw something, anyway.'

'It's a dildo,' Julia said. 'I wish you wouldn't call it a cock.'

'Whatever it is, I believe she threw it,' Farrokh said.

They listened to the tub; it went on gurgling. Below them, on the patio, the sweeper had awakened from his nap beneath the shade of the potted plant; they could hear him discussing the doctor's vomit with Punkaj, the servant boy. Punkaj's opinion was that the culprit was a dog.

It wasn't until Nancy stood in the tub to dry herself that the pain in her foot reminded her of why she'd come to where she was. She welcomed whatever small surgery was required to remove the glass; she was a young woman in a position to find a certain anticipated pain almost purifying.

'Are you a coward, Dieter?' Nancy whispered to herself, just to hear herself say it again; it had been so briefly gratifying.

The small girl on the bus, who was originally from Seattle, turned out to be an ashram groupie who'd traveled through the subcontinent, constantly changing her religion. She said she'd been thrown out of the Punjab for doing something insulting to the Sikhs, although she hadn't understood what it was she'd done. She wore a close-fitting, low-cut tank top; it was evident that she didn't wear a bra. She'd also acquired some silver bangles, which she wore on her wrists; she'd been told that the bangles had been part of someone's dowry. (They weren't the usual dowry material.)

Her name was Beth. She'd lost her fondness for Buddhism when a high-placed bodhisattva had tried to

314

seduce her with chang; Nancy assumed this was something you smoked, but Dieter told her it was Tibetan rice beer, which reputedly made Westerners ill.

In Maharashtra, Beth said, she'd been to Poona, but only to express her contempt for her fellow Americans who were meditating at the Rajneesh ashram. She'd lost her fondness for what she called 'California meditating,' too. No 'lousy export guru' was going to win her over.

Beth was taking a 'scholarly approach' to Hinduism. She wasn't ready to study the Vedas – the ancient spiritual texts, the orthodox Hindu scriptures – under any kind of supervision; Beth would begin with her own interpretations of *The Upanishads*, which she was currently reading. She showed the small book of spiritual treatises to Nancy and Dieter; it was one of those thin volumes in which the Introduction and the Note on the Translations amounted to more pages than the text.

Beth didn't think it odd to pursue her study of Hinduism by journeying to Goa, which attracted more Christian pilgrims than any other kind; she admitted she was going for the beaches, and for the companionship of people like herself. Besides, soon the monsoon would be everywhere, and by then she'd be in Rajasthan; the lakes were lovely during the monsoon – she'd heard about an ashram on a lake. Meanwhile, she was grateful for the company; it was no fun being a woman on your own in India, Beth assured them.

Around her neck was a rawhide thong, from which dangled a polished vulva-shaped stone. Beth explained that this was her yoni, an object of veneration in Shiva temples. The phallic lingam, representing the penis of Lord Shiva, is placed in the vulvate yoni, representing the vagina of Shiva's wife, Parvati. Priests pour a libation over the two symbols; worshipers partake of a kind of communion in the runoff.

After this puzzling account of her unusual necklace, Beth was exhausted and curled up on the seat beside

315

Nancy; she fell asleep with her head in Nancy's lap. Dieter also fell asleep, in the seat across the aisle, but not before saying to Nancy that he thought it would be great fun to show Beth the dildo. 'Let her put *that* lingam in her stupid yoni,' he said crudely. Nancy sat awake, hating him, as the bus moved through Maharashtra.

In the darkness, the most constant sound was the bus driver's tape recorder, which played only Qawwali; the recorder was turned to a low volume, and Nancy found the religious verses soothing. Of course she didn't know that they were Muslim verses, nor would she have cared. Beth's breathing was soft and regular against her thigh; Nancy thought about how long it had been since she'd had a friend — just a friend.

The dawn light in Goa was the color of sand. Nancy marveled at how childlike Beth appeared in her sleep; in both her small hands, the waif clutched the stone vagina as if this yoni were powerful enough to protect her from every evil on the subcontinent — even from Dieter and Nancy.

In Mapusa, they changed buses because their bus from Bombay went on to Panjim. They spent a long day in Calangute while Dieter did his business, which amounted to repeatedly harassing the patrons of the bus stop for any information related to Rahul. Along Baga Road, they also stopped at the bars, the hotels and the stalls for cold drinks; in all these places, Dieter spoke privately with someone while Beth and Nancy waited. Everyone claimed to have heard of Rahul, but no one had ever seen him.

Dieter had arranged for a cottage near the beach. There was only one bathroom, and the toilet and tub needed to be flushed and filled by hand with buckets from an outdoor well, but there were two big beds that looked pretty clean and a standing partition of wooden latticework — it was almost a wall, almost private. They had a propane hot plate for boiling water. A motionless ceiling fan had been installed in the optimistic faith that one day there would also be electricity; and although there were no screens, there were mosquito nets in fair repair on both beds. Outside, there was a cistern of fresh (if not clean) water; the water in the well, with which they flushed the toilet and in which they bathed, was slightly salty. By the cistern was a hut of palm leaves; if they kept the leaves wet, this hut was an adequate cooler for soda and juice and fresh fruit. Beth was disappointed that they were some distance from the beach. Although they could hear the Arabian Sea, especially at night, they had to tramp across an area of dead and rotting palm fronds before they could walk on the sand or even see the water.

Both these luxuries and inconveniences were wasted on Nancy; upon arrival, she was immediately sick. She vomited; she was so weak from diarrhea that Beth had to fetch the water to flush the toilet for her. Beth also filled the tub for Nancy's baths. Nancy had a fever with chills so violent and sweating so profuse that she stayed in bed all day and night, except when Beth stripped the sheets and gave them to the dhobi, who came for the laundry.

Dieter was disgusted with her; he went on about his business of looking for Rahul. Beth fixed her tea and brought her fresh bananas; when Nancy was stronger, Beth cooked her some rice. Because of the fever, Nancy tossed and turned all night and Dieter wouldn't sleep in the same bed with her. Beth slept in a small corner of the bed beside her; Dieter slept behind the lattice-work partition, alone. Nancy told herself that, when she was healthy, she would go to Rajasthan with Beth. She hoped Beth hadn't been revolted by her illness.

Then, one evening, Nancy woke up and felt a little better. She thought her fever was gone because she was so clear-headed; she thought she was past the vomiting and the diarrhea because she was ravenous. Dieter and Beth were out of the cottage; they'd gone to the disco in Calangute. There was a place called something stupid, like Coco Banana, where Dieter

317

asked a lot of questions about Rahul. Dieter said it was cooler to go there with a girl than to look like a loser, which was apparently what you looked like when you went there alone.

There was nothing to eat in the cottage but bananas, and Nancy ate three; then she made herself some tea. After that, she went in and out, drawing water for a bath. She was surprised how tired she was after she'd carried the water, and with her fever gone, the bath felt chilly.

After her bath, she went outside to the palm-hut cooler and drank some bottled sugarcane juice, which she hoped wouldn't bring back her diarrhea. There was nothing to do but wait for Dieter and Beth to come back. She tried reading *The Upanishads*, but it had made more sense to her when she had a fever and Beth read it aloud. Besides, she had lit an oil lamp to read and there were suddenly a million mosquitoes. Also, she encountered an exasperating passage in 'Katha Upanishad'; it repeated, as a refrain, an irritating sentence: 'This in truth is That.' She thought the phrase would drive her crazy if she read it one more time. She blew out the oil lamp and retreated under the mosquito net.

She brought the entrenching tool into the bed beside her because she was frightened to be alone in the cottage at night. There was not only the threat of bandits, of dacoit gangs; there was a gecko that lived behind the bathroom mirror – it often raced across the bathroom walls and ceiling while Nancy took her bath. She hadn't seen the gecko tonight. She wished she knew where it was.

When she'd been feverish, she'd wondered at the shadows cast by the strange gargoyles along the top of the latticework partition; then one night the gargoyles weren't there, and another night there'd been only one. Now that her fever was gone, she realized the 'gargoyles' were in nearly constant motion – they were rats. They favored the vantage point that the partition gave them, to look down upon both beds. Nancy watched them until she fell asleep.

She was beginning to understand that she was a long way from Bombay, which was a long way from anywhere else. Not even young Vijay Patel – Police Inspector, Colaba Station – could help her here.

13. NOT A DREAM

A Beautiful Stranger

When Nancy's fever came back, the sweating didn't wake her but the chills did. She knew she was delirious because it was impossible that a beautiful woman in a sari could be sitting on the bed beside her, holding her hand. At 31 or 32, the woman was at the very peak of her beauty, and her subtle jasmine scent should have told Nancy that the beautiful woman was *not* the result of delirium. A woman with such a wonderful smell could never be dreamed. When the woman spoke, even Nancy had reason to doubt that she was any kind of hallucination at all.

'You're the one who's sick, aren't you?' the woman asked Nancy. 'And they've left you all alone, haven't they?'

'Yes,' Nancy whispered; she was shivering so hard, her teeth were chattering. Although she clutched the entrenching tool, she doubted she could summon the strength to lift it.

Then, as so often happens in dreams, there was no transition, no logic to the order of events, because the beautiful woman unwound her sari – she completely undressed. Even in the ghostly pallor of the moonlight, she was the color of tea; her limbs looked as smooth and hard as fine wood, like cherry. Her breasts were only slightly bigger than Beth's, but much more upright, and when she slipped past the mosquito net and into the bed beside Nancy, Nancy relinquished her grip on the entrenching tool and allowed the beautiful woman to hold her.

'They shouldn't leave you all alone, should they?' the woman asked Nancy.

'No,' Nancy whispered; her teeth had stopped chattering, and her shivers subsided in the beautiful woman's strong arms. At first they lay face-to-face, the woman's firm breasts against Nancy's softer bosom, their legs entwined. Then Nancy rolled onto her other side and the woman pressed herself against Nancy's back; in this position, the woman's breasts touched Nancy's shoulder blades – the woman's breath stirred Nancy's hair. Nancy was impressed by the suppleness of the woman's long, slender waist – how it curved to accommodate Nancy's broad hips and her round bottom. And to Nancy's surprise, the woman's hands, which gently held Nancy's heavy breasts, were even bigger than Nancy's hands.

'This is better, isn't it?' the woman asked her.

'Yes,' Nancy whispered, but her own voice sounded uncharacteristically hoarse and far away. An unshakable drowsiness attended the woman's embrace, or else this was a new stage in Nancy's fever, which signaled the beginning of a sleep deeper than dreams.

Nancy had never slept with a woman's breasts pressed against her back; she marveled at how soothing it was, and she wondered if this was what men felt when they fell asleep this way. Previously, Nancy *had* fallen asleep with that odd sensation of a man's inert and usually small penis brushing against her buttocks. It was upon this awareness, and on the edge of sleep, that Nancy was suddenly aware of an unusual situation, which was surely in the area of dream or delirium or both, because she felt – at the same time! – a woman's breasts pressed against her back *and* a man's sleepy penis curled against her buttocks. Another fever dream, Nancy decided.

'Won't they be surprised, when they get here?' the beautiful woman asked her, but Nancy's mind had drifted too far away for her to answer.

Nancy Is a Witness

When Nancy woke up, she lay alone in the moonlight, smelling the ganja and listening to Dieter and Beth; they were whispering on the other side of the partition. The rats on the latticework were so still that they appeared to be listening, too – or else the rats were stoned, because Dieter and Beth were smoking up a storm.

Nancy heard Dieter ask Beth, 'What is the first sexual experience that you had some confidence in?' Nancy counted to herself in the silence; of course she knew what Beth was thinking. Then Dieter said, 'Masturbation, right?'

Nancy heard Beth whisper, 'Yes.'

'Everyone is different,' Dieter told Beth philosophically. 'You just have to learn what your own best way is.'

Nancy lay watching the rats while she listened to Dieter. He was successful in getting Beth to relax, although Beth did possess the decency to ask, if only once, 'What about Nancy?'

'Nancy is asleep,' Dieter said. 'Nancy won't object.'

'I have to be lying on my tummy,' Beth told Dieter, whose grasp of English vernacular wasn't sound enough for him to understand 'tummy.'

Nancy heard Beth roll over. There was no sound for a while, and then there came a change in Beth's breathing, to which Dieter whispered some encouragement. There was the sound of messy kissing, and Beth panting, and then Beth uttered that special sound, which made the rats run along the top of the latticework partition and caused Nancy to reach for the entrenching tool with her big hands.

While Beth was still moaning, Dieter said to her, 'Just wait right there. I have a surprise for you.'

The surprise for Nancy was that the entrenching tool was gone; she was sure she'd brought it to bed with her. She wanted to crack Dieter in the shins with it, just to drop him to his knees so that she could tell him what

322

she thought of him. She'd give Beth one more chance. As she groped under the mosquito net and along the floor beside the bed, looking for the entrenching tool, Nancy still hoped that she and Beth could go to Rajasthan together.

That was when her hand found the jasmine-scented sari that the beautiful woman in the dream had worn. Nancy pulled the sari into bed with her and breathed it in; the scent of it brought the beautiful woman back to her mind – the woman's unusually large, strong hands . . . the woman's unusually upright, firm breasts. Last came the memory of the woman's unusual penis, which had curled like a snail against Nancy's buttocks as Nancy drifted into sleep.

'Dieter?' Nancy tried to whisper, but her voice made no sound. It was exactly as they'd told Dieter in Bombay: you go to Goa *not* to find Rahul but to let Rahul find you. Dieter had been right about one thing: there *were* chicks with dicks. Rahul wasn't a hijra – he was a zenana, after all.

Nancy could hear Dieter in the bathroom, looking for the dildo in the semidarkness. She heard a bottle break against the stone floor. Dieter must have placed the bottle precariously on the edge of the tub; not much moonlight penetrated the bathroom, and he probably needed to search for the dildo with both hands. Briefly, Dieter cursed; he must have cursed in German because Nancy didn't catch the word.

Beth called out to Dieter – she'd obviously forgotten that Nancy was supposed to be sleeping. 'Did you break your Coke, Dieter?' Beth called; her own question dissolved her into mindless giggles – Dieter was addicted to Coca-Cola.

'*Ssshhh!*' Dieter said from the bathroom.

'*Ssshhh!*' Beth repeated; she made a failed effort to stifle her laughter.

The next sound that Nancy heard was one she'd been fearing, but she'd been unable to find her voice – to warn Dieter that someone else was here. She heard what she was sure was the entrenching tool, the spade end, as it made full-force contact with what sounded like the base of Dieter's skull. A metallic after-ring followed the blow, but surprisingly little noise attended Dieter falling. Then there was the second sound of violent contact, almost as if a spade or a heavy shovel had been swung against the trunk of a tree. Nancy realized that Beth hadn't heard this because Beth was sucking on the ganja pipe as if the fire had died in the bowl and she was trying to revive it.

Nancy lay very still, holding the jasmine-scented sari in her arms. The spectral figure with the small, upright breasts and the little boy's penis passed close to Nancy's bed without a sound. It was no wonder that Rahul was called Pretty, Nancy thought.

'Beth!' Nancy tried to say, but once again her voice had abandoned her.

From the other side of the partition, a sudden light came through the latticework in patches; the shadows of the startled rats were cast upon the ceiling. Nancy could see through the latticing. Beth had completely opened the mosquito net in order to light an oil lamp; she was looking for more ganja for the pipe when the naked tea-colored body appeared beside her bed. Rahul's big hands held the entrenching tool with the handle nestled in the delicate curve of the small of his back, the spade end concealed between his shoulder blades.

'Hi,' Rahul said to Beth.

'Hi. Who are you?' Beth said. Then Beth managed a gasp, which caused Nancy to stop looking through the space between the latticework. Nancy lay on her back with the jasmine-scented sari covering her face; she didn't want to look at the ceiling, either, because she knew that the shadows of the rats would be twitching there.

'Hey, like, what *are* you?' she heard Beth say. 'Are you a boy or a girl?'

'I'm pretty, aren't I?' Rahul said.

'You sure are . . . different,' Beth replied.

From the responding sound of the entrenching tool, Nancy guessed that Rahul was displeased to be called 'different.' Rahul's preferred nickname was 'Pretty.' Nancy pushed the jasmine-scented sari entirely off the bed and outside the mosquito net. She hoped it fell to the floor very close to where Rahul had left it. Then she lay with her eyes open, staring at the ceiling, where the shadows of the rats scurried back and forth; it was almost as if the second and third blows from the entrenching tool were a kind of starting signal for the rats.

Later, Nancy quietly rolled on her side so that she could peek through the latticing and watch what Rahul was doing; he appeared to be performing a kind of surgery on Beth's stomach, but Nancy soon realized that Rahul was drawing a picture on Beth's belly. Nancy shut her eyes and wished that her fever would come back; even though she wasn't feverish, she was so frightened that she began to shiver. It was the shivers that saved her. When Rahul came to her, Nancy's teeth were chattering as uncontrollably as before. Instantly, she felt his lack of sexual interest; he was mocking her, or merely curious.

'Is that bad old fever back again?' Rahul asked her.

'I keep dreaming,' Nancy told him.

'Yes, of course you do, dear,' Rahul said.

'I keep trying to sleep but I keep dreaming,' Nancy said.

'Are they bad dreams?' Rahul asked her.

'Pretty bad,' Nancy said.

'Do you want to tell me about them, dear?' Rahul asked her.

'I just want to sleep,' Nancy told him. To her surprise, he let her. He parted the mosquito net and sat on the bed beside her; he rubbed her between her shoulder blades until the shivers went away and she could imitate the regular breathing of a deep sleep – she even parted her lips and tried to imagine that she was already dead. He kissed her once on the temple, and once on the tip of her nose. At last, she felt Rahul's weight leave the bed. She also felt the entrenching tool, when Rahul gently returned it to her hands. Although she never heard a door open or close, she knew Rahul was gone when she heard the rats racing recklessly through the cottage; they even scampered under the mosquito net and across her bed, as if they were secure in their belief that there were three dead people in the cottage instead of two. That was when Nancy knew it was safe to get up. If Rahul had still been there, the rats would have known.

In the predawn light, Nancy saw that Rahul had used the dhobi pen – and indelible dhobi ink – to decorate Beth's belly. The laundry-marking pen was a crude wooden handle with a simple, broad nib; the ink was black. Rahul had left the ink bottle and the dhobi pen on Nancy's pillow. Nancy recalled that she'd picked up the ink bottle and the dhobi pen before putting them both back on her bed; her fingerprints were also all over the handle of the entrenching tool.

She'd become ill so soon upon her arrival; yet it was Nancy's strong impression that this was a rustic sort of place. She doubted she'd have much success convincing the local police that a beautiful woman with a little boy's penis had murdered Dieter and Beth. And Rahul had been smart enough not to empty Dieter's money belt; he'd taken the money belt with him. There was no evidence of a robbery. Beth's jewelry was untouched, and there was even some money in Dieter's wallet; their passports weren't stolen. Nancy knew that most of the money was in the dildo, which she didn't even try to open because Dieter had bled on it and it was sticky to touch. She wiped it with a wet towel; then she packed it in the rucksack with her things.

She thought Inspector Patel would believe her, provided she could get back to Bombay without the local police finding her first. On the surface, Nancy thought, it would be judged a crime of passion – one of those triangular relationships that had turned a little twisted. And the drawing on Beth's belly gave the murders a hint of diabolism, or at least a flair for sarcasm. The elephant was surprisingly small and unadorned – a frontal view. The head was wider than it was long, the eyes were unmatched, and one was squinting – actually, one eye seemed puckered, Nancy thought. The trunk hung slack, pointing straight down; from the end of the trunk, the artist had drawn several broad lines in the shape of a fan – a childish indication that water sprayed from the elephant's trunk, as from a showerhead or from the nozzle of a hose. These lines extended into Beth's pubic hair. The entire drawing was the size of a small hand.

Then Nancy realized why the drawing was slightly off center, and why one eye seemed 'puckered.' One of the eyes was Beth's navel, outlined in dhobi ink; the other eye was an imperfect imitation of the navel. Because the navel had real depth, the eyes weren't the same; one eye appeared to be winking. Beth's navel was the winking eye. What further contributed to the elephant's mirthful or mocking expression was that one of its tusks drooped in the normal position; the opposing tusk was raised, almost as if an elephant could lift a tusk in the manner that a human being can cock an eyebrow. This was a small, ironical elephant – an elephant with an inappropriate sense of humor, to be sure.

The Getaway

Nancy dressed Beth's body in the tank top that Beth had been wearing when Nancy first met her; at least it covered the drawing. She left Beth's sacred yoni in place, at her throat, as if it might prove itself to be a more successful talisman in the next world than it had demonstrated itself to be in this.

The sun rose inland and a tan light filtered through

the areca and coconut palms, leaving most of the beach in shade, which was a blessing for Nancy, who labored for over an hour with the entrenching tool; yet she managed to dig no better than a shallow pit near the tidemark for high tide. The pit was already half full of water when she dragged Dieter's body along the beach and rolled him into the hole. By the time she'd arranged Beth's body next to his, Nancy was aware of the blue crabs that she'd uncovered with her digging; they were scurrying to bury themselves again. She'd chosen an especially soft stretch of sand, the part of the beach that was nearest the cottage; now Nancy realized why the sand was soft. A tidal inlet cut through the beach and drained into the matted jungle; she'd dug too close to this inlet. Nancy knew the bodies wouldn't stay buried for long.

Worse, in her haste to clean up the broken glass in the bathroom, she'd stepped on the jagged heel of the Coca-Cola bottle; several pieces of glass had broken off in her foot. She was wrong to think she'd picked all the pieces out, but she was in a hurry. She'd bled so heavily on that bathroom mat, she was forced to roll it up and put it (with the broken glass) in the grave; she buried it, together with the rest of Dieter's and Beth's things, including Beth's silver bangles, which were much too small for Nancy, and Beth's beloved copy of *The Upanishads*, which Nancy had no interest in reading herself.

It had surprised Nancy that digging the grave was harder work than dragging Dieter's body to the beach; Dieter was tall, but he weighed less than she'd ever imagined. It crossed her mind that she could have left him anytime she'd wanted to; she could have picked him up and thrown him against a wall. She felt incredibly strong, but as soon as she'd filled the grave, she was exhausted.

A moment of panic nearly overcame Nancy when she discovered that she couldn't find the top half of the silver ballpoint pen that Dieter had given her – the pen with *Made in India* written lengthwise on it in script. The bottom part said *Made in,* the missing part said *India.* Nancy had already discovered the flaw in the pen's design: the pen wouldn't snap securely together if the script wasn't perfectly aligned; the top and the bottom were always getting separated. Nancy looked through the cottage for the missing top; she thought it unlikely that Rahul had taken it – it wasn't the part of the pen that you could write with. Nancy had the part that wrote, and so she kept it; because it was small, it would make its way to the bottom of her rucksack. At least it was real silver.

Nancy knew her fever had finally gone because she was smart enough to take Dieter's and Beth's passports; she also reminded herself that their bodies would be found soon. Whoever rented the cottage to Dieter had known there were three of them. She suspected that the police would assume she'd leave by bus from Calangute or by ferry from Panjim. Nancy's plan was remarkably clear-headed: she would place Dieter's and Beth's passports in a conspicuous place at the bus stand in Calangute, but she would take the ferry from Panjim to Bombay. That way, with any luck – and while she was on the ferry – the police would be looking for her in bus stations.

But Nancy would be the beneficiary of better luck than this. When the bodies were discovered, the landlord who rented the cottage to Dieter admitted that he'd seen Beth and Nancy only at a distance. Since Dieter was German, the landlord assumed the other two were Germans; also, he mistook Nancy for a man. After all, she was so big – especially beside Beth. The landlord would tell the police that they were looking for a German hippie male. When the passports were found in Calangute, the police realized that Beth had been an American; yet they persisted in their belief that the murderer was a German man, traveling by bus.

The grave wouldn't be discovered right away; the

tide eroded the sand near the inlet only a little bit at a time. It would be unclear whether the carrion birds or the pye-dogs were the first to catch wind of something; by then, Nancy was gone.

She waited only for the sun to top the palm trees and flood the beach in white light; it took just a few minutes for the sun to dry the wet sand of the grave. With a palm frond, Nancy wiped smooth the stretch of beach leading to the jungle and the cottage; then she limped on her way. It was still early morning when she left Anjuna. She deemed she'd discovered an isolated pocket of eccentrics when she saw the nude sunbathers and swimmers who were almost a tradition in the area. She'd been sick – she didn't know.

The first day, her foot wasn't too bad, but she had to walk all over Calangute after she placed the passports. There was no doctor staying at Meena's or Varma's. Someone told her that an English-speaking doctor was staying at the Concha Hotel; when she got there, the doctor had checked out. At the Concha, they told her there was an English-speaking doctor in Baga at the Hotel Bardez. The next day, when she went there, they turned her away; by then, her foot was infected.

As she emerged from her endless baths in Dr Daruwalla's tub, Nancy couldn't remember if the murders were two or three days old. She did, however, remember a glaring error in her judgment. She'd already told Dr Daruwalla that she was taking the ferry to Bombay; that was decidedly unwise. When the doctor and his wife helped her onto the table on the balcony, they mistook her silence for anxiety regarding the small surgery, but Nancy was thinking of how to rectify her mistake. She hardly flinched at the anesthetic, and while Dr Daruwalla probed for the broken glass, Nancy calmly said, 'You know, I've changed my mind about Bombay. I'm going south instead. I'll take the bus from Calangute to Panjim, then I'll take the bus to Margao. I want to go to Mysore, where they make the incense – you know? Then I want to go to Kerala. What do you think of that?' she asked the doctor. She wanted him to remember her false itinerary.

'I think you must be a very ambitious traveler!' said Dr Daruwalla. He extracted a surprisingly big, half-moon-shaped piece of glass from her foot; it was probably a piece from the thick heel of a Coke bottle, the doctor told her. He disinfected the smaller cuts once they were free of glass fragments. He packed the larger wound with iodophor gauze. Dr Daruwalla also gave Nancy an antibiotic that he'd brought with him to Goa for his children. She'd have to see a doctor in a few days – sooner, if there was any redness around the wound or if she had a fever.

Nancy wasn't listening; she was worrying how she would pay him. She didn't think it would be proper to ask the doctor to unscrew the dildo; she also didn't think he looked strong enough. Farrokh, in his own way, was also distracted by his thoughts about the dildo.

'I can't pay you very much,' Nancy told the doctor.

'I don't want you to pay me at all!' Dr Daruwalla said. He gave her his card; it was just his habit.

Nancy read the card and said, 'But I told you – I'm not going to Bombay.'

'I know, but if you feel feverish or the infection worsens, you should call me – from wherever you are. Or if you see a doctor who can't understand you, have the doctor call me,' Farrokh said.

'Thank you,' Nancy told him.

'And don't walk on it any more than you have to,' the doctor told her.

'I'll be on the *bus*,' Nancy insisted.

As she was limping to the stairs, the doctor introduced her to John D. She was in no mood to meet such a handsome young man, and although he was very polite to her – he even offered to help her down the stairs – Nancy felt extremely vulnerable to his kind of European superiority. He showed not the slightest spark of sexual interest in her, and this hurt her more

331

than her foot did. But she said good-bye to Dr Daru-walla and allowed John D. to carry her downstairs; she knew she was heavy, but he looked strong. The desire to shock him grew overwhelming. Besides, she knew he was strong enough to unscrew the dildo.

'If it's not too much trouble,' she said to him in the lobby of the hotel, 'you could do me a big favor.' She showed him the dildo without removing it from her rucksack. 'The tip unscrews,' she told him, watching his eyes. 'But I'm just not strong enough.' She con-tinued to regard his face while he gripped the big cock in both hands; she would remember him because of how poised he was.

As soon as he loosened the tip, she stopped him.

'That's enough,' she told him; she didn't want him to see the money. It disappointed her that he seemed unshockable, but she kept trying. She resolved she would look into his eyes until he had to look away. 'I'm going to spare you,' she said softly. 'You don't want to know what's inside the thing.'

She would remember him for his instinctive sneer, for John D. was an actor long before he was Inspector Dhar. She would remember that sneer, the same sneer with which Inspector Dhar would later incense all of Bombay. It was Nancy who had to look away from him; she would remember that, too.

She avoided the bus stand in Calangute; she would try to hitchhike to Panjim, even if it meant she had to walk – or defend herself with the entrenching tool. She hoped she still had a day or two before the bodies were found. But before she located the road to Panjim, she remembered the big piece of glass the doctor had removed from her foot. After showing it to her, he'd put it in an ashtray on a small table near the hammock; probably he would throw it away, she thought. But what if he heard about the broken glass in the hippie grave – it would soon be called the 'hippie grave' – and what if he wondered if the piece of glass from her foot would match?

It was late at night when Nancy returned to the Hotel Bardez. The door to the lobby was locked, and the boy who slept on a rush mat in the lobby all night was still engaged in talking to the dog that spent every night with him; that was why the dog never heard Nancy when she climbed the vine to the Daruwallas' second-floor balcony. Her procaine injection had worn off and her foot throbbed; but Nancy could have screamed in pain and knocked over the furniture and still she would never have awakened Dr Daruwalla.

The doctor's lunch has been described. It would be superfluous to provide similar detail regarding the doctor's dinner; suffice it to say that he substituted the vindaloo-style pork for the fish, and he further indulged in a pork stew called sorpotel, which features pig's liver and is abundantly flavored with vinegar. Yet it was the dried duckling with tamarind that dominated the aroma of his heavy breathing, and his snores were scented with sharp blasts of a raw red wine, which he would deeply regret in the morning. He should have stuck to the beer. Julia was grateful that Dr Daruwalla had elected to sleep in the hammock on the balcony, where only the Arabian Sea – and the lizards and insects that in the night were legion – would be disturbed by the doctor's windy noises. Julia also desired a rest from the passions inspired by Mr James Salter's artistry. For the moment, her private speculations concerning the departed hippie's dildo had cooled Julia's sexual ardor.

As for the insect and lizard life that clung to the mosquito net enclosing the cherubic doctor in his hammock, the gecko and mosquito world appeared to be charmed by both the doctor's music and his vapors. The doctor had bathed just before retiring, and his plump pale-brown body was everywhere dusted with Cuticura powder – from his neck to between his toes. His closely shaven throat and cheeks were refreshed with a powerful astringent redolent of lemons. He'd even shaved his mustache off, leaving only a little clump of a beard on his chin; he was almost as smooth-faced as a baby. Dr Daruwalla was so clean and he smelled so wonderful that Nancy had the impression that only the mosquito net prevented the geckos and mosquitoes from devouring him.

At a level of sleep so deep it seemed to Farrokh that he had died and lay buried somewhere in China, the doctor dreamed that his most ardent admirers were digging up his body – to prove a point. The doctor wished they would leave him undisturbed, for he felt he was at peace; in truth, he'd passed out in the hammock in a stupor of overeating – not to mention the effect of the wine. To dream that he was prey to gravediggers was surely an indication of his overindulgence.

So what if my body is a miracle, he was dreaming – please just leave it alone!

Meanwhile, Nancy found what she was looking for; in the ashtray, where it had left only a spot of dried blood, lay the half-moon-shaped piece of glass. As she took it, she heard Dr Daruwalla cry out, 'Leave me in China!' The doctor thrashed his legs, and Nancy saw that one of his beautiful eggshell-brown feet had escaped the mosquito net and was protruding from the hammock – exposed to the terrors of the night. The disturbance sent the geckos darting in all directions and caused the mosquitoes to swarm.

Well, Nancy thought, the doctor had done her a favor, hadn't he? She stood stock-still until she was sure Dr Daruwalla was sound asleep; she didn't want to wake him up, but it was hard for her to leave him when his gorgeous foot was prey to the elements. Nancy contemplated how she might safely return Farrokh's foot to the mosquito net, but her newfound good sense persuaded her not to risk it. She descended the vine from the balcony to the patio; this required the use of both her hands, and so she delicately held the piece of broken glass in her teeth – careful that it not cut her tongue or her lips. She was limping along the dark road to Calangute when she threw the glass away. It was lost in a dense grove of palms, where it disappeared without a sound – as unseen by any living human eye as Nancy's lost innocence.

The Wrong Toe

Nancy had been fortunate to leave the Hotel Bardez when she had. She never knew that Rahul was a guest there, nor did Rahul know that Nancy had been Dr Daruwalla's patient. This was *extremely* lucky, because Rahul also climbed the vine to the Daruwallas' second-floor balcony – on that very same night. Nancy had come and gone; but when Rahul arrived on the balcony, Dr Daruwalla's poor foot was still vulnerable to the nighttime predators.

Rahul himself had come as a predator. He'd learned from Dr Daruwalla's innocent daughters that John D. usually slept in the hammock on the balcony. Rahul had come to the balcony to seduce John D. The sexually curious may find it interesting to speculate whether or not Rahul would have met with success in his attempted seduction of the beautiful young man, but John D. was spared this test because Dr Daruwalla was sleeping in the hammock on this busy night.

In the darkness – not to mention that he was blinded by his overeagerness – Rahul was confused. The body asleep under the mosquito net was certainly of a desirable fragrance. Maybe it was the moonlight that played tricks with skin color. Possibly it was only the moonlight which gave Rahul the impression that John D. had grown a little clump of a beard. As for the toes of the doctor's exposed foot, they were tiny and hairless, and the foot itself was as small as a young girl's. Rahul found that the ball of the foot was endearingly fleshy and soft, and he thought that the sole of Dr Daruwalla's foot was almost indecently pink – in contrast to the doctor's sleek, brown ankle.

Rahul knelt by the doctor's small foot; he stroked it with his large hand; he brushed his cheek against the doctor's freshly scented toes. Naturally, it would have startled him if Dr Daruwalla had cried out, 'But I don't *want* to be a miracle!'

The doctor was dreaming that he was Francis Xavier, dug up from his grave and taken against his will to the Basilica de Bom Jesus in Goa. More accurately, he was dreaming that he was Francis Xavier's miraculously preserved *body*, and things were about to be done to his body – also against his will. But despite the terror of what was happening to him, in his dream Farrokh couldn't give utterance to his fears; he was so heavily sedated with food and wine that he was forced to suffer in silence – even though he anticipated that a crazed pilgrim was about to eat his toe. After all, he knew the story.

Rahul ran his tongue along the sole of the doctor's fragrant foot, which tasted strongly of Cuticura powder and vaguely of garlic. Because Dr Daruwalla's foot was the single part of him that was unprotected by the mosquito net, Rahul could manifest his powerful attraction to the delicious John D. only by enclosing what he presumed to be the big toe of John D.'s right foot in his warm mouth. Rahul then sucked on this toe with such force that Dr Daruwalla moaned. Rahul at first fought against the desire to bite him, but he gave in to this urge and slowly sank his teeth into the squirming toe; then he once more resisted the compelling impulse to bite – then he weakened and bit down harder. It was torture for Rahul to stop himself from going too far – from swallowing Dr Daruwalla, either whole or in pieces. When he at last released the doctor's foot, both Rahul *and* Dr Daruwalla were gasping. In his dream, the doctor was certain that the obsessed woman had already done her damage; she'd bitten off the sacred relic of his toe, and now there was tragically less of his miraculous body than they had buried.

As Rahul undressed himself, Dr Daruwalla withdrew his maimed foot from the dangerous world; he curled himself tightly into his hammock under the mosquito net, for in his dream he was fearing that the emissaries from the Vatican were approaching – to take his arm to Rome. As Farrokh struggled to give voice to his terror of amputation, Rahul attempted to penetrate the mysteries of the mosquito net.

Rahul thought it would be best if John D. awoke to find his face firmly between Rahul's breasts, for these latter creations were surely to be counted among Rahul's best features. But then, since Rahul thought that the young man appeared to have been aroused by the oddity of having his big toe sucked and bitten, perhaps a bolder approach would succeed. It was frustrating to Rahul that he could proceed with *no* approach until he solved the puzzle of entrance to the mosquito net, which was vexing. And it was at this complicated juncture in Rahul's attempted seduction that Farrokh finally found the voice to express his fears. Rahul, who recognized the doctor's voice, distinctly heard Dr Daruwalla shout, 'I don't *want* to be a saint! I *need* that arm – it's a very good arm!'

At this, the boy's dog in the lobby barked briefly; the boy once more began to talk to the animal. Rahul hated Dr Daruwalla as fervently as he desired John D.; therefore, Rahul was appalled that he'd caressed the doctor's foot, and he was nauseated that he'd sucked and bitten the doctor's big toe. As he hurriedly dressed himself, Rahul was also embarrassed. The taste of Cuticura powder was bitter on his tongue as he climbed down the vine to the patio, where the dog in the lobby heard him spit; the dog barked again, and this time the boy unlocked the door to the lobby and peered anxiously at the misty beach.

The boy heard Dr Daruwalla cry out from the balcony: 'Cannibals! Catholic maniacs!' Even to an inexperienced Hindu boy, this seemed a fearful combination. Then the dog's barking exploded at the door

337

to the lobby, where both the boy and the dog were surprised by the sudden appearance of Rahul.

'Don't lock me out,' Rahul said. The boy let him in and gave him his room key. Rahul wore a loose-fitting skirt of a kind that's easy to put on and take off, and a bright-yellow halter top of a kind that drew the boy's awkward attention to Rahul's well-shaped breasts. There was a time when Rahul would have grabbed the boy's face in both hands and pulled him into his bosom; then he might have played with the boy's little prick, or else he might have kissed him, in which case Rahul would have stuck his tongue so far down the boy's throat that the boy would have gagged. But not now; Rahul wasn't in the mood.

He went upstairs to his room; he brushed his teeth until the taste of Dr Daruwalla's Cuticura powder was gone. Then he undressed and lay down on his bed, where he could look at himself in the mirror. He wasn't in the mood to masturbate. He made some drawings, but nothing worked. Rahul was furious at Dr Daruwalla for being in John D.'s hammock; it made him so angry that he couldn't even arouse himself. In the adjacent room, Aunt Promila was snoring.

Down in the lobby, the boy tried to calm the dog down. He thought it was peculiar that the dog was so agitated; usually, women had no effect on the dog. It was only men who made the dog's fur stand up, or made the dog walk around stiff-legged – sniffing everywhere the men had been. It puzzled the boy that the dog had reacted in this fashion to Rahul. The boy also needed to calm himself down; he'd reacted to Rahul's breasts in his own fashion; he was so aroused that he had a sizable erection – for a boy. And he knew perfectly well that the lobby of the Hotel Bardez was no place for him to indulge his fantasies. There was nothing the boy could do. He lay down on the rush mat, where he at last coaxed the dog to join him, and there he went on speaking to the dog as before.

Farrokh Is Converted

At dawn, on the road to Panjim, Nancy had the good fortune to arouse the sympathy of a motorcyclist who noticed her limp. It wasn't much of a motorcycle, but it would do; it was a 250 cc. Yezdi with red plastic tassles hanging from the handlebars, a black dot painted on the headlight, and a sari-guard mounted on the left-side rear wheel. Nancy was wearing jeans, and she simply straddled the seat behind the skinny teenaged driver. She locked her hands around the boy's waist without a word; she knew he couldn't drive fast enough to scare her.

The Yezdi was equipped with crash bars that protruded from the motorcycle in the manner of a full fairing. In Dr Daruwalla's profession, these so-called crash bars were known as tibial-fracture bars; they were renowned for breaking the tibias of motorcyclists – all for the sake of not denting the gas tank.

Nancy's weight was at first disconcerting to the young driver; she had a dangerously wide effect on his cornering – he held his speed down.

'Can't this thing go any faster?' she asked him. He half-understood her, or else her voice in his ear was thrilling; possibly it hadn't been her limp he'd noticed but the tightness of her jeans, or her blond hair – or even the swaying of her breasts, which the teenager felt pressing against his back. 'That's better,' Nancy told him, after he dared to speed up. Streaming from the handlebars, the red plastic tassles were whipped by the rushing wind; they appeared to beckon Nancy toward the steamer jetty and her chosen destiny in Bombay.

She'd embraced evil; she'd found it lacking. She was the sinner in search of the impossible salvation; she thought that only the uncorrupted and incorruptible policeman could restore her essential goodness. She had spotted something conflicted about Inspector Patel. She believed that he was virtuous and honorable, but also that she could seduce him; her logic was such that she thought of his virtue and his honor as transferable to her. Nancy's illusion was not uncommon – nor is it an illusion limited to women. It is an old belief: that several sexually wrong decisions can be remedied – even utterly erased – by one decision that is sexually right. No one should blame Nancy for trying.

As Nancy rode the Yezdi to the ferry, and to her fate, a dull but persistent pain in the big toe of his right foot awaked Dr Daruwalla from a night of bedlam dreams and indigestion. He freed himself from the mosquito net and swung his legs from the hammock, but when he put only the slightest weight on his right foot, his big toe stabbed him with a sharp pain; for a second, he imagined he was still dreaming he was St Francis's body. In the early light, which was a muted brown – not unlike the color of Dr Daruwalla's skin – the doctor inspected his toe. The skin was unbroken, but deep bruises of a crimson and purple hue clearly indicated the bite marks. Dr Daruwalla screamed.

'Julia! I've been bitten by a *ghost*!' the doctor cried. His wife came running.

'What is it, *Liebchen*?' she asked him.

'Look at my big toe!' the doctor demanded.

'Have you been biting yourself?' Julia asked him with unconcealed distaste.

'It's a *miracle*!' shouted Dr Daruwalla. 'It was the ghost of that crazy woman who bit St Francis!' Farrokh shouted.

'Don't be a blasphemer,' Julia cautioned him.

'I am being a *believer* – not a blasphemer!' the doctor cried. He ventured a step on his right foot, but the pain in his big toe was so wilting that he fell, screaming, to his knees.

'Hush or you'll wake up the children – you'll wake up everybody!' Julia scolded him.

'Praise the Lord,' Farrokh whispered, crawling back to his hammock. 'I believe, God – please don't torture me further!' He collapsed into the hammock, hugging both his arms around his chest. 'What if they come for my arm?' he asked his wife.

Julia was disgusted with him. 'I think it must be something you ate,' she said. 'Or else you've been dreaming about the dildo.'

'I suppose *you've* been dreaming about it,' Farrokh said sullenly. 'Here I've suffered some sort of *conversion* and you're thinking about a big cock!'

'I'm thinking about how you're behaving in a peculiar fashion,' Julia told him.

'But I've had some sort of religious *experience*!' Farrokh insisted.

'I don't see what's religious about it,' Julia said.

'Look at my toe!' the doctor cried.

'Maybe you bit it in your sleep,' his wife suggested.

'Julia!' Farrokh said. 'I thought you were already a Christian.'

'Well, I don't go around yelling and moaning about it,' Julia said.

John D. appeared on the balcony, never realizing that Dr Daruwalla's religious experience was very nearly his own experience – of another kind.

'What's going on?' the young man asked.

'It's apparently unsafe to sleep on the balcony,' Julia told him. 'Something bit Farrokh – some kind of animal.'

'Those are *human* teeth marks!' the doctor declared. John D. examined the bitten toe with his usual detachment.

'Maybe it was a monkey,' he said.

Dr Daruwalla curled himself into a ball in the hammock, deciding to give his wife and his favorite young man the silent treatment. Julia and John D. took their breakfast with the Daruwalla daughters on the patio below the balcony; at times they would raise their eyes and look up the vine in the direction where they presumed Farrokh lay sulking. They were wrong; he wasn't sulking – he was praying. Since the doctor was

341

inexperienced at prayer, his praying resembled an interior monologue of a fairly standard confessional kind – especially that kind which is brought on by a bad hangover.

O God! prayed Dr Daruwalla. *It isn't necessary to take my arm – the toe convinced me. I don't need any more convincing. You got me the first time, God.* The doctor paused. *Please leave the arm alone,* he added.

Later, from the lobby of the Hotel Bardez, the syphilitic tea-server thought he heard voices from the Daruwallas' second-floor balcony. Since Ali Ahmed was known to be almost entirely deaf, it was assumed that he probably always heard 'voices.' But Ali Ahmed had actually heard Dr Daruwalla praying, for by midmorning the doctor was murmuring aloud and the pitch of his prayers was precisely in a register that the syphilitic tea-server could hear.

'I am heartily sorry if I have offended Thee, God!' Dr Daruwalla murmured intensely. 'Heartily sorry – very sorry, really! I never meant to mock anybody – I was only kidding,' he confessed. 'St Francis – you, too – please forgive me!' An unusual number of dogs were barking, as if the pitch of the doctor's prayers were precisely in a register that the dogs could hear, too. 'I am a surgeon, God,' the doctor moaned. 'I *need* my arm – *both* my arms!' Thus did Dr Daruwalla refuse to leave the hammock of his miraculous conversion, while Julia and John D. spent the morning plotting how to prevent the doctor from spending another night on the balcony.

Later in the day, as his hangover abated, Farrokh regained a little of his self-confidence. He said to Julia that he thought it would be enough for him to become a Christian; he meant that perhaps it wasn't necessary for him to become a *Catholic.* Did Julia think that becoming a Protestant would be good enough? Maybe an Anglican would do. By now, Julia was quite frightened by the depth and color of the bite marks on

342

her husband's toe; even though the skin was un-broken, she was afraid of rabies.

'Julia!' Farrokh complained. 'Here I am worrying about my mortal soul, and you're worried about rabies!'

'Lots of monkeys have rabies,' John D. offered.

'*What* monkeys?' Dr Daruwalla shouted. '*I* don't see any monkeys here! Have *you* seen any monkeys?'

While they were arguing, they failed to notice Promila Rai and her nephew-with-breasts checking out of the hotel. They were going back to Bombay, but not tonight; Nancy was again fortunate – Rahul wouldn't be on *her* ferry. Promila knew that Rahul's holiday had been disappointing to him, and so she'd accepted an invitation for them both to spend the night at someone's villa in Old Goa; there would be a costume party, which Rahul might find amusing.

It hadn't been an entirely disappointing holiday for Rahul. His aunt was generous with her money, but she expected him to make his own contribution toward a much-discussed trip to London; Promila would help Rahul financially, but she wanted him to come up with *some* money of his own. There were several thousand Deutsche marks in Dieter's money belt, but Rahul had been expecting more – given the quality and the amount of hashish that Dieter had told everyone he wanted to buy. Of course, there *was* more, *much* more – in the dildo.

Promila thought that her nephew was interested in art school in London. She also knew he was seeking a *complete* sex change, and she knew such operations were expensive; given her loathing for men, Promila was delighted with her nephew's choice – to become her niece – but she was deluding herself if she thought that the strongest motivating factor behind Rahul's proposed move to London was 'art school.'

If the maid who cleaned Rahul's room had looked more carefully at the discarded drawings in the waste-basket, she could have told Promila that Rahul's talent with a pen was of a pornographic persuasion that most art schools would discourage. The self-portraits would have especially disturbed the maid, but all the discarded drawings were nothing but balled-up pieces of paper to her; she didn't trouble herself to examine them.

They were en route to the villa in Old Goa when Promila peered into Rahul's purse and saw Rahul's new, curious money clip; at least he was using it as a money clip – it was really nothing but the top half of a silver pen.

'My dear, you *are* eccentric!' Promila said. 'Why don't you get a *real* money clip, if you like those things?'

'Well, Auntie,' Rahul patiently explained, 'I find that real money clips are too loose, unless you carry a great *wad* of money in them. What I like is to carry just a few small notes outside my wallet – something handy to pay for a taxi, or for tipping.' He demonstrated that the top half of the silver pen possessed a very strong, tight clip – where it was meant to attach itself to a jacket pocket or a shirt pocket – and that this clip was perfect for holding just a few rupees. 'Besides, it's real silver,' Rahul added.

Promila held it in her veinous hand. 'Why so it is, dear,' she remarked. She read aloud the one word, in script, that was engraved on the top half of the pen: '*India* – isn't *that* quaint?'

'*I* certainly thought so,' Rahul remarked, returning the eccentric item to his purse.

Meanwhile, as Dr Daruwalla grew hungrier, he also grew more relaxed about his praying; he cautiously rekindled his sense of humor. After he'd eaten, Farrokh could almost joke about his conversion. 'I wonder what next the Almighty will ask of me!' he said to Julia, who once more cautioned her husband about blasphemy.

What was next in store for Dr Daruwalla would test his newfound faith in ways the doctor would find most disturbing. By the same means that Nancy had dis-covered the doctor's whereabouts, the police also discovered him. They'd found what everyone now called the 'hippie grave' and they needed a doctor to hazard a guess concerning the cause of death of the grave's ghastly occupants. They'd gone looking for a doctor on holiday. A *local* doctor would talk too much about the crime; at least this was what the local police told Dr Daruwalla.

'But I don't do autopsies!' Dr Daruwalla protested; yet he went to Anjuna to view the remains.

It was generally supposed that the blue crabs were the reason the bodies were spoiled for viewing; and if the salt water proved itself to be a modest preserv-ative, it did little to veil the stench. Farrokh easily concluded that several blows to the head had done them both in, but the female's body was messier. Her forearms and the backs of her hands were battered, which suggested that she'd tried to defend herself; the male, clearly, had never known what hit him.

It was the elephant drawing that Farrokh would remember. The murdered girl's navel had been trans-formed to a winking eye; the opposing tusk had been flippantly raised, like the tipping of an imaginary hat. Short, childish lines indicated that the elephant's trunk was spraying – the 'water' fanning over the dead girl's pubic hair. Such intended mockery would remain with Dr Daruwalla for 20 years; the doctor would remember the little drawing too well.

When Farrokh saw the broken glass, he suffered only the slightest discomfort, and the feeling quickly passed. Back at the Hotel Bardez, he was unable to find the piece of glass he'd removed from the young woman's foot. And so what if the glass from the grave had matched? he thought. There were soda bottles everywhere. Besides, the police had already told him that the suspected murderer was a German male.

Farrokh thought that this theory suited the preju-dices of the local police – namely, that only a hippie from Europe or North America could possibly perform a double slaying and then trivialize the murders with a cartoonish drawing. Ironically, these killings and that drawing stimulated Dr Daruwalla's need to be more creative. He found himself fantasizing that *he* was a detective.

The doctor's success in the orthopedic field had given him certain commercial expectations; these considerations doubtless returned the doctor's imagination to that notion of himself as a screenwriter. No *one* movie could have satisfied Farrokh's suddenly insatiable creativity; nothing less than a series of movies, featuring the same detective, would do. Finally, that was how it happened. At the end of his holiday, on the ferry back to Bombay, Dr Daruwalla invented Inspector Dhar.

Farrokh was watching how the young women on board the ferry couldn't take their eyes off the beautiful John D. Suddenly, the doctor could envision the hero that these young women imagined when they looked at a young man like that. The excitement that Mr James Salter's example had inspired was already becoming a moment of the sexual past; it was becoming a part of the second honeymoon that Dr Daruwalla was leaving behind. To the doctor, murder and corruption spoke louder than art. And besides, what a career John D. might have!

It would never have occurred to Farrokh that the young woman with the big dildo had seen the same murder victims he had seen. But 20 years later, even the movie version of that drawing on Beth's belly would ring a bell with Nancy. How could it be a coincidence that the victim's naval was the elephant's winking eye, or that the opposing tusk was raised? In the movie, no pubic hair was shown, but those childish lines indicated to Nancy that the elephant's trunk was still spraying – like a showerhead, or like the nozzle of a hose.

Nancy would also remember the beautiful, unshock-able young man she'd been introduced to by Dr

Daruwalla. When she saw her first Inspector Dhar movie, Nancy would recall the first time she'd seen that knowing sneer. The future actor had been strong enough to carry her downstairs without apparent effort; the future movie star had been poised enough to unscrew the troublesome dildo without appearing to be appalled.

And all of this was what she meant when she left her uncompromising message on Dr Daruwalla's answering machine. 'I know who you really are, I know what you really do,' Nancy had informed the doctor. 'Tell the deputy commissioner – the *real* policeman. Tell him who you are. Tell him what you do,' Nancy had instructed the secret screenwriter, for she'd figured out who Inspector Dhar's creator was.

Nancy knew that no one could have imagined the movie version of that drawing on Beth's belly; Inspector Dhar's creator had to have seen what *she* had seen. And the handsome John D., who now passed himself off as Inspector Dhar – that young man would never have been invited to view the murder victims. That would have been the doctor's job. Therefore, Nancy knew that Dhar hadn't created himself; Inspector Dhar had also been the doctor's job.

Dr Daruwalla was confused. He remembered introducing Nancy to John D., and how gallantly John D. had carried the heavy young woman downstairs. Had Nancy seen an Inspector Dhar movie, or all of them? Had she recognized the more mature John D.? Fine; but how had she made the imaginative leap that the doctor was Dhar's creator? And how could she know 'the *real* policeman,' as she called him? Dr Daruwalla could only assume that she meant Deputy Commissioner Patel. Of course, the doctor didn't realize that Nancy had known Detective Patel for 20 years – not to mention that she was married to him.

The Doctor and His Patient Are Reunited

One might recall that Dr Daruwalla had all this time been sitting in his bedroom in Bombay, where the doctor was alone again. Julia had at last left him sitting there; she'd gone to apologize to John D. – and to be sure that their supper was still warm enough to eat. Dr Daruwalla knew it was an unprecedented rudeness to have kept his favorite young man waiting, but in the light of Nancy's phone message, the doctor felt compelled to speak to D.C.P. Patel. The subject that the deputy commissioner wished to discuss in private with Dr Daruwalla was only a part of what prompted the doctor to make the call; of more interest to Farrokh was where Nancy was now and why she knew 'the *real* policeman.'

Given the hour, Dr Daruwalla phoned Detective Patel at home. Farrokh was thinking that there were Patels all over Gujarat; there were many Patels in Africa, too. He knew both a hotel-chain Patel and a department-store Patel in Nairobi. He was thinking he knew only *one* Patel who was a policeman, when – as luck would have it – Nancy answered the phone. All she said was, 'Hello,' but the one word was sufficient for Farrokh to recognize her voice. Dr Daruwalla was too confused to speak, but his silence was all the identification that Nancy needed.

'Is that the doctor?' she asked in her familiar fashion.

Dr Daruwalla supposed it would be stupid of him to hang up, but for a moment he couldn't imagine what else to do. He knew from the surprising experience of his long and happy marriage to Julia that there was no understanding what drew or held people together. If the doctor had known that the relationship between Nancy and Detective Patel was deeply connected to the dildo, he would have admitted that his understanding of sexual attraction and compatibility was even less than he supposed. The doctor suspected some elements of interracial interest on the part of both parties

348

– Farrokh and Julia had surely felt this. And in the curious case of Nancy and Deputy Commissioner Patel, Dr Daruwalla also guessed that Nancy's bad-girl appearance possibly concealed a good-girl heart; the doctor could easily imagine that Nancy had *wanted* a cop. As for what had attracted the deputy commissioner to Nancy, Farrokh tended to overestimate the value of a light complexion; after all, he adored the fairness of Julia's skin, and Julia wasn't even a blonde. What the doctor's research for the Inspector Dhar movies had failed to uncover was a characteristic common to many policemen – a love of confession. Poor Vijay Patel was prone to enjoy the confessing of crimes, and Nancy had held nothing back. She'd begun by handing him the dildo.

'You were right,' she'd told him. 'It unscrews. Only it was sealed with wax. I didn't know it came apart. I didn't know what was in it. But look what I brought into the country,' she said. As Inspector Patel counted the Deutsche marks, Nancy kept talking. 'There was more,' she said, 'but Dieter spent some, and some of it was stolen.' After a short pause, she added, 'There were two murders, but just one drawing.' Then she told him absolutely everything, beginning with the football players. People have fallen in love for stranger reasons.

Meanwhile, still waiting for the doctor's answer on the telephone, Nancy grew impatient. 'Hello?' she said. 'Is anyone there? *Is that the doctor?'* she repeated.

A born procrastinator, Dr Daruwalla nevertheless knew that Nancy wouldn't be denied; still, he didn't like to be bullied. Countless stupid remarks came to the closet screenwriter's mind; they were smart-ass, tough-guy wisecracks – the usual voice-over from old Inspector Dhar movies. ('Bad things had happened – worse things were happening. The woman was worth it – after all, she might know something. It was time to put all the cards on the table.') After a career of such glibness, it was hard for Dr Daruwalla to know what to say to Nancy. After 20 years, it was difficult to sound casual, but the doctor lamely tried.

'So – it's *you*!' he said.

On her end of the phone, Nancy just waited. It was as if she expected nothing less than a full confession. Farrokh felt he was being treated unfairly. Why should Nancy want to make him feel guilty? He should have known that Nancy's sense of humor wasn't easy to locate, but Dr Daruwalla foolishly kept trying to find it.

'So – how's the foot?' he asked her. 'All better?'

14. TWENTY YEARS

A Complete Woman, but
One Who Hates Women

The hollowness of the doctor's dumb joke contributed to an empty sound that the receiver made against his ear, for Nancy wasn't talking; her silence echoed, as if the phone call were transnational. Then Dr Daruwalla heard Nancy say to someone else, 'It's him.' Her voice was indistinct, although her effort to cover the mouthpiece with her hand had been halfhearted. Farrokh couldn't have known how 20 years had stolen the enthusiasm from many of Nancy's efforts.

And yet, 20 years ago, she'd reintroduced herself to young Inspector Patel with admirable resolve, not only presenting the policeman with the dildo and the sordid particulars of Dieter's crimes, but strengthening her confession with her intention to change. Nancy said she sought a life of righting wrongs, and she declared the extent of her attraction to young Patel in such graphic terms that she gave the proper policeman pause. Also, as Nancy had anticipated, she managed to give the inspector pangs of the severest desire, which he wouldn't act upon, for he was both a highly professional detective and a gentleman – neither an oafish football player nor a jaded European. If the physical attraction that drew Nancy and Inspector Patel together was ever to be acted upon, Nancy knew that *she* would need to initiate the contact.

Although she trusted that, in the end, she would marry the idealistic detective, certain conditions beyond her control contributed to Nancy's delay of the matter. For example, there was the distress caused by the disappearance of Rahul. As a most recent and eager

351

convert to the pursuit of justice, Nancy was deeply disappointed that Rahul could not be found. The allegedly murderous zenana, who'd only briefly achieved a legendary status in the brothel area of Bombay, had vanished from Falkland Road and Grand Road and Kamathipura. Also, Inspector Patel discovered that the transvestite known as Pretty had always been an outsider; the hijras hated him – the few who knew him – and his fellow zenanas hated him, too.

Rahul had sold his services for an uncommonly high price, but what he sold was merely his appearance; his good looks, which were the result of his outstanding femininity in juxtaposition to his dominating physical size and strength, made him an attractive showpiece for any transvestite brothel. Once a customer was lured into the brothel by Rahul's presence, the other zenanas – or the hijras – were the only transvestites who made themselves available for sexual contact. Hence there was to his nickname, Pretty, both an honest appraisal of his powers to attract and a disparagement of his character; for, by his refusal to do more than display himself, Rahul brandished a high-mindedness that insulted the transvestite prostitutes.

They could see he was indifferent to the offense he caused; he was also too big and strong and confident for them to threaten. The hijras hated him because he was a zenana; his fellow zenanas hated him because he'd told them he intended to make himself 'complete.' But *all* the transvestite prostitutes hated Rahul because he wasn't a prostitute.

There prevailed some nasty rumors about Rahul, although any evidence of these allegations eluded Inspector Patel. Some transvestite prostitutes claimed that Rahul frequented a female brothel in Kamathipura; it further outraged the transvestites to imagine that, when Rahul chose to advertise himself in *their* brothels on Falkland Road and Grant Road, he was in reality merely slumming. Also, there were ugly stories concerning how Rahul made use of the female prostitutes in Kamathipura; it was claimed that he never had sex with the girls but that he beat them. There was mention of a flexible rubber billy stick. If these rumors were true, the beaten girls would have nothing but raised red welts to show for their pain; such marks faded quickly and were thought to be insubstantial in comparison to broken bones or the deeper, darker discolorations of those bruises inflicted by a harder weapon. There was no legal recourse for the girls who might have suffered such beatings; whoever Rahul was, he was smart. Shortly after murdering Dieter and Beth, he was also out of the country.

Inspector Patel suspected that Rahul had left India. This was no consolation to Nancy; having chosen goodness over evil, she anticipated resolution. It was a pity that Nancy would wait 20 years for a simple but informative conversation with Dr Daruwalla which would reveal to them both that they'd made acquaintance with the *same* Rahul. However, not even a detective as dogged as D.C.P. Patel could have been expected to guess that a sexually altered killer might have been found at the Duckworth Club. Moreover, for 15 years, Rahul would *not* have been found there – at least not very often. He was more frequently in London, where, after the lengthy and painful completion of his sex-change operation, he was able to give more of his energy and concentration to what he called his art. Alas . . . no excess of energy or concentration would much expand his talent or his range; the cartoon quality of his belly drawings persisted. His tendency toward sexually explicit caricature endured.

It was thematic with Rahul – an inappropriately mirthful elephant with one tusk raised, one eye winking, and water spraying from the end of its downward-pointing trunk. The size and shape of the victims' navels afforded the artist a considerable variety of winking eyes; the amount and color of the victims' pubic hair also varied. The water from the elephant's trunk was constant; the elephant sprayed, with seeming indifference, over all. Many of the murdered prostitutes had shaved their pubic hair; the elephant appeared not to notice, or not to care.

But it wasn't only that his imagination was sexually perverse, for within Rahul a veritable war was being waged over the true identity of his sexual self, which, to his astonishment, was not appreciably clarified by the successful completion of his long-awaited sex change. Now Rahul was to all appearances a woman; if he couldn't bear children, it had never been the desire to bear children that had compelled him to become a her. However, it was Rahul's illusion that a new sexual identity could provide a lasting peace of mind.

Rahul had loathed being a man. In the company of homosexuals, he'd never felt he was one of them, either. But he'd experienced little closeness with his fellow transvestites; in the company of hijras or zenanas, Rahul had felt both different and superior. It didn't occur to him that they were content to be what they were – Rahul had never been content. There's more than one way to be a third gender; but Rahul's uniqueness was inseparable from his viciousness, which extended even toward his fellow transvestites.

He detested the all-too-womanly gestures of most hijras and zenanas; he thought the mischief with which they dressed indicated an all-too-womanly frivolity. As for the traditional powers of the hijras to bless or to curse, Rahul had no belief that they possessed such powers; he believed they tended to parade themselves, either for the smug amusement of boring heterosexuals or for the titillation of more conventional homosexuals. In the homosexual community, at least there were those few – like Subodh, Rahul's late brother – who defiantly stood out; they advertised their sexual orientation *not* for the entertainment of the timid but in order to discomfort the intolerant. Yet Rahul imagined that even those homosexuals who were as bold as Subodh were vulnerable to how slavishly they sought the affections of other homosexuals. Rahul had hated how girlishly Subodh had allowed himself to be dominated by Neville Eden.

Rahul had imagined that it was only as a woman that *she* could dominate both women and men. He'd also imagined that being a woman would make him envy other women less, or not at all; he'd even thought that his desire to hurt and humiliate women would somehow *evanesce*. He was unprepared for how he would continue to hate them and desire to do them harm; prostitutes – and other women of what he presumed to be loose behavior – especially offended him, in part because of how lightly they regarded their sexual favors, and how they took for granted their sexual parts, which Rahul had been forced to acquire through such perseverance and pain.

Rahul had put himself through the rigors of what he believed was necessary to make him happy; yet he still raged. Like some (but fortunately few) *real* women, Rahul was contemptuous of those men who sought his attention, while at the same time he strongly desired those men who remained indifferent to his obvious beauty. And this was only half his problem; the other half was that his need to kill certain women was surprisingly (to him) unchanged. And after he'd strangled or bludgeoned them – he favored the latter form of execution – he couldn't resist creating his signature work of art upon their flaccid bellies; the soft stomach of a dead woman was Rahul's preferred medium, his canvas of choice.

Beth had been the first; killing Dieter was unmemorable to Rahul. But the spontaneity with which he'd struck down Beth and the utter unresponsiveness of her abdomen to the dhobi pen were stimulations so extreme that Rahul continued to yield to them.

In this sense was his tragedy compounded, for his sex change had not enabled him to view other women as companionable human beings. And because Rahul still hated women, he knew he'd failed to become a woman at all. Further isolating him, in London, was the fact that Rahul also loathed his fellow transsexuals. Before his operation, he'd suffered countless psychological interviews; obviously, they were superficial, for Rahul had managed to convey an utter lack of sexual anger. He'd observed that friendliness, which he interpreted as an impulse toward a cloying kind of sympathy, impressed the evaluating psychiatrist and the sex therapist.

There were meetings with other would-be transsexuals, both those applying for the operation and those in the more advanced phase of 'training' for the post-operative women they would soon become. Complete transsexuals also attended these agonizing meetings. It was supposed to be encouraging to socialize with complete transsexuals, just to see what real women they were. This was nauseating to Rahul, who hated it when anyone dared to suggest that he or she was like him; Rahul knew that he wasn't 'like' anyone.

It appalled him that these *complete* transsexuals even shared the names and phone numbers of former boyfriends. These were men, they said, who weren't at all repulsed by women 'like us' – possibly these interesting men were even attracted by them. What a concept! Rahul thought. He wasn't becoming a woman in order to become a member of some transsexual *club*; if the operation was complete, no one would ever know that Rahul had not been born a woman.

But there was one who knew: Aunt Promila. She'd been such a supporter. Gradually, Rahul resented how she sought to control him. She would continue her most generous financial assistance to his life in London, but only if he promised not to forget her – only if he would come pay some attention to her from time to time. Rahul wasn't opposed to these periodic visits to Bombay; he was merely annoyed that his aunt manipulated how often and when he traveled to see her. And as she grew older, she grew more needy; shamelessly, and frequently, she referred to Rahul's elevated status in her will.

Even with Promila's considerable influence, it took Rahul longer to legalize his change of name than it had taken him to change his sex – in spite of the bribes. And although there were many other women's names that he preferred, it was politic of him to choose Promila, which greatly pleased his aunt and assured him an indeed favorable position in her much-mentioned will. Nevertheless, the new name on the new passport left Rahul feeling incomplete. Perhaps he felt that he could never *be* Promila Rai as long as his Aunt Promila was alive. Since Promila was the only person on earth whom Rahul loved, it made him feel guilty that he grew impatient with how long he had to wait for her to die.

Remembering Aunt Promila

He was five or six, or maybe only four; Rahul could never remember. What he did recall was that he thought he was old enough to be going to the men's room by himself. Aunt Promila took him to the ladies' room – she took him with her into the toilet stall, too. He'd told her that there were urinals in the men's room and that the men stood up to pee.

'I know a better way to pee,' she'd told him.

At the Duckworth Club, the ladies' room suffered from an elephant motif; in the men's room, the tiger-hunt decor was far less obtrusive. For example, in the ladies' room toilet stalls, there was a pull-down platform on the inside of the stall door. It was simply a shelf that folded flat against the door when not in use. By means of a handle, the shelf could be pulled down; on this platform, a lady could put her handbag – or whatever else she took with her into the toilet stall. The handle was a ring that passed like an earring through the base of an elephant's trunk.

Promila would lift her skirt and pull down her panties; then she sat on the toilet seat, and Rahul –

who'd also pulled down his pants and his underpants – would sit on her lap.

'Pull down the elephant, dear,' Aunt Promila would tell him, and Rahul would lean forward until he could reach the ring through the elephant's trunk. The elephant had no tusks; Rahul found the elephant generally lacking in realism – for example, there was no opening at the end of the elephant's trunk.

First Promila peed, then Rahul. He sat on his aunt's lap, listening to her. When she wiped herself, he could feel the back of her hand against his bare bum. Then she would reach into his lap and point his little penis down into the toilet. It was difficult for him to pee from her lap.

'Don't miss,' she'd whisper in his ear. 'Are you being careful?' Rahul tried to be careful. When he was finished, Aunt Promila wiped his penis with some toilet paper. Then she felt his penis with her bare hand. 'Let's be sure you're dry, dear', Promila would say to him. She always held him until his penis was stiff. 'What a big boy you are,' she'd whisper.

When they were finished, they washed their hands together.

'The hot water is too hot – it will burn you,' Aunt Promila would warn him. Together they stood at the wildly ornate sink. There was a single faucet in the form of an elephant's head. The water flowed through the elephant's trunk, emerging in a broad spray. You lifted one tusk for the hot water, the other tusk for the cold. 'Just the cold water, dear,' Aunt Promila told him. She let Rahul operate the faucet for both of them; he would raise and lower the tusk for cold water – just one tusk. 'Always wash your hands, dear,' Aunt Promila would say.

'Yes, Auntie,' Rahul answered. He'd supposed his aunt's preference for cold water was a sign of her age; she must have remembered a time before there was hot water.

When he was older, maybe 8 or 9 – he could have

been 10 – Promila sent him to see Dr Lowji Daruwalla. She was concerned with what she called Rahul's inexplicable hairlessness – or so she told the doctor. In retrospect, Rahul realized that he'd disappointed his aunt – and on more than one occasion. Promila's disappointment, Rahul also realized, was sexual; his so-called hairlessness had little to do with it. But there was no way for Promila Rai to complain about the size or the short-lived stiffness of her nephew's penis – certainly not to Dr Lowji Daruwalla! The question of whether or not Rahul was impotent would have to wait until Rahul was 12 or 13; at that time, the examining physician would be old Dr Tata.

In retrospect, Rahul would realize that his aunt was chiefly interested in knowing whether he was impotent or merely impotent with *her*. Naturally, she'd not told Tata that she was having a repeatedly disappointing sexual experience with Rahul; she'd implied that Rahul himself was concerned because he'd failed to maintain an erection with a prostitute. Dr Tata's response had been disappointing to Aunt Promila, too.

'Perhaps it was the prostitute,' old Dr Tata had replied.

Years later, when he thought of his Aunt Promila, Rahul would remember that. Perhaps it was the prostitute, he would think to himself; possibly he'd not been impotent after all. All things considered, now that Rahul was a woman, what did it really matter? He sincerely loved his Aunt Promila. As for washing his hands, the memory of the elephant with one tusk raised would never be lost on Rahul; but he preferred to wash his hands in hot water.

A Childless Couple Searches for Rahul

With hindsight, it is impressive how Deputy Commissioner Patel fathomed Rahul's attachment to family money – in India. The detective thought that a well-to-do relative might explain the killer's few but periodic visits to Bombay. For 15 years, the victims who were decorated with the winking elephant were prostitutes from the Kamathipura brothels or from the brothels on Grant Road and Falkland Road. Their murders occurred in groups of two or three, within two or three weeks' time, and then not again for nearly nine months or a year. There were no murders recorded in the hottest months, just before the monsoon, or during the monsoon itself; the murderer struck at a more comfortable time of the year. Only the first two murders, in Goa, were hot-weather murders.

Detective Patel could find no evidence of murders with elephant drawings in any other Indian city; this was why he had concluded that the killer lived abroad. It wasn't hard to uncover the relatively few murders of this nature in London; although these weren't restricted to the Indian community, the victims were always prostitutes or students – the latter, usually of an artistic inclination, were reputed to have lived in a bohemian or otherwise unconventional way. The more he studied the murderer, and the more deeply he loved Nancy, the more the deputy commissioner realized that Nancy was lucky to be alive.

But with the passage of time, Nancy less and less wore the countenance of a woman who felt herself to be lucky. The Deutsche marks in the dildo – such an excessive amount that, at first, both Nancy and young Inspector Patel had felt quite liberated – were the beginning of Nancy and Patel's feeling that they had been compromised. It made only the smallest dent in the sum for Nancy to send what she'd stolen from the hardware store to her parents. It was, she thought, the best way to erase the past, but her newfound crusade for justice interfered with the purity of her intention. The money was to repay the hardware store, but in sending it to her parents she couldn't resist naming those men (in feed-and-grain supply) who'd made her feel like dirt. If her parents wanted to repay the store after knowing what had happened to their daughter there, that would be *their* decision.

Thus she created a moral dilemma for her parents, which had quite the opposite effect from what Nancy desired. She had *not* erased the past; she'd brought it to life in her parents' eyes, and for almost 20 years (until they died), her parents faithfully described their on-going torment in Iowa to her – all the while begging her to come 'home' but refusing to come visit her. It was never clear to Nancy what they finally did with the money.

As for young Inspector Patel, it made a similarly small dent in the sum of Dieter's Deutsche marks for the previously uncorrupted policeman to engage in his first and last bribe. It was simply the usual and necessary sum required for promotion, for a more lucrative posting – and one must remember that Vijay Patel was not a Maharashtrian. For a Gujarati to make the move from an inspector at the Colaba Station to a deputy commissioner in Crime Branch Headquarters at Crawford Market required what is called greasing the wheel. But – over the years, and in combination with his failure to find Rahul – the bribe had etched itself into a part of the deputy commissioner's vulner-able self-esteem. It had been a reasonable expense, certainly not a lavish amount of money; and contrary to the infuriating fiction represented by the Inspector Dhar movies, there was no significant advancement within the Bombay police force without a *little* bribery.

And although Nancy and the detective were a love story, they were unhappy. It wasn't only that the sheer grimness of serving justice had grown to be a task, nor was it simply that Rahul had escaped unpunished. Both Mr and Mrs Patel assumed that a higher judgment had been made against them; for Nancy was infertile, and they'd spent nearly a decade learning the reason – and then another decade, first trying to adopt a child and finally deciding against adoption.

In the first decade of their efforts to conceive a child, both Nancy and young Patel – she called him Vijay – believed that they were being punished for dipping into the Deutsche marks. Nancy had entirely forgotten a brief period of physical discomfort upon her return to Bombay with the dildo. A slight burning in her urethra and the appearance in her underwear of an insignificant vaginal discharge had contributed to Nancy's delay in initiating a sexual relationship with Vijay Patel. The symptoms were mild, and they over-lapped, to some degree, with cystitis (inflammation of the bladder) and urinary tract infection. She didn't want to imagine that Dieter had given her something venereal, although her memory of that brothel in Kamathipura, and how familiarly Dieter had spoken with the madam, gave Nancy good reason to be worried.

Moreover, at the time, she could plainly see that she and young Patel were falling in love with each other; she wasn't about to ask *him* to recommend a suitable physician. Instead, in that well-worn travel guide, which she still faithfully carried, was an on-the-road recipe for a douche; but she misread the proper proportion of vinegar and gave herself much worse burning than she began with. For a week, there was an even yellower stain in her underwear, which she ascribed to the unwise remedy of her homemade douche. As for the abdominal pain, it closely attended the onset of her period, which was unusually heavy; she had much cramping and even a little chill. She wondered if her body was trying to reject the IUD. And then she completely recovered; she only remembered this episode 10 years later. She was sitting with her husband in the office of a fancy private venereologist, and – with Vijay's help – she was filling out a detailed questionnaire; it was part of the infertility work.

What had happened was that Dieter had given her a dose of gonorrhea, which he'd caught from the 13-year-old prostitute he'd fucked standing up in the hall of that brothel in Kamathipura. It hadn't been true, as the madam had told him, that there were no available cubicles with mattresses or cots; instead, it was the young prostitute's request to have sex standing up, for her case of gonorrhea had advanced to the more uncomfortable symptoms of pelvic inflammatory disease. She was suffering from the so-called chandelier sign, where moving the cervix up and down elicits pain in the tubes and ovaries; in short, it hurt her to have a man's weight pounding on her belly. It was better for her when she stood up.

As for Dieter, he was a fastidious young German who gave himself a shot of penicillin before he left the brothel; a medical student among his friends had told him that this worked well to prevent incubating syphilis. The injection, however, did nothing to abort the pencillinase-producing *Neisseria gonorrhea*. No one had told him that these strains were endemic in the tropics. Besides, less than a week after his contact with the infected prostitute, Dieter was murdered; he'd begun to notice only the slightest symptoms.

And what relatively mild symptoms Nancy had experienced before her spontaneous healing and the scarring were the result of the inflammation spreading from her cervix to the lining of her uterus and her tubes. When the venereologist explained to Mr and Mrs Patel that this was the cause of Nancy's infertility, the distraught couple firmly believed that Dieter's nasty disease – even from the hippie grave – was final proof of the judgment against them. They should never have taken a pfennig of those dirty Deutsche marks in the dildo.

In their ensuing efforts to adopt a child, their experience was not uncommon. The better adoption agencies, which kept prenatal records as well as a history of the natural mother's health, were uncharitable on the issue of their 'mixed' marriage; this wouldn't have deterred the Patels in the end, but it prolonged the process of humiliating interviews and the swamp of petty paperwork. In the interim, while they awaited approval, first Nancy and then Vijay expressed whatever slight doubts they both felt about the disappointment of adopting a child when they'd hoped to have one of their own. If they'd been able to adopt a child quickly, they would have begun to love it before their doubts could have mounted; but in the extended period of waiting, they lost their nerve. It wasn't that they believed they would have loved an adopted child insufficiently; it was that they believed the judgment against them would condemn the child to some unbearable fate.

They'd done something wrong. They were paying for it. They wouldn't ask a child to pay for it, too. And so the Patels accepted childlessness; after almost 15 years of expecting a child, this acceptance came to them at considerable cost. In the way they walked, in the detectable lethargy with which they raised their many cups and glasses of tea, they reflected their own consciousness of this resignation to their fate. About that time, Nancy went to work – first in one of the adoption agencies that had so rigorously interviewed her, then as a volunteer in an orphanage. It wasn't the sort of work she could sustain for very long – it made her think of the child she'd given up in Texas.

And, after 15 years or so, D.C.P. Patel began to believe that Rahul had come back to Bombay, this time to stay. The murders were now evenly spaced over the calendar year; in London, the killings had altogether stopped. What had happened was that Rahul's Aunt Promila had finally died, and her estate on old Ridge Road – not to mention the considerable allowance she'd bestowed upon her only *niece* – had passed into the hands of her namesake, the former Rahul. He had become Promila's heir, or – to be more anatomically correct – *she* had become Promila's *heiress*. And the *new* Promila had not long to wait for her acceptance at the Duckworth Club, where her aunt had faithfully made application for her niece's membership – even before she technically had a niece.

This niece was slow and deliberate about her entry into that society which the Duckworth Club would offer her; she was in no hurry to be seen. Some Duckworthians, upon meeting her, found her a touch crude – and almost all Duckworthians agreed that, although she must have been a great beauty in her prime, she was rather well advanced into that phase called middle age . . . especially for someone who'd never been married. That struck nearly everyone as odd, but before there was time for much talk about it, the *new* Promila Rai – with surprising swiftness, considering that hardly anyone really knew her – was engaged to be married. And to another Duckworthian, an elderly gentleman of such sizable wealth that *his* estate on old Ridge Road was rumored to put the late Promila's place to shame! It was no surprise that the wedding was held at the Duckworth Club, but it was too bad that the wedding took place at a time when Dr Daruwalla was in Toronto, for he – or certainly Julia – might have recognized this *new* Promila who'd so successfully passed herself off as the *old* Promila's niece.

By the time the Daruwallas and Inspector Dhar were back in Bombay, the new Promila Rai was identified by her married name – actually by two names, one of which was never used to her face. Rahul, who'd become Promila, had lately become the beautiful Mrs Dogar, as old Mr Sethna usually addressed her.

Yes, *of course* – the former Rahul was none other than the second Mrs Dogar, and each time Dr Daruwalla felt the stab of pain in his ribs, where she'd collided with him in the foyer of the Duckworth Club, he mistakenly searched his forgetful mind for those now-faded film stars he saw over and over again on so many of his favorite videos. Farrokh would never find her there. Rahul wasn't hiding in the old movies.

The Police Know the Movie Is Innocent

Just when Deputy Commissioner Patel had decided that he would never find Rahul, there was released in Bombay another predictably dreadful Inspector Dhar film. The real policeman had no desire to be further insulted; but when he learned what *Inspector Dhar and the Cage-Girl Killer* was about, the deputy commissioner not only went to see the film – he took Nancy to see it with him the second time. There could be no doubt regarding the source of that elephant drawing. Nancy was sure she knew where the jaunty little elephant had come from. No *two* minds could imagine a dead woman's navel as a winking eye; even in the movie version, the elephant raised just one tusk – it was always the same tusk, too. And the water spraying from the elephant's trunk – who would think of such a thing? Nancy had wondered, for 20 years. A *child* might think of such a thing, the deputy commissioner had told her.

The police had never given out such details to the press; the police preferred to keep their business to themselves – they'd not even informed the public about the existence of such an artistic serial killer. People often killed prostitutes. Why invite the press to sensationalize the presence of a single fiend? So, in truth, the police – most especially Detective Patel – *knew* that these murders had long predated the release of such a fantasy as *Inspector Dhar and the Cage-Girl Killer.* The movie merely drew the public's attention to the real murders. The media assumed, wrongly, that the movie was to blame.

It had been Deputy Commissioner Patel's idea to allow the misunderstanding to pass; the deputy commissioner wanted to see if the movie might inspire some jealousy on the part of Rahul, for the detective was of the opinion that, if his wife recognized the source of the inspiration of Inspector Dhar's creator, so would the real murderer. The killing of Mr Lal –

especially the interesting two-rupee note in his mouth – indicated that the deputy commissioner had been right. Rahul must have seen the movie – assuming that *Rahul* wasn't the screenwriter.

What puzzled the detective was that the note said MORE MEMBERS DIE IF DHAR REMAINS A MEMBER. Since Nancy had been smart enough to figure out that only a doctor would have been shown Beth's decorated body, surely Rahul would know as well that it wasn't Dhar himself who'd seen one of Rahul's works of art; it could only be the doctor who was so frequently in Dhar's company.

The matter that Detective Patel wished to speak of with Dr Daruwalla in private was simply this. The detective wanted the doctor to confirm Nancy's theories – that he was Dhar's true creator and had seen the drawing on Beth's belly. But the deputy commissioner also wanted to warn Dr Daruwalla. MORE MEMBERS DIE . . . this could mean that the doctor might be Rahul's future target. Detective Patel and Nancy believed that Farrokh was a more likely target than Dhar himself.

On the telephone, such complicated news took time for the policeman to deliver and for the doctor to comprehend. And since Nancy had passed the telephone to her husband, that element of the real murderer being a transvestite, or even a thoroughly convincing *woman*, wasn't a part of Detective Patel's conversation with Farrokh. Unfortunately, the name Rahul was never mentioned. It was simply agreed that Dr Daruwalla would come to Crime Branch Headquarters, where the deputy commissioner would show him photographs of the elephants drawn on the murdered women – this for the sake of mere confirmation – and that both Dhar and the doctor should exercise extreme caution. The real murderer had seemingly been provoked by *Inspector Dhar and the Cage-Girl Killer* – if not exactly in the way that the public and many angry prostitutes believed.

367

A View of Two Marriages at a
Vulnerable Hour

As soon as Dr Daruwalla hung up the phone, he carried his agitation to the dinner table, where Roopa apologized for the utter deterioration of the mutton, which was her way of saying that this mushy meat in her beloved dhal was all the doctor's fault, which of course it was. Dhar then asked the doctor if he'd read the new hate mail – Farrokh had not. A pity, John D. said, because it might well be the last of the mail from those infuriated prostitutes. Balraj Gupta, the director, had informed John D. that the new Inspector Dhar movie (*Inspector Dhar and the Towers of Silence*) was being released tomorrow. After that, John D. said ironically, the hate mail would most likely be from all the offended Parsis.

'Tomorrow!' cried Dr Daruwalla.

'Well, actually, after midnight tonight,' Dhar said.

Dr Daruwalla should have known. Whenever Balraj Gupta called him and asked to discuss with him something that the director wanted to do, it invariably meant that the director had already done it.

'But no more of this trivia!' Farrokh said to his wife and John D. The doctor took a deep breath; then he informed them of everything that Deputy Commissioner Patel had told him.

All Julia asked was, 'How many murders has this killer managed – how many victims are there?'

'Sixty-nine,' said Dr Daruwalla. Julia's gasp was less surprising than John D.'s inappropriate calm.

'Does that count Mr Lal?' Dhar asked.

'Mr Lal makes seventy – *if* Mr Lal is truly connected,' Farrokh replied.

'Of course he's *connected*,' said Inspector Dhar, which irritated Dr Daruwalla in the usual way. Here was his fictional creation once again sounding like an authority; but what Farrokh failed to acknowledge was that Dhar was a good and well-trained actor. Dhar had

faithfully studied the role and taken many com-
ponents of the part into himself; instinctually, he'd
become quite a good detective – Dr Daruwalla had
only made up the character. Dhar's character was an
utter fiction to Farrokh, who could scarcely remember
his research on various aspects of police work from
screenplay to screenplay; Dhar, on the other hand,
rarely forgot either these finer points or his less-
than-original lines. As a screenwriter, Dr Daruwalla
was at best a gifted amateur, but Inspector Dhar was
closer to the real thing than either Dhar or his creator
knew.

'May I go with you to see the photographs?' Dhar
asked his creator.

'I believe that the deputy commissioner wished me
to see them privately,' the doctor replied.

'I'd like to see them, Farrokh,' John D. said.

'He should see them if he wants to!' Julia snapped.

'I'm not sure the police would agree,' Dr Daruwalla
began to say, but Inspector Dhar gave a most familiar
and dismissive wave of his hand, a perfect gesture of
contempt. Farrokh felt his exhaustion draw close to
him – like old friends and family gathering around his
imagined sickbed.

When John D. retired to the balcony to sleep, Julia
was quick to change the subject – even before Farrokh
had managed to undress for bed.

'You didn't *tell* him!' she cried.

'Oh, please stop it about the damnable *twin* business!' he said to her. 'What makes you think that's such
a priority? Especially now!'

'I think that the arrival of his twin might be *more*
of a priority to John D.,' Julia remarked decisively.
She left her husband alone in the bedroom while she
used the bathroom. Then, after Farrokh had had his
turn in the bathroom, he noted that Julia had already
fallen asleep – or else she was pretending to be
asleep.

At first he tried to sleep on his side, which was his

usual preference, but in that position he was conscious of the soreness in his ribs; on his stomach, the pain was more evident. Flat on his back – where he struggled in vain to fall asleep, and where he was inclined to snore – he wracked his overexcited brain for the precise image of the movie actress he was sure he was reminded of when he'd shamelessly stared at the second Mrs Dogar. Despite himself, he grew sleepy. The names of actresses came to and left his lips. He saw Neelam's full mouth, and Rekha's nice mouth, too; he thought of Sridevi's mischievous smile – and almost everything there was to think about Sonu Walia, too. Then he half-waked himself and thought, No, no . . . it's no one contemporary, and she's probably not even Indian. Jennifer Jones? he wondered. Ida Lupino? Rita Moreno? Dorothy Lamour! No, no . . . what was he thinking? It was someone whose beauty was much more cruel than the beauty of any of these. This insight nearly woke him. Had he awakened simultaneously with the reminder caused by the pain in his ribs, he might have got it. But although the hour was now late, it was still too soon for him to know.

There was more communication in the marriage bed of Mr and Mrs Patel at this very same late hour. Nancy was crying; her tears, as they often were, were a mix of misery and frustration. Deputy Commissioner Patel was trying, as he often did, to be comforting.

Nancy had suddenly remembered what had happened to her – maybe two weeks after the last of her symptoms of gonorrhea had disappeared. She'd broken out in a terrible rash, red and sore and with unbearable itching, and she'd assumed that this was a new phase of something venereal she'd caught from Deiter. Furthermore, there was no hiding *this* phase from her beloved policeman; young Inspector Patel had straightaway brought her to a doctor, who informed her that she'd been taking too many antimalarial pills – she was simply suffering from an allergic reaction. But how this had frightened her! And she only now remembered the goats.

For all these years, she'd thought about the goats in the brothels, but she'd not remembered how she'd first feared that it was something from the goats that had given her such a hideous rash and such uncontrollable itching. That had been her worst fear. For 20 years, when she'd thought about those brothels and the women who'd been murdered there, she'd forgotten the men Dieter had told her about – the terrible men who fucked goats. Maybe Dieter had fucked goats, too. No wonder she'd at least *tried* to forget this.

'But nobody is fucking those goats,' Vijay just now informed her.

'What?' Nancy said.

'Well, I don't presume to know about the United States – or even about certain rural areas of India – but no one in Bombay is fucking goats,' her husband assured her.

'What?' Nancy said. 'Dieter *told* me that they fucked the goats.'

'Well, it's not at all true,' the detective said. 'Those goats are pets. Of course some of them give milk. This is a bonus – for the children, I suppose. But they're pets, just pets.'

'Oh, Vijay!' Nancy cried. He had to hold her. 'Oh, Dieter *lied* to me!' she cried. 'Oh, how he lied to me . . . all those years I *believed* it! Oh, that *fucker*!' The word was so sharply spoken, it caused a dog in the alley below them to stop rooting through the garbage and bark. Over their heads, the ceiling fan barely stirred the close air, which seemed always to smell of the perpetually blocked drains, and of the sea, which in their neighborhood was not especially clean or fresh-smelling. 'Oh, it was another lie!' Nancy screamed. Vijay went on holding her, although to do so for long would make them both sweat. The air was unmoving where they lived.

The goats were just pets. Yet, for 20 years, what Dieter had told her had hurt her so badly; at times, it had made her physically sick. And the heat, and the sewer smell, and the fact that, whoever Rahul was, he was still getting away with it – all this Nancy had accepted, but in the fashion that she'd accepted her childlessness, which she'd accepted so slowly and only after what had felt to her like a lingering and merciless defeat.

What the Dwarf Sees

It was late. While Nancy cried herself to sleep and Dr Daruwalla failed to realize that the second and beautiful Mrs Dogar had reminded him of Rahul, Vinod was driving one of Mr Garg's exotic dancers home from the Wetness Cabaret.

She was a middle-aged Maharashtrian with the English name of Muriel – not her real name but her exotic-dancing name – and she was upset because one of the patrons of the Wetness Cabaret had thrown an orange at her while she was dancing. The clientele of the Wetness Cabaret was vile, Muriel had decided. Even so, she rationalized, Mr Garg was a gentleman. Garg had recognized that Muriel was upset by the episode with the orange; he'd personally engaged Vinod's 'luxury' taxi to drive Muriel home.

Although Vinod had praised Mr Garg's humanitarian efforts on behalf of runaway child prostitutes, the dwarf wouldn't have gone so far as to call Mr Garg a gentleman; possibly Garg was more of a gentleman with middle-aged women. With younger girls, Vinod wasn't sure. The dwarf didn't entirely share Dr Daruwalla's suspicions of Mr Garg, but Vinod and Deepa had occasionally encountered a child prostitute who seemed in need of rescuing *from* Garg. Save this poor child, Mr Garg seemed to be saying; save her from *me*, Garg might have meant.

It wouldn't have helped Vinod and Deepa's child-rescue operations to have Dr Daruwalla treating Garg like a criminal. The new runaway, the boneless one – a potential plastic lady – was a case in point. Although she'd appeared to be more personally involved with Mr Garg than she should have been, such implications wouldn't help her cause with Dr Daruwalla; the doctor had to pronounce her healthy or the Great Blue Nile wouldn't take her.

Vinod now noted that the middle-aged woman with the exotic-dancing name of Muriel had fallen asleep; she slept with a somewhat sour expression, her mouth disagreeably open and her hands resting on her fat breasts. The dwarf thought that it made more sense to throw an orange at her than it did to watch her dance. But Vinod's humanitarian instincts extended even to middle-aged strippers; he slowed down because the streets were bumpy, seeing no reason to wake the poor woman before she was home. In her sleep, Muriel suddenly cringed. She was ducking oranges, the dwarf imagined.

After Vinod dropped off Muriel, it was too late for him to go anywhere but back to the brothel area; the red-light district was the only part of Bombay where people needed a taxi at 2:00 in the morning. Soon the international travelers would be arriving at the Oberoi and the Taj, but no one who'd just flown in from Europe or North America would have the slightest inclination to cruise around the city.

Vinod thought he'd wait for the end of the last show at the Wetness Cabaret; one of Mr Garg's other exotic dancers might want a safe ride home. It amazed Vinod that the Wetness Cabaret, the building itself, was 'home' to Mr Garg; the dwarf couldn't imagine sleeping there. He supposed there were rooms upstairs, above the slick bar and the sticky tables and the sloping stage. Vinod shivered to think of the dimly lit bar, the bright lit stage, the darkened tables where the men sat – some of them masturbating, although the dominant odor of the Wetness Cabaret was one of urine. How could Garg sleep in such a place, even if he slept above it?

But as distasteful as it was to Vinod – to cruise the brothel area, as if he carried a potential customer in the Ambassador's back seat – the dwarf had decided that he might as well stay awake. Vinod was fascinated by that hour when most of the brothels switched over; in Kamathipura, on Falkland Road and Grant Road, there came an hour of the early morning when most of the brothels would accept only all-night customers. In the dwarf's opinion, these were different and desperate men. Who else would want to spend *all night* with a prostitute?

Vinod grew alert and edgy at this hour, as if – particularly in those little lanes in Kamathipura – he might spot a man who wasn't entirely human. When he got tired, the dwarf dozed in his car; his car was more home to him than home, at least when Deepa was away at the circus. And when he was bored, Vinod would cruise past the transvestite brothels on Falkland Road and Grant Road. Vinod liked the hijras; they were so bold and so outrageous – they also seemed to like dwarfs. Possibly the hijras thought that *dwarfs* were outrageous.

Vinod was aware that some of the hijras *didn't* like him; they were the ones who knew that the dwarf was Inspector Dhar's driver – the ones who hated *Inspector Dhar and the Cage-Girl Killer*. Lately, Vinod had to be a little careful in the brothel area; the prostitute murders had made Dhar *and* Dhar's dwarf more than a little unpopular. Thus that hour when most of the brothels 'switched over' made Vinod more alert and edgy than usual.

While he cruised, the dwarf was among the first to notice what had changed about Bombay; the change was being enacted before Vinod's very eyes. Gone was the movie poster of his most famous client, that larger-than-life image of Inspector Dhar which Vinod and all of Bombay had grown so used to – the huge hoardings, the overhead billboards that advertised *Inspector Dhar and the Cage-Girl Killer*. Dhar's handsome face, albeit bleeding slightly; the torn white shirt, open to expose Dhar's muscular chest; the pretty, ravaged young woman slung over Dhar's strong shoulder; and, always, the blue-gray semi-automatic pistol held in Dhar's hard right hand. In its place, everywhere in Bombay, was a brand-new poster. Vinod thought that only the semi-automatic was the same, although Inspector Dhar's sneer was remarkably familiar. *Inspector Dhar and the Towers of Silence;* this time, the young woman slung over Dhar's shoulder was noticeably dead – more noticeably, she was a Western hippie.

It was the only safe time to put the posters up; if people had been awake, they would doubtless have attacked the poster-wallas. The old posters in the brothel area had long ago been destroyed; tonight, perhaps, the prostitutes left the poster-wallas unharmed because the prostitutes were happy to see that *Inspector Dhar and the Cage-Girl Killer* was being replaced with a new offense – this time, to somebody else.

But, upon closer inspection, Vinod noted that not so much was different about the new poster as he'd first observed. The posture of the young woman over Dhar's shoulder was quite the same, alive or dead; and again, albeit from a slightly different spot, Inspector Dhar's cruel, handsome face was bleeding. The longer Vinod looked at the new poster, the more he found it to resemble the previous poster; it seemed to the dwarf that Dhar even wore the same torn shirt. This possibly explained why the dwarf had driven around Bombay for more than two hours before he'd noticed that a new Inspector Dhar film had been born into the world. Vinod couldn't wait to see it.

The unspeakable life of the red-light district teemed all around him – the bartering and the betrayals and the frightening, unseen beatings – or so the excited dwarf imagined. About the most hopeful thing that could be said is that throughout the brothel area of Bombay, no one – truly no one – was fucking a goat.

15. DHAR'S TWIN

Three Old Missionaries Fall Asleep

That week between Christmas and New Year's, when the first American missionary was due to arrive at St Ignatius in Mazagaon, the Jesuit mission prepared a celebration in honor of 1990. St Ignatius was a Bombay landmark; it would soon be 125 years old – in all these years, it had faithfully managed its holy and secular tasks without the assitance of an American. The management of St Ignatius was a threesome of responsibility, and these three had been almost as successful as the Blessed Trinity. The Father Rector (Father Julian, who was 68 years old and English), the senior priest (Father Cecil, who was 72 and Indian), and Brother Gabriel (who was around 75 and had fled Spain after the Civil War) were a triumvirate of authority that was seldom questioned and never overruled; they were also unanimous in their opinion that St Ignatius could continue to serve mankind and the heavenly kingdom without the aid of *any* American – yet one had been offered. To be sure, they would have preferred another Indian, or at least a European, but since these three wise men were of an average age of 71 years and eight months, they were attracted to one aspect of the 'young' scholastic, as they called him. At 39, Martin Mills was no kid. Only Dr Daruwalla would have judged 'young' Martin to be unsuitably old for a man who was still in training to be a priest. That the so-called scholastic was almost 40 was at least mildly comforting to Father Julian and Father Cecil and Brother Gabriel, although they shared the conviction that the mission's 125th jubilee was diminished by their obligation to welcome the former Californian, who was allegedly fond of Hawaiian shirts.

They knew of this laughable eccentricity from the otherwise impressive dossier of Martin Mills, whose letters of recommendation were glowing. However, the Father Rector said that when it came to Americans, one must read between the lines. For example, Father Julian pointed out, Martin Mills had evidently eschewed his native California, although nowhere in his dossier did it say so. He'd been schooled elsewhere in the United States and had taken a teaching job in Boston, which was about as far away from California as one could get. Clearly, said Father Julian, this indicated that Martin Mills had come from a troubled family. Perhaps it was his own mother or father whom he'd 'eschewed.'

And along with young Martin's unexplained attraction to the garish, which Father Julian concluded was the root cause of the scholastic's reported fondness for Hawaiian shirts, there was mention in the dossier of Martin Mills's success with apostolic work – even as a novice, and especially with young people. Bombay's St Ignatius was a good school, and Martin Mills was expected to be a good teacher; most of the students weren't Catholics – many weren't even Christians. 'It won't do to have a crazed American proselyte-hunting among our pupils,' the Father Rector warned, although there was no mention in the dossier of Martin Mills being either 'crazed' or a proselyte-hunter.

The dossier did say that he'd undertaken a six-week pilgrimage as part of his novitiate, and that during this pilgrimage he'd spent no money – not a penny. He'd managed to find places to live and work in return for humanitarian services; these included soup kitchens for the homeless, hospitals for handicapped children, homes for the elderly, shelters for AIDS patients and a clinic for babies suffering from fetal alcohol syndrome – this was on a Native American reservation.

Brother Gabriel and Father Cecil were inclined to

view Martin Mills's dossier in a positive light. Father Julian, on the other hand, quoted from Thomas à Kempis's *Imitation of Christ:* 'Be rarely with young people and strangers.' The Father Rector had read through Martin Mills's dossier as if it were a code to be deciphered. The task of teaching at St Ignatius, and otherwise serving the mission, was a part of the typical three-year service in preparation for the priesthood; it was called regency, and it was followed by another three years of theological study. Ordination followed theology; Martin Mills would complete a fourth year of theological study after his ordination.

He'd completed the two-year Jesuit novitiate at St Aloysius in Massachusetts, which Father Julian said was an extremist's choice because of the reputed harshness of its winters. This suggested a proneness to self-flagellation and other chastisements of the flesh – even an inclination to fasting, which the Jesuits discouraged; they encouraged fasting only in moderation. But, once again, the Father Rector seemed to be searching through Martin Mills's dossier for some hidden evidence of the scholastic's flawed character. Brother Gabriel and Father Cecil pointed out to Father Julian that Martin had joined the New England Province of the Society of Jesus while he was teaching in Boston. The province's novitiate was in Massachusetts; it was only natural for Martin Mills to have been a novice at St Aloysius – it hadn't really been a 'choice.'

But why had he taught for 10 years in a dismal parochial school in Boston? His dossier didn't say that the school was 'dismal'; however, it was admitted that the school was not accredited. Actually, it was a kind of reform school, where young criminals were encouraged to give up their delinquent behavior; as far as the Father Rector could tell, the means by which this was accomplished was theatrical. Martin Mills had directed *plays* wherein all the roles were acted by former felons and miscreants and thugs! In such an environment Martin Mills had first felt his vocation – namely, he'd felt Christ's presence and had been drawn to the priesthood. But why did it take 10 years? Father Julian questioned. After completing his novitiate, Martin Mills was sent to Boston College to study philosophy; that met with the Father Rector's approval. But then, in the midst of his regency, young Martin had requested a three-month 'experiment' in India. Did this mean that the scholastic had suffered doubts about his vocation? Father Julian asked.

'Well, we'll soon see,' Father Cecil said. 'He seems perfectly all right to *me*.' Father Cecil had almost said that Martin Mills seemed perfectly 'Loyola-like,' but he'd thought better of it because he knew how the Father Rector distrusted those Jesuits who too consciously patterned their behavior on the life of St Ignatius Loyola – the founder of the Jesuit order, the Society of Jesus.

Even a pilgrimage could be a fool's errand when undertaken by a fool. The *Spiritual Exercises* of St Ignatius Loyola is a handbook for the retreat master, not for the retreatant; it was never intended to be published, much less memorized by would-be priests – not that Martin Mills's dossier suggested that the missionary had followed the *Spiritual Exercises* to such an excess. Once again, the Father Rector's suspicion of Martin Mills's extreme piety was intuitive. Father Julian suspected all Americans of an unflagging fanaticism, which the Father Rector believed was emboldened by a frightening reliance on self-education – or 'reading on a deserted island,' as Father Julian called an American education. Father Cecil, on the other hand, was a kindly man – of that school which said Martin Mills should be given a chance to prove himself.

The senior priest chided the Father Rector for his cynicism: 'You don't know for a fact that our Martin wanted to be a novice at St Aloysius because he *sought* the harshness of a New England winter.' Father Cecil further implied that Father Julian was only guessing that Martin Mills had hoped to attend St Aloysius as a form of penitential practice, to chastise his flesh. Indeed, Father Julian was wrong. Had he known the *real* reason why Martin Mills wanted St Aloysius for his novitiate, the Father Rector *really* would have been worried, for Martin Mills had desired to be a novice at St Aloysius solely because of his identification with St Aloysius Gonzaga, that avid Italian whose chastity was so fervent that he refused to look upon his own mother after taking his permanent vows.

This was Martin Mills's favorite example of that 'custody of the senses' which every Jesuit sought to attain. To Martin's thinking, there was much to admire in the very notion of never again seeing one's own mother. His mother, after all, was Veronica Rose, and to deny himself even a farewell glimpse of *her* would certainly be enhancing to his Jesuitical goal of keeping his voice, his body and his curiosity in check. Martin Mills was very much held in check, and both his pious intentions and the life that had fueled them were more fanatically shot through and through with zeal than Father Julian could have guessed.

And now Brother Gabriel – that 75-year-old icon collector – had lost the scholastic's letter. If they didn't know when the new missionary was arriving, how could they meet his plane?

'After all,' Father Julian said, 'it seems that our Martin *likes* challenges.'

Father Cecil thought that this was cruel of the Father Rector. For Martin Mills to arrive in Bombay at that dead-of-night hour when the international flights landed in Sahar, and then to have to find his own way to the mission, which would be locked up and virtually impenetrable until the early-morning Mass . . . this was worse than any pilgrimage the missionary had previously undertaken.

'After all,' Father Julian said with characteristic sarcasm, 'St Ignatius Loyola managed to find his way to Jerusalem. No one met *his* plane.'

It was unfair, Father Cecil thought. And so he'd

called Dr Daruwalla to ask the doctor if he knew when Martin Mills was arriving. But the senior priest had reached only the doctor's answering machine, and Dr Daruwalla hadn't returned his call. And so Father Cecil prayed for Martin Mills in general. In particular, Father Cecil prayed that the missionary would not have too traumatic a first encounter upon his arrival in Bombay.

Brother Gabriel also prayed for Martin Mills in general. In particular, Brother Gabriel prayed that he might yet find the scholastic's lost letter. But the letter was never found. Long before Dr Daruwalla drifted into sleep, in the midst of his efforts to locate a movie star who resembled the second Mrs Dogar, Brother Gabriel gave up looking for the letter and went to bed, where he also fell asleep. When Vinod drove Muriel home – it was while the dwarf and the exotic dancer were considering the vileness of the clientele at the Wetness Cabaret – Father Cecil stopped praying, and then he fell asleep, too. And shortly after Vinod noticed that *Inspector Dhar and the Towers of Silence* was about to be launched upon the sleeping city, Father Julian locked the cloister gate and the school-bus gate and the gate that admitted entrance to St Ignatius Church. And shortly after that, the Father Rector was sound asleep as well.

Early Indications of Mistaken Identity

At approximately 2:00 in the morning – that very same hour when the poster-wallas were plastering the advertisements for the new Inspector Dhar movie all over Bombay, and when Vinod was cruising by the brothels in Kamathipura – the airplane carrying Dhar's twin landed safely in Sahar. Dhar himself was at that moment sleeping on Dr Daruwalla's balcony.

However, the customs official who looked back and forth from the intense expression of the new missionary to the utterly bland passport photograph of Martin Mills was convinced that he stood face-to-face with Inspector Dhar. The Hawaiian shirt was a mild surprise, for the customs official couldn't imagine why Dhar would attempt to conceal himself as a tourist; similarly, shaving off the identifying Dhar mustache was a lame disguise – with the upper lip exposed, something of the inimitable Dhar sneer was even more pronounced.

It was a U.S. passport – *that* was clever! thought the customs official – but the passport admitted that this so-called Martin Mills had been born in Bombay. The customs official pointed to this evidence in the passport; then he winked at the missionary, as a way of indicating to Inspector Dhar that *this* customs official was nobody's fool.

Martin Mills was very tired; it had been a long flight, which he'd spent studying Hindi and otherwise informing himself of the particulars of 'native behavior.' He knew all about the salaam, for example, but the customs official had distinctly *winked* at him – he had not salaamed – and Martin Mills hadn't encountered any information regarding the wink in his reading about native behavior. The missionary didn't wish to be impolite; therefore, he winked back, and he salaamed a little, too, just to be sure.

The customs official was very pleased with himself. He'd seen the wink in a recent Charles Bronson movie, but he was uncertain if it would be a cool thing to do to Inspector Dhar; above all, in dealing with Dhar, the customs official wanted to be perceived as cool. Unlike most Bombayites and all policemen, the customs official *loved* Inspector Dhar movies. So far, no customs officials had been portrayed in the films; therefore, none had been offended. And prior to his service as a customs official, he'd been rejected for police work; therefore, the constant mockery of the police – the prevalence of bribe taking, which was basic to every Inspector Dhar movie – was adored by the customs official.

Nevertheless, it was most irregular for someone to be entering the country under a false identity, and the customs official wanted Dhar to know that he was hip to Dhar's disguise, while at the same time he would do nothing to interfere with the creative genius who stood before him. Besides, Dhar didn't look well. His color was poor – he was mostly pale and blotchy – and he appeared to have lost a lot of weight.

'Is this your first time in Bombay since your birth?' the customs official asked Martin Mills. Thereupon the official winked again and smiled.

Martin Mills smiled and winked back. 'Yes,' he said. 'But I'm going to stay here for at least three months.'

This was an absurdity to the customs official, but he insisted on being cool about it. He saw that the missionary's visa was 'conditional'; it was possible to extend it for three months. The examination of the visa elicited more winking. It was also expected of the customs official that he looked through the missionary's belongings. For a visit of three months, the scholastic had brought only a single suitcase, albeit a large and heavy one, and in his ungainly luggage were some surprises: the black shirts with the white detachable collars – for although Martin Mills wasn't an ordained priest, he was permitted to wear such clerical garb. There was also a wrinkled black suit and about a half-dozen more Hawaiian shirts, and then came the *culpa* beads and the foot-long whip with the braided cords, not to mention the leg iron that was worn around the thigh; the wire prongs pointed inward, toward the flesh. But the customs official remained calm; he just kept smiling and winking, despite his horror at the instruments of self-torture.

The Father Rector, Father Julian, would also have been horrified to see such antiquities of mortification as these; they were artifacts of an earlier time – even Father Cecil would have been horrified, or else much amused. Whips and leg irons had never been notable parts of the Jesuit 'way of perfection.' Even the *culpa*

384

beads were an indication that Martin Mills might not have a true Jesuit vocation.

As for the customs official, the scholastic's books contributed further to the authenticity of Inspector Dhar's 'disguise,' which is what the customs official took all of this to be – an actor's elaborate props. Doubtless Dhar was preparing himself for yet another challenging role. This time he plays a *priest?* the customs official wondered. He looked over the books – all the while winking and smiling in ceaseless approval, while the baffled missionary kept winking and smiling back. There was the 1988 edition of the *Catholic Almanac* and many pamphlets of something called *Studies in the Spirituality of Jesuits;* there was a *Pocket Catholic Catechism* and a *Compact Dictionary of the Bible;* there was both a Bible and a Lectionary, and a thin book called *Sadhana: A Way to God* by Anthony de Mello, S.J.; there was *The Autobiography of St Ignatius Loyola* and a copy of the *Spiritual Exercises* – there were many other books, too. Altogether, there were more books than there were Hawaiian shirts and clerical collars combined.

'And where will you be staying – for three months?' the customs official asked Martin Mills, whose left eye was growing tired from all the winking.

'At St Ignatius in Mazagaon,' the Jesuit replied.

'Oh, of course!' said the customs official. 'I greatly admire your work!' he whispered. Then he gave the surprised Jesuit one more wink for the road.

A fellow Christian where one least expected to meet one! the new missionary thought.

All this winking would leave poor Martin Mills ill prepared for the 'native behavior' of most Bombayites, who find winking an exceptionally aggressive, suggestive and rude thing to do. But thus did the scholastic pass through customs and into the shit-smelling night air – all the while expecting a friendly greeting from one of his brother Jesuits.

Where were they? the new missionary wondered.

Delayed in traffic? Outside the airport there was much confusion; at the same time, there was little traffic. There were many standing taxis, all parked at the edge of an immense darkness, as if the airport were not huge and teeming (as Martin Mills had first thought), but a fragile wilderness outpost in a vast desert, where unseen fires were dying out and unseen squatters were defecating, without interruption, thoughout the night.

Then, like flies, the taxi-wallas lighted on him; they pecked at his clothes, they tugged at his suitcase, which – although it was extremely heavy – he would not relinquish.

'No, thank you, I'm being met,' he said. He realized that his Hindi had abandoned him, which was just as well; he spoke it very poorly, anyway. The weary missionary suspected himself of suffering from that paranoia which is commonplace to first-time travelers to the East, for he grew increasingly apprehensive of the way the taxi-wallas looked at him. Some were in utter awe; others appeared to want to kill him. They assumed he was Inspector Dhar, and although they flitted near to him like flies, and darted away from him like flies, they seemed entirely too dangerous for flies.

After an hour, Martin Mills was still standing there, warding off newly arrived flies; the old flies hovered at a distance, still watching him but not bothering to approach him again. The missionary was so tired, he got the idea that the taxi-wallas were of the hyena class of animal, and that they were waiting for him to exhibit a loss of vital signs before they swarmed over him en masse. A prayer fluttered to his lips, but he was too exhausted to utter it. He was thinking that the other missionaries were perhaps too old to have met his plane, for he'd been informed of their advanced ages. He also knew about the jubilee celebration that was pending; surely the proper recognition of 125 years of service to God and to humanity was more worthwhile than meeting a newcomer's plane. This was Martin Mills in a nutshell: he practiced self-deprecation to such a degree that it had become a vanity with him.

He shifted the suitcase from one hand to the other; he wouldn't allow it to rest on the pavement, not only because this sign of weakness would invite the lingering taxi-wallas to approach him but also because the weight of the suitcase was steadily becoming a welcome chastisement of his flesh. Martin Mills found a certain focus, a pleasing purpose, to the specificity of such pain. It was neither as exquisite nor as unending a pain as the leg iron when properly tightened around the thigh; it wasn't as sudden or breathtaking a pain as the whip on his bare back. Yet he greeted the pain of the suitcase warmly, and the suitcase itself bore a reminder of the ongoing task of Martin's formation, of his search for God's will and the strength of his self-denial. Inscribed in the old leather was the Latin *Nostris* ('Ours') – meaning *us Jesuits*, meaning 'the Life' (as it was called) in the Society of Jesus.

The suitcase itself called to memory Martin's two years in the novitiate at St Aloysius; his room had only a table, a straight-backed chair, a bed and a two-inch-high wooden kneeler. As his lips formed the word *Nostris*, he could summon to his memory the little bell that signaled *flagellatio;* he recalled the 30 days of his first silent retreat. He still took strength from these two years: pray, shave, work, be silent, study, pray. His was no fit of devotion but an orderly submission to rules: perpetual poverty, chastity, obedience. Obedience to a religious superior, yes; but, more important, obedience to a community life. Such rules made him feel free. Yet, on the matter of obedience, it haunted him that his previous superior had once criticized him on the grounds that Martin Mills seemed more suited to a monastic order – a *stricter* order, such as the Carthusians. Jesuits are meant to go out into the world; if not on our terms 'worldly,' they are also not monks.

'I am *not* a monk,' Martin Mills said aloud. The nearby taxi-wallas understood this as a summons; once again, they swarmed around him.

'Avoid worldliness,' Martin cautioned himself. He smiled tolerantly at the milling taxi-wallas. There had been an admonition in Latin above his bed at St Aloysius; it was an indirect reminder that a man should make his own bed – *etiam si sacerdotes sint* ('even if they be priests'). Therefore, Martin Mills decided, he would get himself into Bombay.

The Wrong Taxi-Walla

Of the taxi-wallas, there was only one who looked strong enough to handle the suitcase. He was tall and bearded, with a swarthy complexion and an exceedingly sharp, aggressive thrust to his nose.

'St Ignatius, Mazagaon,' Martin said to this taxi-walla, who struck the missionary as a university student with a demanding night job – an admirable young man, probably paying his way through school.

With a savage glare, the young man took the suitcase and hurled it into his waiting taxi. All the taxi-wallas had been waiting for the Ambassador with the thug dwarf driver, for none of them had really believed that Inspector Dhar would stoop to use any other cab. There'd been many depictions of taxi-wallas in Inspector Dhar films; they were always portrayed as reckless and crazy.

The particular taxi-walla who'd seized the missionary's suitcase and now watched Martin Mills slide into the back seat was a violent-minded young man named Bahadur. He'd just been expelled from a hotel-management school for cheating on a food-services exam – he'd plagiarized the answer to a simple question about catering. ('Bahadur' means 'brave.') He'd also just driven to the airport from Bombay and had seen the posters advertising *Inspector Dhar and the Towers of Silence*, which had greatly offended his loyal sensibilities. Although taxi driving wasn't his preferred profession, Bahadur was grateful to his present

388

employer, Mr Mirza. Mr Mirza was a Parsi; doubtless *Inspector Dhar and the Towers of Silence* would be monstrously offensive to Mr Mirza. Bahadur felt honor-bound to represent the feelings of his boss.

Not surprisingly, Bahadur had hated all the earlier Dhar films. Before the release of this new offense, Bahadur had been hoping that Inspector Dhar would be murdered by offended hijras or offended female prostitutes. Bahadur generally favored the notion of murdering famous people, for he found it offensive to *un*famous people that only very few people were famous. Moreover, he felt that driving a taxi was beneath him; he was doing it only to prove to a rich uncle that he was capable of 'mingling with the masses.' It was Bahadur's expectation that this uncle would soon send him off to another school. The present interim was unfortunate, but one could do worse than work for Mr Mirza; like Vinod, Mr Mirza operated a privately owned taxi company. Meanwhile, in his spare time, Bahadur was seeking to improve his English by concentrating on vulgar and profane expressions. Should he ever encounter a famous person, Bahadur wished to have such expressions on the tip of his tongue.

The reputations of famous people were entirely inflated, Bahadur knew. He'd heard stories of how tough Inspector Dhar was supposed to be, also that Dhar was a weight lifter! One look at the missionary's scrawny arms proved this to be a typical lie. Movie hype! Bahadur thought. He liked to drive by the film studios, hoping to give actresses a ride. But no one important ever chose his taxi, and at Asha Pictures – and at Rajkamal Studio and Famous Studio and Central Studio – he'd been accosted by the police for loitering. *Fuck* these film people! Bahadur thought.

'I suppose you know where St Ignatius is,' Martin Mills said nervously, once they were under way. 'It's a Jesuit mission, a church, a school,' he added, looking for some sign of recognition in the glare of the taxi-walla. When the scholastic saw that the young man was watching him in the rearview mirror, Martin did the friendly thing – at least he presumed it was the native-behavior thing to do. He winked.

That does it! Bahadur thought. Whether the wink was condescending, or whether it was the lewd invitation of a homosexual, Bahadur had made up his mind. Inspector Dhar should *not* be allowed to get away with the violent farce he made of Bombay life. In the middle of the night, Dhar wanted to go to St Ignatius! What was he going to do there? Pray?

In addition to everything else that was fake about Inspector Dhar, Bahadur decided that the man was a fake Hindu, too. Inspector Dhar was a bleeding Christian!

'You're supposed to be a Hindu,' Bahadur told the Jesuit.

Martin Mills was thrilled. His first religious confrontation in the missionary kingdom – his first Hindu! He knew they were the majority religion here.

'Well . . . well,' Martin said cheerfully. 'Men of all faiths must be brothers.'

'Fuck your Jesus, and fuck you,' Bahadur remarked coldly.

'Well . . . well,' Martin said. Possibly there was a time to wink and a time *not* to wink, the new missionary thought.

Proselyte-Hunting Among the Prostitutes

Through the smoldering, reeking darkness, the taxi careened, but darkness had never intimidated Martin Mills. In crowds, he could be anxious, but the black of night did not menace him. Nor did it concern the missionary that he was in danger of some violence. He meditated on the unfulfilled dream of the Middle Ages, which was to win back Jerusalem for Christ. He contemplated that St Ignatius Loyola's own pilgrimage to

Jerusalem had been a journey fraught with endless dangers and accidents. Ignatius's attempted conquest of the Holy Land was a failure, for he was sent back; yet the saint's desire to rescue unsaved souls remained ardent. It was always the Ignatian purpose to conform to the will of God. It was no coincidence that, to this end, the *Spiritual Exercises* of St Ignatius began with a vivid representation of hell in all its horror. The fear of God was purifying; it had long been so to Martin Mills. To see both the fires of hell and a union with God in mystical ecstasy, one needed only to follow the *Spiritual Exercises* and call upon 'the eye of the imagination,' for the missionary had no doubt that this was the clearest eye of all.

'Toil and will,' Martin Mills said aloud. This was his creed.

'I said, *fuck* your Jesus, and *fuck you*!' the taxi-walla repeated.

'Bless you,' Martin said. 'Even you, and whatever you do to me, is God's will – though you know not what you do.'

Most of all, Martin admired Ignatius Loyola's notable encounter with the Moor on a mule and their ensuing discussion of the Holy Virgin. The Moor said he could believe that Our Lady had conceived without a man, but he could *not* believe that she'd remained a virgin after giving birth. After the Moor rode on, young Ignatius thought that he should hurry after the Muslim and kill him. He felt obliged to defend Our Lady's honor. The defaming of the Virgin's postbirth vaginal condition was gross and unacceptable behavior. Ignatius, as always, sought God's will on the matter. Where the road parted, he let his own mule's reins go slack; if the animal followed the Moor, Ignatius would kill the infidel. But the mule chose the other road.

'And *fuck* your St Ignatius!' the taxi-walla shouted.

'St Ignatius is where I would like to go,' Martin replied calmly. 'But take me where you will.' Where they went, the missionary believed, would be God's will. Martin Mills was just the passenger.

He thought of the late Father de Mello's renowned book *Christian Exercises in Eastern Form;* so many of these exercises had helped him in the past. For example, there was that exercise which concerned the 'healing of hurtful memories.' Whenever Martin Mills was troubled by the shame his parents had caused him, or by his seeming inability to love and forgive and honor his parents, he followed Father de Mello's exercise verbatim. 'Return to some unpleasant event'; such events were never hard to recall, but the selection of *which* horror to revisit was always an arduous decision. 'Now place yourself before Christ Crucified' – that always had a certain power. Even the depravities of Veronica Rose paled before such an agony; even the self-destruction of Danny Mills seemed a trifling pain. 'Keep commuting between the unpleasant event and the scene of Jesus on the Cross'; for years, Martin Mills had engaged in such commuting. Father de Mello was a hero to him. He had been born in Bombay, and until his death was the director of the Sadhana Institute of Pastoral Counseling (near Poona); it had been Father de Mello who had inspired Martin Mills to come to India.

Now, as the embracing darkness gradually yielded to the lights of Bombay, the bodies of the sidewalk sleepers appeared in mounds. The moonlight glinted off Mahim Bay. Martin couldn't smell the horses as the taxi rocketed past the Mahalaxmi Race Course, but he could see the dark silhouette of Haji Ali's Tomb; the slender minarets stood out against the fish-scale glint of the Arabian Sea. Then the taxi veered away from the moonlit ocean, and the missionary saw the sleeping city come to life – if the eternal sexual activity of Kamathipura could fairly be called life. It wasn't a life that Martin Mills had ever known – it was nothing he'd ever imagined – and he prayed that his brief glimpse of the Muslim mausoleum wouldn't be the last holy edifice he'd see in his allotted time on this mortal earth.

He saw the brothels overflowing into the little lanes. He saw the sex-stoned faces of the men let loose from the Wetness Cabaret; the last show was over, and the men who couldn't yet bear to go home were wandering. And just when Martin Mills thought he'd encountered a greater evil than St Ignatius Loyola had met on the streets of Rome, the taxi-walla jostled and edged his way into a darker hell. There were suddenly those prostitutes in human cages on Falkland Road.

'Won't the cage girls just love to get a look at *you*!' cried Bahadur, who saw himself as Inspector Dhar's designated persecutor.

Martin Mills remembered how Ignatius had raised money among rich people and founded an asylum for fallen women. It was in Rome where the saint had announced that he would sacrifice his life if he could prevent the sins of a single prostitute on a single night.

'Thank you for bringing me here,' the missionary said to the taxi-walla, who screeched to a halt in front of a compelling display of eunuch-transvestites in their cages. Bahadur assumed that the hijra prostitutes were by far the angriest at Inspector Dhar. But, to the taxi-walla's surprise, Martin Mills cheerfully opened the rear door and stepped into Falkland Road with a look of eager anticipation. He took his heavy suitcase from the trunk; and when the taxi-walla hurled the money for the fare at the missionary's feet and spat on it – for the trip from the airport had been prepaid – Martin retrieved the wet money and handed it back to Bahadur.

'No, no – you've done your job. I am where I should be,' the missionary said. A circle of pickpockets and street prostitutes with their pimps were slowly surrounding the scholastic, but Bahadur wanted the hijras to be certain to see their enemy, and so he pushed against the gathering crowd.

'Dhar – Inspector *Dhar*! Dhar! Dhar!' the taxi-walla cried. But this was entirely unnecessary, for the word that Dhar was on Falkland Road had traveled ahead of the taxi-walla's cries. Martin Mills quite easily made his own way through the crowd; the degraded women in those cages were the ones he wished to address. (It never occurred to him, of course, that they weren't really women.)

'Please, let me speak with you,' the missionary said to a transvestite in his cage. Most of the hijras were, at first, too stunned to attack the hated actor. 'Surely you must know of the diseases – nowadays, of the certain death you are exposing yourselves to! But I tell you, if you want to be saved, that is all you need – to *want* to be.'

Two pickpockets and several pimps were fighting over the money that Martin had tried to give back to the taxi-walla. Bahadur had already been beaten to his knees, and several street prostitutes continued to kick at him. But Martin Mills was oblivious to what was behind him. The apparent women in the cages faced him, and it was only to them that he spoke. 'St Ignatius,' he said. 'In Mazagaon? You must know it. I can always be found there. You have only to come there.'

It is intriguing to imagine how Father Julian and Father Cecil might have responded to this generous invitation, for surely the mission's 125th jubilee would be a much more colorful celebration with the added presence of several eunuch-transvestite prostitutes in search of salvation. Unfortunately, the Father Rector and the senior priest were not on hand to witness Martin Mills's extraordinary proposition. Did Martin suppose that if the prostitutes arrived at St Ignatius during school hours, the schoolchildren might benefit from the visible conversion of these fallen women?

'If you feel but the slightest remorse, you must take this as a sign that you can be saved,' the scholastic told them.

It wasn't a hijra who struck the first blow, but one of the street prostitutes; probably she was feeling ignored.

She shoved Martin in the small of his back and he stumbled forward on one knee; then the pimps and pickpockets pulled his suitcase away from him – that was when the hijras became involved. After all, Dhar had been speaking to *them;* they didn't want their territory, or their vengeance, trespassed on – certainly not by this common rabble off the street. The transvestite prostitutes easily beat away the street prostitutes and their pimps, and not even the pickpockets could escape with the heavy suitcase, which the hijras opened for themselves.

They wouldn't touch the wrinkled black suit and the black shirts or the clerical collars – these weren't their style – but the Hawaiian shirts were appealing to them, and they quickly took these. Then one of them stripped the shirt off Martin Mills, being careful not to tear it, and when the missionary was naked above his waist, one of the hijras discovered the whip with the braided cords, which was too tempting to ignore. With the first of the stinging lashes from the whip, Martin lay on his stomach; then he curled himself into a ball. He wouldn't cover his face, for it mattered too much to him that he clasped his hands together in prayer; thus he maintained the extreme conviction that even such a beating as this was *ad majorem Dei Gloriam* ('to the greater glory of God').

The tranvestite prostitutes were respectful of all the assembled evidence of education that was contained in the suitcase; even in their excitement to each take a turn with the whip, they wouldn't tear or wrinkle a page of a single book. The leg iron, however, was misinterpreted by them, as were the *culpa* beads; a transvestite prostitute tried to eat the beads before he threw them away. As for the leg iron, the hijras didn't know it went around the thigh – or else they simply thought it would be more suitable to attach the device around Inspector Dhar's neck, which they did. It wasn't too tight a fit, but the wire prongs had raked the missionary's face – the hijras were so impatient that

they'd scraped the leg iron over their victim's head –
and now the prongs dug into Martin's throat, which
caused a multitude of minor cuts. The missionary's
torso was striped with blood.

Gamely, he tried to stand. As he kept trying, he faced
the whip. The transvestites stepped away from him, for
he wasn't behaving as they'd expected. He didn't fight
back; he didn't beg for his life, either. 'It is you, and
everything that happens to you, that I care for!' Martin
Mills called to them. 'Though you revile me, and I am
nothing, I want only for you to save yourselves. I can
show you how, but only if you let me.'

The hijras passed the whip, but there was noticeably
less enthusiasm among them. When one would hold it,
he would quickly pass it on, without taking a whack.
The raised red welts covered Martin's exposed flesh –
they were especially startling on his face – and the
blood from the wrongly placed leg iron streaked his
chest. He protected not himself but his books! He
closed the suitcase safely around these treasures of his
learning, and *still* he beseeched the prostitutes to join
him.

'Take me to Mazagaon,' he said to them. 'Take me to
St Ignatius, and you shall also be welcome there.' To
those few of them who understood what he said, the
concept was preposterous. To their surprise, the man
before them was a physical weakling, but his courage
seemed unsurpassed; it wasn't the kind of toughness
they'd anticipated. Suddenly, no one wanted to hurt
him. They hated him; yet he made them feel ashamed.

But the street prostitutes and their pimps, and the
pickpockets – they would have made short work of
him, just as soon as the hijras left him. This was
precisely when that familiar off-white Ambassador,
which all night had cruised between Kamathipura and
Grant Road and Falkland Road, cruised by them again.
In the driver's-side window, soberly looking them
over, was the driver they all thought of as Dhar's thug
dwarf.

One can imagine Vinod's surprise upon seeing his famous client stripped of half his clothes and bloodied. The wretched villains had even shaved off Inspector Dhar's mustache! This was a humiliation beyond the obvious pain that the beloved movie star had suffered. And what ghastly instrument of torture had the filthy prostitutes fitted around the actor's neck? It looked like a dog's collar, only the spikes were on the inside. Furthermore, poor Dhar was as pale and scrawny as a cadaver. It looked like Vinod's famous client had lost 20 pounds!

A pimp with a big brass ring of keys scratched a key against the driver's-side door of the Ambassador – all the while meeting Vinod's eyes, straight on. He didn't see Vinod reach under his specially constructed car seat, where the dwarf driver kept a ready supply of squash-racquet handles. There was confusion regarding what happened next. Some claimed that the dwarf's taxi swerved and deliberately ran over the pimp's foot; others explained that the Ambassador jumped the curb and that it was the panicked crowd that pushed the pimp – either way, his foot was run over by the car. All agreed that Vinod was hard to see in the crowd; he was so much shorter than everyone else. His presence could be detected by the wary, however, for everywhere people were dropping from sight, clutching their knees or their wrists and writhing on the garbage-strewn pavement. Vinod swung the squash-racquet handles at a level equal to most people's knees. Their cries commingled with the cries of the cage girls on Falkland Road continuously hawking their wares.

When Martin Mills saw the grim face of the dwarf who was whacking his way toward him, the scholastic thought that his time had come. He repeated what Jesus said to Pilate [John 18:36], 'My kingdom is not of this world.' Then he turned to face the oncoming dwarf. 'I forgive you,' Martin said; he bowed his head, as if awaiting the executioner's blow. It didn't occur to him that if he *hadn't* bowed his head, Vinod never could have reached his head with the racquet handles.

But Vinod simply grabbed the missionary by the rear pocket of his pants and steered him to the taxi. When Martin was rescued – pinned under the weight of his suitcase in the back seat of the car – the scholastic foolishly struggled, albeit briefly, to return to Falkland Road.

'Wait!' he cried. 'I want my whip – that's *my* whip!'

Vinod had already swung a racquet handle and cracked the wrist of the unfortunate hijra who was the last to hold the whip. The dwarf easily retrieved Martin Mills's mortification toy and handed it to him. 'Bless you!' the scholastic said. The doors of the Ambassador slammed solidly around him; the sudden acceleration pressed him against the seat. 'St Ignatius,' he told the brutal driver. Vinod thought that Dhar was praying, which was dismaying to the dwarf because he'd never thought of Dhar as a religious man.

At the intersection of Falkland Road and Grant Road, a boy who was a tea-server for one of the brothels threw a glass of tea at the passing taxi. Vinod just kept going, although his stubby fingers reached under the car seat to reassure himself that the squash-racquet handles were properly in place.

Before the taxi turned onto Marine Drive, Vinod stopped the car and lowered the rear windows; he knew how Dhar enjoyed the smell of the sea. 'You sure are fooling me,' Vinod said to his battered client. 'I am thinking you are sleeping the whole night on Daru-walla's balcony!' But the missionary was asleep. In the rearview mirror, the sight of him took Vinod's breath away. It wasn't the lash marks on his swollen face, or even his bare, bloodied torso; it was the spiked leg iron around his neck, for the dwarf had seen the terrible depictions that the Christians worshiped – their gory versions of Christ on the Cross – and to Vinod it appeared that Inspector Dhar had undertaken the role of Christ. However, his crown of thorns had slipped; the cruel device gripped the famous actor by his throat.

All Together – in One Small Apartment

As for Dhar, the *real* Dhar, a smog the consistency and color of egg whites had rolled over Dr Daruwalla's balcony, where the actor was still sleeping. Had he looked, he couldn't have seen through this soup – at least not six floors below him to the predawn sidewalk, where Vinod struggled with the movie star's semi-conscious twin. Nor did Dhar hear the predictable eruption from the first-floor dogs. Vinod allowed the missionary to lean heavily on him, while the dwarf dragged the suitcase carrying Martin Mills's education across the lobby to the forbidden lift. A first-floor apartment owner, a member of the Residents' Society, got a glimpse of the thug driver and his mangled companion before the elevator door closed.

Martin Mills, even as mauled and mindless of his surroundings as he was, was surprised by the elevator and the modernity of the apartment building, for he knew that the mission school and its venerable church were 125 years old. The sound of savage dogs seemed out of place.

'St Ignatius?' the missionary asked the Good Samaritan midget.

'You are not needing a saint – you are needing a doctor!' the dwarf told him.

'Actually, I *know* a doctor in Bombay. He's a friend of my mother and father – a certain Dr Daruwalla,' Martin Mills said.

Vinod was truly alarmed. The lashes from the whip and even the bleeding from the leg iron around the poor man's neck seemed superficial; but this incomprehensible muttering about Dr Daruwalla was an indication to Vinod that the movie star was suffering from some sort of amnesia. A serious head injury, perhaps!

'Of *course* you are knowing Dr Daruwalla!' Vinod shouted. 'We are going to see Dr Daruwalla!'

'Ah, so you know him, *too*?' said the astonished scholastic.

'Try to not be moving your head,' the worried dwarf replied.

In a reference to the echoing dogs, which Vinod completely failed to grasp, Martin Mills said, 'It sounds like a veterinarian's – I thought he was an orthopedist.'

'Of *course* he is being an orthopedist!' Vinod cried. Standing on tiptoe, the dwarf tried to peer into Martin's ears, as if he were expecting to see some stray brain matter there. But Vinod wasn't tall enough.

Dr Daruwalla woke to the distant orchestra of the dogs. From the sixth floor, their barks and howls were muted but nonetheless identifiable; the doctor had no doubt as to the cause of their cacophony.

'That damn dwarf!' he said aloud, to which Julia didn't respond; she was familiar with the many things her husband said in his sleep. But when Farrokh got out of bed and put on his robe, Julia was instantly awake.

'Is it Vinod again?' she asked him.

'I assume so,' Dr Daruwalla replied.

It was a little before 5:00 in the morning when the doctor crept past the closed sliding-glass doors that led to the balcony, which was completely enveloped in a mournful-looking mist. The smog had mingled with a dense sea fog. The doctor couldn't see Dhar's cot or the Tortoise mosquito coils with which the actor surrounded himself whenever he slept on the balcony. In the foyer, Farrokh seized a dusty umbrella; he was hoping to give Vinod a good scare. Then the doctor opened his apartment door. The dwarf and the missionary had just exited from the lift; when Dr Daruwalla first saw Martin Mills, the doctor feared that Dhar had violently shaved off his mustache in the smog – thus inflicting on himself a multitude of razor cuts – and then, doubtless depressed, the much-reviled actor had jumped off the sixth-floor balcony.

As for the missionary, he was taken aback to see a man in a black kimono holding a black umbrella – an ominous image. But the umbrella was undaunting to

Vinod, who slipped close to Dr Daruwalla and whispered, 'I am finding him preaching to transvestite prostitutes – the hijras are almost killing him!'

Farrokh knew who Martin Mills was as soon as the missionary spoke; 'I believe you've met my mother and father – my name is Martin, Martin Mills.'

'Please come in – I've been expecting you,' Dr Daruwalla said, taking the beaten man's arm.

'You *have*?' said Martin Mills.

'There is being brain damage!' Vinod whispered to the doctor, who supported the wobbly missionary into the bathroom, where he told Martin to strip. Then the doctor prepared an Epsom-salts bath. While the bath was filling, Farrokh got Julia out of bed and told her to get rid of Vinod.

'Who's taking a bath at this hour?' she asked her husband.

'It's John D.'s twin,' Dr Daruwalla said.

Free Will

Julia had managed to coax Vinod no farther than the foyer when the phone rang. She answered quickly. Vinod could hear the entire conversation because the man on the other end of the phone was screaming. It was Mr Munim, the first-floor member of the Residents' Society.

'I saw him getting on the lift! He woke all the dogs! I saw him – your dwarf!' Mr Munim shouted.

Julia said, 'I beg your pardon – we don't own a dwarf.'

'You don't fool me!' Mr Munim hollered. 'That movie star's dwarf – that's who I mean!'

'We don't own a movie star, either,' Julia told him.

'You are violating a stated rule!' Mr Munim screamed.

'I don't know what you mean – you must be out of your mind,' Julia replied.

'The taxi-walla used the lift – that midget thug!' Mr Munim cried.

'Don't make me call the police,' Julia said; then she hung up.

'I am using the stairs, but they are making me limp – the whole six floors,' Vinod said. Martyrdom strangely suited him, Julia thought, but she realized that Vinod was lingering in the foyer for a purpose. 'There are being *five* umbrellas in your umbrella stand,' the dwarf observed.

'Would you like to borrow one, Vinod?' Julia asked him.

'Only for helping me on the stairs,' Vinod replied. 'I am needing a cane.' He'd left the squash-racquet handles in his taxi; were he to encounter either a first-floor dog or Mr Munim, Vinod wanted a weapon. Therefore, he took an umbrella with him; Julia let him out the kitchen door, which led to the back stairs.

'Maybe you are never seeing me again,' Vinod told her. As the dwarf peered down the stairwell, Julia noticed that he was slightly shorter than the umbrella that he'd chosen; Vinod had taken the biggest umbrella.

In the bathtub, Martin Mills looked as if he welcomed the stings from his raised red welts, and he never flinched while Dr Daruwalla sponged off the multitude of minor wounds caused by the gruesome leg iron; the doctor thought that the missionary appeared to miss the leg iron after it had been removed, and Martin twice expressed concern that he'd left his whip in the heroic dwarf's car.

'Vinod will surely return it to you,' Dr Daruwalla said. The doctor was not as amazed by the missionary's story as the missionary himself was amazed; given the magnitude of the mistaken identity, Dr Daruwalla was astonished that Martin Mills was still alive – not to mention that his wounds were minor. And the more the missionary babbled on and on about his experience, the less he bore any resemblance, in

Farrokh's eyes, to his taciturn twin. Dhar didn't babble.

'Well, I mean I *knew* I wasn't among Christians,' Martin Mills said, 'but still I hardly expected the *violent* hostility toward Christianity that I encountered.'

'Now, now – I wouldn't jump to *that* conclusion,' Dr Daruwalla cautioned the agitated scholastic. 'There is some sensitivity, however, toward proselytizing . . . of any kind.'

'Saving souls is *not* proselytizing,' Martin Mills said defensively.

'Well, as you say, you were not exactly in Christian territory,' Dr Daruwalla replied.

'How many of those prostitutes are carrying the AIDS virus?' Martin asked.

'I'm an orthopedist,' the doctor reminded the scholastic, 'but people who know say forty percent – some say sixty.'

'Either way,' said Martin Mills, 'that's Christian territory.'

For the first time, Farrokh considered that the madman before him posed a threat to himself that might exceed the danger presented by his striking resemblance to Inspector Dhar.

'But I thought you were an English teacher,' said Dr Daruwalla. 'As a former student of the place, I can assure you, St Ignatius is first and foremost a *school*.' The doctor knew the Father Rector; Dr Daruwalla could well anticipate that this was precisely what Father Julian would have to say about the matter of saving prostitutes' souls. But as Farrokh watched Martin step naked from the bath – whereupon, unmindful of his wounds, the missionary began to vigorously towel himself dry – the doctor further anticipated that the Father Rector and all the aged defenders of the faith at St Ignatius would have a hard time convincing such a zealous scholastic as this that his duties were restricted to improving the English of

403

the upper classes. For as he rubbed and rubbed the towel against his lash marks until his face and torso were striped as bright red as when the whip had only just struck him, Martin Mills was all the while thinking of a reply. Like the crafty Jesuit that he was, he began his answer with a question.

'Aren't you a Christian?' the missionary asked the doctor. 'I believe my father said you were converted, but that you're not a Roman Catholic.'

'Yes, that's true,' Dr Daruwalla replied cautiously. He gave Martin Mills a clean pair of his best silk pajamas, but the scholastic preferred to stand naked.

'Are you familiar with the Calvinist, Jansenist position in regard to free will?' Martin asked Farrokh. 'I'm greatly oversimplifying, but this was that dispute born of Luther and those Protestant divines of the Reformation – namely, the idea that we're doomed by original sin and can expect salvation only through divine grace. Luther denied that good works could contribute to our salvation. Calvin further denied that our faith could save us. According to Calvin, we are all predestined to be saved – or not. Do you believe that?'

By the way the logic of the Jesuit was leaning, Farrokh guessed that he should *not* believe that, and so he said, 'No – not exactly.'

'Well, good – then you're not a Jansenist,' the scholastic said. 'They were very discouraging – their doctrine of grace over that of free will was quite defeatist, really. They made us all feel that there was absolutely nothing we could do to be saved – in short, why bother with good works? And so what if we sin?'

'Are you still oversimplifying?' asked Dr Daruwalla. The Jesuit regarded the doctor with sly respect; he also took this interruption as a useful time in which to put on the doctor's silk pajamas.

'If you're suggesting that it's almost impossible to reconcile the concept of free will with our belief in an omnipotent and omniscient God, I agree with you – it's difficult,' Martin said. 'The question of the relationship between human will and divine omnipotence ... is that your question?'

Dr Daruwalla guessed that this *should* be his question, and so he said, 'Yes – something like that.'

'Well, that really *is* an interesting question,' the Jesuit said. 'I just hate it when people try to reduce the spiritual world with purely mechanical theories – those behaviorists, for example. Who cares about Loeb's plant-lice theories or Pavlov's dog?' Dr Daruwalla nodded, but he didn't dare speak; he'd never heard of plant lice. He'd heard of Pavlov's dog, of course; he could even recall what made the dog salivate and what the saliva meant.

'We must seem excessively strict to you – we Catholics to you Protestants, I mean,' Martin said. Dr Daruwalla shook his head. 'Oh, yes we do!' the missionary said. 'We are a theology of rewards and punishments, which are meted out in the life after death. Compared to you, we make much of sin. We Jesuits, however, tend to minimize those sins of thought.'

'As opposed to those of deed,' interjected Dr Daruwalla, for although this was obvious and totally unnecessary to say, the doctor felt that only a fool would have nothing to say, and he'd been saying nothing.

'To us – to us Catholics, I mean – you Protestants appear, at times, to overemphasize the human propensity toward evil ...' And here the missionary paused; but Dr Daruwalla, unsure whether he should nod or shake his head, just stared stupidly at the bathwater spiraling down the drain, as if the water were his own thoughts, escaping him.

'Do you know Leibniz?' the Jesuit suddenly asked him.

'Well, in university ... but that was years ago,' the doctor said.

'The Leibniz assumption is that man's freedom was not taken from him by his fall, which makes Leibniz

405

quite a friend of ours – of us Jesuits, I mean,' Martin said. 'There is some Leibniz I can never forget, such as, "Although the impulse and the help come from God, they are at all times accompanied by a certain co-operation of man himself; if not, we could not say that we had acted" – but you agree, don't you?'

'Yes, of course,' said Dr Daruwalla.

'Well, you see, that's why I can't be *just* an English teacher,' the Jesuit replied. 'Naturally, I shall endeavor to improve the children's English – and to the most perfect degree possible. But, given that I am free to act – "although the impulse and the help come from God," of course – I must do what I can, not only to save *my* soul but to rescue the souls of others.'

'I see,' said Dr Daruwalla, who was also beginning to understand why the enraged transvestite prostitutes had failed to make much of a dent in the flesh *or* the indomitable will of Martin Mills.

Furthermore, the doctor found that he was standing in his own living room and watching Martin lie down on the couch, without the slightest recollection of having left the bathroom. That was when the missionary handed the leg iron to the doctor, who received the instrument reluctantly.

'I can see I will not be needing this here,' the scholastic said. 'There will be sufficient adversity without it. St Ignatius Loyola also changed his mind in regard to these weapons of mortification.'

'He did?' said Farrokh.

'I think he overused them – but only out of a positive abhorrence of his earlier sins,' the Jesuit said. 'In fact, in the later version of the *Spiritual Exercises*, St Ignatius urges against such scourges of the flesh – he is also opposed to heavy fasting.'

'So am I,' said Dr Daruwalla, who didn't know what to do with the cruel leg iron.

'Please throw it away,' Martin said to him. 'And perhaps you'd be so kind as to tell the dwarf to keep the whip – I don't want it.'

Dr Daruwalla knew all about Vinod's racquet handles; the prospect of what use the dwarf might make of the whip was chilling. Then the doctor noticed that Martin Mills had fallen asleep. With his fingers interlocked on his chest, and with an utterly beatific expression, the missionary resembled a martyr en route to the heavenly kingdom.

Farrokh brought Julia into the living room to see him. At first, she wouldn't approach past the glass-topped table – she viewed him as one might view a contaminated corpse – but the doctor encouraged her to take a closer look. The nearer Julia drew to Martin Mills, the more relaxed she became. It was as if – at least, when he was alseep – Martin had a pacifying effect on everyone around him. Eventually, Julia sat on the floor beside the couch. She would say later that he reminded her of John D. as a much younger, more carefree man, although Farrokh maintained that Martin Mills was simply the result of no weight lifting and no beer – meaning that he had no muscles but that he had no belly, either.

Without remembering when he sat down, the doctor found himself on the floor beside his wife. They were both sitting beside the couch, as if transfixed by the sleeping body, when Dhar came in from the balcony to have a shower and to brush his teeth; from Dhar's perspective, Farrokh and Julia appeared to be praying. Then the movie star saw the dead person – at least, the person looked dead to Dhar – and without taking too close a look, he said, 'Who's that?'

Farrokh and Julia were shocked that John D. didn't immediately recognize his twin; after all, an actor is especially familiar with his own facial features – and under a variety of makeup, including the radical altering of his age – but Dhar had never seen such an expression on his own face. It's doubtful that Dhar's face ever reflected beatification, for not even in his sleep had Inspector Dhar imagined the happiness of heaven. Dhar had many expressions, but none of them was saintly.

Finally, the actor whispered, 'Well, okay, I see *who* it is, but what's he doing here? Is he going to die?'

'He's trying to be a priest,' Farrokh whispered.

'Jesus Christ!' John D. said. Either he should have whispered or else the particular name he spoke was one that Martin Mills was prone to hear; a smile of such immense gratitude crossed the missionary's sleeping face that Dhar and the Daruwallas felt suddenly ashamed. Without a word to one another, they tiptoed into the kitchen, as if they were unanimously embarrassed that they'd been spying on a sleeping man; what truly had disturbed them, and had made them feel as if they didn't belong where they were, was the utter contentment of a man momentarily at peace with his soul – although none of them could have identified what it was that so upset them.

'What's wrong with him?' Dhar asked.

'Nothing's wrong with him!' Dr Daruwalla said; then he wondered why he'd said that about a man who'd been whipped and beaten while he was proselytizing among transvestite prostitutes. 'I should have told you he was coming,' the doctor added sheepishly, to which John D. merely rolled his eyes; his anger was often understated. Julia rolled her eyes, too.

'As far as I'm concerned,' Farrokh said to John D., 'it's entirely your decision as to whether or not you want to let him know that you exist. Although I don't know if *now* would be the right time to tell him.'

'Forget about now,' Dhar said. 'Tell me what he's like.'

Dr Daruwalla could not utter the first word that came to his lips – the word was 'crazy.' On second thought, he almost said, Like *you*, except that *he* talks. But this was such a contradictory concept – the very idea of a Dhar who talked might be insulting to Dhar.

'I said, what's he like?' John D. repeated.

'I saw him only when he was asleep,' Julia told John D. Both of them were staring at Farrokh, whose mind – on the matter of what Martin Mills was 'like' – was

408

truly blank. Not a single picture came to his mind, although the missionary had managed to argue with him, lecture to him and even educate him – and most of this had transpired while the zealot was naked.

'He's somewhat zealous,' the doctor offered cautiously.

'Zealous?' said Dhar.

'*Liebchen*, is that all you can say?' Julia asked Farrokh. 'I heard him talking and talking in the bathroom. He must have been saying *something*!'

'In the bathroom?' John D. asked.

'He's very determined,' Farrokh blurted.

'I guess that would follow from being "zealous,"' said Inspector Dhar; he was at his most sarcastic.

It was exasperating to Dr Daruwalla that they expected him to be able to summarize the Jesuit's character on the basis of this one peculiar meeting.

The doctor didn't know the history of that other zealot – the greatest zealot of the 16th century, St Ignatius Loyola – who had so inspired Martin Mills. When Ignatius died without ever having permitted a portrait of himself to be painted, the brothers of the order sought to have a portrait made of the dead man. A famous painter tried and failed. The disciples declared that the death mask, which was the work of an unknown, was also not the true face of the father of the Jesuits. Three other artists tried and failed to capture him, but they had only the death mask for their model. It was finally decided that God did not wish for Ignatius Loyola, His servant, to be painted. Dr Daruwalla couldn't have known how greatly Martin Mills loved this story, but it doubtless would have pleased the new missionary to see how the doctor struggled to describe even such a fledgling servant of God as this mere scholastic. Farrokh felt the right word come to his lips, but then it escaped him.

'He's well educated,' Farrokh managed to say. Both John D. and Julia groaned. 'Well, damn it, he's *complicated*!' Dr Daruwalla shouted. 'It's too soon to know what he's like!'

'*Ssshhh!* You'll wake him up,' Julia told Farrokh.

'If it's too soon to know what he's like,' John D. said, 'then it's too soon for me to know if I want to meet him.'

Dr Daruwalla was irritated; he felt that this was a typical Inspector Dhar thing to say.

Julia knew what her husband was thinking. 'Hold your tongue,' she told him. She made coffee for herself and John D. – for Farrokh, she made a pot of tea. Together, the Daruwallas watched their beloved movie star leave by the kitchen door. Dhar liked to use the back stairs so that he wouldn't be seen; the early morning – it wasn't quite 6:00 – was one of the few times he could walk from Marine Drive to the Taj without being recognized and surrounded. At that hour, only the beggars would hassle him; they hassled everyone equally. It simply didn't matter to the beggars that he was Inspector Dhar; many beggars went to the cinema, but what did a movie star matter to them?

Standing Still: An Exercise

At exactly 6:00 in the morning, when Farrokh and Julia were sharing a bath together – she soaped his back, he soaped her breasts, but there was no more extensive hanky-panky than that – Martin Mills awoke to the soothing sounds of Dr Aziz, the praying urologist. 'Praise be to Allah, Lord of Creation' – Dr Aziz's incantations to Allah drifted upward from his fifth-floor balcony and brought the new missionary instantly to his feet. Although he'd been asleep for less than an hour, the Jesuit felt as refreshed as a normal man who had slept the whole night through; thus invigorated, he bounded to Dr Daruwalla's balcony, where he could oversee the morning ritual that Urology Aziz enacted on his prayer rug. From the vantage point of the Daruwallas' sixth-floor apartment, the view of Back Bay was stunning. Martin Mills could see Malabar Hill and Nariman Point; in the distance, a small city of people had already congregated on Chowpatty Beach. But the Jesuit had not come to Bombay for the view. He followed the prayers of Dr Aziz with the keenest concentration. There was always something one could learn from the holiness of others.

Martin Mills did not take prayer for granted. He knew that prayer wasn't the same as thinking, nor was it an escape from thinking. It was never as simple as mere asking. Instead, it was the seeking of instruction; for to know God's will was Martin's heart's desire, and to attain such a state of perfection – a union with God in mystical ecstasy – required the patience of a corpse.

Watching Urology Aziz roll up his prayer rug, Martin Mills knew it was the perfect time for him to practice another exercise of Father de Mello's *Christian Exercises in Eastern Form* – namely, 'stillness.' Most people didn't appreciate how impossible it was to stand absolutely still; it could be painful, too, but Martin was good at it. He stood so still that, 10 minutes later, a passing fork-tailed kite almost landed on his head. It wasn't because the missionary so much as blinked that the bird suddenly veered away from him; the light that was reflected in the brightness of the missionary's eyes frightened the bird away.

Meanwhile, Dr Daruwalla was tearing through his hate mail, wherein he found a troubling two-rupee note. The envelope was addressed to Inspector Dhar in care of the film studio; typed on the serial-number side of the money, in capital letters, was this warning: YOU'RE AS DEAD AS LAL. The doctor would show this to Deputy Commissioner Patel, of course, but Farrokh felt he didn't need the detective's confirmation in order to know that the typist was the same lunatic who'd typed the message on the money found in Mr Lal's mouth.

Then Julia burst into the bedroom. She'd peeked into the living room to see if Martin Mills was still

411

sleeping, but he wasn't on the couch. The siding-glass doors to the balcony were open, but she'd not seen the missionary on the balcony – he was standing so still, she'd missed him. Dr Daruwalla stuffed the two-rupee note into his pocket and rushed to the balcony.

By the time the doctor got there, the missionary had moved ahead to a new prayer tactic – this one being one of Father de Mello's exercises in the area of 'body sensations' and 'thought control.' Martin would lift his right foot, move it forward, then put it down. As he did this, he would chant, 'Lifting . . . lifting . . . lifting,' and then (naturally) 'Moving . . . moving . . . moving,' and (finally) 'Placing . . . placing . . . placing.' In short, he was merely walking across the balcony, but with an exaggerated slowness – all the while exclaiming aloud his exact movements. To Dr Daruwalla, Martin Mills resembled a patient in physical therapy – someone recovering from a recent stroke – for the missionary appeared to be teaching himself how to speak and walk at the same time, with only modest success.

Farrokh tiptoed back to the bedroom and Julia.

'Perhaps I've underestimated his injuries,' the doctor said. 'I'll have to take him to the office with me. At least for a while, it's best to keep an eye on him.'

But when the Daruwallas cautiously approached the Jesuit, he was dressed in clerical garb. He was looking through his suitcase.

'They took only my *culpa* beads and my casual clothes,' Martin remarked. 'I'll have to buy some cheap local wear – it would be ostentatious to show up at St Ignatius looking like this!' Whereupon he laughed and plucked at his startlingly white collar.

It certainly won't do to have him walking around Bombay like this, Dr Daruwalla thought. What was required was the sort of clothing that would allow the madman somehow to fit in. Possibly I could arrange to shave his head, the doctor thought. Julia simply gaped at Martin Mills, but as soon as he began to relate (again!) the tale of his introduction to the city, he completely charmed her, and she became as alternately flirtatious and shy as a schoolgirl. For a man who'd taken a vow of chastity, the Jesuit was remarkably at ease with women – at least with an older woman, Dr Daruwalla thought.

The complexities of the day ahead for Dr Daruwalla were almost as frightening to the doctor as the thought of spending the next 12 hours in the missionary's discarded leg iron – or being followed around by Vinod, with the angry dwarf wielding the missionary's whip.

There was no time to lose. While Julia fixed a cup of coffee for Martin, Farrokh glanced hurriedly at the library collected in the Jesuit's suitcase. Father de Mello's *Sadhana: A Way to God* drew a particularly covert look, for in it Farrokh found a dog-eared page and an assertively underlined sentence: 'One of the biggest enemies to prayer is nervous tension.' I guess that's why I can't do it, Dr Daruwalla thought.

In the lobby, the doctor and the missionary didn't escape the notice of that first-floor member of the Residents' Society, the murderous Mr Munim.

'So! There is your movie star! Where is your dwarf?' Mr Munim shouted.

'Pay no attention to this man,' Farrokh told Martin. 'He's completely crazy.'

'The dwarf is in the suitcase!' Mr Munim cried. Thereupon he kicked the scholastic's suitcase, which was ill considered, because he was wearing only a floppy pair of the most insubstantial sandals; from the instant expression of pain on Mr Munim's face, it was clear that he'd made contact with one of the more solid tomes in Martin Mills's library – maybe the *Compact Dictionary of the Bible*, which was compact but not soft.

'I assure you, sir, there is no dwarf in this suitcase,' Martin Mills began to say, but Dr Daruwalla pulled him on. The doctor was beginning to realize that it was the new missionary's most basic inclination to talk to anyone.

413

In the alley, they found Vinod asleep in the Ambassador; the dwarf had locked the car. Leaning against the driver's-side door was the exact 'anyone' whom Dr Daruwalla most feared, for the doctor imagined there was no one more inspiring of missionary zeal than a crippled child . . . unless there'd been a child missing both arms and both legs. By the shine of excitement in the scholastic's eyes, Farrokh could tell that the boy with the mangled foot was sufficiently inspiring to Martin Mills.

Bird-Shit Boy

It was the beggar from the day before – the boy who stood on his head at Chowpatty Beach, the cripple who slept in the sand. The crushed right foot was once again an offense to the doctor's standard of surgical neatness, but Martin Mills was fatally drawn to the rheumy discharge about the beggar's eyes; to his missionary mind, it was as if the stricken child already clutched a crucifix. The scholastic only momentarily took his eyes off the boy – to glance heavenward – but that was long enough for the little beggar to fool Martin with the infamous Bombay bird-shit trick.

In Dr Daruwalla's experience, it was a filthy trick, usually performed in the following fashion: while one hand pointed to the sky – to the nonexistent passing bird – the other hand of the little villain squirted your shoe or your pants. The instrument that applied the presumed 'bird shit' was similar to a turkey baster, but any kind of bulb with a syringelike nozzle would suffice. The fluid it contained was some whitish stuff – often curdled milk or flour and water – but on your shoe or your pants, it appeared to be bird shit. When you looked down from the sky, having failed to see the bird, there was the shit – it had already hit you – and the sneaky little beggar was wiping it off your shoe or your pants with a handy rag. You then rewarded him with at least a rupee or two.

But in this instance Martin Mills didn't comprehend that a reward was expected. He'd looked in a heavenly direction without the boy needing to point; thereupon the beggar had drawn out the syringe and squirted the Jesuit's scuffed black shoe. The cripple was so quick on the draw and so smooth at concealing the syringe under his shirt that Dr Daruwalla had seen neither the quick draw nor the shot – only the slick return to the shirt. Martin Mills believed that a bird had uncer-emoniously shat on his shoe, and that the tragically mutilated boy was wiping off this bird shit with the tattered leg of his baggy shorts. To the missionary, this maimed child was definitely heaven-sent.

With that in mind, there in the alley, the scholastic dropped to his knees, which wasn't the usual response that was made to the outstretched hand of the beggar. The boy was frightened by the missionary's embrace. 'O God – thank you!' Martin Mills cried, while the cripple looked to Dr Daruwalla for help. 'This is your lucky day,' the missionary told the greatly bewildered beggar. 'That man is a *doctor*,' Martin Mills told the lame boy. 'That man can fix your foot.'

'I can't fix his foot!' Dr Daruwalla cried. 'Don't tell him that!'

'Well, certainly you can make it look better than this!' Martin replied. The cripple crouched like a cor-nered animal, his eyes darting back and forth between the two men.

'It's not as if I haven't already thought of it,' Farrokh said defensively. 'But I'm sure I can't give him a foot that works. And what do you think a boy like this cares for the appearance of the thing? He'll still limp!'

'Wouldn't you like your foot to be *cleaner-looking*?' Martin Mills asked the cripple. 'Wouldn't you like it to look less like a *hoe* or a *club*?' As he spoke, he cupped his hand near the bony fusion of ankle and foot, which the beggar awkwardly rested on the heel. Close up, the doctor could confirm his earlier suspicion: he would have to saw through bone. There would be little chance of success, a greater chance of risk.

'Primum non nocere,' Farrokh said to Martin Mills. 'I presume you know Latin.'

'"Above all, do no harm,"' the Jesuit replied.

'He was stepped on by an elephant,' Dr Daruwalla explained. Then Farrokh remembered what the cripple had said. Dr Daruwalla repeated this to the missionary, but the doctor looked at the boy when he spoke: 'You can't fix what elephants do.' The boy nodded, albeit cautiously.

'Do you have a mother or a father?' the Jesuit asked. The beggar shook his head. 'Does anyone look after you?' Martin asked. The cripple shook his head again. Dr Daruwalla knew it was impossible to understand how much the boy understood, but the doctor remembered that the boy's English was better than he was letting on – a clever boy.

'There's a gang of them at Chowpatty,' the doctor said. 'There's a kind of pecking order to their begging.' But Martin Mills wasn't listening to him; although the zealot manifested a certain 'modesty of the eyes,' which was encouraged among the Jesuits, there was nonetheless an intensity to his gazing into the rheumy eyes of the crippled child. Dr Daruwalla realized that the boy was mesmerized.

'But there *is* someone looking after you,' the missionary said to the beggar. Slowly, the cripple nodded.

'Do you have any other clothes but these?' the missionary asked.

'No clothes,' the boy instantly said. He was undersized, but hardened by the street life. Maybe he was 8, or 10.

'And how long has it been since you've had any food – since you've had a *lot* of food?' Martin asked him.

'Long time,' the beggar said. At the most, he might have been 12.

'You can't do this, Martin,' Farrokh said. 'In Bombay, there are more boys like this than would fit into all of St Ignatius. They wouldn't fit in the school or in the church or in the cloister – they wouldn't fit in the schoolyard, or in the parking lot! There are too many boys like this – you can't begin your first day here by *adopting* them!'

'Not "them" – just this one,' the missionary replied. 'St Ignatius said that he would sacrifice his life if he could prevent the sins of a single prostitute on a single night.'

'Oh, I see,' said Dr Daruwalla. 'I understand you've already *tried* that!'

'It's very simple, really,' said Martin Mills. 'I was going to buy clothes – I'll buy half as many for me, and the rest for him. I presume that I will eat something sometime later today. I'll eat half as much as I normally would have eaten . . .'

'And – don't tell me! – the rest is for *him*,' Dr Daruwalla said angrily. 'Oh, this is brilliant. I wonder why *I* didn't think of it years ago!'

'Everything is just a start,' the Jesuit calmly replied. 'Nothing is overwhelming if you take one step at a time.' Then he stood up with the child in his arms, leaving his suitcase for Dr Daruwalla to deal with. He walked with the boy, circling Vinod's taxi as the dwarf slept on and on. 'Lifting . . . lifting . . . lifting,' Martin Mills said. 'Moving . . . moving . . . moving,' he repeated. 'Placing . . . placing . . . placing,' the missionary said. The boy thought this was a game – he laughed.

'You see? He's happy,' Martin Mills announced. 'First the clothes, then the food, then – if not the foot – you can at least do something about his eyes, can't you?'

'I'm not an eye doctor,' Dr Daruwalla replied. 'Eye diseases are common here. I could refer him to someone . . .'

'Well, that's a start, isn't it?' Martin said. 'We're just

417

going to get you *started*,' he told the cripple.

Dr Daruwalla pounded on the driver's-side window, startling Vinod awake; the dwarf's stubby fingers were groping for his squash-racquet handles before he recognized the doctor. Vinod hurried to unlock the car. If, in the light of day, the dwarf saw that Martin Mills bore a less-than-exact resemblance to his famous twin, Vinod gave no indication of any suspicion. Not even the missionary's clerical collar appeared to faze the dwarf. If Dhar looked different to Vinod, the dwarf assumed this was the result of being beaten by transvestite whores. Furiously, Farrokh threw the fool's suitcase into the trunk.

There was no time to lose. The doctor realized that he had to get Martin Mills to St Ignatius as soon as he could. Father Julian and the others would lock him up. Martin would have to obey them – after all, wasn't that what a vow of obedience meant? The doctor's advice to the Father Rector would be simple enough: keep Martin Mills in the mission, or keep him in school. *Don't* let him loose in the rest of Bombay! The chaos he could cause was inconceivable!

As Vinod backed the Ambassador out of the alley, Dr Daruwalla saw that both the scholastic and the crippled child were smiling. That was when Farrokh thought of the word that had escaped him; it floated to his lips, in belated answer to John D.'s question regarding what Martin Mills was like. The word was 'dangerous.' The doctor couldn't stop himself from saying it.

'You know what you are?' Dr Daruwalla asked the missionary. 'You're *dangerous*.'

'Thank you,' the Jesuit said.

There was no further conversation until the dwarf was struggling to park the taxi on that busy stretch of Cross Maidan near the Bombay Gymkhana. Dr Daruwalla was taking Martin Mills and the cripple to Fashion Street, where they could buy the cheapest cotton clothes – factory seconds, with small defects –

when the doctor caught sight of the gob of fake bird shit that had hardened on the strap of his right sandal; Farrokh could feel that a bit of the stuff had also dried between his bare toes. The boy must have squirted Dr Daruwalla while the doctor and the scholastic had been arguing, although the doctor supposed there was a slim possibility that the bird shit was authentic.

'What's your name?' the missionary asked the beggar.

'Ganesh,' the boy replied.

'After the elephant-headed god – the most popular god in Maharashtra,' Dr Daruwalla explained to Martin Mills. It was the name of every other boy on Chowpatty Beach.

'Ganesh – may I call you Bird-Shit Boy?' Farrokh asked the beggar. But there was no reading the deep-black eyes that flashed in the cripple's feral face; either he didn't understand or he thought it was politic to remain silent – a clever boy.

'You certainly shouldn't call him Bird-Shit Boy!' the missionary protested.

'Ganesh?' said Dr Daruwalla. 'I think *you* are danger-ous, too, Ganesh.' The black eyes moved quickly to Martin Mills; then they fixed once again on Farrokh.

'Thank you,' Ganesh said.

Vinod had the last word; unlike the missionary, the dwarf was not automatically moved to pity cripples.

'You, Bird-Shit Boy,' Vinod said. 'You are definitely being dangerous,' the dwarf told him.

419

16. MR GARG'S GIRL

A Little Something Venereal

Deepa had taken the night train to Bombay; she'd
traveled from somewhere in Gujarat – from wherever
the Great Blue Nile was playing. She'd arranged to
bring the runaway child prostitute to Dr Daruwalla's
office at the Hospital for Crippled Children, intending
to shepherd the girl through her examination – it was
the child's first doctor's visit. Deepa didn't expect
there would be anything wrong; she planned to take
the girl back to the Great Blue Nile with her. It was true
that the child had run away from a brothel, but –
according to Mr Garg – she'd managed to run away
when she was still a virgin. Dr Daruwalla didn't think
so.

Her name was Madhu, which means 'honey.' She
had the floppy, oversized hands and feet and the dis-
proportionately small body of a large-pawed puppy, of
the kind one always assumes will become a big dog.
But in Madhu's case this was a sign of malnutrition;
her body had failed to develop in proportion to her
hands and feet. Also, Madhu's head wasn't as large as
it appeared at first glance. Her long, oval face was
simply unmatched to her petite body. Her protuberant
eyes were the tawny yellow of a lion's, but remote with
distraction; her lips were full and womanly and
entirely too grown-up for her unformed face, which
was still the face of a child.

It was her child-woman appearance that must have
been Madhu's particular appeal in the brothel she'd
run away from; her undersized body reflected this
disquieting ambivalence. She had no hips – that is, she
had the hips of a boy – but her breasts, which were

absurdly small, were nonetheless as fully formed and womanly as her compelling mouth. Although Garg had told Deepa that the child was prepubescent, Dr Daruwalla guessed that Madhu had not yet had her period because she'd never had enough to eat and she was overworked; furthermore, it was not that the girl hadn't grown any underarm or pubic hair – someone had skillfully shaved her. Farrokh made Deepa feel the faint stubble that was growing in Madhu's armpits.

The doctor's memory of his accidental encounter with Deepa's pudenda surfaced at the oddest times. The sight of the dwarf's wife touching the hollow of the young girl's armpit gave Farrokh the shivers. It was the wiry strength of the former flyer's hand that the doctor remembered – how she'd grabbed his chin as he'd struggled to raise the bridge of his nose off her pubic bone, how she'd simply wrenched his head out of her crotch. And he was off balance, his forehead pressing into her belly and the scratchy sequins on her singlet, so that a good portion of his weight rested on her; yet Deepa had cranked on his chin with only one hand and had managed to lift him. Her hands were strong from the trapeze work. And now the sight of Deepa's sinewy hand in the girl's armpit was enough to make Farrokh turn away – not from the exposed girl but from Deepa.

Farrokh realized that probably there remained more innocence in Deepa than what innocence, if any, remained in Madhu; the dwarf's wife had never been a prostitute. The indifference with which Madhu had undressed for Dr Daruwalla's cursory examination made the doctor feel that the girl was probably an *experienced* prostitute. Farrokh knew how awkwardly most children Madhu's age undressed. After all, it wasn't only that he was a doctor; he had daughters.

Madhu was silent; perhaps she didn't comprehend the reason for her physical exam, or else she was ashamed. When she covered her breasts and held her hand over her mouth, Madhu looked like an 8-year-old child. But Dr Daruwalla believed that the girl was at least 13 or 14.

'I'm sure it was someone else who shaved her – she didn't shave herself,' Farrokh told Deepa. From his research for *Inspector Dhar and the Cage-Girl Killer*, the doctor knew a few things about the brothels. In the brothels, virginity was a term of sale – not one of accuracy. Maybe in order to *look* like a virgin, one had to be shaved. The doctor knew that most of the older prostitutes were also shaved. Pubic hair, like under-arm hair, was simply an invitation to lice.

The dwarf's wife was disappointed; she'd hoped that Dr Daruwalla was going to be the first and last doctor whom Madhu would be required to see. Dr Daruwalla didn't think so. He found Madhu disturbingly mature; not even to please Deepa could he give the girl a clean bill of health, not without first making Madhu see Gynecology Tata – Tata Two, as he was more commonly known.

Dr Tata (the son) was not the best OB/GYN in Bombay, but – like his father before him – he saw any referral from any other physician immediately. It had long been Dr Daruwalla's suspicion that these referrals were the heart of Tata Two's business. Farrokh doubted that many patients were inclined to see Tata Two twice. Despite removing the adjectival 'best' and 'most famous' from his clinic's description – it was now called DR TATA'S CLINIC FOR GYNECOLOGICAL & MATERNITY NEEDS – the clinic was the most steadfastly mediocre in the city. If one of his orthopedic patients had a problem of an OB/GYN nature, Dr Daruwalla never would have referred her to Tata Two. But for a routine examination – for a simple certificate of health, or a standard venereal-disease screening – Tata Two would do, and Tata Two was fast.

He was remarkably fast in Madhu's case. While Vinod drove Deepa and Madhu to Dr Tata's office, where Dr Tata would keep them waiting only a short time, Farrokh attempted to restrain Martin Mills from playing too zealous a role in embracing that cause which the dwarf and his wife practiced like a religion. Having observed the scholastic's compassion for the elephant-footed beggar, Vinod had wasted little time in enlisting the famous Inspector Dhar's services. Unfortunately, it had been impossible to conceal from the missionary that the only *un*crippled child in Dr Daruwalla's waiting room was, or had been, a child prostitute.

Even before Dr Daruwalla could complete his examination of Madhu, the damage had been done: Martin Mills had been totally swayed by Vinod and Deepa's insane idea that every runaway from the brothels of Bombay could become an acrobat in the circus. To Martin, sending child prostitutes to the circus was a step en route to saving their souls. Farrokh feared what was coming next – that is, as soon as it occurred to Martin. It was only a matter of time before the missionary would decide that Ganesh, the elephant-footed boy, could save *his* little soul at the circus, too. Dr Daruwalla knew there weren't enough circuses for all the children that the Jesuit believed he could rescue.

Then Dr Tata called with the news about Madhu.

'Yes, she is certainly sexually active – too many previous partners to count! – and yes, she has a little something venereal,' said Tata Two. 'But, under the circumstances, it could be a lot worse.'

'And you'll check if she's HIV-positive?' asked Dr Daruwalla.

'We're checking – we'll let you know,' Dr Tata said.

'So what have you found?' Farrokh asked. 'Is it gonorrhea?'

'No, but there's some inflammation of the cervix, and a slight discharge,' Dr Tata explained. 'She doesn't complain of any urethritis – the inflammation in her urethra is so mild, it may go unnoticed. I'm guessing it's chlamydia. I'll put her on a course of tetracycline. But it's difficult to diagnose a chlamydial infection – as you know, chlamydiae are not visible under the microscope.'

'Yes, yes,' said Dr Daruwalla impatiently; he *didn't* know this about chlamydiae, but he didn't care to know. He had been lectured to enough for one day, commencing with a rehashing of the Protestant Reformation and the Jesuitical approach to free will. All he wanted to know was if Madhu was sexually active. And might there be something venereal that he could pin on the acid-scarred Mr Garg? *All* of Mr Garg's previous discoveries had carried something venereal; the doctor would have loved to attribute the blame for this to Garg himself. Farrokh didn't believe that the cause of the sexually transmitted disease was always the brothel that the girl was running away from. Most of all – and the doctor couldn't have explained why – it was Deepa and Vinod's seemingly good opinion of Mr Garg that Dr Daruwalla wished he could change. Why didn't the dwarf and his wife see that Mr Garg was egregiously slimy?

'So, if she's *not* HIV-positive, you'll call her clean?' Farrokh asked Tata Two.

'After the course of tetracycline, *and* provided no one lets her return to the brothel,' Dr Tata said.

And provided Deepa doesn't take the girl back to the Wetness Cabaret, or to Mr Garg, Farrokh thought. Dr Daruwalla understood that Deepa would need to return to the Great Blue Nile before the doctor knew the results of Madhu's HIV test. Vinod would have to look after Madhu and keep her away from Garg; the girl would be safe with the dwarf.

Meanwhile, the doctor could observe that the morally meddlesome nature of Martin Mills had been momentarily curbed; the missionary was enthralled by Farrokh's favorite circus photograph – the doctor always kept it on his office desk. It was a picture of Pratap Singh's adopted sister, Suman, the star of the Great Royal Circus. Suman was in her costume for the Peacock Dance; she stood in the wing of the main tent, helping two little girls into their peacock costumes. The peacocks were always played by little girls. Suman was putting on their peacock heads; she was tucking their hair under the blue-green feathers of the long peacock necks.

The Peacock Dance was performed in all the Indian circuses. (The peacock is the national bird of India.) In the Great Royal, Suman always played the legendary woman whose lover has been cast under a spell to make him forget her. In the moonlight, she dances with two peacocks, she wears bells on her ankles and wrists.

But what haunted Dr Daruwalla about the Peacock Dance was neither Suman's beauty nor the little girls in their peacock costumes. Instead, it always seemed to him that the little girls (the peacocks) were about to die. The music for the dance was soft and eerie, and the lions were audible in the background. In the darkness outside the ring, the lions were being moved from their cages and into the holding tunnel, which was a long, tubular cage that led to the ring. The lions hated the holding tunnel. They fought among themselves because they were pressed too low to the ground; they could neither go back to the cages nor advance into the ring. Farrokh had always imagined that a lion would escape. When the peacock girls were finished with their dance and running back to their troupe tent – there in the dark avenue, the escaped lion would catch them and kill them.

After the Peacock Dance, the roustabouts set up the cage for the lions in the ring. To distract the audience from the tedious assembly of the cage and the setting up of the hoops of fire, a motorcycle act was performed in the open wing of the main tent. It was so insanely loud, no one would hear the peacock girls screaming if a lion was loose. The motorcycles raced in opposite directions inside a steel-mesh ball; this was called the Globe of Death, because *if* the motorcycles ever collided, it was possible that both riders could be killed. But Dr Daruwalla imagined it was called the Globe of Death because the sound of the motorcycles concealed the fate of the peacock girls.

The first time he'd seen Suman, she was helping the little girls into their peacock costumes; she seemed to be a mother to them, although she had no children of her own. But it also seemed to Farrokh that Suman was dressing the little girls for the last time. They would run out of the ring, the Globe of Death would begin and the escaped lion would already be waiting for them in the dark avenue of the troupe tents.

Maybe, if she wasn't HIV-positive, Madhu would become one of the peacock girls at the Great Blue Nile. Either way, whether she was HIV-positive or a peacock girl, Dr Daruwalla thought that Madhu's chances were pretty slim. Garg's girls were always in need of more than a dose of tetracycline.

Martin Luther Is Put to Dubious Use

Martin Mills had insisted on observing Dr Daruwalla at his doctor's chores, for the zealot had proclaimed – even before he saw a single one of Dr Daruwalla's patients – that the doctor was performing 'the Lord's work.' After all, what activity was nearer to Jesus than healing crippled children? It was right up there with saving their little souls, Farrokh guessed. Dr Daruwalla had allowed the missionary to follow him as closely as his own shadow, but only because he wanted to observe how the zealot was recovering from his beating. The doctor had alertly anticipated any indications that the scholastic might have suffered a serious head injury, but Martin Mills was ploddingly disproving this theory. Martin's particular madness seemed in no way trauma-related; rather, it appeared to be the result of blind convictions and a systematic education. Furthermore, after their experience on Fashion Street, Dr Daruwalla didn't dare let Martin Mills wander freely in Bombay; yet the doctor hadn't found the time to deliver the madman to the presumed safety of St Ignatius.

On Fashion Street, Martin Mills had been completely unaware of that giant likeness of Inspector Dhar which was freshly plastered above the stalls of the clothes bazaar. The missionary had noticed the other movie advertisement; side by side with *Inspector Dhar and the Towers of Silence* was a poster for *Death Wish*, with a sizeable likeness of Charles Bronson.

'That looks like Charles Bronson!' the Jesuit had observed.

'That *is* Charles Bronson,' Farrokh had informed him. But of himself, in the image of Inspector Dhar, the missionary saw no resemblance. The clothes vendors, however, looked upon the Jesuit with baleful eyes. One refused to sell him anything; the scholastic assumed that the merchant had nothing in the right size. Another screamed at Martin Mills that his appearance on Fashion Street was nothing but a film-publicity stunt. This was probably because the missionary insisted on carrying the crippled beggar. The accusation had been made in Marathi, and the elephant-footed boy had enlivened the exchange by spitting on a rack of the merchant's clothes.

'Now, now – even though they revile you, simply smile,' Martin Mills had told the crippled boy. 'Show them charity.' The Jesuit must have assumed it was Ganesh and his crushed foot that had caused the outburst.

It was a wonder they'd escaped from Fashion Street with their lives; Dr Daruwalla had also managed to persuade Martin Mills to get his hair cut. It was short enough to begin with, but the doctor had said something about the weather growing hotter and hotter, and that in India many ascetics and holy men shaved their heads. The haircut that Farrokh had arranged – with one of those three-rupee curbside barbers who hang out at the end of the clothing stalls on Fashion Street –

had been as close to a shaven head as possible. But even as a 'skinhead,' Martin Mills exhibited something of Inspector Dhar's aggressive quality. The resemblance went well beyond the propensity for the family sneer.

John D. had little to say; yet he was unstoppably opinionated – and when he was acting, he always knew his lines. Martin Mills, on the other hand, never shut up; but wasn't what Martin had to say also a recitation? Weren't they the lines of another kind of actor, the ceaseless intervening of a true believer? Weren't *both* twins unstoppably opinionated? Certainly they were both stubborn.

The doctor was fascinated that barely a majority of Bombayites appeared to recognize Inspector Dhar in Martin Mills; there was almost as many individuals who seemed to see no resemblance whatsoever. Vinod who knew Dhar well, never doubted that Martin was Dhar. Deepa also knew Dhar, and she was indifferent to the movie star's fame; because she'd never seen an Inspector Dhar movie, the character meant nothing to her. When Deepa met the missionary in Dr Daruwalla's waiting room, she instantly took Martin Mills for what he was: an American do-gooder. But this had long been her opinion of *Dhar.* If the dwarf's wife had never seen an Inspector Dhar movie, she had seen Dhar's TV appearance on behalf of the Hospital for Crippled Children. Dhar had always struck Deepa as a do-gooder *and* a non-Indian. On the other hand, Ranjit wasn't fooled. The medical secretary saw only the slightest resemblance to Dhar in the frail missionary. Ranjit didn't even suspect the two of being twins; his only comment, which he whispered to Dr Daruwalla, was that he'd never known Dhar had a brother. Given Martin Mills's ravaged condition, Ranjit assumed he was Dhar's *older* brother.

Dr Daruwalla's first concern was to keep Martin Mills in the dark; once the doctor could get the missionary to St Ignatius, Martin would be kept in perpetual darkness – or so the doctor hoped. Farrokh wanted it to be John D.'s decision whether to know his twin or not. But in the doctor's office, and in the waiting room, it had been awkward to keep Martin Mills separated from Vinod and Deepa. Short of telling the dwarf and his wife that the missionary was Dhar's twin, Dr Daruwalla didn't know what to do or how to keep them apart.

It was upon Vinod's initiative that Madhu and Ganesh were introduced to each other, as if a 13-year-old child prostitute and a 10-year-old beggar who'd allegedly been stepped on by an elephant would instantly have worlds in common. To Dr Daruwalla's surprise, the children appeared to hit it off. Madhu was excited to learn that the ugly problem with Ganesh's eyes – if not the ugly foot – might soon be corrected. Ganesh imagined that he could do very well for himself in the circus, too.

'With that foot?' Farrokh said. 'What could you do in the circus with that foot?'

'Well, there are things he can do with his *arms*,' Martin Mills replied. Dr Daruwalla feared that the Jesuit had been schooled to refute any defeatist argument.

'Vinod,' Farrokh said beseechingly. 'Could the boy even be a roustabout with a limp like that? Do you see them letting him shovel the elephant shit? He could limp after the wheelbarrow, I suppose . . .'

'Clowns are limping,' Vinod replied. '*I* am limping,' the dwarf added.

'So you're saying that he can limp and be laughed at, like a clown,' said Dr Daruwalla.

'There's always working in the cook's tent,' Vinod said stubbornly. 'He could be kneading and rolling out the dough for the chapati. He could be chopping up the garlic and the onions for the dhal.'

'But why would they take *him*, when there are countless boys with two good feet to do that?' Dr Daruwalla asked. The doctor kept his eye on Bird-Shit

Boy, knowing that his discouraging arguments might meet with the beggar's disapproval and a corresponding measure of bird shit.

'We could tell the circus that they had to take the two of them together!' Martin cried. 'Madhu *and* Ganesh – we could say that they're brother and sister, that one looks after the other!'

'We could *lie*, in other words,' said Dr Daruwalla.

'For the good of these children, *I* could lie!' the missionary said.

'I'll bet you could!' Farrokh cried. He was frustrated that he couldn't remember his father's favorite condemnation of Martin Luther. What had old Lowji said about Luther's justification for lying? Farrokh wished he could surprise the scholastic with what he recalled as a fitting quotation, but it was Martin Mills who surprised him.

'You're a Protestant, aren't you?' the Jesuit asked the doctor. 'You should be advised by what your old friend Luther said: "What wrong can there be in telling a downright good lie for a good cause . . ."'

'Luther is *not* my old friend!' Dr Daruwalla snapped. Martin Mills had left something out of the quotation, but Farrokh couldn't remember what it was. What was missing was the part about this downright good lie being not only for a good cause but also 'for the advancement of the Christian Church.' Farrokh knew he'd been fooled, but he lacked the necessary information to fight back; therefore, he chose to fight with Vinod instead.

'And I suppose you're telling me that Madhu here is another Pinky – is that it?' Farrokh asked the dwarf.

This was a sore point between them. Because Vinod and Deepa had been Great Blue Nile performers, they were sensitive to Dr Daruwalla's preference for the performers of the Great Royal. There was a 'Pinky' in the Great Royal Circus; she was a star. She'd been bought by the circus when she was only three or four. She'd been trained by Pratap Singh and his wife, Sumi.

430

By the time Pinky was seven or eight, she could balance on her forehead at the top of a 10-foot-high bamboo pole; the pole was balanced on the forehead of a bigger girl, who stood on another girl's shoulders . . . the act was that kind of impossible thing. It was an item that called for a girl whose sense of balance was one in a million. Although Deepa and Vinod had never performed for the Great Royal Circus, they knew which circuses had high standards – at least higher than the standards at the Great Blue Nile. Yet Deepa brought the doctor these wrecked little whores from Kamathipura and proclaimed them circus material; at best, they were Great Blue Nile material.

'Can Madhu even stand on her head?' Farrokh asked Deepa. 'Can she walk on her hands?'

The dwarf's wife suggested that the child could learn. After all, Deepa had been sold to the Great Blue Nile as a boneless girl, a future plastic lady; she had learned to be a trapeze artist, a flyer.

'But you fell,' the doctor reminded Deepa.

'She is merely falling into a net!' Vinod exclaimed.

'There isn't always a net,' Dr Daruwalla said. 'Did *you* land in a net, Vinod?' Farrokh asked the dwarf.

'I am being fortunate in other ways,' Vinod replied. 'Madhu won't be working with clowns – or with elephants,' the dwarf added.

But Farrokh had the feeling that Madhu was clumsy; she *looked* clumsy – not to mention the dubious coordination of the limping garlic-and-onion chopper, Madhu's newly appointed brother. Farrokh felt certain that the elephant-footed boy would find another elephant to step on him. Dr Daruwalla imagined that the Great Blue Nile might even conceive of a way to display the cripple's mashed foot; Ganesh would become a minor sideshow event – the elephant boy, they would call him.

That was when the missionary, on the evidence of less than one day's experience in Bombay, had said to Dr Daruwalla, 'Whatever the dangers in the circus, the circus will be better for them than their present situation – we know the alternatives to their being in the circus.'

Vinod had remarked to Inspector Dhar that he was looking surprisingly well recovered from his nightmarish experience on Falkland Road. (Farrokh thought the missionary looked awful.) To keep the dwarf and the missionary from talking further to each other, which Dr Daruwalla knew would be confusing to them both, the doctor pulled Vinod aside and informed him that he should humor Dhar – 'and by no means contradict him' – because the dwarf had correctly diagnosed the movie star. There *had* been brain damage; it would be delicate to assess how much.

'Are you having to delouse him, too?' Vinod had whispered to Farrokh. The dwarf was referring to the reason for the scholastic's horrible haircut, but Dr Daruwalla had solemnly agreed. Yes, there had been lice *and* brain damage.

'Those are being filthy prostitutes!' Vinod had explained.

What a morning it had been already! Dr Daruwalla thought. He'd finally gotten rid of Vinod and Deepa – by sending them with Madhu to Dr Tata. Dr Daruwalla had not expected Tata Two to send them back so soon. Farrokh barely had time to get rid of Martin Mills; the doctor wanted the scholastic out of the office and the waiting room before Vinod and Deepa and Madhu returned. What's more, Dr Daruwalla wanted time to be alone; the deputy commissioner expected the doctor to come to Crime Branch Headquarters. Doubtless the doctor's viewing of the photographs of the murdered prostitutes would serve to undermine the collected optimism of the Jesuit, the dwarf and the dwarf's wife. But before Farrokh could slip away to Crawford Market, where he was meeting Deputy Commissioner Patel, it was necessary for the doctor to create an errand for Martin Mills; if only for an hour or two, the missionary was in need of a mission.

Another Warning

The elephant boy was a problem. Ganesh had behaved badly in the exercise yard, where many of the post-operative patients among the crippled children were engaged in their various physical-therapy assignments. Ganesh took this opportunity to squirt several of the more defenseless children with the bird-shit syringe; when Ranjit took the syringe away from the aggressive boy, Ganesh bit Dr Daruwalla's faithful secretary on the hand. Ranjit was offended that he'd been bitten by a beggar; dealing with the unruly likes of the elephant-footed boy wasn't a suitable use of the medical secretary's training.

On a day that had barely begun, Dr Daruwalla was already exhausted. Nevertheless, the doctor made quick and clever use of the biting episode. If Martin Mills was so sure that Bird-Shit Boy was capable of contributing to the daily chores of a circus, perhaps the missionary could be persuaded to take some responsibility for the little beggar. Martin Mills was eager to take responsibility for the elephant boy; the zealot would be likely to claim responsibility for a world of cripples, Farrokh imagined. Thereupon Dr Daruwalla assigned Martin Mills the task of taking Ganesh to Parsi General Hospital; the doctor wanted the crippled beggar to be examined by Eye, Ear, Nose and Throat Jeejeebhoy – Double E-NT Jeejeebhoy, as he was called. Dr Jeejeebhoy was an expert on the eye problems that were epidemic in India.

Although there was a rheumy discharge and Ganesh had said that his eyelids were gummed shut every morning, there wasn't that softness of the eyeballs that Dr Daruwalla thought of as end-stage or 'white' eyes; then the cornea is dull and opaque, and the patient is blind. Farrokh hoped that, whatever was wrong with Ganesh, it was in an early stage. Vinod had admitted that the circus wouldn't take a boy who was going blind – not even the Great Blue Nile.

But before Farrokh could hurry the elephant boy and the Jesuit on their way to Parsi General, which wasn't far, Martin Mills had spontaneously come to the aid of a woman in the waiting room. She was the mother of a crippled child; the missionary had dropped to his knees at her feet, which Farrokh found to be an irritating habit of the zealot. The woman was frightened by the gesture. Also, she wasn't in need of aid; she was *not* bleeding from her lips and gums, as the scholastic had declared – she was merely eating betel nut, which the Jesuit had never seen.

Dr Daruwalla ushered Martin from the waiting room to his office, where the doctor believed that the missionary could do slightly less harm. Dr Daruwalla insisted that Ganesh come with them, for the doctor was fearful that the dangerous beggar might bite someone else. Thereupon Farrokh calmly told Martin Mills what paan was – the local version of betel. The areca nut is wrapped in a betel leaf. Other common ingredients are rose syrup, aniseed, lime paste . . . but people put almost everything in the betel leaf, even cocaine. The veteran betel-nut eater had red-stained lips and teeth and gums. The woman the missionary had alarmed was *not* bleeding; she was merely eating paan.

Finally, Farrokh was able to free himself from Martin Mills. Dr Daruwalla hoped that Double E-NT Jeejeebhoy would take forever to examine Ganesh's eyes.

By midmorning, the day's confusion had achieved a lunatic pace. It was already a day that brought to Farrokh's mind those white-faced, dark-skinned girls in their purple tutus; it was a Load Cycle kind of day, as if everyone in the doctor's office and waiting room were riding bicycles to cancan music. As if to empha- size this chaos, Ranjit walked into the office without knocking; the medical secretary had just read Dr Daruwalla's mail. Although the envelope that Ranjit handed to Dr Daruwalla was addressed to the doctor,

434

not to Inspector Dhar, there was something familiar about the cold neutrality of the typescript; even before the doctor looked inside the envelope and saw the two-rupee note, he knew what he'd find. Farrokh was nevertheless stunned to read the message typed in capital letters on the serial-number side of the money. This time the warning said, YOU'RE AS DEAD AS DHAR.

Madhu Uses Her Tongue

There was a telephone call that added to the general confusion; in his distress, Ranjit made a mistake. The secretary thought the caller was Radiology Patel – it was a question regarding when Dr Daruwalla would come to view the photographs. Ranjit assumed that the 'photographs' were X rays, and he answered abruptly that the doctor was busy; either Ranjit or the doctor would call back with the answer. But after the secretary hung up, he realized that the caller hadn't been *Radiology* Patel. It had been Deputy Commissioner Patel, of course.

'There was a . . . Patel on the phone for you,' Ranjit told Farrokh in an offhand fashion. 'He wants to know when you're coming to see the photographs.'

And now there were *two* two-rupee notes in Dr Daruwalla's pocket; there was the warning to Dhar (YOU'RE AS DEAD AS LAL) and the warning to the doctor (YOU'RE AS DEAD AS DHAR). Farrokh felt certain that these threats would enhance the grimness of the photographs that the deputy commissioner wanted to show him.

Farrokh knew that John D., who was good at concealing his anger, was already angry with him for not forewarning the actor of the arrival of his bothersome twin. Dhar would be even angrier if Dr Daruwalla saw the photographs of the elephants drawn on the murdered prostitutes without him, but the doctor thought it unwise to bring Dhar to Crime Branch Headquarters

435

– nor would it be advisable to bring Martin Mills. The particular police station was near St Xavier's College, another Jesuit institution; this one was coeducational – St Ignatius admitted only boys. Martin Mills would doubtless attempt to persuade his fellow Jesuits to admit Madhu to their school in case she wasn't acceptable to the circus. The madman would probably insist that St Xavier's offer scholarships to other available child prostitutes! The scholastic had already announced that he would approach the Father Rector of St Ignatius on Ganesh's behalf. Dr Daruwalla couldn't wait to hear Father Julian's response to the notion of St Ignatius School attempting to educate a crippled beggar from Chowpatty Beach!

While the doctor was speculating in this fashion, and as he was hurrying to examine his remaining patients, Vinod and Deepa returned with Madhu and the tetracycline. Before he could abscond to the police station, Farrokh felt obliged to set a trap for Mr Garg. The doctor told Deepa to tell Garg that Madhu was being treated for a sexually transmitted disease; that sounded vague enough. If Mr Garg had diddled the child, he would need to call Dr Daruwalla to find out *which* disease – in order to learn the prescribed cure.

'And tell him we're checking to see if she's HIV-positive,' Farrokh said. *That* ought to make the bastard squirm, Dr Daruwalla thought.

The doctor wanted Deepa and Vinod to understand that Madhu must be kept away from the Wetness Cabaret, and away from Garg. The dwarf would drive his wife to the train station – Deepa had to return to the Great Blue Nile – but Vinod had to keep Madhu with him.

'And, remember, she's *not* clean until she's taken all the tetracycline,' the doctor told the dwarf.

'I am remembering,' Vinod said.

Then the dwarf asked about Dhar. Where was he? Was he all right? And didn't Dhar need his faithful driver? Dr Daruwalla explained to Vinod that Dhar was suffering from the common post-trauma delusion that he was someone else.

'Who is he being?' the dwarf inquired.

'A Jesuit missionary in training to be a priest,' the doctor replied.

Vinod was instantly sympathetic to this delusion. The actor was even more brain-damaged than the dwarf had first suspected! The key to dealing with Dhar, the doctor explained, was to expect him to be one person one minute and another person the next. The dwarf gravely nodded his big head.

Then Deepa kissed the doctor good-bye. There always lingered on her lips the sticky sweetness of those lemon drops she liked. Any physical contact with the dwarf's wife made Dr Daruwalla blush.

Farrokh could feel himself blush, but he'd never known if his blushes were visible. He knew he was dark-skinned for a Parsi, although he was fair-skinned in comparison to many other Indians – certainly, say, to a Goan or to a South Indian. In Canada, of course, the doctor was well aware that he was usually perceived as a man 'of color,' but when it came to blushing, he never knew whether or not he could blush undetected. Naturally, his embarrassment was communicated by other signals quite unrelated to his complexion and utterly unknown to him. For example, in the aftermath of Deepa's kiss, he averted his eyes but his lips remained parted, as if he'd forgotten something he was about to say. Thus he was caught all the more off guard when Madhu kissed him.

He wanted to believe that the child was merely imitating the dwarf's wife, but the girl's kiss was too lush and knowing – Deepa had *not* inserted her tongue. Farrokh felt Madhu's tongue flick his own tongue, dartingly. And the girl's breath was redolent of some dark spice – not lemon drops, possibly cardamom or clove. As Madhu withdrew from him, she flashed her first smile, and Dr Daruwalla saw the blood-red edge to her teeth at the gum line. For Farrokh to realize that the child prostitute was a veteran betel-nut eater was only a mild surprise, even anticlimactic. The doctor presumed that an addiction to paan was the least of Madhu's problems.

A Meeting at Crime Branch Headquarters

The inappropriately lewd encounter with Madhu left Dr Daruwalla in no mood to be tolerant of the photographic record of Rahul's artistry on the bellies of the murdered whores. The subject matter was no less limited than what the doctor had seen depicted on Beth's belly 20 years ago, nor had the intervening years imparted to the artist any measurable subtlety of style. The ever-mirthful elephant winked its eye and raised the opposite tusk. The water from the end of the elephant's trunk continued to spray the pubic hair – in many cases, the shaved pubic area – of the dead women. Not even the passing of so many years, not to mention the horror of so many murders, was sufficient to inspire Rahul beyond the first act of his imagination – namely, that the victim's navel was always the winking eye. The differences among the women's navels provided the only variety in the many photographs. Detective Patel remarked that both the drawings and the murders gave new meaning to that tired old phrase 'a one-track mind.' Dr Daruwalla, who was too appalled to speak, could only nod that he agreed.

Farrokh showed the deputy commissioner the threatening two-rupee notes, but D.C.P. Patel was unsurprised; he'd been expecting more warnings. The deputy commissioner knew that the note in Mr Lal's mouth had been just the beginning; no murderer the detective had ever known was content to threaten potential victims only once. Either killers didn't warn you or they repeatedly warned you. Yet, for 20 years, *this* killer hadn't given anyone a warning; only now, beginning with Mr Lal, had there emerged a kind of

438

vendetta against Inspector Dhar and Dr Daruwalla. It seemed unlikely to the deputy commissioner that the sole motivation for this change in Rahul had been a stupid movie. Something about the Daruwalla-Dhar connection must have infuriated Rahul – both personally *and* for a long time. It was the deputy commissioner's suspicion that *Inspector Dhar and the Cage-Girl Killer* had simply exacerbated Rahul's longstanding hatred.

'Tell me – I'm just curious,' said Detective Patel to Dr Daruwalla. 'Do you know any hijras – I mean *personally*?' But as soon as he saw that the doctor was thinking about the question – the doctor had been unable to answer spontaneously – the detective added, 'In your movie, you made a hijra the murderer. Whatever gave you such an idea? I mean, in *my* experience, the hijras *I* know are reasonably gentle – they're mostly nice people. The hijra prostitutes may be bolder than the female prostitutes, yet I don't think of them as dangerous. But possibly you knew one – someone who wasn't very nice. I'm just curious.'

'Well, *someone* had to be the murderer,' Dr Daruwalla said defensively. 'It was nothing personal.'

'Let me be more specific,' said the deputy commissioner. It was a line that got Dr Daruwalla's attention, because the doctor had often written that line for Inspector Dhar. 'Did you ever know somebody with a woman's breasts and a boy's penis? It was a rather small penis, from all reports,' the detective added. 'I don't mean a hijra. I mean a zenana – a transvestite with a penis, but with breasts.'

That was when Farrokh felt a flutter of pain in the area of his heart. It was his injured rib, trying to remind him of Rahul. The rib was crying out to him that Rahul was the second Mrs Dogar, but the doctor mistook the pain for an actual signal from his heart. His heart said, *Rahul!* But Rahul's connection to Mrs Dogar still eluded Dr Daruwalla.

'Yes, or maybe – I mean, I knew a man who was trying to become a woman,' Farrokh replied. 'He'd

obviously taken estrogens, maybe he'd even had surgical implants – he definitely had a woman's breasts.
But whether he'd been castrated, or if he'd had other
surgery, I don't know – I mean, I *presumed* he had a
penis because he was interested in the *complete*
operation . . . a total sex change.'

'And did he have this operation?' the deputy commissioner asked.

'I wouldn't know,' the doctor replied. 'I haven't seen
him, or her, for twenty years.'

'That would be the right number of years, wouldn't
it?' the detective asked. Again, Farrokh felt the twinge
in his rib that he confused with his excited heart.

'He was hoping to go to London for the operation,'
Farrokh explained. 'In those days, I believe it would
have been very difficult to get a complete sex-change
operation in India. They're still illegal here.'

'I believe that our murderer also went to London,'
Patel informed the doctor. 'Obviously, and only recently, he – or she – came back.'

'The person I knew was interested in going to art
school . . . in London,' Farrokh said numbly. The
photographs of the drawings on the bellies of the murdered prostitutes grew clearer in his mind, although
the photographs lay facedown on the deputy commissioner's desk. It was Patel who picked one up and
looked at it again.

'Not a very good art school would have taken him, I
suspect,' the detective said.

He never shut his office door, which opened on an
outdoor balcony; there were a dozen such offices off
this balcony, and it was the deputy commissioner's
policy that no one ever closed a door – except in the
monsoon rains, and then only when the wind was
wrong. With the doors open, no one being interrogated
could later claim that they'd been beaten. Also, the
sound of the police secretaries typing their officers'
reports was a sound that the deputy commissioner
enjoyed; the cacophony of typewriters implied both

industry and order. He knew that many of his fellow policemen were lazy and their secretaries were sloppy; the typed reports themselves were rarely as orderly as the clacking of the keys. On his desk, Deputy Commissioner Patel faced three reports in need of rewriting, and an additional report in greater need, but he pushed these four reports aside in order to spread out the photographs of the murdered whores' bellies. The elephant drawings were so familiar to him that they calmed him; he didn't want the doctor to sense his eagerness.

'And would this person that you knew have had a common sort of name, a name like Rahul?' the detective asked. It was a delivery worthy of the insincerity of Inspector Dhar.

'Rahul Rai,' said Dr Daruwalla; it was almost a whisper, but this didn't lessen the deputy commissioner's quickening pleasure.

'And would this Rahul Rai have been in Goa . . . perhaps visiting the beaches . . . at or about the time when the German and the American – those bodies you saw – were murdered?' Patel asked. The doctor was slumped in his chair as if bent by indigestion.

'At my hotel – at the Bardez,' Farrokh replied. 'He was staying with his aunt. And the thing is, if Rahul *is* in Bombay, he is certainly familiar with the Duckworth Club – his aunt was a member!'

'*Was?*' the detective said.

'She's dead,' Dr Daruwalla said. 'I would presume that Rahul, he or she, inherited her fortune.'

D.C.P. Patel touched the raised tusk of the elephant in one of the photographs; then he stacked the photos in a single neat pile. He'd always known there was family money in India, but the Duckworth Club connection was a surprise. What had misled him for 20 years was Rahul's brief notoriety in the transvestite brothels on Falkland Road and Grant Road; these were hardly the usual haunts of a Duckworthian.

'Of course I know that you know my wife,' the

441

detective said. 'I must put you together with her. She knows your Rahul, too, and it might help me to hear you compare notes – so to speak.'

'We could have lunch at the club. Someone there might know more about Rahul,' Farrokh suggested.

'Don't *you* ask any questions!' the deputy commissioner suddenly shouted. It offended Dr Daruwalla to be yelled at, but the detective was quickly tactful, if not exactly mollifying. 'We wouldn't want to warn Rahul, would we?' Patel said, as if he were speaking to a child.

The rising dust from the courtyard had coated the leaves of the neem trees; the rail of the balcony was also coated with dust. In the detective's office, the dull brass ceiling fan labored in an effort to push the motes of dust back out the open door. The darting shadows of fork-tailed kites occasionally moved across the deputy commissioner's desk. The one open eye of the topmost elephant in the stack of photos seemed to notice all these things, which the doctor knew he would never forget.

'Lunch *today?*' suggested the detective.

'Tomorrow is better for me,' Dr Daruwalla said. His pending obligation to deliver Martin Mills into the hands of the Jesuits at St Ignatius was a welcome intrusion; he also needed to talk to Julia, and he wanted the time to tell Dhar – Dhar should be at the lunch with the wounded hippie. Farrokh knew that John D. had a superior memory, maybe even of Rahul.

'Tomorrow is fine,' said the deputy commissioner, but his disappointment was evident. The words his wife had used to describe Rahul were constantly with him. Also with him was the size of Rahul's big hands, which had held his wife's big breasts; also, the erectness and the shapeliness of Rahul's breasts, which Nancy had felt against her back; also, the small, silky little boy's penis, which his wife had felt against her buttocks. Nancy had said he was condescending, mocking, teasing – certainly sophisticated, probably cruel.

Because Dr Daruwalla had only begun the struggle to compose a written report on Rahul Rai, the detective couldn't quite leave him alone. 'Give me one word for Rahul,' Patel asked Farrokh. 'The first word that comes to your mind – I'm just curious,' the detective said.

'Arrogant,' the doctor replied. After 20 years, it was visible on Detective Patel's face that this was unsatisfactory.

'Please try another,' the detective said.

'Superior,' said Dr Daruwalla.

'You're getting closer,' Patel replied.

'Rahul is a tease,' Farrokh explained. 'He condescends to you, he mocks you, he bullies you with a sort of self-satisfied sophistication. Like his late aunt, he uses his sophistication as a weapon. I think he is basically a cruel person.' The doctor paused in his description because the detective had closed his eyes and sat smiling at his desk. All the while, Deputy Commissioner Patel articulated his fingers as if he were typing up another report, but his fingers weren't tapping the keys of his typewriter; the detective had once more spread out the photographs – they covered his desk – and he typed on the many heads of the mocking elephants, his fingers finding the navels of the murdered prostitutes ... all those ceaselessly winking eyes.

Down the balcony, from another detective's office, a man was screaming that he was telling the truth, while a policeman calmly contradicted him with the almost harmonious repetition of the word 'lies.' From the courtyard kennel came a corresponding clamor – the police attack dogs.

After Dr Daruwalla had completed his written report on Rahul, the doctor wandered onto the balcony to have a look at the dogs; they'd barked themselves out. The late-morning sun was now beating down on the courtyard; the police dogs, all Dobermans, were asleep in the only shady corner of their kennel, which was obscured from Farrokh's view by a clump of neem trees. On the balcony itself, however, was a small cage with a newspaper floor, and the doctor knelt to play with a Doberman pinscher puppy – a prisoner in a portable pen. The puppy wriggled and whined for Farrokh's attention. It thrust its sleek black muzzle through a square of the wire mesh; it licked the doctor's hand – its needle-sharp teeth nipped his fingers.

'Are you a good dog?' Farrokh asked the puppy. Its wild eyes were ringed with the rusty-brown markings of its breed, which is preferred for police work in Bombay because the Doberman's short hair is suitable for the hot weather. The dogs were large and powerful and fast; they had the terrier's jaws and tenacity, although they weren't quite as intelligent as German Shepherds.

A subinspector, a junior officer, came out of an office where at least three typewriters were resounding, and this young, officious policeman spoke aggressively to Dr Daruwalla . . . something to the effect that 'spoiling' the Doberman puppy would make it untrainable for police business, something about not treating a future attack dog as a pet. Whenever anyone spoke Hindi this abruptly to the doctor, Farrokh felt frozen by his lack of fluency in the language.

'I'm sorry,' Dr Daruwalla said in English.

'No, don't *you* be sorry!' someone suddenly shouted. It was Deputy Commissioner Patel; he'd popped out of his office onto the balcony, where he stood clutching Farrokh's written statement in his hands. 'Go on – play with the puppy all you want to!' the deputy commissioner shouted.

The junior policeman realized his error and quickly apologized to Dr Daruwalla. 'I'm sorry, saar,' he said. But before the subinspector could slip back into his office and the safe din of the typewriters, he was barked at by Detective Patel, too.

444

'You *should* be sorry – speaking to *my* witness!' the deputy commissioner yelled.

So I am a 'witness,' Farrokh realized. He'd made a small fortune satirizing the police; now he knew he was in utter ignorance of even a matter as trivial as the pecking order among policemen.

'Go on – play with the puppy!' Patel repeated to the doctor, and so Farrokh once more turned his attention to the Doberman. Since the little dog had just dropped a surprisingly large turd on the newspaper floor of its cage, Dr Daruwalla's attention was momentarily attracted to the turd. That was when he saw that the newspaper was today's edition of *The Times of India*, and that the Doberman's turd had fallen on the review of *Inspector Dhar and the Towers of Silence*. It was a bad review, of such a hostile nature that its surliness seemed enhanced by the smell of dog shit.

The turd prevented all but a partial reading of the review, which was just as well; Farrokh was angered enough. There was even a gratuitous swipe taken at Dhar's perceived weight problem. The reviewer asserted that Inspector Dhar sported too protrusive a beer belly to justify the film studio's claim that Dhar was the Charles Bronson of Bombay.

By the nearby flutter of pages, Dr Daruwalla realized that the deputy commissioner had finished reading the doctor's statement. The detective also stood close enough to the puppy's cage to observe what Farrokh had been reading; Detective Patel was the one who had put the newspaper there.

'I'm afraid it's not a very good review,' the deputy commissioner observed.

'They never are,' Farrokh said. He followed Patel back to his office. Dr Daruwalla could feel that the detective wasn't altogether pleased by the doctor's written report.

'Sit down,' Detective Patel said, but when the doctor moved to the chair he'd sat in before, the detective caught his arm and steered him around the desk. 'No, no – you sit where *I* usually sit!' And so Farrokh seated himself in the deputy commissioner's chair. It was higher than the doctor's previous seat; the photographs of the murdered prostitutes were easier to see, or else harder to ignore. The doctor remembered the day at Chowpatty Beach when little John D. had been so frightened by the festival mob, by all the elephant heads being carried into the sea. 'They're drowning the elephants!' the child had cried. 'Now the elephants will be angry!'

In his written statement, Farrokh had said that he believed the hateful phone calls about his father's assassination had been from Rahul; after all, it was the voice of a woman trying to sound like a man, and this might suit whatever voice Rahul had ended up with. Twenty years ago, Rahul's voice had been a work-in-progress; it had been sexually undecided. But although Detective Patel found this speculation interesting, the detective was disturbed by Dr Daruwalla's conclusion: that Rahul had been old Lowji's assassin. This was too imaginative – it was too big a leap. This was the kind of conjecture that marred the doctor's written report and made it, in the deputy commissioner's opinion, 'amateurish.'

'Your father was blown up by professionals,' D.C.P. Patel informed Farrokh. 'I was still an inspector at the Colaba Station – only the duty officer. The Tardeo Police Station answered that call. I wasn't allowed at the scene of the crime, and then the investigation was turned over to the government. But I know for a fact that Lowji Daruwalla was exploded by a team. For a while, I heard that they thought the head mali might have been involved.'

'The Duckworth Club gardener?' cried Dr Daruwalla; he'd always disliked the head mali, without knowing why.

'There was a different head mali then . . . you will remember,' the detective said.

'Oh,' Farrokh said. He was feeling more and more amateurish by the minute.

'Anyway, Rahul is possibly the one making the phone calls – that's as good a guess as any,' Patel said. 'But he's no car-bomb expert.'

The doctor sat dismally still, looking at the photographic history of the murdered women. 'But why would Rahul hate me – *or* Dhar?' Dr Daruwalla asked.

'*That* is the question you don't answer, or even ask, in your written statement,' said D.C.P. Patel. 'Why, indeed?'

Thus were both men left with this unanswered question – Dr Daruwalla as he took a taxi uptown to meet Martin Mills, and Detective Patel as he reclaimed his desk chair. There the deputy commissioner once more faced the winking elephants on the slack bellies of the brutalized women.

No Motive

The deputy commissioner reflected that the mystery of Rahul's hatred was probably unsolvable. There would be no end to the conjecture on this subject, which would remain unsatisfactorily answered, probably forever. The matter of what motivated Rahul's hatred would remain incomplete. What was truly implausible in all the Inspector Dhar films was that *all* the murderers' motives were plainly established; the reasons for this or that hatred, which would lead to this or that violence, were always clear. Detective Patel regretted that Rahul Rai wasn't in a movie.

In addition to Dr Daruwalla's written statement, the detective had secured a letter from the doctor, for it hadn't escaped Patel's attention that Dr Daruwalla was guest chairman of the Membership Committee at the Duckworth Club. On behalf of Deputy Commissioner Patel, the Duckworth Club was requested to release the names of its new members – 'new' as of the last 20 years. The deputy commissioner sent a subinspector to the club with the letter of requisition; the subinspector was instructed not to leave the Duckworth Club without the list of names. Detective Patel doubted that he would need to peruse the names of all 6,000 members; with any luck, a recent membership to a relative of the late Promila Rai would be easy to spot. It was hard for the deputy commissioner to contain himself while he waited for the subinspector to bring him the list.

At his desk, Detective Patel sat among the dust motes that danced in the movement of the ceiling fan, which was silent not because it was truly noiseless, but because the constant orchestra of the secretaries' typewriters concealed the fan's faint whirs and ticks. At first, the deputy commissioner had been enthusiastic about the information he'd received from Dr Daruwalla. The detective had never been this close to Rahul; now he thought it was inevitable that the killer would be apprehended – an arrest seemed imminent. Yet Detective Patel couldn't bring himself to share his enthusiasm with his wife; he would hate to see her disappointed if there remained something inconclusive. There was always something inconclusive, the detective knew.

'But why would Rahul hate me – *or* Dhar?' Dr Daruwalla had asked. To the deputy commissioner, this question had been a typical inanity from the creator of Inspector Dhar; even so, the detective – the *real* detective – had encouraged the doctor to keep asking himself that same inane question.

Detective Patel had lived with the photographs for too long; that little elephant with its cocky tusk and its mischievous eyes had gotten to him, not to mention those murdered women with their unresponsive stomachs. There would never be a satisfactory motive for such hatred, the deputy commissioner believed. Rahul's *real* crime was that he didn't have sufficient justification for his actions. Something about Rahul would remain uncaptured; the horror about murders

like his was that they were never sufficiently motivated. And so it seemed to Detective Patel that his wife
was destined to be disappointed; he wouldn't call her
because he didn't want to get her hopes up. As he
might have guessed, Nancy called him.

'No, sweetie,' the detective said.

From the adjacent office, the sound of typing ceased;
then, from the next office, the typing also stopped –
and so on, all along the baclony.

'No, I would have told you, sweetie,' the deputy
commissioner said.

For 20 years, Nancy had called him almost every
day. She always asked him if he'd caught Beth's killer.

'Yes, of course I promise, sweetie,' the detective said.

Below, in the courtyard, the big Dobermans were
still asleep, and the police mechanic had mercifully
stopped his infernal revving of the patrolmen's motorcycles. The tuning of these ancient engines was so
constant, the dogs usually slept through it. But even
this sound had ceased, as if the mechanic – in spite of
his throttling up and throttling down – had managed to
hear the typing stop. The motorcycle mechanic had
joined the speechless typewriters.

'Yes, I showed the doctor the photographs,' Patel
told Nancy. 'Yes, of course you were right, sweetie,'
the deputy commissioner told his wife.

There was a new sound in Detective Patel's office;
the detective looked all around, trying to identify it.
Gradually, he became aware of the absence of typing.
Then he looked up at the revolving ceiling fan and
realized that it was the fan's whirring and ticking that
he heard. It was so quiet, he could hear the rusted iron
wheels of the hot-lunch wagons that were pushed by
hand along Dr Dadabhai Navroji Road; the dabba-
wallas were on their way to deliver hot lunches to the
office workers uptown.

Deputy Commissioner Patel knew that his fellow
policemen and their secretaries were listening to every
word of his conversation, and so he whispered into the

phone. 'Sweetie,' the detective said, 'it is slightly better than you first believed. The doctor didn't merely see the bodies, the doctor also knows Rahul. Both Daruwalla and Dhar – they actually know who he is . . . or at least who he, or she, *was*.' Patel paused, and then he whispered. 'No, sweetie – they haven't *seen* him, or her . . . not for twenty years.'

Then the detective once more listened to his wife – and to the ceiling fan, and to the grinding wheels of the dabba-wallas' faraway wagons.

When the deputy commissioner spoke again, it was an outburst, not a whisper. 'But I *never* dismissed your theories!' he cried into the phone. Then there entered into his voice a familiar tone of resignation; it so pained his fellow policemen, who all admired him and could no more fathom the *motive* for the extreme love that Detective Patel felt for his wife than there was any fathoming the motivation for Rahul's extreme hatred. There was simply no determining where either a love or a hate like that came from, and this mystery compelled the officers and their secretaries to listen. All along the balcony, it overwhelmed them to hear the intensity of what appeared to them to be a groundless, irrational love.

'No, of course I'm not angry,' Patel told Nancy. 'I'm sorry if I *sounded* angry, sweetie.' The detective sounded drained; the officers and their secretaries wished only that they could help him. They weren't eavesdropping for information related to those murdered prostitutes; they knew that the evidence of what had been done to those women was never farther away from the deputy commissioner than the top drawer of his desk. It was the pathetic sound of Detective Patel's love for his wretched wife that removed the hand of the motorcycle mechanic from the throttle.

In his office, Patel was painstakingly returning the photographs to his top drawer; he always returned them one by one, just as he reviewed them faithfully and in the exact order in which the crimes had been

discovered. 'I love you, *too*, sweetie,' the detective said
into the phone. He always waited for Nancy to hang up
first. Then he slammed shut the top drawer of his desk
and rushed to the balcony. He caught his fellow
policemen and their secretaries by surprise; not one of
them was fast enough to start typing before the deputy
commissioner started shouting.

'Have you run out of things to describe?' he hollered.
'Have your fingers all fallen off?' he screamed. 'Are
there no more murders? Is crime a thing of the past?
Have you all gone on holiday? Have you nothing better
to do than listen to *me*?'

The typing began again, although Detective Patel
knew that most of these first words would be meaningless. Below him, in the courtyard, the Doberman
pinschers started barking witlessly; he could see them
lunging in their kennel. Also below him, the police
mechanic had mounted the nearest motorcycle and
was jumping again and again, but without success, on
the kick starter. The engine made a dry, gasping
sound, like the catching of a pawl against a ratchet
wheel.

'Bleed the carburetor – there's too much air!' Patel
shouted to the mechanic, who quickly fussed with the
carburetor; his tireless leg continued to flail the kick
starter. When the engine caught and the mechanic
revved the throttle so loudly that the barking Dobermans were drowned out of hearing, the deputy
commissioner returned to his office and sat at his desk
with his eyes closed. Gradually, his head began to bob,
as if he'd found a followable rhythm, if not a melody,
among the staccato outbursts from the police secretaries' typewriters.

He'd not exactly neglected to tell Nancy that they
would have lunch tomorrow at the Duckworth Club
with Dr Daruwalla – probably with Inspector Dhar,
too. He'd purposefully withheld this information from
his wife. He knew it would worry her, or bring her to
tears – or at least cause her another long night of

sleeplessness and helpless sorrowing. Nancy hated to go out in public. Moreover, she'd developed a point-less dislike of both Inspector Dhar's creator and Dhar himself. Detective Patel understood that his wife's dislike was no more logical than her blaming both men for failing to comprehend how savagely she'd been traumatized in Goa. With equal illogic, the detec-tive anticipated, Nancy would be ashamed of herself in both Daruwalla and Dhar's company, for she couldn't bear the thought of encountering anyone who'd known her *then*.

He would tell her about lunch at the Duckworth Club in the morning, the detective thought; that way, his wife might have a fair night's sleep. Also, once he'd read over the names of the new members at the club, the deputy commissioner hoped he might know who Rahul was – or who he or she was pretending to be nowadays.

Patel's fellow policemen and their secretaries didn't relax until they heard the sound of his typewriter contributing its tedious music to their own. This was a welcome boredom, they knew, for with the flat clacking of the deputy commissioner's keys, Patel's colleagues were relieved to know that the deputy commissioner had returned to sanity – if not to peace of mind. It even comforted his junior officers to know that Patel was rewriting their own botched reports. They also knew they could expect that sometime in the afternoon Detective Patel would have their original reports back on their desks; the revised reports would be prefaced by a creative array of insults directed to their myriad inabilities – for none of them, in Detective Patel's opinion, knew how to write a proper report. And the secretaries would be taken to task for their typing errors. He was so disdainful of the secretaries, the deputy commissioner did his own typing.

Trachoma, which is one of the leading causes of blindness in the world, is easily treatable at its earliest phase – a chlamydial infection of the conjunctiva. In Ganesh's case, there was no scarring of the cornea. Double E-NT Jeejeebhoy had prescribed three weeks of tetracycline orally, together with a tetracycline ointment. Sometimes, multiple courses of treatment were needed, Dr Jeejeebhoy had said; the elephant boy's weepy eyes would likely clear up.

'You see?' Martin Mills asked Dr Daruwalla. 'We've already done the boy some good. It wasn't hard, was it?'

It seemed disloyal of the doctor that they were riding in a taxi, *not* driven by Vinod; it wasn't even a taxi from the dwarf's company. It also seemed dangerous, for the decrepit driver had warned them that he was unfamiliar with Bombay. Before they proceeded to the mission in Mazagaon, they dropped the beggar at Chowpatty Beach, where he said he wanted to go. Dr Daruwalla couldn't resist saying to Martin Mills that the little cripple was doubtless eager to sell his Fashion Street clothes.

'You're so cynical,' the scholastic said.

'He'll probably sell the tetracycline, too,' Farrokh replied. 'He'll probably be blind before he gets to see the circus.'

As he escorted the missionary to St Ignatius, Farrokh felt sufficiently overwhelmed to have reached the stage of making bitter resolutions to himself. Dr Daruwalla had resolved that he would never write another Inspector Dhar movie; the doctor had resolved that he would call a press conference, at which he would take the full blame for Dhar's creation upon himself.

Thus distracted, and always a nervous passenger in Bombay – even when Vinod was at the wheel, and the dwarf was a decent driver – Dr Daruwalla was frightened to see that their taxi had nearly mowed down a pedestrian. The near-accident had no effect on Martin Mills's impromptu lecture on Jainism. 'A pre-Buddhist offshoot of Hinduism,' Martin declared. The Jains were absolutely pure, the missionary explained . . . not just no meat, but no eggs; kill nothing, not even flies; bathe every morning. He would love to meet a Jain, Martin said. Just that quickly was the chaos of the morning behind him, if not entirely forgotten.

Apropos of nothing, the missionary then moved on to the well-worn subject of Gandhi. Farrokh reflected on how he might derail this conversation; possibly the doctor could say he preferred the warrior Shivaji to Gandhi – none of this turn-the-other-cheek shit for Shivaji! But before the doctor could deflate so much as a sentence of the scholastic's zeal for Gandhi, Martin Mills once more changed the subject.

'Pesonally, I'm more interested in Shirdi Sai Baba,' the missionary said.

'Ah, yes – the Jesus of Maharashtra,' Farrokh replied facetiously. Sai Baba was a patron saint of many circus performers; the acrobats wore little Shirdi Sai Baba medallions around their necks – the Hindu equivalents of St Christopher medals. There were Shirdi Sai Baba calendars hanging in the troupe tents of the Great Royal and the Great Blue Nile. The saint's shrine was in Maharashtra.

'The parallels to Jesus are understandable,' Martin Mills began, 'although Sai Baba was a teenager before he gained attention and he was an old man, in his eighties, when he died . . . I believe in 1918.'

'From his pictures, I always thought he looked a little like Lee Marvin . . . the Lee Marvin of Maharashtra,' Farrokh said.

'Lee Marvin! *Not* Shirdi Sai Baba . . .' the missionary protested.

And here, in an effort to interrupt the zealot's upcoming lecture on the parallels between Christianity and the cult of Sai Baba worship, the doctor launched into a description of the terrible teeterboard item that bore responsibility for Vinod's aerial assault of the surprised audience at the less-than-great Blue Nile Circus. Dr Daruwalla made it clear that such careless elephant-stamping acts would likely be in store for the less-than-innocent Madhu and the elephant-footed Ganesh. But the doctor's calculated pessimism failed to bait the missionary into repeating his claim that the perils of the circus – of *any* circus – paled in comparison to the hardships facing a prostitute or a beggar in Bombay. As swiftly as he'd dropped Gandhi for Sai Baba, Martin Mills now abandoned the Jesus of Maharashtra, too.

The missionary's new and sudden interest was prompted by a billboard they were passing, an advertisement for Close-Up.

DO YOU MOUTHWASH WHEN YOU TOOTHPASTE?

'Look at that!' cried Martin Mills. Their taxi's startled driver barely avoided being broadsided by a Thums Up cola truck; it was as big and bright red as a fire engine. 'English usage is *so* important,' the scholastic declared. 'What worries me about those children is that their English will deteriorate in the circus. Perhaps we could insist that someone in the circus tutor them!'

'How will speaking English serve them in the circus?' Farrokh asked. He knew it was nonsense to think that Madhu possessed enough English for her grasp of the language to 'deteriorate.' It was still a mystery to Dr Daruwalla that the elephant boy's spoken English and his apparent understanding of the language were as good as they were; perhaps someone had already tutored him. Maybe the missionary would suggest that Ganesh tutor Madhu! But Martin Mills didn't wait for the doctor to elaborate on his thesis that English would never provide these children with any advantage – not in the circus.

'Speaking English serves anyone well,' said the

455

English teacher. 'One day, English will be the language of the world.'

'*Bad* English is already the language of the world,' said Dr Daruwalla despairingly. That the children might be mashed by elephants was not the missionary's concern, but the moron wished proper English usage on them!

Passing Dr Vora's Gynecological and Maternity Hospital, Farrokh realized that their decrepit driver was lost; the wretch made a sudden turn and was almost sideswiped by a careening olive-drab van belonging to the Spastics' Society of India. Only a moment later – or so it seemed; it was longer – the doctor realized that his own sense of direction had deserted him, for they were passing the Times of India Building when Martin Mills announced, 'We could give the children a subscription to *The Times of India* and have it sent to them at the circus. We'd have to insist that they give it at least an hour a day of their attention, of course.'

'Of course . . .' said Dr Daruwalla. The doctor thought he might faint with frustration, for their troubled driver had missed the turn he should have taken – there went Sir J.J. Road.

'I'm planning to read the newspaper myself, daily,' the missionary went on. 'When you're a foreigner, there's nothing like a local newspaper to orient you.' The thought of anyone becoming oriented by *The Times of India* made Farrokh feel that a head-on collision with an approaching double-decker bus might be an improvement on the scholastic's continued conversation. Then, in the next instant, they'd plunged into Mazagaon – St Ignatius was now very near – and the doctor, for no calculated reason, instructed their driver to take a slight detour through the slum on Sophia Zuber Road.

'A part of this slum was once a movie set,' Dr Daruwalla explained to Martin Mills. 'It was in this very slum that your mother fainted when she was sneezed on, and then licked, by a cow. Of course, she was pregnant with you at the time – I suppose you've heard the story . . .'

'Please stop the car!' the missionary cried.

When their driver braked, but before the taxi came to a complete halt, Martin Mills opened the rear door and vomited into the moving street. Because nothing in a slum goes unseen, this episode attracted the attention of several slum dwellers, who began to jog beside the slowing car. Their frightened driver speeded up in order to get away from them.

'After your mother fainted, there was a riot,' Farrokh continued. 'Apparently, there was massive confusion concerning who licked whom . . . your mother or the cow.'

'Please stop – *not* the car. Please don't mention my mother,' Martin said.

'I'm sorry,' said Dr Daruwalla, who was secretly excited. At last Farrokh had found a subject that gave him the upper hand.

A Half-Dozen Cobras

It would be no less long a day for Deputy Commissioner Patel than it would be for Dr Daruwalla, but the level of confusion in the detective's day would be slightly less overwhelming. The deputy commissioner easily revised the first botched report that awaited his attention – a suspected murder at the Suba Guest House. It turned out to be a suicide. The report had to be rewritten because the duty officer had misinterpreted the young man's suicide note as a clue left behind by the presumed murderer. Later, the victim's mother had identified her son's handwriting. The deputy commissioner could sympathize with the duty officer's mistake, for it wasn't much of a suicide note.

Had sex with a woman who smelled like meat.
Not very pure.

457

As for the second report in need of rewriting, the deputy commissioner was less sympathetic with the subinspector who'd been summoned to the Alexandria Girls' English Institution. A young student had been discovered in the lavatory, presumably raped and murdered. But when the subinspector arrived at the school, he found the girl to be very much alive; she was totally recovered from her own murder and indignant at the suggestion that she'd been raped. It turned out she'd suffered her first period, and – withdrawing to the lavatory to look more closely at what was happening to her – she'd fainted at the sight of her own blood. There a hysterical teacher had found her, mistaking the blood as proof of the rape of a virgin. The teacher also assumed that the girl was dead.

The reason the report had to be rewritten was that the subinspector couldn't bring himself to mention that the poor girl had suffered her 'period'; it was, he said upon interrogation, as morally impossible for him to write this word as it would be for him to write the word 'menstruation,' which (he added) was very nearly a morally impossible word for him even to say. And so the erroneously reported rape and murder was called, in writing, 'a case of first female bleeding.' Detective Patel needed to remind himself that his 20 years with Nancy had made it easy for him to recognize the tortured morality of many of his colleagues; he restrained himself from too harsh a judgment of the subinspector.

The third report that needed to be revised was Dhar-related; it had never been reported as a crime at all. There'd been a perplexing brouhaha on Falkland Road in the wee hours. Dhar's dwarf bodyguard – that cocky thug! – had beaten up a half-dozen hijras. Two were still hospitalized, and one of the four who'd been released was wearing a cast on a broken wrist. Two of the transvestite prostitutes had been persuaded not to press charges against Dhar's dwarf, whom the investigating officer referred to by the name many policemen used for Vinod: 'the half-bodyguard.' But the report was stupidly written because the part about Inspector Dhar being under attack, and Vinod coming to his rescue, was merely a footnote; there was no mention of what Dhar had been doing in the neighborhood in the first place – the report was too unfinished for submission.

The deputy commissioner made a note to inquire of Dhar what had possessed the actor to approach the hijra prostitutes. If the fool wanted to fuck a prostitute, surely an expensive call girl would be within his financial reach – and safer. The incident struck the detective as highly out of character for the circumspect celebrity. Wouldn't it be funny if Inspector Dhar was a homosexual? the deputy commissioner thought.

There was at least some humor in the deputy commissioner's day. The fourth report had come to Crime Branch Headquarters from the Tardeo Police Station. At least six snakes were loose near the Mahalaxmi temple, but there were no reported bitings – meaning, none yet. The duty officer from the Tardeo Station had taken photographs. Detective Patel recognized the broad expanse of stairs leading to the Mahalaxmi. At the top of the steps, where the temple loomed, there was a wide pavilion where the worshipers bought coconut and flowers for their offerings; this was also where the worshipers left their sandals and shoes. But, in the photos, the deputy commissioner could see that the stairs leading to the temple were dotted with stray sandals and shoes – indicating that a panicked crowd had only recently fled up or down the steps. In the aftermath of riots, the ground was always strewn with sandals and shoes, people had run right out of them or up the backs of other people's heels.

The temple steps were usually crowded; now they were deserted – the flower stalls and the coconut shops were empty of people, too. Everywhere there were only scattered sandals and shoes! At the bottom of the temple stairs, Detective Patel noted the tall woven baskets where the cobras were kept; the baskets were overturned, presumably empty. The snake charmers had fled with everyone else. But where had the cobras gone?

It must have been quite a scene, the deputy commissioner imagined. The worshipers running and screaming, the snakes slithering away. Detective Patel thought that most of the cobras belonging to snake charmers had no venom, although they could still bite.

The puzzle in the photographs was what was missing from the pictures. What had been the crime? Had one snake charmer thrown his cobra at another snake charmer? Had a tourist tripped over one of the cobra baskets? In one second the snakes were loose, in another second people were running out of their shoes. But what was the crime?

Deputy Commissioner Patel sent the snake report back to the Tardeo Police Station. The escaped cobras were their problem. *Probably* the snakes were venomless; if they were snake charmers' snakes, at least they were tame. The detective knew that a half-dozen cobras in Mahalaxmi weren't half as dangerous as Rahul.

At the Mission, Farrokh Is Inspired

It was a surprisingly subdued missionary whom Farrokh delivered to the Jesuits at St Ignatius. Inside the cloister, Martin Mills exhibited the obedience of a well-trained dog; the once-admired 'modesty of the eyes' became a fixed feature of his face – he looked more like a monk than a Jesuit. The doctor couldn't have known that the Father Rector and Father Cecil and Brother Gabriel had been expecting a loud clown in a Hawaiian shirt; Dr Daruwalla was disappointed at the almost reverential greeting the scholastic received. In his unpressed Fashion Street shirt – not to mention his haunted, scratched face and his concentration-camp haircut – the new missionary made a serious first impression.

Dr Daruwalla unaccountably lingered at the mission. Farrokh supposed that he was hoping for an opportunity to warn Father Julian that Martin Mills was a madman; but the doctor was of a considerably mixed mind when it came to involving himself to a greater extent in the newcomer's future. Furthermore, Farrokh found that it was impossible to get the Father Rector alone. They'd arrived just after the schoolboys had finished lunch. Father Cecil and Brother Gabriel – with not fewer than a combined 145 years between them – insisted on struggling with the scholastic's suitcase, and this left Father Julian to conduct Martin's first tour of St Ignatius. Dr Daruwalla followed behind.

Since his own school days, Farrokh had spent only intermittent time at the place. He reviewed the examination scrolls in the entrance hall with a detached curiosity. The Indian Certificate of Secondary Education (I.C.S.E.) marked the completion of junior high school. In the Examination Certificate of 1973, St Ignatius demonstrated its Spanish connection by commemorating the death of Picasso; this must have been Brother Gabriel's idea. A photograph of the artist was among the photos of that year's graduates, as if Picasso had also passed the requisite exam; and there were these few words: PICASSO PASSES AWAY. In 1975, the 300th anniversary of Shivaji's Coronation was commemorated; in '76, the Montreal Olympics was observed; in '77, the deaths of both Charlie Chaplin and Elvis were mourned – they were also pictured among the graduates. This yearbook-minded sentimentality was intermixed with religious and nationalistic fervor. The centerpiece of the entrance hall was a larger-than-life statue of the Virgin Mary standing on the head of the serpent with the apple in its mouth, as if she thus circumvented or had altered the Old Testament. And over the entranceway itself were side-by-side portraits

– one of the pope of the moment, the other of Nehru as a young man.

Haunted by nostalgia, but more strongly disturbed by a culture that had never become his, Farrokh felt himself losing his faint resolve. Why warn the Father Rector about Martin Mills? Why try to warn *any* of them? The whole place, perhaps owing its inspiration to St Ignatius Loyola himself, spoke of survival – not to mention a humbling instinct for repentance. As for the Jesuits' success in Bombay and the rest of India, Farrokh assumed that the Indian stress on mother-worship gave the Catholics a certain advantage. The cult of the Virgin Mary was just more mother-worship, wasn't it? Even in an all-boys' school, the Holy Mother dominated the statuary.

Only a scattering of English names appeared on the examination scrolls, yet passable English was an admissions requirement and fluency in the language was expected of any St Ignatius graduate; it was the classroom language throughout the school, and the only language posted in writing.

At the student canteen, in the courtyard, was a photograph of the junior school's most recent trip: there were the boys in their white shirts with navy-blue ties; they wore navy-blue shorts and kneesocks, too – and black shoes. The caption to this photo said: OUR JUNIORS, INC. OUR MIDGETS AND OUR SUB-MIDGETS. (Dr Daruwalla disapproved of abbreviations.)

In the first-aid room, a boy with a stomach ache lay curled on a cot, above which was tacked a photo of the stereotypical sunset at Haji Ali's Tomb. The caption that accompanied this sunset was as egregious a non sequitur as any that had thus far been uttered by Martin Mills: YOU ONLY LIVE ONCE, BUT IF YOU LIVE RIGHT, ONCE IS ENOUGH.

Moving on to the music parlor, the doctor was struck by the tunelessness of the piano, which, in combination with the abrasive singing of the untalented music teacher, made it hard for Dr Daruwalla to recognize even as oft-droned a dirge as 'Swing Low, Sweet Chariot.' She was an English teacher, a certain Miss Tanuja and Farrokh overheard Father Julian explaining to Martin Mills that this time-honored method of teaching a language through song lyrics was still popular with the younger children. Since very few of the children were contributing more than mumbles to Miss Tanuja's braying voice, Farrokh doubted the Father Rector on this point; maybe the problem wasn't the method but Miss Tanuja.

She struck Dr Daruwalla as one of those Indian women who remain uncontained by Western clothes, which Miss Tanuja was wearing with special grace-lessness and folly. Perhaps the children couldn't sing 'Swing Low, Sweet Chariot' because they were distracted by the riotous array of Miss Tanuja's ensemble; the doctor observed that even Martin Mills appeared to be distracted by her. Farrokh cruelly assumed that Miss Tanuja was desperate to marry. She was very found-faced and of a medium, milk-chocolate complexion, and she wore very sharply angled glasses – of the kind with upward-sweeping wing tips embedded with small, bright gems. Perhaps Miss Tanuja thought that these eye-glasses contrasted pleasingly with the smoothness and roundness of her face.

She had the plump, youthful figure of a high-school voluptuary, but she wore a dark skirt that hugged her hips too tightly and was the wrong length for her. Miss Tanuja was short and the dress chopped her legs off at midcalf, which gave Dr Daruwalla the impression that her thick ankles were wrists and her fat little feet were hands. Her blouse had a reflecting luminosity of a blue-green nature, as if flecked with algae dredged from a pond; and although the woman's most pleasing quality was an overall curvaceousness, she'd chosen a bra that served her badly. From what little Dr Daruwalla knew of bras, he judged it to be the old-fashioned pointy type – one of those rigidly constructed halters more suitable for protecting women from fencing injuries than for enhancing their natural shapeliness. And between Miss Tanuja's outrageously uplifted and sharply pointed breasts, there hung a crucifix, as if the Christ on Miss Tanuja's cross – in addition to his other agonies – were expected to endure the misery of bouncing on the teacher's ample but spear-headed bosoms.

'Miss Tanuja has been with us for many years,' Father Julian whispered.

'I see,' said Dr Daruwalla, but Martin Mills merely stared.

Then they passed a classroom of smaller children in I-3. The kids were napping with their heads on their desks – either 'midgets' or 'sub-midgets,' Farrokh guessed.

'Do you play the piano?' the Father Rector was asking the new missionary.

'I always wanted to learn,' Martin said. Maybe the madman could practice the piano between bouts of orienting himself in *The Times of India*, Dr Daruwalla thought.

And to change the subject from his lack of musical skills, the scholastic asked Father Julian about the sweepers, for there were everywhere about the mission an abundance of men and women who were sweeping – they also cleaned the toilets – and the missionary assumed that these sweepers were people from the untouchable castes.

The Father Rector used the words 'bhangee' and 'maitrani,' but Martin Mills was a man with more of a mission than Father Julian supposed. Martin asked the Father Rector directly: 'And do *their* children attend this school?' All of a sudden, Dr Daruwalla liked him.

'Well, no – that wouldn't be suitable, you see,' Father Julian was saying, but Farrokh was impressed by how gracefully Martin Mills interrupted the Father Rector. The scholastic simply breezed into a description of 'rescuing' the crippled beggar and the child prostitute; it was Martin's one-step-at-a-time method, and the missionary virtually waltzed the Father Rector through the steps. First the circus – instead of begging, or the brothel. Then the mastery of the English language – 'so civilizing as to be essential' – and *then* 'the intelligent conversion'; Martin Mills also called this 'the informed life in Christ.'

A class of seniors, on recess, was enjoying a savage, silent dirt fight in the courtyard, but Dr Daruwalla marveled how the Jesuits were undistracted by this minor violence; they spoke and listened with the concentration of lions stalking a kill.

'But surely, Martin, you wouldn't credit *yourself* with these children's conversion?' Father Julian said. 'That is, should they eventually be converted.'

'Well, no . . . what do you mean?' Martin asked.

'Only that I never know if *I* have converted anyone,' the Father Rector replied. 'And if these children were converted, how could you presume it happened because of you? Don't be too proud. If it happens, it was God. It wasn't you.'

'Why, no – of course not!' said Martin Mills. 'If it happens, it was God!'

Was this 'obedience'? Dr Daruwalla wondered.

When Father Julian led Martin to his cubicle, which Dr Daruwalla imagined as a kind of prison cell with built-in instruments to chastise the flesh, the doctor continued to roam; he wanted to look at the sleeping children again, because that image of sleeping with his head on his desk was more appealing than anything else he could remember about attending St Ignatius School – it had been so many years ago. But when he peered into I-3 again, a teacher he hadn't seen before regarded him sternly, as if his presence in the doorway would disturb the children. And this time the doctor noticed the exposed wiring for the fluorescent lights, which were off, and the exposed wiring for the ceiling fan, which was on. Suspended over the blackboard like a puppet on tangled, immobile strings was yet another statue of the Virgin Mary. From Farrokh's

Canadian perspective, this particular Holy Mother was covered with frost, or a light snow; but it was only rising chalk dust from the blackboard that had settled on the statue.

Dr Daruwalla amused himself by reading as many printed messages and announcements as he could find. There was a plea from the Social Concern Group – 'to help less fortunate brothers and sisters.' Prayers were offered for the Souls in Purgatory. There was the pleasing juxtaposition of the Minimax fire extinguisher that was mounted on the wall beside the statue of Christ with the sick child; in fire-extinguisher language, a short list of instructions was printed next to a page from a lined notebook on which a child's handwriting proclaimed, 'Thanks to Infant Jesus and Our Lady of Perpetual Help.' Farrokh felt somewhat more comforted by the presence of the fire extinguisher. The great stone mission had been erected in 1865; the fluorescent lights, the ceiling fans, the vast network of haphazard wiring – these had been added later. The doctor concluded that an electrical fire was entirely possible.

Farrokh tried to familiarize himself with all the meetings that a good Christian could go to. There was an announced Meeting of Liturgical Readers, and the Meeting of the Members of the Cross – 'to make parish members more politically conscious.' The present topic of proposed conversation in the Adult Catholic Education Program was 'The Christian Today in the World of Non-Christian Religions.' This month, the Hope Alive Center was conducted by Dr Yusuf Merchant. Dr Daruwalla wondered what 'conduct by' meant. There was a Get to Know Each Other Party for the Altar Service Corps, which Farrokh suspected would be a grim gathering.

Under the archway of the second-floor balcony, the doctor was struck by the unfinished irregularity of the pieces of stained glass – as if the very notion of God were this fragmented, this incomplete. In the Icon

Chapel, the doctor abruptly closed a hymnal upon encountering the hymn called 'Bring Me Oil.' Then he read the bookmark that he'd removed from the hymnal; the bookmark celebrated St Ignatius's upcoming jubilee year – 'a labour of love in building youth for 125 years.' There was also the word 'world-affirming'; Dr Daruwalla had never had the slightest idea what this implied. Farrokh peeked into the hymnal again, but even the name of the thing offended him; it was called the 'Song Book of the Charismatic Renewal in India' – he hadn't known that there *was* any charismatic renewal! And so he exchanged the hymnal for a prayer book, wherein he looked no further than the opening line of the first prayer: 'Keep us, Lord, as the apple of Your eye.'

Dr Daruwalla then discovered the Holy Father's Intentions for 1990. For January, it was advised that the dialogue between the Catholic and Anglican communities continue in the quest for Christian unity. For February, prayers were offered for those Catholics who, in many parts of the world, suffered either verbal or physical persecution. For March, the parishioners were exhorted to give a more authentic witness for support of the needy – and fidelity to the poverty of the Gospels. Dr Daruwalla couldn't read past March, for the phrase 'poverty of the Gospels' stopped him. Farrokh felt surrounded by too much that was meaningless to him.

Even Brother Gabriel's fastidious collecting of icons meant little to the doctor, and the icon-collection room at St Ignatius was famous in Bombay. To Farrokh, the depictions were lugubrious and obscure. There was a 16th-century Adoration of the Magi, of the Ukrainian School; there was a 15th-century Decapitation of John the Baptist, of the Central Northern School. In the Passing of Our Lord category, there was a Last Supper, a Crucifixion, a Deposition (the taking of Christ's body from the cross), an Entombment, a Resurrection and an Ascension; they were all icons from the 14th through the 18th centuries, and they varied among the

467

Novgorod School, the Byzantine School, the Moscow School ... and so on. There was one called the Dormition of the Virgin, and that did it for Dr Daruwalla; the doctor didn't know what the Dormition was.

From the icons, the doctor roamed to the Father Rector's office, where something resembling a cribbage board was nailed to the closed door; by means of holes and pegs, Father Julian could indicate his whereabouts or availability – 'back soon' or 'do not disturb,' 'rec. room' or 'back late,' 'back for supper' or 'out of Bombay.' That was when Dr Daruwalla considered that *he* should be 'out of Bombay'; that he'd been born here didn't mean that he belonged here.

When he heard the bell signifying the end of school, Farrokh realized that it was already 3:00 in the afternoon. He stood on the second-floor balcony and watched the schoolboys racing through the dusty courtyard. Cars and buses were taking them away; either their mothers or their ayahs were coming to fetch them home. From the perspective of the balcony, Dr Daruwalla determined that they were the fattest children he'd ever seen in India. This was uncharitable; not half the children at St Ignatius were half as plump as Farrokh. Nevertheless, the doctor knew that he would no more interfere with the new missionary's zeal than he would choose to leap from the balcony and kill himself in front of these blameless children.

Farrokh also knew that almost no one of rank at the mission would mistake Martin Mills for Inspector Dhar. The Jesuits weren't known for their appreciation of so-called Bollywood, the trashy Hindi film scene; young women in soaking-wet saris weren't their thing. Superheroes and fiendish villains, violence and vulgarity, tawdriness and corniness – and the occasional descending god, intervening in pathetic, merely human affairs ... Inspector Dhar was *not* famous at St Ignatius. Among the schoolboys, however, more than one student of Martin Mills might note the resemblance. Inspector Dhar was popular with schoolboys.

Dr Daruwalla still lingered; he had things to do, but he couldn't make himself leave. He didn't know that he was *writing*; it had never begun quite like this before. When the children were gone, he went inside St Ignatius Church – but not to pray. A huge wheel of unlit candles hung above the center table, which resembled a refectory table only in its shape; in fact, it was a folding table of a household kind – better suited, say, for sorting laundry. The pulpit, to the right of this table (as Farrokh faced the altar), was equipped with an inappropriately shiny microphone; upon this pulpit a Lectionary lay open, from which the doctor assumed that the lector would be reading – possibly at the evening Mass. Dr Daruwalla couldn't resist snooping. The Lectionary was open to the Second Epistle of Paul to the Corinthians.

'Therefore, since we have this ministry, as we have received mercy, we do not lose heart [II Corinthians 4:1],' wrote the converted one. Skipping ahead, the doctor read: '*We are* hard pressed on every side, yet not crushed; *we are* perplexed, but not in despair; persecuted, but not forsaken; struck down, but not destroyed – always carrying about in the body the dying of the Lord Jesus, that the life of Jesus may also be manifested in our body' [4:8–10].

Dr Daruwalla felt small. He ventured into a pew in one of the side aisles – as if he wasn't significant enough, in his lack of faith, to sit in a center-aisle seat. His own conversion seemed trifling, and very far behind him; in his daily thoughts, he barely honored it – perhaps he *had* been bitten by a monkey, he concluded. He noted that the church was without an organ; another, probably tuneless piano stood to the left of the folding table – another inappropriately shiny microphone stood on it.

From far outside the church, the doctor was aware of the constantly passing mopeds – the snarling of their low-powered engines, the duck-like quacking of their infernal horns. The highly staged altarpiece drew the doctor's eye; there was Christ on the Cross and those two familiar women forlornly flanking him. Mother Mary and Mary Magdalen, Dr Daruwalla presumed. The life-sized figures of the saints, all in stone, were mounted on the columns that defined the aisles; these massive pillars each supported a saint, and at the saints' feet were tilted oscillating fans – pointed down, in order to cool the congregation.

Blasphemously, Dr Daruwalla noticed that one of the stone saints had worked herself loose from her pillar; a thick chain had been secured around the saint's neck, and this chain was attached to the pillar by a sizable steel grommet. The doctor wished he knew which saint she was; he thought that all the female saints too closely resembled the Virgin Mary – at least as statues. Whoever this saint was, she appeared to have been hung in effigy; but without the chain around her neck, she might have toppled into a pew. Dr Daruwalla judged that the stone saint was big enough to kill a pew of worshipers.

Finally, Farrokh said his good-byes to Martin Mills and the other Jesuits. The scholastic suddenly begged to hear the details of Dr Daruwalla's conversion. The doctor supposed that Father Julian had given Martin a cunning and sarcastic rendition of the story.

'Oh, it was nothing,' Farrokh replied modestly. This probably concurred with the Father Rector's version.

'But I should love to hear about it!' Martin said.

'If you tell him yours, I'm sure he'll tell you *his*,' Father Julian said to Farrokh.

'Maybe another time,' Dr Daruwalla said. Never had he so much desired to flee. He had to promise that he'd attend Martin's lecture at the YWCA, although he had no intentions of attending; he would rather die than attend. He'd heard quite enough lecturing from Martin Mills!

'It's the YWCA at Cooperage, you know,' Father Cecil informed him. Since Dr Daruwalla was sensitive to those Bombayites who assumed that he barely knew

470

his way around the city, the doctor was snappish in his reply.

'I *know* where it is!' Farrokh said.

Then a little girl appeared, out of nowhere. She was crying because she'd come to St Ignatius with her mother, to pick up her brother after school, and somehow they'd left without her. There'd been other children in the car. It wasn't a crisis, the Jesuits decided. The mother would realize what had happened and return to the school. It was merely necessary to comfort the child, and someone should call the mother so that she'd not drive recklessly in fear that her daughter was lost. But there was another problem: the little girl confided to them that she needed to pee. Brother Gabriel declared to Dr Daruwalla that there was 'no official peeing place for girls' at St Ignatius.

'But where does Miss Tanuja pee?' Martin Mills asked.

Good for him! Dr Daruwalla thought. He's going to drive them all crazy.

'And I saw several women among the sweepers,' Martin added.

'There must be three or four women teachers, aren't there?' Dr Daruwalla asked innocently.

Of *course* there was a peeing place for girls! These old men simply didn't know where it was.

'Someone could see if a men's room is unoccupied,' Father Cecil suggested.

'Then one of us could guard the door,' Father Julian advised.

When Farrokh finally left them all, they were still discussing this awkward necessity to bend the rules. The doctor presumed that the little girl still needed to pee.

Tetracycline

Dr Daruwalla was on his way back to the Hospital for Crippled Children when he realized that he'd started

471

another screenplay; he knew that this one would *not* be starring Inspector Dhar. In his mind's eye, he saw a beggar working the Arab hotels along Marine Drive; he saw the Queen's Necklace at night . . . that string of yellow smog lights . . . and he heard Julia saying that yellow wasn't the proper color for the necklace of a queen. For the first time, Farrokh felt that he understood the start of a story – the characters were set in motion by the fates that awaited them. Something of the authority of an ending was already contained in the beginning scene.

He was exhausted; he had much to talk about with Julia, and he had to talk to John D. Dr Daruwalla and his wife were having an early dinner at the Ripon Club. Then the doctor had planned to write a first draft of a little speech he would be giving soon; he'd been invited to say something to the Society for the Rehabilitation of Crippled Children – they were such faithful sponsors of the hospital. But now he knew he would write all night – and not his speech. At last, he thought, he had a screenplay in him that justified the telling. In his mind's eye, he saw the characters arriving at Victoria Terminus, but this time he knew where they were going; he wondered if he'd ever been so excited.

The familiar figure in Dr Daruwalla's waiting room distracted the doctor from the story he'd imagined; among the waiting children, the tall man indeed stood out. Even seated, his military erectness immediately captured Farrokh's attention. The taut sallow skin and the slack mouth; the lion-yellow eyes; the acid-shriveled ear and the raw pink smear that had burned a swath along his jawline and down the side of his throat, where it disappeared under the collar of Mr Garg's shirt – all this captured Dr Daruwalla's attention, too.

One look at the nervously wriggling fingers of Mr Garg's locked hands confirmed Farrokh's suspicions. It was clear to the doctor that Garg was itching to know the specific nature of Madhu's 'sexually transmitted disease'; Dr Daruwalla felt only an empty triumph. To see Garg – guilty and ready to grovel, and reduced to waiting his turn among the crippled children – would be the full extent of the doctor's slight victory, for Dr Daruwalla knew, even at this very moment, that something more than professional confidentiality would prevent him from disclosing Mr Garg's guilt to Deepa and Vinod. Besides, how could the dwarf and his wife not already know that Garg diddled young girls? It may have been Garg's guilt that compelled him to allow Deepa and Vinod to attempt their circus rescues of so many of these children. Surely the dwarf and his wife already knew what Farrokh was only beginning to guess: that many of these little prostitutes would have preferred to stay with Mr Garg. Like the circus, even the Great Blue Nile, maybe Garg was better than a brothel.

Mr Garg stood and faced Farrokh. The eyes of every crippled child in Dr Daruwalla's waiting room were fixed on the acid scar, but the doctor looked only at the whites of Garg's eyes, which were a jaundice-yellow – and at the deeper, tawny lion-yellow of Garg's irises, which offset his black pupils. Garg had the same eyes as Madhu. The doctor passingly wondered if they might be related.

'I was here first – before any of them,' Mr Garg whispered.

'I'll bet you were,' said Dr Daruwalla.

If it was guilt that had flickered in Garg's lion eyes, it seemed to be fading; a shy smile tightened his usually slack lips, and something conspiratorial crept into his voice. 'So . . . I guess you know about Madhu and me,' Mr Garg said.

What can one say to such a man? Dr Daruwalla thought. The doctor realized that Deepa and Vinod and even Martin Mills were right: let *every* girl-child be an acrobat in the circus, even in the Great Blue Nile – even if they fall and die. Let them be eaten by lions! For it

was true that Madhu was both a child and a prostitute
– worse, she was Mr Garg's girl. There was truly
nothing to say to such a man. Only a strictly professional question came to Dr Daruwalla's mind, and
he put it to Garg as bluntly as he could.

'Are you allergic to tetracycline?' the doctor asked
him.

17. STRANGE CUSTOMS

Southern California

Because he had a history of suffering in unfamiliar bedrooms, Martin Mills lay awake in his cubicle at the mission of St Ignatius. At first he followed the advice of St Teresa of Avila – her favorite spiritual exercise, which allowed her to experience the love of Christ – but not even this remedy would permit the new missionary to fall asleep. The idea was to imagine that Christ saw you. *'Mira que te mira,'* St Teresa said. 'Notice him looking at you.' But try as he might to notice such a thing, Martin Mills wasn't comforted; he couldn't sleep.

He loathed his memory of the many bedrooms that his awful mother and pathetic father had exposed him to. This was the result of Danny Mills overpaying for a house in Westwood, which was near the U.C.L.A. campus but which the family could rarely afford to live in; it was perpetually rented so that Danny and Vera could live off the rent. This also provided their decaying marriage with frequent opportunities for them not to live with each other. As a child, Martin Mills was always missing clothes and toys that had somehow become the temporary possessions of the tenants of the Westwood house, which he only vaguely could remember.

He remembered better the U.C.L.A. student who was his babysitter, for she used to drag him by his arm across Wilshire Boulevard at high speed, and usually not at the proper crosswalks. She had a boyfriend who ran around and around the U.C.L.A. track; she'd take Martin to the track and they'd watch the boyfriend run and run. She made Martin's fingers ache, she held his

475

hand so tightly. If the traffic on Wilshire had forced an uncommonly hasty crossing of the boulevard, Martin's upper arm would throb.

Whenever Danny and Vera went out in the evening, Vera insisted that Martin sleep in the other twin bed in the babysitter's bedroom; the rest of her quarters consisted only of a tiny kitchenette — a kind of breakfast nook where a black-and-white television shared the small countertop with a toaster. Here the babysister sat on one of two barstools, because there wasn't enough space for chairs and a table.

Often, when he lay in the bedroom with the babysitter, Martin Mills could hear her masturbating; because the room was sealed and permanently air-conditioned, more often he would wake up in the morning and detect that she *had* masturbated by the smell, which was on the fingers of her right hand when she stroked his face and told him it was time for him to get up and brush his teeth. Then she'd drive him to school, which she did in a manner of recklessness equivalent to her habit of dragging him across Wilshire Boulevard. There was an exit from the San Diego Freeway that seemed to draw out of the babysitter a dramatic catching of her breath, which reminded Martin Mills of the sound she made while masturbating; just before this exit, Martin would always close his eyes.

It was a good school, an accelerated progam conducted by the Jesuits at Loyola Marymount University, which was a fair drive from Westwood. But although the traveling to school and back was hazardous, the fact that Martin Mills was first educated in facilities also used by university students seemed to have an austere effect on the boy. Befitting an experiment in early-childhood education — the program was discontinued after a few years — even the chairs were grownup-sized, and the classrooms were not festooned with children's crayon drawings or animals wearing the letters of the alphabet. In the men's room used by these gifted children, the smaller boys stood on a stool to pee – these were the days before there were urinals at wheelchair level for the handicapped. Thus, both at the towering urinals and in the undecorated class-rooms, it was as if these special children had been granted the opportunity to skip over childhood. But if the classrooms and the urinals spoke of the seriousness of the business at hand, they also suffered from the anonymity and impersonality of the many bedrooms in young Martin's life.

Whenever the Westwood house was rented, Danny and Vera also lost the services of the U.C.L.A. baby-sitter. Then – from other, unfamiliar parts of town – Danny would be the designated driver who spirited Martin Mills to his accelerated education at Loyola Marymount. Driving with Danny was no less danger-ous than the trip from and to Westwood with the U.C.L.A. babysitter. Danny would be hungover at the early-morning hour, if he wasn't still inebriated, and by the time Martin was ready to be picked up after school, Danny would have begun to drink again. As for Vera, she didn't drive. The former Hermione Rosen had never learned to drive, which is not unusual among people who pass their teenage years in Brook-lyn or Manhattan. Her father, the producer Harold Rosen, had also never learned to drive; he was a frequent limousine-user, and once – for several months, when Danny Mills had lost his driver's license to a DWI conviction – Harold had sent a limo to take Martin Mills to school.

On the other hand, Vera's uncle, the director Gordon Hathaway, was a veteran speedster behind the wheel, and his penchant for speed in combination with his permanently purple ears (of varying deafness) would result in the periodic suspension of his driver's license. Gordon never yielded to fire trucks or ambulances or police cars; as for his own horn, since he couldn't hear it, he never used it, and he was utterly oblivious to the warning blasts that emanated from other vehicles.

He would meet his Maker on the Santa Monica Free-way, where he rear-ended a station wagon full of surfers. Gordon was killed instantly by a surfboard; maybe it flew off the roof rack of the station wagon, or out of the open tailgate – either way, it came through Gordon's windshield. There were ensuing vehicular collisions spanning four lanes, in two directions, and involving eight automobiles and a motorcycle; only Gordon was killed. Surely the director had a second or two to see his death coming, but at his memorial service his renowned C. of M. sister, who was Harold Rosen's wife and Vera's mother, remarked that Gordon's deafness had at least spared him the *noise* of his own death, for it was generally agreed that the sounds of a nine-vehicle collision must have been considerable.

Nevertheless, Martin Mills survived the harrowing trips to his advanced schooling at Loyola Marymount; it was the bedrooms – their foreignness, their dis-orientation – that got to him. The quintessential sellout, Danny had rashly bought the Westwood house with the money he'd received for a three-screenplay deal; unfortunately, at the time he took the money the screenplays were unwritten – none would be pro-duced. Then, as always, there were more deals based on unfinished work. Danny would have to rent Westwood. This depressed him; he drank to blur his self-disgust. This also led him to live in other people's houses; these were usually the houses of producers or directors or actors to whom Danny owed a finished screenplay. Since these philanthropic souls could stand neither the spectacle nor the company of the desperate writer, they would vacate their houses and run off to New York or Europe. Sometimes, Martin Mills learned later, Vera would run off with them.

Writing a script under such pressure was a process Danny Mills referred to as 'ball-busting,' which had long been a favorite expression of Gordon Hathaway's. As Martin Mills lay awake in his cubicle at St Ignatius, the new missionary couldn't stop himself from remembering these houses belonging to strangers, who were always people in a position of power over his feckless father.

There'd been the house belonging to a director in Beverly Hills; it was on Franklin Canyon Drive, and Danny lost the privilege of living there because the driveway was so steep – that was how Danny put it. What happened was, he came home drunk; he left the director's car in neutral (with the brake off) and the garage door open, and the car rolled over a grapefruit tree and into the swimming pool. This wouldn't have been so damaging had Vera not been having an affair with the director's maid, who the next morning dove naked into the swimming pool and broke her jaw and collarbone against the submerged windshield of the car. This happened while Danny was calling the police to report that the car had been stolen. Naturally, the maid sued the director for having a car in his pool. The movie that Danny was writing at the time was never produced, which was not an infrequent conclusion to Danny busting his balls.

Martin Mills had liked that house, if not that maid. In retrospect, Martin regretted that his mother's sexual preference for young women had been passing; her appetite for young men was messier. As for Martin's particular bedroom in the house on Franklin Canyon Drive, it had seemed nicer than the rest. It was a corner room with enough natural ventilation that he could sleep without the air conditioner; that was why he'd heard the car sinking into the swimming pool – first the splash, then all the bubbles. But he'd not gotten out of bed to look because he assumed it was his drunken father; by the sound, Martin suspected that Danny was cavorting with about a dozen drunken men – they were belching and farting underwater, he deduced. He had no idea a *car* had been involved.

In the morning, up early (as always), Martin had been only mildly surprised to see the car resting on the bottom of the deep end. Slowly it occurred to him that his father might be trapped inside. Martin was naked and crying when he ran downstairs to the swimming pool, where he found the naked maid; she was drowning under the diving board. Martin would never be credited with rescuing her. He picked up the long pole with the net on one end, which was used for skimming frogs and salamanders out of the water, and he extended this to the brown, feral-looking little woman of Mexican descent, but she couldn't speak (because her jaw was broken) and she couldn't lift herself out of the pool (because her collarbone was broken, too). She held fast to the pole while Martin towed her to the pool curb, and there she clung; she looked beseechingly at Martin Mills, who covered his genitals with his hands. From the depths of the pool, the sunken car emitted another bubble.

That was when Martin's mother exited the maid's bungalow, which was next to the shed for pool toys. Wrapped in a towel, Vera saw Martin standing naked by the deep end, but she failed to see her floundering lover of the night before.

'Martin, you know what I think of skinny-dipping,' Vera told the boy. 'Go put on your trunks before Maria sees you.' Maria, of course, was also skinny-dipping.

As for putting on his clothes, that was the moment when Martin Mills identified one of his dislikes for his repeated use of someone else's bedroom; *their* clothes were in the drawers – at best, the bottommost drawers had been emptied for Martin – and *their* clothes hung lifelessly but prepossessingly in the closets. Their old toys filled up a chest; their baby pictures were on the walls. Sometimes their tennis trophies or horse-riding ribbons were displayed. Often there were shrines to their first dogs or cats, apparently deceased; this could be discerned by the presence of a glass jar that contained a dog's toenail or a tuft from a cat's tail. And when Martin would carry his little triumphs 'home' from school – his 'A' papers and other evidence of his accelerated education – he wasn't allowed to display these on *their* walls.

Then, in Los Angeles, there'd been an actor's virtually unlived-in house on South Lorraine – a huge, grandly conceived mansion with many small, musty bedrooms all boasting blurry, enlarged photographs of unknown children of a conspicuously similar age. It seemed to Martin that the children who grew up there had died when they were six or eight, or that they'd uniformly become uninteresting subjects for photography upon reaching this approximate age; but there had simply been a divorce. In the house, time had stopped – Martin had hated it there – and Danny had at last outworn his welcome by falling alseep while smoking on the couch in front of the TV. The smoke alarm woke him, but he was drunk; he called the police instead of the fire department, and by the time that confusion was sorted out, the entire living room was consumed in flames. Danny took Martin to the pool, where he paddled about on an inflated raft in the form of Donald Duck – another relic of the permanently six- and eight-year-old children.

Danny waded back and forth in the shallow end of the pool, although he wore long trousers and a wrinkled dress shirt instead of a bathing suit, and he held the pages of his screenplay-in-progress against his chest; clearly, he didn't want the pages to get wet. Together, father and son watched the firefighters subduing the disaster.

The actor, who was almost famous and whose living room was ruined, came home much later – after the fire was out and the firemen had left. Danny and Martin Mills were still playing in the swimming pool.

'Let's wait up for Mommy, so you can tell her all about the fire,' Danny had suggested.

'Where's Mommy?' Martin had asked.

'Out,' Danny had replied. She was 'out' with the actor. When Vera and the actor returned together, Martin imagined that his father was slightly pleased with the smoldering wreck he'd made of the living room. The screenplay wasn't going too well; it was to be an opportunity for the actor to do something 'timely' – it was a story about a younger man with an older woman . . . 'something bittersweet,' the actor had suggested. Vera was hoping for the role of the older woman. But that screenplay was never made into a movie, either. Martin Mills was not sorry to leave those permanently six- and eight-year-old children on South Lorraine.

In his stark cubicle at St Ignatius in Mazagaon, the missionary was now looking for his copy of the *Pocket Catholic Catechism;* he hoped that these essentials of his faith might rescue him from reliving every bedroom he'd ever slept in in California. But he couldn't find the reassuring little paperback; he presumed he'd left it on Dr Daruwalla's glass-topped table – in fact, he had. Dr Daruwalla had already put it to use. Farrokh had read up on Extreme Unction, the Sacrament of the Anointing of the Sick, for this fit rather neatly into the new screenplay that the doctor was dying to begin; he'd also skimmed a passage about the crucifixion – he thought that he might make some sly use of it. The doctor was feeling mischievous, and the earlier hours of the evening had seemed interminable to him because nothing mattered to him as much as beginning this suddenly important piece of writing. Had Martin Mills known that Dr Daruwalla was about to re-create him as a character in a romantic comedy, the unfortunate missionary might have welcomed the distraction of remembering his itinerant childhood in Los Angeles.

There'd been another L.A. house, on Kings Road, and Martin had cautiously loved that one; it had a fish pond, and the producer-owner kept rare birds, which were unfortunately Danny's responsibility while he lived and wrote there. On the very first day, Martin had observed that the house had no screens. The rare birds weren't caged; they were chained to their perches. One evening, during a dinner party, a hawk flew inside the house – and then another hawk flew inside – and to the considerable alarm of the assembled dinner guests, the rare birds fell victims to these visiting birds of prey. While the rare birds were shrieking and dying, Danny was so drunk that he insisted on finishing his version of how he was evicted from his favorite beach-view duplex in Venice. It was a story that never failed to bring tears to Martin's eyes, because it concerned the death of his only dog. Meanwhile, the hawks swooped and killed; and the dinner guests – at first, just the women – put their heads under the dining-room table. Danny kept telling the story.

It had not yet occurred to young Martin that the declining fortunes of his father's screenwriting career would occasionally result in low-rent housing. Although this was a step down from freeloading in the generally well-to-do homes of directors and producers and almost-famous actors, the cheap rentals were at least free of other people's clothes and toys; in this sense, these rentals seemed a step *up* to Martin Mills. But not Venice. It had also not occurred to young Martin that Danny and Vera were simply waiting for their son to be old enough to send away to school. They presumed this would spare the child the continuing embarrass-ment of his parents' lives – their virtually separate existences, even within the confines of the same residence, their coping with Vera's affairs and with Danny's drinking. But Venice was too low-rent for Vera; she chose to spend the time in New York, while Danny was pounding the keys of a portable typewriter and dangerously driving Martin to and from Loyola Marymount. In Venice, they'd shared the ground-floor half of a shocking-pink duplex on the beach.

'It was the best place we ever lived, because it was so fucking real!' Danny explained to his cowering dinner guests. 'Isn't that right, Marty?' But young Martin was silent; he was noticing the death agonies of a mynah – the bird was succumbing to a hawk, very near where

483

the uneaten hors d'oeuvres still occupied a coffee table in the living room.

In truth, Martin thought, Venice had seemed rather *un*real to him. There were drugged hippies on South Venice Boulevard; Martin Mills was terrified of such an environment, but Danny touched and surprised him by giving him a dog for a pre-Christmas present. It was a beagle-sized mongrel from the pound – 'Saved from death!' Danny said. He named it 'Whiskey,' because of its color and in spite of Martin's protests. This must have condemned the dog, to name it after booze.

Whiskey slept with Martin, and Martin was allowed to put his own things on the ocean-damp walls. When he came 'home' from school, he waited until the lifeguards were off-duty before he took Whiskey walking on the beach, where for the first time he imagined he was the envy of those children who can always be found in public playgrounds – in this case, those children who stood in line to use the slide on Venice Beach. Surely they would have liked a dog of their own to walk on the sand.

For Christmas, Vera visited – albeit briefly. She refused to stay in Venice. She claimed a suite of rooms at a plain but clean hotel on Ocean Avenue in Santa Monica; there she ate a Christmas breakfast with Martin – the first of many lonely meals he would remember with his mother, whose principal measure of luxury was drawn from her qualified praise of room service. Veronica Rose repeatedly said that she would be happier living on reliable room service than in a house of her own – throw the towels on the floor, leave the dishes on the bed, that kind of thing. She gave young Martin a dog collar for Christmas, which profoundly moved him because he could remember no other instance of apparent collaboration between his mother and father; in this isolated case, Danny must have communicated with Vera – at least enough for Vera to know that Danny had given the boy a dog.

But on New Year's Eve, a roller skater (who lived in the turquoise duplex next door) fed the dog a big plate of marijuana lasagna. When Danny and Martin took Whiskey out for a walk after midnight, the stoned runt attacked a weight lifter's Rottweiler; Whiskey was killed by the first snap and shake.

The Rottweiler's owner was a contrite sort of muscle man wearing a tank top and a pair of gym shorts; Danny fetched a shovel, and the apologetic weight lifter dug an enormous grave in the vicinity of the children's slide. No one was permitted to bury a dead dog on Venice Beach; some civic-minded observer called the police. Martin was awakened by two cops very early on New Year's morning, when Danny was too hungover to assist him and there was no weight lifter available to help him dig the dead dog up. When Martin had finished stuffing Whiskey in a trash bag, one of the cops put the body in the trunk of the police car and the other cop, at the moment he handed Martin his fine, asked the boy where he went to school.

'I'm part of an accelerated educational program at Loyola Marymount,' Martin Mills explained to the cop.

Not even this distinction would prevent the landlord from evicting Danny and Martin shortly thereafter, out of fear of further trouble with the police. By the time they left, Martin Mills had changed his mind about the place. Almost every day, he'd seen the weight lifter with his murderous Rottweiler; and – either entering or leaving the turquoise duplex next door – the roller skater with a fondness for marijuana lasagna was a daily presence, too. Once again, Martin wasn't sorry to go.

It was Danny who mindlessly loved the story. In the producer's house on Kings Road, Danny seemed to prolong the telling of the tale, almost as if the ongoing bird deaths were an enhancement to the suddenness of poor Whiskey's demise. 'What a great fucking neighborhood that was!' Danny was shouting to his dinner guests. By now, all the men had put their heads under the table with the women. Both sexes were fearful that the swooping hawks would mistake them for rare birds.

'Daddy, there are *hawks* in the house!' Martin had cried. 'Daddy – the *birds*!'

'This is Hollywood, Marty,' Danny Mills had replied. 'Don't worry about the birds – the birds don't matter. This is Hollywood. The *story* is all that matters.'

That screenplay wasn't made into a movie, either; this was almost a refrain for Danny Mills. The bill for the rare, dead birds would reintroduce the Millses to more low-rent housing.

It was at this juncture in his memories that Martin Mills struggled to stop remembering; for if young Martin's familiarity with his father's shortcomings was well established *before* the boy was sent away to school, it was *after* he'd been sent away that his mother's moral unconcern became more apparent and struck young Martin as more odious than any weakness to be found in Danny.

Alone in his cubicle in Mazagaon, the new missionary now sought *any* means by which he might halt further memories of his mother. He thought of Father Joseph Moriarity, S.J.; he'd been young Martin's mentor at Loyola Marymount, and when Martin had been sent to Massachusetts – where he was *not* enrolled in Jesuit (or even in Catholic) schools – it had been Father Joe who'd answered the boy's religious questions, by mail. Martin Mills also thought of Brother Brennan and Brother LaBombard, his *coadjutores*, or 'fellow workers,' in his novice years at St Aloysius. He even remembered Brother Flynn inquiring if nocturnal emissions were 'allowed' – for was this not the impossible? Namely, sex without sin. Was it Father Toland or Father Feeney who'd implied that a nocturnal emission was in all likelihood an unconscious act of masturbation? Martin was certain that it was either Brother Monahan or Brother Dooley who'd inquired if the act of masturbation was still forbidden in the case of it being 'unconscious.'

'Yes, always,' Father Gannon had said. Father Gannon was bonkers, of course. No priest in his right mind would call an involuntary nocturnal emission an act of masturbation; nothing unconscious is ever a sin, since 'sin' implies freedom of choice. Father Gannon would one day be taken bodily from his classroom at St Aloysius, for his ravings were considered to lend credence to those 19th-century antipapist tracts in which convents are depicted as brothels for priests.

But how Martin Mills had approved of Father Gannon's answer; *that* will separate the men from the boys, he'd thought. It was a rule he'd been able to live with – no nocturnal emissions, unconscious or otherwise. He never touched himself.

But Martin Mills knew that even his triumph over masturbation would lead him to thinking of his mother, and so he tried to think of something else – of *anything* else. He repeated 100 times the date of August 15, 1534; it was the day St Ignatius Loyola, in a chapel in Paris, had taken the vow to go to Jerusalem. For 15 minutes, Martin Mills concentrated on the correct pronunciation of Montmartre. When this didn't work – when he found himself seeing the way his mother brushed her hair before she went to bed – Martin opened his Bible to Genesis, Chapter 19, for the Lord's destruction of Sodom and Gomorrah always calmed him, and within the story of God's wrath was also deftly planted that lesson in obedience which Martin Mills much admired. It was terribly human of Lot's wife . . . that she should look back, even though the Lord had commanded all of them, 'Do not look behind you . . . ,' but Lot's wife was nevertheless turned to a pillar of salt for her disobedience. As well she *should* have been, thought Martin Mills. But even his pleasure at the Lord's destruction of those cities that flaunted their depravities did not spare the missionary from his keenest memories of being sent away to school.

Turkey (Bird and Country)

Veronica Rose and Danny Mills had agreed that their academically gifted son should attend a New England prep school, but Vera didn't wait for young Martin to be of high-school age; in Vera's view, the boy was becoming too religious. As if it wasn't enough that the Jesuits were educating him, they'd managed to put it in the boy's head that he should attend Mass on Sunday and get himself to Confession, too. 'What does *this* kid have to confess?' Vera would ask Danny. She meant that young Martin was far too well behaved for a normal boy. As for Mass, Vera said that it 'screwed up' her weekends, and so Danny took him. A free Sunday morning was wasted on Danny, anyway; with hangovers like his, he might as well have been sitting and kneeling at a Mass.

They sent young Martin first to the Fessenden School in Massachusetts; it was strict but not religious, and Vera liked it because it was close to Boston. When she visited Martin, she could stay at the Ritz-Carlton and not in some dreary motel or a cutesy-quaint country inn. Martin started Fessenden in the sixth grade and would stay through the ninth grade, which was the school's final year; he didn't feel especially sorry for himself – there were even younger boarders at the school, although the majority of boarders were of the five-day variety, which meant that they went home every weekend. The seven-day boarders, like Martin, included many foreign students, or Americans whose families were in diplomatic service in unfriendly countries. Some of the foreign students, like Martin's roommate, were the children of diplomats in residence in Washington or New York.

Despite the roommate, for Martin Mills would rather have had a single room, young Martin enjoyed the crowded cubicle; he was allowed to put his own things on the walls, provided that this could be done without damage to the walls and that the subject matter was not obscene. Obscene subject matter wouldn't have tempted Martin Mills, but young Martin's roommate was tempted.

His name was Arif Koma, and he was from Turkey; his father was with the Turkish Consulate in New York. Arif stashed a calendar of women in bathing suits between his mattress and the bedsprings. Arif didn't offer to share his calendar with Martin, and the Turk usually waited until he thought Martin was asleep before he made masturbatory use of the 12 women. Often a full half hour after the required lights out, Martin would notice Arif's flashlight – the glow emerging from under the sheets and blanket – and the corresponding creak of Arif's bedsprings. Martin had looked at the calendar privately – when Arif was in the shower, or otherwise out of the cubicle – and it appeared (from the more abused pages) that Arif preferred March and August to the other women, although Martin couldn't fathom why. But Martin didn't observe the calendar in great detail, or for long; there was no door on the cubicle he shared with Arif – there was only a curtain – and should a faculty member have found him with the swimsuit calendar, the women (all 12 months of them) would have been confiscated. Martin would have considered this unfair to Arif.

It was less out of growing friendship than out of some silent, mutual respect that the two boys continued to be roommates into their final year at Fessenden. The school assumed that if you didn't complain about your roommate, you must like him. Furthermore, the boys had attended the same summer camp. In the spring of his first year at Fessendon, when Martin was sincerely missing his father and actually looking forward to what residential horrors he might encounter in the summer months, back in L.A., Vera had sent the boy a summer-camp brochure. This was where he was going; it was a matter that had already been decided – it wasn't a question – and as Martin leafed through the brochure, Arif looked at the pictures with him.

'I might as well go to that one, too,' the Turk had told Martin. 'I mean, I'll have to go *somewhere*.'

But there was another reason they stayed together; they were both unathletic, and neither was inclined to assert any physical superiority over the other. At a school like Fessenden, where sports were compulsory and the boys grew feverishly competitive, Arif and Martin could protect their lack of athletic interest only by remaining roommates. They joked to each other that Fessenden's most rabidly despised athletic rivals were schools named Fay and Fenn. They found it comic that these were other 'F' schools, as if the letter *F* signified a conspiracy of athleticism – a 'frenzy' of the competitive spirit. Having concurred on this observation, the two roommates devised a private way to indicate their contempt of Fessenden's obsessively athletic vigor; Arif and Martin resolved not only to remain unathletic – they would use an 'F' word for all the things they found distasteful about the school.

To the dominant colors of the faculty dress shirts, which were a button-down variety of pinks and yellows, the boys would say 'fashionable.' Of an unattractive faculty wife, 'far from fetching.' To the school rule that the top button of the shirt must always be buttoned when wearing a tie, they would respond with 'fastidious.' Other favorites, for varying encounters with the faculty and their fellow students, included 'faltering,' 'fascistic,' 'fatuous,' 'fawning,' 'featherbrained,' 'fecal,' 'fervid,' 'fiendish,' 'fishy,' 'flatulent,' 'fogyish,' 'forbidding,' 'foul,' 'fraudulent,' 'freakish,' 'frigid,' 'fulsome' and 'fussy.'

These one-word adjectival signals amused them; Martin and Arif became, like many roommates, a secret society. Naturally, this led other boys to call them 'fags,' 'faggots,' 'fruits,' 'flits' and 'fairies,' but the only sexual activity that took place in their shared cubicle was Arif's regular masturbation. By the time they were ninth graders, they were given a room with a door. This inspired Arif to take fewer pains to conceal his flashlight.

With this memory, the 39-year-old missionary, who was alone and wide awake in his cubicle at St Ignatius, realized that the subject of masturbation was insidious. In a desperate effort to distact himself from where he knew this subject would lead him – namely, to his mother – Martin Mills sat bolt upright on his cot, turned on his light and began to read at random in *The Times of India*. It wasn't even a recent issue of the newspaper; it was at least two weeks old and rolled into a tube, and it was kept under the cot, where it was handy for killing cockroaches and mosquitoes. But thus it happened that the new missionary began the first of the exercises with which he intended to orient himself in Bombay. A more important matter – that being whether there was anything in *The Times of India* that could defuse Martin's memory of his mother and her connection to the unwelcome theme of masturbation – would remain, for the moment, unresolved.

As Martin's luck would have it, his eyes fell first upon the matrimonials. He saw that a 32-year-old public-school teacher, in search of a bride, confessed to a 'minor squint in one eye'; a government servant (with his own house) admitted to a 'slight skewness in the legs,' but he maintained that he was able to walk perfectly – he would also accept a handicapped spouse. Elsewhere, a '60-ish issueless widower of wheatish complexion' sought a 'slim beautiful homely wheatish non-smoker teetotaller vegetarian under 40 with sharp features'; on the other hand, the widower tolerantly proclaimed, caste, language, state and education were 'no bar' to him (this was one of Ranjit's ads, of course). A bride seeking a groom advertised herself as having 'an attractive face with an Embroidery Diploma'; another 'slim beautiful homely girl,' who said she was planning to study computers, sought an independent young man who was 'sufficiently educated not to have the usual hang-ups about fair complexion, caste and dowry.'

About all that Martin Mills could conclude from these self-advertisements, and these desires, was that 'homely' meant well suited for domestic life and that a 'wheatish' complexion meant reasonably fair-skinned – probably a pale yellow-brown, like Dr Daruwalla. Martin couldn't have guessed that the '60-ish issueless widower of wheatish complexion' was Ranjit; he'd met Ranjit, who was dark-skinned – definitely not 'wheat-ish.' To the missionary, any matrimonial advertise-ment – any expressed longing to be a couple – seemed merely desperate and sad. He got off his cot and lit another mosquito coil, not because he'd noticed any mosquitoes but because Brother Gabriel had lit the last coil for him and Martin wanted to light one for himself.

He wondered if his former roommate, Arif Koma, had had a 'wheatish' complexion. No; Arif was darker than wheat, Martin thought, remembering how clear the Turk's complexion had been. In one's teenage years, a clear complexion was more remarkable than any color. In the ninth grade, Arif already needed to shave every day, which made his face appear much more mature than the faces of the other ninth graders; yet Arif was utterly boyish in his lack of body hair – his hairless chest, his smooth legs, his girlishly unhairy bum . . . such attributes as these connoted a feminine sleekness. Although they'd been roommates for three years, it wasn't until the ninth grade that Martin began to think of Arif as beautiful. Later, he would realize that even his earliest perception of Arif's beauty had been planted by Vera. 'And how is your pretty room-mate – that beautiful boy?' Martin's mother would ask him whenever she called.

It was customary in boarding schools for visiting parents to take their children out to dinner; often room-mates were invited along. Understandably, Martin Mills's parents never visited him together; like a divorced couple, although they weren't divorced, Vera

492

and Danny saw Martin separately. Danny usually took Martin and Arif to an inn in New Hampshire for the Thanksgiving holiday; Vera was more inclined to visits of a single night.

During the Thanksgiving break in their ninth-grade year, Arif and Martin were treated to the inn in New Hampshire with Danny *and* to a one-night visit with Vera – that being the Saturday night of the long weekend. Danny returned the boys to Boston, where Vera was waiting for them at the Ritz. She had arranged a two-bedroom suite. Her quarters were rather grand, with a king-sized bed and a sumptuous bathroom; the boys received a smaller bedroom, with two twin beds and an adjacent shower and toilet.

Martin had enjoyed the time at the inn in New Hampshire. There'd been a similar arrangement of rooms, but different; at the inn, Arif was given a bedroom and a bathroom of his own, while Danny had shared a room with twin beds with his son. For this enforced isolation, Danny was apologetic to Arif. 'You get to have him as your roommate all the time,' Danny explained to the Turk.

'Sure – I understand,' Arif had said. After all, in Turkey, seniority was the basic criterion for relationships of superiority and deference. 'I'm used to deference to seniority,' Arif had added pleasantly.

Sadly, Danny drank too much; he fell almost instantly asleep and snored. Martin was disappointed that there'd been little conversation between them. But before Danny passed out, and as they both lay awake in the dark, the father had said to the son, 'I hope you're happy. I hope you'll confide in me if you're ever *not* happy – or just tell me what you're thinking, in general.' Before Martin could think of what to say, he'd heard his father's snores. Nevertheless, the boy had appreciated the thought. In the morning, to have witnessed Danny's affection and pride, one would have presumed that the father and son had talked intimately.

Then, in Boston on Saturday night, Vera wanted to stray no farther than the dining room at the Ritz; her heaven was a good hotel, and she was already in it. But the dress code in the Ritz dining room was even more severe than Fessenden's. The captain stopped them because Martin was wearing white athletic socks with his loafers. Vera said simply, 'I was going to mention it, darling – now someone else has.' She gave him the room key, to go change his socks, while she waited with Arif. Martin had to borrow a pair of Arif's calf-length black hose. The incident drew Vera's attention to how much more comfortably Arif wore 'proper' clothes; she waited for Martin to rejoin them in the dining room before making her observation known.

'It must be your exposure to the diplomatic life,' Martin's mother remarked to the Turk. 'I suppose there are all sorts of dress-up occasions at the Turkish Embassy.'

'The Turkish Consulate,' Arif corrected her, as he had corrected her a dozen times.

'I'm frightfully uninterested in details,' Vera told the boy. 'I challenge you to make the difference between an embassy and a consulate interesting – I give you one minute.'

This was embarrassing to Martin, for it seemed to him that his mother had only recently learned to talk this way. She'd been such a vulgar young woman, and she'd gained no further education since that trashy time of her life; yet, in the absence of acting jobs, she'd learned to imitate the language of the educated upper classes. Vera was clever enough to know that trashiness was less appealing in older women. As for the adverb 'frightfully,' and the prefatory phrase 'I challenge you,' Martin Mills was ashamed to know where Vera had acquired this particular foppery.

There was a pretentious Brit in Hollywood, just another would-be director who'd failed to get a film made; Danny had written the unsuccessful script. To console himself, the Brit had made a series of moisturizer commercials; they were aimed at the older woman who was making an effort to preserve her skin, and Vera had been the model.

Shamelessly, there was his mother in a revealing camisole, seated in front of a makeup mirror – the kind that was framed with bright balls of light. Super-imposed, the titles read: VERONICA ROSE, HOLLYWOOD ACTRESS. (To Martin's knowledge, this commercial had been his mother's first acting job in years.)

'I'm frightfully opposed to dry skin,' Vera is saying to the makeup mirror (and to the camera). 'In this town, only the youthful last.' The camera closes on the corners of her mouth; a pretty finger applies the moisturizing lotion. Are those the telltale lines of age we see? Something appears to pucker the skin of her upper lip where it meets the well-defined edge of her mouth, but then the lip is miraculously smooth again; possibly this is only our imagination. 'I challenge you to tell me I'm getting old,' the lips say. It was a trick with the camera, Martin Mills was sure. Before the close-up, that was his mother; yet those lips, up close, were unfamiliar to him – someone else's *younger* mouth, Martin guessed.

It was a favorite TV commercial among the ninth-grade boys at Fessenden; when they gathered to watch an occasional television show in one of the dorm masters' apartments, the boys were always ready to answer the question that the close-up lips posed: 'I challenge you to tell me I'm getting old.'

'You're *already* old!' the boys would shout. Only two of them knew that Veronica Rose the Hollywood actress was Martin's mother. Martin would never have identified her, and Arif Koma was a loyal roommate.

Arif always said, 'She looks young enough to *me*.'

So it was doubly embarrassing, in the Ritz dining room, when Martin's mother said to Arif, 'I'm frightfully uninterested in details. I challenge you to make the difference between an embassy and a consulate interesting – I give you one minute.' Martin knew that

495

Arif must have known that the 'frightfully' and the 'I challenge you' had come from the moisturizer commercial.

In the roommates' secret language, Martin Mills suddenly said, 'Frightfully.' He thought Arif would understand; Martin was indicating that his own mother merited an 'F' word. But Arif was taking Vera seriously.

'An embassy is entrusted with a mission to a government and is headed by an ambassador,' the Turk explained. 'A consulate is the official premises of a consul, who is simply an official appointed by the government of one country to look after its commercial interests and the welfare of its citizens in another country. My father is the consul general in New York – New York being a place of commercial importance. A consul general is a consular officer of the highest rank, in charge of lower-ranking consular agents.'

'That took just thirty seconds,' Martin Mills informed his mother, but Vera was paying no attention to the time.

'Tell me about Turkey,' she said to Arif. 'You have thirty seconds.'

'Turkish is the mother tongue of more than ninety percent of the population, and we are more than ninety-nine percent Muslims.' Here Arif Koma paused, for Vera had shivered – the word 'Muslims' made her shiver every time. 'Ethnically, we are a melting pot,' the boy continued. 'Turks may be blond and blue-eyed; we may be of Alpine stock – that is, round-headed with dark hair and dark eyes. We may be of Mediterranean stock, dark, but long-headed. We may be Mongoloid, with high cheekbones.'

'What are you?' Vera interrupted.

'That was only twenty seconds,' Martin pointed out, but it was as if he weren't there at the dinner table with them; just the two of them were talking.

'I'm mostly Mediterranean,' Arif guessed. 'But my cheekbones are a little Mongoloid.'

'I don't think so,' Vera told him. 'And where do your eyelashes come from?'

'From my mother,' Arif replied shyly.

'What a lucky mother,' said Veronica Rose.

'Who's going to have what?' asked Martin Mills; he was the only one looking at the menu. 'I think I'm going to have the turkey.'

'You must have some strange customs,' Vera said to Arif. 'Tell me something strange – I mean, sexually.'

'Marriage is permitted between close kin – under the incest rules of Islam,' Arif answered.

'Something stranger,' Vera demanded.

'Boys are circumcised at any age from about six to twelve,' Arif said; his dark eyes were downcast, roaming the menu.

'How old were you?' Vera asked him.

'It's a public ceremony,' the boy mumbled. 'I was ten.'

'So you must remember it very clearly,' Vera said.

'I think I'll have the turkey, too,' Arif said to Martin.

'What do you remember about it, Arif?' Vera asked him.

'How you behave during the operation reflects on your family's reputation,' Arif replied, but as he spoke he looked at his roommate – not at his roommate's mother.

'And how did *you* behave?' Vera asked.

'I didn't cry – it would have dishonored my family,' the boy told her. 'I'll have the turkey,' he repeated.

'Didn't you two have turkey two days ago?' Vera asked them. 'Don't have the turkey *again* – how boring! Have something different!'

'Okay – I'll have the lobster,' Arif replied.

'That's a good choice – I'll have the lobster, too,' Vera said. 'What are you having, Martin?'

'I'll take the turkey,' said Martin Mills. The sudden strength of his own will surprised him; in the power of his will there was already something Jesuitical.

This particular recollection gave the missionary the

strength to return his attention to *The Times of India*, wherein he read about a family of 14 who'd been burned alive; their house had been set on fire by a rival family. Martin Mills wondered what a 'rival family' was; then he prayed for the 14 souls who'd been burned alive.

Brother Gabriel, who'd been awakened by roosting pigeons, could see the light shining under Martin's door. Another of Brother Gabriel's myriad responsibilities at St Ignatius was to foil the pigeons in their efforts to roost at the mission; the old Spaniard could detect pigeons roosting in his sleep. The many columns of the second-floor outdoor balcony afforded the pigeons almost unlimited access to the overhanging cornices. One by one, Brother Gabriel had fenced in the cornices with wire. After he'd shooed away these particular pigeons, he left the step-ladder leaning against the column; that way, he would know which cornice to re-enclose with wire in the morning.

When Brother Gabriel passed by Martin Mills's cubicle again, on his way back to bed, the new missionary's light was *still* on. Pausing by the cubicle door, Brother Gabriel listened; he feared that 'young' Martin might be ill. But to his surprise and eternal comfort, Brother Gabriel heard Martin Mills praying. Such late-night litanies suggested to Brother Gabriel that the new missionary was a man very strongly in God's clutches; yet the Spaniard was sure he'd misunderstood what he heard of the prayer. It must be the American accent, old Brother Gabriel thought, for although the tone of voice and the repetition was very much in the nature of a prayer, the words made no sense at all.

To remind himself of the power of his will, which surely was evidence of God's will within him, Martin Mills was repeating and repeating that long-ago proof of his inner courage. 'I'll take the turkey,' the missionary was saying. 'I'll take the turkey,' he said again. He knelt on the stone floor beside his cot, clutching the rolled-up copy of *The Times of India* in his hands.

A prostitute had tried to eat his *culpa* beads, then she'd thrown them away; a dwarf had his whip; he'd rashly told Dr Daruwalla to dispose of his leg iron. It would take a while for the stone floor to hurt his knees, but Martin Mills would wait for the pain – worse, he would welcome it. 'I'll take the turkey,' he prayed. He saw so clearly how Arif Koma was unable to raise his dark eyes to meet Vera's fixed stare, which so steadily scrutinized the circumcised Turk.

'It must have been frightfully painful,' Vera was saying. 'And you honestly didn't cry?'

'It would have dishonored my family,' Arif said again. Martin Mills could tell that his roommate was about to cry; he'd seen Arif cry before. Vera could tell, too.

'But it's all right to cry now,' she was saying to the boy. Arif shook his head, but the tears were coming. Vera used her handkerchief to pat Arif's eyes. For a while, Arif completely covered his face with Vera's handkerchief; it was a strongly scented handkerchief, Martin Mills knew. His mother's scent could sometimes make him gag.

'I'll take the turkey, I'll take the turkey, I'll take the turkey,' the missionary prayed. It was such a steady-sounding prayer, Brother Gabriel decided; oddly, it reminded him of the pigeons, maniacally roosting on the cornices.

Two Different Men, Both Wide Awake

It was a different issue of *The Times of India* that Dr Daruwalla was reading – it was the current day's issue. If the sleeplessness of this night seemed full of the torments of hell for Martin Mills, Dr Daruwalla was exhilarated to feel so wide awake. Farrokh was merely using *The Times of India*, which he hated, as a means to energize himself. Nothing enlivened him with such loathing as reading the review of a new Inspector Dhar film. USUAL INSPECTOR DHAR IDIOM, the headline said. Farrokh found this typically infuriating. The reviewer was the sort of cultural commissar who'd never stoop to say a single favorable word about *any* Inspector Dhar film. That dog turd which had prevented Dr Daruwalla from more than a partial reading of this review had been a blessing; it was a form of foolish self-punishment for the doctor to read the entire thing. The first sentence was bad enough: 'The problem with Inspector Dhar is his tenacious umbilical bindings with his first few creations.' Farrokh felt that this sentence alone would provide him with the desired fury to write all night.

'Umbilical bindings!' Dr Daruwalla cried aloud. Then he cautioned himself not to wake up Julia; she was already angry with him. He made further use of *The Times of India* by putting it under his typewriter; the newspaper would keep the typewriter from rattling against the glass-topped table. He had set up his writing materials in the dining room; his writing desk, which was in the bedroom, was out of the question at this late hour.

But he'd never tried to write in the dining room before. The glass-topped table was too low. It had never been a satisfactory dining-room table; it was more like a coffee table – to eat at it, one sat on cushions on the floor. Now, in an effort to make himself more comfortable, Farrokh tried sitting on *two* cushions; he rested his elbows on either side of the typewriter. As an orthopedist, Dr Daruwalla was aware that this position was unwise for his back; also, it was distracting to peer through the glass-topped table at his own crossed legs and bare feet. For a while, the doctor was additionally distracted by what he thought was the unfairness of Julia's being angry with him.

Their dinner at the Ripon Club had been hasty and quarrelsome. It was a difficult day to summarize, and Julia was of the opinion that her husband was condensing too much interesting material in his recitation of the day; she was ready to speculate all night on the subject of Rahul Rai as a serial killer. Moreover, she was perturbed with Farrokh that he thought her presence at the Duckworth Club lunch with Detective Patel and Nancy would be 'inappropriate'; after all, John D. was going to be there.

'I'm asking him to be present because of his memory,' Dr Daruwalla had claimed.

'I suppose I don't have a memory,' Julia had replied.

Even more frustrating was that Farrokh had not been successful in reaching John D. He'd left messages at both the Taj and the Oberoi concerning an important lunch at the Duckworth Club, but Dhar hadn't returned his calls; probably the actor was still miffed about the unannounced-twin business, not that he would deign to admit it.

As for the efforts now under way to send poor Madhu and the elephant-footed Ganesh to the Great Blue Nile Circus, Julia had questioned the wisdom of Farrokh involving himself in 'such dramatic intervention,' as she called it; she wondered why he'd never so directly undertaken the dubious rescue of maimed beggars and child prostitutes before. Dr Daruwalla was irritated because he already suffered from similar misgivings. As for the screenplay that the doctor was dying to begin, Julia expressed further criticism: she was surprised that Farrokh could be so self-centred at such a time – implying that it was selfish of him to be thinking of his own writing when so much that was violent and traumatic was happening in the lives of others.

They'd even had a spat about what to listen to on the radio. Julia chose those channels with programs that made her sleepy; 'song miscellany' and 'regional light music' were her favorites. But Dr Daruwalla became caught up in the last stages of an interview with some complaining writer who was incensed that there was

501

'no follow-through' in India. 'Everything is left incomplete!' the writer was complaining. 'We get to the bottom of nothing!' he cried. 'As soon as we poke our noses into something interesting, we take our noses away again!' The writer's anger interested Farrokh, but Julia flipped to a channel featuring 'instrumental music'; by the time Dr Daruwalla found the complaining writer again, the writer's anger was being directed at a news story he'd heard today. A rape and murder had been reported at the Alexandria Girls' English Institution. The account that the writer had heard went as follows: 'There was no rape and no murder, as previously and erroneously reported, at the Alexandria Girls' English Institution today.' This was the kind of thing that drove the writer crazy; Farrokh guessed it was what he meant by 'no follow-through.'

'It's truly ridiculous to listen to this!' Julia had said, and so he'd left her with her 'instrumental music.'

Now Dr Daruwalla put all this behind him. He thought about limps – all the different kinds he'd seen. He wouldn't use Madhu's name; he would call the girl in his screenplay Pinky, because Pinky was a real star. He would also make the girl much younger than Madhu; that way, nothing sexual could threaten her – not in Dr Daruwalla's story.

Ganesh was the right name for the boy, but in the movie the boy would be older than the girl. Farrokh would simply reverse the ages of the *real* children. He would give *his* Ganesh a bad limp, too, but not nearly so grotesquely crushed a foot as the real Ganesh had; it would be too hard to find a child actor with such a nasty deformity. And the children should have a mother, because the screenwriter had already planned how he would take their mother away. Storytelling was a ruthless business.

Briefly Dr Daruwalla considered that he'd not only failed to understand the country of his origin; he'd also failed to love it. He realized he was about to invent an India he could both comprehend and love – a simplified version. But his self-doubt passed – as self-doubt must, in order to begin a story.

It was a story set in motion by the Virgin Mary, Farrokh believed. He meant the stone statue of the unnamed saint in St Ignatius Church – the one that needed to be restrained with a chain and a steel grommet. She wasn't really the Blessed Mother, but she had nevertheless become the Virgin Mary to Dr Daruwalla. He liked the phrase well enough to write it down – 'a story set in motion by the Virgin Mary.' It was a pity that it wouldn't work as a title. For a title, he would need to find something shorter; but the simple repetition of this phrase enabled him to begin. He wrote it down again, and then again – 'a story set in motion by the Virgin Mary.' Then he crossed out every trace of this phrase, so that not even he could read it. Instead, he said it aloud – repeatedly.

Thus, in the dead of night, while almost five million residents of Bombay were fast asleep on the sidewalks of the city, these two men were wide awake and mumbling. One spoke only to himself – 'a story set in motion by the Virgin Mary' – and this allowed him to get started. The other spoke not only to himself but to God; understandably, his mumbles were a little louder. He was saying, 'I'll take the turkey,' and his repetitions – he hoped – would prevent him from being consumed by that past which everywhere surrounded him. It was the past that had given him his tenacious will, which he believed was the will of God within him; yet how he feared the past.

'I'll take the turkey,' said Martin Mills. By now his knees were throbbing. 'I'll take the turkey, I'll take the turkey, I'll take the turkey.'

18. A STORY SET IN MOTION BY THE VIRGIN MARY

Limo Roulette

In the morning, Julia found Farrokh slumped over the glass-topped table as if he'd fallen asleep while looking through the glass at the big toe of his right foot. Julia knew this was the same toe that had been bitten by a monkey, for which the family had suffered some religious disruption; she was thankful that the effects of the monkey bite had been neither fanatical nor long-lasting, but to observe her husband in the apparent position of praying to this same toe was disconcerting.

Julia was relieved to see the pages of the screenplay-in-progress, which she realized had been the true object of Farrokh's scrutiny – not his toe. The typewriter had been pushed aside; the typed pages had many penciled corrections written on them, and the doctor still held the pencil in his right hand. It appeared to Julia that her husband's own writing had served him as a soporific. She assumed she was a witness to the genesis of yet another Inspector Dhar disaster, but she saw at a glance that Dhar was not the voice-over character; after reading the first five pages, she wondered if Dhar was even in the movie. How odd! she thought. Altogether, there were about 25 pages. She took them into the kitchen with her; there she made coffee for herself and tea for Farrokh.

The voice-over was that of a 12-year-old boy who'd been crippled by an elephant. Oh, no – it's *Ganesh*! Julia thought. She knew the beggar. Whenever she left the apartment building, he was there to follow her; she'd bought him many things, most of which he'd sold, but his unusually good English had charmed her. Unlike Dr Daruwalla, Julia knew *why* Ganesh's English was so polished.

Once, when he'd been begging at the Taj, an English couple had spotted him; they were traveling with a shy, lonely boy a little younger than Ganesh, and the child had requested that they find him someone to play with. There was also a nanny in tow, and Ganesh had traveled with this family for over a month. They fed him and clothed him and kept him atypically clean – they had him examined by a doctor, to be sure he wasn't carrying any infectious diseases – just so he could be a playmate for their lonely child. The nanny taught Ganesh English during the several hours of every day that she was under orders to give language instruction to the English boy. And when it was time for the family to return to England, they simply left Ganesh where they'd found him – begging at the Taj. He quickly sold the unnecessary clothes. For a time, Ganesh said, he'd missed the nanny. The story had touched Julia. It also struck her as highly unlikely. But why would the beggar have made it up? Now here was her husband, putting the poor cripple in a movie!

And Farrokh had given Ganesh a sister, a six-year-old girl named Pinky; she was a gifted street acrobat, a sidewalk beggar who performed various tricks. This didn't fool Julia. Julia knew the real Pinky – she was a circus star. It was also obvious that another inspiration for the fictional Pinky was Madhu, Deepa and Vinod's newest child prostitute; in the movie, Farrokh had made Pinky totally innocent. These fictional children were also fortunate to have a mother. (Not for long.)

The mother is a sweeper at St Ignatius, where the Jesuits have not only employed her – they've converted her. Her children are strict vegetarian Hindus; they're quite disgusted by their mother's conversion, but especially by the concept of Holy Communion. The idea that the wine really *is* Christ's blood, and the

505

bread really *is* his body . . . well, understandably, this is nauseating to the little vegetarians.

It shocked Julia to see that her husband, as a writer, was such a shameless borrower, for she knew he'd robbed the memoir of a nun; it was a terrible story that had long amused him – and old Lowji before him. The nun was working hard to convert a tribe of former cannibals. She had a difficult time explaining the concept of the body and blood of Jesus in the Eucharist. Since there were many former cannibals in the tribe who could still remember eating human flesh, the theological notion of Holy Communion pushed a lot of buttons for them.

Julia saw that her husband was up to his usual blasphemies. But where was Inspector Dhar?

Julia half-expected to see Dhar come to the children's rescue, but the story went on without him. The mother is killed in St Ignatius Church, while genuflecting. A statue of the Virgin Mary falls from a pedestal and crushes her; she is given Extreme Unction on the spot. Ganesh does not mourn her passing greatly. 'At least she was happy,' says his voice-over. 'It is not every Christian who is fortunate enough to be instantly killed by the Blessed Virgin.' If there was ever a time for Dhar to come to the rescue, now's the time, Julia thought. But Dhar didn't come.

Instead, the little beggars begin to play a game called 'limo roulette.' All the street children in Bombay know there are two special limousines that cruise the city. In one is a scout for the circus – a dwarf named Vinod, of course. The dwarf is a former circus clown; his job is looking for gifted acrobats. Pinky is so gifted, the crippled Ganesh believes that Vinod would let him go to the circus *with* Pinky – so that he could look after her. The problem is, there's another scout. He's a man who steals children for the freak circus. He's called Acid Man because he pours acid on your face. The acid is so disfiguring that your own family wouldn't recognize you. Only the circus for freaks will take care of you.

506

So Farrokh was after Mr Garg again, Julia thought. What an appalling story! Even without Inspector Dhar, good and evil were once more plainly in position. Which scout would find the children first? Would it be the Good Samaritan dwarf, or would it be Acid Man?

The limos move around at night. We see a sleek car pass the children, who run after it. We see the brake lights flicker, but then the dark car drives on; other children are chasing after it. We see a limousine stopped at the curb, motor running; the children approach it cautiously. The driver's-side window opens a crack; we see the stubby fingers on the edge of the glass, like claws. When the window is rolled down, there is the dwarf's big head. This is the right limo – this is Vinod.

Or else it's the wrong limo. The back door opens, a kind of frost escapes; it's as if the car's air-conditioning is too cold – the car is like a freezer or a meat locker. Possibly the acid must be preserved at such a temperature; maybe Acid Man himself must be kept this cold, or else he'll rot.

Apparently, the poor children wouldn't be forced to play 'limo roulette' if the Virgin Mary hadn't toppled off a pedestal and murdered their mother. What was her husband thinking? Julia wondered. She was used to reading Farrokh's first drafts, his raw beginnings. Normally, she felt she wasn't invading her husband's privacy; he always shared with her his work-in-progress. But Julia was worried that this screenplay was something he'd never share with her. There was something desperate about it. Probably it suffered from the potential disappointment of attempted art – a vulnerability that had certainly been lacking in the doctor's Inspector Dhar scripts. It occurred to Julia that Farrokh might care too much about this one.

It was this reasoning that led her to return the manuscript to its previous position on the glass-topped table, more or less between the typewriter and her husband's head. Farrokh was still asleep, although a smile of drooling-idiot proportions indicated that he was dreaming, and he emitted a nasal humming – an unfollowable tune. The awkward position of the doctor's head on the glass-topped table allowed him to imagine that he was a child again, napping at St Ignatius School with his head on his desk in I-3.

Suddenly, Farrokh snorted in his sleep. Julia could tell that her husband was about to wake up, but she was startled when he woke up screaming. She thought he'd had a nightmare but it turned out to be a cramp in the arch of his right foot. He looked so disheveled, she was embarrassed for him. Then her anger with him returned . . . that he'd thought it 'inappropriate' for her to attend the interesting lunch with the deputy commissioner and the limping hippie from 20 years ago. Worse, Farrokh drank his tea without mentioning his screenplay-in-progress; he even attempted to conceal the pages in his doctor's bag.

Julia remained aloof when he kissed her good-bye, but she stood in the open doorway of the apartment and watched him push the button for the lift. If the doctor was demonstrating the early symptoms of an artistic temperament, Julia thought she should nip such an ailment in the bud. She waited until the elevator door opened before she called to him.

'If that ever was a movie,' Julia said, 'Mr Garg would sue you.'

Dr Daruwalla stood dumbfounded while the elevator door closed on his doctor's bag, and then opened; the door kept opening and closing on his bag as he stared indignantly at his wife. Julia blew him a kiss, just to make him cross. The elevator door grew more aggressive; Farrokh was forced to fight his way inside. He hadn't time to retort to Julia before the door closed and he was descending; he'd never successfully kept a secret from her. Besides, Julia was right: Garg *would* sue him! Dr Daruwalla wondered if the creative process had eclipsed his common sense.

In the alley, another blow to his common sense

awaited him. When Vinod opened the door of the Ambassador for him, the doctor saw the elephant-footed beggar asleep in the back seat. Madhu had chosen to sit up front, beside the dwarf driver. Except for the crusty exudation on his eyelashes, the sleeping boy looked angelic. His crushed foot was covered with one of the rags he carried for wiping off the fake bird shit; even in his sleep, Ganesh had managed to conceal his deformity. This wasn't a make-believe Ganesh, but a real boy; nevertheless, Farrokh found himself looking at the cripple as he might stand back and take pride in one of his fictional creations. The doctor was still thinking about his story; he was thinking that what would happen next to Ganesh was entirely a matter of the screenwriter's imagination. But the *real* beggar had found a benefactor; until the circus took him, the back seat of Vinod's Ambassador would do – it was already better than what he was used to.

'Good morning, Ganesh,' the doctor said. The boy was instantly awake, as alert as a squirrel.

'What are we doing today?' the beggar asked.

'No more bird-shit tricks,' the doctor said.

The beggar registered his understanding with a tight-lipped smile. 'But what are we doing?' the boy repeated.

'We're going to my office,' Dr Daruwalla said. 'We're waiting for some test results for Madhu, before we make our plans. And this morning you will be kind enough *not* to practice the bird-shit trick on those postoperative children in the exercise yard.' The boy's black eyes kept darting with the movements of the traffic. The doctor could see Madhu's face reflected in the rearview mirror; she'd not responded – she'd not even glanced in the mirror at the mention of her name.

'What concerns me, about the *circus* . . .' Dr Daruwalla said; he paused deliberately. The emphasis he'd given to the word had gained Ganesh's full attention, but not Madhu's.

'My arms are the best – very strong. I could ride a

509

pony – no legs necessary with hands as strong as mine,' Ganesh suggested. 'I could do lots of tricks – hang by my arms from an elephant's trunk, maybe ride a lion.'

'But what concerns me is that they won't *let* you do tricks – no tricks,' Dr Daruwalla replied. 'They'll give you all the bad jobs, all the hard work. Scooping up the elephant shit, for example – not hanging from their trunks.'

'I'll have to show them', Ganesh said. 'But what do you do to the lions to make them stand on those little stools?'

'*Your* job would be to wash the lion piss off the stools,' Farrokh told him.

'And what do you do with tigers?' Ganesh asked.

'What *you* would do with tigers is clean their cages – tiger shit!' said Dr Daruwalla.

'I'll have to show them,' the boy repeated. 'Maybe something with their tails – tigers have long tails.'

The dwarf entered the roundabout that the doctor hated. There were too many easily distracted drivers who stared at the sea and at the worshipers milling in the mudflats around Haji Ali's Tomb; the rotary was near Tardeo, where Farrokh's father had been blown to smithereens. Now, in the midst of this round-about, the traffic swerved to avoid a lunatic cripple; a legless man in one of those makeshift wheelchairs powered by a hand crank was navigating the rotary against the flow of other vehicles. The doctor could follow Ganesh's roaming gaze; the boy's black eyes either ignored or avoided the wheelchair madman. The little beggar was probably still thinking about the tigers.

Dr Daruwalla didn't know the exact ending of his screenplay; he had only a general idea of what would happen to *his* Pinky, to *his* Ganesh. Caught in the roundabout, the doctor realized that the fate of the real Ganesh – in addition to Madhu's fate – was out of his hands. But Farrokh felt responsible for beginning *their* stories, just as surely as he'd begun the story he was making up.

In the rearview mirror, Dr Daruwalla could see that Madhu's lion-yellow eyes were following the movements of the legless maniac. Then the dwarf needed to brake sharply; he brought his taxi to a full stop in order to avoid the crazed cripple in the wrong-way wheelchair. The wheelchair sported a bumper sticker opposed to horn blowing.

PRACTICE THE VIRTUE OF PATIENCE

A battered oil truck loomed over the wheelchair lunatic; in a fury, the oil-truck driver repeatedly blew his horn. The great cylindrical body of the truck was covered with foot-high lettering the color of flame.

WORLD'S FIRST CHOICE
– GULF ENGINE OILS

The oil truck also sported a bumper sticker, which was almost illegible behind flecks of tar and splattered insects.

KEEP A FIRE EXTINGUISHER IN YOUR GLOVE
COMPARTMENT

Dr Daruwalla knew that Vinod didn't have one.

As if it wasn't irritating enough to be obstructing traffic, the cripple was begging among the stopped cars. The clumsy wheelchair bumped against the Ambassador's rear door. Farrokh was incensed when Ganesh rolled down the rear window, toward which the wheelchair madman extended his arm.

'Don't give that idiot anything!' the doctor cried, but Farrokh had underestimated the speed of Bird-Shit Boy. Dr Daruwalla never saw the bird-shit syringe, only the look of surprise on the face of the crazed cripple in the wheelchair; he quickly withdrew his arm

– his palm, his wrist, his whole forearm dripping bird shit. Vinod cheered.

'Got him,' Ganesh said.

A passing paint truck nearly obliterated the wheel-chair lunatic. Vinod cheered for the paint truck, too.

CELEBRATE WITH ASIAN PAINTS

When the paint truck was gone from view, the traffic moved again – the dwarf's taxi taking the lead. The doctor remembered the bumper sticker on Vinod's Ambassador.

HEY YOU WITH THE EVIL EYE,
MAY YOUR FACE TURN BLACK!

'I said no more bird-shit tricks, Ganesh,' Farrokh told the boy. In the rearview mirror, Dr Daruwalla could see Madhu watching him; when he met her eyes, she looked away. Through the open window, the air was hot and dry, but the pleasure of a moving car was new to the boy, if not to the child prostitute. Maybe nothing was new to her, the doctor feared. But for the beggar, if not for Madhu, this was the start of an adventure.

'Where *is* the circus?' Ganesh asked. 'Is it far?'

Farrokh knew that the Great Blue Nile might be anywhere in Gujarat. The question that concerned Dr Daruwalla was not *where* the circus was, but whether it would be safe.

Ahead, the traffic slowed again; probably ped-estrians, Dr Daruwalla thought – shoppers from the nearby chowk, crowding into the street. Then the doctor saw the body of a man in the gutter; his legs extended into the road. The traffic was squeezed into one lane because the oncoming drivers didn't want to drive over the dead man's feet or ankles. A crowd was quickly forming; soon there would be the usual chaos. For the moment, the only concession made to the dead man was that no one drove over him.

'Is the circus *far?*' Ganesh asked again.

'Yes, it's far – it's a world apart,' said Dr Daruwalla. 'A world apart' was what he hoped for the boy, whose bright black eyes spotted the body in the road. Ganesh quickly looked away. The dwarf's taxi inched past the dead man; once more, Vinod moved ahead of the traffic.

'Did you see that?' Farrokh asked Ganesh.

'See what?' the cripple said.

'There is a man being dead,' Vinod said.

'They are nonpersons,' Ganesh replied. 'You think you see them but they are not really being there.'

O God, keep this boy from becoming a nonperson! Dr Daruwalla thought. His fear surprised him; he couldn't bring himself to seek the cripple's hopeful face. In the rearview mirror, Madhu was watching the doctor again. Her indifference was chilling. It had been quite a while since Dr Daruwalla had prayed, but he began.

India wasn't limo roulette. There were no good scouts or bad scouts for the circus; there was no freak circus, either. There were no right-limo, wrong-limo choices. For these children, the real roulette would begin after they got to the circus – *if* they got there. At the circus, no Good Samaritan dwarf could save them. At the Great Blue Nile, Acid Man – a comic-book villain – wasn't the danger.

Mother Mary

In the new missionary's cubicle, the last mosquito coil had burned out just before dawn. The mosquitoes had come with the early gray light and had departed with the first heat of the day – all but the mosquito that Martin Mills had mashed against the white wall above his cot. He'd killed it with the rolled-up issue of *The Times of India* after the mosquito was full of blood; the bloodstain on the wall was conspicuous and only a

513

few inches below the crucifix that hung there, which gave Martin the gruesome impression that a sizable drop of Christ's blood had spotted the wall.

In his inexperience, Martin had lit the last mosquito coil too close to his cot. When his hand trailed on the floor, his fingers must have groped through the dead ashes. Then, in his brief and troubled sleep, he'd touched his face. This was the only explanation for the surprising view of himself that he saw in the pitted mirror above the sink; his face was dotted with fingerprints of ash, as if he'd meant to mock Ash Wednesday – or as if a ghost had passed through his cubicle and fingered him. The marks struck him as a sarcastic blessing, or else they made him look like an insincere penitent.

When he'd filled the sink and wet his face to shave, he held the razor in his right hand and reached for the small sliver of soap with his left. It was a jagged-shaped piece of such an iridescent blue-green color that it was reflected in the silver soap dish; it turned out to be a lizard, which leaped into his hair before he could touch it. The missionary was frightened to feel the reptile race across his scalp. The lizard launched itself from the top of Martin's head to the crucifix on the wall above the cot; then it jumped from Christ's face to the partially open slats of the window blind, through which the light from the low sun slanted across the floor of the cubicle.

Martin Mills had been startled; in an effort to brush the lizard out of his hair, he'd slashed his nose with the razor. An imperceptible breeze stirred the ashes from the mosquito coils, and the missionary watched himself bleed into the water in the sink. He'd long ago given up shaving lather; plain soap was good enough. In the absence of soap, he shaved himself in the cold, bloody water.

It was only 6:00 in the morning. Martin Mills had to survive another hour before Mass. He thought it would be a good idea to go to St Ignatius Church early; if the church wasn't locked, he could sit quietly in one of the pews – that usually helped. But his stupid nose kept bleeding; he didn't want to bleed all over the church. He'd neglected to pack any handkerchiefs – he'd have to buy some – and so for now he chose a pair of black socks; although they were of a thin material, not very absorbent, at least they wouldn't show the bloodstains. He soaked the socks in fresh cold water in the sink; he wrung them out until they were merely damp. He balled up a sock in each hand and, first with one hand and then the other, he restlessly dabbed at the wound on his nose.

Someone watching Martin Mills dress himself might have suspected the missionary of being in a deep trance; a less kind observer might have concluded that the zealot was semiretarded, for he wouldn't put down the socks. The awkward pulling on of his trousers – when he tied his shoes, he held the socks in his teeth – and the buttoning of his short-sleeved shirt . . . these normally simple tasks were turned arduous, almost athletic; these clumsy feats were punctuated by the ceaseless dabbing at his nose. In the second buttonhole of his shirt, Martin Mills affixed a silver cross like a lapel pin, and together with this adornment he left a thumbprint of blood on his shirt, for the socks had already stained his hands.

St Ignatius Church was unlocked. The Father Rector unlocked the church at 6:00 every morning, and so Martin Mills had a safe place to sit and wait for Mass. For a while, he watched the altar boys setting up the candles. He sat in a center-aisle pew, alternately praying and dabbing at his bleeding nose. He saw that the kneeling pad was hinged. Martin didn't like hinged kneelers because they reminded him of the Protestant school where Danny and Vera had sent him after Fessenden.

St Luke's was an Episcopalian place; as such, in Martin's view, it was barely a religious school at all. The morning service was only a hymn and a prayer and a virtuous thought for the day, which was followed by a curiously secular benediction – hardly a blessing, but some sage advice about studying relentlessly and never plagiarizing. Sunday church attendance was required, but in St Luke's Chapel the service was of such a *low* Episcopalian nature that no one knelt for prayers. Instead, the students slumped in their pews; probably they weren't sincere Episcopalians. And whenever Martin Mills would attempt to lower the hinged kneeling pad – so that he could properly kneel to pray – his fellow students in the pew would firmly hold the hinged kneeler in the upright, nonpraying position. They insisted on using the kneeling pad as a footrest. When Martin complained to the school's headmaster, the Reverend Rick Utley informed the underclassman that only *senior* Catholics and *senior* Jews were permitted to attend worship services in their churches and synagogues of choice; until Martin was a senior, St Luke's would have to do – in other words, no kneeling.

In St Ignatius Church, Martin Mills lowered the kneeling pad and knelt in prayer. In the pew was a rack that held the hymnals and prayer books; whenever Martin bled on the binding of the nearest hymnal, he dabbed at his nose with one sock and wiped the hymnal with the other. He prayed for the strength to love his father, for merely pitying him seemed insufficient. Although Martin knew that the task of loving his mother was an insurmountable one, he prayed for the charity to forgive her. And he prayed for the soul of Arif Koma. Martin had long ago forgiven Arif, but every morning he prayed that the Holy Virgin would forgive Arif, too. The missionary always began this prayer in the same way.

'O Mother Mary, it was *my* fault!' Martin prayed. In a way, the new missionary's story had also been set in motion by the Virgin Mary – in the sense that Martin held her in higher esteem than he held his own Mother. Had Vera been killed by a falling statue of the

Blessed Virgin – especially if such good riddance had occurred when the zealot was of a tender, unformed age – Martin might never have become a Jesuit at all.

His nose was still bleeding. A drop of his blood dripped on the hymnal; once more the missionary dabbed at his wound. Arbitrarily, he decided *not* to wipe the song book; perhaps he thought that blood-stains would give the hymnal character. After all, it was a religion steeped in blood – Christ's blood and the blood of saints and martyrs. It would be glorious to be a martyr, Martin thought. He looked at his watch. In just half an hour, if he could make it, the missionary knew he would be saved by the Mass.

Is There a Gene for It, Whatever It Is?

In his stepped-up efforts to save Madhu from Mr Garg, Dr Daruwalla placed a phone call to Tata Two. But the OB/GYN's secretary told Farrokh that Dr Tata was already in surgery. The poor patient, whoever she was, Dr Daruwalla thought. Farrokh wouldn't want a woman he knew to be subjected to the uncertain scalpel of Tata Two, for (fairly or unfairly) Farrokh assumed that the surgical procedures of the second Dr Tata were second-rate, too. It was quickly apparent to Dr Daruwalla that Tata Two's medical secretary lived up to the family reputation for mediocrity, because the doctor's simple request for the quickest possible results of Madhu's HIV test were met with suspicion and condescension. Dr Tata's secretary had already identified himself, rather arrogantly, as *Mister* Subhash.

'You are wanting a rush job?' Mr Subhash asked Dr Daruwalla. 'Are you being aware that you are paying more for it?'

'Of course!' Farrokh said.

'It is normally costing four hundred rupees,' Mr Subhash informed Dr Daruwalla. 'A rush job is costing you a thousand rupees. Or is the patient paying?'

517

'No, *I'm* paying. I want the quickest possible results,' Farrokh replied.

'It is normally taking ten days or two weeks,' Mr Subhash explained. 'It is most conveniently being done in *batches*. We are normally waiting until we are having forty specimens.'

'But I don't want you to wait in this case,' Dr Daruwalla replied. 'That's why I called – I know how it's normally done.'

'If the ELISA is being positive, we are normally confirming the results by Western Blot. The ELISA is having a lot of false positives, you know,' Mr Subhash explained.

'I know,' said Dr Daruwalla. 'If you get a positive ELISA, please send it on for a Western Blot.'

'This is prolonging the turnaround time for a positive test,' Mr Subhash explained.

'Yes, I *know*,' Dr Daruwalla replied.

'If the test is being negative, you are having the results in two days,' Mr Subhash explained. 'Naturally, if it is being positive . . .'

'Then it would take longer – I *know*!' Dr Daruwalla cried. 'Please just order the test immediately. That's why I called.'

'Only Dr Tata is ordering the testing,' Mr Subhash said. 'But of course I am telling him what you are wanting.'

'Thank you,' Dr Daruwalla replied.

'Is there anything else you are wanting?' Mr Subhash asked.

There *had* been something else, but Farrokh had forgotten what it was that he'd meant to ask Tata Two. Doubtless it would come back to him.

'Please just ask Dr Tata to call me,' Farrokh replied.

'And what is being the subject you are wishing to discuss with Dr Tata?' Mr Subhash asked.

'It is a subject of discussion between *doctors*,' Dr Daruwalla said.

'I am telling him,' Mr Subhash said testily.

Dr Daruwalla resolved that he would never again complain about the nincompoopish matrimonial activities of Ranjit. Ranjit was competent and he was polite. Moreover, Dr Daruwalla's secretary had steadfastly maintained his enthusiasm for the doctor's dwarf-blood project. No one else had ever encouraged the doctor's genetic studies – least of all, the dwarfs. Dr Daruwalla had to admit that even his own enthusiasm for the project was slipping.

The ELISA test for HIV was simple in comparison to Farrokh's genetic studies, for the latter had to be performed on cells (rather than on serum). Whole blood needed to be sent for the studies, and the unclotted blood had to be transported at room temperature. Blood specimens could cross international boundaries, although the paperwork was formidable; the specimens were usually shipped on dry ice, to preserve the proteins. But in the case of a genetic study, shipping dwarf blood from Bombay to Toronto was risky; it was likely that the cells would be killed before reaching Canada.

Dr Daruwalla had solved this problem with the help of an Indian medical school in Bombay; the doctor let their research lab perform the studies and prepare the slides. The lab gave Farrokh finished sets of photographs of the chromosomes; it was easy to carry the photographs back to Toronto. But there the dwarf-blood project had stalled. Through a close friend and colleague – a fellow orthopedic surgeon at the Hospital for Sick Children in Toronto – Farrokh had been introduced to a geneticist at the university. Even this contact proved fruitless, for the geneticist maintained that there was no identifiable genetic marker for this type of dwarfism.

The geneticist at the University of Toronto was quite emphatic to Farrokh: it was far-fetched to imagine that he would find a genetic marker for this autosomal dominant trait – achondroplasia is transmitted by a single autosomal dominant gene. This was a type of dwarfism that resulted from a spontaneous mutation. In the case of a spontaneous mutation, unaffected parents of dwarf childen have essentially no further risk of producing another dwarf child; the unaffected brothers and sisters of an achondroplastic dwarf are similarly not at risk – they won't necessarily produce dwarfs, either. The dwarfs themselves, on the other hand, are quite likely to pass the trait on to their children – half their children will be dwarfs. As for a genetic marker for this dominant characteristic, none could be found.

Dr Daruwalla doubted that he knew enough about genetics to argue with a geneticist; the doctor simply continued to draw samples of the dwarfs' blood, and he kept bringing the photographs of the chromosomes back to Toronto. The U. of T. geneticist was discouraging but fairly friendly, if not sympathetic. He was also the boyfriend of Farrokh's friend and colleague at the Hospital for Sick Children – Sick Kids, they called the hospital in Toronto. Farrokh's friend and the geneticist were gay.

Dr Gordon Macfarlane, who was the same age as Dr Daruwalla, had joined the orthopedic group at the Hospital for Sick Children in the same year as Farrokh; their hospital offices were next door to each other. Since Farrokh hated to drive, he often rode back and forth to work with Macfarlane; they both lived in Forest Hill. Early on in their relationship, there'd been those comic occasions when Julia and Farrokh had tried to interest Mac in various single or divorced women. Eventually, the matter of Macfarlane's sexual orientation grew clear; in no time, Mac was bringing his boyfriend to dinner.

Dr Duncan Frasier, the gay geneticist, was renowned for his research on the so-called (and elusive) gay chromosomes; Frasier was used to being teased about it. Biological studies of homosexuality generally irritate everyone. The debate as to whether homosexuality is present at birth or is a learned behavior is always inflamed with politics. Conservatives reject scientific suggestions that sexual orientation is biological; liberals anguish over the possible medical misuse of an identifiable genetic marker for homosexuality – should one be found. But Dr Frasier's research had led him to a fairly cautious and reasonable conclusion. There were only two 'natural' sexual orientations among humans – one in the majority, one in the minority. Nothing he'd studied about homosexuality, nor anything he'd personally experienced or had ever felt, could persuade Dr Frasier that either homosexuality *or* heterosexuality was a matter of choice. Sexual orientation wasn't a 'life-style.'

'We are born with what we desire – whatever it is,' Frasier liked to say.

Farrokh found it an interesting subject. But if the search for gay genes was so fascinating to Dr Frasier, it discouraged Dr Daruwalla that the gay geneticist would entertain no hope of finding a genetic marker for Vinod's dwarfism. Sometimes Dr Daruwalla was guilty of thinking that Frasier had no personal interest in dwarfs, whereas gays got the geneticist's full attention. Nevertheless, Farrokh's friendship with Macfarlane was unshakable; soon Farrokh was admitting to his gay friend how he'd always disliked the word 'gay' in its current, commonplace homosexual sense. To Farrokh's surprise, Mac had agreed; he said he wished that something as important to him as his homosexuality had a word of its own – a word that had no other meaning.

'"Gay" is such a frivolous word,' Macfarlane had said.

Dr Daruwalla's dislike of the contemporary usage of the word was more a generational matter than a matter of prejudice – or so the doctor believed. It was a word his mother, Meher, had loved but overused. 'We had a gay time,' she would say. 'What a gay evening we had – even your father was in a gay mood.'

It disheartened Dr Daruwalla to see this old-fashioned

adjective – a synonym for 'jolly' or 'merry' or 'frolic-some' or 'blithe' – take on a much more serious meaning.

'Come to think of it, "straight" isn't an original word, either,' Farrokh had said.

Macfarlane laughed, but his longtime companion, Frasier, responded with a touch of bitterness. 'What you're telling us, Farrokh, is that you accept gays when we're so quiet about it that we might as well still be in the closet – *and* provided that we don't dare call ourselves gay, which offends you. Isn't that what you're saying?' But this wasn't what Farrokh meant.

'I'm not criticizing your orientation,' Dr Daruwalla replied. 'I just don't like the word for it.'

There lingered an air of dismissiveness about Dr Frasier; the rebuke reminded Dr Daruwalla of the geneticist's dismissal of the notion that the doctor might find a genetic marker for the most common type of dwarfism.

The last time Dr Daruwalla had brought Dr Frasier the photographs of the dwarf's chromosomes, the gay geneticist had been more dismissive than usual. 'Those dwarfs must be bleeding to death, Farrokh,' Frasier told him. 'Why don't you leave the little buggers alone?'

'If *I* used the word "bugger," you would be offended,' Farrokh said. But what did Dr Daruwalla expect? Dwarf genes or gay genes, genetics was a touchy subject.

All this left Farrokh feeling full of contempt for his own lack of follow-through on his dwarf-blood project. Dr Daruwalla didn't realize that his notion of 'follow-through' (or lack thereof) had originated with the radio interview he'd briefly overheard the previous evening – that silliness with the complaining writer. But, at last, the doctor stopped brooding on the dwarf-blood subject.

Farrokh now made the morning's second phone call.

It was early to call John D., but Dr Daruwalla hadn't told him about Rahul; the doctor also wanted to stress the importance of John D.'s attending the lunch at the Duckworth Club with Detective Patel and Nancy. To Farrokh's surprise, it was an alert Inspector Dhar who answered the phone in his suite at the Taj.

'You sound awake!' Dr Daruwalla said. 'What are you doing?'

'I'm reading a play – actually, two plays,' John D. replied. 'What are *you* doing? Isn't it time you were cutting open someone's knee?'

This was the famous distant Dhar; the doctor felt he'd created this character, cold and sarcastic. Farrokh immediately launched into the news about Rahul – that he had a female identity these days; that, in all likelihood, the complete sex change had been accomplished. But John D. seemed barely interested. As for participating in the lunch at the Duckworth Club, not even the prospect of taking part in the capture of a serial murderer (or murderess) could engage the actor's enthusiasm.

'I have a lot of reading to do,' John D. told Farrokh.

'But you can't read all day,' the doctor said. '*What* reading?'

'I told you – two plays,' said Inspector Dhar.

'Oh, you mean homework,' Farrokh said. He assumed that John D. was studying his lines for his upcoming parts at the Schauspielhaus Zürich. The actor was thinking of Switzerland, of his day job, the doctor supposed. John D. was thinking of going home. After all, what was keeping him here? If, under the present threat, he gave up his membership at the Duckworth Club, what would he do with himself? Stay in his suite at the Taj, or at the Oberoi? Like Farrokh, John D. *lived* at the Duckworth Club when he was in Bombay.

'But now that the murderer is *known*, it's absurd to

resign from the club!' Dr Daruwalla cried. 'Any day now, they're going to catch him!'

'Catch *her*,' Inspector Dhar corrected the doctor.

'Well, him *or* her,' Farrokh said impatiently. 'The point is, the police know who they're looking for. There won't be any more killings.'

'I suppose seventy *is* enough,' John D. said. He was in a simply infuriating mood, Dr Daruwalla thought.

'So, what are these plays?' Farrokh asked, in exasperation.

'I have only two leading roles this year,' John D. replied. 'In the spring, it's Osborne's *Der Entertainer* – I'm Billy Rice – and in the fall I'm Friedrich Hofreiter in Schnitzler's *Das weite Land.*'

'I see,' Farrokh said, but this was all foreign to him. He knew only that John Daruwalla was a respected professional as an actor, and that the Schauspielhaus Zürich was a sophisticated city theater with a reputation for performing both classical and modern plays. In Farrokh's opinion, they gave short shrift to slapstick; he wondered if there were more slapstick comedies performed at the Bernhard or at the Theater am Hechtplatz – he didn't really know Zürich.

The doctor knew only what his brother, Jamshed, had told him, and Jamshed was no veteran theatergoer – he went to see John D. In addition to Jamshed's possibly philistine opinions, there was what little information Farrokh could force out of the guarded Dhar. The doctor didn't know if two leading roles a year were enough, or if John D. had chosen only two such roles. The actor went on to say that he had smaller parts in something by Dürrenmatt and something by Brecht. A year ago, he'd made his directing debut – it was something by Max Frisch – and he'd played the eponymous Volpone in the Ben Jonson play. Next year, John D. had said, he hoped to direct Gorki's *Wassa Schelesnowa.*

It was a pity that everything had to be in German, Dr Daruwalla thought.

Except for his outstanding success as Inspector Dhar, John D. had never acted in films; he never auditioned. Was he lacking in ambition? Dr Daruwalla wondered, for it seemed a mistake for Dhar not to take advantage of his perfect English. Yet John D. said he detested England, and he refused to set foot in the United States; he ventured to Toronto only to visit Farrokh and Julia. The actor wouldn't even stray to Germany to audition for a film!

Many of the guest performers at the Schauspielhaus Zürich were German actors and actresses – Katharina Thalbach, for example. Jamshed had once told Farrokh that John D. had been romantically linked with the German actress, but John D. denied this. Dhar never appeared in a German theater, and (to Farrokh's knowledge) there was no one at the Schauspielhaus Zürich to whom the actor had ever been 'romantically linked.' Dhar was a friend of the famous Maria Becker, but not *romantically* a friend. Besides, Dr Daruwalla guessed, Maria Becker would be a little too old for John D. And Jamshed had reported seeing John D. out to dinner at the Kronenhalle with Christiane Hörbiger, who was also famous – and closer to John D.'s age, the doctor speculated. But Dr Daruwalla suspected that this sighting was no more significant than spotting John D. with any other of the regular performers at the Schauspielhaus. John D. was also friends with Fritz Schediwy and Peter Ehrlich and Peter Arens. Dhar was seen dining, on more than one occasion, with the pretty Eva Rieck. Jamshed also reported that he frequently saw John D. with the director Gerd Heinz – and as often with a local terror of the avant-garde, Matthias Frei.

John D., as an actor, eschewed the avant-garde; yet, apparently, he was on friendly terms with one of Zürich's elder statesmen of such theater. Matthias Frei was a director and occasional playwright, a kind of deliberately underground and incomprehensible fellow – or so Dr Daruwalla believed. Frei was about the doctor's age, but he looked older, more rumpled; he was certainly wilder. Jamshed had told Farrokh that John D. even split the expense of renting a flat or a chalet in the mountains with Matthias Frei; one year they would rent something in the Grisons, another year they'd try the Bernese Oberland. Supposedly, it was agreeable for them to share a place because John D. preferred the mountains in the ski season and Matthias Frei liked the hiking in the summer; also, Dr Daruwalla presumed, Frei's friends would be people of a different generation from John D.'s friends.

But, once again, Farrokh's view of the culture John D. inhabited was marginal. As for the actor's love life, there was no understanding his aloofness. He'd appeared to have a long relationship with someone in a publishing house – a publicist, or so Farrokh remembered her. She was an attractive, intelligent younger woman. They'd occasionally traveled together, but not to India; for Dhar, India was strictly business. They'd never lived together. And now, Farrokh was told, this publicist and John D. were 'just good friends.'

Julia surmised that John D. didn't want to have children, and that this would eventually turn most younger women away. But now, at 39, John D. might meet a woman his own age, or a little older – someone who would accept childlessness. Or, Julia had said, perhaps he'd meet a nice divorced woman who'd already had her children – someone whose children would be grownups. That would be ideal for John D., Julia had decided.

But Dr Daruwalla didn't think so. Inspector Dhar had never exhibited a nesting instinct. The rentals in the mountains, a different one each year, utterly suited John D. Even in Zürich, he made a point of owning very little. His flat – which was within walking distance of the theater, the lake, the Limmat, the Kronenhalle – was also rented. He didn't want a car. He seemed proud of his framed playbills, and even an Inspector Dhar poster or two; in Zürich, Dr Daruwalla supposed, these Hindi cinema advertisements were probably amusing to John D.'s friends. They could never have imagined that such craziness translated into a raving audience beyond the wildest dreams of the Schauspielhaus.

In Zürich, Jamshed had observed, John D. was infrequently recognized; he was hardly the best-known of the Schauspielhaus troupe. Not exactly a character actor, he was also no star. In restaurants around town, theatergoers might recognize him, but they wouldn't necessarily know his name. Only schoolchildren, after a comedy, would ask for his autograph; the children simply held out their playbills to anyone in the cast.

Jamshed said that Zürich had no money to give to the arts. There'd recently been a scandal because the city wanted to close down the Schauspielhaus Keller; this was the more avant-garde theater, for younger theatergoers. John D.'s friend Matthias Frei had made a big fuss. As far as Jamshed knew, the theater was always in need of money. Technical personnel hadn't been given an annual raise; if they quit, they weren't replaced. Farrokh and Jamshed speculated that John D.'s salary couldn't be very significant. But of course he didn't need the money; Inspector Dhar was rich. What did it matter to Dhar that the Schauspielhaus Zürich was inadequately subsidized by the city, by the banks, by private donations?

Julia also implied that the theater somewhat complacently rested on its illustrious history in the 1930's and '40's, when it was a refuge for people fleeing from Germany, not only Jews but Social Democrats and Communists – or anyone who'd spoken out against the Nazis and as a result either weren't permitted to work or were in danger. There'd been a time when a production of *Wilhelm Tell* was defiant, even revolutionary – a symbolic blow against the Nazis. Many Swiss had been afraid to get involved in the war, yet the Schauspielhaus Zürich had been courageous at a time when any performance of Goethe's *Faust* might

527

have been the last. They'd also performed Sartre, and von Hofmannsthal, and a young Max Frisch. The Jewish refugee Kirt Hirschfeld had found a home there. But nowadays, Julia thought, there were many younger intellectuals who might find the Schauspiel-haus rather staid. Dr Daruwalla suspected that 'staid' suited John D. What mattered to him was that in Zürich he was *not* Inspector Dhar.

When the Hindi movie star was asked where he lived, because it was obvious that he spent very little time in Bombay, Dhar always replied (with character-istic vagueness) that he lived in the Himalayas – 'the abode of snow.' But John D.'s abode of snow was in the Alps, and in the city on the lake. The doctor thought that Dhar was probably a Kashmiri name, but neither Dr Daruwalla nor Inspector Dhar had ever been to the Himalayas.

Now, on the spur of the moment, the doctor decided to tell John D. his decision.

'I'm not writing another Inspector Dhar movie,' Farrokh informed the actor. 'I'm going to have a press conference and identify myself as the man responsible for Inspector Dhar's creation. I want to call an end to it, and let you off the hook – so to speak. If you don't mind,' the doctor added uncertainly.

'Of course I don't mind,' John D. said. 'But you should let the real policeman find the real murderer – you don't want to interfere with that.'

'Well, I won't!' Dr Daruwalla said defensively. 'But if you'd only come to lunch . . . I just thought you might remember something. You have an eye for detail, you know.'

'What sort of detail have you got in mind?' John D. asked.

'Well, anything you might remember about Rahul, or about that time in Goa. I don't know, really – just *anything*!' Farrokh said.

'I remember the hippie,' said Inspector Dhar. He began with his memory of her weight; after all, he'd

528

carried her down the stairs of the Hotel Bardez and into the lobby. She was very solid. She'd looked into his eyes the whole time, and there was her fragrance – he knew she'd just had a bath.

Then in the lobby, she'd said, 'If it's not too much trouble, you could do me a big favor.' She'd showed him the dildo without removing it from her rucksack; Dhar remembered its appalling size, and the head of the thing pointing at him. 'The tip unscrews,' Nancy had told him; she was still watching his eyes. 'But I'm just not strong enough.' It was screwed together so tightly, he needed to grip the big cock in both hands. And then she stopped him, as soon as he'd loosened the tip. 'That's enough,' she told him. 'I'm going to spare you,' she said too softly. 'You don't want to know what's inside the thing.'

It had been quite a challenge – to meet her eyes, to stare her down. John D. had focused on the idea of the big dildo inside her; he believed that she would see in his eyes what he was thinking. What he thought he'd seen in Nancy's eyes was that she'd courted danger before – maybe it had even thrilled her – but that she wasn't so sure about danger anymore. Then she'd looked away.

'I can't imagine what's become of the hippie!' Dr Daruwalla blurted out suddenly. 'It's inconceivable – a woman like that, with Deputy Commissioner Patel!'

'Lunch *is* tempting, if only to see what she looks like . . . after twenty years,' said Inspector Dhar.

He's just acting, thought Dr Daruwalla. Dhar didn't care what Nancy looked like; something else was on the actor's mind.

'So . . . you'll come to lunch?' the doctor asked.

'Sure. Why not?' the actor said. But Dr Daruwalla knew that John D. wasn't as indifferent as he seemed.

As for Inspector Dhar, he'd never intended to miss the lunch at the Duckworth Club, and he thought he would rather be murdered by Rahul than resign his membership under a threat so coarse that it had to be left in a dead man's mouth. It was not how Nancy looked that mattered to him; he was an actor – a professional – and even 20 years ago he'd known that Nancy had been acting. She wasn't the young woman she'd pretended to be. Twenty years ago, even the young John D. could tell that Nancy had been terrified, that she'd been bluffing.

Now the actor wanted to see if Nancy was still bluffing, if she was still pretending. Maybe now, Dhar thought, Nancy had stopped acting; maybe now, after 20 years, she simply let her terror show.

Something Rather Odd

It was 6:45 in the morning when Nancy awoke in her husband's arms. Vijay was holding her the way she loved to be held; it was the best way for her to wake up, and she was astonished at what a good night's sleep she'd had. She felt Vijay's chest against her back; his delicate hands held her breasts, his breath slightly stirred her hair. Detective Patel's penis was quite stiff, and Nancy could feel its light but insistent pulse against the base of her spine. Nancy knew she was fortunate to have such a good husband, and such a kind one. She regretted how difficult she was to live with; Vijay took such pains to protect her. She began to move her hips against him; it was one of the ways he liked to make love to her – to enter her from behind while she was on her side. But the deputy commissioner didn't respond to the rolling motion of his wife's hips, although he truly worshiped her nakedness – her whiteness, her blondness, her voluptuousness. The policeman let go of Nancy's breasts, and simultaneously (with his retreating from her) she noticed that the bathroom door was open; they always went to sleep with the door closed. The bedroom smelled fresh, like soap; her husband had already had his morning shower. Nancy turned to face Vijay – she

530

touched his wet hair. He couldn't meet her eyes.

'It's almost seven o'clock,' the detective told her.

Detective Patel was normally out of bed before 6:00; he usually left for Crime Branch Headquarters before 7:00. But this morning he'd let her sleep; he'd showered and then he'd got back into bed beside her. He'd merely been waiting for her to wake up, Nancy thought; yet he hadn't been waiting to have sex.

'What are you going to tell me?' Nancy asked him. 'What have you *not* told me, Vijay?'

'It's really nothing – just a little lunch,' Patel replied.

'Who's having lunch?' Nancy asked him.

'*We* are – at the Duckworth Club,' the policeman told her.

'With the doctor, you mean,' Nancy said.

'With the actor, too, I imagine,' the detective said.

'Oh, Vijay. No . . . not Dhar!' she cried.

'I think Dhar will be there,' Vijay told her. 'They both know Rahul,' he explained. It sounded crude to him, to put it the way he'd said it yesterday, to the doctor ('to compare notes'), and so he said, 'It could be valuable, just to hear what all of you remember. There might be some details that would help me . . .' His voice trailed off. He hated to see his wife so withdrawn. Then she was suddenly wracked with sobs.

'We're not *members* of the Duckworth Club!' Nancy cried.

'We've been invited – we're guests,' Patel told her.

'But they'll *see* me, they'll think I'm horrible,' Nancy moaned.

'They know you're my wife. They just want to help,' the deputy commissioner replied.

'What if Rahul sees me?' Nancy asked him. She was always raising this question.

'Would you recognize Rahul?' Patel asked. The detective thought it was unlikely that any of them would recognize Rahul, but the question was spurious; Nancy wasn't in disguise.

'I don't think so, but maybe,' Nancy said.

Deputy Commissioner Patel dressed himself and left her while she was still naked in the bedroom; Nancy was aimlessly searching through her clothes. The dilemma of what she should wear to the Duckworth Club was gradually overwhelming her. Vijay had told her that he would come home from the police station to drive her to the Duckworth Club; Nancy wouldn't have to get herself there. But the detective doubted that she'd heard him. He'd have to come home early, because he suspected she would still be naked in the bedroom; possibly she'd have progressed to trying on her clothes.

Sometimes (on her 'good days') she wandered into the kitchen, which was the only room where the sun penetrated the apartment, and she would lie on the countertop in a long patch of sunlight; the sun came through the open window for only two hours of the morning, but it was enough to give her a sunburn if she didn't apply some protection to her skin. Once, she'd stretched herself out on the countertop, completely naked, and a woman from a neighboring flat had called the police. The caller had described Nancy as 'obscene.' After that, she'd always worn something, even if it was only one of Vijay's shirts. Sometimes she wore sunglasses, too, although she liked to have a nice tan and the sunglasses gave her 'raccoon eyes,' she said.

She never shopped for food, because she said the beggars assailed her. Nancy was a decent cook but Vijay did the shopping. They didn't believe in grocery lists; he brought home something that appealed to him and she would think of a way to prepare it. Once or twice a month, she went out to buy books. She preferred shopping curbside, along Churchgate and at the intersection of Mahatma Gandhi and Hornby roads. She liked secondhand books best, especially memoirs; her favorite was *A Combat Widow of the Raj* – a memoir that ended with a suicide note. She also bought a lot of remaindered American novels; for one of these novels, she rarely paid more than 15 rupees –

sometimes as little as 5. She said that beggars didn't bother people who bought books.

Once or twice a week, Vijay took her out to dinner. Although they'd still not spent all of the dildo money, they thought they couldn't afford the hotel restaurants, which were the only places where Nancy could feel she was anonymous – among foreigners. Only once had they argued about it; Vijay had told her that he suspected she preferred the hotel restaurants because she could imagine that she was only a tourist, just passing through. He'd accused her of wishing that she didn't live in India – of wanting to be back in the States. She'd showed him. The next time they went to their regular restaurant – a Chinese place called Kamling, at Churchgate – Nancy had summoned the owner to their table. She'd asked the owner if he knew that her husband was a deputy commissioner; indeed, the Chinese gentleman knew this – Crime Branch Headquarters was nearby, just opposite Crawford Market.

'Well, then,' Nancy wanted to know, 'how come you never offer us a free meal?'

After that, they always ate there for free; they were treated splendidly, too. Nancy said that, with the money they'd saved, they could afford to go to one of the hotel restaurants – or at least to one of the hotel bars – but they rarely did so. On those few occasions, Nancy mercilessly criticized the food; she would also pick out the Americans and say hateful things about them.

'Don't you dare tell me that I want to go back to the States, Vijay,' she said; she only had to say it once. The deputy commissioner never suggested it again, and Nancy could tell he was pleased; all of it had needed saying. This was how they lived, with a delicate passion – with something usually held back. They were so careful. Nancy felt it was unfair that a lunch at the Duckworth Club could completely undo her.

She put on one of the dresses that she knew she

would never wear to the club; she didn't bother with underwear, because she supposed she would just keep changing it. Nancy went into the kitchen and made some tea for herself. Then she found her sunglasses and she stretched out on her back in the long patch of sunlight on the countertop. She'd forgotten to put any sunscreen on her face – it was hard to find sunscreen in Bombay – but she told herself that she would lie there for only an hour; in a half hour, she'd take the sunglasses off. She didn't want 'raccoon eyes,' but she wanted Dr Daruwalla and Inspector Dhar to see that she was healthy, that she took care of herself.

Nancy wished the apartment had a view; she would have liked to see a sunrise or a sunset. (What were they saving the dildo money *for?*) Coming from Iowa, Nancy would have especially appreciated a view of the Arabian Sea, which was the view to the west. Instead, she stared out the open window; she could see other women in the windows of other apartments, but they were constantly in motion, too busy to notice her. One day, Nancy hoped she might spot the woman who'd called the police and told them that she was 'obscene.' But Nancy didn't know how she would ever recognize the anonymous caller.

This thought led her to wondering if she would recognize Rahul; it was of more concern to Nancy that Rahul might recognize *her*. What if she was alone, just buying a book, and Rahul saw her and knew who she was?

She lay on the countertop, staring at the sun until it was blocked by an adjacent building. Now I'll have raccoon eyes, she told herself, but another thought obsessed her; that she would one day be standing right next to Rahul and she wouldn't know who Rahul was; yet Rahul would know who she was. That was her fear.

Nancy removed the sunglasses but she remained motionless, on her back on the countertop. She was thinking about the curl to Inspector Dhar's lip. He had an almost perfect mouth, and she recalled how the curl to his lip had first struck her as friendly, even inviting; then she'd realized he was sneering at her.

Nancy knew she was attractive to men. In 20 years, she'd gained 15 pounds, but only a woman would have been troubled by the way she'd put on the weight. The 15 pounds had spread themselves over her generously; they hadn't all ended up in her face, or on the backs of her thighs. Nancy's face had always been round, but it was still firm; her breasts had always been good – now, for most men, they were better. Certainly, they were bigger. Her hips were a little fuller, her waist a little thicker; the exaggerated curvaceousness of her body lent to her overall figure a voluptuous definition. Her waist, however thickened, still went in; her breasts and her hips still stood out. She was about Dhar's age, not quite 40, but it was not only her blondness or the fairness of her skin that made her seem younger; it was her nervousness. She was as awkward as a teenager who believes everyone is staring at her. This was because she was convinced that Rahul was watching her, everywhere she went.

Unfortunately, in a crowd, or in a new place where people would look at her – and people tended to look at her, both men and women – Nancy became so self-conscious that she found it difficult to speak. She thought that people stared at her because she was grotesque; on her good days, she thought she was merely fat. And whenever she was around strangers, she would recall Dhar's sneer. She'd been a pretty girl then, but he hadn't noticed; she'd shown him a huge dildo, and she'd asked him (quite suggestively) to unscrew it for her. She'd added that she was sparing him . . . to not let him see what was inside the thing. Yet, in his sneer, there'd not been the smallest measure of attraction to her; Nancy believed that she'd disgusted him.

She wandered back into the bedroom, where she removed the unsuitable dress; once again, she stood naked. She was surprised at herself for wanting to look

her best for Inspector Dhar; she thought she hated him.
But the strangest conviction was compelling her to
dress herself for him. She knew he wasn't a *real*
inspector, but Nancy believed that Dhar had certain
powers. Nancy believed that it would *not* be her
beloved husband, Vijay Patel, who would catch the
killer; nor would the funny doctor be the hero. There
was no reason for it – none beyond the authority of an
actor's sneer – but Nancy believed that Inspector Dhar
would be Rahul's undoing.

But what exactly did Dhar like? He must like
something rather odd, Nancy decided. A faint ridge of
blond fuzz extended from her pubic hair to her navel,
which was especially long and deep. When Nancy
rubbed her belly with coconut oil, this blond streak of
fur would darken slightly and become more noticeable. If she wore a sari, she could leave her navel bare.
Maybe Dhar would like her furry navel. Nancy knew
that Vijay liked it.

19. OUR LADY OF VICTORIES

Another Author in Search of an Ending

The second Mrs Dogar also suspected Dhar of unconventional sexual interests. It was frustrating to the former Rahul that Inspector Dhar had not returned the recently married woman's attentions. And although both the disapproving Mr Sethna and Dr Daruwalla had observed the unrequited flirtations of Mrs Dogar, neither gentleman had truly appreciated the seriousness of Mrs Dogar's designs. The former Rahul did not suffer rejection lightly.

While Farrokh had been struggling to begin his first artistic screenplay, his first quality picture, the second Mrs Dogar had also undertaken the first draft of a story-in-progress; she had hatched a plot. Last night at the Duckworth Club, the second Mrs Dogar had loudly denounced her husband for having had too much to drink. Mr Dogar had had no more than his usual one whiskey and two beers; he was surprised at his wife's accusations.

'This is *your* night to drive – this is *my* night to drink!' Mrs Dogar had said.

She'd spoken distinctly, and deliberately in the presence of the ever-disapproving Mr Sethna – one waiter and one busboy had overheard her, too – and she'd chosen to utter her criticism at a lull in the other conversations in the Ladies' Garden, where the grieving Bannerjees were the only Duckworthians still dining.

The Bannerjees had been having a late, sober dinner; the murder of Mr Lal had upset Mrs Bannerjee too much to cook, and her intermittent conversation with her husband had concerned what efforts they might make to comfort Mr Lal's widow. The Bannerjees

537

would never have guessed that the second Mrs Dogar's rude outburst was as premeditated as her intentions to soon join Mrs Lal in the state of widowhood. Rahul had married Mr Dogar out of eagerness to become his widow.

Also deliberately, Mrs Dogar had turned to Mr Sethna and said, 'My dear Mr Sethna, would you kindly call us a taxi? My husband is in no condition to drive us home.'

'Promila, *please* . . .' Mr Dogar began to say.

'Give me your keys,' Mrs Dogar commanded him. 'You can take a taxi with me or you can call your own taxi, but you're *not* driving a car.'

Sheepishly, Mr Dogar handed her his ring of keys.

'Now just *sit* here – don't get up and wander around,' Mrs Dogar told him. Mrs Dogar herself stood up. 'Wait for me,' she ordered her husband – the rejected designated driver. When Mr Dogar was alone, he glanced at the Bannerjees, who looked away; not even the waiter would look at the condemned drunk, and the busboy had slunk into the circular driveway to smoke a cigarette.

Rahul timed how long everything took. He – or, rather, *she* (if outward anatomy is the measure of a man or a woman) – walked into the men's room by the door from the foyer. She knew no one could be in the men's room, for none of the wait-staff were permitted to use it – except Mr Sethna, who so disapproved of peeing with the hired help that he made uncontested use of the facilities marked FOR MEMBERS ONLY. The old steward was more in charge of the Duckworth Club than any member. But Mrs Dogar knew that Mr Sethna was busy calling a taxi.

Since she'd become a woman, Mrs Dogar didn't regret not using the men's room at the Duckworth Club; its decor wasn't as pleasing to her as the ladies' room – Rahul loathed the men's room wallpaper. She found the tiger-hunting motif brutal and stupid.

She moved past the urinals, the toilet stalls, the sinks

for shaving, and into the darkened locker room, which extended to the clubhouse and the clubhouse bar; these latter facilities were never in use at night, and Mrs Dogar wanted to be sure that she could navigate their interiors in darkness. The big windows of frosted glass admitted the moonlight that reflected from the tennis courts and the swimming pool, which was presently under repair and not in service; it was an empty cement-lined hole with some construction debris in the deep end, and the members were already betting that it wouldn't be ready for use in the hotter months ahead.

Mrs Dogar had sufficient moonlight to unlock the rear door to the clubhouse; she found the right key in less than a minute – then she relocked the door. This was just a test. She also found Mr Dogar's locker and unlocked it; it took the smallest key on the ring, and Mrs Dogar discovered that she could easily find this key by touch. She unlocked and relocked the locker by touch, too, although she could see everything in the moonlight; one night, she might not have the moon.

Rahul could quite clearly make out the shrine of old golf clubs displayed on the wall. These were the clubs of famous Golfers Past and of some living, less famous Duckworthians who had retired from active play. Mrs Dogar needed to assure herself that these clubs could be easily removed from the wall. After all, it had been a while since Rahul had visited the men's locker room; she hadn't been there since she'd been a boy. When she'd handled a few of the clubs to her satisfaction, she went back into the men's room – after assuring herself that neither Mr Sethna nor Mr Bannerjee was using the facilities. She knew her husband wouldn't leave the table in the Ladies' Garden; he did what he was told.

When she could see (from the men's room) that there was no one in the foyer, she returned to the Ladies' Garden. She went directly to the Bannerjees' table –

they weren't friends of the Dogars's – and she whispered to them, 'I'm sorry for my outspokenness. But when he's like this, he's virtually a baby – he's so senile, he's not to be trusted. And not only in a car. One night, after dinner – he had all his clothes on – I stopped him just before he dove into the club pool.'

'The *empty* pool?' said Mr Bannerjee.

'I'm glad you understand,' Mrs Dogar replied. 'That's what I'm talking about. If I don't treat him like a child, he'll hurt himself!'

Then she went to her husband, leaving the Bannerjees with this impression of Mr Dogar's senility and self-destructiveness – for her husband being found dead in the deep end of the club's empty pool was one of the possible outcomes for the first draft that the second Mrs Dogar was hard at work on. She was merely foreshadowing, as any good storyteller does. She also knew that she should set up other options, and these alternative endings were already in her mind.

'I hate to treat you like this, darling, but just sit tight while I see about our cab,' Mrs Dogar told her husband. He was bewildered. Although his second wife was in her fifties, she was a young woman in comparison to what Mr Dogar had been used to; the old gentleman was in his seventies – he'd been a widower for the last 10 years. He supposed these swings of mood were characteristic among younger women. He wondered if perhaps he *had* drunk too much. He *did* remember that his new wife had lost a brother to an automobile accident in Italy; he just couldn't recall if alcohol had been the cause of the wreck.

Now Rahul was off whispering to Mr Sethna, who disapproved of women whispering to men – for whatever reason.

'My dear Mr Sethna,' the second Mrs Dogar said. 'I *do* hope you'll forgive my aggressive behavior, but he's simply not fit to wander about the club – much less drive a car. I'm sure he's the one who's been killing the flowers.'

Mr Sethna was shocked by this allegation, but he was also eager to believe it was true. Something or someone *was* killing the flowers. An undiagnosed blight had struck patches of the bougainvillea. The head mali was stymied. Here, at last, was an answer. Mr Dogar had been pissing on the flowers!

'He's . . . incontinent?' Mr Sethna inquired.

'Not at all,' said Mrs Dogar. 'He's doing it deliberately.'

'He wants to kill the flowers?' Mr Sethna asked.

'I'm glad you understand,' Mrs Dogar replied. 'Poor man.' With a wave, she indicated the surrounding golf course. 'Naturally, he wanders out there only after dark. Like a dog, he always goes to the same spots!'

'Territorial, I suppose,' said Mr Sethna.

'I'm glad you understand,' Mrs Dogar said. 'Now, where's our cab?'

In the taxi, old Mr Dogar looked as if he wasn't sure if he should apologize or complain. But, before he could decide, his younger wife once more surprised him.

'Oh, darling, never let me treat you like that again – at least not in public. I'm so ashamed!' she cried. 'They'll think I bully you. You mustn't let me. If I *ever* tell you that you can't drive a car again, here's what you must do . . . are you listening, or are you too drunk?' Mrs Dogar asked him.

'No . . . I mean *yes*, I'm listening,' Mr Dogar said. 'No, I'm *not* too drunk,' the old man assured her.

'You must *throw* the keys on the floor and make me pick them up, as if I were your servant,' Mrs Dogar told him.

'What?' he asked.

'Then tell me that you always carry an extra set of keys and that you'll drive the car home, when and if you choose. Then tell me to *go* – tell me you wouldn't drive me home if I *begged* you!' Mrs Dogar cried.

'But, Promila, I would never . . .' Mr Dogar began to say, but his wife cut him off.

'Just promise me one thing – never back down to me,' she told him. Then she seized his face in her hands and kissed him on his mouth. 'First, you should tell me to take a taxi – you just carry on sitting at the dinner table, as if you're smoldering with rage. Then you should go to the men's room and wash your face.'

'Wash my face?' said Mr Dogar with surprise.

'I can't stand the smell of food on your face, darling,' Mrs Dogar told her husband. 'Just wash your face – soap and warm water. *Then* come home to me. I'll be waiting for you. That's how I want you to treat me. Only you must wash your face first. Promise me.'

It had been years since Mr Dogar had been so aroused, nor had he ever been so confused. It was difficult to understand a younger woman, he decided – yet surely worth it.

This was a pretty good first draft, Rahul felt certain. The next time, Mr Dogar would do as he was told. He would be abusive to her and tell her to go. But she would take the taxi no farther than the access road to the Duckworth Club, or perhaps three quarters of the length of the driveway – just out of the reach of the overhead lamps. She'd tell the driver to wait for her because she'd forgotten her purse. Then she'd cross the first green of the golf course and enter the clubhouse through the rear door, which she would have previously unlocked. She'd take off her shoes and cross the dark locker room and wait there until she heard her husband washing his face. She'd either kill him with a single blow from one of the 'retired' golf clubs in the locker room, or (if possible) kill him by lifting his head by his hair and smashing his skull against the sink. Her preference for the latter method was because she preferred the swimming-pool ending. She'd be careful to clean the sink; then Mrs Dogar would drag her husband's body out the rear door of the clubhouse and dump him in the deep end of the empty pool. She wouldn't keep her taxi waiting long – at the most, 10 minutes.

But killing him with a golf club would certainly be easier. After she had clubbed her husband to death, she would put a two-rupee note in his mouth and stuff his body in his locker. The note, which Mrs Dogar already carried in her purse, displayed a typed message on the serial-number side of the money.

... BECAUSE DHAR IS STILL A MEMBER

It was an intriguing decision – which ending Rahul would choose – for although she liked the appearance of the 'accidental' death in the deep end of the pool, she also favored the attention-getting murder of another Duckworthian, especially if Inspector Dhar didn't give up his membership. The second Mrs Dogar was quite sure that Dhar *wouldn't* resign, at least not without another killing to coax him into it.

The Way It Happened to Mr Lal

It was an embarrassed and exhausted-looking Mr Dogar who appeared at the Duckworth Club before 7:00 the next morning, looking every inch the portrait of a hangover. But it wasn't alcohol that had wrecked him. Mrs Dogar had made violent love to him the previous night; she'd scarcely waited for the taxi to depart their driveway, or for Mr Dogar to unlock the door – she'd given him back his keys. They were fortunate that the servants didn't mistake them for intruders, for Mrs Dogar had pounced on her husband in the front hall; she'd torn the clothes off both of them while they were still on the first floor of the house. Then she'd made the old man run up the stairs after her, and she'd straddled him on the bedroom floor; she wouldn't let him crawl a few feet farther so that they could do it on the bed – nor had she once volunteered to relinquish the top position.

This was, of course, another first-draft possibility . . . that old Mr Dogar would suffer a heart attack while Rahul was deliberately overexciting him. But the second Mrs Dogar had resolved that she wouldn't wait as long as a year for this 'natural' ending to occur. It was simply too boring. If it happened soon, fine. If not, there was always the golf-club, locker-room ending; in this version, it amused the second Mrs Dogar to imagine how they might finally find the body.

She would report that her husband had not come home for the night. They would find his car in the Duckworth Club parking lot. The wait-staff would relate what had transpired after the Dogars had eaten their dinner; doubtless, Mr Sethna would convey more intimate information. It was possible that no one would think to look for Mr Dogar in his locker until the body began to stink.

But the swimming-pool version also intrigued Rahul. The Bannerjees would confide to the authorities that such a dive in the pool was reputed to be the old fool's inclination. Mrs Dogar herself could always say, 'I told you so.' For Rahul, the hard part about this version would be maintaining a straight face. And the rumor that old Mr Dogar was pissing on the bougain-villea was already established.

When the ashamed Mr Dogar appeared at the Duckworth Club to claim his car, he spoke in apolo-getic tones to the disapproving Mr Sethna, to whom the very idea of urinating outdoors was repugnant.

'Did I seem especially drunk to you, Mr Sethna?' Mr Dogar asked the venerable steward. 'I'm really very sorry . . . if I behaved insensitively.'

'Nothing happened, really,' Mr Sethna replied coldly. He'd already spoken to the head mali about the bou-gainvillea. The fool gardener confirmed that there were only isolated patches of the blight. The dead spots in the bougainvillea bordered the greens at the fifth and the ninth holes; both these greens were out of sight of the Duckworth Club dining room and the club-house – also, they couldn't be seen from the Ladies' Garden. As for that bougainvillea which surrounded the Ladies' Garden, there was only one dead patch and it was suspiciously in a spot that was out of sight from any of the club's facilities. Mr Sethna surmised that this gave credence to Mrs Dogar's urine theory – poor old Mr Dogar *was* peeing on the flowers!

It would never have occurred to the old steward that a *woman* – not even as vulgar a member of the species as Mrs Dogar – could be the pissing culprit. But the killer was no amateur at foreshadowing. She'd been systematically murdering the bougainvillea for months. One of many things that the new Mrs Dogar liked about wearing dresses was that it was comfortable not to wear underwear. The only thing Rahul missed about having a penis was how convenient it had been to pee outdoors. But her penchant for pissing on certain out-of-the-way plots of the bougainvillea was not whimsical. While in the pursuit of this odd habit, Mrs Dogar had been mindful of her larger work-in-progress. Even before the unfortunate Mr Lal had happened upon her while she was squatting in the bougainvillea by the fatal ninth hole (which had long been Mr Lal's nemesis), Rahul had already made a plan.

In her purse, for weeks, she'd carried the two-rupee note with her first typed message to the Duckworth-ians: MORE MEMBERS DIE IF DHAR REMAINS A MEMBER. She'd always assumed that the easiest Duckworthian to murder would be someone who stumbled into her in one of her out-of-the-way peeing places. She'd thought it would happen at night – in the darkness. She'd imagined a younger member than Mr Lal, probably someone who'd drunk too much beer and wandered out on the nighttime golf course – drawn by the same need that had drawn Mrs Dogar there. She'd imagined a brief flirtation – they were the best kind.

'So! You had to pee, too? If you tell me what you like about doing it outdoors, I'll tell you *my* reasons!' Or maybe: 'What *else* do you like to do outdoors?'

Mrs Dogar had also imagined that she might indulge in a kiss and a little fondling; she liked fondling. Then she would kill him, whoever he was, and she'd stick the two-rupee note in his mouth. She'd never strangled a man; with her hand strength, she didn't doubt she could do it. She'd never much liked strangling women – not as much as she enjoyed the pure strength of a blow from a blunt instrument – but she was looking forward to strangling a man because she wanted to see if that old story was true . . . if men got erections and ejaculated when they were close to choking to death.

Disappointingly, old Mr Lal had afforded Mrs Dogar neither the opportunity for a brief flirtation nor the novelty of a strangulation. Rahul was so lazy, she rarely made breakfast for herself. Although he was officially retired, Mr Dogar left early for his office, and Mrs Dogar often indulged in an early-morning pee on the golf course – before even the most zealous golfers were on the fairways. Then she'd have her tea and some fruit in the Ladies Garden and go to her health club to lift weights and skip rope. She'd been surprised by old Mr Lal's early-morning assault on the bougain-villea at the ninth green.

Rahul had only just finished peeing; she rose up out of the flowers, and there was the old duffer plodding off the green and tripping through the vines. Mr Lal was searching for a challenging spot in this jungle in which to deposit the stupid golf ball. When he looked up from the flowers, the second Mrs Dogar was stand-ing directly in front of him. She'd startled him so – for a moment, she thought it would be unnecessary to kill him. He clutched his chest and staggered away from her.

'Mrs Dogar!' he cried. 'What's happened to you? Has someone . . . *molested* you?' Thus he gave her the idea; after all, her dress was still hiked up to her hips.

Clearly distraught, she wriggled her dress down. (She would change into a sari for lunch.)

'Oh, Mr Lal! Thank God it's you!' she cried. 'I've been . . . taken advantage of!' she told him.

'What a world, Mrs Dogar! But how may I assist you? *Help!*' the old man shouted out.

'Oh no, please! I couldn't bear to see anyone else – I'm so ashamed!' she confided to him.

'But how may I help you, Mrs Dogar?' Mr Lal inquired.

'It's painful for me to walk,' she confessed. 'They hurt me.'

'*They!*' the old man shouted.

'Perhaps if you would lend me one of your clubs . . . if I could just use it as a cane,' Mrs Dogar suggested. Mr Lal was on the verge of handing her his nine iron, then changed his mind.

'The putter would be best!' he declared. Poor Mr Lal was out of breath from the short trot to his golf bag and his stumbling return to her side through the tangled vines, the destroyed flowers. He was much shorter than Mrs Dogar; she was able to put one of her big hands on his shoulder – the putter in her other hand. That way, she could see over the old man's head to the green and the fairway; no one was there.

'You could rest on the green while I fetch you a golf cart,' Mr Lal suggested.

'Yes, thank you – you go ahead,' she told him. He tripped purposefully forward, but she was right behind him; before he reached the green, she had struck him senseless – she hit him just behind one ear. After he'd fallen, she bashed him directly in the temple that was turned toward her, but his eyes were already open and unmoving when she struck him the second time. Mrs Dogar suspected he'd been killed by the first blow.

In her purse, she had no difficulty finding the two-rupee note. For 20 years, she'd clipped her small bills to the top half of that silver ballpoint pen which she'd stolen from the beach cottage in Goa. She even kept this silly memento well polished. The clip – the 'pocket clasp,' as her Aunt Promila had called it – continued to maintain the perfect tension on a small number of bills, and the polished silver made the top half of the pen easy to spot in her purse; she hated how small things could become lost in purses.

She'd inserted the two-rupee note in Mr Lal's gaping mouth; to her surprise, when she closed his mouth, it opened again. She'd never tried to close a dead person's mouth before. She'd assumed that the body parts of the dead would be fairly controllable; that had certainly been her experience with manipulating limbs – sometimes an elbow or a knee had been in the way of her belly drawing, and she'd easily rearranged it.

The distracting detail of Mr Lal's mouth was what caused her to be careless. She'd returned the remaining small notes to her purse, but *not* the top half of the well-traveled pen; it must have fallen in the bougainvillea. She hadn't been able to find it later, and there in the bougainvillea was the last place she recalled holding it in her hand. Mrs Dogar assumed that the police were presently puzzling over it; with the widow Lal's help, they'd probably determined that the top half of the pen hadn't belonged to Mr Lal. Mrs Dogar speculated that the police might even conclude that no Duckworthian would be caught dead with such a pen; that it was made of real silver was somehow negated by the sheer tackiness of the engraved word, *India*. Rahul found tacky things amusing. It also amused Rahul to imagine how aimlessly the police must be tracking her, for Mrs Dogar believed that the half-pen would be just another link in a chain of meaningless clues.

Some Small Tragedy

It was after Mr Dogar had apologized to Mr Sethna and retrieved his car from the Duckworth Club parking lot that the old steward received the phone call from Mrs

Dogar. 'Is my husband still there? I suppose not. I'd meant to remind him of something to attend to – he's so forgetful.'

'He was here, but he's gone,' Mr Sethna informed her.

'Did he remember to cancel our reservation for lunch? I suppose not. Anyway, we're *not* coming,' Rahul told the steward. Mr Sethna prided himself in his daily memorizing of the reservations for lunch and dinner; he knew that there'd been no reservation for the Dogars. But when he informed Mrs Dogar of this fact, she surprised him. 'Oh, the poor man!' she cried. 'He forgot to cancel the reservation, but he was so drunk last night that he forgot to *make* the reservation in the first place. This would be comic if it weren't also so tragic, I suppose.'

'I suppose . . .' Mr Sethna replied, but Rahul could tell that she'd achieved her goal. One day Mr Sethna would be an important witness to Mr Dogar's utter frailty. Foreshadowing was simply necessary preparation. Rahul knew that Mr Sethna would be unsurprised when Mr Dogar became a victim – either of a murder in the locker room *or* of a swimming-pool mishap.

In some ways, this was the best part of a murder, Rahul believed. In the first draft of a work-in-progress, you had so many options – more options than you would end up with in the final act. It was only in the planning phase that you saw so many possibilities, so many variations on the outline. In the end, it was always over too quickly; that is, if you cared about neatness, you couldn't prolong it.

'The poor man!' Mrs Dogar repeated to Mr Sethna. The poor man, indeed! Mr Sethna thought. With a wife like Mrs Dogar, Mr Sethna presumed it might even be a comfort to already have one foot in the grave, so to speak.

The old steward had just hung up the phone when Dr Daruwalla called the Duckworth Club to make a reservation. There would be four for lunch, the doctor informed Mr Sethna; he hoped no one had already taken his favourite table in the Ladies' Garden. There was plenty of room, but Mr Sethna disapproved of making a reservation for lunch on the morning of the same day; people shouldn't trust in plans that were so spur-of-the-moment.

'You're in luck – I've just had a cancellation,' the steward told the doctor.

'May I have the table at noon?' Farrokh asked.

'One o'clock would be better,' Mr Sethna instructed him, for the steward also disapproved of the doctor's inclination to eat his lunch early. Mr Sethna theorized that early lunch-eating contributed to the doctor's being overweight. It was most unsightly for *small* men to be overweight, Mr Sethna thought.

Dr Daruwalla had just hung up the phone when Dr Tata returned his call. Farrokh remembered instantly what he'd wanted to ask Tata Two.

'Do you remember Rahul Rai and his Aunt Promila?' Farrokh asked.

'Doesn't everybody remember them?' Tata Two replied.

'But this is a professional question,' Dr Daruwalla said. 'I believe your father examined Rahul when he was twelve or thirteen. That would have been in 1949. *My* father examined Rahul when he was only eight or ten. It was his Aunt Promila's request – the matter of his hairlessness was bothering her. My father dismissed it, but I believe Promila took Rahul to see your father. I was wondering if the alleged hairlessness was still the issue.'

'Why would anyone see your father *or* mine about hairlessness?' asked Dr Tata.

'A good question,' Farrokh replied. 'I believe that the real issue concerned Rahul's sexual identity. Possibly a sex change would have been requested.'

'My father didn't do sex changes!' said Tata Two. 'He was a gynecologist, an obstetrician . . .'

550

'I know what he was,' said Dr Daruwalla. 'But he might have been asked to make a diagnosis ... I'm speaking of Rahul's reproductive organs, whether there was anything peculiar about them that would have warranted a sex-change operation – at least in the boy's mind, or in his aunt's mind. If you've kept your father's records – I have *my* father's.'

'Of course I've kept his records!' Dr Tata cried. 'Mr Subhash can have them on my desk in two minutes. I'll call you back in five.' So ... even Tata Two called his medial secretary *Mister*; perhaps, like Ranjit, Mr Subhash was a medical secretary who'd remained in the family. Dr Daruwalla reflected that Mr Subhash had sounded (on the phone) like a man in his eighties!

Ten minutes later, when Dr Tata had not called him back, Farrokh also reflected on the presumed chaos of Tata Two's record keeping; apparently, old Dr Tata's file on Rahul wasn't exactly at Mr Subhash's fingertips. Or maybe it was the diagnosis of Rahul that gave Tata Two pause? Regardless, Farrokh told Ranjit that he would take no calls except one he was expecting from Dr Tata.

Dr Daruwalla had one office appointment before his much-anticipated lunch at the Duckworth Club, and he told Ranjit to cancel it. Dr Desai, from London, was in town; in his spare time from his own surgical practice, Dr Desai was a designer of artificial joints. He was a man with a theme; joint replacement was his only topic of conversation. This made it hard on Julia whenever Farrokh tried to converse with Dr Desai at the Duckworth Club. It was easier to deal with Desai in the office. 'Should the implant be fixated to the skeleton with bone cement or is biological fixation the method of choice?' This was typical of Dr Desai's initial conversation; it was what Dr Desai said instead of, 'How are your wife and kids?' For Dr Daruwalla to cancel an office appointment with Dr Desai was tantamount to his admitting a lack of interest in his chosen orthopedic field; but the doctor had his mind on his new screenplay – he wanted to write.

To this end, Farrokh sat on the opposite side of his desk, eliminating his usual view; the doctor found the exercise yard of the Hospital for Crippled Children distracting – the physical therapy for some of his postoperative patients was hard for him to ignore. Dr Daruwalla was more enticed by a make-believe world than he was drawn to confront the world he lived in.

For the most part, Inspector Dhar's creator was unaware of the real-life dramas that teemed all around him. Poor Nancy, with her raccoon eyes, was dressing herself for Inspector Dhar. The famous actor, even offstage and off-camera, was still acting. Mr Sethna, who so strongly disapproved of everything, had discovered (to his deep distaste) that human urine was killing the bougainvillea. And that wasn't the only murder-in-progress at the Duckworth Club, where Rahul was already envisioning herself as the widow Dogar. But Dr Daruwalla was still untouched by these realities. Instead, for his inspiration, the doctor chose to stare at the circus photograph on his desk.

There was the beautiful Suman – Suman the sky-walker. The last time Dr Daruwalla had seen her, she'd been unmarried – a 29-year-old star acrobat, the idol of all the child acrobats in training. The screenwriter was presuming that Suman was 29, and that it was high time for her to be wed; she should be engaged in more practical activities than walking upside down across the roof of the main tent, 80 feet from the ground, with no net. A woman as wonderful as Suman should definitely be married, the screenwriter thought. Suman was an acrobat, not an actress. The screenwriter intended to give his circus characters very little responsibility in the way of acting. The boy, Ganesh, would be an accomplished actor, but his sister, Pinky, would be the *real* Pinky – from the Great Royal Circus. Pinky would perform as an acrobat; it wouldn't be necessary to have her talk.

(Keep her dialogue to a minimum, the screenwriter thought.)

Farrokh was getting ahead of himself; he was already casting the movie. In his screenplay, he still had to get the children to the circus. That was when Dr Daruwalla thought of the new missionary; in the screenplay, the doctor wouldn't call him Martin Mills – the name Mills was too boring. The screenwriter would call him simply 'Mr Martin.' The Jesuit mission would take charge of these children because their mother was killed in St Ignatius Church by an unsafe statue of the Holy Virgin; St Ignatius would certainly bear some responsibility for that. And so the children would manage to be picked up by the *right* limousine, by Vinod; the so-called Good Samaritan dwarf would still need to get the Jesuits' permission to take the kids to the circus. Oh, this is brilliant! thought Dr Daruwalla. That would be how Suman and Mr Martin meet. The morally meddlesome missionary takes the children to the circus, and the fool falls in love with the skywalker!

Why not? The Jesuit would soon find Suman preferable to chastity. The fictional Mr Martin would have to be a skilled actor, and the screenwriter would provide the character with a far more winning personality than that of Martin Mills. In the screenplay, the seduction of Mr Martin would be an *un*conversion story. There was no small measure of mischief in the screenwriter's next idea: that John D. would play a perfect Mr Martin. How happy he'd be – to not be Inspector Dhar!

What a screenplay this was going to be – what an improvement on reality! That was when Dr Daruwalla realized that nothing was preventing him from putting himself in the movie. He wouldn't presume to make himself a hero – perhaps a minor character with admirable intentions would suffice. But how should he describe himself? Farrokh wondered. The screenwriter didn't know he was handsome, and to speak of himself as 'highly intelligent' sounded defensive; also, in movies, you could only describe how one *appeared*.

There was no mirror in the doctor's office and so he saw himself as he often looked in the full-length mirror in the foyer of the Duckworth Club, which doubtless conveyed to Dr Daruwalla a Duckworthian sense of himself as an elegant gentleman. Such a gentlemanly doctor could play a small but pivotal role in the screenplay, for the character of the do-gooder missionary would naturally be obsessed with the idea that Ganesh's limp could be fixed. Ideally, the character of Mr Martin would bring the boy to be examined by none other than Dr Daruwalla. The doctor would announce the hard truth: there were exercises that Ganesh could do – these would strengthen his legs, including the crippled leg – but the boy would always limp. (A few scenes of the crippled boy struggling bravely to perform these exercises would be excellent for audience sympathy, the screenwriter believed.)

Like Rahul, Dr Daruwalla enjoyed this phase of storytelling – namely, plot. The thrill of exploring one's options! In the beginning, there were always so many.

But euphoria, in the case of murder *and* in the case of writing, is short-lived. Farrokh began to worry that his masterpiece had already been reduced to a romantic comedy. The two kids escape in the right limo; the circus is their salvation. Suman gives up skywalking to marry a missionary, who gives up being a missionary. Even Inspector Dhar's creator suspected that this ending was too happy. Surely something *bad* should happen, the screenwriter thought.

Thus the doctor sat pondering in his office at the Hospital for Crippled Children, with his back to the exercise yard. In such a setting one might imagine that Dr Daruwalla must have felt ashamed of himself for trying to imagine some small tragedy.

Not a Romantic Comedy

Contrary to Rahul's opinion, the police had *not* found the top half of the silver pen with *India* inscribed on it. Rahul's money clip had no longer been in the bougain-villea when the deputy commissioner had examined Mr Lal's body. The silver was so shiny in the morning sun, it had caught a crow's sharp eyes. It was the half-pen that led the crow to discover the corpse. The crow had begun by pecking out one of Mr Lal's eyes; the bird was busy at the open wound behind Mr Lal's ear and at the wound at Mr Lal's temple when the first of the vultures settled on the ninth green. The crow had stood its ground until more vultures came; after all, it had found the body first. And before taking flight, the crow had stolen the silver half-pen. Crows were always stealing shiny objects. That this crow had promptly lost its prize in the ceiling fan in the Duckworth Club dining room was not necessarily a comment on the bird's overall intelligence, but the blade of the fan (at that time of the morning) had moved in and out of the sunlight; the fan had also caught the crow's sharp eyes. It was a silly place for a crow to land, and a waiter had rudely shooed the shitting bird away.

As for the shiny object that the crow had held so tenaciously in its beak, it had been left where it occasionally disturbed the mechanism of the ceiling fan. Dr Daruwalla had observed one such disturbance; the doctor had also observed the landing of the shitting crow upon the fan. And so the top half of the silver pen existed only in the crowded memory of Dr Daruwalla, and the doctor had already forgotten that the second Mrs Dogar had reminded him of someone else – an old movie star. Farrokh had also forgotten the pain of his collision with Mrs Dogar in the foyer of the Duckworth Club. That shiny something, which first Nancy and then Rahul and then the crow had lost, might now be lost forever, for its discovery lay within the limited abilities of Dr Daruwalla. Frankly, both the memory and the powers of observation of a closet screenwriter are not the best. One might more sensibly rely on the mechanism of the ceiling fan to spit out the half-pen and present it, as a miracle, to Detective Patel (or to Nancy).

An unlikely miracle of that coincidental kind was exactly what was needed to rescue Martin Mills, for the Mass had been celebrated too late to save the missionary from his worst memories. There were times when every church reminded Martin of Our Lady of Victories. When his mother was in Boston, Martin always went to Mass at Our Lady of Victories on Isabella Street; it was only an eight-minute walk from the Ritz. That Sunday morning of the long Thanksgiving weekend of his ninth-grade year, young Martin slipped out of the bedroom he shared with Arif Koma without waking the Turk up. In the living room of the two-bedroom suite at the hotel, Martin saw that the door to his mother's bedroom was ajar; this struck the boy as indicative of Vera's carelessness, and he was about to close the door – before he left the suite to go to Mass – when his mother spoke to him.

'Is that you, Martin?' Vera asked. 'Come kiss me good-morning.'

Dutifully, although he was loath to see his mother in the strongly scented disarray of her boudoir, Martin went to her. To his surprise, both Vera and her bed were unrumpled; he had the impression that his mother had already bathed and brushed her teeth and combed her hair. The sheets weren't in their usual knot of apparent bad dreams. Also, Vera's nightgown was a pretty, almost girlish thing; it was revealing of her dramatic bosom but not sluttishly revealing, as was often the case. Martin cautiously kissed her cheek.

'Off to church?' his mother asked him.

'To Mass – yes,' Martin told her.

'Is Arif still sleeping?' Vera inquired.

'Yes, I think so,' Martin replied. Arif's name on his

mother's lips reminded Martin of the painful embarrassment of the night before. 'I don't think you should ask Arif about such . . . personal things,' Martin said suddenly.

'Personal? Do you mean *sexual*?' Vera asked her son. 'Honestly, Martin, the poor boy has probably been *dying* to talk to someone about his terrible circumcision. Don't be such a prude!'

'I think Arif is a very private person,' Martin said. 'Also,' he added stubbornly, 'I think he might be a bit . . . disturbed.'

Vera sat up in her bed with new interest. '*Sexually* disturbed?' she asked her son. 'What gives you that idea?'

It didn't seem a betrayal, not at the time; Martin thought he was speaking to his mother in order to protect Arif. 'He masturbates,' Martin said quietly.

'Goodness, I should *hope* so!' Vera exclaimed. 'I certainly hope that *you* do!'

Martin wouldn't take this bait, but he replied, 'I mean that he masturbates a *lot* – almost every night.'

'The poor boy!' Vera remarked. 'But you sound so disapproving, Martin.'

'I think it's . . . excessive,' her son told her.

'*I* think masturbation is quite healthy for boys your age. Have you discussed masturbation with your father?' Vera asked him.

'Discussed' wasn't the right word. Martin had listened to Danny go on and on in reassuring tones in regard to all the desires Danny presumed that Martin was experiencing – how such desires were perfectly natural . . . that was Danny's theme.

'Yes,' Martin told his mother. 'Dad thinks masturbation is . . . normal.'

'Well, there – you see?' Vera said sarcastically. 'If your sainted father says it's normal, I suppose we should *all* be trying it!'

'I'll be late for Mass,' Martin said.

'Run along, then,' his mother replied. Martin was

about to close the door to her bedroom behind him when his mother gave him a parting shot. 'Personally, dear, I think masturbation would be better for you than Mass. And please leave the door open – I like it that way.' Martin remembered to take the room key in case Arif was still sleeping when he came back from Mass – in case his mother was in the bathroom or talking on the telephone.

When Mass was over, he looked briefly at a window display of men's suits in a Brooks Brothers store; the mannequins wore Christmas-tree neckties, but Martin was struck by the smoothness of the mannequins' skin – it reminded him of Arif's perfect complexion. Except for his pausing at this window, Martin came straight back to the suite at the Ritz. When he unlocked the door, he was happy he'd brought the room key because he thought his mother was talking on the phone; it was a one-sided conversation – all Vera. But then the awful words themselves were clear to him.

'I'm going to make you squirt again,' his mother was saying. 'I absolutely know you can squirt again – I can feel you. You're going to squirt again *soon* – aren't you? Aren't you?' The door to his mother's bedroom was still open – a little wider open than the way she liked it – and Martin Mills could see her naked back, her naked hips and the crack in her shapely ass. She was riding Arif Koma, who lay wordlessly under her; Martin was grateful that he couldn't see his room-mate's face.

He quietly let himself out of the suite as his mother continued to urge Arif to squirt. On the short walk back to Isabella Street, Martin wondered if it had been his own revelation of Arif's penchant for masturbation that had given Vera the idea; probably his mother had already had the seduction in mind, but the masturbation story must have provided her with greater incentive.

Martin Mills had sat as stupefied in Our Lady of Victories Church as he'd sat waiting for the Mass at

St Ignatius. Brother Gabriel was worried about him. First the late-night prayers – 'I'll take the turkey, I'll take the turkey' – and then, even after Mass was over, the missionary knelt on the kneeling pad as if he were waiting for the *next* Mass. That was exactly what he'd done in Our Lady of Victories on Isabella Street; he'd waited for the next Mass, as if one Mass hadn't been enough.

What also troubled Brother Gabriel were the blood-stains on the missionary's balled-up fists. Brother Gabriel couldn't have known about Martin's nose, for the wound had stopped bleeding and was almost entirely concealed by a small scab on one nostril; but Brother Gabriel wondered about the bloody socks that Martin Mills clutched in his hands. The blood had dried between his knuckles and under his nails, and Brother Gabriel feared that the source of the bleeding might have been the missionary's palms. That's all we need to make our jubilee year a success, Brother Gabriel thought – an outbreak of stigmata!

But later, when Martin attended the morning classes, he seemed back on track, so to speak; he was lively with the students, humble with the other teachers – although, as a teacher, he'd had more experience than many of the staff at St Ignatius School. Watching the new scholastic interact with both the pupils and the staff, the Father Rector suspended his earlier anxieties that the American might be a crazed zealot. And Father Cecil found Martin Mills to be every bit as charming and dedicated as he'd hoped.

Brother Gabriel kept silent about the turkey prayer and the bloody socks; but he noted the haunted, far-away smile that occasionally stole over the scholastic's repertoire of otherwise earnest expressions. Martin seemed to be struck by some remembrance, possibly inspired by a face among the upper-school boys, as if the smooth, dark skin of one of the 15-year-olds had called to mind someone he'd once known . . . or so Brother Gabriel guessed. It was an innocent, friendly smile – almost too friendly, Brother Gabriel thought.

But Martin Mills was just remembering. Back in school, at Fessenden, after the long Thanksgiving weekend, he'd waited until the lights were out before saying what he wanted to say.

'Fucker,' Martin quietly said.

'What's that?' Arif asked him.

'I said "fucker," as in motherfucker,' Martin said.

'Is this a game?' Arif inquired after too long a pause.

'You know what I mean, you *motherfucker*,' said Martin Mills.

After another long pause, Arif said, 'She made me do it – sort of.'

'You'll probably get a disease,' Martin told his roommate. Martin didn't really mean it, nor would he have said it had it occurred to him that Arif might have fallen in love with Vera. He was surprised when Arif pounced on him in the dark and began to hit his face.

'Don't ever say that . . . about your mother!' the Turk cried. 'Not about your mother! She's *beautiful*!'

Mr Weems, the dorm master, broke up the fight; neither of the boys was hurt – neither of them knew how to fight. Mr Weems was kindly; with rougher boys, he was entirely ineffectual. He was a music teacher, and – with hindsight, that is easy to say – most likely a homosexual, but no one thought of him that way (except a few of the brassier faculty wives, women of the type who thought that *any* unmarried man over 30 was a queer). Mr Weems was well liked by the boys, despite his taking no part in the school's prevailing athleticism. In his report to the Discipline Committee, the dorm master would dismiss the altercation between Martin and Arif as a 'spat.' This unfortunate choice of a word would have grave consequences.

Later, when Arif Koma was diagnosed as suffering from gonorrhea – and when he wouldn't tell the school doctor where he might have acquired it – the suspicion fell on Martin Mills. That word 'spat' connoted a lover's quarrel – at least to the more manly members of the Discipline Committee. Mr Weems was instructed to ask the boys if they were homosexuals, if they'd been doing it. The dorm master was more sympathetic to the notion that Arif and Martin might be 'doing it' than any of the faculty jocks would have been.

'If you boys are lovers, then you should see the doctor, too, Martin,' Mr Weems explained.

'Tell him!' Martin said to Arif.

'We're not lovers,' Arif said.

'That's right – we're not lovers,' Martin repeated. 'But go on – tell him. I dare you,' Martin said to Arif.

'Tell me what?' the dorm master asked.

'He hates his mother,' Arif explained to Mr Weems. Mr Weems had met Vera; he could understand. 'He's going to tell you that I got the disease from his mother – that's how much he hates her.'

'He fucked my mother – or, rather, she fucked him,' Martin told Mr Weems.

'You see what I mean?' Arif Koma said.

At most private schools, the faculty is composed of truly saintly people and incompetent ogres. Martin and Arif were fortunate that their dorm master was a teacher of the saintly category; yet Mr Weems was *so* well-meaning, he was perhaps more blind to depravity than a normal person.

'Please, Martin,' the dorm master said. 'A sexually transmitted disease, especially at an all-boys' school, is not something to lie about. Whatever your feelings are for your mother, what we hope to learn here is the truth – not to punish anyone, but only so that we may advise you. How can we instruct you, how can we tell you what we think you should do, if you won't tell us the truth?'

'My mother fucked him when she thought I was at Mass,' Martin told Mr Weems. Mr Weems shut his eyes and smiled; he did this when he was counting, which he did to summon patience.

'I was trying to protect you, Martin,' Arif Koma said, 'but I can see it's no use.'

'Boys, please . . . one of you is lying,' the dorm master said.

'Okay – so we tell him,' Arif said to Martin. 'What do you say?'

'Okay,' Martin replied. He knew that he liked Arif; for three years Arif had been his only friend. If Arif wanted to say they'd been lovers, why not go along with it? There was no one else Martin Mills wanted to please as much as he wanted to please Arif. 'Okay,' Martin repeated.

'Okay *what*?' Mr Weems asked.

'Okay, we're lovers,' said Martin Mills.

'I don't know why he doesn't have the disease,' Arif explained. 'He *should* have it. Maybe he's immune.'

'Are we going to get thrown out of school?' Martin asked the dorm master. He hoped so. It might teach his mother something, Martin thought; at 15, he still thought Vera was educable.

'All we did was *try* it,' Arif said. 'We didn't *like* it.'

'We don't do it anymore,' Martin added. This was the first and last time that he'd lied; it made him feel giddy – it was almost as if he were drunk.

'But one of you must have caught this disease from someone else,' Mr Weems reasoned. 'I mean, it couldn't have *originated* here, with you . . . not if each of you has had no other sexual contact.'

Martin Mills knew that Arif Koma had been phoning Vera and that she wouldn't talk to the Turk; Martin knew that Arif had written to Vera, too – and that she'd not written the boy back. But it was only now that Martin realized how far his friend would go to protect Vera. He must have been absolutely gaga about her.

'I paid a prostitute. I caught this disease from a whore,' Arif told Mr Weems.

'Where would you ever see a whore, Arif?' the dorm master asked.

'You don't know Boston?' Arif Koma asked him. 'I stayed with Martin and his mother at the Ritz. When they were asleep, I left the hotel. I asked the doorman

562

to get me a taxi. I asked the taxi driver to find me a hooker. That's the way you do it in New York, too,' Arif explained. 'Or at least that's the only way *I* know how to do it.'

And so Arif Koma was booted from the Fessenden School for catching a venereal disease from a whore. There was a statute in the school's book of rules, something pertaining to morally reprehensible behavior with women or girls being punishable by dismissal; under this rubric, the Discipline Committee (despite Mr Weems's protestations) expelled Arif. It was judged that having sex with a prostitute was not a gray area when it came to 'morally reprehensible behavior with women or girls.'

As for Martin, Mr Weems also pleaded on his behalf. His homosexual encounter was a single episode of sexual experimentation; the incident should be forgotten. But the Discipline Committee insisted that Vera and Danny should know. Vera's first response was to reiterate that masturbation was preferable for boys Martin's age. All Martin said to his mother – naturally, *not* in Danny's hearing – was, 'Arif Koma has gonorrhea and so do you.'

There was barely time to talk to Arif before he was sent home. The last thing Martin said to the Turk was, 'Don't hurt yourself trying to protect my mother.'

'But I also like your father,' Arif explained. Once again, Vera had gotten away with murder because no one wanted to hurt Danny.

Arif's suicide was the bigger shock. The note to Martin didn't arrive in his Fessenden mailbox until two days after Arif had jumped out of the 10th-floor window of his parents' apartment on Park Avenue. *Dishonored my family* – that was all the note said. Martin recalled that it was for the purpose of *not* dishonoring his parents, or reflecting ill on his family's reputation, that Arif hadn't shed a tear at his own circumcision.

There was no blaming Vera for it. The first time she

was alone with Martin, Vera said, 'Don't try to tell me that it's *my* fault, dear. You told me he was disturbed – sexually disturbed. You said so yourself. Besides, you don't want to do anything that would hurt your father, do you?'

Actually, it had hurt Danny quite a bit to hear that his son had dabbled in a homosexual experience, even if it was only a single episode. Martin assured his father that he'd only tried it, and that he hadn't liked it. Still, Martin realized that this was the sole impression Danny had of his son's sexuality: he'd screwed his Turkish roommate when both boys were only 15 years old. It didn't occur to Martin Mills that the *truth* about his sexuality might have been even more painful for Danny – namely, that his son was a 39-year-old virgin who'd never even masturbated. Nor had it occurred to Martin that he might actually have been in love with Arif Koma; certainly this was more plausible, not to mention more justifiable, than Arif falling in love with Vera.

Now here was Dr Daruwalla 'inventing' a missionary called Mr Martin. The screenwriter knew that he needed to provide motives for Mr Martin's decision to become a priest; even in a movie, Farrokh felt that a vow of chastity required *some* explanation. Having met Vera, the screenwriter should have guessed that the *real* missionary's motives in taking a vow of chastity and becoming a priest were not made of the material usually found in a romantic comedy.

A Make-Believe Death; the Real Children

The screenwriter had the good sense to know he was stalling. The problem was, who was going to die? In real life, it was the doctor's hope that Madhu and Ganesh would be saved by the circus. In the screenplay, it simply wasn't realistic for both children to live happily ever after. The more believable story was that only one of them would be a survivor. Pinky was the acrobat, the star. The crippled Ganesh could hope for no role more important than that of a cook's helper – the circus's servant boy, the circus's sweeper. The circus would surely start him out at the bottom; he'd be scooping up the elephant shit and washing the lion piss off the stools. From such a shit-and-piss beginning, Ganesh would be fortunate to be promoted to the cook's tent; cooking food, or serving it, would represent a form of graduation – probably the best that the crippled boy could hope for. This was true for the real Ganesh *and* for the character in the screenplay – this was realism, Dr Daruwalla believed.

It should be Pinky who dies, the screenwriter decided. The only reason that the circus accepted the crippled brother in the first place was that they wanted the talented sister; the brother was part of the deal. That was the premise of the story. But if Pinky was to die, why wouldn't the circus get rid of Ganesh? What use does the circus have for a cripple? Now this is a *better* story, Farrokh imagined. The burden of performance is suddenly shifted to the cripple; Ganesh must come up with something to do so that the circus will find him worth keeping. A boy without a limp can shovel the elephant shit faster.

But it was the bane of the screenwriter to always be rushing ahead of himself. Before he found something for Ganesh to do at the circus, wasn't it necessary to determine *how* Pinky would die? Well, she's an acrobat – she could always fall, the doctor prematurely decided. Maybe she's trying to learn Suman's Skywalk item and she simply falls. But, realistically, Pinky wouldn't be learning to skywalk from the roof of the main tent. At the Great Royal, Pratap Singh always taught the Skywalk from the roof of the family troupe tent; the rope rungs of the ladder weren't 80 feet in the air – the upside-down skywalker wasn't more than a foot or two above the ground. If Farrokh wanted to use the real Great Royal Circus, which he did – and if he

565

wanted to use his actual favorite performers (Pinky and Suman and Pratap, principally) – then the screen-writer could *not* have a death attributed to carelessness or to some cheap accident. Farrokh meant only to praise the Great Royal and circus life – not to condemn them. No; Pinky's death couldn't be the responsibility of the circus – that wasn't the right story.

That was when Dr Daruwalla thought of Mr Garg, the real-life Acid Man. After all, Acid Man was already an established villain in the screenplay; why not use him? (The threat of a lawsuit seemed remote in these moments when sheer invention struck.) Acid Man could be so enthralled by Pinky's loveliness and ability, he simply can't bear her rising stardom – or that she's escaped disfigurement of his special kind. Having lost Pinky to the Great Royal, the fiend per-forms acts of sabotage at the circus. One of the lion cubs is burned with acid, or maybe one of the dwarf clowns. Poor Pinky is killed by a lion that escapes its cage because Acid Man has burned off the lock.

Great stuff! the screenwriter thought. The irony mo-mentarily eluded Dr Daruwalla: here he was, plotting the death of his fictional Pinky while at the same time he awaited the *real* results of Madhu's HIV test. But Farrokh had once more got ahead of himself; he was try-ing to imagine what Ganesh could do to make himself irreplaceable to the circus. The boy is a lowly cripple, a mere beggar; he's clumsy, he'll always limp – the only stunt he can perform is the bird-shit trick. (The screen-writer made a hasty note to put the bird-shit trick in the screenplay; more comic relief was necessary, now that Pinky was going to be killed by a lion.)

At that moment, Ranjit put through the phone call from Dr Tata. Farrokh's forward momentum, his entire train of thought, was interrupted. Farrokh was even more annoyed by the nature of Dr Tata's information.

'Oh, dear – dear old Dad,' said Tata Two. 'I'm rather afraid he blew this one!'

It wouldn't have surprised Dr Daruwalla to learn

that the senior Dr Tata had blown many a diagnosis; after all, the old fool had not known (until the delivery) that Vera was giving birth to twins. What is it *this* time? Farrokh was tempted to ask. But he more politely inquired, 'So he *did* see Rahul?'

'You bet he did!' said Dr Tata. 'It must have been an exciting examination – Promila claimed that the boy had proved himself to be impotent in an alleged single episode with a prostitute! But I suspect the diagnosis was a bit premature.'

'What *was* the diagnosis?' Dr Daruwalla asked.

'Eunuchoidism!' cried Tata Two. 'Nowadays, we would use the term hypogonadism. But, call it what you will, this is merely a symptom or syndrome with several possible causes. Rather like the syndrome of headache or dizziness . . .'

'Yes, yes,' Dr Daruwalla said impatiently. He could tell that Tata Two had been doing a little research, or perhaps he'd been talking to a better OB/GYN; most OB/GYNs tended to know more about this sort of thing than other doctors – because they were well versed in hormones, Farrokh supposed. 'What conditions might cause you to suspect hypogonadism?' Dr Daruwalla asked Tata Two.

'If I saw a boy or a man with long limbs and an arm span – when he stretches his arms out – that is two inches more than his height. Also, his pubis-to-floor height being greater than his pubis-to-crown height,' Dr Tata replied. He *must* be reading from a book, Dr Daruwalla thought. 'And if this boy or man also had absent secondary sexual characteristics . . .' Tata Two continued, '. . . you know – voice, muscular development, phallic development, extension of pubic hair up the belly in a diamond pattern . . .'

'But how could you assess such secondary sexual characteristics as being incomplete, unless the boy is over fifteen or so?' Dr Daruwalla asked.

'Well, that's the problem – you really couldn't,' said Tata Two.

'Rahul was only twelve or thirteen in 1949!' Farrokh cried. It was preposterous that Promila had pronounced the boy impotent because he hadn't been able to get an erection, or keep an erection, with a prostitute; it was more preposterous that old Dr Tata had believed her!

'Well, that's what I mean by the diagnosis being a bit premature,' Tata Two admitted. 'The process of maturation begins at eleven or twelve ... is heralded by the hardening of the testes and is usually completed within five years – although some things, like the growth of chest hair, may take another decade.' With the word 'heralded,' Dr Daruwalla was certain that Tata Two was reading from a book.

'In short, you mean that Rahul's puberty might simply have been delayed. It was entirely too soon to call him a kind of *eunuch*!' Farrokh cried.

'Well, now, to say "eunuchoidism" isn't really calling someone "a kind of eunuch," ' Dr Tata explained.

'To a twelve- or thirteen-year-old boy, this diagnosis would have come at an impressionable age – wouldn't you agree?' asked Dr Daruwalla.

'That's true,' Tata Two replied. 'It might be a more appropriate diagnosis in the case of an eighteen-year-old with a microphaullus.'

'Jesus Christ,' said Dr Daruwalla.

'Well, we must remember that all the Rais were rather strange,' Dr Tata reasoned.

'Just the sort of family to make the most out of a misdiagnosis,' Dr Daruwalla remarked.

'I wouldn't call it a "misdiagnosis" – just a bit early to know for sure,' Tata Two said defensively. It was understandable why Dr Tata then wanted to change the subject. 'Oh, I have an answer for you about the girl. Mr Subhash told me you wanted a rush job.' Actually, Mr Subhash had told Dr Daruwalla that the HIV test would take at least two days – more, if the first phase was positive. 'Anyway, she's okay. The test was negative,' Dr Tata said.

'That was fast,' Dr Daruwalla replied. 'This is the girl who's named Madhu? Her name is Madhu?'

'Yes, yes,' said Dr Tata; it was his turn to sound impatient. 'I'm looking at the results! The name is Madhu. The test was negative. Mr Subhash just put the file on my desk.'

How *old* is Mr Subhash? Dr Daruwalla wanted to ask, but he was annoyed enough for one conversation; at least he could get the girl out of town. He thanked Tata Two, then hung up the phone. He wanted to go back to his screenplay, but first he called Ranjit into his office and asked the secretary to notify Mr Garg that Madhu was *not* HIV-positive; the doctor himself didn't want to give Garg the satisfaction.

'That was fast,' Ranjit said; but the screenplay was still occupying the majority of Dr Daruwalla's thoughts. At the moment, he was giving more of his attention to *those* children than to the children in his charge.

The doctor did remember to ask Ranjit to contact the dwarf's wife; Deepa should be told that Madhu and Ganesh were coming to the circus – and that Dr Daruwalla needed to know where (in all of Gujarat) the circus was. Farrokh should also have called the new missionary – to forewarn the Jesuit that they would be spending the weekend traveling to the circus with the children – but the screenplay beckoned to him; the fictional Mr Martin was more compelling to Dr Daruwalla than Martin Mills.

Unfortunately, the more vividly the screenwriter recalled and described the acts of the Great Royal Circus, the more he dreaded the disappointment he was certain he'd feel when he and Martin Mills delivered the *real* children to the Great Blue Nile.

20. THE BRIBE

Time to Slip Away

As for Martin Mills and how he compared to the
fictional Mr Martin, Farrokh felt only the slightest
guilt; the screenwriter suspected he'd created a light-
weight fool out of a heavyweight lunatic, but this was
only the faintest suspicion. In the screenplay, the first
time the missionary visits the children in the circus, he
slips and falls in elephant shit. It hadn't yet crossed Dr
Daruwalla's mind that the *real* missionary had possibly stepped into a worse mess than elephant shit.

As for *Elephant Shit*, it wouldn't work as a title.
Farrokh had written it in the margin of the page where
the phrase first appeared, but now he crossed this out.
A film of that title would be banned in India. Besides,
who would want to go to a movie called *Elephant
Shit*? People wouldn't bring their children, and it was
a movie *for* children, Dr Daruwalla hoped – if it was
for anybody, he thought darkly. Thus did self-doubt,
the screenwriter's old enemy, assail him; he seemed to
welcome it as a friend.

The screenwriter baited himself with other bad-title
possibilities. *Limo Roulette* was the arty choice. Farrokh
worried that dwarfs the world over would be offended
by the film, no matter what the title was. In his closet
career as a screenwriter, Dr Daruwalla had managed to
offend almost everyone else. Rather than worry about
offending dwarfs, the doctor took up the even smaller
task of wondering which movie magazine would be
the first to misunderstand and mock his efforts. The
two he detested most were *Stardust* and *Cine Blitz*. He
thought they were the most scandalous and libelous of
the film-gossip press.

The mere thought of these media goons, this journalistic slime, set Farrokh to worrying about the press conference at which he intended to announce an end to Inspector Dhar. It occurred to Farrokh that if *he* called for a press conference, no one would attend; the screenwriter would have to ask Dhar to call for such a conference, and Dhar would have to be there – otherwise, it would look like a hoax. Worse, Dhar himself would have to do the talking; after all, he was the movie star. The trashy journalists would be less interested in Dr Daruwalla's motives for perpetrating this fraud than in the reasons for Dhar's complicity. Why had Dhar gone along with the fiction that the actor was his own creator? As always, even at such a revealing press conference as Farrokh had imagined, Dhar would deliver the lines that the screenwriter had written.

The truth would simply be another acting job; moreover, the most important truth would never be told – that it was out of love for John D. that Dr Daruwalla had invented Inspector Dhar. Such a truth would be wasted on the media sleaze. Farrokh knew that he wouldn't want to read what mockery would be made of such a love, especially in *Stardust* or *Cine Blitz*.

Dhar's last press conference had been deliberately conducted as a farce. Dhar had chosen the swimming pool at the Taj as the site, for he said he enjoyed the bewildered gaping of foreigners. The journalists were instantly irritated because they'd expected a more intimate environment. 'Are you trying to emphasize that *you* are a foreigner, that you aren't really Indian at all?' That had been the first question; Dhar had responded by diving into the pool. He'd meant to splash the photographers; that had been no accident. He'd answered only what he wanted to and ignored the rest. It was an interview puncutated by Dhar repeatedly diving into the pool. The journalists said insulting things about him while he was underwater.

Farrokh presumed that John D. would be happy to be free of the role of Inspector Dhar; the actor had enough money, and he clearly preferred his Swiss life. Yet Dr Daruwalla suspected that, deep down, Dhar had cherished the loathing he'd inspired among the media scum; earning the hatred of the cinema-gossip journalists might have been John D.'s best performance. With that in mind, Farrokh thought he knew what John D. would prefer: no press conference, no announcement. 'Let them wonder,' Dhar would say – Dhar had often said.

There was another line that the screenwriter remembered; after all, he'd not only written it – it was repeated in every Inspector Dhar movie near the end of the story. There was always the temptation for Dhar to do something more – to seduce one more woman, to gun down one more villain – but Inspector Dhar knew when to stop. He knew when the action was over. Sometimes to a scheming bartender, sometimes to a fellow policeman of a generally dissatisfied nature, sometimes to a pretty woman who'd been waiting impatiently to make love to him, Inspector Dhar would say, 'Time to slip away.' Then he would.

In this case, facing the facts – that he wanted to call an end to Inspector Dhar *and* that he wanted to finally leave Bombay – Farrokh knew what John D.'s advice would be. 'Time to slip away,' Inspector Dhar would say.

Bedbugs Ahead

In the old days, before the doctors' offices and the examining rooms of the Hospital for Crippled Children were air-conditioned, there'd been a ceiling fan over the desk where Dr Daruwalla now sat thinking, and the window to the exercise yard was always open. Nowadays, with the window closed and the hum of the air-conditioning a reassuring constant, Farrokh was cut off from the sound of children crying in the exercise yard. When the doctor walked through the yard, or when he was called to observe the progress of one of his postoperative patients in physical therapy, the crying children did not greatly upset him. Farrokh associated some pain with recovery; a joint, after surgery – *especially* after surgery – had to be moved. But in addition to the cries of pain, there were the whines that children made in anticipation of their pain, and this piteous mewling affected the doctor strongly.

Farrokh turned and faced the closed window with its view of the exercise yard; from the soundless expressions of the children, the doctor could still discern the difference between those children who were in pain and those who were pitifully frightened of the pain they expected. Soundlessly, the therapists were coaxing the children to move; there was the recent hip replacement being told to stand up, there was the new knee being asked to step forward – and the first rotation of the new elbow. The landscape of the exercise yard was timeless to Dr Daruwalla, who reflected that his ability to hear that which was soundless was the only measure of his humanity that he was certain of. Even with the air-conditioning on, even with the window closed, Dr Daruwalla could hear the whimpering. Time to slip away, he thought.

He opened the window and leaned outside. The heat at midday was oppressive in the rising dust, although (for Bombay) the weather had remained relatively cool and dry. The cries of the children commingled with the car horns and the chainsaw clamor of the mopeds. Dr Daruwalla breathed it all in. He squinted into the dusty glare. He gave the exercise yard an almost detached appraisal; it was a good-bye look. Then the doctor called Ranjit for his messages.

It was no surprise to Dr Daruwalla that Deepa had already negotiated with the Great Blue Nile; the doctor hadn't expected the dwarf's wife to get a better deal.

573

The circus would attempt to train the talented 'sister.' They would commit themselves to this effort for three months; they'd feed her, clothe her, shelter her and care for her crippled 'brother.' If Madhu could be trained, the Great Blue Nile would keep both children; if she was untrainable, the circus would let them go.

In Farrokh's screenplay, the Great Royal paid Pinky three rupees a day while they trained her; the fictional Ganesh worked without pay for his food and shelter. At the Great Blue Nile, Madhu's training was considered a privilege; she wouldn't be paid at all. And for a real boy with a crushed foot, it was enough of a privilege to be fed and sheltered; the real Ganesh would work, too. At the parents' expense – or, in the case of orphans, it was the obligation of the children's 'sponsors' – Madhu and Ganesh would be brought to the site of the Great Blue Nile's present location. At this time, the circus was performing in Junagadh, a small city of about 100,000 people in Gujarat.

Junagadh! It would take a day to get there, another day to get back. They would have to fly to Rajkot and then endure a car ride of two or three hours to the smaller town; a driver from the circus would meet their plane – doubtless a reckless roustabout. But the train would be worse. Farrokh knew that Julia hated him to be away overnight, and in Junagadh there would probably be nowhere to stay but the Government Circuit House; lice were likely, bedbugs a certainty. There would be 48 hours of conversation with Martin Mills, and no time to keep writing the screenplay. It had also occurred to the screenwriter that the *real* Dr Daruwalla was part of a parallel story-in-progress.

Raging Hormones

When Dr Daruwalla phoned St Ignatius School to alert the new missionary to their upcoming journey, the doctor wondered if his writing was prophetic. He'd already described the fictional Mr Martin as 'the most popular teacher at the school'; now here was Father Cecil telling the screenwriter that Martin Mills, on the evidence of his first morning of visiting the classrooms, had instantly made 'a most popular impression.' Young Martin, as Father Cecil still called him, had even persuaded the Father Rector to permit the teaching of Graham Greene to the upper-school boys; although controversial, Graham Greene was one of Martin Mills's Catholic heroes. 'After all, the novelist popularized Catholic issues,' Father Cecil said.

Farrokh, who considered himself an old fan of Graham Greene, asked suspiciously, 'Catholic issues?'

'Suicide as a mortal sin, for example,' Father Cecil replied. (Apparently, Father Julian was allowing Martin Mills to teach *The Heart of the Matter* to the upper school.) Dr Daruwalla felt briefly uplifted; on the long trip to Junagadh and back, perhaps the doctor would be able to steer the missionary's conversation to Graham Greene. Who were some of the zealot's *other* heroes? the doctor wondered.

Farrokh hadn't had a good discussion of Graham Greene in quite a while. Julia and her literary friends were happier discussing more contemporary authors; they found it old-fashioned of Farrokh to prefer rereading those books he regarded as classics. Dr Daruwalla was intimidated by Martin Mills's education, but possibly the doctor and the scholastic would discover a common ground in the novels of Graham Greene.

Dr Daruwalla couldn't have known that the subject of suicide was of more interest to Martin Mills than the craft of Graham Greene as a writer. For a Catholic, suicide was a violation of God's dominion over human life. In the case of Arif Koma, Martin reasoned, the Muslim hadn't been in full possession of his faculties; falling in love with Vera surely suggested a loss of faculties, or a vastly different set of faculties altogether.

The denial of ecclesiastical burial was a horror to Martin Mills; however, the Church permitted suicides among those who'd lost their senses or were unaware that they were killing themselves. The missionary hoped that God would judge the Turk's suicide as an out-of-his-head kind. After all, Martin's mother had fucked the boy's brains out. How could Arif have made a sane decision after that?

But if Dr Daruwalla would be unprepared for Martin Mill's Catholic interpretation of the doctor's much-admired author, Farrokh was also in the dark regarding the unwelcome disturbance that had shaken St Ignatius School in the late morning, to which Father Cecil made incoherent references. The mission had been disrupted by an unruly intruder; the police had been forced to subdue the violent individual, whose violence Father Cecil attributed to 'raging hormones.'

Farrokh liked the phrase so much that he wrote it down.

'It was a transvestite prostitute, of all things,' Father Cecil whispered into the phone.

'Why are you whispering?' Dr Daruwalla asked.

'The Father Rector is still upset about the episode,' Father Cecil confided to Farrokh. 'Can you imagine? A *hijra* coming here – and during school hours!'

Dr Daruwalla was amused at the presumed spectacle. 'Perhaps he, or she, wanted to be better educated,' the doctor suggested to Father Cecil.

'It claimed it had been invited,' Father Cecil replied.

'*It!*' Dr Daruwalla cried.

'Well, he or she – whatever it was, it was big and strong. A rampaging prostitute, a crazed cross-dresser!' Father Cecil whispered. 'They give themselves hormones, don't they?'

'Not hijras,' Dr Daruwalla replied. 'They don't take estrogens; they have their balls and their penises removed – with a single cut. The wound is then cauterized with hot oil. It resembles a vagina.'

'Goodness – don't tell me!' Father Cecil said.

'Sometimes, but not usually, their breasts are surgically implanted,' Dr Daruwalla informed the priest.

'This one was implanted with *iron*!' Father Cecil said enthusiastically. 'And young Martin was busy teaching. The Father Rector and I, and poor Brother Gabriel, had to deal with the creature by ourselves – until the police came.'

'It sounds exciting,' Farrokh remarked.

'Fortunately, none of the children saw it,' Father Cecil said.

'Aren't transvestite prostitutes allowed to convert?' asked Dr Daruwalla, who enjoyed teasing any priest.

'Raging hormones,' Father Cecil repeated. 'It must have just given itself an overdose.'

'I told you – they don't usually take estrogens,' the doctor said.

'This one was taking something,' Father Cecil insisted.

'May I speak with Martin now?' Dr Daruwalla asked. 'Or is he still busy teaching?'

'He's eating his lunch with the midgets, or maybe he's with the submidgets today,' Father Cecil replied.

It was almost time for the doctor's lunch at the Duckworth Club. Dr Daruwalla left a message for Martin Mills, but Father Cecil struggled with the message to such a degree that the doctor knew he'd have to call again. 'Just tell him I'll call him back,' Farrokh finally said. 'And tell him we're definitely going to the circus.'

'Oh, won't that be fun!' Father Cecil said.

The Hawaiian Shirt

Detective Patel had wanted to compose himself before his lunch at the Duckworth Club; however, there was the interruption of this incident at St Ignatius. It was merely a misdemeanor, but the episode had been brought to the deputy commissioner's attention because it fell into the category of Dhar-related crimes.

The perpetrator was one of the transvestite prostitutes who'd been injured by Dhar's dwarf driver in the fracas on Falkland Road; it was the hijra whose wrist had been broken by a blow from one of Vinod's squash-racquet handles. The eunuch-transvestite had shown up at St Ignatius, clubbing the old priests with his cast; his story was that Inspector Dhar had told all the transvestite prostitutes that they'd be welcome at the mission. Also, Dhar had told the hijras that they could always find him there.

'But it wasn't Dhar,' the hijra told Detective Patel in Hindi. 'It was someone being a Dhar imposter.' It would have been laughable to Patel, to hear a transvestite complaining that someone else was an 'imposter,' if the detective had been in a laughing mood; instead, the deputy commissioner looked at the hijra with impatience and scorn. He was a tall, broad-shouldered, bony-faced hooker whose small breasts were showing because the top two buttons of his Hawaiian shirt were unbuttoned and the shirt was too loose for him; the looseness of his shirt and the tightness of his scarlet miniskirt were an absurd combination – hijra prostitutes usually wore saris. Also, they generally made more of an effort to be feminine than this one was making; his breasts (what the deputy commissioner could see of them) were shapely – in fact, they were very well formed – but there were whiskers on his chin and the noticeable shadow of a mustache on his upper lip. Possibly the hijra had thought that the colors of the Hawaiian shirt were feminine, not to mention the parrots and flowers; yet the shirt did little for his figure.

D.C.P. Patel continued the interrogation in Hindi. 'Where'd you get that shirt?' the detective asked.

'Dhar was wearing it,' the prostitute replied.

'Not likely,' said the deputy commissioner.

'I told you he was being an imposter,' the prostitute said.

'What sort of fool would pretend to be Dhar, and

dare show his face on Falkland Road?' Patel asked.

'He looked like he didn't know he was Dhar,' the hijra replied.

'Oh, I see,' said Detective Patel. 'He was an imposter but he didn't *know* he was an imposter.' The hijra scratched his hooked nose with the cast on his wrist. Patel was bored with the interrogation; he kept the hijra sitting there only because the preposterous sight of him helped the detective to focus on Rahul. Of course Rahul would be 53 or 54 now, and she wouldn't stand out as someone who was making a half-assed effort to *look* like a woman.

It had occurred to the deputy commissioner that this might be one of the ways that Rahul managed to commit so many murders in the same area of Bombay. Rahul could enter a brothel as a man and leave looking like a hag; she could also leave looking like an attractive, middle-aged woman. And until this waste-of-time hijra had interrupted him, Patel had been enjoying a fairly profitable morning's work; the deputy commissioner's research on Rahul was progressing rather nicely. The list of new members at the Duck-worth Club had been helpful.

'Did you ever hear of a zenana by the name of Rahul?' Patel asked the hijra.

'That old question,' the transvestite said.

'Only she'd be a *real* woman now – the complete operation,' the detective added. He knew there were some hijras who envied the very idea of a *complete* transsexual, but not most; most hijras were exactly what they wanted to be – they had no use for a fully fashioned vagina.

'If I knew of there being someone like that, I'd probably kill her,' the hijra said good-naturedly. 'For her *parts*,' he added with a smile; he was just kidding, of course. Detective Patel knew more about Rahul than this hijra did; in the last 24 hours, the detective had learned more about Rahul than he'd known for 20 years.

'You may go now,' said the deputy commissioner. 'But leave the shirt. By your own admission, you stole it.'

'But I have nothing else to wear!' the hijra cried.

'We'll find you something you can wear,' the policeman said. 'It just may not match your miniskirt.'

When Detective Patel left Crime Branch Headquarters for his lunch at the Duckworth Club, he took a paper bag with him; in it was the Hawaiian shirt that had belonged to Dhar's imposter. The deputy commissioner knew that not every question would or could be answered over one lunch, but the question posed by the Hawaiian shirt seemed a relatively simple one.

The Actor Guesses Right

'No,' said Inspector Dhar. 'I would never wear a shirt like that.' He'd glanced quickly and indifferently into the bag, not bothering to draw out the shirt – not even touching the material.

'It has a California label,' Detective Patel informed the actor.

'I've never been to California,' Dhar replied.

The deputy commissioner put the paper bag under his chair; he seemed disappointed that the Hawaiian shirt had not served as an icebreaker to their conversation, which had halted once again. Poor Nancy hadn't spoken at all. Worse, she'd chosen to wear a sari, wound up in the navel-revealing fashion; the golden hairs that curled upward in a sleek line to her belly button were as worrisome to Mr Sethna as the unsightly paper bag the policeman had placed under his chair. It was the kind of bag that a bomb would be in, the old steward thought. And how he disapproved of Western women in Indian attire! Furthermore, the fair skin of this particular woman's midriff clashed with her sunburned face. She must have been lying in the sun with tea saucers over her eyes, Mr Sethna thought; any evidence of women lying on their backs disturbed him.

As for the ever-voyeuristic Dr Daruwalla, his eyes were repeatedly drawn to Nancy's furry navel; since she'd pulled her chair snugly to their table in the Ladies' Garden, the doctor was restless because he could no longer see this marvel. Farrokh found himself glancing sideways at Nancy's raccoon eyes instead. The doctor made Nancy so nervous that she took her sunglasses out of her purse and put them on. She had the look of someone who was trying to gather herself together for a performance.

Inspector Dhar knew how to handle sunglasses. He simply stared into them with a satisfied expression on his face, which implied to Nancy that her sunglasses were no impediment to *his* vision – that he could see her clearly nonetheless. Dhar knew this would soon cause her to take the sunglasses off.

Oh, great – they're *both* acting! Dr Daruwalla thought.

Mr Sethna was disgusted with all of them. They were as socially graceless as teenagers. Not one of them had glanced at a menu; none of them had so much as raised an eyebrow to a waiter to suggest an aperitif, and they couldn't even talk to one another! Mr Sethna was also full of indignation at the explanation that was now before him of why Detective Patel spoke such good English: the policeman's wife was a slatternly American! Needless to say, Mr Sethna considered this a 'mixed marriage,' of which he strongly disapproved. And the old steward was no less outraged that Inspector Dhar should have brashly presented himself at the Duckworth Club so soon after the warning in the late Mr Lal's mouth; the actor was recklessly endangering other Duckworthians! That Mr Sethna had come by this information through the relentlessness and the practiced stealth of his eavesdropping didn't cause the old steward to consider that he might not know the whole story. To a man with Mr Sethna's readiness to disapprove, a mere shred of information was sufficient to form a full opinion.

But of course Mr Sethna had another reason to be outraged with Inspector Dhar. As a Parsi and a practicing Zoroastrian, the old steward had reacted predictably to the posters for the newest Inspector Dhar absurdity. Not since his days at the Ripon Club, and his famous decision to pour hot tea on the head of the man wearing the wig, had Mr Sethna felt so aroused to righteous anger. He'd seen the work of the poster-wallas on his way home from the Duckworth Club, and he blamed *Inspector Dhar and the Towers of Silence* for giving him uncharacteristically lurid dreams.

He'd suffered a vision of a ghostly-white statue of Queen Victoria that resembled the one they took away from Victoria Terminus, but in his dream the statue was levitating; Queen Victoria was hovering about a foot off the floor of Mr Sethna's beloved fire-temple, and all the Parsi faithful were bolting for the doorway. Were it not for the blasphemous cinema poster, Mr Sethna believed he would never have had such a blasphemous dream. He'd promptly woken up and donned his prayer cap, but the prayer cap fell off when he suffered another dream. He was riding in the Parsi Panchayat Hearse to the Towers of Silence; although he was already a dead body, he could smell the rites attendant to his own death – the scent of burning sandalwood. Suddenly the stink of putrefaction, which clung to the vultures' beaks and talons, was choking him; he woke again. His prayer cap was on the floor, where he mistook it for a waiting hunchbacked crow; pathetically, he'd tried to shoo the imagined crow away.

Dr Daruwalla glanced only once at Mr Sethna. From the steward's withering stare, the doctor wondered if another hot-tea incident was brewing. Mr Sethna interpreted the doctor's glance as a summons.

'An aperitif before lunch, perhaps?' the steward asked the awkward foursome. Since 'aperitif' wasn't a word much used in Iowa – nor had Nancy heard it from Dieter, nor was it ever spoken in her life with Vijay Patel – she made no response to Mr Sethna, who was looking directly at her. (If anywhere, Nancy might have encountered the word in one or another of the remaindered American novels she'd read, but she wouldn't have known how to pronounce 'aperitif' and she would have assumed that the word was inessential to understanding the plot.)

'Would the lady enjoy something to drink before her lunch?' Mr Sethna asked, still looking at Nancy. No one at the table could hear what she said, but the old steward understood that she'd whispered for a Thums Up cola. The deputy commissioner ordered a Gold Spot orange soda, Dr Daruwalla asked for a London Diet beer and Dhar wanted a Kingfisher.

'Well, this should be lively,' Dr Daruwalla joked. 'Two teetotalers and two beer drinkers!' This lead balloon lay on the table, which inspired the doctor to discourse, at length, on the history of the lunch menu.

It was Chinese Day at the Duckworth Club, the culinary low point of the week. In the old days, there'd been a Chinese chef among the kitchen staff, and Chinese Day had been an epicure's delight. But the Chinese chef had left the club to open his own restaurant, and the present-day collection of cooks could not concoct Chinese; yet, one day a week, they tried.

'It's probably safest to stick with something vegetarian,' Farrokh recommended.

'By the time you saw the bodies,' Nancy suddenly began, 'I suppose they were pretty bad.'

'Yes – I'm afraid the crabs had found them,' Dr Daruwalla replied.

'But I guess the drawing was still clear, or you wouldn't have remembered it,' Nancy said.

'Yes – indelible ink, I'm sure,' said Dr Daruwalla.

'It was a laundry-marking pen – a dhobi pen,' Nancy told him, although she appeared to be looking at Dhar. With her sunglasses on, who knew where she was looking? 'I buried them, you know,' Nancy went on. 'I didn't see them die, but I heard them. The sound of the spade,' she added.

Dhar continued to stare at her, his lip not quite sneering. Nancy took her sunglasses off and returned them to her purse. Something she saw in her purse made her pause; she held her lower lip in her teeth for three or four seconds. Then she reached in her purse and brought out the bottom half of the silver ballpoint pen, which she'd carried with her, everywhere she'd gone, for 20 years.

'He stole the other half of this – he or she,' Nancy said. She handed the half-pen to Dhar, who read the interrupted inscription.

' "Made in" *where*?' Dhar asked her.

'India,' said Nancy. 'Rahul must have stolen it.'

'Who would want the top half of a pen?' Farrokh asked Detective Patel.

'Not a writer,' Dhar replied; he passed the half-pen to Dr Daruwalla.

'It's real silver,' the doctor observed.

'It needs to be polished,' Nancy said. The deputy commissioner looked away; he knew his wife had polished the thing only last week. Dr Daruwalla couldn't see any indication that the silver was dull or blackened; everything was shiny, even the inscription. When he handed the half-pen to Nancy, she didn't put it back in her purse; instead, she placed it alongside her knife and spoon – it was brighter than both. 'I use an old toothbrush to polish the lettering,' she said. Even Dhar looked away from her; that he couldn't meet her eyes gave her confidence. 'In real life,' Nancy said to the actor, 'have you ever taken a bribe?' She saw the sneer she'd been looking for; she'd been expecting it.

'No, never,' Dhar told her. Now Nancy had to look away from him; she looked straight at Dr Daruwalla.

584

'How come you keep it a secret . . . that you write all his movies?' Nancy asked the doctor.

'I already have a career,' Dr Daruwalla replied. 'The idea was to create a career for *him*.'

'Well, you sure did it,' Nancy told Farrokh. Detective Patel reached for her left hand, which was on the table by her fork, but Nancy put her hand in her lap. Then she faced Dhar.

'And how do you like it? Your *career* . . .' Nancy asked the actor. He responded with his patterned shrug, which enhanced his sneer. Something both cruel and merry entered his eyes.

'I have a day job . . . another life,' Dhar replied.

'Lucky you,' Nancy told him.

'Sweetie,' said the deputy commissioner; he reached into his wife's lap and took her hand. She seemed to go a little limp in the rattan chair. Even Mr Sethna could hear her exhale; the old steward had heard almost everything else, too, and what he hadn't actually heard he'd fairly accurately surmised from reading their lips. Mr Sethna was good lip-reader, and for an elderly man he could move spryly around a conversation; a table for four posed few problems for him. It was easier to pick up conversation in the Ladies' Garden than in the main dining room, because only the bower of flowers was overhead; there were no ceiling fans.

From Mr Sethna's point of view, it was already a much more interesting lunch than he'd anticipated. Dead bodies! A stolen part of a pen? And the most startling revelation – that Dr Daruwalla was the actual author of that trash which had elevated Inspector Dhar to stardom! In a way, Mr Sethna believed that he'd known it all along; the old steward had always sensed that Farrokh wasn't the man his father was.

Mr Sethna glided in with the drinks; then he glided away. The venomous feelings that the old steward had felt for Dhar were now what Mr Sethna was feeling for Dr Daruwalla. A Parsi writing for the Hindi cinema! And making fun of other Parsis! How dare he? Mr

Sethna could barely restrain himself. In his mind, he could hear the sound that his silver serving tray would make off the crown of Dr Daruwalla's head; it sounded like a gong. The steward had needed all his strength to resist the temptation to cover that appalling woman's fuzzy navel with her napkin, which was carelessly lumped in her lap. A belly button like hers should be clothed – if not banned! But Mr Sethna quickly calmed himself, for he didn't want to miss what the real policeman was saying.

'I should like to hear the three of you describe what Rahul would look like today, assuming that Rahul is now a woman,' said the deputy commissioner. 'You first,' Patel said to Dhar.

'Vanity and an overall sense of physical superiority would keep her looking younger than she is,' Dhar began.

'But she would be fifty-three or fifty-four,' Dr Daruwalla interjected.

'You're next. Please let him finish,' said Detective Patel.

'She wouldn't *look* fifty-three or fifty-four, except maybe very early in the morning,' Dhar continued. 'And she would be very fit. She has a predatory aura. She's a stalker – I mean sexually.'

'I think she was quite hot for him when he was a boy!' Dr Daruwalla remarked.

'Who *wasn't*?' Nancy asked bitterly. Only her husband looked at her.

'Please let him finish,' Patel said patiently.

'She's also the sort of woman who enjoys making you want her, even if she intends to reject you,' Dhar said. He made a point of looking at Nancy. 'And I would assume that, like her late aunt, she has a caustic manner. She would always be ready to ridicule someone, or some idea – anything.'

'Yes, yes,' said Dr Daruwalla impatiently, 'but don't forget, she is also a *starer*.'

'Excuse me – a *what*?' asked Detective Patel.

586

'A family trait – she stares at everyone. Rahul is a compulsive *starer*!' Farrokh replied. 'She does it because she's deliberately rude but also because she has a kind of uninhibited curiosity. That was her aunt, in spades! Rahul was brought up that way. No modesty whatsoever. Now she would be very feminine, I suppose, but not with her eyes. She is a *man* with her eyes – she's always looking you over and staring you down.'

'Were you finished?' the deputy commissioner asked Dhar.

'I think so,' the actor replied.

'I never saw her clearly,' Nancy said suddenly. 'There was no light, or the light was bad – only an oil lamp. I got just a peek at her, and I was sick – I had a fever.' She toyed with the bottom half of the ballpoint pen on the table, turning it at a right angle to her knife and spoon, then lining it up again. 'She smelled good, and she felt very silky – but strong,' Nancy added.

'Talk about her *now*, not then,' Patel said. 'What would she be like now?'

'The thing is,' Nancy said, 'I think she feels like she can't control something in herself, like she just *needs* to do things. She can't stop herself. The things she wants are just too strong.'

'What things?' asked the detective.

'You know. We've talked about it,' Nancy told him.

'Tell *them*,' her husband said.

'She's horny – I think she's horny all the time,' Nancy told them.

'That's unusual for someone who's fifty-three or fifty-four,' Dr Daruwalla observed.

'That's just the feeling she gives you – believe me,' Nancy said. 'She's awfully horny.'

'Does this remind you of someone you know?' the detective asked Inspector Dhar, but Dhar kept looking at Nancy; he didn't shrug. 'Or *you*, Doctor – are you reminded of anyone?' the deputy commissoner asked Farrokh.

'Are you talking about someone we've actually met – as a woman?' Dr Daruwalla asked the deputy commissioner.

'Precisely,' said Detective Patel.

Dhar was still looking at Nancy when he spoke. 'Mrs Dogar,' Dhar said. Farrokh put both his hands on his chest, exactly where the familiar pain in his ribs was suddenly sharp enough to take his breath away.

'Oh, very good – very *impressive*,' said Detective Patel. He reached across the table and patted the back of Dhar's hand. 'You wouldn't have made a bad policeman, even if you don't take bribes,' the detective told the actor.

'Mrs Dogar!' Dr Daruwalla gasped. 'I *knew* she reminded me of someone!'

'But there's something wrong, isn't there?' Dhar asked the deputy commissioner. 'I mean, you haven't arrested her – have you?'

'Quite so,' Patel said. 'Something is wrong.'

'I *told* you he'd know who it was,' Nancy told her husband.

'Yes, sweetie,' the detective said. 'But it's not a crime for Rahul to be Mrs Dogar.'

'How did you find out?' Dr Daruwalla asked the deputy commissioner. 'Of course – the list of new members!'

'It was a good place to start,' said Detective Patel. 'The estate of Promila Rai was inherited by her niece, not her nephew.'

'I never knew there was a niece,' Farrokh said.

'There wasn't,' Patel replied. 'Rahul, her nephew, went to London. He came back as her niece. He even gave himself her name – Promila. It's perfectly legal to change your sex in England. It's perfectly legal to change your name – even in India.'

'Rahul Rai married Mr Dogar?' Farrokh asked.

'That was perfectly legal, too,' the detective replied. 'Don't you see, Doctor? The fact that you and Dhar could verify that Rahul was there in Goa, at the Hotel

Bardez, does *not* confirm that Rahul was ever at the scene of the crime. And it would *not* be believable for Nancy to physically identify Mrs Dogar as the Rahul of twenty years ago. As she told you, she hardly saw Rahul.'

'Besides, he had a penis then,' Nancy said.

'But, in all these killings, are there no fingerprints?' Farrokh asked.

'In the cases of the prostitutes, there are *hundreds* of fingerprints,' D.C.P. Patel replied.

'What about the putter that killed Mr Lal?' Dhar asked.

'Oh, very good!' the deputy commissioner said. 'But the putter was wiped clean.'

'Those drawings!' Dr Daruwalla said. 'Rahul always fancied himself an artist. Surely Mrs Dogar must have some drawings around.'

'That would be convenient,' Patel replied. 'But this very morning I sent someone to the Dogar house – to bribe the servants.' The detective paused and looked directly at Dhar. 'There *were* no drawings. There wasn't even a typewriter.'

'There must be ten typewriters in this club,' Dhar said. 'The typed messages on the two-rupee notes – were they all typed on the same machine?'

'Oh, what a very good question,' said Detective Patel. 'So far, three messages – two different typewriters. Both in this club.'

'Mrs Dogar!' Dr Daruwalla said again.

'Be quiet, please,' the deputy commissioner said. He suddenly pointed to Mr Sethna. The old steward attempted to hide his face with his silver serving tray, but Detective Patel was too fast for him. 'What is that old snoop's name?' the detective asked Dr Daruwalla.

'That's Mr Sethna,' Farrokh said.

'Please come here, Mr Sethna,' the deputy commissioner said. He didn't raise his voice or look in the steward's direction; when Mr Sethna pretended that he

589

hadn't heard, the detective said, 'You heard me.' Mr Sethna did as he was told.

'Since you've been listening to us – Wednesday you listened to my telephone conversation with my wife – you will kindly give me your assistance,' Detective Patel said.

'Yes, sir,' Mr Sethna said.

'Every time Mrs Dogar is in this club, you call me,' the deputy commissioner said. 'Every reservation she makes, lunch or dinner, you let me know about it. Every little thing you know about her, I want to know, too – am I making myself clear?'

'Perfectly clear, sir,' said Mr Sethna. 'She said her husband is peeing on the flowers and that one night he'll try to dive into the empty pool,' Mr Sethna babbled. 'She said he's senile – and a drunk.'

'You can tell me later,' Detective Patel said. 'I have just three questions. Then I want you to go far enough away from this table so that you don't hear another word.'

'Yes, sir,' Mr Sethna said.

'On the morning of Mr Lal's death . . . I don't mean lunch, because I already know that she was here for lunch, but in the morning, well before lunch . . . did you see Mrs Dogar here? That's the first question,' the deputy commissioner said.

'Yes, she was here for a bit of breakfast – very early,' Mr Sethna informed the detective. 'She likes to walk on the golf course before the golfers are playing. Then she has a little fruit before she does her fitness training.'

'Second question,' Patel said. 'Between breakfast and lunch, did she change what she was wearing?'

'Yes, sir,' the old steward replied. 'She was wearing a dress, rather wrinkled, at breakfast. For lunch she wore a sari.'

'Third question,' the deputy commissioner said. He handed Mr Sethna his card – his telephone number at Crime Branch Headquarters and his home number.

590

'Were her shoes wet? I mean, for breakfast?'

'I didn't notice,' Mr Sethna admitted.

'Try to improve your noticing,' Detective Patel told the old steward. 'Now, go far away from this table – I mean it.'

'Yes, sir,' said Mr Sethna, already doing what he did best – gliding away. Nor did the prying old steward approach the Ladies' Garden again during the four-some's solemn lunch. But even at a considerable distance, Mr Sethna was able to observe that the woman with the fuzzy navel ate very little; her rude husband ate half her food and all his own. At a proper club, people would be forbidden to eat off one another's plates, Mr Sethna thought. He went into the men's room and stood in front of the full-length mirror, in which he appeared to be trembling. He held the silver serving tray in one hand and pounded it against the heel of his other hand, but he felt little satisfaction from the sound it made – a muffled bonging. He *hated* policemen, the old steward decided.

Farrokh Remembers the Crow

In the Ladies' Garden, the early-afternoon sun had slanted past the apex of the bower and no longer touched the lunchers' heads; the rays of sunlight now penetrated the wall of flowers only in patches. The tablecloth was mottled by this intermittent light, and Dr Daruwalla watched a tiny diamond of the sun – it was reflected in the bottom half of the ballpoint pen. The brilliantly white point of light shone in the doctor's eye as he pecked at his soggy stir-fry; the limp, dull-colored vegetables reminded him of the monsoon.

At that time of year, the Ladies' Garden would be strewn with torn petals of the bougainvillea, the skeletal vines still clinging to the bower – with the brown sky showing through and the rain coming through. All the wicker and rattan furniture would be heaped upon itself in the ballroom, for there were no balls in the monsoon season. The golfers would sit drinking in the clubhouse bar, forlornly staring out the streaked windows at the sodden fairways. Wild clumps of the dead garden would be blowing across the greens.

The food on Chinese Day always depressed Farrokh, but there was something about the winking sun that was reflected in the bottom half of the silver ballpoint pen, something that both caught and held the doctor's attention; something flickered in his memory. What was it? That reflected light, that shiny something . . . it was as small and lonely but as absolutely a presence as the far-off light of another airplane when you were flying across the miles of darkness over the Arabian Sea at night.

Farrokh stared into the dining room and at the open veranda, through which the shitting crow had flown. Dr Daruwalla looked at the ceiling fan where the crow had landed; the doctor kept watching the fan, as if he were waiting for it to falter, or for the mechanism to catch on something – that shiny something which the shitting crow had held in its beak. Whatever it was, it was too big for the crow to have swallowed, Dr Daruwalla thought. He took a wild guess.

'I know what it was,' the doctor said aloud. No one else had been talking; the others just looked at him as he left the table in the Ladies' Garden and walked into the dining room, where he stood directly under the fan. Then he drew an unused chair away from the nearest table; but when he stood on it, he was still too short to reach over the top of the blades.

'Turn the fan off!' Dr Daruwalla shouted to Mr Sethna, who was no stranger to the doctor's eccentric behavior – and his father's before him. The old steward shut off the fan. Almost everyone in the dining room had stopped eating.

Dhar and Detective Patel rose from their table in the Ladies' Garden and approached Farrokh, but the doctor waved them away. 'Neither of you is tall enough,' he told them. 'Only *she* is tall enough.' The doctor was pointing at Nancy. He was also following the good advice that the deputy commissioner had given to Mr Sethna. ('Try to improve your noticing.')

The fan slowed; the blades were unmoving by the time the three men helped Nancy to stand on the chair.

'Just reach over the top of the fan,' the doctor instructed her. 'Do you feel a groove?' Her full figure above them in the chair was quite striking as she reached into the mechanism.

'I feel something,' she said.

'Walk your fingers around the groove,' said Dr Daruwalla.

'What am I looking for?' Nancy asked him.

'You're going to feel it,' he told her. 'I think it's the top half of your pen.'

They had to hold her or she would have fallen, for her fingers found it almost the instant that the doctor warned her what it was.

'Try not to handle it – just hold it very lightly,' the deputy commissioner said to his wife. She dropped it on the stone floor and the detective retrieved it with a napkin, holding it only by the pocket clasp.

' "India," ' Patel said aloud, reading that inscription which had been separated from *Made in* for 20 years.

It was Dhar who lifted Nancy down from the chair. She felt heavier to him than she had 20 years before. She said she needed a moment to be alone with her husband; they stood whispering together in the Ladies' Garden, while Farrokh and John D. watched the fan start up again. Then the doctor and the actor went to join the detective and his wife, who'd returned to the table.

'Surely now you'll have Rahul's fingerprints,' Dr Daruwalla told the deputy commissioner.

'Probably,' said Detective Patel. 'When Mrs Dogar comes to eat here, we'll have the steward save us her fork or her spoon – to compare. But her fingerprints on the top of the pen don't place her at the crime.'

Dr Daruwalla told them all about the crow. Clearly the crow had brought the pen from the bougainvillea at the ninth green. Crows are carrion eaters.

'But what would Rahul have been doing with the top of the pen – I mean *during* the murder of Mr Lal?' Detective Patel asked.

In frustration, Dr Daruwalla blurted out, 'You make it sound as if you have to witness another murder – or do you expect Mrs Dogar to offer you a full confession?'

'It's only necessary to make Mrs Dogar think that we know more than we know,' the deputy commissioner answered.

'That's easy,' Dhar said suddenly. 'You tell the murderer what the murderer *would* confess, if the murderer were confessing. The trick is, you've got to make the murderer think that you really *know* the murderer.'

'Precisely,' Patel said.

'Wasn't that in *Inspector Dhar and the Hanging Mali*?' Nancy asked the actor; she meant that it was Dr Daruwalla's line.

'Very good,' Dr Daruwalla told her.

Detective Patel didn't pat the back of Dhar's hand; he tapped Dhar on one knuckle – just once, but sharply – with a dessert spoon. 'Let's be serious,' said the deputy commissioner. 'I'm going to offer you a bribe – something you've always wanted.'

'There's nothing I want,' Dhar replied.

'I think there is,' the detective told him. 'I think you'd like to play a *real* policeman. I think you'd like to make a *real* arrest.'

Dhar said nothing – he didn't even sneer.

'Do you think you're still attractive to Mrs Dogar?' the detective asked him.

'Oh, absolutely – you should see how she looks him over!' cried Dr Daruwalla.

'I'm asking *him*,' said Detective Patel.

'Yes, I think she wants me,' Dhar replied.

'Of course she does,' Nancy said angrily.

'And if I told you how to approach her, do you think you could do it – I mean *exactly* as I tell you?' the detective asked Dhar.

'Oh, yes – you give him *any* line, he can deliver it!' cried Dr Daruwalla.

'I'm asking *you*,' the policeman said to Dhar. This time, the dessert spoon rapped his knuckle hard enough for Dhar to take his hand off the table.

'You want to set her up – is that it?' Dhar asked the deputy commissioner.

'Precisely,' Patel said.

'And I just follow your instructions?' the actor asked him.

'That's it – *exactly*,' said the deputy commissioner.

'You can do it!' Dr Daruwalla declared to Dhar.

'That's not the question,' Nancy said.

'The question is, do you *want* to do it?' Detective Patel asked Dhar. 'I think you really want to.'

'All right,' Dhar said. 'Okay. Yes, I want to.'

For the first time in the course of the long lunch, Patel smiled. 'I feel better, now that I've bribed you,' the deputy commissioner told Dhar. 'Do you see? That's all a bribe is, really – just something you want, in exchange for something else. It's no big deal, is it?'

'We'll see,' Dhar said. When he looked at Nancy, she was looking at him.

'You're not sneering,' Nancy said.

'Sweetie,' said Detective Patel, taking her hand.

'I need to go to the ladies' room,' she said. 'You show me where it is,' she said to Dhar. But before his wife or the actor could stand up, the deputy commissioner stopped them.

'Just a trivial matter, before you go,' the detective said. 'What is this nonsense about you and the dwarf brawling with prostitutes on Falkland Road – what is this nonsense about?' Detective Patel asked Dhar.

'That wasn't him,' said Dr Daruwalla quickly.

'So there's some truth to the rumor of a Dhar imposter?' the detective asked.

'Not an imposter – a twin,' the doctor replied.

'You have a *twin*?' Nancy asked the actor.

'Identical,' said Dhar.

'That's hard to believe,' she said.

'They're not at all alike, but they're identical,' Farrokh explained.

'It's not the best time for you to have a twin in Bombay,' Detective Patel told the actor.

'Don't worry – the twin is totally out of it. A missionary!' Farrokh declared.

'God help us,' Nancy said.

'Anyway, I'm taking the twin out of town for a couple of days – at least overnight,' Dr Daruwalla told them. The doctor started to explain about the children and the circus, but no one was interested.

'The ladies' room,' Nancy said to Dhar. 'Where is it?'

Dhar was about to take her arm when she walked past him untouched; he followed her to the foyer. Almost everyone in the dining room watched her walk – the woman who'd stood on a chair.

'It will be nice for you to get out of town for a couple of days,' the deputy commissioner said to Dr Daruwalla. Time to slip away, Farrokh was thinking; then he realized that even the moment of Nancy leaving the Ladies' Garden with Dhar had been planned.

'Was there something you wanted her to say to him, something only she could say – alone?' the doctor asked the detective.

'Oh, what a very good question,' Patel replied. 'You're learning, Doctor,' the deputy commissioner added. 'I'll bet you could write a better movie now.'

A Three-Dollar Bill?

In the foyer, Nancy said to Dhar, 'I've thought about you almost as much as I've thought about Rahul. Sometimes, you upset me more.'

'I never intended to upset you,' Dhar replied.

'What *have* you intended? What *do* you intend?' she asked him.

When he didn't answer her, Nancy asked him, 'How did you like lifting me? You're always carrying me. Do I feel heavier to you?'

'We're both a little heavier than we were,' Dhar answered cautiously.

'I weigh a ton, and you know it,' Nancy told him. 'But I'm not trash – I never was.'

'I never thought you were trash,' Dhar told her.

'You should never look at people the way you look at me,' Nancy said. He did it again; there was his sneer. 'That's what I mean,' she told him. 'I hate you for it – the way you make me feel. Later, after you've gone, it makes me keep thinking about you. I've thought about you for twenty years.' She was about three inches taller than the actor; when she reached out suddenly and touched his upper lip, he stopped sneering. 'That's better. Now say something,' Nancy told him. But Dhar was thinking about the dildo – if she still had it. He couldn't think of what to say. 'You know, you really should take some responsibility for the effect you have on people. Do you ever think about that?'

'I think about it all the time – I'm *supposed* to have an effect,' Dhar said finally. 'I'm an actor.'

'You sure are,' Nancy said. She could see him stop himself from shrugging; when he wasn't sneering, she liked his mouth more than she thought was possible. 'Do you *want* me? Do you ever think about *that*?' she asked him. She saw him thinking about what to say, so she didn't wait. 'You don't know how to read what *I* want, do you?' she asked him. 'You're going to have to be better than this with Rahul. You can't tell me what I want to hear because you don't really know if I want you, do you? You're going to have to read Rahul better than you can read me,' Nancy repeated.

'I can read you,' Dhar told her. 'I was just trying to be polite.'

'I don't believe you – you don't convince me,' Nancy

said. 'Bad acting,' she added, but she believed him.

In the ladies' room, when she washed her hands in the sink, Nancy saw the absurd faucet – the water flowing from the single spigot, which was an elephant's trunk. Nancy adjusted the degree of hot and cold water, first with one tusk, then the other. Twenty years ago, at the Hotel Bardez, not even four baths had made her feel clean; now Nancy felt unclean again. She was at least relieved to see that there was no winking eye; that much Rahul had imagined, with the help of many murdered women's navels.

She'd also noticed the pull-down platform on the inside of the toilet-stall door; the handle that lowered the shelf was a ring through an elephant's trunk. Nancy reflected on the psychology that had compelled Rahul to select one elephant and reject the other.

When Nancy returned to the Ladies' Garden, she offered only a matter-of-fact comment on her discovery of what she believed to be the source of inspiration for Rahul's belly drawings. The deputy commissioner and the doctor rushed off to the ladies' room to see the telltale elephant for themselves; their opportunity to view the Victorian faucet was delayed until the last woman had vacated the ladies' room. Even from a considerable distance – from the far side of the dining room – Mr Sethna was able to observe that Inspector Dhar and the woman with the obscene navel had nothing to say to each other, although they were left alone in the Ladies' Garden for an uncomfortable amount of time.

Later, in the car, Detective Patel spoke to Nancy – before they'd left the driveway of the Duckworth Club. 'I have to go back to headquarters, but I'll take you home first,' he told her.

'You should be more careful about what you ask me to do, Vijay,' Nancy said.

'I'm sorry, sweetie,' Patel replied. 'But I wanted to know your opinion. Can I trust him?' The deputy commissioner saw that his wife was about to cry again.

'You can trust *me*!' Nancy cried.

'I *know* I can trust you, sweetie,' Patel said. 'But what about *him*? Do you think he can do it?'

'He'll do anything you tell him, if he knows what you want,' Nancy answered.

'And you think Rahul will go for him?' her husband asked.

'Oh, yes,' she said bitterly.

'Dhar is a pretty cool customer!' said the detective admiringly.

'Dhar is as queer as a three-dollar bill,' Nancy told him.

Not being from Iowa, Detective Patel had some difficulty with the concept of how 'queer' a three-dollar bill was – not to mention that, in Bombay, they call a bill a note. 'You mean that he's gay – a homosexual?' her husband asked.

'No doubt about it. You can trust me,' Nancy repeated. They were almost home before she spoke again. 'A *very* cool customer,' she added.

'I'm sorry, sweetie,' said the deputy commissioner, because he saw that his wife couldn't stop crying.

'I *do* love you, Vijay,' she managed to say.

'I love you, *too*, sweetie,' the detective told her.

Just Some Old Attraction-Repulsion Kind of Thing

In the Ladies' Garden, the sun now slanted sideways through the latticework of the bower; the same shade of pinkness from the bougainvillea dappled the table-cloth, which Mr Sethna had brushed free of crumbs. It seemed to the old steward that Dhar and Dr Daruwalla would never leave the table. They'd long ago stopped talking about Rahul – or, rather, Mrs Dogar. For the moment, they were both more interested in Nancy.

'But exactly what do you think is *wrong* with her?' Farrokh asked John D.

'It appears that the events of the last twenty years have had a strong effect on her,' Dhar answered.

'Oh, elephant shit!' cried Dr Daruwalla. 'Can't you just once say what you're really feeling?'

'Okay,' Dhar replied. 'It appears that she and her husband are a real couple . . . very much in love, and all of that.'

'Yes, that does appear to be the main thing about them,' the doctor agreed. But Farrokh realized that this observation didn't greatly interest him; after all, he was still very much in love with Julia and he'd been married longer than Detective Patel. 'But what was happening between the two of you – between you and her?' the doctor asked Dhar.

'It was just some old attraction-repulsion kind of thing,' John D. answered evasively.

'The next thing you'll tell me is that the world is round,' Farrokh said, but the actor merely shrugged. Suddenly, it was not Rahul (or Mrs Dogar) who frightened Dr Daruwalla; it was *Dhar* the doctor was afraid of, and only because Dr Daruwalla felt that he didn't really know Dhar – not even after all these years. As before – because he felt that something unpleasant was pending – Farrokh thought of the circus; yet when he mentioned again his upcoming journey to Junagadh, he saw that John D. still wasn't interested.

'You probably think it's doomed to fail – just another save-the-children project,' said Dr Daruwalla. 'Like coins in a wishing well, like pebbles in the sea.'

'It sounds as if *you* think it's doomed to fail,' Dhar told him.

It was truly time to slip away, the doctor thought. Then Dr Daruwalla spotted the Hawaiian shirt in the paper bag; Detective Patel had left the package under his chair. Both men were standing, ready to leave, when the doctor pulled the loud shirt out of the bag.

'Well, look at that. The deputy commissioner actually forgot something. How uncharacteristic,' John D. remarked.

'I doubt that he forgot it. I think he wanted you to have it,' Dr Daruwalla said. Impulsively, the doctor held up the riotous display of parrots in palm trees; there were flowers, too – red and orange and yellow against a jungle of impossible green. Farrokh placed the shoulders of the shirt against Dhar's shoulders. 'It's the right size for you,' the doctor observed. 'Are you sure you don't want it?'

'I have all the shirts I need,' the actor told him. 'Give it to my fucking twin.'

601

21. ESCAPING MAHARASHTRA

Ready for Rabies

This time, Julia found him in the morning with his face pressing a pencil against the glass-topped table in the dining room. An ongoing title search was evident from Farrokh's last jottings. There was *Lion Piss* (crossed out, blessedly) and *Raging Hormones* (also crossed out, she was happy to see), but the one that appeared to have pleased the screenwriter before he fell asleep was circled. As a movie title, Julia had her doubts about it. It was *Limo Roulette*, which reminded Julia of one of those French films that defy common sense – even when one manages to read every word of the subtitles.

But this was far too busy a morning for Julia to take the time to read the new pages. She woke up Farrokh by blowing in his ear; while he was in the bathtub, she made his tea. She'd already packed his toilet articles and a change of clothes, and she'd teased her husband about his habit of taking with him a medical-emergency kit of an elaborately paranoid nature; after all, he was going to be away only one night.

But Dr Daruwalla never traveled anywhere in India without bringing with him certain precautionary items: erythromycin, the preferred antibiotic for bronchitis; Lomotil, for diarrhea. He even carried a kit of surgical instruments, including sutures and iodophor gauze – and both an antibiotic powder and an ointment. In the usual weather, infection thrived in the simplest wound. And the doctor would never travel without a sample selection of condoms, which he freely dispensed without invitation. Indian men were renowned for not using condoms. All Dr Daruwalla had to do was meet a man who so much as joked about prostitutes; in the doctor's mind, this amounted to a confession. 'Here – next time try one of these,' Dr Daruwalla would say.

The doctor also toted with him a half-dozen sterile disposable needles and syringes – just in case anyone needed any kind of shot. At a circus, people were always being bitten by dogs and monkeys. Someone had told Dr Daruwalla that rabies was endemic among chimpanzees. For this trip, especially, Farrokh brought along three starter-doses of rabies vaccine, together with three 10mL vials of human rabies immune globulin. Both the vaccine and the immune globulin required refrigeration, but for a journey of less than 48 hours a thermos with ice would be sufficient.

'Are you expecting to be bitten by something?' Julia had asked him.

'I was thinking of the new missionary,' Farrokh had replied; for he believed that, if *he* were a rabid chimpanzee at the Great Blue Nile, he would certainly be inclined to bite Martin Mills. Yet Julia knew that he'd packed enough vaccine and immune globulin to treat himself and the missionary and both children – just in case a rabid chimpanzee attacked them all.

Lucky Day

In the morning, the doctor longed to read and revise the new pages of his screenplay, but there was too much to do. The elephant boy had sold all the clothes that Martin Mills had bought for him on Fashion Street. Julia had anticipated this; she'd bought the ungrateful little wretch more clothes. It was a struggle to get Ganesh to take a bath – at first because he wanted to do nothing but ride in the elevator, and then because he'd never been in a building with a balcony overlooking Marine Drive; all he wanted to do was stare at the view. Ganesh also objected to wearing a sandal on his good foot, and even Julia doubted the

603

wisdom of concealing the mangled foot in a clean white sock; the sock wouldn't stay clean or white for long. As for the lone sandal, Ganesh complained that the strap across the top of his foot hurt him so much, he could scarcely walk.

When the doctor had kissed Julia good-bye, he steered the disgruntled boy to Vinod's waiting taxi; there, in the front seat beside the dwarf, was the sullen Madhu. She was irritated by Dr Daruwalla's difficulty in understanding her languages. She had to try both Marathi and Hindi before the doctor understood that Madhu was displeased with the way Vinod had dressed her; Deepa had told the dwarf how to dress the girl.

'I'm not a child,' the former child prostitute said, although it was clear that it had been Deepa's intention to make the little whore *look* like a child.

'The circus wants you to look like a child,' Dr Daruwalla told Madhu, but the girl pouted; nor did she respond to Ganesh in a sisterly fashion.

Madhu glanced briefly, and with disgust, at the boy's viscid eyes; there was a film of tetracycline ointment, which had been recently applied – it tended to give Ganesh's eyes a glazed quality. The boy would need to continue the medication for a week or more before his eyes looked normal. 'I thought they were fixing your eyes,' Madhu said cruelly; she spoke in Hindi. It had been Farrokh's impression, when he'd been alone with Madhu or alone with Ganesh, that both children endeavored to speak English; now that the kids were together, they lapsed into Hindi and Marathi. At best, the doctor spoke Hindi tentatively – and Marathi hardly at all.

'It's important that you behave like a brother and sister,' Farrokh reminded them, but the cripple's mood was as sulky as Madhu's.

'If she were my sister, I'd beat her up,' Ganesh said.

'Not with that foot, you wouldn't,' Madhu told him.

'Now, now,' said Dr Daruwalla; he'd decided to

speak English because he was almost certain that Madhu, as well as Ganesh, could understand him, and he presumed that in English he commanded more authority. 'This is your lucky day,' he told them.

'What's a lucky day?' Madhu asked the doctor.

'It doesn't mean anything,' Ganesh said.

'It's just an expression,' Dr Daruwalla admitted, 'but it does mean something. It means that today it is your good fortune to be leaving Bombay, to be going to the circus.'

'So you mean that *we're* lucky – not the day,' the elephant-footed boy replied.

'It's too soon to say if we're lucky,' said the child prostitute.

On that note, they arrived at St Ignatius, where the single-minded missionary had been waiting for them. Martin Mills climbed into the back seat of the Ambassador, an air of boundless enthusiasm surrounding him. 'This is your lucky day!' the zealot announced to the children.

'We've been through that,' said Dr Daruwalla. It was only 7:30 on a Saturday morning.

Out of Place at the Taj

It was 8:30 when they arrived at the terminal for domestic flights in Santa Cruz, where they were told that their flight to Rajkot would be delayed until the end of the day.

'Indian Airlines!' Dr Daruwalla exclaimed.

'At least they are admitting it,' Vinod said.

Dr Daruwalla decided that they could wait somewhere more comfortable than the Santa Cruz terminal. But before Farrokh could usher them all back inside the dwarf's taxi, Martin Mills had wandered off and bought the morning newspaper; on their way back to Bombay, in rush-hour traffic, the missionary treated them to snippets from *The Times of India*. It would be

10:30 before they arrived at the Taj. (It was Dr Daruwalla's eccentric decision that they should wait for their flight to Rajkot in the lobby of the Taj Mahal Hotel.)

'Listen to this,' Martin began. ' "Two brothers stabbed . . . The police have arrested one assailant while two other accused are absconding on a scooter in a rash manner." An unexpected use of the present tense, not to mention "rash," ' the English teacher observed. 'Not to mention "absconding." '

' "Absconding" is a very popular word here,' Farrokh explained.

'Sometimes it is the police who are absconding,' Ganesh said.

'What did he say?' the missionary asked.

'When a crime happens, often the police abscond,' Farrokh replied. 'They're embarrassed that they couldn't prevent the crime, or that they can't catch the criminal, so they run away.' But Dr Daruwalla was thinking that this pattern of behavior didn't apply to Detective Patel. According to John D., the deputy commissioner intended to spend the day in the actor's suite at the Oberoi, rehearsing the best way to approach Rahul. It hurt Farrokh's feelings that he'd not been invited to participate, or that they hadn't offered to hold up the rehearsal until the screenwriter returned from the circus; after all, there would be dialogue to imagine and to compose, and although dialogue wasn't part of the doctor's day job, it was at least his other business.

'Let me be sure that I understand this,' Martin Mills said. 'Sometimes, when there's a crime, both the criminals *and* the police are "absconding." '

'Quite so,' replied Dr Daruwalla. He was unaware that he'd borrowed this expression from Detective Patel. The screenwriter was distracted by pride; he was thinking how clever he'd been, for he'd already made similar disrespectful use of *The Times of India* in his screenplay. (The fictional Mr Martin is always reading

606

something stupid aloud to the fictional children.)

Life imitates art, Farrokh was thinking, when Martin Mills announced, 'Here's a refreshingly frank opinion.' Martin had found the Opinion section of *The Times of India*; he was reading one of the letters. 'Listen to this,' the missionary said. ' "Our culture will have to be changed. It should start in primary schools by teaching boys not to urinate in the open." '

'Catch them young, in other words,' said Dr Daruwalla.

Then Ganesh said something that made Madhu laugh.

'What did he say?' Martin asked Farrokh.

'He said there's no place to pee *except* in the open,' Dr Daruwalla replied.

Then Madhu said something that Ganesh clearly approved of.

'What did *she* say?' the missionary asked.

'She said she prefers to pee in parked cars – particularly at night,' the doctor told him.

When they arrived at the Taj, Madhu's mouth was full of betel juice; the blood-red spittle overflowed the corners of her mouth.

'No betel chewing in the Taj,' the doctor said. The girl spat the lurid mess on the front tire of Vinod's taxi; both the dwarf and the Sikh doorman observed, with disgust, how the stain extended into the circular driveway. 'You won't be allowed any paan at the circus,' the doctor reminded Madhu.

'We're not at the circus yet,' said the sullen little whore.

The circular driveway was overcrowded with taxis and an array of expensive-looking vehicles. The elephant-footed boy said something to Madhu, who was amused.

'What did he say?' the missionary asked Dr Daruwalla.

'He said there are lots of cars to pee in,' the doctor replied. Then he overhead Madhu telling Ganesh that she'd been in a car like one of the expensive-looking cars before; it didn't sound like an empty boast, but Farrokh resisted the temptation to translate this information for the Jesuit. As much as Dr Daruwalla enjoyed shocking Martin Mills, it seemed prurient to speculate on what a child prostitute had been doing in such an expensive-looking car.

'What did Madhu say?' Martin asked Farrokh.

'She said she would use the ladies' room, instead,' Dr Daruwalla lied.

'Good for you!' Martin told the girl. When she parted her lips to smile at him, her teeth were brightly smeared from the paan; it was as if her gums were bleeding. The doctor hoped that it was only his imagination that he saw something lewd in Madhu's smile. When they entered the lobby, Dr Daruwalla didn't like the way the doorman followed Madhu with his eyes; the Sikh seemed to know that she wasn't the sort of girl who was permitted at the Taj. No matter how Deepa had told Vinod to dress her, Madhu didn't look like a child.

Ganesh was already shivering from the air-conditioning; the cripple looked anxious, as if he thought the Sikh doormen might throw him out. The Taj was no place for a beggar and a child prostitute, Dr Daruwalla was thinking; it was a mistake to have brought them here.

'We'll just have some tea,' Farrokh assured the children. 'We'll keep checking on the plane,' the doctor told the missionary. Like Madhu and Ganesh, Martin appeared overwhelmed by the opulence of the lobby. In the few minutes it took Dr Daruwalla to arrange for special treatment from the assistant manager, some lesser official among the hotel staff had already asked the Jesuit and the children to leave. When that misunderstanding was cleared up, Vinod appeared in the lobby with the paper bag containing the Hawaiian shirt. The dwarf was dutifully observing, without comment, what he thought were Inspector Dhar's delusions – namely, that the famous actor was a Jesuit missionary in training to be a priest. Dr Daruwalla had meant to give the Hawaiian shirt to Martin Mills, but the doctor had forgotten the bag in the dwarf's taxi. (Not just any taxi-walla would have been permitted in the lobby of the Taj, but Vinod was known as Inspector Dhar's driver.)

When Farrokh presented the Hawaiian shirt to Martin Mills, the missionary was excited.

'Oh, it's wonderful!' the zealot cried. 'I used to have one just like it!'

'Actually, this is the one you used to have,' Farrokh admitted.

'No, no,' Martin whispered. 'The shirt I used to have was stolen from me – one of those prostitutes took it.'

'The prostitute gave it back,' Dr Daruwalla whispered.

'She *did*? Why, that's remarkable!' said Martin Mills. 'Was she contrite?'

'*He*, not she,' said Dr Daruwalla. 'No – he wasn't contrite, I think.'

'What do you mean? *He* . . .' the missionary said.

'I mean that the prostitute was a *him*, not a her,' the doctor told Martin Mills. 'He was a eunuch-transvestite – all of them were men. Well, *sort* of men.'

'What do you mean? *Sort of* . . .' the missionary said.

'They're called hijras – they've been emasculated,' the doctor whispered. A typical surgeon, Dr Daruwalla liked to describe the procedure in exact detail – including the cauterizing of the wound with hot oil, and not forgetting that part of the female anatomy which the puckered scar resembled when it healed.

When Martin Mills came back from the men's room, he was wearing the Hawaiian shirt, the brilliant colors of which were a contrast to his pallor. Farrokh assumed that the paper bag now contained the shirt that the missionary had been wearing, upon which poor Martin had been sick.

'It's a good thing that we're getting these children

out of this city,' the zealot gravely told the doctor, who once more happily entertained the notion that life was imitating art. Now, if only the fool would shut up so that the screenwriter could read over his new pages!

Dr Daruwalla knew that they couldn't spend the whole day at the Taj. The children were already restless. Madhu might proposition stray guests at the hotel, and the elephant boy would probably steal something – those silver trinkets from the souvenir shop, the doctor supposed. Dr Daruwalla didn't dare leave the children with Martin Mills while he phoned Ranjit to check his messages; he wasn't expecting any messages, anyway – nothing but emergencies happened on Saturday, and the doctor wasn't on call this weekend.

The girl's posture further upset Farrokh; Madhu more than slouched in the soft chair – she lolled. Her dress was hiked up nearly to her hips and she stared into the eyes of every man who passed. This certainly detracted from her looking like a child. Worse, Madhu seemed to be wearing perfume; she smelled a little like Deepa to Dr Daruwalla. (Doubtless Vinod had allowed the girl some access to Deepa's things, and Madhu had liked the perfume that the dwarf's wife wore.) Also, the doctor believed that the air-conditioning at the Taj was too comfortable – in fact, it was too cold. At the Government Circuit House in Junagadh, where Dr Daruwalla had arranged for them all to spend the night, there wouldn't be any air-conditioning – just ceiling fans – and in the circus, where the children would spend the following night (and every night thereafter), there would be only tents. No ceiling fans . . . and probably the mosquito netting would be in disrepair. Every second they stayed in the lobby of the Taj, Dr Daruwalla realized that he was making it harder for the children to adjust to the Great Blue Nile.

Then a most irksome thing happened. A messenger boy was paging Inspector Dhar. The method for paging at the Taj was rudimentary; some thought it quaint. The messenger tramped through the lobby with a chalkboard that dangled brass chimes, treating everyone in the lobby to an insistent dinging. The messenger boy, who thought that he'd recognized Inspector Dhar, stopped in front of Martin Mills and shook the board with its incessant chimes. Chalked on the board was MR DHAR.

'Wrong man,' Dr Daruwalla told the messenger boy, but the boy continued to shake the chimes. 'Wrong man, you moron!' the doctor shouted. But the boy was no moron; he wouldn't leave without a tip. Once he got it, he strolled casually away, still chiming. Farrokh was furious.

'We're going now,' he said abruptly.

'Going where?' Madhu asked him.

'To the circus?' asked Ganesh.

'No, not yet – we're just going somewhere else,' the doctor informed them.

'Aren't we comfortable here?' the missionary asked.

'*Too* comfortable,' Dr Daruwalla replied.

'Actually, a tour of Bombay would be nice – for me,' the scholastic said. 'I realize the rest of you are familiar with the city, but possibly there's something you wouldn't mind showing me. Public gardens, perhaps. I also like marketplaces.'

Not a great idea, Farrokh knew – to be dragging Dhar's twin through public places. Dr Daruwalla was thinking that he could take them all to the Duckworth Club for lunch. It was certain that they wouldn't run into Dhar at the Taj, because John D. was rehearsing with Detective Patel at the Oberoi; it was therefore likely that they wouldn't run into John D. at the club, either. As for the outside chance that they might encounter Rahul, it didn't bother Dr Daruwalla to contemplate having another look at the second Mrs Dogar; the doctor would do nothing to arouse her suspicions. But it was too early to go to lunch at the Duckworth Club, and he had to phone for a reservation; without one, Mr Sethna would be rude to them.

Back in the Ambassador, the doctor instructed Vinod to drive them to the Asiatic Society Library, opposite Horniman Circle; this was one of those oases in the teeming city – not unlike the Duckworth Club or St Ignatius – where the doctor was hoping that Dhar's twin would be safe. Dr Daruwalla was a member of the Asiatic Society Library; he'd often dozed in the cool, high-ceilinged reading rooms. The larger-than-life statues of literary geniuses had barely noticed the screenwriter's quiet ascending and descending of the magnificent staircase.

'I'm taking you to the grandest library in Bombay,' Dr Daruwalla told Martin Mills. 'Almost a million books! Almost as many bibliophiles!'

Meanwhile, the doctor told Vinod to drive the children 'around and around.' He also told the dwarf that it was important not to let the kids out of the car. They liked riding in the Ambassador, anyway – the anonymity of cruising the city, the secrecy of staring at the passing world. Madhu and Ganesh were unfamiliar with taxi riding; they stared at everyone as if they themselves were invisible – as if the dwarf's crude Ambassador were equipped with one-way windows. Dr Daruwalla wondered if this was because they knew they were safe with Vinod; they'd never been safe before.

The doctor had caught just a departing glimpse of the children's faces. At that moment, they'd looked frightened – frightened of what? It certainly wasn't that they feared they were being abandoned with a dwarf; they weren't afraid of Vinod. No; on their faces Farrokh had seen a greater anxiety – that the circus they were supposedly being delivered to was only a dream, that they would never get out of Bombay.

Escaping Maharashtra: it suddenly struck him as a better title than *Limo Roulette*. But maybe not, Farrokh thought.

'I'm quite fond of bibliophiles,' Martin Mills was saying as they climbed the stairs. For the first time, Dr Daruwalla was aware of how loudly the scholastic spoke; the zealot was too loud for a library.

'There are over eight hundred thousand volumes here,' Farrokh whispered. 'This includes ten thousand manuscripts!'

'I'm glad we're alone for a moment,' the missonary said in a voice that rattled the wrought iron of the loggia.

'*Ssshhh!*' the doctor hissed. The marble statues frowned down upon them; 80 or 90 of the library staffers had long ago assumed the frowning air of the statuary, and Dr Daruwalla foresaw that the zealot with his booming voice would soon be rebuked by one of the slipper-clad, scolding types who scurried through the musty recesses of the Asiatic Society Library. To avoid a confrontation, the doctor steered the scholastic into a reading room with no one in it.

The ceiling fan had snagged the string that turned the fan on and off, and only the slight ticking of the string against the blades disturbed the silence of the moldering air. The dusty books sagged on the carved teak shelves; numbered cartons of manuscripts were stacked against the bookcases; wide-bottomed, leather-padded chairs surrounded an oval table that was strewn with pencils and pads of notepaper. Only one of these chairs was on castors; it was tilted, for it was four-legged and had only three castors – the missing castor, like a paperweight, held down one of the pads of notepaper.

The American zealot, as if compelled by his countrymen's irritating instinct to appear handy with all things, instantly undertook the task of repairing the broken chair. There were a half-dozen other chairs that the doctor and the missionary could have sat in, and Dr Daruwalla suspected that the chair with the detached castor had probably maintained its disabled condition, untouched, for the last 10 or 20 years; perhaps the

613

chair had been partially destroyed in celebration of Independence – more than 40 years ago! Yet here was this fool, determined to make it right. Is there no place in town I can take this idiot? Farrokh wondered. Before the doctor could stop the zealot, Martin Mills had upended the chair on the oval table, where it made a loud thump.

'Come on – you must tell me,' the missionary said. 'I'm dying to hear the story of your conversion. Naturally, the Father Rector has told me about it.'

Naturally, Dr Daruwalla thought; Father Julian had doubtless made the doctor come off as a deluded, false convert. Then, suddenly, to Farrokh's surprise, the missionary produced a knife! It was one of those Swiss Army knives that Dhar liked so much – a kind of toolbox unto itself. With something that resembled a leather-punch, the Jesuit was boring a hole into the leg of the chair. The rotting wood fell on the table.

'It just needs a new screw hole,' Martin exclaimed. 'I can't believe no one knew how to fix it.'

'I suppose people just sat in the other chairs,' Dr Daruwalla suggested. While the scholastic wrestled with the chair leg, the nasty little tool on the knife suddenly snapped closed, neatly removing a hunk of Martin's index finger. The Jesuit bled profusely onto a pad of notepaper.

'Now, look, you've cut yourself . . .' Dr Daruwalla began.

'It's nothing,' the zealot said, but it was evident that the chair was beginning to make the man of God angry. 'I want to hear your story. Come on. I know how it starts . . . you're in Goa, aren't you? You've just gone to visit the sainted remains of our Francis Xavier . . . what's left of him. And you go to sleep thinking of that pilgrim who bit off St Francis's toe.'

'I went to sleep thinking of nothing at all!' Farrokh insisted, his voice rising.

'*Ssshhh!* This is a library,' the missionary reminded Dr Daruwalla.

'I *know* it's a library!' the doctor cried – too loudly, for they weren't alone. At first unseen but now emerging from a pile of manuscripts was an old man who'd been sleeping in a corner chair; it was another chair on castors, for it wheeled their way. Its disagreeable rider, who'd been roused from the depths of whatever sleep his reading material had sunk him into, was wearing a Nehru jacket, which (like his hands) was gray from transmitted newsprint.

'*Ssshhh!*' the older reader said. Then he wheeled back into his corner of the room.

'Maybe we should find another place to discuss my conversion,' Farrokh whispered to Martin Mills.

'I'm going to fix this chair,' the Jesuit replied. Now bleeding onto the chair and the table *and* the pad of notepaper, Martin Mills jammed the rebellious castor into the inverted chair leg; with another dangerous-looking tool, a stubby screwdriver, he struggled to affix the castor to the chair. 'So . . . you went to sleep . . . your mind an absolute blank, or so you're telling me. And then what?'

'I dreamt I was St Francis's corpse . . .' Dr Daruwalla began.

'Body dreams, very common,' the zealot whispered.

'*Ssshhh!*' said the old man in the Nehru jacket, from the corner.

'I dreamt that the crazed pilgrim was biting off my toe!' Farrokh hissed.

'You *felt* this?' Martin asked.

'Of *course* I felt it!' hissed the doctor.

'But corpses don't feel, do they?' the scolastic said. 'Oh, well . . . so you *felt* the bite, and then?'

'When I woke up, my toe was *throbbing*. I couldn't stand on that foot, much less walk! And there were bite marks – not broken skin, mind you, but actual teeth marks! Those marks were *real*! The *bite* was real!' Farrokh insisted.

'Of course it was real,' the missionary said. 'Something real bit you. What could it have been?'

615

'I was on a balcony – I was in the *air*!' Farrokh whispered hoarsely.

'Try to keep it down,' the Jesuit whispered. 'Are you telling me that this balcony was utterly unapproachable?'

'Through locked doors ... where my wife and children were asleep ...' Farrokh began.

'Ah, the *children*!' Martin Mills cried out. 'How old were they?'

'I wasn't bitten by my own children!' Dr Daruwalla hissed.

'Children *do* bite, from time to time – or as a prank,' the missionary replied. 'I've heard that children go through actual *biting ages* – when they're especially prone to bite.'

'I suppose my wife could have been hungry, too,' Farrokh said sarcastically.

'There were no trees around the balcony?' Martin Mills asked; he was now both bleeding and sweating over the stubborn chair.

'I see it coming,' Dr Daruwalla said. 'Father Julian's monkey theory. Biting apes, swinging from vines – is that what you think?'

'The point is, you were *really* bitten, weren't you?' the Jesuit asked him. 'People get so confused about miracles. The miracle wasn't that something bit you. The miracle is that you believe! Your *faith* is the miracle. It hardly matters that it was something ... common that triggered it.'

'What happened to my toe wasn't *common*!' the doctor cried.

The old reader in the Nehru jacket shot out of his corner on his chair on castors. '*Ssshhh!*' the old man hissed.

'Are you trying to read or trying to *sleep*?' the doctor shouted at the old gentleman.

'Come on – you're disturbing him. He was here first,' Martin Mills told Dr Daruwalla. 'Look!' the scholastic said to the old man, as if the angry reader were a child.

'See this chair? I've fixed it. Want to try it?' The missionary set the chair on all four castors and rolled it back and forth. The gentleman in the Nehru jacket eyed the zealot warily.

'He has his own chair, for God's sake,' Farrokh said.

'Come on – give it a try!' the missionary urged the old reader.

'I have to find a telephone,' Dr Daruwalla pleaded with the zealot. 'I should make a reservation for lunch. And we should stay with the children – they're probably bored.' But, to his dismay, the doctor saw that Martin Mills was staring up at the ceiling fan; the tangled string had caught the handyman's eye.

'That string is annoying – if you're trying to read,' the scholastic said. He climbed up on the oval table, which accepted his weight reluctantly.

'You'll break the table,' the doctor warned him.

'I won't break the table – I'm thinking of fixing the fan,' Martin Mills replied. Slowly and awkwardly, the Jesuit went from kneeling to standing.

'I can see what you're thinking – you're crazy!' Dr Daruwalla said.

'Come on – you're just angry about your miracle,' the missionary said. 'I'm not trying to take your miracle away from you. I'm only trying to make you see the *real* miracle. It is simply that you believe – not the silly thing that made you believe. The biting was only a vehicle.'

'The *biting* was the miracle!' Dr Daruwalla cried.

'No, no – that's where you're wrong,' Martin Mills managed to say, just before the table collapsed under him. Falling, he reached for – and fortunately missed – the fan. The gentleman in the Nehru jacket was the most astonished; when Martin Mills fell, the old reader was cautiously trying out the newly repaired chair. The collapse of the table and the missonary's cry of alarm sent the old man scrambling. The chair leg with the freshly bored hole rejected the castor. While both the old reader and the Jesuit lay on the floor, Dr

Daruwalla was left to calm down the outraged library staffer who'd shuffled into the reading room in his slippers.

'We were just leaving,' Dr Daruwalla told the librarian. 'It's too noisy here to concentrate on anything at all!'

Sweating and bleeding and limping, the missionary followed Farrokh down the grand staircase, under the frowning statues. To relax himself, Dr Daruwalla was chanting, 'Life imitates art. Life imitates art.'

'What's that you say?' asked Martin Mills.

'*Ssshhh!*' the doctor told him. 'This is a library.'

'Don't be angry about your miracle,' the zealot said.

'It was long ago. I don't think I believe in anything anymore,' Farrokh replied.

'Don't say that!' the missionary cried.

'*Ssshhh!*' Farrokh whispered to him.

'I know, I know,' said Martin Mills. 'This is a library.'

It was almost noon. Outside, in the glaring sunlight, they stared into the street without seeing the taxi that was parked at the curb. Vinod had to walk up to them; the dwarf led them to the car as if they were blind. Inside the Ambassador, the children were crying. They were sure that the circus was a myth or a hoax.

'No, no – it's real,' Dr Daruwalla assured them. 'We're going there, we really are – it's just that the plane is delayed.' But what did Madhu or Ganesh know about airplanes? The doctor assumed that they'd never flown; flying would be another terror for them. And when the children saw that Martin Mills was bleeding, they were worried that there'd been some violence. 'Only to a chair,' Farrokh said. He was angry at himself, for in the confusion he'd forgotten to reserve his favorite table in the Ladies' Garden. He knew that Mr Sethna would find a way to abuse him for this oversight.

618

A Misunderstanding at the Urinal

As punishment, Mr Sethna had given the doctor's table
to Mr and Mrs Kohinoor and Mrs Kohinoor's noisy,
unmarried sister. The latter woman was so shrill, not
even the bower of flowers in the Ladies' Garden could
absorb her whinnies or brays. Probably on purpose,
Mr Sethna had seated Dr Daruwalla's party at a table in
a neglected corner of the garden, where the waiters
either ignored you or failed to see you from their
stations in the dining room. A torn vine of the bougainvillea hung down from the bower and brushed the
back of Dr Daruwalla's neck like a claw. The good
news was it wasn't Chinese Day. Madhu and Ganesh
orderd vegetarian kabobs; the vegetables were broiled
or grilled on skewers. It was a dish that children
sometimes ate with their fingers. While the doctor
hoped that Madhu's and Ganesh's unfamiliarity with
knives and forks would go unnoticed, Mr Sethna
speculated on whose children they were.

The old steward observed that the cripple had
kicked his one sandal off; the calluses on the sole of
the boy's good foot were as thick as a beggar's. The
foot the elephant had stepped on was still concealed
by the sock, which was already gray-brown, and it
didn't fool Mr Sethna, who could tell that the hidden
foot was oddly flattened – the boy had limped on his
heel. On the ball of the bad foot, the sock was still
mostly white.

As for the girl, the steward detected something
lascivious in her posture; furthermore, Mr Sethna
concluded that Madhu had never been in a restaurant
before – she stared too openly at the waiters. Dr
Daruwalla's grandchildren would have been better
behaved than this; and although Inspector Dhar had
proclaimed to the press that he would sire only Indian
babies, these children bore no resemblance to the
famous actor.

As for the actor, he looked *awful*, Mr Sethna

thought. Possibly he'd forgotten to wear his makeup. Inspector Dhar looked pale and in need of sleep; his gaudy shirt was outrageous, there was blood on his pants and overnight his physique had deteriorated – he must be suffering from acute diarrhea, the old steward determined. How else does one manage to lose 15 or 20 pounds in a day? And had the actor's head been shaved by muggers, or was his hair falling out? On second thought, Mr Sethna suspected that Dhar was the victim of a sexually transmitted disease. In a sick culture, where movie actors were revered as demigods, a lifestyle contagion was to be expected. That will bring the bastard down to earth, Mr Sethna thought. Maybe Inspector Dhar has AIDS! The old steward was sorely tempted to place an anonymous phone call to *Stardust* or *Cine Blitz*; surely either of these film-gossip magazines would be intrigued by such a rumor.

'I wouldn't marry him if he owned the Queen's Necklace and he offered me *half*!' cried Mrs Kohinoor's unmarried sister. 'I wouldn't marry him if he gave me all of *London*!'

If you were *in* London, I could still hear you, thought Dr Daruwalla. He picked at his pomfret; the fish at the Duckworth Club was unfailingly overcooked – Farrokh wondered why he'd ordered it. He envied how Martin Mills attacked his meat kabobs. The meat kept falling out of the flatbread; because Martin had stripped the skewers and tried to make a sandwich, the missionary's hands were covered with chopped onions. A dark-green flag of mint leaf was stuck between the zealot's upper front teeth. As a polite way of suggesting that the Jesuit take a look at himself in a mirror, Farrokh said, 'You might want to use the men's room here, Martin. It's more comfortable than the facilities at the airport.'

Throughout lunch, Dr Daruwalla couldn't stop glancing at his watch, even though Vinod had called Indian Airlines repeatedly; the dwarf predicted a late-afternoon departure at the earliest. They were in no hurry. The doctor had called his office only to learn that there were no messages of any importance; there'd been just one call for him, and Ranjit had handled the matter competently. Mr Garg had phoned for the mailing address, in Junagadh, of the Great Blue Nile Circus; Garg had told Ranjit that he wanted to send Madhu a letter. It was odd that Mr Garg hadn't asked Vinod or Deepa for the address, for the doctor had obtained the address from the dwarf's wife. It was odder still how Garg imagined that Madhu could read a letter, or even a postcard; Madhu couldn't read. But the doctor guessed that Mr Garg was euphoric to learn that Madhu was *not* HIV-positive; maybe the creep wanted to send the poor child a thank-you note, or merely give her good-luck wishes.

Now, short of telling him that he wore a mint leaf on his front teeth, there seemed no way to compel Martin Mills to visit the men's room. The scholastic took the children to the card room; there he tried in vain to teach them crazy eights. Soon the cards were speckled with blood; the zealot's index finger was still bleeding. Rather than unearth his medical supplies from his suitcase, which was in the Ambassador – besides, the doctor had packed nothing as simple as a Band-Aid – Farrokh asked Mr Sethna for a small bandage. The old steward delivered the Band-Aid to the card room with characteristic scorn and inappropriate ceremony; he presented the bandage to Martin Mills on the silver serving tray, which the steward extended at arm's length. Dr Daruwalla took this occasion to tell the Jesuit, 'You should probably wash that wound in the men's room – *before* you bandage it.'

But Martin Mills washed and bandaged his finger without once looking in the mirror above the sink, or in the full-length mirror – except at some distance, and only to appraise his lost-and-found Hawaiian shirt. The missionary never spotted the mint leaf on his

621

teeth. He did, however, notice a tissue dispenser near the flush handle for the urinal, and he noted further that every flush handle had a tissue dispenser in close proximity to it. These tissues, when used, were *not* carelessly deposited in the urinals; rather, there was a silver bucket at the end of the lineup of urinals, something like an ice bucket without ice, and the used tissues were deposited in it.

This system seemed exceedingly fastidious and ultra-hygienic to Martin Mills, who reflected that he'd never wiped his penis with a tissue before. The process of urinating was made to seem more important, certainly more solemn, by the expectation of wiping one's penis after the act. At least, this is what Martin Mills *assumed* the tissues were for. It troubled him that no other Duckworthians were urinating at any of the other urinals; therefore, he couldn't be *sure* of the purpose of the tissue dispensers. He was about to finish peeing as usual – that is, without wiping himself – when the unfriendly old steward who had presented the Jesuit with his Band-Aid entered the men's room. The silver serving tray was stuck in one armpit and rested against the forearm of the same arm, as if Mr Sethna were carrying a rifle.

Because someone was watching him, Martin Mills thought he should use a tissue. He tried to wipe himself as if he always completed a responsible act of urination in this fashion; but he was so unfamiliar with the process, the tissue briefly caught on the end of his penis and then fell into the urinal. What was the protocol in the case of such a mishap? Martin wondered. The steward's beady eyes were fastened on the Jesuit. As if inspired, Martin Mills seized several fresh tissues, and with these held between his bandaged index finger and his thumb, he plucked the lost tissue from the urinal. With a flourish, he deposited the bunch of tissues in the silver bucket, which tilted suddenly, and almost toppled; the missionary had to steady it with both hands. Martin tried to smile reassuringly to Mr

Sethna, but he realized that because he'd grabbed the silver bucket with both hands, he'd neglected to return his penis to his pants. Maybe this was why the old steward looked away.

When Martin Mills had left the men's room, Mr Sethna gave the missionary's urinal a wide berth; the steward peed as far away as possible from where the diseased actor had peed. It was definitely a sexually transmitted disease, Mr Sethna thought. The steward had never witnessed such a grotesque example of urination. He couldn't imagine the medical necessity of dabbing one's penis every time one peed. The old steward didn't know for certain if there were other Duckworthians who made the same use of the tissue dispensers as Martin Mills had made. For years, Mr Sethna had assumed that the tissues were for wiping one's *fingers*. And now, after he'd wiped his fingers, Mr Sethna accurately deposited his tissue in the silver bucket, ruefully reflecting on the fate of Inspector Dhar. Once a demigod, now a terminal patient. For the first time since he'd poured hot tea on the head of that fop wearing the wig, the world struck Mr Sethna as fair and just.

In the card room, while Martin Mills had been experimenting at the urinal, Dr Daruwalla realized why the children had such difficulty in grasping crazy eights, or any other card game. No one had ever taught them their numbers; not only could they not read, they couldn't count. The doctor was holding up his fingers with the corresponding playing card – three fingers with the three of hearts – when Martin Mills returned from the men's room, still sporting the mint leaf on his front teeth.

Fear No Evil

Their plane to Rajkot took off at 5·10 in the afternoon, not quite eight hours after its scheduled departure. It was a tired-looking 737. The inscription on the fusel-age was legible but faded.

Dr Daruwalla quickly calculated that the plane had first been put in service in India in 1987. Where it had flown before then was anybody's guess.

Their departure was further delayed by the need of the petty officials to confiscate Martin Mill's Swiss Army knife – a potential terrorist's tool. The pilot would carry the 'weapon' in his pocket and hand it over to Martin in Rajkot.

'Well, I suppose I'll never see it again,' the mission-ary said; he didn't say this stoically, but more like a martyr.

Farrokh wasted no time in teasing him. 'It can't matter to you,' the doctor told him. 'You've taken a vow of poverty, haven't you?'

'I know what you think about my vows,' Martin replied. 'You think that, because I've accepted poverty, I must have no fondness for material things. This shirt, for example – my knife, my books. And you think that, because I've accepted chastity, I must be free of sexual desire. Well, I'll tell you: I resisted the commitment to become a priest not only because of how much I *did* like my few things, but also because I imagined I was in love. For ten years, I was smitten. I not only suffered from sexual desire; I'd embraced a sexual obsession. There was absolutely no getting this person out of my mind. Does this surprise you?'

'Yes, it does,' Dr Daruwalla admitted humbly. He was also afraid of what the lunatic might confess in front of the children, but Ganesh and Madhu were too enthralled with the airplane's preparations for takeoff to pay the slightest attention to the Jesuit's confession.

'I continued to teach at this wretched school – the students were delinquents, not scholars – and all because I had to test myself,' Martin Mills told Dr

624

Daruwalla. 'The object of my desire was there. Were I to leave, to run away, I would never have known if I had the strength to resist such a temptation. And so I stayed. I forced myself into the closest possible proximity to this person, only to see if I had the courage to withstand such an attraction. But I know what you think of priestly denial. You think that priests are people who simply don't feel these ordinary desires, or who feel them less strongly than you do.'

'I'm not judging you!' said Dr Daruwalla.

'Yes you are,' Martin replied. 'You think you know all about me.'

'This person that you were in love with . . .' the doctor began.

'It was another teacher at the school,' the missionary answered. 'I was crippled by desire. But I kept the object of my desire *this* close to me!' And here the zealot held his hand in front of his face. 'Eventually, the attraction lessened.'

'*Lessened?*' Farrokh repeated.

'Either the attraction went away or I overcame it,' said Martin Mills. 'Finally, I won.'

'*What* did you win?' Farrokh asked.

'Not freedom from desire,' the would-be priest declared. 'It is more like freedom from the fear of desire. Now I know I can resist it.'

'But what about *her*?' Dr Daruwalla asked.

'*Her?*' said Martin Mills.

'I mean, what were *her* feelings for *you*?' the doctor asked him. 'Did she even know how you felt about her?'

'*Him*,' the missionary replied. 'It was a *he*, not a she. Does that surprise you?'

'Yes, it does,' the doctor lied. What surprised him was how *un*surprised he was by the Jesuit's confession. The doctor was upset without understanding why; Farrokh felt greatly disturbed, without knowing the reason.

But the plane was taxiing, and even its lumbering

movement on the runway was sufficient to panic Madhu; she'd been sitting across the aisle from Dr Daruwalla and the missionary – now she wanted to move over and sit with the doctor. Ganesh was happily ensconced in the window seat. Awkwardly, Martin Mills changed places with Madhu; the Jesuit sat with the enraptured boy, and the child prostitute slipped into the aisle seat next to Farrokh.

'Don't be frightened,' the doctor told her.

'I don't want to go to the circus,' the girl said; she stared down the aisle, refusing to look out the windows. She wasn't alone in her inexperience; half the passengers appeared to be flying for the first time. One hand reached to adjust the flow of air; then 35 other hands were reaching. Despite the repeated announcement that carry-on baggage be stowed under the seats, the passengers insisted on piling their heavy bags on what the flight attendant kept calling the hat rack, although there were few hats on board. Perhaps the fault lay with the long delay, but there were many flies on board; they were treated with a vast indifference by the otherwise excited passengers. Someone was already vomiting, and they hadn't even taken off. At last, they took off.

The elephant boy believed *he* could fly. His animation appeared to be lifting the plane. The little beggar will ride a lion if they tell him to; he'll wrestle a tiger, Dr Daruwalla thought. How suddenly the doctor felt afraid for the cripple! Ganesh would climb to the top of the tent – the full 80 feet. Probably in compensation for his useless foot, the boy's hands and arms were exceptionally strong. What instincts will protect him? the doctor wondered, while in his arms he felt Madhu tremble; she was moaning. In her slight bosom, the beating of her heart throbbed against Farrokh's chest.

'If we crash, do we burn or fly apart in little pieces?' the girl asked him, her mouth against his throat.

'We *won't* crash, Madhu,' he told her.

'You don't know,' she replied. 'At the circus, I could

be eaten by a wild animal or I could fall. And what if they can't train me or if they beat me?'

'Listen to me,' said Dr Daruwalla. He was a father again. He remembered his daughters – their nightmares, their scrapes and bruises and their worst days at school. Their awful first boyfriends, who were beyond redemption. But the consequences for the crying girl in his arms were greater. 'Try to look at it this way,' the doctor said. 'You are *escaping*.' But he could say no more; he knew only what she was escaping – not what she was fleeing to. Out of the jaws of one kind of death, into the jaws of another . . . I hope not, was all the doctor thought.

'Something will get me,' Madhu replied. With her hot, shallow breathing against his neck, Farrokh instantly knew why Martin Mills's admission of homosexual desire had distressed him. If Dhar's twin was fighting against his sexual inclination, what was John D. doing?

Dr Duncan Frasier had convinced Dr Daruwalla that homosexuality was more a matter of biology than of conditioning. Frasier had once told Farrokh that there was a 52 percent chance that the identical twin of a gay male would also be gay. Furthermore, Farrokh's friend and colleague Dr Macfarlane had convinced him that homosexuality was immutable. ('If homosexuality is a learned behavior, how come it can't be *un*learned? Mac had said.)

But what upset Dr Daruwalla was *not* the doctor's sudden conviction that John D. must also be a homosexual; rather, it was all the years of John D.'s aloofness and the remoteness of his Swiss life. Neville, not Danny, must have been the twins' father, after all! And what does it say about *me* that John D. wouldn't tell me? the doctor wondered.

Instinctively (as if *she* were his beloved John D.), Farrokh hugged the girl. Later, he supposed that Madhu only did as she'd been taught to do; she hugged him back, but in an inappropriately wriggling fashion.

It shocked him; he pulled away from her when she began to kiss his throat.

'No, please . . .' he began to say.

Then the missionary spoke to him. Clearly, the elephant boy's delight with flying had delighted Martin Mills. 'Look at him! I'll bet he'd try to walk on the wing, if we told him it was safe!' the zealot said.

'Yes, I'll bet he would,' said Dr Daruwalla, whose gaze never left Madhu's face. The fear and confusion of the child prostitute were a mirror of Farrokh's feelings.

'What do you want?' the girl whispered to him.

'No, it's not what you think . . . I want you to *escape*,' the doctor told her. The concept meant nothing to her; she didn't respond. She continued to stare at him; in her eyes, trust still lingered with her confusion. At the blood-red edge of her lips, the unnatural redness once more overflowed her mouth; Madhu was eating paan again. Where she'd kissed Farrokh, his throat was marked with the lurid stain, as if a vampire had bitten him. He touched the mark and his fingertips came away with the color on them. The Jesuit saw him staring at his hand.

'Did you cut yourself?' Martin Mills asked.

'No, I'm fine,' Dr Daruwalla replied, but he wasn't. Farrokh was admitting to himself that he knew even less about desire than the would-be priest did.

Probably sensing his confusion, Madhu once more pressed herself against the doctor's chest. Once again, in a whisper, she asked him, 'What do you want?' It horrified the doctor to realize that Madhu was asking him a sexual question.

'I want you to be a child, because you *are* a child,' Farrokh told the girl. 'Please, won't you try to be a child?' There was such an eagerness in Madhu's smile that, for a moment, the doctor believed the girl had understood him. Quite like a child, she walked her fingers over his thigh; then, unlike a child, Madhu pressed her small palm firmly on Dr Daruwalla's penis. There'd been no groping for it; she'd known exactly where it was. Through the summer-weight material of his pants, the doctor felt the heat of Madhu's hand.

'I'll try what you want – anything you want,' the child prostitute told him. Instantly, Dr Daruwalla pulled her hand away.

'Stop that!' Farrokh cried.

'I want to sit with Ganesh,' the girl told him. Farrokh let her change seats with Martin Mills.

'There's a matter I've been pondering,' the missionary whispered to the doctor. 'You said we had two rooms for the night. Only two?'

'I suppose we could get more . . .' the doctor began. His legs were shaking.

'No, no – that's not what I'm getting at,' Martin said. 'I mean, were you thinking the children would share one room, and we'd share the other?'

'Yes,' Dr Daruwalla replied. He couldn't stop his legs from shaking.

'But – well, I know you'll think this is silly, *but* – it would seem prudent to me to not allow them to sleep together. I mean, not in the same room,' the missionary added. 'After all, there is the matter of what we can only guess has been the girl's orientation.'

'Her *what*?' the doctor asked. He could stop one leg from shaking, but not the other.

'Her sexual experience, I mean,' said Martin Mills. 'We must assume she's had some . . . sexual contact. What I mean is, what if Madhu is inclined to *seduce* Ganesh? Do you know what I mean?'

Dr Daruwalla knew very well what Martin Mills meant. 'You have a point,' was all the doctor said in reply.

'Well, then, suppose the boy and I take one room, and you and Madhu take the other? You see, I don't think the Father Rector would approve of someone in my position sharing a room with the girl,' Martin explained. 'It might seem contradictory to my vows.'

629

'Yes . . . your vows,' Farrokh replied. Finally, his other leg stopped shaking.

'Do you think I'm being totally silly?' the Jesuit asked the doctor. 'I suppose you think it's idiotic of me to suggest that Madhu might be so *inclined* – just because the poor child was . . . what she was.' But Farrokh could feel that he still had an erection, and Madhu had touched him so briefly.

'No, I think you're wise to be a little worried about her . . . inclination,' Dr Daruwalla answered. He spoke slowly because he was trying to remember the popular psalm. 'How does it go – the twenty-third psalm?' the doctor asked the scholastic. '"Yea, though I walk through the valley of the shadow of death . . ."'

'"I will fear no evil . . ."' said Martin Mills.

'Yes – that's it. "I will fear no evil,"' Farrokh repeated.

Dr Daruwalla assumed that the plane had left Maharashtra; he guessed they were already flying over Gujarat. Below them, the land was flat and dry-looking in the late-afternoon haze. The sky was as brown as the ground. *Limo Roulette* or *Escaping Maharashtra* – the screenwriter couldn't make up his mind between the two titles. Farrokh thought: It depends on what happens – it depends on how the story ends.

22. THE TEMPTATION
OF DR DARUWALLA

On the Road to Junagadh

At the airport in Rajkot, they were testing the loud-speaker system. It was a test without urgency, as if the loudspeaker were of no real importance – as if no one believed there could be an emergency.

'One, two, three, four, five,' said a voice. 'Five, four, three, two, one.' Then the message was repeated. Maybe they *weren't* testing the loudspeaker system, thought Dr Daruwalla; possibly they were testing their counting skills.

While the doctor and Martin Mills were gathering the bags, their pilot appeared and handed the Swiss Army knife to the missionary. At first Martin was embarrassed – he'd forgotten that he'd been forced to relinquish the weapon in Bombay. Then he was ashamed, for he'd assumed the pilot was a thief. While this demonstration of social awkwardness was unfolding, Madhu and Ganesh each ordered and drank two glasses of tea; Dr Daruwalla was left to haggle with the chai vendor.

'We'll have to be stopping all the way to Junagadh, so you can pee,' Farrokh told the children. Then they waited nearly an hour in Rajkot for their driver to arrive. All the while, the loudspeaker system went on counting up to five and down to one. It was an annoying airport, but Madhu and Ganesh had plenty of time to pee.

Their driver's name was Ramu. He was a roustabout who'd joined the Great Blue Nile Circus in Maharashtra, and this was his second round trip between

631

Junagadh and Rajkot today. He'd been on time to meet the plane in the morning; when he learned that the flight was delayed, he drove back to the circus in Junagadh – only because he liked to drive. It was nearly a three-hour trip one way, but Ramu proudly told them that he usually covered the distance in under two hours. They soon saw why.

Ramu drove a battered Land Rover, spattered with mud (or the dried blood of unlucky pedestrians and animals). He was a slight young man, perhaps 18 or 20, and he wore a baggy pair of shorts and a begrimed T-shirt. Most notably, Ramu drove barefoot. The padding had worn off the clutch and brake pedals – their smooth metal surfaces looked slippery – and the doubtlessly overused accelerator pedal had been replaced by a piece of wood; it looked as flimsy as a shingle, but Ramu never took his right foot off it. He preferred to operate both the clutch and the brake with his left foot, although the latter pedal received little attention.

Through Rajkot, they roared into the twilight. They passed a water tower, a women's hospital, a bus station, a bank, a fruit market, a statue of Gandhi, a telegraph office, a library, a cemetery, the Havmore Restaurant and the Hotel Intimate. When they raced through the bazaar area, Dr Daruwalla couldn't look anymore. There were too many children – not to mention the elderly, who weren't as quick to get out of the way as the children; not to mention the bullock carts and the camel wagons, and the cows and donkeys and goats; not to mention the mopeds and the bicycles and the bicycle rickshaws and the three-wheeled rickshaws, and of course there were cars and trucks and buses, too. At the edge of town, off the side of the road, Farrokh was sure that he spotted a dead man – another 'nonperson,' as Ganesh would say – but at the speed they were traveling, there was no time for Dr Daruwalla to ask Martin Mills to verify the shape of death with the frozen face that the doctor saw.

Once they were out of town, Ramu drove faster. The roustabout subscribed to the open-road school of driving. There were no rules about passing; in the lane of oncoming traffic, Ramu yielded only to those vehicles that were bigger. In Ramu's mind, the Land Rover was bigger than anything on the road – except for buses and a highly selective category of heavy-duty trucks. Dr Daruwalla was grateful that Ganesh sat in the passenger seat; both the boy and Madhu had wanted that seat, but the doctor was afraid that Madhu would distract the driver – a high-speed seduction. So the girl sulked in the back with the doctor and the missionary while the elephant boy chatted nonstop with Ramu.

Ganesh had probably expected that the driver would speak only Gujarati; to discover that Ramu was a fellow Maharashtrian who spoke Marathi and Hindi inspired the beggar. Although Farrokh found their conversation difficult to follow, it seemed that Ganesh wanted to list all the possible circus-related activities that a cripple with one good foot might do. For his part, Ramu was discouraging; he preferred to talk about driving while demonstrating his violent technique of upshifting and downshifting (instead of using the brakes), assuring Ganesh that it would be impossible to match his skill as a driver without a functioning right foot.

To Ramu's credit, he didn't look at Ganesh when he talked; thankfully, the driver was transfixed by the developing madness on the road. Soon it would be dark; perhaps then the doctor could relax, for it would be better not to see one's own death approaching. After nightfall, there would be only the sudden nearness of a blaring horn and the blinding, onrushing headlights. Farrokh imagined the entanglement of bodies in the rolling Land Rover; a foot here, a hand there, the back of someone's head, a flailing elbow – and not knowing who was who, or in which direction the ground was, or the black sky (for the headlights would surely be shattered, and in one's hair there would be fragments of glass, as fine as sand). They would smell the gasoline; it would be soaking their clothes. At last, they would see the ball of flame.

'Distract me,' Dr Daruwalla said to Martin Mills. 'Start talking. Tell me anything at all.' The Jesuit, who'd spent his childhood on the Los Angeles freeways, seemed at ease in the careening Land Rover. The burned-out wrecks off the side of the road were of no interest to him – not even the occasional upside-down car that was still on fire – and the carnage of animals that dotted the highway interested him only when he couldn't identify their remains.

'What was that? Did you see that?' the missionary asked, his head whipping around.

'A dead bullock,' answered Dr Daruwalla. 'Please talk to me, Martin.'

'I know it was dead,' said Martin Mills. 'What's a bullock?'

'A castrated bull – a steer,' Farrokh replied.

'There's another one!' the scholastic cried, his head turning again.

'No, that was a cow,' the doctor said.

'I saw a camel earlier,' Martin remarked. 'Did you see the camel?'

'Yes, I saw it,' Farrokh answered him. 'Now tell me a story. It will be dark soon.'

'A pity – there's so much to see!' said Martin Mills.

'*Distract* me, for God's sake!' Dr Daruwalla cried. 'I know you like to talk – tell me anything at all.'

'Well . . . what do you want me to tell you about?' the missionary asked. Farrokh wanted to kill him.

The girl had fallen asleep. They'd made her sit between them because they were afraid she'd lean against one of the rear doors; now she could lean only against them. Asleep, Madhu seemed as frail as a rag doll; they had to press against her and hold her shoulders to keep her from flopping around.

Her scented hair brushed against Dr Daruwalla's

throat at the open collar of his shirt; her hair smelled like clove. Then the Land Rover would swerve and Madhu would slump against the Jesuit, who took no notice of her. But Farrokh felt her hip against his. As the Land Rover again pulled out to pass, Madhu's shoulder ground against the doctor's ribs; her hand, which was limp, dragged across his thigh. Sometimes, when Farrokh could feel Madhu breathe, he held his breath. The doctor wasn't looking forward to the awkwardness of spending the night in the same room with her. It was not only from Ramu's reckless driving that Farrokh sought some distraction.

'Tell me about your mother,' Dr Daruwalla said to Martin Mills. 'How *is* she?' In the failing but lingering light, the doctor could see the missionary's neck tighten; his eyes narrowed. 'And your father – how's Danny doing?' the doctor added, but the damage had already been done. Farrokh could tell that Martin hadn't heard him the second time; the Jesuit was searching the past. The landscape of hideously slain animals flew by, but the zealot no longer noticed.

'All right, if that's what you want. I'm going to tell you a little story about my mother,' said Martin Mills. Somehow, Dr Daruwalla knew that the story wouldn't be 'little.' The missionary wasn't a minimalist; he favored description. In fact, Martin left out no detail; he told Farrokh absolutely everything he could remember. The exquisiteness of Arif Koma's complexion, the different odors of masturbation – not only Arif's, but also the smell that lingered on the U.C.L.A. babysitter's fingers.

Thus they hurtled through the darkened countryside and the dimly lit towns, where the reek of cooking and excrement assailed them – together with the squabbling of chickens, the barking of dogs and the savage threats of the shouting, almost-runover pedestrians. Ramu apologized that his driver's-side window was missing; not only did the rushing night air grow cooler, but the back-seat passengers were struck by flying insects. Once, something the size of a humming-bird smacked against Martin's forehead; it must have stung, and for five minutes or more it lay buzzing and whirring on the floor before it died – whatever it was. But the missionary's story was unstoppable; nothing could deter him.

It took him all the way to Junagadh to finish. As they entered the brightly lit town, the streets were teeming; two crowds were surging against each other. A loud-speaker on a parked truck played circus music. One crowd was coming from the early-evening show, the other hurrying to line up for the show that was to start later on.

I should tell the poor bastard everything, Dr Daru-walla was thinking. That he has a twin, that his mother was always a slut, that Neville Eden was probably his real father. Danny was too dumb to be the father; both John D. and Martin Mills were smart. Neville, although Farrokh had never liked him, had been smart. But Martin's story had struck Farrokh speechless. More-over, the doctor believed that these revelations should be John D.'s decision. And although Dr Daruwalla wanted to punish Vera in almost any way that he could, the one thing that Martin had said about Danny contributed further to the doctor's silence. 'I love my father – I just wish I didn't pity him.'

The rest of the story was all about Vera; Martin hadn't said another word about Danny. The doctor decided that it wasn't a good time for the Jesuit to hear that his probable father was a two-timing, bisexual shit named Neville Eden. This news would not help Martin to pity Danny any less.

Besides, they were almost at the circus. The elephant-footed boy was so excited, he was kneeling on the front seat and waving out the window at the mob. The circus music, which was blaring at them over the loud-speaker, had managed to wake up Madhu.

'Here's your new life,' Dr Daruwalla told the child prostitute. 'Wake up and see it.'

Although Ramu never stopped blowing the horn, the Land Rover barely crawled through the crowd. Several small boys clung to the door handles and the rear bumper, allowing themselves to be dragged along the road. Everyone stared into the back seat. Madhu was mistaken to be anxious; the crowd wasn't staring at her. It was Martin Mills who drew their attention; they were unused to white men. Junagadh wasn't a tourist town. The missionary's skin was as pale as dough in the glare from the streetlights. Because they were forced to move ahead so slowly, it grew hot in the car, but when Martin rolled his rear window down, people reached inside the Land Rover just to touch him.

Far ahead of them, a dwarf clown on stilts was leading the throng. It was even more congested at the circus because it was too early to let the crowd in; the Land Rover had to inch its way through the well-guarded gate. Once inside the compound, Dr Daruwalla appreciated a familiar sensation: the circus was a cloister, a protected place; it was as exempt from the mayhem of Junagadh as St Ignatius stood, like a fort, within the chaos of Bombay. The children would be safe here, provided that they gave the place a chance – provided that the circus gave *them* a chance.

But the first omen was inhospitable: Deepa didn't meet them; the dwarf's wife and son were sick – confined to their tent. And, almost immediately, Dr Daruwalla could sense how the Great Blue Nile compared unfavorably to the Great Royal. There was no owner of the charm and dignity of Pratap Walawalkar; in fact, the owner of the Great Blue Nile was away. No dinner was waiting for them in the owner's tent, which they never saw. The ringmaster was a Bengali named Das; there was no food in Mr Das's tent, and the sleeping cots were all in a row, as in a spartan barracks; a minimum of ornamentation was draped on the walls. The dirt floor was completely covered with rugs; bolts of brightly colored fabric, for costumes, were hung high in the apex of the tent, out of everyone's way, and the trappings of a temple were prominently displayed alongside the TV and the VCR.

A cot like all the others was identified as Madhu's; Mr Das was putting her between two older girls, who (he said) would mind her. Mrs Das, the ringmaster assured them, would 'mind' Madhu, too. As for Mrs Das, she didn't get off her cot to greet them. She sat sewing sequins on a costume, and only as they were leaving the tent did she speak to Madhu.

'I am meeting you tomorrow,' she told the girl.

'What time shall we come in the morning?' Dr Daruwalla asked, but Mrs Das – who manifested something of the victimized severity of an unexpectedly divorced aunt – didn't answer him. Her head remained lowered, her eyes on her sewing.

'Don't come too early, because we'll be watching television,' Mr Das told the doctor.

Well, naturally . . . Dr Daruwalla thought.

Ganesh's cot would be set up in the cook's tent, where Mr Das escorted them – and where he left them. He said he had to prepare for the 9:30 show. The cook, whose name was Chandra, assumed that Ganesh had been sent to help him; Chandra began to identify his utensils to the cripple, who listened indifferently – Dr Daruwalla knew that the boy wanted to see the lions.

'Kadhai,' a wok. 'Jhara,' a slotted spoon. 'Kisni,' a coconut grater. From outside the cook's tent, in the darkness, they also listened to the regular coughs of the lions. The crowd still hadn't been admitted to the main tent but they were present in the darkness, like the lions, as a kind of background murmur.

Dr Daruwalla didn't notice the mosquitoes until he began to eat. The doctor and the others ate standing up, off stainless-steel plates – curried potatoes and eggplant with too much cumin. Then they were offered a plate of raw vegetables – carrots and radishes, onions and tomatoes – which they washed down with warm orange soda. Good old Gold Spot. Gujarat was a dry state, because Gandhi was born there – the tedious teetotaler. Farrokh reflected that he would probably be awake all night. He'd been counting on beer to keep him away from his screenplay, to help him sleep. Then he remembered that he'd be sharing a room with Madhu; in that case, it would be best to stay awake all night and to *not* have any beer.

Throughout their hasty, unsatisfying meal, Chandra progressed to naming vegetables to Ganesh, as if the cook assumed the boy had lost his language in the same accident that had mangled his foot. ('Aloo,' potato. 'Chawli,' a white pea. 'Baingan,' eggplant.) As for Madhu, she appeared neglected, and she was shivering. Surely she had a shawl or a sweater in her small bag, but all their bags were still in the Land Rover, which was parked God knew where; Ramu, their driver, was God knew where, too. Besides, it was almost time for the late show.

When they stepped into the avenue of troupe tents, they saw that the performers were already in costume; the elephants were being led down the aisle. In the wing of the main tent, the horses were standing in line. A roustabout had already saddled the first horse. Then a trainer prodded a big chimpanzee with a stick, launching the animal into what appeared to be a vertical leap of at least five feet. The horse had started forward, just a nervous step or two, when the chimpanzee landed on the saddle. There the chimp squatted on all fours; when the trainer touched the saddle with his stick, the chimpanzee performed a front flip on the horse's back – and then another.

The band was already on the platform stage above the arena, which was still filling with the crowd. The visitors would be in the way if they stood in the wing, but Mr Das, the ringmaster, hadn't appeared; there was no one to show them to their seats. Martin Mills suggested that they find seats for themselves before the tent was full; Dr Daruwalla resented such informality. While the doctor and the missonary were arguing about what to do, the chimp doing front flips on the horse grew distracted. Martin Mills was the distraction.

The chimpanzee was an old male named Gautam, because even as a baby he'd demonstrated a remarkable similarity to Buddha; he could sit in the same position and stare at the same thing for hours. As he'd aged, Gautam had extended his capacity for meditation to include certain repetitive exercies; the front flips on the horse's back were but one example. Gautam could repeat the move tirelessly; whether the horse was galloping or standing still, the chimpanzee always landed on the saddle. There was, however, a diminished enthusiasm to Gautam's front flips, and to his other activities as well. His trainer, Kunal, attributed Gautam's emotional decline to the big chimp's infatuation with Mira, a young female chimpanzee. Mira was new to the Great Blue Nile, and Gautam could be observed pining for her – often at inappropriate times.

If he saw Mira when he was doing front flips, Gautam would miss not only the saddle but the whole horse. Hence Mira rode a horse far back in the procession of animals that paraded around the main tent during the Grand Entry. It was only when Gautam was warming up in the wing that the old chimpanzee could spot Mira; she was kept near the elephants, because Gautam was afraid of elephants. At some trancelike distance in Gautam's mind, this view of Mira – as the big chimp waited for the curtains to open and the Grand Entry music to begin – satisfied him. He kept doing front flips, mechanically, almost as if the jumps were triggered by a mild electrical shock, at about five-second intervals. In the corner of Gautam's eye, Mira was a faraway presence; nevertheless, she was enough of a presence to soothe him.

Gautam became extremely unhappy if his view of Mira was blocked. Only Kunal was allowed to pass between the chimp and his view of Mira. Kunal never stood anywhere near Gautam without a stick in his hand. Gautam was big for a chimp; according to Kunal, the ape weighed 145 pounds and was almost five feet tall.

Simply put, Martin Mills was standing in the wrong place at the wrong time. After the attack, Kunal speculated that Gautam might have imagined that the missionary was another male chimpanzee; not only had Martin blocked Gautam's view of Mira, but Gautam might have assumed that the missionary was seeking Mira's affection – for Mira was a very affectionate female, and her friendliness (to male chimpanzees) was something that regularly drove Gautam insane. As for *why* Gautam might have mistaken Martin Mills for an ape, Kunal suggested that the paleness of the scholastic's skin would surely have struck Gautam as unnatural for a human being. If Martin's skin color was a novelty to the people of Junagadh – who, after all, had gawked at him and pawed him over in the passing Land Rover – Martin's skin was only slightly less foreign to Gautum's experience. Since, to Gautam, Martin Mills didn't look like a human being, the ape probably thought that the missionary was a male chimpanzee.

It was with a logic of this kind that Gautam interrupted his front flips on the horse's back. The chimpanzee screamed once and bared his fangs; then he vaulted from the rump of the horse and over the back of another horse, landing on Martin's shoulders and chest and driving the missionary to his back on the ground. There Gautam sunk his teeth into the side of the surprised Jesuit's neck. Martin was fortunate to have protected his throat with his hand, but this meant that his hand was bitten, too. When it was over, there was a deep puncture wound in Martin's neck and a slash wound from the heel of his hand to the ball of his thumb; and a small piece of the missonary's right earlobe was missing. Gautam was too strong to be pulled off the struggling scholastic, but Kunal was able to beat the ape away with his stick. The whole time Mira was shrieking; it was hard to tell if her cries signified requited love or disapproval.

The discussion of whether the chimp attack had been racially motivated or sexually inspired, or both, continued throughout the late-evening show. Martin Mills refused to allow Dr Daruwalla to attend to his wounds until the performance was concluded; the Jesuit insisted that the children would learn a valuable lesson from his stoicism, which the doctor regarded as a *stupid* stoicism of the show-must-go-on variety. Both Madhu and Ganesh were distracted by the missionary's missing earlobe and the other gory evidence of the savage biting that the zealot had suffered; Madhu hardly watched the circus at all. Farrokh, however, paid close attention. The doctor was content to let the missionary bleed. Dr Daruwalla didn't want to miss the performance.

A Perfect Ending

The better acts had been borrowed from the Great Royal – in particular, an item called Bicycle Waltz, for which the band played 'The Yellow Rose of Texas.' A thin, muscular woman of an obvious sinewy strength performed the Skywalk at a fast, mechanical pace. The audience was unfrightened for her; even without a safety net, there was no palpable fear that she could fall. While Suman looked beautiful and vulnerable – as could be expected of a young woman hanging upside down at 80 feet – the skywalker at the Great Blue Nile resembled a middle-aged robot. Her name was Mrs Bhagwan, and Farrokh recognized her as the knife thrower's assistant; she was also his wife.

In the knife-throwing item, Mrs Bhagwan was

spread-eagled on a wooden wheel; the wheel was painted as a target, with Mrs Bhagwan's belly covering the bull's-eye. Throughout the act, the wheel revolved faster and faster, and Mr Bhagwan hurled knives at his wife. When the wheel was stopped, the knives were stuck every which way in the wood; not even the crudest pattern could be discerned, except that there were no knives sticking in Mrs Bhagwan's spread-eagled body.

Mr Bhagwan's other specialty was the item called Elephant Passing, which almost every circus in India performs. Mr Bhagwan lies in the arena, sandwiched between mattresses that are then covered with a plank; an elephant walks this plank, over Mr Bhagwan's chest. Farrokh observed that this was the only act that *didn't* prompt Ganesh to say he could learn it, although being crippled wouldn't have interfered with the boy's ability to lie under a passing elephant.

Once, when Mr Bhagwan had been stricken with acute diarrhea, Mrs Bhagwan had replaced her husband in the Elephant Passing item. But the woman was too thin for the Elephant Passing. There was a story that she'd bled internally for days and that, even after she'd recovered, she was never the same again; both her diet and her disposition had been ruined by the elephant.

Of Mrs Bhagwan, Farrokh understood that her version of the Skywalk and her passive contribution to the knife-throwing act were one and the same; it was less a skill she had learned, or even a drama to be enacted, than a mechanical submission to her fate. Her husband's errant knife or the fall from 80 feet – they were one and the same. Mrs Bhagwan *was* a robot, Dr Daruwalla believed. Possibly the Elephant Passing had done this to her.

Mr Das confided this feeling to Farrokh. When the ringmaster briefly joined them in the audience – to apologize for Gautam's rude attack, and to add his own ideas to the doctor's and the Jesuit's speculations

643

regarding the ape's racism and/or sexual jealousy – Mr Das attributed Mrs Bhagwan's lackluster performance to her elephant episode.

'But in other ways it's better since she's been married,' Mr Das admitted. Before Mrs Bhagwan's marriage, she'd complained bitterly about her menstrual cycle – how hanging upside down when she was bleeding was unusually uncomfortable. 'And before she was married, of course it wasn't proper for her to use a tampon,' Mr Das added.

'No, of course not,' said Dr Daruwalla, who was appalled.

When there were lulls in the acts, which there often were – or when the band was resting between items – they could hear the sounds of the chimp being beaten. Kunal was 'disciplining' Gautam, Mr Das explained. In some of the towns where the Great Blue Nile played, there might be other white males in the audience; they couldn't allow Gautam to think that white males were fair game.

'No, of course not,' said Dr Daruwalla. The big ape's screams and the sounds of Kunal's stick were carried to them in the still night air. When the band played, no matter how badly, the doctor and the missionary and the children were grateful.

If Gautam was rabid, the ape would die; better to beat him, in case he wasn't rabid and he lived – this was Kunal's philosophy. As for treating Martin Mills, Dr Daruwalla knew it was wise to assume the chimp was rabid. But, for now, the children were laughing.

When one of the lions pissed violently on its stool and then stamped in the puddle, both Madhu and Ganesh laughed. Yet Farrokh felt obliged to remind the elephant boy that washing this same stool might be his first job.

There was a Peacock Dance, of course – two little girls played the peacocks, as always – and the screenwriter thought that his Pinky character should be in a peacock costume when the escaped lion kills her.

Farrokh thought it would be best if the lion kills her because the lion thinks she *is* a peacock. More poignant that way ... more sympathy for the lion. Thus would the screenwriter act out his old presentiment – that the restless lions in the holding tunnel were restless because their act was next and the peacock girls were temptingly in sight. When Acid Man applied his acid to the locked cage, the lion that got loose would be in an agitated, antipeacock mood. Poor Pinky!

There was an encore to the Skywalk item. Mrs Bhagwan didn't climb all the way to the top of the tent to repeat the Skywalk, which had left the audience largely unimpressed the first time. She climbed to the top of the tent only to repeat her descent on the dental trapeze. It was the dental trapeze that the audience had liked; more specifically, it was Mrs Bhagwan's *neck* that they had liked. She had an extremely muscular neck, overdeveloped from all her dental-trapezing, and when she descended – twirling, from the top of the tent, with the trapeze clamped tightly in her teeth – her neck muscles bulged, the spotlight turning from green to gold.

'I could do that,' Ganesh whispered to Dr Daruwalla. 'I have a strong neck. And strong teeth,' he added.

'And I suppose you could hang, and walk, upside down,' the doctor replied. 'You have to hold both feet rigid, at right angles – your ankles support all your weight.' As soon as he spoke, Farrokh realized his error. The cripple's crushed foot was permanently fused at his ankle – a perfect right angle. It would be no problem for him to keep that foot in a rigid right-angle position.

There was an idiotic finale in progress in the ring – chimps and dwarf clowns riding mopeds. The lead chimp was dressed as a Gujarati milkman, which the local crowd loved. The elephant-footed boy was smiling serenely in the semidarkness.

'So it would be only my *good* foot that I would have

to make stronger – is that what you are telling me?' the cripple asked.

'What I'm telling you, Ganesh, is that *your* job is with the lion piss and the elephant shit. And maybe, if you're lucky,' Farrokh told the boy, 'you'll get to work with the food.'

Now the ponies and the elephants entered the ring, as in the beginning, and the band played loudly; it was impossible to hear Gautam being beaten. Not once had Madhu said, 'I could do that' – not about a single act – but here was the elephant-footed boy, already imagining that he could learn to walk on the sky.

'Up there,' Ganesh told Dr Daruwalla, pointing to the top of the tent, 'I wouldn't walk with a limp.'

'Don't even think about it,' the doctor said.

But the screenwriter couldn't stop thinking about it, for it would be the perfect ending to his movie. After the lion kills Pinky – and justice is done to Acid Man (perhaps acid could accidentally be spilled in the villain's crotch) – Ganesh knows that the circus won't keep him unless he can make a contribution. No one believes he can be a skywalker – Suman won't give the crippled boy lessons, and Pratap won't let him practice on the ladder in the troupe tent. There is nowhere he can learn to skywalk, except in the main tent; if he's going to try it, he must climb up to the real device and do the real thing – at 80 feet, with no net.

What a great scene! the screenwriter thought. The boy slips out of the cook's tent in the predawn light. There's no one in the main tent to see him climb the trapeze rope to the top. 'If I fall, death happens,' his voice-over says. 'If no one sees you die, no one says any prayers for you.' Good line! Dr Daruwalla thought; he wondered if it was true.

The camera is 80 feet below the boy when he hangs upside down from the ladder; he holds the sides of the ladder with both hands as he puts his good foot and then his bad one into the first two loops. There are 18 loops of rope running the length of the ladder; the

Skywalk requires 16 steps. 'There is a moment when you must let go with your hands,' Ganesh's voice-over says. 'I do not know whose hands I am in then.'

The boy lets go of the ladder with both hands; he hangs by his feet. (The trick is, you have to start swinging your body; it's the momentum you gather, from swinging, that allows you to step forward – one foot at a time, out of the first loop and into the next one, still swinging. Never stop the momentum . . . keep the forward motion constant.) 'I think there is a moment when you must decide where you belong,' the boy's voice-over says. Now the camera approaches him, from 80 feet away; the camera closes in on his feet. 'At that moment, you are in no one's hands,' the voice-over says. 'At that moment, everyone walks on the sky.'

From another angle, we see that the cook has discovered what Ganesh is doing; the cook stands very still, looking up – he's counting. Other performers have come into the tent – Pratap Singh, Suman, the dwarf clowns (one of them still brushing his teeth). They follow the crippled boy with their eyes; they're all counting – they all know how many steps there are in the Skywalk.

'Let other people do the counting,' Ganesh's voice-over says. 'What I tell myself is, I am just walking – I don't think *skywalking*, I think *just walking*. That's my little secret. Nobody else would be much impressed by the thought of just walking. Nobody else could concentrate very hard on that. But for me the thought of *just walking* is very special. What I tell myself is, I am walking without a limp.'

Not bad, Dr Daruwalla thought. And there should be a scene later, with the boy in full costume – a singlet sewn with blue-green sequins. As he descends on the dental trapeze, spinning in the spotlight, the gleaming sequins throw back the light. Ganesh should never quite touch the ground; instead, he descends into Pratap's waiting arms. Pratap lifts the boy up to the cheering crowd. Then Pratap runs out of the ring with

Ganesh in his arms – because after a cripple has walked on the sky, no one should see him limp.

It could work, the screenwriter thought.

After the performance, they managed to find where Ramu had parked the Land Rover, but they couldn't find Ramu. The four of them required two rickshaws for the trip across town to the Government Circuit House; Madhu and Farrokh followed the rickshaw carrying Ganesh and Martin Mills. These were the three-wheeled rickshaws that Dr Daruwalla hated; old Lowji had once declared that a three-wheeled rickshaw made as much sense as a moped towing a lawn chair. But Madhu and Ganesh were enjoying the ride. As their rickshaw bounced along, Madhu tightly gripped Farrokh's knee with one hand. It was a child's grip – not sexual groping, Dr Daruwalla assured himself. With her other hand, Madhu waved to Ganesh. Looking at her, the doctor kept thinking: Maybe the girl will be all right – maybe she'll make it.

On the mud flaps of the rickshaw ahead of them, Farrokh saw the face of a movie star; he thought it might be a poor likeness of either Madhuri Dixit or Jaya Prada – in any case, it wasn't Inspector Dhar. In the cheap plastic window of the rickshaw, there was Ganesh's face – the *real* Ganesh, the screenwriter reminded himself. It was such a perfect ending, Farrokh was thinking – all the more remarkable because the *real* cripple had given him the idea.

In the window of the bouncing rickshaw, the boy's dark eyes were shining. The headlight from the following rickshaw kept crossing the cripple's smiling face. Given the distance between the two rickshaws and the fact that it was night, Dr Daruwalla observed that the boy's eyes looked healthy; you couldn't see the slight discharge or the cloudiness from the tetracycline ointment. From such a partial view, you couldn't tell that Ganesh was crippled; he looked like a happy, normal boy.

How the doctor wished it were true.

There was nothing to do about the missing piece of Martin's earlobe. Altogether, Dr Daruwalla used two 10mL vials of the human rabies immune globulin; he injected a half-vial directly into each of the three wound areas – the earlobe, the neck, the hand – and he administered the remaining half-vial by a deep intramuscular injection in Martin's buttocks.

The hand was the worst – a slash wound, which the doctor packed with iodophor gauze. A bite should drain, and heal from the inside, so Dr Daruwalla wouldn't stitch the wound – nor did the doctor offer anything for the pain. Dr Daruwalla had observed that the missionary was enjoying his pain. However, the zealot's limited sense of humor didn't permit him to appreciate Dr Daruwalla's joke – that the Jesuit appeared to suffer from 'chimpanzee stigmata.' The doctor also couldn't resist pointing out to Martin Mills that, on the evidence of the scholastic's wounds, whatever had bitten Farrokh (and converted him) in Goa was certainly *not* a chimp; such an ape would have consumed the whole toe – maybe half the foot.

'Still angry about your miracle, I see,' Martin replied.

On that testy note, the two men said their goodnights. Farrokh didn't envy the Jesuit the task of calming Ganesh down, for the elephant boy was in no mood to sleep; the cripple couldn't wait for his first full day at the circus to begin. Madhu, on the other hand, seemed bored and listless, if not exactly sleepy.

Their rooms at the Government Circuit House were adjacent to each other on the third floor. Off Farrokh and Madhu's bedroom, two glass doors opened onto a small balcony covered with bird droppings. They had their own bathroom with a sink and a toilet, but no door; there was just a rug hung from a curtain rod – it didn't quite touch the floor. The toilet could be flushed only with a bucket, which was conveniently positioned under a faucet that dripped. There was also a shower, of sorts; an open-ended pipe, without a showerhead, poked out of the bathroom wall. There was no curtain for the shower, but there was a sloped floor leading to an open drain, which (upon closer inspection) appeared to be the temporary residence of a rat; Farrokh saw its tail disappearing down the hole. Very close to the drain was a diminished bar of soap, the edges nibbled.

In the bedroom, the two beds were too close together – and doubtless infested. Both mosquito nets were yellowed and stiff, and one was torn. The one window that opened had no screen, and little air was inclined to move through it. Dr Daruwalla thought they might as well open the glass doors to the balcony, but Madhu said she was afraid that a monkey would come inside.

The ceiling fan had only two speeds: one was so slow that the fan had no effect at all, and the other was so fast that the mosquito nets were blown away from the beds. Even in the main tent at the circus, the night air had felt cool, but the third floor of the Government Circuit House was hot and airless. Madhu solved the problem by using the bathroom first; she wet a towel and wrung it out, and then she lay naked under the towel – on the better bed, the one with the untorn mosquito net. Madhu was small, but so was the towel; it scarcely covered her breasts and left her thighs exposed. A deliberate girl, the doctor thought.

Lying there, she said, 'I'm still hungry. There was nothing sweet.'

'You want a dessert?' Dr Daruwalla asked.

'If it's sweet,' she said.

The doctor carried the thermos with the rest of the rabies vaccine and the immune globulin down to the lobby; he hoped there was a refrigerator, for the thermos was already tepid. What if Gautam bit someone else tomorrow? Kunal had informed the doctor that the chimpanzee was 'almost definitely' rabid. Rabid or not, the chimp shouldn't be beaten; in the doctor's opinion, only a second-rate circus beat its animals.

In the lobby, a Muslim boy was tending the desk, listening to the Qawwali on the radio; he appeared to be eating ice cream to the religious verses – his head nodding while he ate, the spoon conducting the air between the container and his mouth. But it wasn't ice cream, the boy told Dr Daruwalla; he offered the doctor a spoon and invited him to take a taste. The texture differed from that of ice cream – a cardamom-scented, saffron-colored yogurt, sweetened with sugar. There was a refrigerator full of the stuff, and Farrokh took a container and spoon for Madhu. He left the vaccine and the immune globulin in the refrigerator, after assuring himself that the boy knew better than to eat it.

When the doctor returned to his room, Madhu had discarded the towel. He tried to give her the Gujarati dessert without looking at her; probably on purpose, she made it awkward for him to hand her the spoon and container – he was sure she was pretending that she didn't know where the mosquito net opened. She sat naked in bed, eating the sweetened yogurt and watching him while he arranged his writing materials.

There was an unsteady table, a thick candle affixed by wax to a dirty ashtray, a packet of matches alongside a mosquito coil. When Farrokh had spread out his pages and smoothed his hand over the pad of fresh paper, he lit the candle and the mosquito coil and turned off the overhead light. At high speed, the ceiling fan would have disturbed his work and Madhu's mosquito net, so the doctor kept the fan on low; although this was ineffectual, he hoped that the movement of the blade might make Madhu sleepy.

'What are you doing?' the child prostitute asked him.

'Writing,' he told her.

'Read it to me,' Madhu asked him.

'You wouldn't understand it,' Farrokh replied.

'Are you going to be sleeping?' the girl asked.

'Maybe later,' said Dr Daruwalla.

He tried to block her out of his mind, but this was difficult. She kept watching him; the sound of her spoon in the container of yogurt was as regular as the drone of the fan. Her purposeful nakedness was oppressive, but not because he was actually tempted by her; it was more that the pure evil of having sex with her (the very *idea* of it) was suddenly his obsession. He didn't *want* to have sex with her – he felt only the most passing desire for her – but the sheer obviousness of her availability was numbing to his other senses. It struck him that an evil this pure, something so clearly wrong, wasn't often presented without consequence; the horror was that it seemed there could be no harmful result of sex between them. If he permitted her to seduce him, nothing would come of it – nothing beyond what he would remember and feel guilty for, forever.

The lucky girl was not HIV-positive; besides, he happened to be traveling in India, as usual – with condoms. And Madhu wasn't a girl who would ever tell anyone; she wasn't a talker. In her present situation, she might never have the occasion to tell anyone. It was not only the child's tarnished innocence that convinced him of the purity of this evil, like almost no other evil he'd ever imagined; it was also her strident amorality – whether this had been acquired in the brothel or, hideously, taught to her by Mr Garg. Whatever one did to her, one wouldn't pay for it – not in this life, or only in the torments of one's soul. These were the darkest thoughts that Dr Daruwalla had ever had, but he nevertheless thought his way through them; soon he was writing again.

By the movement of his pen (for she'd never stopped watching him), Madhu seemed to sense that she'd lost him. Also, her dessert was gone. She got out of the bed and walked naked to him; she peered over his shoulder, as if she knew how to read what he was writing. The screenwriter could feel her hair against his cheek and neck.

'Read it to me – just that part,' Madhu said. She leaned more firmly against him as she reached and touched the paper with her hand; she touched his last sentence. The cardamom-scented yogurt smelled sickly on her breath, and there was something like the smell of dead flowers – possibly the saffron.

The screenwriter read aloud to her: ' "Two stretcher bearers in white dhotis are running with the body of Acid Man, who is curled in a fetal position on the stretcher – his face glazed in pain, smoke still drifting from the area of his crotch." '

Madhu made him read it again; then she said, 'In *what* position?'

'Fetal,' said Dr Daruwalla. 'Like a baby inside its mother.'

'Who is Acid Man?' the child prostitute asked him.

'A man who's been scarred by acid – like Mr Garg,' Farrokh told her. At the mention of Garg's name, there wasn't even a flicker of recognition in the girl's face. The doctor refused to look at her naked body, although Madhu still clung to his shoulder; where she pressed against him, he felt himself begin to sweat.

'The smoke is coming from *what* area?' Madhu asked.

'From his crotch,' the screenwriter replied.

'Where's that?' the child prostitute asked him.

'You know where that is, Madhu – go back to bed,' he told her.

She raised one arm to show him her armpit. 'The hair is growing back,' she said. 'You can feel it.'

'I can see that it's growing back – I don't need to feel it,' Farrokh replied.

'It's growing back everywhere,' Madhu said.

'Go back to bed,' the doctor told her.

He could tell from the change in her breathing; he knew the moment when she finally fell asleep. Then he thought it was safe to lie down on the other bed.

Although he was exhausted, he'd not yet fallen asleep when he felt the first of the fleas or the bedbugs. They didn't seem to jump like fleas, and they were invisible; probably they were bedbugs. Evidently, Madhu was used to them – she hadn't noticed.

Farrokh decided that he would rather try to sleep among the bird droppings on the balcony; possibly it was cool enough outside so there wouldn't be any mosquitoes. But when the doctor stepped out on his balcony, there on the adjacent balcony was a wide-awake Martin Mills.

'There are a million things in my bed!' the missionary whispered.

'In mine, too,' Farrokh replied.

'I don't know how the boy manages to sleep through all the biting and crawling!' the scholastic said.

'There are probably a million fewer things here than he's used to in Bombay,' Dr Daruwalla said.

The night sky was yielding to the dawn; soon the sky would be the same milky-tea color as the ground. Against such gray-brown tones, the white of the missionary's new bandages was startling – his mittened hand, his wrapped neck, his patched ear.

'You're quite a sight,' the doctor told him.

'You should see yourself,' the missionary replied. 'Have you slept at all?'

Since the children were sleeping so soundly – and they'd only recently fallen asleep – the two men decided to take a tour of the town. After all, Mr Das had warned them not to come to the circus too early, or else they'd interrupt the television watching. It being a Sunday, the doctor presumed that the televisions in all the troupe tents would be tuned to the *Mahabharata*; the popular Hindu epic had been broadcast every Sunday morning for more than a year – altogether, there were 93 episodes, each an hour long, and the great journey to the gates of heaven (where the epic ends) wouldn't be over until the coming summer. It was the world's most successful soap opera, depicting

654

religion as heroic action; it was a legend with countless homilies, not to mention blindness and illegitimate births, battles and women-stealing. A record number of robberies had occurred during the broadcasts because the thieves knew that almost everyone in India would be glued to the TV. The missionary would be consumed with Christian envy, Dr Daruwalla thought.

In the lobby, the Muslim boy was no longer eating to the Qawwali on the radio; the religious verses had put him to sleep. There was no need to wake him. In the driveway of the Government Circuit House, a half-dozen three-wheeled rickshaws were parked for the night; their drivers, all but one, were asleep in the passenger seats. The one driver who was awake was finishing his prayers when the doctor and the missionary hired his services. Through the sleeping town, they rode in the rickshaw; such peacefulness was improbable in Bombay.

By the Junagadh railroad station, they saw a yellow shack where several early risers were renting bicycles. They passed a coconut plantation. They saw a sign to the zoo, with a leopard on it. They passed a mosque, a hospital, the Hotel Relief, a vegetable market and an old fort; they saw two temples, two water tanks, some mango groves and what Dr Daruwalla said was a baobab tree – Martin Mills said it wasn't. Their driver took them to a teak forest. This was the start of the climb up Girnar Hill, the driver told them; from this point on, they would have to proceed on foot. It was a 600-meter ascent up 10,000 stone steps; it would take them about two hours, their driver said.

'Why on earth does he think we want to climb ten thousand steps for two hours?' Martin asked Farrokh. But when the doctor explained that the hill was sacred to the Jains, the Jesuit wanted to climb it.

'It's just a bunch of temples!' Dr Daruwalla cried. The place would probaby be crawling with sadhus, practicing yoga. There would be unappetitizing refreshment stalls and scavenging monkeys and the repugnant evidence of human feces along the way. (There would be eagles soaring overhead, their rickshaw driver informed them.)

There was no stopping the Jesuit from his holy climb; the doctor wondered if the arduous trek was a substitute for Mass. The climb took them barely an hour and a half, largely because the scholastic walked so fast. There were monkeys nearby, and these doubtless made the missionary walk faster; after his chimp experience, Martin was wary of ape-related animals — even small ones. They saw only one eagle. They passed several sadhus, who were climbing up the holy hill as the doctor and the Jesuit were walking down. It was too early for most of the refreshment stalls to be open; at one stall, they split an orange soda between them. The doctor had to agree that the marble temples near the summit were impressive, especially the largest and the oldest, which was a Jain temple from the 12th century.

By the time they descended, they were both panting, and Dr Daruwalla remarked that his knees were killing him; no religion was worth 10,000 steps, Farrokh said. The occasional encounters with human feces had depressed him, and during the entire hike he'd worried that their driver would abandon them and they'd be forced to walk back to town. If Farrokh had tipped the driver too much before their climb, there would be no incentive for the driver to stay; if Farrokh had tipped him too little, the driver would be too insulted to wait for them.

'It will be a miracle if our driver hasn't absconded,' Farrokh told Martin. But their driver was not only waiting for them; as they came upon him, they saw that the faithful man was cleaning his rickshaw.

'You really should restrict your use of this word "miracle,"' the missionary said; his neck bandage was beginning to unravel because the hike had made him sweat.

It was time to wake the children and take them to the circus. It vexed Farrokh that Martin Mills had waited until now to say the obvious. The scholastic would say it only once. 'Dear God,' the Jesuit said, 'I hope we're doing the right thing.'

23. LEAVING THE CHILDREN

Not Charlton Heston

For weeks after the unusual foursome had departed from the Government Circuit House in Junagadh, the rabies vaccine and the vial of immune globulin, which Dr Daruwalla had forgotten, remained in the lobby refrigerator. One night, the Muslim boy who regularly ate the saffron-colored yogurt remembered that the unclaimed package was the doctor's medicine; everyone was afraid to touch it, but someone mustered the courage and threw it out. As for the one sock and the lone left-footed sandal, which the elephant boy had intentionally left behind, these were donated to the town hospital, although it was improbable that anyone there could use them. At the circus, Ganesh knew, neither the sock nor the sandal would be of any value to him; they weren't necessary for a cook's helper, or for a skywalker.

The cripple was a barefoot boy when he limped into the ringmaster's troupe tent on Sunday morning; it was still before 10:00, and Mr and Mrs Das (and at least a dozen child acrobats) were sitting cross-legged on the rugs, watching the *Mahabharata* on TV. Despite their hike up Girnar Hill, the doctor and the missionary had brought the children to the circus too early. No one greeted them, which made Madhu instantly awkward; she bumped into a bigger girl, who still paid no attention to her. Mrs Das, without taking her eyes from the television, waved both her arms – a confusing signal. Did she mean for them to go away or should they sit down? The ringmaster cleared up the matter. 'Sit – anywhere!' Mr Das commanded.

Ganesh and Madhu were immediately riveted to the

658

TV; the seriousness of the *Mahabharata* was obvious to them. Even beggars knew the Sunday-morning routine; they often watched the program through store-front windows. Sometimes people without televisions assembled quietly outside the open windows of those apartments where the TV was on; it didn't matter if they couldn't see the screen – they could still hear the battles and the singing. Child prostitutes, too, the doctor assumed, were familiar with the famous show. Only Martin Mills was perplexed by the visible reverence in the troupe tent; the zealot failed to recognize that everyone's attention had been captured by a religious epic.

'Is this a popular musical?' the Jesuit whispered to Dr Daruwalla.

'It's the *Mahabharata* – be quiet!' Farrokh told him.

'The *Mahabharata* is on television?' the missionary cried. 'The whole thing? It must be ten times as long as the Bible!'

'Ssshhh!' the doctor replied. Mrs Das waved both her arms again.

There on the screen was Lord Krishna, 'the dark one' – an avatar of Vishnu. The child acrobats gaped in awe; Ganesh and Madhu were transfixed. Mrs Das rocked back and forth; she was quietly humming. Even the ringmaster hung on Krishna's every word. The sound of weeping was in the background of the scene; apparently Lord Krishna's speech was emotionally stirring.

'Who's that guy?' Martin whispered.

'Lord Krishna,' whispered Dr Daruwalla.

There went both of Mrs Das's arms again, but the scholastic was too excited to keep quiet. Just before the show was over, the Jesuit whispered once more in the doctor's ear; the zealot felt compelled to say that Lord Krishna reminded him of Charlton Heston.

But Sunday morning at the circus was special for more reasons than the *Mahabharata*. It was the only morning in the week when the child acrobats didn't practice their acts, or learn new items, or even do their strength and flexibility exercises. They did do their chores; they would sweep and neaten their bed areas, and they swept and cleaned the tiny kitchen in the troupe tent. If there were sequins missing from their costumes, they would get out the old tea tins that were filled with sequins – one color per tin – and sew new sequins on their singlets.

Mrs Das wasn't unfriendly as she introduced Madhu to these chores; nor were the other girls in the troupe tent unwelcoming to Madhu. An older girl went through the costume trunks, pulling out the singlets that she thought might fit the child prostitute. Madhu was interested in the costumes; she was even eager to try them on.

Mrs Das confided to Dr Daruwalla that she was happy Madhu wasn't from Kerala. 'Kerala girls want too much,' said the ringmaster's wife. 'They expect good food all the time, and coconut hair oil.'

Mr Das spoke to Dr Daruwalla in hushed confidentiality; Kerala girls were reputed to be a hot lay, a virtue negated by the fact that these girls would attempt to unionize everyone. The circus was no place for a Communist-party revolt; the ringmaster concurred with his wife – it was a good thing Madhu wasn't a Kerala girl. This was as close as Mr and Mrs Das could come to sounding reassuring – by expressing a common prejudice against people from somewhere else.

The child acrobats were not unkind to Ganesh; they simply ignored him. Martin Mills in his bandages was more interesting to them; they'd all heard about the chimp attack – many of them had seen it. The elaborately bandaged wounds excited them, although they were disappointed that Dr Daruwalla refused to unwrap the ear; they wanted to see what was missing.

'How much? This much?' one of the acrobats asked the missionary.

'Actually,' Martin replied, 'I didn't see how much was missing.'

660

This conversation deteriorated into speculation about whether or not Gautam had swallowed the piece of earlobe. Dr Daruwalla observed that none of the child acrobats appeared to notice how the missionary resembled Inspector Dhar, although Hindi films were a part of their world. Their interest was in the missing piece of Martin's earlobe, and whether or not the ape had eaten it.

'Chimps aren't meat eaters,' said an older boy. 'If Gautam swallowed it, he'd be sick this morning.' Some of them, those who'd finished their chores, went to see if Gautam was sick; they insisted that the missionary come with them. Dr Daruwalla realized that he shouldn't linger; it wouldn't do Madhu any good.

'I'll say good-bye now,' the doctor told the child prostitute. 'I hope that your new life is happy. Please be careful.'

When she put her arms around his neck, Farrokh flinched; he thought she was going to kiss him, but he was mistaken. All she wanted to do was whisper in his ear. 'Take me home,' Madhu whispered. But what was 'home' – what could she mean? the doctor wondered. Before he could ask her, she told him. 'I want to be with Acid Man,' she whispered. Just that simply, Madhu had adopted Dr Daruwalla's name for Mr Garg. All the screenwriter could do was take her arms from his neck and give her a worried look. Then the older girl distracted Madhu with a brightly sequined singlet – the front was red, the back orange – and Farrokh was able to slip away.

Chandra had built a bed for the elephant boy in a wing of the cook's tent; Ganesh would sleep surrounded by sacks of onions and rice – a wall of tea tins was the makeshift headboard for his bed. So that the boy wouldn't be homesick, the cook had given him a Maharashtrian calendar; there was Parvati with her elephant-headed son, Ganesh – Lord Ganesha, 'the lord of hosts,' the one-tusked deity.

It was hard for Farrokh to say good-bye. He asked

the cook's permission to take a walk with the elephant-footed boy. They went to look at the lions and tigers, but it was well before meat-feeding time; the big cats were either asleep or cranky. Then the doctor and the cripple strolled in the avenue of troupe tents. A dwarf clown was washing his hair in a bucket, another was shaving; Farrokh was relieved that none of the clowns had tried to imitate Ganesh's limp, although Vinod had warned the boy that this was sure to happen. They paused at Mr and Mrs Bhagwan's tent; in front was a display of the knife thrower's knives – apparently it was knife-sharpening day for Mr Bhagwan – and in the doorway Mrs Bhagwan was unbraiding her long black hair, which reached nearly to her waist.

When the skywalker saw the cripple, she called him to her. Dr Daruwalla followed shyly. Everyone who limps needs extra protection, Mrs Bhagwan was telling the elephant boy; therefore, she wanted him to have a Shirdi Sai Baba medallion – Sai Baba, she said, was the patron saint of all people who were afraid of falling. 'Now he won't be afraid,' Mrs Bhagwan explained to Dr Daruwalla. She tied the trinket around the boy's neck; it was a very thin piece of silver on a rawhide thong. Watching her, the doctor could only marvel at how, as an unmarried woman, she'd once suffered the Skywalk while bleeding from her period – before it was proper for her to use a tampon. Now she mechanically submitted to the Skywalk, and to her husband's knives.

Although Mrs Bhagwan wasn't pretty, her hair was shiny and beautiful; yet Ganesh wasn't looking at her hair – he was staring into her tent. Along the roof was the practice model for the Skywalk, the ladderlike device, complete with exactly 18 loops. Not even Mrs Bhagwan could skywalk without practice. Also hanging from the roof of the troupe tent was a dental trapeze; it was as shiny as Mrs Bhagwan's hair – the doctor imagined that it might still be wet from her mouth.

Mrs Bhagwan saw where the boy was looking.

'He's got this foolish idea that he wants to be a skywalker,' Farrokh explained.

Mrs Bhagwan looked sternly at Ganesh. 'That *is* a foolish idea,' she said to the cripple. She took hold of her gift, the boy's Sai Baba medallion, and tugged it gently in her gnarled hand. Dr Daruwalla realized that Mrs Bhagwan's hands were as large and powerful-looking as a man's; the doctor was unpleasantly reminded of his last glimpse of the second Mrs Dogar's hands – how they'd restlessly plucked at the table-cloth, how they'd looked like paws. 'Not even Shirdi Sai Baba can save a skywalker from falling,' Mrs Bhagwan told Ganesh.

'What saves *you* then?' the boy asked her.

The skywalker showed him her feet; they were bare under the long skirt of her sari, and they were oddly graceful, even delicate, in comparison to her hands. But the tops of her feet and the fronts of her ankles were so roughly chafed that the normal skin was gone; in its place was hardened scar tissue, wrinkled and cracked.

'Feel them,' Mrs Bhagwan told the boy. 'You, too,' she said to the doctor, who obeyed. He'd never touched the skin of an elephant or a rhino before; he'd only imagined their tough, leathery hides. The doctor couldn't help speculating that there must be an oint-ment or a lotion that Mrs Bhagwan could put on her poor feet to help heal the cracks in her hardened skin; then it occurred to him that if the cracks were healed, her skin would be too callused to allow her to feel the loops chafing against her feet. If her cracked skin gave her pain, the pain was also her guide to knowing that her feet were securely in the loops – the right way. Without pain, Mrs Bhagwan would have to rely on her sense of sight alone; when it came to putting her feet in the loops, two senses (pain *and* sight) were probably better than one.

Ganesh didn't appear to be discouraged by the look

and feel of Mrs Bhagwan's feet. His eyes were healing – they looked clearer every day – and in the cripple's alert face there was that radiance which reflected his unchanged belief in the future. He knew he could master the Skywalk. One foot was ready to begin; it was merely a matter of bringing the other foot along.

Jesus in the Parking Lot

Meanwhile, the missionary had provoked mayhem in the area of the chimp cages. Gautam was infuriated to see him – the bandages being even whiter than the scholastic's skin. On the other hand, the flirtatious Mira reached her long arms through the bars of her cage as if she were beseeching Martin for an embrace. Gautam responded by forcefully urinating in the missionary's direction. Martin believed he should remove himself from the chimpanzees' view rather than stand there and encourage their apery, but Kunal wanted the missionary to stay. It would be a valuable lesson to Gautam, Kunal reasoned: the more violently the ape reacted to the Jesuit's presence, the more Kunal beat the ape. To Martin's mind, the psychology of disciplining Gautam in this fashion seemed flawed; yet the Jesuit obeyed the trainer's instructions.

In Gautam's cage, there was an old tire; the tread was bald and the tire swung from a frayed rope. In his anger, Gautam hurled the tire against the bars of his cage; then he seized the tire and sank his teeth into the rubber. Kunal responded by reaching through the bars and jabbing Gautam with a bamboo pole. Mira rolled onto her back.

When Dr Daruwalla finally found the missionary, Martin Mills was standing helplessly before this apish drama, looking as guilty and as compromised as a prisoner.

'For God's sake – why are you standing here?' the

doctor asked him. 'If you just walked away, all this would stop!'

'That's what *I* think,' the Jesuit replied. 'But the trainer told me to stay.'

'Is he *your* trainer or the chimps' trainer?' Farrokh asked Martin.

Thus the missionary's good-byes to Ganesh were conducted with the racist ape's shrieks and howls in the background; it was hard to imagine this as a learning experience for Gautam. The two men followed Ramu to the Land Rover. The last cages they passed were those of the sleepy, disgruntled lions; the tigers looked equally listless and out of humor. The reckless driver ran his fingers along the bars of the big cats' cages; occasionally a paw (claws extended) flicked out, but Ramu confidently withdrew his hand in time.

'One more hour until meat-feeding time,' Ramu sang to the lions and tigers. 'One whole hour.'

It was unfortunate that such a note of mockery, if not an underlying cruelty, described their departure from the Great Blue Nile. Dr Daruwalla looked only once at the elephant boy's retreating figure. Ganesh was limping back to the cook's tent. In the cripple's unsteady gait, his right heel appeared to bear the weight of two or three boys; like a dewclaw on a dog or a cat, the ball of the boy's right foot (and his toes) never touched the ground. No wonder he wanted to walk on the sky.

As for Farrokh and Martin, their lives were once again in Ramu's hands. Their drive to the airport in Rajkot was in daylight. Both the highway's carnage and the Land Rover's near misses could be clearly seen. Once again, Dr Daruwalla sought to be distracted from Ramu's driving, but the doctor found himself up front in the passenger seat this time, and there was no seat belt. Martin clung to the back of the front seat, his head over Farrokh's shoulder, which probably blocked whatever view Ramu might have had in the rearview mirror – not that Ramu would even glance at what might be coming up behind him, or that anything could be fast enough to be coming up from behind.

Because Junagadh was the jumping-off point for visits to the Gir Forest, which was the last habitat of the Asian lion, Ramu wanted to know if they'd seen the forest – they hadn't – and Martin Mills wanted to know what Ramu had said. This would be a long trip, the doctor imagined – Ramu speaking Marathi and Hindi, Farrokh struggling to translate. The missionary was sorry that they hadn't seen the Gir lions. Maybe when they returned to visit the children, they could see the forest. By then, the doctor suspected, the Great Blue Nile would be playing in another town. There were a few Asian lions in the town zoo, Ramu told them; they could have a quick look at the lions and still manage to catch their plane in Rajkot. But Farrokh wisely vetoed this idea; he knew that any delay in their departure from Junagadh would make Ramu drive to Rajkot all the faster.

Nor was a discussion of Graham Greene as distracting as Farrokh had hoped. The Jesuit's 'Catholic interpretation' of *The Heart of the Matter* wasn't at all what the doctor was looking for; it was infuriating. Not even a novel as profoundly about faith as *The Power and the Glory* could or should be discussed in strictly 'Catholic' terms, Dr Daruwalla argued; the doctor quoted, from memory, that passage which he loved. '"There is always one moment in childhood when the door opens and lets the future in."'

'Perhaps you'll tell me what is especially Catholic about that,' the doctor challenged the scholastic, but Martin skillfully changed the subject.

'Let us pray that this door opens and lets the future in for our children at the circus,' the Jesuit said. What a sneaky mind he had!

Farrokh didn't dare ask him anything more about his mother; not even Ramu's driving was as daunting as the possibility of another story about Vera. What Farrokh desired to hear was more about the homosexual inclinations of Dhar's twin; the doctor was chiefly curious to learn whether or not John D. was so inclined, but Dr Daruwalla felt uncertain of how to inspire such a subject of conversation with John D.'s twin. However, it would be an easier subject to broach with Martin than with John D.

'You say you were in love with a man, and that your feelings for him finally *lessened*,' the doctor began.

'That's correct,' the scholastic said stiffly.

'But can you point to any moment or to any single episode that marked the end of your infatuation?' Farrokh asked. 'Did anything happen – was there an incident that convinced you? What made you decide you could resist such an attraction and become a priest?' This was beating around the bush, Dr Daruwalla knew, but the doctor had to begin somewhere.

'I saw how Christ existed for me. I saw that Jesus had never abandoned me,' the zealot said.

'Do you mean you had a *vision?*' Farrokh asked.

'In a way,' the Jesuit said mysteriously. 'I was at a low point in my relationship with Jesus. And I'd reached a very cynical decision. There is no lack of resistance that is as great a giving-up as fatalism – I'm ashamed to say I was totally fatalistic.'

'Did you actually see Christ or didn't you?' the doctor asked him.

'Actually, it was only a *statue* of Christ,' the missionary admitted.

'You mean it was real?' Farrokh asked.

'Of course it was real – it was at the end of a parking lot, at the school where I taught. I used to see it every day – twice a day, in fact,' Martin said. 'It was just a white stone statue of Christ in a typical pose.' And there, in the back seat of the speeding Land Rover, the zealot rotated both his palms toward heaven, apparently to demonstrate the pose of the supplicant.

'It sounds truly tasteless – Christ in a parking lot!' Dr Daruwalla remarked.

'It wasn't very artistic,' the Jesuit replied. 'Occasionally, as I recall, the statue was vandalized.'

'I can't imagine why,' Farrokh muttered.

'Well, anyway, I had stayed at the school quite late one night – I was directing a school play, another musical . . . I can't remember which one. And this man who'd been such an obsession for me . . . he was also staying late. But his car wouldn't start – he had an awful car – and he asked me for a ride home.'

'Uh-oh,' said Dr Daruwalla.

'My feelings for him had already lessened, as I've said, but I was still not immune to his attractiveness,' the missionary admitted. 'Here was such a sudden opportunity – the *availability* of him was painfully apparent. Do you know what I mean?'

Dr Daruwalla, who was remembering his disturbing night with Madhu, said, 'Yes – of course I know. What happened?'

'This is what I mean by how cynical I was,' the scholastic said. 'I was so totally fatalistic, I decided that if he made the slightest advance toward me, I would respond. I wouldn't initiate such an advance, but I knew I would respond.'

'And did you? Did *he?*' the doctor asked.

'Then I couldn't find my car – it was a huge parking lot,' Martin said. 'But I remembered that I always tried to park near Christ . . .'

'The statue, you mean . . .' Farrokh interrupted.

'Yes, the statue, of course – I had parked right in front of it,' the Jesuit explained. 'When I finally found my car, it was so dark I couldn't see the statue, not even when I was sitting inside my car. But I knew exactly where Christ was. It was a funny moment. I was waiting for this man to touch me, but all the while I was looking into the darkness at that exact spot where Jesus was.'

'Did the guy touch you?' Farrokh asked.

'I turned on the headlights before he had a chance,' Martin Mills replied. 'And there was Christ – he stood

668

out very brightly in the headlights. He was exactly where I knew he would be.'

'Where *else* would a statue be?' Dr Daruwalla cried. 'Do statues move around in your country?'

'You belittle the experience to focus on the statue,' the Jesuit said. 'The statue was just the vehicle. What I felt was the presence of God. I felt a oneness with Jesus, too – not with the statue. I felt I'd been shown what believing in Christ was like – for me. Even in the darkness – even as I sat expecting something horrible to happen to me – there was a certainty that he was there. Christ was there for me; he'd not abandoned me. I could still see him.'

'I guess I'm not making the necessary leap,' said Dr Daruwalla. 'I mean, your belief in Christ is one thing. But wanting to be a priest . . . how did you get from Jesus in the parking lot to wanting to be a priest?'

'Well, that's different,' Martin confessed.

'That's the part I don't get,' Farrokh replied. Then he said it: 'And was that the end of all such desires? I mean, was your homosexuality ever again engaged . . . so to speak . . .'

'Homosexuality?' said the Jesuit. 'That's not the point. I'm not a homosexual, nor am I a heterosexual. I am simply not a sexual entity – not anymore.'

'Come on,' the doctor said. 'If you *were* to be sexually attracted, it would be a homosexual attraction, wouldn't it?'

'That's not a relevant question,' the scholastic replied. 'It isn't that I'm without sexual feelings, but I have resisted sexual attraction. I will have no problem continuing to resist it.'

'But what you're resisting is a *homosexual* inclination, isn't it?' Farrokh asked. 'I mean, let us speculate – you can speculate, can't you?'

'I don't speculate on the subject of my vows,' the Jesuit said.

'But, please indulge me, if something happened – if for *any* reason you decided *not* to be a priest – then wouldn't you be a homosexual?' Dr Daruwalla asked.

'Mercy! You are the most stubborn person!' Martin Mills cried out good-naturedly.

'*I* am stubborn?' the doctor shouted.

'I am neither a homosexual nor a heterosexual,' the Jesuit calmly stated. 'The terms don't necessarily apply to *inclinations*, or do they? I had a passing inclination.'

'It has passed? Completely? Is that what you're saying?' Dr Daruwalla asked.

'Mercy,' Martin repeated.

'You become a person of no identifiable sexuality on the basis of an encounter with a statue in a parking lot; yet you deny the possibility that I was bitten by a ghost!' Dr Daruwalla cried. 'Am I following your reasoning correctly?'

'I don't believe in ghosts, per se,' the Jesuit replied.

'But you believe you experienced a oneness with Jesus. You felt the presence of God – in a parking lot!' Farrokh shouted.

'I believe that our conversation – that is, if you continue to raise your voice – is a distraction to our driver,' said Martin Mills. 'Perhaps we should resume discussion of this subject after we've safely arrived at the airport.'

They were still nearly an hour from Rajkot, with Ramu dodging death every few miles; then there would be the wait at the airport, not to mention a likely delay, and finally the flight itself. On a Sunday afternoon or evening, the taxi from Santa Cruz into Bombay could take another 45 minutes or an hour. Worse, it was a special Sunday; it was December 31, 1989, but neither the doctor nor the missionary knew it was New Year's Eve – or if they knew, they'd forgotten.

At St Ignatius, the jubilee celebration was planned for New Year's Day, which Martin Mills had also forgotten, and the New Year's Eve party at the Duckworth Sports Club was a black-tie occasion of uncharacteristic merriment; there would be dancing to a live band and a splendid midnight supper – not to mention the unusual, once-a-year quality of the champagne. No Duckworthian in Bombay would willingly miss the New Year's Eve party.

John D. and Deputy Commissioner Patel were sure that Rahul would be there – Mr Sethna had already informed them. They'd spent much of the day rehearsing what Inspector Dhar would say when he and the second Mrs Dogar danced. Julia had pressed Farrokh's tuxedo, which needed a lengthy airing on the balcony to rid it of its mothball aroma. But both New Year's Eve and the Duckworth Club were far from Farrokh's mind. The doctor was focused on what remained of his journey to Rajkot, after which he still had to travel to Bombay. If Farrokh couldn't endure another minute of Martin's arguments, he had to initiate a different conversation.

'Perhaps we should change the subject,' Dr Daruwalla suggested. 'And keep our voices down.'

'As you wish. I promise to keep *mine* down,' the missionary said with satisfaction.

Farrokh was at a loss to know what to talk about. He tried to think of a long personal story, something which would allow him to talk and talk, and which would render the missionary speechless – powerless to interrupt. The doctor could begin, 'I know your twin'; that would lead to quite a long personal story. *That* would shut Martin Mills up! But, as before, Farrokh felt it wasn't his place to tell this story; that was John D.'s decision.

'Well, *I* can think of something to say,' the scholastic said; he'd been politely waiting for Dr Daruwalla to begin, but he hadn't waited long.

'Very well – go ahead,' the doctor replied.

'I think that you shouldn't go witch-hunting for homosexuals,' the Jesuit began. 'Not *these* days. Not when there is understandable sensitivity toward anything remotely homophobic. What do you have against homosexuals, anyway?'

'I have *nothing* against homosexuals. I'm *not*

homophobic,' Dr Daruwalla snapped. 'And you haven't exactly changed the subject!'

'You're not exactly keeping your voice down,' Martin said.

Little India

At the airport in Rajkot, the loudspeaker system had progressed to a new test; more advanced counting skills were being demonstrated. 'Eleven, twenty-two, thirty-three, forty-four, fifty-five,' said the tireless voice. There was no telling where this would lead; it hinted at infinity. The voice was without emotion; the counting was so mechanical that Dr Daruwalla thought he might go mad. Instead of listening to the numbers or enduring the Jesuitical provocations of Martin Mills, Farrokh chose to tell a story. Although it was a true story – and, as the doctor would soon discover, painful to tell – it suffered from the disadvantage that the storyteller had never told it before; even true stories are improved by revision. But the doctor hoped that his tale would illustrate how the missionary's allegations of homophobia were false, for Dr Daruwalla's favorite colleague in Toronto was a homosexual. Gordon Macfarlane was also Farrokh's best friend.

Unfortunately, the screenwriter began the story in the wrong place. Dr Daruwalla should have started with his earliest acquaintance of Dr Macfarlane, including how the two had concurred on the misuse of the word 'gay'; that they'd generally agreed with the findings of Mac's boyfriend, the gay geneticist – regarding the biology of homosexuality – was also interesting. Had Dr Daruwalla started with a discussion of this subject, he might not have prejudiced Martin Mills against him. But, at the airport in Rajkot, he'd made the mistake of inserting Dr Macfarlane in the form of a flashback – as if Mac were only a minor character and not a friend who was often foremost on Farrokh's mind.

He'd begun with the wrong story, about the time he'd been abducted by a crazed cab driver, for Farrokh's training as a writer of action films had pre-conditioned him to begin any story with the most violent action he could imagine (or, in this case, re-member). But to begin with an episode of racial abuse was misleading to the missionary, who concluded that Farrokh's friendship with Gordon Macfarlane was sec-ondary to the doctor's outrage at his own mistreatment as an Indian in Toronto. This was inept storytelling, for Farrokh had meant only to convey how his mistreat-ment as an obvious immigrant of color in Canada had further solidified his friendship with a homosexual, who was no stranger to discrimination of another kind.

It was a Friday in the spring; many of Farrokh's colleagues left their offices early on Friday afternoons because they were cottagers, but the Daruwallas enjoyed their weekends in Toronto – their second home was in Bombay. Farrokh had had a cancellation; hence he was free to leave early – otherwise, he would have asked Macfarlane for a ride home or called a cab. Mac also spent his weekends in Toronto and kept late office hours on Friday.

Since it wasn't yet rush hour, Farrokh thought he'd walk for a while and then hail a taxi from the street, probably in front of the museum. For some years he'd avoided the subway; an uncomfortable racial incident had happened there. Oh, there'd been shouts from the occasional passing car – no one had ever called him a Parsi; in Toronto, few people knew what a Parsi was. What they called out was 'Paki bastard!' or 'Wog!' or 'Babu!' or 'Go home!' His pale-brown coloring and jet-black hair made it difficult for them; he wasn't as identifiable as many Indians. Sometimes they called him an Arab – twice he'd been called a Jew. It was his Persian ancestry; he could pass for a Middle Easterner. But whoever the shouters were, they knew he was foreign – racially different.

Once he'd even been called a Wop! At the time, he'd

wondered what sort of idiot could mistake him for an Italian. Now he knew that it wasn't *what* he was that bothered the shouters; it was only that he wasn't one of them. But most often the theme of the slurs subscribed to that view of him which can only clumsily be expressed as 'an immigrant of color.' In Canada, it seemed, the prejudice against the *immigrant* composition of his features was as strong as whatever prejudice existed of the *of-color* kind.

He stopped taking the subway after an episode with three teenage boys. At first, they hadn't seemed so threatening – more mischievous. There was a hint of menace only because they sat so deliberately close to him; there were many other places for them to sit. One sat on either side of him, the third across the aisle. The boy to the doctor's left nudged his arm. 'We've got a bet going,' the boy said. 'What *are* you?'

Dr Daruwalla realized later that the only reason he'd found them unthreatening was that they wore their school blazers and ties. After the incident, he could have called their school; he never did.

'I said what *are* you?' the boy repeated. That was the first moment Farrokh felt threatened.

'I'm a doctor,' Dr Daruwalla replied.

The boys on either side of him looked decidedly hostile; it was the boy across the aisle who saved him. 'My dad's a doctor,' the boy stupidly remarked.

'Are you going to be a doctor, too?' Farrokh asked him.

The other two got up; they pulled the third boy along with them.

'Fuck you,' the first boy said to Farrokh, but the doctor knew this was a harmless bomb – already defused.

He never took the subway again. But after his worst episode, the subway incident seemed mild. After his worst episode, Farrokh was so upset, he couldn't remember whether the taxi driver had pulled over before or after the intersection of University and

Gerrard; either way, he'd just left the hospital and he was daydreaming. What was odd, he remembered, was that the driver already had a passenger, and that the passenger was riding in the front seat. The driver said, 'Don't mind him. He's just a friend with nothing to do.'

'I'm not a fare,' the driver's friend said.

Later, Farrokh remembered only that it wasn't one of Metro's taxis or one of Beck's – the two companies he most often called. It was probably what they call a gypsy cab.

'I said where are you going?' the driver asked Dr Daruwalla.

'Home,' Farrokh replied. (It struck him as pointless to add that he'd intended to walk for a while. Here was a taxi. Why not take it?)

'Where's "home"?' the friend in the front seat asked.

'Russell Hill Road, north of St Clair – just north of Lonsdale,' the doctor answered; he'd stopped walking – the taxi had stopped, too. 'Actually, I was going to stop at the beer store – and then go home,' Farrokh added.

'Get in, if you want,' the driver said.

Dr Daruwalla didn't feel anxious until he was settled in the back seat and the taxi began to move. The friend in the front seat belched once, sharply, and the driver laughed. The windshield visor in front of the driver's friend was pushed flat against the windshield, and the glove-compartment door was missing. Farrokh couldn't remember if these were the places where the driver's certification was posted – or was it usually on the Plexiglas divider between the front and back seats? (The Plexiglas divider itself was unusual; in Toronto, most taxis didn't have these dividers.) Anyway, there was no visible driver's certification inside the cab, and the taxi was already moving too fast for Dr Daruwalla to get out – maybe at a red light, the doctor thought. But there were no red lights for a while and the taxi ran the first red light it came to; that was when the driver's friend in the front seat turned around and faced Farrokh.

'So where's your *real* home?' the friend asked.

'Russell Hill Road,' Dr Daruwalla repeated.

'Before that, asshole,' the driver said.

'I was born in Bombay, but I left India when I was a teenager. I'm a Canadian citizen,' Farrokh said.

'Didn't I tell you?' the driver said to his friend.

'Let's take him home,' the friend said.

The driver glanced in the rearview mirror and made a sudden U-turn. Farrokh was thrown against the door.

'We'll show you where your home is, babu,' the driver said.

At no time could Dr Daruwalla have escaped. When they crawled slowly ahead in the traffic, or when they were stopped at a red light, the doctor was too afraid to attempt it. They were moving fairly fast when the driver slammed on the brakes. The doctor's head bounced off the Plexiglas shield. Dr Daruwalla was pressed back into the seat when the driver accelerated. Farrokh felt the tightness of the instant swelling; by the time he gently touched his puffy eyebrow, blood was already running into his eye. Four stitches, maybe six, the doctor's fingers told him.

The area of Little India is not extensive; it stretches along Gerrard from Coxwell to Hiawatha – some would say as far as Woodfield. Everyone would agree that by the time you get to Greenwood, Little India is over; and even in Little India, the Chinese community is interspersed. The taxi stopped in front of the Ahmad Grocers on Gerrard, at Coxwell; it was probably no coincidence that the grocer was diagonally across the street from the offices of the Canadian Ethnic Immigration Services – this was where the driver's friend dragged Farrokh out of the back seat. 'You're home now – better stay here,' the friend told Dr Daruwalla.

'Better yet, babu – go back to Bombay,' the driver added.

As the taxi pulled away, the doctor could see it

clearly out of only one eye; he was so relieved to be free of the thugs that he paid scant attention to the identifying marks of the car. It was red – maybe red and white. If Farrokh saw any printed names or numbers, he wouldn't remember them.

Little India appeared to be mostly closed on Friday. Apparently, no one had seen the doctor roughly pulled out of the taxi; no one approached him, although he was dazed and bleeding – clearly disoriented. A small, pot-bellied man in a dark suit – his white shirt was ruined from the blood that flowed from his split eyebrow – he clutched his doctor's bag in one hand. He began to walk. On the sidewalk, dancing in the spring air, kaftans were hanging on a clothes rack. Later, Farrokh struggled to remember the names of the places. Pindi Embroidery? Nirma Fashions? There was another grocery with fresh fruits and vegetables – maybe the Singh Farm? At the United Church, there was a sign saying that the church also served as the Shri Ram Hindu Temple on Sunday evenings. At the corner of Craven and Gerrard, a restaurant claimed to be 'Indian Cuisine Specialists.' There was also the familiar advertisement for Kingfisher lager – INSTILLED WITH INNER STRENGTH. A poster, promising an ASIA SUPERSTARS NITE, displayed the usual faces: Dimple Kapadia, Sunny Deol, Jaya Prada – with music by Bappi Lahiri.

Dr Daruwalla never came to Little India. In the storefront windows, the mannequins in their saris seemed to rebuke him. Farrokh saw few Indians in Toronto; he had no close Indian friends there. Parsi parents would bring him their sick children – on the evidence of his name in the telephone directory, Dr Daruwalla supposed. Among the mannequins, a blonde in her sari struck Farrokh as sharing his own disorientation.

At Raja Jewellers, someone was staring out the window at him, probably noticing that the doctor was bleeding. There was a South Indian 'Pure Vegetarian Restaurant' near Ashdale and Gerrard. At the Chaat

Hut, they advertised 'all kinds of kulfi, faluda and paan.' At the Bombay Bhel, the sign said FOR TRUE AUTHENTIC GOL GUPPA ... ALOO TIKKI ... ETC. They served Thunderbolt beer, SUPER STRONG LAGER ... THE SPIRIT OF EXCITEMENT. More saris were in a window at Hiawatha and Gerrard. And at the Shree Groceries, a pile of ginger root overflowed the store, extending onto the sidewalk. The doctor gazed at the India Theater ... at the Silk Den.

At J. S. Addison Plumbing, at the corner of Wood-field and Gerrard, Farrokh saw a fabulous copper bathtub with ornate faucets; the handles were tiger heads, the tigers roaring – it was like the tub he'd bathed in as a boy on old Ridge Road, Malabar Hill. Dr Daruwalla began to cry. Staring at the display of copper sinks and drains and other bathroom Victor-iana, he was suddenly aware of a man's concerned face staring back at him. The man came out on the side-walk.

'You've been hurt – may I help you?' the man asked; he wasn't an Indian.

'I'm a doctor,' said Dr Daruwalla. 'Please just call me a taxi – I know where to go.' He had the taxi take him back to the Hospital for Sick Children.

'You sure you want Sick Kids, mon?' the driver asked; he was a West Indian, a black man – very black. 'You don't look like a sick kid to me.'

'I'm a doctor,' Farrokh said. 'I work there.'

'Who done that to you, mon?' the driver asked.

'Two guys who don't like people like me – or like you,' the doctor told him.

'I know them – they everywhere, mon,' the driver said.

Dr Daruwalla was relieved that his secretary and his nurse had gone home. He kept a change of clothes in his office; after he was stitched up, he would throw the shirt away ... he'd ask his secretary to have the suit dry-cleaned.

He examined the split wound on his eyebrow; using

the mirror, he shaved around the gash. This was easy, but he was used to shaving in a mirror; then he contemplated the procaine injection and the sutures – to do these properly in the mirror was baffling to him, especially the sewing. Farrokh called Dr Macfarlane's office and asked the secretary to have Mac stop by when he was ready to go home.

Farrokh first tried to tell Macfarlane that he'd hit his head in a taxi because of a reckless driver, the brakes throwing him forward into the Plexiglas divider. Although it was the truth, or only a lie of omission, his voice trailed off; his fear, the insult, his anger – these things were still reflected in his eyes.

'Who did this to you, Farrokh?' Mac asked.

Dr Daruwalla told Dr Macfarlane the whole story – beginning with the three teenagers on the subway and including the shouts from the passing cars. By the time Mac had stitched him up – it required five sutures to close the wound – Farrokh had used the expression 'an immigrant of color' more times than he'd ever uttered it aloud before, even to Julia. He would never tell Julia about Little India, either; that Mac knew was comfort enough.

Dr Macfarlane had his own stories. He'd never been beaten up, but he'd been threatened and intimidated. There were phone calls late at night; he'd changed his number three times. There were also phone calls to his office; two of his former secretaries had resigned, and one of his former nurses. Sometimes letters or notes were shoved under his office door; perhaps these were from the parents of former patients, or from his fellow doctors, or from other people who worked at Sick Kids.

Mac helped Farrokh rehearse how he would describe his 'accident' to Julia. It sounded more plausible if it wasn't the taxi driver's fault. They decided that an idiot woman had pulled out from the curb without looking; the driver had had no choice but to hit the brakes. (A blameless woman driver had been blamed again.) As soon as he realized he was cut and bleeding, Farrokh had asked the driver to take him back to the hospital; fortunately, Macfarlane was still there and had stitched him up. Just five sutures. His white shirt was a total loss, and he wouldn't know about the suit until it came back from the cleaner's.

'Why not just tell Julia what happened?' Mac asked.

'She'll be disappointed in me – because I didn't do anything,' Farrokh told him.

'I doubt that,' Macfarlane said.

'*I'm* disappointed that I didn't do anything,' Dr Daruwalla admitted.

'That can't be helped,' Mac said.

On the way home to Russell Hill Road, Farrokh asked Mac about his work at the AIDS hospice – there was a good one in Toronto.

'I'm just a volunteer,' Macfarlane explained.

'But you're a *doctor*,' Dr Daruwalla said. 'I mean, it must be interesting there. But exactly what can an orthopedist do?'

'Nothing,' Mac said. 'I'm not a doctor there.'

'But of course you're a doctor – you're a doctor anywhere!' Farrokh cried. 'There must be patients with bed sores. We know what to do with bed sores. And what about pain control?' Dr Daruwalla was thinking of morphine, a wonderful drug; it disconnects the lungs from the brain. Wouldn't many of the deaths in an AIDS hospice be respiratory deaths? Wouldn't morphine be especially useful there? The respiratory distress is unchanged, but the patient is unaware of it. 'And what about muscular wasting, from being bed-ridden?' Farrokh added. 'Surely you could instruct families in passive range-of-motion exercises, or dispense tennis balls for the patients to squeeze . . .'

Dr Macfarlane laughed. 'The hospice has its own doctors. They're AIDS doctors,' Macfarlane said. 'I'm absolutely not a doctor there. That's something I like about it – I'm just a volunteer.'

'What about the catheters?' Farrokh asked. 'They

680

must get blocked, the skin tunnels get inflamed . . .'
His voice fell away; he was wondering if you could
unplug them by flushing them with an anticoagulant,
but Macfarlane wouldn't let him finish the thought.

'I don't do anything medical there,' Mac told him.

'Then what *do* you do?' Dr Daruwalla asked.

'One night I did all the laundry,' Macfarlane replied.
'Another night I answered the phone.'

'But anyone could do that!' Farrokh cried.

'Yes – any volunteer,' Mac agreed.

'Listen. There's a seizure, a patient seizes from uncontrolled infection,' Dr Daruwalla began. 'What do
you do? Do you give intravenous Valium?'

'I call the doctor,' Dr Macfarlane said.

'You're kidding me!' said Dr Daruwalla. 'And what
about the feeding tubes? They slip out. Then what? Do
you have your own X ray facilities or do you have to
take them to a hospital?'

'I call the doctor,' Macfarlane repeated. 'It's a
hospice – they're not there to get well. One night I read
aloud to someone who couldn't sleep. Lately, I've been
writing letters for a man who wants to contact his
family and his friends – he wants to say good-bye, but
he never learned how to write.'

'Incredible!' Dr Daruwalla said.

'They come there to die, Farrokh. We try to help
them control it. We can't help them like we're used to
helping most of our patients,' Macfarlane explained.

'So you just go there, you show up,' Farrokh began.
'You check in . . . tell someone you've arrived. Then
what?'

'Usually a nurse tells me what to do,' Mac said.

'A nurse tells the doctor what to do!' cried Dr Daruwalla.

'Now you're getting it,' Dr Macfarlane told him.

There was his home on Russell Hill Road. It was a
long way from Bombay; it was a long way from Little
India, too.

'Honestly, if you want to know what *I* think,' said

681

Martin Mills, who'd interrupted Farrokh's story only a half-dozen times, '*I* think you must drive your poor friend Macfarlane crazy. Obviously, you like him, but on whose terms? On *your* terms – on your heterosexual doctor terms.'

'But that's what I *am*!' Dr Daruwalla shouted. 'I'm a heterosexual doctor!' Several people in the Rajkot airport looked mildly surprised.

'Three thousand, eight hundred and ninety-four,' the voice on the loudspeaker said.

'The point is, could you empathize with a *raving* gay man?' the missionary asked. '*Not* a doctor, and some-one not even in the least sympathetic to *your* problems – someone who couldn't care less about racism, or what happens to immigrants of color, as you say? You think you're not homophobic, but how much could you care about someone like that?'

'Why *should* I care about someone like that?' Farrokh screamed.

'That's my point about you. Do you see what I mean?' the missionary asked. 'You're a typical homo-phobe.'

'Three thousand, nine hundred and forty-nine,' the voice on the loudspeaker droned.

'You can't even listen to a story,' Dr Daruwalla told the Jesuit.

'Mercy!' said Martin Mills.

They were delayed in boarding the plane because the authorities again confiscated the scholastic's dangerous Swiss Army knife.

'Couldn't you have remembered to pack the damn knife in your bag?' Dr Daruwalla asked the scholastic.

'Given the mood you're in, I'd be foolish to answer questions of that kind,' Martin replied. When they were finally on board the aircraft, Martin said, 'Look. We're both worried about the children – I know that. But we've done the best we can for them.'

'Short of adopting them,' Dr Daruwalla remarked.

'Well, we weren't in a position to do that, were we?'

the Jesuit asked. 'My point is, we've put them in a position where at least they can help themselves.'

'Don't make me throw up,' Farrokh said.

'They're safer in the circus than where they were,' the zealot insisted. 'In how many weeks or months would the boy have been blind? How long would it have taken the girl to contract some horrible disease – even the worst? Not to mention what she would have endured before that. Of *course* you're worried. So am I. But there's nothing more we can do.'

'Is this fatalism I hear?' Farrokh asked.

'Mercy, no!' the missionary replied. 'Those children are in God's hands – that's what I mean.'

'I guess that's why I'm worried,' Dr Daruwalla replied.

'You weren't bitten by a monkey!' Martin Mills shouted.

'I *told* you I wasn't,' Farrokh said.

'You must have been bitten by a snake – a *poisonous* snake,' the missionary said. 'Or else the Devil himself bit you.'

After almost two hours of silence – their plane had landed and Vinod's taxi was navigating the Sunday traffic from Santa Cruz to Bombay – Martin Mills thought of something to add. 'Furthermore,' the Jesuit said, 'I get the feeling you're keeping something from me. It's as if you're always stopping yourself – you're always biting your tongue.'

I'm not telling you *half*! the doctor almost hollered. But Farrokh bit his tongue again. In the slanting light of the late afternoon, the lurid movie posters displayed the confident image of Martin Mills's twin. Many of the posters for *Inspector Dhar and the Towers of Silence* were already defaced; yet through the tatters and the muck flung from the street, Dhar's sneer seemed to be assessing them.

In reality, John D. had been rehearsing a different role, for the seduction of the second Mrs Dogar was out of Inspector Dhar's genre. Rahul wasn't the usual cinema bimbo. If Dr Daruwalla had known who'd bitten him in his hammock at the Hotel Bardez, the doctor would have agreed with Martin Mills, for Farrokh truly had been bitten by the Devil himself . . . by the Devil *herself*, the second Mrs Dogar would prefer.

As the dwarf's taxi came into Bombay, it was momentarily stalled near an Iranian restaurant – of a kind not quite in a class with Lucky New Moon or Light of Asia, Dr Daruwalla was thinking. The doctor was hungry. Towering over the restaurant was a nearly destroyed Inspector Dhar poster; the movie star was ripped open from his cheek to his waist, but his sneer was undamaged. Beside the mutilated Dhar was a poster of Lord Ganesha; the elephant-headed deity might have been advertising an upcoming religious festival, but the traffic began to move before Farrokh could translate the announcement.

The god was short and fat, but surpassingly beautiful to his believers; Lord Ganesha's elephant face was as red as a China rose and he sported the lotus smile of a perpetual daydreamer. His four human arms swarmed with bees – doubtless attracted by the perfume of the ichor flowing in his godly veins – and his three all-seeing eyes looked down upon Bombay with a benevolence that challenged Dhar's sneer. Lord Ganesha's pot belly hung almost to his human feet; his toenails were as long and brightly painted as a woman's. In the sharply angled light, his one unbroken tusk gleamed.

'That elephant is everywhere!' exlaimed the Jesuit. 'What happened to its other tusk?'

The myth that Farrokh had loved best as a child was that Lord Ganesha broke off his own tusk and threw it at the moon; the moon had mocked the elephant-headed god for his portliness and for being clumsy. Old Lowji had liked this story; he'd told it to Farrokh and Jamshed when they were small boys. Only now did Dr Daruwalla wonder if this was a real myth, or if it was only Lowji's myth; the old man wasn't above making up a myth of his own.

There were other myths; there was more than one story about Ganesh's birth, too. In a South Indian version, Parvati saw the sacred syllable 'Om,' and her mere glance transformed it into two coupling elephants, who gave birth to Lord Ganesha and then resumed the form of the sacred syllable. But in a dark version, which attests to the reputed sexual antagonism between Parvati and her husband, Lord Shiva, a considerable jealousy attended Shiva's feelings for Parvati's son, who – not unlike the baby Jesus – was never described as being born from Parvati in the 'natural' manner.

In the darker myth, it was Shiva's evil eye that beheaded the newborn Ganesh, who wasn't born with an elephant's head. The only way the child could live was if someone else's head – someone facing north – was found and attached to the headless boy. What was found, after a great battle, was an unfortunate elephant, and in the violent course of the elephant's beheading, one tusk was broken.

But because he'd first heard it as a boy, Farrokh preferred the myth of the moon.

'Excuse me – did you hear me?' Martin asked the doctor. 'I was inquiring what happened to that elephant's other tusk.'

'He broke it himself,' Dr Daruwalla replied. 'He got pissed off and threw it at the moon.' In the rearview mirror, the dwarf gave the doctor the evil eye; a good Hindu, Vinod wasn't amused by Dr Daruwalla's blasphemy. Surely Lord Ganesha was never 'pissed off,' which was strictly a mortal weakness.

The missionary's sigh was intended to convey his long-suffering patience with whatever vexatious mood the doctor was in. 'There you go again,' the Jesuit said. 'Still keeping something from me.'

24. THE DEVIL HERSELF

Getting Ready for Rahul

Although Deputy Commissioner Patel had insulted Mr
Sethna, the disapproving steward relished his new role
as a police informant, for self-importance was Mr
Sethna's middle name; also, the deputy com-
missioner's stated objective of entrapping the second
Mrs Dogar greatly pleased the old Parsi. Nonetheless,
Mr Sethna faulted Detective Patel for not trusting him
more completely; it irritated the steward that he was
given his instructions without being informed of the
overall plan. But the extent of the intrigue against
Rahul was contingent on how Rahul responded to
John D.'s sexual overtures. In rehearsing Inspector
Dhar's seduction of Mrs Dogar, both the real policeman and the actor were forced to consider more than
one outcome. That was why they'd been waiting for
Farrokh to come back from the circus; not only did
they want the screenwriter to provide Dhar with some
dialogue – Dhar also needed to know some alternative
conversation, in case his first advances were rebuffed.

This was vastly more demanding dialogue than Dr
Daruwalla was accustomed to writing, for it was not
just that he was required to anticipate the various
responses that Rahul might make; the screenwriter
also needed to guess what Mrs Dogar might *like* – that
is, sexually. Would she be more attracted to John D. if
he was gentlemanly or if he was crude? For flirtation,
did she favor the discreet approach or the explicit? A
screenwriter could only suggest certain directions in
which the dialogue might roam; Dhar could charm
her, tease her, tempt her, shock her, but the particular
approach that the actor chose would necessarily be a

spontaneous decision. John D. had to rely on his instincts for what would work. After Dr Daruwalla's most revealing conversations with Dhar's twin, the doctor could only wonder what John D.'s 'instincts' were.

Farrokh wasn't prepared to find Detective Patel and Inspector Dhar waiting for him in his Marine Drive apartment. To begin with Dr Daruwalla wondered why they were so well dressed; he still didn't realize it was New Year's Eve – not until he saw what Julia was wearing. Then it puzzled him why everyone had dressed for New Year's Eve so early; no one ever showed up for the party at the Duckworth Club before 8:00 or 9:00.

But no one had wanted to waste time dressing when they could be rehearsing, and they couldn't properly rehearse Dhar's options for dialogue until *after* the screenwriter was home from the circus and had written the lines. Farrokh felt flattered – having first suffered the keenest disappointment for being left out of the process – but he was also overwhelmed; he'd been writing for the last three nights, and he feared he might be written-out. And he hated New Year's Eve; the night seemed to prey on his natural inclination toward nostalgia (especially at the Duckworth Club), although Julia did enjoy the dancing.

Dr Daruwalla expressed his regret that there wasn't time to tell them what had happened at the circus; interesting things had transpired there. That was when John D. said something insensitive by stating that preparing himself for the seduction of the second Mrs Dogar was 'no circus'; those were the disparaging words he used – meaning that the doctor should save his silly circus stories for another, more frivolous time.

Detective Patel came to the point even more bluntly. The top half of the silver ballpoint pen had not only revealed Rahul's fingerprints; a speck of dried blood had been removed from the pocket clasp – it was human blood, of Mr Lal's type. 'May I remind you,

Doctor,' said the deputy commissioner, 'it is still necessary to determine what Rahul would have been doing with the top half of the pen ... *during* the murder of Mr Lal.'

'It's also necessary for Mrs Dogar to admit that the top half of the pen is hers,' John D. interrupted.

'Yes, thank you,' Patel said, 'but the top half of the pen isn't incriminating evidence – at least not by itself. What we really need to establish is that no one else could have made those drawings. I'm told that drawings like those are as identifiable as a signature, but it's necessary to induce Mrs Dogar to *draw*.'

'If there was a way for me to suggest to her that she should *show* me what it might be like ... between us,' Dhar told the screenwriter. 'Maybe I could ask her to give me just a hint of what she preferred – I mean, sexually. Or I could ask her to tease me with something – I mean, something sexually explicit,' the actor said.

'Yes, yes – I get the picture,' Dr Daruwalla said impatiently.

'And then there are the two-rupee notes,' the real policeman said. 'If Rahul is thinking of killing anyone else, perhaps there exist some notes with the appropriate warnings or messages already typed on the money.'

'Surely *that* would be incriminating evidence, as you call it,' Farrokh said.

'I would prefer all three – a connection to the top half of the pen, a drawing *and* something typed on the money,' Patel replied. 'That would be evidence enough.'

'How fast do you want to go?' Farrokh asked. 'In a seduction, there's usually the setting up – some kind of mutual sexual spark is ignited. Then there's the assignation – or at least a discussion of the trysting place, if not the actual tryst.'

It was of small comfort to the screenwriter when Inspector Dhar said ambiguously, 'I think I'd prefer to avoid the actual tryst, if it's possible – if things don't have to go that far.'

'You *think*! You don't *know*?' Dr Daruwalla cried.

'The point is, I need dialogue to cover every contingency,' the actor said.

'Precisely,' said Detective Patel.

'The deputy commissioner showed me the photographs of those drawings,' John D. said; his voice dropped away. 'There must also be private drawings – things she keeps secret.' Again Farrokh was reminded of the boy who'd cried out, 'They're drowning the elephants! Now the elephants will be angry!'

Julia went to help Nancy finish dressing. Nancy had brought a suitcase of her clothes to the Daruwallas', for she couldn't make up her mind about what to wear to the New Year's Eve party – not without Julia's help. The two women decided on something surprisingly demure; it was a gray sleeveless sheath with a mandarin collar, with which Nancy wore a simple string of pearls. Dr Daruwalla recognized the necklace because it was Julia's. When the doctor retired to his bedroom and his bath, he brought a clipboard and a pad of lined paper with him; he also brought a bottle of beer. He was so tired, the hot bath and the cold beer made him instantly sleepy, but even with his eyes closed he was seeing the possible options for dialogue between John D. and the second Mrs Dogar – or was he writing for Rahul and Inspector Dhar? That was a part of the problem; the screenwriter felt he didn't know the characters he was writing dialogue for.

Julia told Farrokh how Nancy had become so agitated – trying to decide what to wear – that the poor woman had worked herself into a sweat; she'd had to take a bath in the Daruwallas' tub, a concept that caused the screenwriter's mind to wander. There was a lingering scent in the bathroom – probably not a perfume or a bath oil but something unfamiliar, *not* Julia's – and the strangeness of it mingled with the doctor's memory of that time in Goa. The foremost issue to resolve, in order to initiate the opening line of Inspector Dhar's dialogue, was whether or not to have John D.

know that Mrs Dogar was Rahul. Shouldn't he tell her that he knew who she was – that he knew her former self – and shouldn't this be the first phase of the seduction? ('I always wanted you' – that kind of thing.)

The decision to have Nancy dress so demurely – she even wore her hair pulled up, off her neck – had sprung from Nancy's desire not to be recognized by Rahul. Although the deputy commissioner had repeatedly told his wife that he very much doubted Rahul would recognize her, Nancy's fear of being recognized persisted. The only time Rahul had seen her, Nancy had been naked and her hair was down. Now Nancy wanted her hair up; she'd told Julia that her choice of dress was 'the opposite of naked.'

But if the gray sheath was severe, there was no hiding the heavy womanliness of Nancy's hips and breasts; also, her heavy hair, which usually rested on her shoulders, was too thick and not quite long enough to be held neatly up and kept off her neck – especially if she danced. Strands of her hair would come loose; Nancy would soon look uncontained. The screenwriter decided that he wanted Nancy to dance with Dhar; after that, the possible scenes began to flow.

Farrokh put a towel around his waist and poked his head into the dining room, where Julia was serving some snacks; although it would be a long time before the midnight supper at the Duckworth Club, no one really wanted to eat. The doctor decided to send Dhar down to the alley, where the dwarf was waiting in the Ambassador. Dr Daruwalla knew that Vinod was acquainted with many of the exotic dancers at the Wetness Cabaret; possibly there was one who owed the dwarf a favor.

'I want to get you a date,' Farrokh told John D.

'With a stripper?' John D. asked.

'Tell Vinod the more tarted up she is, the better,' the screenwriter replied. He guessed that New Year's Eve was an important night at the Wetness Cabaret; whoever the exotic dancer was, she'd have to leave the

Duckworth Club early. That was fine with Farrokh; he wanted the woman to make something of a production over leaving before midnight. Whoever she was, the screenwriter knew that her choice of dress would be the opposite of demure – she certainly wouldn't look very Duckworthian. She'd be sure to get everyone's attention.

On such short notice, Vinod wouldn't have a wide range of choices; of the women at the Wetness Cabaret, the dwarf picked the one with the exotic-dancing name of Muriel. She'd impressed Vinod as being more sensitive than the other strippers. After all, someone in the audience had thrown an orange at her; such blatant disrespect had upset her. To be hired for a little dancing at the Duckworth Club – particularly, to be asked to dance with Inspector Dhar – would be quite a step up in the world for Muriel. Short notice or not, Vinod delivered the exotic dancer to the Durawallas' apartment in a hurry.

When Dr Daruwalla had finished dressing, there was barely time for John D. to rehearse the dialogue. Both Nancy and Muriel needed coaching, and Detective Patel had to get Mr Sethna on the phone; the detective recited quite a long list of instructions to the steward, which doubtless left the old eavesdropper with a surfeit of disapproval. Vinod would drive Dhar and the exotic dancer to the Duckworth Club; Farrokh and Julia would follow with the Patels.

John D. managed to pull Dr Daruwalla aside; the actor steered the screenwriter out on the balcony. When they were alone, Dhar said, 'I've got a question regarding my character, Farrokh, for you seem to have given me some dialogue that is sexually ambiguous – at best.'

'I was just trying to cover every contingency, as you would say,' the screenwriter replied.

'But I gather that I'm supposed to be interested in Mrs Dogar as a woman – that is, as a man would be interested in her,' Dhar said. 'While at the same time, I seem to be implying that I was once interested in Rahul as a man – that is, as a man is interested in another man.'

'Yes,' Farrokh said cautiously. 'I'm trying to imply that you're sexually curious, and sexually aggressive – a bit of a bisexual, maybe . . .'

'Or even strictly a homosexual whose interest in Mrs Dogar is, in part, because of how interested I *was* in Rahul,' John D. interrupted. 'Is that it?'

'Something like that,' said Dr Daruwalla. 'I mean, we think Rahul was once attracted to you – we think Mrs Dogar is *still* attracted to you. Beyond that, what do we really know?'

'But you've made my character a kind of sexual mystery,' the actor complained. 'You've made me *odd*. It's as if you're gambling that the weirder I am, the more Mrs Dogar will go for me. Is that it?'

Actors are truly impossible, the screenwriter thought. What Dr Daruwalla wanted to say was this: Your twin has experienced decidedly homosexual inclinations. Does this sound familiar to you? Instead, what Farrokh said was this: 'I don't know how to shock a serial killer. I'm just trying to attract one.'

'And I'm just asking you for a fix on my character,' Inspector Dhar replied. 'It's always easier when I know who I'm supposed to be.'

There was the old Dhar, Dr Daruwalla thought – sarcastic to the core. Farrokh was relieved to see that the movie star had regained his self-confidence.

That was when Nancy came out on the balcony. 'I'm not interrupting anything, am I?' she asked, but she went straight to the railing and leaned on it; she didn't wait for an answer.

'No, no,' Dr Daruwalla mumbled.

'That's west, isn't it?' Nancy asked. She was pointing to the sunset.

'The sun usually sets in the west,' Dhar said.

'And if you went west across the sea – from Bombay straight across the Arabian Sea – what would you come to?' Nancy asked. 'Make it west and a little north,' she added.

'Well,' Dr Daruwalla said cautiously. 'West and a little north from here is the Gulf of Oman, then the Persian Gulf . . .'

'Then Saudi Arabia,' Dhar interrupted.

'Keep going,' Nancy told him. 'Keep going west and a little north.'

'That would take you across Jordan . . . into Israel, and into the Mediterranean,' Farrokh said.

'Or across North Africa,' said Inspector Dhar.

'Well, yes,' Dr Daruwalla said. 'Across Egypt . . . what's after Egypt?' he asked John D.

'Libya, Tunisia, Algeria, Morocco,' the actor replied. 'You could pass through the Straits of Gibraltar, or touch the coast of Spain, if you like.'

'Yes – that's the way I want to go,' Nancy told him. 'I touch the coast of Spain. Then what?'

'Then you're in the North Atlantic,' Dr Daruwalla said.

'Go west,' Nancy said. 'And a little north.'

'New York?' Dr Daruwalla guessed.

'I know the way from there,' Nancy said suddenly. 'From there I go straight west.'

Both Dhar and Dr Daruwalla didn't know what Nancy would come to next; they weren't familiar with the geography of the United States.

'Pennsylvania, Ohio, Indiana, Illinois,' Nancy told them. 'Maybe I'd have to go through New Jersey before I got to Pennsylvania.'

'Where are you going?' Dr Daruwalla asked.

'Home,' Nancy answered. 'Home to Iowa – Iowa comes after Illinois.'

'Do you want to go home?' John D. asked her.

'Never,' Nancy said. 'I never want to go home.'

The screenwriter saw that the zipper of the gray sheath dress was a straight line down her back; it clasped at the top of her high mandarin collar.

'If you wouldn't mind,' Farrokh said to her, 'perhaps

693

you could have your husband unfasten the zipper of your dress. If it were unzipped just a little – down to somewhere between your shoulder blades – that would be better. When you're dancing, I mean,' the doctor added.

'Wouldn't it be better if *I* unzipped it?' the actor asked. 'I mean, when we're dancing?'

'Well, yes, that would be best,' Dr Daruwalla said.

Still looking west into the sunset, Nancy said, 'Just don't unzip me too far. I don't care what the script says – if you unzip me too far, I'll let you know it.'

'It's time,' said Detective Patel. No one was sure how long he'd been on the balcony.

In departing, it was fortunate that none of them really looked at one another; their faces conveyed a certain dread of the event, like mourners preparing to attend the funeral of a child. The deputy commissioner was almost avuncular; he affectionately patted Dr Daruwalla's shoulder, he warmly shook Inspector Dhar's hand, he held his troubled wife at her waist – his fingers familiarly spreading to the small of her back, where he knew she felt some occasional pain. It was his way of saying, I'm in charge – everything's going to be okay.

But there was that interminable period when they had to wait in the policeman's car; Vinod had taken Dhar and Muriel ahead. As the driver, the deputy commissioner sat up front with the screenwriter, who wanted Dhar and Muriel to be already dancing when the Daruwallas and their guests, the Patels, arrived. In the back seat, Julia sat with Nancy. The detective avoided his wife's eyes in the rearview mirror; Patel also tried not to grip the steering wheel too tightly – he didn't want any of them to see how nervous he was.

The passing headlights flowed like water along Marine Drive, and when the sun finally dipped into the Arabian Sea, the sea turned quickly from pink to purple to burgundy to black, like the phases of a bruise. The doctor said, 'They must be dancing by now.' The detective started the car, easing them into the flow of traffic.

In a misguided effort to sound positive, Dr Daruwalla said, 'Let's go get the bitch, let's put her away.'

'Not tonight,' Detective Patel said quietly. 'We won't catch her tonight. Let's just hope she takes the bait.'

'She'll take it,' Nancy said from the back seat.

There was nothing the deputy commissioner wanted to say. He smiled. He hoped he looked confident. But the real policeman knew there was really no getting ready for Rahul.

Just Dancing

Mr Sethna had to wonder what was going on; wonderment was not among the few expressions that the old Parsi favored. To anyone who observed the steward's sour, intolerant visage, Mr Sethna was simply expressing his contempt for New Year's Eve; he thought the party at the Duckworth Club was superfluous. Pateti, the Parsi New Year, comes in the late summer or the early fall; it is followed a fortnight later by the anniversary of the prophet Zarathustra's birth. By the time of the New Year's Eve party at the Duckworth Club, Mr Sethna had already celebrated *his* New Year. As for the Duckworthian version of New Year's Eve, Mr Sethna viewed it as a tradition for Anglophiles. It was also morbid that New Year's Eve at the Duckworth Club was doubly special to those many Duckworthians who enjoyed the party as an anniversary – this year it was the 90th anniversary – of Lord Duckworth's suicide.

The steward also thought that the events of the evening were foolishly ordered. Duckworthians, in general, were an older crowd, especially at this time of year; with a 22-year waiting list for membership, one would expect the members to be 'older,' but this was also the result of the younger Duckworthians being away at school – for the most part, in England. In the summer months, when the student generation was back in India, Duckworthians appeared to be younger. But now here were all these older people, who should be eating their dinners at a reasonable hour; they were expected to drink and dance until the midnight supper was served – an ass-backward order of events, Mr Sethna believed. Feed them early and *then* let them dance – if they're able. The effects of too much champagne on empty stomachs were particularly deleterious to the elderly. Some couples lacked the stamina to last until the midnight supper. And wasn't the point of the silly evening – apparently, the only point – to last until midnight?

From the way he was dancing, Dhar couldn't last until midnight, Mr Sethna presumed; yet the steward was impressed at how the actor had rebounded from his dreadful appearance of the day before. On Saturday, the diseased man had been ghostly pale and dabbing at his penis over the urinal – a sickening sight. Now here he was on Sunday night, tanned and looking positively beefy; he was dancing up a storm. Perhaps the actor's sexually transmitted disease was in re-mission, Mr Sethna speculated, as Dhar continued to hurl Muriel around the dance floor. And where had the movie-star slime found a woman like that?

Once, there'd been a banner draped from the marquee of the Bombay Eros Palace, and the woman painted on that banner had looked like Muriel, Mr Sethna remembered. (The woman had actually been Muriel, of course; the Wetness Cabaret was a step down from the Bombay Eros Palace.) Mr Sethna had never seen a Duckworthian in such a costume as Muriel wore. The glitter of her turquoise sequins, her plunging neckline, her miniskirt at midthigh ... her dress hugged her bum so tightly, Mr Sethna ex-pected that some of her sequins would pop off and litter the dance floor. Muriel had maintained the high, hard athletic bum of a dancer; and although she was certainly a few years older than Inspector Dhar, she looked as if she could both outdance and outsweat him. Their dancing lacked the element of courtship; they were brutally aggressive – astonishingly rough with each other – which implied to the disapproving steward that dancing was merely the public forum in which they lewdly hinted at the violence of their more private lovemaking.

Mr Sethna also observed that everyone was watching them. By design, Mr Sethna knew, they kept to that portion of the dance floor which was visible from the main dining room, forcing numerous couples to see them perform their gyrations. Nearest to this view of the ballroom was the table Mr Sethna had reserved for Mr and Mrs Dogar; the steward had followed Detective Patel's instructions to the letter, taking care that the second Mrs Dogar was shown to the chair that offered her the very best view of Dhar dancing.

From the Ladies' Garden, the Daruwallas' table looked in upon the main dining room; from where the doctor and the detective were seated, they could observe Mrs Dogar but not the ballroom. It wasn't Dhar they wanted to see. Blessedly, the big blonde had hidden her unusual navel, Mr Sethna observed; Nancy was dressed like the headmistress of a school – or a nanny, or a clergyman's wife – but the steward nevertheless detected her lawlessness, her penchant for unpredictable or inexplicable behavior. She sat with her back to Mrs Dogar, staring into the gathering darkness beyond the trellis; at this hour, the bougainvillea had the luster of velvet. The exposed nape of Nancy's neck – the downy blond hair that looked so soft there – reminded Mr Sethna of her furry navel.

The doctor's sleek tuxedo and black silk tie clashed with the deputy commissioner's badly wrinkled Nehru suit; Mr Sethna determined that most Duckworthians were never in contact with that element of society which could recognize policemen by their clothes. The steward approved of Julia's gown, which was a proper gown – the long skirt almost brushing the floor, the long sleeves ruffled at the cuffs, the neckline not a mandarin choker but a decent distance above any discernible cleavage. Ah, the old days, Mr Sethna mourned; as if anticipating his thoughts, the band responded with a slower number.

Dhar and Muriel, breathing hard, relaxed a little too languidly into each other's arms; she hung on his neck, his hand resting possessively on the hard beaded sequins at her hip. She appeared to be whispering to him – actually, she was just singing the words to the song, for Muriel knew every song that this band knew, and many more besides – while Inspector Dhar smiled knowingly at what she was saying. There was his sneer, which was almost a smirk – that look of disdain, which was at once decadent and bored. Actually, Dhar was amused by Muriel's accent; he thought the stripper was very funny. But what the second Mrs Dogar saw did not amuse her. She saw John D. dancing with a tart, a presumably loose woman – and one close to Mrs Dogar's age. Women like that were so easy; surely Dhar could do better, Rahul thought.

On the dance floor, the staid Duckworthians who dared to dance – they'd been waiting for a slow number – kept their distance from Dhar and Muriel, who was clearly no lady. Mr Sethna, the old eavesdropper and lip-reader *extraordinaire*, easily caught what Mr Dogar said to his wife. 'Has the actor brought an actual prostitute to the party? I must say she looks like a whore.'

'I think she's a stripper,' said Mrs Dogar – Rahul had honed a sharp eye for such social details.

'Perhaps she's an actress,' Mr Dogar said.

'She's acting, but she's no actress,' Mrs Dogar replied.

From what Farrokh could see of Rahul, the transsexual had inherited the reptilian scrutiny of her Aunt Promila; it was as if, when she looked at you, she were seeing a different life form – certainly not a fellow human being.

'It's hard to tell from here,' said Dr Daruwalla. 'I don't know if she's attracted to him or if she wants to kill him.'

'Maybe with her,' said the deputy commissioner, 'the feeling is one and the same.'

'Whatever else she feels, she's attracted,' Nancy said. Her back was the only part of her that Rahul could see, if Rahul had been looking. But Rahul had eyes for John D. only.

When the band played a faster number, Dhar and Muriel grew even rougher with each other, as if invigorated by the slower interlude or by their closer contact. A few of the cheap sequins were torn from Muriel's dress; they glittered on the dance floor, reflecting the light from the ballroom chandelier – when Dhar or Muriel stepped on them, they crunched. A constant rivulet of sweat ran its course in Muriel's cleavage, and Dhar was bleeding slightly from a scratch on his wrist; the cuff of his white shirt was dotted with blood. Because of how tightly he held Muriel at her waist, a sequin had scratched him. He paid the scratch only passing attention, but Muriel took his wrist in her hands and covered the cut with her mouth. In this way, with his wrist to her lips, they kept dancing. Mr Sethna had seen such things only in the movies. The steward didn't realize that this was what he was seeing: a screenplay by Farrokh Daruwalla, a movie starring Inspector Dhar.

When Muriel left the Duckworth Club, she made a fuss over her departure. She danced one last dance (another slow one) with her shawl on; she downed a nearly full glass of champagne in the foyer. Then the exotic dancer leaned on Vinod's head while the dwarf walked her to the Ambassador.

'A to-do worthy of a slut,' said Mr Dogar. 'I suppose she's going back to the brothel.'

But Rahul merely glanced at the time. The second

Mrs Dogar was a close observer of Bombay's low life; she knew that the hour for the first show at the Eros Palace was fast approaching, or maybe Dhar's tart worked at the Wetness Cabaret – the first show there was 15 minutes later.

When Dhar asked the Sorabjee daughter to dance, a new tension could be felt throughout the main dining room and the Ladies' Garden. Even with her back to the action, Nancy knew that something unscripted had happened.

'He's asked someone else to dance, hasn't he?' she said; her face and the nape of her neck were flushed.

'Who's that young girl? She's not part of our plan!' said Detective Patel.

'Trust him – he's a great improviser,' the screen-writer said. 'He always understands who he is and what his role is. He knows what he's doing.'

Nancy was pinching a pearl on her necklace; her thumb and index finger were white. 'You bet he knows,' she said. Julia turned around, but she couldn't see the ballroom – only the look of loathing that was unconcealed on Mrs Dogar's face.

'It's little Amy Sorabjee – she must be back from school,' Dr Daruwalla informed his wife.

'She's only a teenager!' Julia cried.

'I think she's a little older,' the real policeman replied.

'It's a brilliant move!' the screenwriter said. 'Mrs Dogar doesn't know *what* to think!'

'I know how she feels,' Nancy told him.

'It'll be all right, sweetie,' the deputy commissioner told his wife. When he took her hand, she pulled it away.

'Am I next?' Nancy asked. 'Do I wait in line?'

Almost every face in the main dining room was turned toward the ballroom. They watched the unstoppable sweating movie star with his bulky shoulders and his beer belly; he was twirling little Amy Sorabjee around as if she were no heavier than her clothes.

Although the Sorabjees and the Daruwallas were old friends, Dr and Mrs Sorabjee had been surprised at Dhar's spur-of-the-moment invitation – and that Amy had accepted. She was a silly girl in her twenties, a former university student who hadn't merely come home for the holiday; she'd been withdrawn from school. Granted, Dhar wasn't mashing her; the actor was behaving like a proper gentleman – excessively charming, possibly, but the young lady seemed delighted. Theirs was a different kind of dancing from Dhar's performance with Muriel; the friskiness of the youthful girl was appealingly offset by the sure, smooth quality of the older man's gestures.

'Now he's seducing children!' Mr Dogar announced to his wife. 'He's going to dance his way through all the women – I'm sure he'll ask you, too, Promila!'

Mrs Dogar was visibly upset. She excused herself for the ladies' room, where she was reminded of how she hated this aspect of being a woman – waiting to pee. There was too long a line; Rahul slipped through the foyer and into the closed and darkened administrative offices of the old club. There was enough moonlight for her to type by, and she rolled a two-rupee note into the typewriter that was nearest a window. On the money, the typed message was as spontaneous as her feelings at the moment.

A MEMBER NO MORE

This was a message meant for Dhar's mouth, and Mrs Dogar slipped it into her purse where it could keep company with the message she'd already typed for her husband.

... BECAUSE DHAR IS STILL A MEMBER

It comforted Mrs Dogar to have these two-rupee notes in place; she always felt better when she was prepared for every contingency. She slipped back through the foyer and into the ladies' room, where the line ahead of her wasn't so long. When Rahul returned to her table in the main dining room, Dhar was dancing with a new partner.

Mr Sethna, who'd been happily monitoring the conversation between the Dogars, was thrilled to note Mr Dogar's observation to his coarse wife. 'Now Dhar's dancing with that hefty Anglo who came with the Daruwallas. I think she's the white half of a mixed marriage. Her husband looks like a pathetic civil servant.'

But Mrs Dogar was prevented from seeing the new dancers. Dhar had wheeled Nancy into the part of the ballroom that wasn't visible from the main dining room. Only intermittently did a glimpse of them appear. Earlier, Rahul had taken little notice of the big blonde. When Mrs Dogar glanced at the Daruwallas' table, the Daruwallas were bent in conversation with the out-of-place 'pathetic civil servant,' as her husband had described him. Maybe he was a minor magistrate, Rahul guessed – or some controlling little guru who'd met his Western wife in an ashram.

Then Dhar and the heavy woman danced into view. Mrs Dogar sensed the strength with which they gripped each other – the woman's broad hand held fast to Dhar's neck, and the biceps of his right arm was locked in her armpit (as if he were trying to lift her up). She was taller than he was; from the way she grasped his neck, it was impossible for Rahul to tell if Nancy was pulling Dhar's face into the side of her throat or if she was struggling to prevent him from nuzzling her. What was remarkable was that they were whispering fiercely to each other; neither one of them was listening, but they were talking urgently and at the same time. When they danced out of her sight again, Rahul couldn't stand it; Mrs Dogar asked her husband to dance.

'He's got her! I told you he could do it,' said Dr Daruwalla.

'This is only the beginning,' the deputy commissioner replied. 'This is just the dancing.'

Happy New Year

Fortunately for Mr Dogar, it was a slow dance. His wife steered him past several faltering couples, who were disconcerted that Muriel's fallen sequins still crunched underfoot. Mrs Dogar had Dhar and the big blonde in her sights.

'Is this in the script?' Nancy was whispering to the actor. 'This isn't in the script, you bastard!'

'We're supposed to make something of a scene – like an old lovers' quarrel,' Dhar whispered.

'You're embracing me!' Nancy told him.

'You're squeezing me back,' he whispered.

'I wish I was killing you!' Nancy whispered.

'She's here,' Dhar said softly. 'She's following us.'

With a pang, Rahul observed that the blond wench had gone limp in Dhar's arms – and she'd been resisting him; that had been obvious. Now it appeared to Mrs Dogar that Dhar was supporting the heavy woman; the blonde might otherwise have fallen to the dance floor, so lifelessly was she draped on the actor. She'd thrown her arms over his shoulders and locked her hands behind his back; her face was buried in his neck – awkwardly, because she was taller. Rahul could see that Nancy was shaking her head while Dhar went on whispering to her. The blonde had that pleasing air of submission about her, as if she'd already given up; Rahul was reminded of the kind of woman who'd let you make love to her or let you kill her without a breath of complaint – like someone with a high fever, Rahul thought.

'Does she recognize me?' Nancy was whispering; she trembled, and then stumbled. Dhar had to hold her up with all his strength.

'She can't recognize you, she *doesn't* recognize you

703

– she's just curious about what's between us,' the actor replied.

'What *is* between us?' Nancy whispered. Where her hands were locked together, he felt her dig her knuckles into his spine.

'She's coming closer,' Dhar warned Nancy. 'She doesn't recognize you. She just wants to look. I'm going to do it now,' he whispered.

'Do what?' Nancy asked; she'd forgotten – she was so frightened of Rahul.

'Unzip you,' Dhar said.

'Not too far,' Nancy told him.

The actor turned her suddenly; he had to stand on tiptoe to look over her shoulder, but he wanted to be sure that Mrs Dogar saw his face. John D. looked straight at Rahul and smiled; he gave the killer a sly wink. Then he unzipped the back of Nancy's dress while Rahul watched. When he felt the clasp of Nancy's bra, he stopped; he spread his palm between her bare shoulder blades – she was sweating and he felt her shudder.

'Is she watching?' Nancy whispered. 'I hate you,' she added.

'She's right on top of us,' Dhar whispered. 'I'm going to go right at her. We're changing partners now.'

'Zip me up first!' Nancy whispered. 'Zip me up!'

With his right hand, John D. zipped Nancy up; with his left, he reached out and took the second Mrs Dogar by the wrist – her arm was cool and dry, as sinewy as a strong rope.

'Let's switch partners for the next number!' said Inspector Dhar. But it was still the slow dance that played. Mr Dogar staggered briefly; Nancy, who was relieved to be out of Dhar's arms, forcefully drew the old man to her chest. A lock of her hair had come undone; it hid her cheek. No one saw her tears, which might have been confused with her sweat.

'Hi,' Nancy said. Before Mr Dogar could respond, she palmed the back of his head; his cheek was pressed flat between her shoulder and her collarbone. Nancy moved the old man resolutely away from Dhar and Rahul; she wondered how long she had to wait until the band changed to a faster number.

What was left of the slow dance suited Dhar and Rahul. John D.'s eyes were level with a thin blue vein that ran the length of Mrs Dogar's throat; something deep-black and polished, like onyx – a single stone, set in silver – rested in the perfect declivity where her throat met her sternum. Her dress, which was an emerald green, was cut low but it fit her breasts snugly; her hands were smooth and hard, her grip surprisingly light. She was light on her feet, too; no matter where John D. moved, she squared her shoulders to him – her eyes locked onto his eyes, as if she were reading the first page of a new book.

'That was rather crude – and clumsy, too,' the second Mrs Dogar said.

'I'm tired of trying to ignore you,' the actor told her. 'I'm sick of pretending that I don't know who you are . . . who you *were*,' Dhar added, but her grip maintained its even, soft pressure – her body obediently followed his.

'Goodness, you *are* provincial!' Mrs Dogar said. 'Can't a man become a woman if she wants to?'

'It's certainly an exciting idea,' said Inspector Dhar.

'You're not sneering, are you?' Mrs Dogar asked him.

'Certainly not! I'm just remembering,' the actor replied. 'Twenty years ago, I couldn't get up the nerve to approach you – I didn't know how to begin.'

'Twenty years ago, I wasn't *complete*,' Rahul reminded him. 'If you *had* approached me, what would you have done?'

'Frankly, I was too young to think of *doing*,' Dhar replied. 'I think I just wanted to *see* you!'

'I don't suppose that *seeing* me is all you have in mind today,' Mrs Dogar said.

'Certainly not!' said Inspector Dhar, but he couldn't

muster the courage to squeeze her hand; she was everywhere so dry and cool and light of touch, but she was also very hard.

'Twenty years ago, I *tried* to approach you,' Rahul admitted.

'It must have been too subtle for me – at least I missed it,' John D. remarked.

'At the Bardez, I was told you slept in the hammock on the balcony,' Rahul told him. 'I went to you. The only part of you that was outside the mosquito net was your foot. I put your big toe in my mouth. I sucked it – actually, I bit you. But it wasn't you. It was Dr Daruwalla. I was so disgusted, I never tried again.'

This was not the conversation Dhar had expected. John D.'s options for dialogue didn't include a response to this interesting story, but while he was at a loss for words, the band saved him; they changed to a faster number. People were leaving the dance floor in droves, including Nancy with Mr Dogar. Nancy led the old man to his table; he was almost breathless by the time she got him seated.

'Who are you, dear?' he managed to ask her.

'Mrs Patel,' Nancy replied.

'Ah,' the old man said. 'And your husband . . .' What Mr Dogar meant was, *What does he do*? He wondered: *Which sort of civil-service employee is he?*

'My husband is Mr Patel,' Nancy told him; when she left him, she walked as carefully as possible to the Daruwallas' table.

'I don't think she recognized me,' Nancy told them, 'but I couldn't look at her. She looks the same, but ancient.'

'Are they dancing?' Dr Daruwalla asked. 'Are they talking too?'

'They're dancing *and* they're talking – that's all I know,' Nancy told the screenwriter. 'I couldn't look at her,' she repeated.

'It's all right, sweetie,' the deputy commissioner said. 'You don't have to do anything more.'

'I want to be there when you catch her, Vijay,' Nancy told her husband.

'Well, we may not catch her in a place where you want to be,' the detective replied.

'Please let me be there,' Nancy said. 'Am I zipped up?' she asked suddenly; she rotated her shoulders so that Julia could see her back.

'You're zipped up perfectly, dear,' Julia told her.

Mr Dogar, alone at his table, was gulping champagne and catching his breath, while Mr Sethna plied him with hors d'oeuvres. Mrs Dogar and Dhar were dancing in that part of the ballroom where Mr Dogar couldn't see them.

'There was a time when I wanted you,' Rahul was telling John D. 'You were a beautiful boy.'

'I still want you,' Dhar told her.

'It seems you want everybody,' Mrs Dogar said. 'Who's the stripper?' she asked him. He had no dialogue for this.

'Just a stripper,' Dhar answered.

'And who's the fat blonde?' Rahul asked him. This much Dr Daruwalla had prepared him for.

'She's an old story,' the actor replied. 'Some people can't let go.'

'You can have your choice of women – younger women, too,' Mrs Dogar told him. 'What do you want with me?' This introduced a moment in the dialogue that the actor was afraid of; this required a quantum leap of faith in Farrokh's script. The actor had little confidence in his upcoming line.

'I need to know something,' Dhar told Rahul. 'Is your vagina really made from what used to be your penis?'

'Don't be crude,' Mrs Dogar said; then she started laughing.

'I wish there was another way to ask the question,' John D. admitted. When she laughed more uncontrollably, her hands gripped him harder; he could feel the strength of her hands for the first time. 'I suppose I could have been more indirect,' Dhar continued, for her laughter encouraged him. 'I could have said, "What sort of sensitivity do you have in that vagina of yours, anyway? I mean, does it feel sort of like a penis?"' The actor stopped; he couldn't make himself continue. The screenwriter's dialogue wasn't working – Farrokh was frequently hit-or-miss with dialogue.

Besides, Mrs Dogar had stopped laughing. 'So you're just curious – is that it?' she asked him. 'You're attracted to the oddity of it.'

Along the thin blue vein at Rahul's throat, there appeared a cloudy drop of sweat; it ran quickly between her taut breasts. John D. thought that they hadn't been dancing that hard. He hoped it was the right time. He took her around her waist with some force, and she followed his lead; when they crossed that part of the dance floor which made them visible to Mrs Dogar's husband – and to Mr Sethna – Dhar saw that the old steward had understood his signal. Mr Sethna turned quickly from the dining room toward the foyer, and the actor again wheeled Mrs Dogar into the more private part of the ballroom.

'I'm an actor,' John D. told Rahul. 'I can be anyone you want me to be – I can do absolutely anything you like. You just have to draw me a picture.' (The actor winced; he had Farrokh to thank for that clunker, too.)

'What an eccentric presumption!' Mrs Dogar said. 'Draw you a picture of *what*?'

'Just give me an idea of what appeals to you. Then I can do it,' Dhar told her.

'You said, "Draw me a picture" – I heard you say it,' Mrs Dogar said.

'I meant, just tell me what you like – I mean sexually,' the actor said.

'I know what you *mean*, but you said "draw,"' Rahul replied coldly.

'Didn't you used to be an artist? Weren't you going to art school?' the actor asked. (What the hell is Mr Sethna doing? Dhar was thinking. John D. was afraid that Rahul smelled a rat.)

'I didn't learn anything in art school,' Mrs Dogar told him.

In the utility closet, off the foyer, Mr Sethna had discovered that he couldn't read the writing in the fuse box without his glasses, which he kept in a drawer in the kitchen. It took the steward a moment to decide whether or not to kill all the fuses.

'The old fool has probably electrocuted himself!' Dr Daruwalla was saying to Detective Patel.

'Let's try to keep calm,' the policeman said.

'If the lights don't go out, let Dhar improvise – if he's such a great improviser,' Nancy said.

'I want you *not* as a curiosity,' Dhar said suddenly to Mrs Dogar. 'I know you're strong, I think you're aggressive – I believe you can assert yourself.' (It was the worst of Dr Daruwalla's dialogue, the actor thought – it was sheer groping.) 'I want you to tell me what you like. I want you to tell me what to do.'

'I want you to submit to me,' Rahul said.

'You can tie me up, if you want to,' Dhar said agreeably.

'I mean more than that,' Mrs Dogar said. Then the ballroom and the entire first floor of the Duckworth Club were pitched into darkness. There was a communal gasp and a fumbling in the band; the number they were playing persisted through a few more toots and thumps. From the dining room came an artless clapping. Noises of chaos could be heard from the kitchen. Then the knives and forks and spoons began their impromptu music against the water glasses.

'Don't spill the champagne!' Mr Bannerjee called out.

The girlish laughter probably came from Amy Sorabjee.

When John D. tried to kiss her in the darkness, Mrs Dogar was too fast; his mouth was just touching hers when he felt her seize his lower lip in her teeth. While she held him thus, by the lip, her exaggerated breathing was heavy in his face; her cool, dry hands unzipped him and fondled him until he was hard.

Dhar put his hands on her buttocks, which she instantly tightened. Still she clamped his lower lip between her teeth; her bite was hard enough to hurt him but not quite deep enough to make him bleed. As Mr Sethna had been instructed, the lights flashed briefly on and then went out again; Mrs Dogar let go of John D. – both with her teeth and with her hands. When he took his hands off her to zip up his fly, he lost her. When the lights came on, Dhar was no longer in contact with Mrs Dogar.

'You want a picture? I'll show you a picture,' Rahul said quietly. 'I could have bitten your lip off.'

'I have a suite at both the Oberoi and the Taj,' the actor told her.

'No – I'll tell you where,' Mrs Dogar said. 'I'll tell you at lunch.'

'At lunch here?' Dhar asked her.

'Tomorrow,' Rahul said. 'I could have bitten your nose off, if I'd wanted to.'

'Thank you for the dance,' John D. said. As he turned to leave her, he was uncomfortably aware of his erection and the throbbing in his lower lip.

'Careful you don't knock over any chairs or tables,' Mrs Dogar said. 'You're as big as an elephant.' It was the word 'elephant' – coming from Rahul – that most affected John D.'s walk. He crossed the dining room, still seeing the cloudy drop of her quickly disappearing sweat – still feeling her cool, dry hands. And the way she'd breathed into his open mouth when his lip was trapped . . . John D. suspected he would never forget that. He was thinking that the thin blue vein in her throat was so very still; it was as if she didn't have a pulse, or that she knew some way to suspend the normal beating of her heart.

When Dhar sat down at the table, Nancy couldn't look at him. Deputy Commissioner Patel didn't look at him, either, but that was because the policeman was more interested in watching Mr and Mrs Dogar. They were arguing – Mrs Dogar wouldn't sit down, Mr

Dogar wouldn't stand up – and the detective noticed something extremely simple but peculiar about the two of them; they had almost exactly the same haircut. Mr Dogar wore his wonderfully thick hair in a vain pompadour; it was cut short at the back of his neck, and it was tightly trimmed over his ears, but a surprisingly full and cocky wave of his hair was brushed high off his forehead – his hair was silver, with streaks of white. Mrs Dogar's hair was black with streaks of silver (probably dyed), but her hairdo was the same as her husband's, albeit more stylish. It gave her a slightly Spanish appearance. A pompadour! Imagine that, thought Detective Patel. He saw that Mrs Dogar had persuaded her husband to stand.

Mr Sethna would later inform the deputy commissioner of what words passed between the Dogars, but the policeman could have guessed. Mrs Dogar was complaining that her husband had already slurped too much champagne; she wouldn't tolerate a minute more of his drunkenness – she would have the servants fix them a midnight supper at home, where at least she would not be publicly embarrassed by Mr Dogar's ill-considered behavior.

'They're leaving!' Dr Daruwalla observed. 'What happened? Did you agitate her?' the screenwriter asked the actor.

Dhar had a drink of champagne, which made his lip sting. The sweat was rolling down his face – after all, he'd been dancing all night – and his hands were noticeably shaky; they watched him exchange the champagne glass for his water glass. Even a sip of water caused him to wince. Nancy had had to force herself to look at him; now she couldn't look away.

The deputy commissioner was still thinking about the haircuts. The pompadour had a feminizing effect on old Mr Dogar, but the same hairdo conveyed a mannishness to his wife. The detective concluded that Mrs Dogar resembled a bullfighter; Detective Patel had never seen a bullfighter, of course.

Farrokh was dying to know which dialogue John D. had used. The sweating movie star was still fussing with his lip. The doctor observed that Dhar's lower lip was swollen; it had the increasingly purplish hue of a contusion. The doctor waved his arms for a waiter and asked for a tall glass of ice – just ice.

'So she kissed you,' Nancy said.

'It was more like a bite,' John D. replied.

'But what did you *say*?' Dr Daruwalla cried.

'Did you arrange a meeting?' Detective Patel asked Dhar.

'Lunch here, tomorrow,' the actor replied.

'Lunch!' the screenwriter said with disappointment.

'So you've made a start,' the policeman said.

'Yes, I think so. It's something, anyway – I'm not sure what,' Dhar remarked.

'So she *responded*?' Farrokh asked. He felt frustrated, for he wanted to hear the dialogue between them – word for word.

'Look at his lip!' Nancy told the doctor. 'Of *course* she responded!'

'Did you ask her to draw you a picture?' Farrokh wanted to know.

'That part was scary – at least it got a little strange,' Dhar said evasively. 'But I think she's going to show me something.'

'At *lunch*?' Dr Daruwalla asked. John D. shrugged; he was clearly exasperated with all the questions.

'Let him talk, Farrokh. Stop putting words in his mouth,' Julia told him.

'But he's *not* talking!' the doctor cried.

'She said she wanted me to submit to her,' Dhar told the deputy commissioner.

'She wants to tie him up!' Farrokh shouted.

'She said she meant more than that,' Dhar replied.

'What's "more than that"?' Dr Daruwalla asked.

The waiter brought the ice and John D. held a piece to his lip.

'Put the ice in your mouth and suck on it,' the doctor told him, but John D. kept applying the ice in his own way.

'She bit me inside and out,' was all he said.

'Did you get to the part about her sex-change operation?' the screenwriter asked.

'She thought that part was funny,' John D. told them. 'She laughed.'

By now the indentations on the outside of Dhar's lower lip were easier to see, even in the candelight in the Ladies' Garden; the teeth marks had left such deep bruises, the discolored lip was turning from a pale purple to a dark magenta, as if Mrs Dogar's teeth had left a stain.

To her husband's surprise, Nancy helped herself to a second glass of champagne; Detective Patel had been mildly shocked that his wife had accepted the first glass. Now Nancy raised her glass, as if she were toasting everyone in the Ladies' Garden.

'Happy New Year,' she said, but to no one in particular.

'Auld Lang Syne'

Finally, they served the midnight supper. Nancy picked at her food, which her husband eventually ate. John D. couldn't eat anything spicy because of his lip; he didn't tell them about the erection Mrs Dogar had given him, or how – or about how she'd said he was as big as an elephant. Dhar decided he'd tell Detective Patel later, when they were alone. When the policeman excused himself from the table, John D. followed him to the men's room and told him there.

'I didn't like the way she looked when she left here.' That was all the detective would say.

Back at their table, Dr Daruwalla told them that he had a plan to 'introduce' the top half of the pen; Mr Sethna was involved – it sounded complicated. John D.

repeated that he hoped Rahul was going to make him a drawing.

'That would do it, wouldn't it?' Nancy asked her husband.

'That would help,' the deputy commissioner said. He had a bad feeling. He once again excused himself from the table, this time to call Crime Branch Headquarters. He ordered a surveillance officer to watch the Dogars' house all night; if Mrs Dogar left the house, he wanted the officer to follow her – and he wanted to be told if she left the house, whatever the hour.

In the men's room, Dhar had said that he'd never felt it was Rahul's intention to bite his lip off, nor even that taking his lip in her teeth was a deliberate decision – it wasn't something she'd done merely to scare him, either. The actor believed that Mrs Dogar hadn't been able to stop herself; and all the while she'd held his lip, he'd felt that the transsexual was unable to let go.

'It wasn't that she *wanted* to bite me,' Dhar had told the detective. 'It was that she couldn't help it.'

'Yes, I understand,' the policeman had said; he'd resisted the temptation to add that only in the movies did every murderer have a clear motive.

Now, as he hung up the phone, a dreary song reached the deputy commissioner in the foyer. The band was playing 'Auld Lang Syne'; the drunken Duckworthians were murdering the lyrics. Patel crossed the dining room with difficulty because so many of the maudlin members were leaving their tables and traipsing to the ballroom, singing as they staggered forth. There went Mr Bannerjee, sandwiched between his wife and the widow Lal; he appeared to be manfully intent on dancing with them both. There went Dr and Mrs Sorabjee, leaving little Amy alone at their table.

When the detective returned to the Daruwallas' table, Nancy was nagging Dhar. 'I'm sure that little girl is dying to dance with you again. And she's all alone. Why don't you ask her? Imagine how she feels. You started it,' Nancy told him. She'd had three glasses of champagne, her husband calculated; this wasn't much, but she never drank – and she'd eaten next to nothing. Dhar was managing not to sneer; he was trying to ignore Nancy instead.

'Why don't you ask *me* to dance?' Julia asked John D. 'I think Farrokh has forgotten to ask me.'

Without a word, Dhar led Julia to the ballroom; Amy Sorabjee watched them all the way.

'I like your idea about the top half of the pen,' Detective Patel told Dr Daruwalla.

The screenwriter was taken aback by this unexpected praise. 'You *do*?' Farrokh said. 'The problem is, Mrs Dogar's got to think that it's been in her purse – that it's *always* been there.'

'I agree that if Dhar can distract her, Mr Sethna can plant the pen.' That was all the policeman would say.

'You *do*?' Dr Daruwalla repeated.

'It would be nice if we found other things in her purse,' the deputy commissioner thought aloud.

'You mean the money with the typewritten warnings – or maybe even a drawing,' the doctor said.

'Precisely,' Patel said.

'Well, I wish I could write *that*!' the screenwriter replied.

Suddenly Julia was back at the table; she'd lost John D. as a dance partner when Amy Sorabjee had cut in.

'The shameless girl!' Dr Daruwalla said.

'Come dance with me, *Liebchen*,' Julia told him.

Then the Patels were alone at the table; in fact, they were alone in the Ladies' Garden. In the main dining room, an unidentified man was sleeping with his head on one of the dinner tables; everyone else was dancing, or they were standing in the ballroom – apparently for the morbid pleasure of singing 'Auld Lang Syne.' The waiters were beginning to scavenge the abandoned tables, but not a single waiter disturbed Detective Patel and Nancy in the Ladies' Garden; Mr Sethna had instructed them to respect the couple's privacy.

Nancy's hair had come down, and she had trouble unfastening the pearl necklace; her husband had to help her with the clasp.

'They're beautiful pearls, aren't they?' Nancy asked. 'But if I don't give them back to Mrs Daruwalla now, I'll forget and wear them home. They might get lost or stolen.'

'I'll try to find you a necklace like this,' Detective Patel told her.

'No, it's too expensive,' Nancy said.

'You did a good job,' her husband told her.

'We're going to catch her, aren't we, Vijay?' she asked him.

'Yes, we are, sweetie,' he replied.

'She didn't recognize me!' Nancy cried.

'I told you she wouldn't, didn't I?' the detective said.

'She didn't even see me! She looked right through me – like I didn't exist! All these years, and she didn't even remember me,' Nancy said.

The deputy commissioner held her hand. She rested her head on his shoulder; she felt so empty, she couldn't even cry.

'I'm sorry, Vijay, but I don't think I can dance. I just can't,' Nancy said.

'That's all right, sweetie,' her husband said. 'I don't dance – remember?'

'He didn't have to unzip me – it was unnecessary,' Nancy said.

'It was part of the overall effect,' Patel replied.

'It was unnecessary,' Nancy repeated. 'And I didn't like the way he did it.'

'The idea was, you weren't supposed to like it,' the policeman told her.

'She must have tried to bite his whole lip off!' Nancy cried.

'I believe she barely managed to stop herself,' the deputy commissioner said. This had the effect of releasing Nancy from her emptiness; at last, she was able to cry on her husband's shoulder. It seemed that the band would never stop playing the tiresome old song.

'"We'll drink a cup of kindness yet ..."' Mr Bannerjee was shouting.

Mr Sethna observed that Julia and Dr Daruwalla were the most stately dancers on the floor. Dr and Mrs Sorabjee danced nervously; they didn't dare take their eyes off their daughter. Poor Amy had been brought home from England, where she hadn't been doing very well. Too much partying, her parents suspected – and, more disturbing, a reputed attraction to older men. At university, she was notoriously opposed to romances with her fellow students; rather, she'd thrown herself at one of her professors – a married chap. He'd not taken advantage of her, thank goodness. And now Dr and Mrs Sorabjee were tortured to see the young girl dancing with Dhar. From the frying pan to the fire! Mrs Sorabjee thought. It was awkward for Mrs Sorabjee, being a close friend of the Daruwallas' and therefore unable to express her opinion of Inspector Dhar.

'Do you know you're available in England – on videocassette?' Amy was telling the actor.

'*Am* I?' he said.

'Once we had a wine tasting and we rented you,' Amy told him. 'People who aren't from Bombay don't know what to make of you. The movies seem terribly odd to them.'

'Yes,' said Inspector Dhar. 'To me, too,' he added.

This made her laugh; she was an easy girl, he could tell – he felt a little sorry for her parents.

'All that music, mixed in with all the murders,' Amy Sorabjee said.

'Don't forget the divine intervention,' the actor remarked.

'Yes! And all the women – you *do* gather up a lot of women,' Amy observed.

'Yes, I do,' Dhar said.

'"We'll drink a cup of kindness yet for the days

717

of auld lang syne!'" the old dancers brayed; they sounded like donkeys.

'I like *Inspector Dhar and the Cage-Girl Killer* the best – it's the sexiest,' said little Amy Sorabjee.

'I don't have a favorite,' the actor confided to her; he guessed she was 22 or 23. He found her a pleasant distraction, but it irritated him that she kept staring at his lip.

'What happened to your lip?' she finally asked him in a whisper – her expression still girlish but sly, even conspiratorial.

'When the lights went out, I danced into a wall,' Dhar told her.

'I think that horrid woman did it to you,' Amy Sorabjee dared to say. 'It looks like she bit you!'

John D. just kept dancing; the way his lip had swollen, it hurt to sneer.

'Everyone thinks she's a horrid woman, you know,' Amy said; Dhar's silence had made her less sure of herself. 'And who was that first woman you were with?' Amy asked him. 'The one who left?'

'She's a stripper,' said Inspector Dhar.

'Go on – not really!' Amy cried.

'Yes, really,' John D. replied.

'And who is the blond lady?' Amy asked. 'I thought she looked about to cry.'

'She's a former friend,' the actor answered; he was tired of the girl now. A young girl's idea of intimacy was getting answers to all her questions.

John D. was sure that Vinod would already be waiting outside; surely the dwarf had returned from taking Muriel to the Wetness Cabaret. Dhar wanted to go to bed, alone; he wanted to put more ice on his lip, and he wanted to apologize to Farrokh, too. It had been unkind of the actor to imply that preparing himself for the seduction of Mrs Dogar was 'no circus'; John D. knew what the circus meant to Dr Daruwalla – the actor could have more charitably said that getting ready for Rahul was 'no picnic.' And now here was the insatiable Amy Sorabjee, trying to get him (and herself) into some unnecessary trouble. Time to slip away, the actor thought.

Just then, Amy took a quick look over Dhar's shoulder; she wanted to be exactly sure where her parents were. A doddering threesome had blocked Dr and Mrs Sorabjee from Amy's view – Mr Bannerjee was struggling to dance with his wife and the widow Lal – and Amy seized this moment of privacy, for she knew she was only briefly free of her parents' scrutiny. She brushed her soft lips against John D.'s cheek; then she whispered overbreathlessly in the actor's ear. 'I could kiss that lip and make it better!' she said.

John D., smoothly, just kept dancing. His unresponsiveness made Amy feel insecure, and so she whispered more plaintively – at least more matter-of-factly – 'I prefer older men.'

'*Do* you?' the movie star said. 'Why, so do I,' Inspector Dhar told the silly girl. 'So do I!'

That got rid of her; it always worked. At last, Inspector Dhar could slip away.

25. JUBILEE DAY

No Monkey

It was January 1, 1990, a Monday. It was also Jubilee Day at St Ignatius School in Mazagaon – the start of the mission's 126th year. Well-wishers were invited to a high tea, which amounted to a light supper in the early evening; this was scheduled to follow a special late-afternoon Mass. This was also the occasion that would formally serve to introduce Martin Mills to the Catholic community in Bombay; therefore, Father Julian and Father Cecil regretted that the scholastic had returned from the circus in such mutilated condition. The previous night, Martin had frightened Brother Gabriel, who mistook the mauled figure with his bloodstained and unraveling bandages for the wandering spirit of a previously persecuted Jesuit – some poor soul who'd been tortured and then put to death.

Earlier that same night, the zealot had prevailed upon Father Cecil to hear his confession. Father Cecil was so tired, he fell asleep before he could give Martin absolution. Typically, Martin's confession seemed unending – nor had Father Cecil caught the gist of it before he nodded off. It struck the old priest that Martin Mills was confessing nothing more serious than a lifelong disposition to complain.

Martin had begun by enumerating his several disappointments with himself, beginning with the period of his novitiate at St Aloysius in Massachusetts. Father Cecil tried to listen closely, for there was a tone of urgency in the scholastic's voice; yet young Martin's capacity for finding fault with himself was vast – the poor priest soon felt that his participation in Martin's confession was superfluous. For example, as a novice at St Aloysius, Martin confessed, a significantly holy event had been entirely wasted on him; Martin had been unimpressed by the visit of the sacred arm of St Francis Xavier to the Massachusetts novitiate. (Father Cecil didn't think this was so bad.)

The acolyte bearing the saint's severed arm was the famous Father Terry Finney, S.J.; Father Finney had selflessly undertaken the task of carrying the golden reliquary around the world. Martin confessed that, to him, the holy arm had been nothing but a skeletal limb under glass, like something partially eaten – like a leftover, Martin Mills had observed. Only now could the scholastic bear to confess having had such blasphemous thoughts. (By this time, Father Cecil was fast asleep.)

There was more; it troubled Martin that the issue of Divine Grace had taken him years to resolve to his satisfaction. And sometimes the scholastic felt he was merely making a conscious effort not to think about it. Old Father Cecil really should have heard this, for Martin Mills was dangerously full of doubt. The confession would eventually lead young Martin to his present disappointment with himself, which was the way he'd behaved on the trip to and from the circus.

The scholastic said he was guilty of loving the crippled boy more than he loved the child prostitute; his abhorrence of prostitution caused him to feel almost resigned to the girl's fate. And Dr Daruwalla had provoked the Jesuit on the sensitive matter of homosexuality; Martin was sorry that he'd spoken to the doctor in an intellectually arrogant fashion. At this point, Father Cecil was sleeping so soundly, the poor priest never woke when he slumped forward in the confessional and his nose poked between the latticework where Martin Mills could see it.

When Martin saw the old priest's nose, he knew that Father Cecil was dead to the world. He didn't want to embarrass the poor man; however, it wasn't right to leave him sleeping in such an uncomfortable position.

721

That was why the missionary crept away and went looking for Brother Gabriel: that was when poor Brother Gabriel mistook the wildly bandaged scholastic for a persecuted Christian from the past. After his fear had subsided, Brother Gabriel went to wake up Father Cecil, who thereafter suffered a sleepless night; the priest couldn't remember what Martin Mills had confessed, or whether or not he'd given the zealot absolution.

Martin slept blissfully. Even without absolution, it had felt good to say all those things against himself; tomorrow was soon enough for someone to hear his full confession – perhaps he'd ask Father Julian this time. Although Father Julian was scarier than Father Cecil, the Father Rector was also a bit younger. Thus, with his conscience clear and no bugs in his bed, Martin would sleep through the night. Full of doubt one minute, brimming with conviction the next, the missionary was a walking contradiction – he was dependably unreliable.

Nancy also slept through the night; one couldn't claim that she slept 'blissfully,' but at least she slept. Surely the champagne helped. She wouldn't hear the ringing of the phone, which Detective Patel answered in the kitchen. It was 4:00 on the morning of New Year's Day, and at first the deputy commissioner was relieved that the call was *not* from the surveillance officer who'd been assigned to watch the Dogars' house on old Ridge Road, Malabar Hill; it was a homicide report from the red-light district in Kamathipura – a prostitute had been murdered in one of the arguably better brothels. Ordinarily, no one would have awakened the deputy commissioner with such a report, but both the investigating officer and the medical examiner were certain that the crime was Dhar-related. Once again, there was the elephant drawing on the belly of the murdered whore, but there was also a fearsome new twist to this killing, which the caller was sure Detective Patel would want to see.

As for the surveillance officer, the subinspector who was watching the Dogars' house, he might as well have slept through the night, too. He swore that Mrs Dogar had never left her house; only *Mr* Dogar had left. The subinspector, whom the deputy commissioner would later reassign to something harmless, like answering letters of complaint, declared that he knew it was Mr Dogar because of the old man's characteristic shuffle; also, the figure was stooped. Then there was the matter of the baggy suit, which was gray. It was a man's suit of an exeedingly loose fit – not what Mr Dogar had worn to the new New Year's Eve party at the Duckworth Club – and with it Mr Dogar wore a white shirt, open at the throat. The old man climbed into a taxi at about 2:00 A.M.; he returned to his house, in another taxi, at 3:45 A.M. The surveillance officer (whom the deputy commissioner would also later demote from subinspector to constable) had smugly assumed that Mr Dogar was visiting either a mistress or a prostitute.

Definitely a prostitute, thought Detective Patel. Unfortunately, it hadn't been *Mr* Dogar.

The madam at the questionably better brothel in Kamathipura told the deputy commissioner that it was her brothel's policy to turn out the lights at 1:00 or 2:00 A.M., depending on the volume of customers or the lack thereof. After the lights were out, she accepted only all-night visitors; to spend the night with one of her girls, the madam charged from 100 rupees on up. The 'old man' who'd arrived after 2:00 A.M., when the brothel was dark, had offered 300 rupees for the madam's smallest girl.

Detective Patel first thought the madam must have meant her *youngest* girl, but the madam said she was sure that the gentleman had requested her 'smallest'; in any case, that's what he got. Asha was a very small, delicate girl – about 15, the madam declared. About 13, the deputy commissioner guessed.

Because the lights were out and there were no other girls in the hallway, no one but the madam and Asha saw the alleged old man – he wasn't *that* old, the madam believed. He wasn't at all stooped, either, the madam recalled, but (like the soon-to-be-demoted surveillance officer) she noted how loosely the suit fit him and that it was gray. 'He' was very clean-shaven, except for a thin mustache – the latter was false, Detective Patel assumed – and an unusual hairdo . . . here the madam held her hands high above her forehead and said, 'But it was cut short in the back, and over the ears.'

'Yes, I know – a pompadour,' Patel said. He knew that the hair would not have been silver, streaked with white, but he asked the question anyway.

'No, it was black, streaked with silver,' the madam said.

And no one had seen the 'old man' leave. The madam had been awakened by the presence of a nun. She'd heard what she thought was someone trying to open the door from the street; when she went to see, there was a nun outside the door – it must have been about 3:00 in the morning.

'Do you see a lot of nuns in this district at that hour?' the deputy commissioner asked her.

'Of course not!' the madam cried. She'd asked the nun what she wanted, and the nun had replied that she was searching for a Christian girl from Kerala; the madam responded that she had no Kerala Christians in her house.

'And what color was the nun's habit?' Patel asked, although he knew the answer would be 'gray,' which it was. It wasn't an unusual color for a habit of tropical weight, but it was also something that could have been fashioned from the same gray suit that Mrs Dogar had worn when she came to the brothel. The baggy suit had probably fitted over the habit; then, in turn, the habit fit over the suit, or parts of the habit and the suit were one and the same – at least the same fabric. The white shirt could have various uses; maybe it was rolled, like a high collar, or else it could cover the head, like a kind of cowl. The detective presumed that the alleged nun didn't have a mustache. ('Of course not!' the madam declared.) And because the nun had covered her head, the madam wouldn't have noticed the pompadour.

The only reason the madam had found the dead girl so soon was that she'd been unable to fall back asleep; first, one of the all-night customers was shouting, and then, when it was finally quiet, the madam had heard the sound of water boiling, although it wasn't time for tea. In the dead girl's cubicle, a pot of water had come to a boil on a heating coil; that was how the madam discovered the body. Otherwise, it might have been 8:00 or 9:00 in the morning before the other prostitutes would have noticed that tiny Asha wasn't up and about.

The deputy commissioner asked the madam about the sound of someone trying to open the door from the street – the sound that had awakened her. Wouldn't the door have made the same sound if it had been opened from the *inside*, and then closed *behind* the departing nun? The madam admitted that this would have made the same sound; in short, if the madam hadn't heard the door, she never would have seen the nun. And by the time Mrs Dodger took a taxi home, she was no longer a nun at all.

Detective Patel was exceedingly polite in asking the madam a most obvious question: 'Would you consider the idea that the not-so-old man and the nun were in fact the same person?' The madam shrugged; she doubted she could identify either of them. When the deputy commissioner pressed her on this point, all the madam would add was that she'd been sleepy; both the not-so-old man and the nun had woken her up.

Nancy was still not awake when Detective Patel returned to his flat; he'd already typed a scathing report, demoting the surveillance officer and consigning him to the mailroom of Crime Branch Headquarters.

The deputy commissioner wanted to be home when his wife woke up; he also didn't want to call Inspector Dhar and Dr Daruwalla from the police station. Detective Patel thought he'd let them all sleep a little longer.

The deputy commissioner determined that Asha's neck had been broken so cleanly for two reasons. One, she was small; two, she'd been completely relaxed. Rahul must have coaxed her over onto her stomach, as if to prepare her for sex in that position. But of course there'd been no sex. The deep fingerprint bruises in the prostitute's eye sockets – and on her throat, just below her jaw – suggested that Mrs Dogar had grabbed Asha's face from behind; she'd wrenched the small girl's head back and to one side, until Asha's neck snapped.

Then Rahul had rolled Asha onto her back in order to make the drawing on her belly. Although the drawing was of the usual kind, it was of less than the usual quality; it suggested undue haste, which was strange – there was no urgency for Mrs Dogar to leave the brothel. Yet something had compelled Rahul to hurry. As for the fearsome 'new twist' to this killing, it sickened Detective Patel. The dead girl's lower lip was bitten clean through. Asha could not have been bitten so savagely while she was alive; her screams would have awakened the entire brothel. No; the bite had occurred after the murder and after the drawing. The minimal amount of bleeding indicated that Asha had been bitten after her heart had stopped. It was the idea of biting the girl that had made Mrs Dogar hurry, the policeman thought. She couldn't wait to finish the drawing because Asha's lower lip was so tempting to her.

Even such slight bleeding had made a mess, which was uncharacteristic of Rahul. It must have been Mrs Dogar who put the pot of water on the heating coil; her own face, at least her mouth, must have been marked with the prostitute's blood. When the water was warm, Rahul dipped some of the dead girl's clothes in the pot and used them to wash the blood off herself. Then she left – as a nun – forgetting that the heating coil was on. The boiling water had brought the madam. Although the nun had been a smart idea, this had otherwise been a sloppy job.

Nancy woke up about 8:00; she had a hangover, but Detective Patel didn't hesitate to tell her what had happened. He could hear her being sick in the bathroom; he called the actor first, then the screenwriter. He told Dhar about the lip, but not the doctor; with Dr Daruwalla, the deputy commissioner wanted to emphasize the importance of a good script for Dhar's lunch with Mrs Dogar. Patel told them both that he would have to arrest Rahul today; he hoped he had enough circumstantial evidence to arrest her. Whether or not he had enough evidence to *keep* her – that was another story. That was what he was counting on the actor and the screenwriter for: they had to make something happen over lunch.

Deputy Commissioner Patel was encouraged by one thing that the gullible surveillance officer had told him. After the disguised Mrs Dogar had shuffled out of the taxi and into her house, the lights were turned on in a ground-floor room – not a bedroom – and these lights remained on well after daybreak. The deputy commissioner hoped that Rahul had been drawing.

As for Dr Daruwalla, his first good night's sleep – for five nights, and counting – had been interrupted rather early. He had no surgeries scheduled for New Year's Day, and no office appointments, either; he'd been planning to sleep in. But upon hearing from Detective Patel, the screenwriter called John D. immediately. There was a lot to do before Dhar's lunch at the Duckworth Club; there would be much rehearsing – some of it would be awkward, because Mr Sethna would have to be involved. The deputy commissioner had already notified the old steward.

It was from John D. that Farrokh heard about Asha's lower lip.

'Rahul must have been thinking of *you!*' Dr Daruwalla cried.

'Well, we know she has a thing about biting,' Dhar told the doctor. 'In all likelihood, it started with *you*.'

'What do you mean?' Dr Daruwalla asked, for John D. hadn't told him that Mrs Dogar had confessed to gnawing on the doctor's toe.

'It all started with the big toe of your right foot, in Goa,' John D. began. 'That was Rahul who bit you. You were right all along – it was no monkey.'

The Wrong Madhu

That Monday, well before meat-feeding time at the Great Blue Nile Circus in Junagadh, the elephant-footed boy would wake up to the steady coughs of the lions; their low roars rose and fell as regularly as breathing. It was a cold morning in that part of Gujarat. For the first time in his life, Ganesh could see his own breath; the huffs of breath from the lions were like blasts of steam escaping from their cages.

The Muslims delivered the meat in a wooden wagon, dotted with flies; the entire floor of the wagon was lifted from the cart and placed on the ground between the cook's tent and the big cats' cages – the raw beef was piled on this slab of rough wood, which was the appproximate size of a double door. Even in the cold morning air, the flies hovered over the meat, which Chandra sorted. Sometimes there was mutton mixed in with the beef, and the cook wanted to rescue it; mutton was too expensive for lions and tigers.

The big cats were bellowing now; they could smell the meat, and some of them could see the cook separating the choicer pieces of mutton. If the elephant boy was frightened by how savagely the lions and tigers devoured the raw beef, Dr Daruwalla would never learn of it; nor would the doctor ever know if the sight of the lions slipping in the meat grease upset the cripple. At the circus, it was one of the few things that always upset the doctor.

The same Monday, someone proposed to marry Madhu. The proposal, as was only proper, was first offered to Mr and Mrs Das; the ringmaster and his wife were surprised. Not only had they not begun to train the girl, but, because Madhu was untrained, she wasn't in evidence among the performers; yet the marriage proposal was offered by a gentleman who claimed to have been in the audience for the late-evening show on Sunday. Here he was, the following morning, professing his instant devotion!

The Bengali ringmaster and his wife had children of their own; their kids had rejected the circus life. But Mr and Mrs Das had trained many other children to be circus acrobats; they were kind to these adopted kids and especially protective of the girls. After all, when these girls were properly trained, they were of some value – not only to the circus. They had acquired a little glamour; they'd even earned some money, which they'd had no occasion to spend – hence the ringmaster and his wife were used to keeping dowries for them.

Mr and Mrs Das conscientiously advised the girls whether or not a marriage proposal was worthy of acceptance or negotiation, and they routinely gave up these adopted daughters – always to decent marriages, and often making their own contributions to the girls' dowries. In many cases, the ringmaster and his wife had grown so fond of these children that it broke their hearts to see them go. Almost all the girls would eventually leave the circus; the few who stayed became trainers.

Madhu was very young and totally unproven, and she had no dowry. Yet here was a gentleman of means, well dressed, clearly a city person – he owned property and managed an entertainment business in Bombay – and was offering Madhu a marriage proposal that Mr and Mrs Das found extremely generous; he would take the poor girl *without* a dowry. Doubtless, in these

729

premarital negotiations, there would have been some substantive discussion of the remuneration that the ringmaster and his wife deserved, for (who knows?) Madhu might have become a star of the Great Blue Nile. From Mr and Mrs Das's point of view, they were offered a sizable payment for a sullen girl who might never prove herself to be any kind of acrobat at all. It wasn't as if they were being asked to part with a young woman they'd grown fond of; they'd barely had time to talk with Madhu.

It may have crossed the Bengalis' minds to consult the doctor or the missionary; Mr and Mrs Das at least should have discussed the would-be marriage with Deepa, but the dwarf's wife was still sick. So what if Deepa was the one who'd spotted Madhu as a future boneless girl? The dwarf's wife was still confined to her tent. Moreover, the ringmaster held a grudge against Vinod. Mr Das was envious of the dwarf's car-driving business; since Vinod had left the Great Blue Nile, the dwarf hadn't hesitated to exaggerate his success. And the ringmaster's wife felt herself to be vastly superior to the dwarf's wife; to consult with Deepa was beneath Mrs Das – even if Deepa were healthy. Besides, Mrs Das quickly persuaded her husband that Madhu's marriage proposal was a good deal. (It was certainly a good deal for them.)

If Madhu wasn't interested, they'd keep the silly child in the circus; but if the unworthy girl had the wisdom to recognize her good fortune, the ringmaster and his wife would let her go, with their blessings. As for the crippled brother, the gentleman from Bombay appeared to know nothing about him. Mr and Mrs Das felt some responsibility for the fact that the elephant-footed boy would be left on his own; they had considered it prudent to promise Dr Daruwalla and Martin Mills that Ganesh would be given every chance to succeed. The ringmaster and his wife saw no reason to discuss Ganesh with Deepa; the cripple hadn't been a discovery of hers – she'd only claimed to discover the boneless girl. And what if the dwarf's wife had something contagious?

A phone call to the doctor or the missionary would have been an appreciated courtesy – if nothing more. But there were no telephones at the circus; a trip to either the post office or the telegraph office would have been required, and Madhu surprised the ringmaster and his wife by her immediate and unrestrained acceptance of the marriage proposal. She didn't feel that the gentleman was too old for her, as Mr Das had feared; nor was Madhu repelled by the gentleman's physical appearance, which had been the primary concern of Mrs Das. The ringmaster's wife was repulsed by the gentleman's disfiguring scar – some sort of burn, she supposed – but Madhu made no mention of it, nor did she otherwise seem to mind such a hideous flaw.

Probably sensing, in advance, Dr Daruwalla's disapproval, the ringmaster would wisely send a telegram to Martin Mills; the missionary had struck Mr and Mrs Das as the more relaxed of the two – by which they meant the more accepting. Furthermore, the Jesuit had seemed slightly less concerned for Madhu's prospects – or else the doctor's concern had been more apparent. And because it was Jubilee Day at St Ignatius, the school offices were closed; it would be Tuesday before anyone handed the telegram to Martin. Mr Garg would already have brought his young wife back to the Wetness Cabaret.

Naturally, it was in the Bengali's best interests to make his telegram sound upbeat.

THAT GIRL MADHU / IT IS BEING HER LUCKY DAY / VERY ACCEPTABLE MATRIMONIAL MADE BY MIDDLE-AGED BUT MOST SUCCESSFUL BUSINESSMAN / IT IS WHAT SHE IS WANTING EVEN IF SHE ISN'T LOVING HIM EXACTLY AND IN SPITE OF HIS SCAR / MEANWHILE THE CRIPPLE IS BEING AFFORDED EVERY OPPORTUNITY OF WORKING HARD HERE / REST BEING ASSURED / DAS

731

By the time Dr Daruwalla would hear the news, the doctor would be kicking himself; he should have known all along – for why else would Mr Garg have asked Ranjit for the address of the Great Blue Nile? Surely Mr Garg, like Dr Daruwalla, knew that Madhu couldn't read; Acid Man had never intended to send the girl a letter. And when Ranjit gave Farrokh the message (that Garg had requested the circus's address), the faithful secretary failed to inform the doctor that Garg had also inquired *when* the doctor was returning from Junagadh. That same Sunday, when Dr Daruwalla left the circus, Mr Garg went there.

Farrokh wouldn't be persuaded by Vinod's notion – that Garg was so smitten by Madhu, he couldn't let her go. Maybe Mr Garg had been unprepared for how much he would miss Madhu, the dwarf said. Deepa insisted on the importance of the fact that Acid Man had actually *married* Madhu; surely Garg had no intentions of sending the girl back to a brothel – not after he'd married her. The dwarf's wife would add that perhaps it *was* Madhu's 'lucky day.'

But this particular news wouldn't find its way to Dr Daruwalla on Jubilee Day. This news would wait. Waiting with it was worse news. Ranjit would hear it first, and the medical secretary would elect to spare the doctor such bad tidings; they were unsuitable tidings for New Year's Day. But the busy office of Tata Two was in full operation on this holiday Monday – there were no holidays for Tata Two. It was Dr Tata's ancient secretary, Mr Subhash, who informed Ranjit of the problem. The two old secretaries conversed in the manner of hostile but toothless male dogs.

'I am having information for the doctor only,' Mr Subhash began, without bothering to identify himself.

'Then you'll have to wait until tomorrow,' Ranjit informed the fool.

'This is Mr Subhash, in Dr Tata's office,' the imperious secretary said.

'You'll still have to wait until tomorrow,' Ranjit told him. 'Dr Daruwalla isn't here today.'

'This is being important information – the doctor is definitely wanting to know it as soon as possible,' Mr Subhash said.

'Then tell me,' Ranjit replied.

'Well . . . she is having it,' Mr Subhash announced dramatically.

'You've got to be clearer than that,' Ranjit told him.

'That girl, Madhu – she is testing positive for HIV,' Mr Subhash said. Ranjit knew this contradicted the information he'd seen in Madhu's file; Tata Two had already told Dr Daruwalla that Madhu's test was negative. If the girl was carrying the AIDS virus, Ranjit assumed that Dr Daruwalla wouldn't have allowed her to go to the circus.

'The ELISA is being positive, and this is being confirmed by Western Blot,' Mr Subhash was saying.

'But Dr Tata himself told Dr Daruwalla that Madhu's test was *negative*,' Ranjit said.

'That was definitely the wrong Madhu,' old Mr Subhash said dismissively. '*Your* Madhu is being HIV-positive.'

'This is a serious mistake,' Ranjit remarked.

'There is being no *mistake*,' Mr Subhash said indignantly. 'This is merely a matter of there being two Madhus.' But there was nothing 'merely' about the matter.

Ranjit transcribed his phone conversation with Mr Subhash into a neatly typed report, which he placed on Dr Daruwalla's desk; from the existing evidence, the medical secretary concluded that Madhu and Mr Garg might be sharing something a little more serious than chlamydia. What Ranjit couldn't have known was that Mr Garg had gone to Junagadh and retrieved Madhu from the circus; probably Garg had made his plans to bring the girl back to Bombay only after he'd been told that Madhu was *not* HIV-positive – but maybe not. In the world of the Wetness Cabaret, and throughout the brothels in Kamathipura, a certain fatalism was the norm.

The news about the wrong Madhu would wait for Dr Daruwalla, too. What was the point of hurrying evil tidings? After all, Ranjit believed that Madhu was still with the circus in Junagadh. As for Mr Garg, Dr Daruwalla's secretary wrongly assumed that Acid Man had never left Bombay. And when Martin Mills called Dr Daruwalla's office, Ranjit saw no reason to inform the missionary that Madhu was carrying the AIDS virus. The zealot wanted his bandages changed; he'd been advised by the Father Rector that clean bandages would be more suitable for the Jubilee Day celebration. Ranjit told Martin that he'd have to call the doctor at home. Because Farrokh was hard at work – rehearsing for Rahul, with John D. and old Mr Sethna – Julia took the message. She was surprised to hear that Dhar's twin had been bitten by a presumed-to-be-rabid chimpanzee. Martin was surprised, and his feelings were hurt, to hear that Dr Daruwalla hadn't informed his wife of the painful episode.

Julia graciously accepted the Jesuit's invitation to the high tea in honor of Jubilee Day; she promised that she'd bring Farrokh to St Ignatius before the start of the festivities so that the doctor would have plenty of time to change Martin's bandages. The scholastic thanked Julia, but when he hung up the phone, he felt overcome by the sheer foreignness of his situation. He'd been in India less than a week; suddenly, everything that was unfamiliar was exacting a toll.

To begin with, the zealot had been taken aback by Father Julian's response to his confession. The Father Rector had been impatient and argumentative; his absolution had been grudging and abrupt – and it had been hastily followed by Father Julian's insistence that Martin do something about his soiled and bloody bandages. But the priest and the scholastic had encountered a fundamental misunderstanding. At that point in his confession when Martin Mills had admitted to loving the crippled boy more than he could ever love the child prostitute, Father Julian had interrupted him and told him to be less concerned with his own capacity for love, by which the Father Rector meant that Martin should be *more* concerned with God's love and God's will – and that he should be more humble about his own, merely human role. Martin was a member of the Society of Jesus, and he should behave accordingly; he wasn't just another egocentric social worker – a do-gooder who was constantly evaluating, criticizing and congratulating himself.

'The fate of these children isn't in your hands,' Father Julian told the scholastic, 'nor will one of them suffer, more or less, because of *your* love for them – or your *lack* of love for them. Try to stop thinking so much about yourself. You're an instrument of God's will – you're not your own creation.'

This not only struck the zealot as blunt; Martin Mills was confused. That the Father Rector saw the children as already consigned to their fate seemed remarkably Calvinistic for a Jesuit; Martin feared that Father Julian might also be suffering from the influence of Hinduism, for this notion of the children's 'fate' had a karmic ring. And what was wrong with being a social worker? Hadn't St Ignatius Loyola himself been a social worker of unflagging zeal? Or did the Father Rector mean only that Martin shouldn't take the fate of the circus children too *personally*? That the scholastic had intervened on the children's behalf did *not* mean he was responsible for every little thing that might happen to them.

It was in such a spiritual fog that Martin Mills took a walk in Mazagaon; he hadn't wandered far from the mission before he encountered that slum which Dr Daruwalla had first shown to him – the former movie-set slum where his evil mother had fainted when she was stepped on and licked by a cow. Martin remembered that he'd vomited from the moving car.

At midmorning, on this busy Monday, the slum was

teeming, but the missionary found that it was better to focus on such abjectness in a microcosmic fashion; rather than look up the length of Sophia Zuber Road for as far as he could see, Martin kept his eyes cast down – at his slowly moving feet. He never allowed his gaze to wander above ground level. Most of the slum dwellers were thus cut off at their ankles; he saw only the children's faces – naturally, the children were begging. He saw the paws and the inquiring noses of scavenging dogs. He saw a moped that had fallen or crashed in the gutter; a garland of marigolds was entwined on its handlebars, as if the moped were being prepared for cremation. He came upon a cow – a whole cow, not just the hooves, because the cow was lying down. It was hard to navigate around the cow. But when Martin Mills stopped walking, even though he'd been walking slowly, he found himself quickly surrounded; it should be stated clearly in every guidebook for tourists – never stand still in a slum.

The cow's long sad dignified face gazed up at him; its eyes were rimmed with flies. On the cow's tawny flank, a patch of the smooth hide was abraded – the raw spot was no bigger than a human fist, but it was encrusted with flies. This apparent abrasion was actually the entrance to a deep hole that had been made in the cow by a vehicle transporting a ship's mast; but Martin hadn't witnessed the collision, nor did the milling crowd permit him a comprehensive view of the cow's mortal wound.

Suddenly, the crowd parted; a procession was passing – all Martin saw was a lunatic mob of flower throwers. When the worshipers had filed by, the cow lay sprinkled with rose petals; some of the flowers were stuck to the wound, alongside the flies. One of the cow's long legs was extended, for the animal was lying on its side; the hoof almost reached the curb. There in the gutter, within inches of the hoof but entirely untouched, was (unmistakably) a human turd. Beyond the serenely undisturbed turd was a vendor's stall.

They were selling something that looked purposeless
to Martin Mills; it was a vivid scarlet powder, but the
missionary doubted that it was a spice or anything
edible. Some of it spilled into the gutter, where its
dazzling red particles coated both the cow's hoof and
the human turd.

That was Martin's microcosm of India; the mortally
wounded animal, the religious ritual, the incessant
flies, the unbelievably bright colors, the evidence of
casual human shit – and of course the confusion
of smells. The missionary had been forewarned: if he
couldn't see beyond such abjectness, he would be of
scant use to St Ignatius – or to any mission in such a
world. Shaken, the scholastic wondered if he had the
stomach to be a priest. So vulnerable was his state of
mind, Martin Mills was fortunate that the news about
Madhu was still a day away.

Take Me Home

In the Ladies' Garden at the Duckworth Club, the noon
sun shimmered above the bower. So dense was the
bougainvillea, the sun shot through the flowers in
pinholes; these beads of bright light dappled the tablecloths like sprinkled diamonds. Nancy passed her
hands under the needle-thin rays. She was playing
with the sun, trying to reflect its light in her wedding
ring, when Detective Patel spoke to her. 'You don't
have to be here, sweetie,' her husband said. 'You can
go home, you know.'

'I want to be here,' Nancy told him.

'I just want to warn you – don't expect this to be
satisfying,' the deputy commissioner said. 'Somehow,
even when you catch them, it's never quite satisfying.'

Dr Daruwalla, who kept looking at his watch, then
remarked, 'She's late.'

'They're *both* late,' Nancy said.

'Dhar is *supposed* to be late,' the policeman reminded her.

Dhar was waiting in the kitchen. When the second Mrs Dogar arrived, Mr Sethna would observe the increasing degrees of her irritation; when the steward saw that she was clearly agitated, he would send Dhar to her table. Dr Daruwalla was operating on the theory that agitation inspired Rahul to act rashly.

But when she arrived, they almost didn't recognize her. She was wearing what Western women familiarly call a little black dress; the skirt was short, with a slight flare, the waist very long and slimming. Mrs Dogar's small, high breasts were displayed to good effect. If she'd worn a black-linen jacket, she would have looked almost businesslike, Dr Daruwalla believed; without a jacket, the dress was more suitable for a cocktail party in Toronto. As if intended to offend Duckworthians, the dress was sleeveless, with spaghetti straps; the brawniness of Rahul's bare shoulders and upper arms, not to mention the breadth of her chest, hulked ostentatiously. She was too muscular for a dress like that, Farrokh decided; then it occurred to him that this was what she thought Dhar liked.

Yet Mrs Dogar didn't move as if she were at all conscious that she was a woman of great strength or noticeable size. Her entry into the Duckworth Club dining room wasn't in the least aggressive. Her attitude was shy and girlish; rather than stride to her table, she allowed old Mr Sethna to escort her on his arm — Dr Daruwalla had never seen her this way. This wasn't a woman who would ever pick up a spoon or a fork and ring it against her water glass; this was an extremely feminine woman — she would rather starve at her table than cause herself any unflattering attention. She would sit smiling and waiting for Dhar until the club closed and someone sent her home. Apparently, Detective Patel was prepared for this change in her, because the deputy commissioner spoke quickly to the screenwriter; Mrs Dogar had barely been seated at her table.

'Don't bother to keep her waiting,' the policeman said. 'She's a different woman today.'

Farrokh summoned Mr Sethna – to have John D. 'arrive' – but all the while the deputy commissioner was watching what Mrs Dogar did with her purse. It was a table for four, as the screenwriter had suggested; this had been Julia's idea. When there were only two people at a table for four, Julia said, a woman usually put her purse on one of the empty chairs – not on the floor – and Farrokh had wanted the purse on a chair.

'She put it on the floor, anyway,' Detective Patel observed.

Dr Daruwalla had been unable to prevent Julia from attending *this* lunch; now Julia said, 'That's because she's not a real woman.'

'Dhar will take care of it,' the deputy commissioner said.

All Farrokh could think was that the change in Mrs Dogar was terrifying.

'It was the murder, wasn't it?' the doctor asked the policeman. 'I mean, the murder has totally calmed her – it's had a completely soothing effect on her, hasn't it?'

'It appears to have made her feel like a young girl,' Patel replied.

'She must have a hard time feeling like a young girl,' Nancy remarked. 'What a lot to do – just to feel like a young girl.'

Then Dhar was there, at Mrs Dogar's table; he didn't kiss her. He approached her unseen, from behind, and he put both his hands on her bare shoulders; perhaps he leaned on her, because she appeared to stiffen, but he was only trying to kick her purse over. When he managed to do this, she picked her purse up and put it on an empty chair.

'We're forgetting to talk among ourselves,' the deputy commissioner said. 'We can't simply be staring at them and saying nothing.'

'Please kill her, Vijay,' Nancy said.

'I'm not carrying a gun, sweetie,' the deputy commissioner lied.

'What will the law do to her?' Julia asked the policeman.

'Capital punishment exists in India,' the detective said, 'but the death penalty is rarely enacted.'

'Death is by hanging,' Dr Daruwalla said.

'Yes, but there's no jury system in India,' Patel said. 'A single judge decides the prisoner's fate. Life imprisonment and hard labor are much more common than the death penalty. They won't hang her.'

'You should kill her now,' Nancy repeated.

They could see Mr Sethna hovering around Mrs Dogar's table like a nervous ghost. They couldn't see Dhar's left hand – it was under the table. Speculation was rife that his hand was on Rahul's thigh, or in her lap.

'Let's just keep talking,' Patel told them cheerfully.

'Fuck you, fuck Rahul, fuck Dhar,' Nancy told Patel. 'Fuck you, too,' she said to Farrokh. 'Not you – I like you,' she told Julia.

'Thank you, dear,' Julia replied.

'Fuck, fuck, fuck,' Nancy said.

'Your poor lip,' Mrs Dogar was saying to John D. This much Mr Sethna understood; they would understand this much from the Ladies' Garden, too, because they saw Rahul touch Dhar's lower lip with her long index finger – it was just a brief, feather-light touch. Dhar's lower lip was a luminous navy blue.

'I hope you're not in a biting mood today,' John D. told her.

'I'm in a very good mood today,' Mrs Dogar replied. 'I want to know where you're going to take me, and what you're going to do to me,' she said coquettishly. It was embarrassing how young and cute she seemed to think she was. Her lips were pursed, which exaggerated the deep wrinkles at the corners of her savage mouth; her smile was small and coy, as if she were blotting lipstick in a mirror. Although her makeup mostly concealed the mark, there was a tiny inflamed cut across the green-tinted eyelid of one of her eyes; it caused her to blink, as if the eye itself were sore. But it was only a small irritation, the tiniest scratch; it was all that the prostitute named Asha had been able to do to her – to flick back one hand, to poke at Rahul's eye – maybe a second or two before Rahul broke her neck.

'You've scratched your eye, haven't you?' Inspector Dhar observed, but he felt no stiffening in Mrs Dogar's thighs; under the table, she gently pressed her thighs together on his hand.

'I must have been thinking of you in my sleep,' she said dreamily. When she closed her eyes, her eyelids had the silver-green iridescence of a lizard; when she parted her lips, her long teeth were wet and shiny – her warm gums were the color of strong tea.

It made John D.'s lip throb to look at her, but he continued to press his palm against the inside of her thigh. He hated this part of the script. Dhar suddenly said, 'Did you draw me a picture of what you want?' He felt the muscles in both her thighs grip his hand tightly – her mouth was also tightly closed – and her eyes opened wide and fixed on his lip.

'You can't expect me to show you *here*,' Mrs Dogar said.

'Just a peek,' John D. begged her. 'Otherwise, I'll be in too much of a hurry to eat.'

Had he not been so easily offended by vulgarity, Mr Sethna would have been in eavesdropper heaven; yet the steward was trembling with disapproval and responsibility. It struck the old Parsi as an awkward moment to bring them the menus, but he knew he needed to be near her purse.

'It's disgusting how much people eat – I loathe eating,' Mrs Dogar said. Dhar felt her thighs go slack; it was as if her concentration span were shorter than a child's – as if she were losing her sexual interest, and for no better reason than the merest mention of food.

741

'We don't have to eat at all – we haven't ordered,' Dhar reminded her. 'We could just go – now,' he suggested, but even as he spoke he was prepared to hold her in her chair (if need be) with his left hand. The thought of being alone with her, in a suite at either the Oberoi or the Taj, would have frightened John D., except that he knew Detective Patel would never allow Rahul to leave the Duckworth Club. But Mrs Dogar was almost strong enough to stand up, despite the downward pressure of Dhar's hand. 'Just one picture,' the actor pleaded with her. 'Just show me something.'

Rahul exhaled thinly through her nose. 'I'm in too good a mood to be exasperated with you,' she told him. 'But you're a very naughty boy.'

'Show me,' Dhar said. In her thighs, he thought he felt those seemingly involuntary shivers that are visible on the flanks of a horse. When she turned to her purse, John D. raised his eyes to Mr Sethna, but the old Parsi appeared to be suffering from stage fright; the steward clutched the menus in one hand, his silver serving tray in the other. How could the old fool upend Mrs Dogar's purse if he didn't have a free hand? John D. wondered.

Rahul took the purse into her lap; Dhar could feel the bottom of it, for it briefly rested on his wrist. There was more than one drawing, and Mrs Dogar appeared to hesitate before she withdrew all three; but she still didn't show him any of them. She held the drawings protectively in her right hand; with her left hand, she returned her purse to the empty chair – that was when Mr Sethna sprang into erratic action. He dropped the serving tray; there was a resounding silvery clatter upon the dining room's stone floor. Then the steward stepped on the tray – he actually appeared to trip over it – and the menus flew from his hand into Mrs Dogar's lap. Instinctively, she caught them, while the old Parsi staggered past her and collided with the all-important chair. There went her purse, upside down on the floor, but nothing spilled out of it until Mr Sethna clumsily attempted to pick the purse up; then everything was everywhere. Of the three drawings, which Rahul had left unattended on the table, John D. could see only the one on top. It was enough.

The woman in the picture bore a striking resemblance to what Mrs Dogar might have looked like as a young girl. Rahul had never exactly been a young girl, but this portrait reminded John D. of how she had looked in Goa 20 years ago. An elephant was mounting her, but this elephant had two trunks. The first trunk – it was in the usual place for an elephant's trunk – was deeply inside the young woman's mouth; in fact, it had emerged through the back of her head. The second trunk, which was the elephant's preposterous penis, had penetrated the woman's vagina; it was this trunk that had burst between the woman's shoulder blades. Approximately at the back of the woman's neck, John D. could see that the elephant's two trunks were touching each other; the actor could also see that the elephant was winking. Dhar would never see the other two drawings; he wouldn't want to. The movie star stepped quickly behind Mrs Dogar's chair and pushed the fumbling Mr Sethna out of the way.

'Allow me,' Dhar said, bending to the spilled contents of her purse. Mrs Dogar's mood had been so improved by her recent killing, she was remarkably unprovoked by the apparent accident.

'Oh, purses! They're *such* a nuisance!' Rahul said. Flirtatiously, she allowed her hand to touch the back of Inspector Dhar's neck. He was kneeling between her chair and the empty chair; he was gathering the contents of her purse, which he then put on the table. Quite casually, the actor pointed to the top half of the silver ballpoint pen, which he'd placed between a mirror and a jar of moisturizer.

'I don't see the bottom half of this,' the actor said. 'Maybe it's still in your purse.' Then he handed her the purse, which was easily half full, and he pretended to look under the table for the bottom half of the silver

743

ballpoint pen – that part which Nancy had kept so well polished these 20 years.

When John D. lifted his face to her, he was still kneeling; as such, his face was level with her small, well-shaped breasts. Mrs Dogar was holding the top half of the pen. 'A rupee for your thoughts,' said Inspector Dhar; it was something he said in all his movies.

Rahul's lips were parted; she looked quizzically down at Dhar – her scratched eye blinking once, and then again. Her lips softly closed and she once more exhaled thinly through her nose, as if such controlled breathing helped her to think.

'I thought I'd lost this,' Mrs Dogar said slowly.

'It appears you've lost the other half,' John D. replied; he stayed on his knees because he imagined that she liked looking down on him.

'This is the only half I ever had,' Rahul explained.

Dhar stood up and walked behind her chair; he didn't want her to grab the drawings. When John D. returned to his seat, Rahul was staring at the half-pen.

'You might as well have lost *that* half,' John D. told her. 'You can't use it for anything.'

'But you're wrong!' Mrs Dogar cried. 'It's really marvelous as a money clip.'

'A money clip,' the actor repeated.

'Look here,' Rahul began. There was no money among the spilled contents of her purse, which John D. had spread on the table; she had to search in her purse. 'The problem with money clips,' Mrs Dogar told him, 'is that they're conceived for a big *wad* of money . . . the sort of wad of money that men are always flashing out of their pockets, you know.'

'Yes, I know,' said Inspector Dhar. He watched her fishing in her purse for some smaller bills. She pulled out a 10-rupee note, and two 5's, and when the actor saw the two 2-rupee notes with the unnatural typing on them, he raised his eyes to Mr Sethna and the old steward began his hurried shuffle across the dining room to the Ladies' Garden.

744

'Look here,' Rahul repeated. 'When you have just a few small notes, which most women must carry – for tipping, for the odd beggar – this is the perfect money clip. It holds just a few notes, but quite snugly . . .' Her voice trailed away because she saw that Dhar had covered the drawings with his hand; he was sliding the three drawings across the tablecloth when Rahul reached out and grabbed his pinky finger, which she sharply lifted, breaking it. John D. still managed to pull the drawings into his lap. The pinky finger of his right hand pointed straight up, as if it grew out of the back of his hand; it was dislocated at the big knuckle joint. With his left hand, Dhar was able to protect the drawings from Mrs Dogar's grasp. She was still struggling with him – she was trying to get the drawings away from him with her right hand – when Detective Patel hooked her neck in the crook of his elbow and pinned her left arm behind her chair.

'You're under arrest,' the deputy commissioner told her.

'The top half of the pen is a money clip,' said Inspector Dhar. 'She uses it for small notes. When she put the note in Mr Lal's mouth, the makeshift money clip must have fallen by the body – you know the rest. There's some typing on those two-rupee notes,' Dhar told the real policeman.

'Read it to me,' Patel said. Mrs Dogar held herself very still; her free right hand, which had ceased struggling with John D. for the drawings, floated just above the tablecloth, as if she were about to give them all her blessing.

'"A member no more,"' Dhar read aloud.

'That one was for you,' the deputy commissioner told him.

'". . . because Dhar is still a member,"' Dhar read.

'Who was that one for?' the policeman asked Rahul, but Mrs Dogar was frozen in her chair, her hand still conducting an imaginary orchestra above the table-cloth; her eyes had never left Inspector Dhar. The top

drawing had become wrinkled in the tussle, but John
D. smoothed all three drawings against the tablecloth.
He was careful not to look at them.

'You're quite an artist,' the deputy commissioner
told Rahul, but Mrs Dogar just kept staring at Inspector
Dhar.

Dr Daruwalla regretted that he looked at the drawings; the second was worse than the first, and the third
was the worst of all. He knew he would go to his grave
still thinking of them. Julia alone had the sense to
remain in the Ladies' Garden; she knew there was no
good reason to come any closer. But Nancy must have
felt compelled to confront the Devil herself; it would be
uncomfortable for her later to recall the last words
between Dhar and Rahul.

'I really wanted you – I wasn't kidding,' Mrs Dogar
said to the actor.

To Dr Daruwalla's surprise, John D. said to Mrs
Dogar, 'I wasn't kidding, either.'

It must have been hard for Nancy to feel that the
focus of her victimization had shifted so far from
herself; it still galled her that Rahul didn't remember
who she was.

'I was in Goa,' Nancy announced to the killer.

'Don't say anything, sweetie,' her husband told her.

'Say anything you feel like saying, sweetie,' Rahul
said.

'I had a fever and you crawled into bed with me,'
Nancy said.

Mrs Dogar appeared to be thoughtfully surprised.
She stared at Nancy as she had previously stared at the
top half of the pen, her recognition traveling over time.
'Why, is it really *you*, dear?' Rahul asked Nancy. 'But
what on earth has happened to you?'

'You should have killed me when you had the
chance,' Nancy told her.

'You look already dead to me,' Mrs Dogar said.

'Please kill her, Vijay,' Nancy said to her husband.

'I told you this wouldn't be very satisfying, sweetie.'

That was all the deputy commissioner would say to her.

When the uniformed constables and the subinspectors came, Detective Patel told them to put away their weapons. Rahul was not resisting arrest. The deep and unknown satisfactions of the previous night's murder seemed to radiate from Mrs Dogar; she was no more violent on this New Year's Monday than whatever brief impulse had urged her to break John D.'s pinky finger. The serial killer's smile was serene.

Understandably, the deputy commissioner was worried about his wife. He told her he'd have to go directly to Crime Branch Headquarters, but surely she could get a ride home. Dhar's dwarf driver had already made his presence known; Vinod was prowling the foyer of the Duckworth Club. Detective Patel suggested that perhaps Dhar wouldn't mind taking Nancy home in his private taxi.

'Not a good idea.' That was all Nancy would say to her husband.

Julia said that she and Dr Daruwalla would bring Nancy home. Dhar offered to have Vinod drive Nancy home – just the dwarf, alone. That way, she wouldn't have to talk to anyone.

Nancy preferred this plan. 'I'm safe around dwarfs,' she said. 'I like dwarfs.'

When she'd gone with Vinod, Detective Patel asked Inspector Dhar how he liked being a real policeman. 'It's better in the movies,' the actor replied. 'In the movies, things happen the way they should happen.'

After the deputy commissioner had departed with Rahul, John D. let Dr Daruwalla snap his pinky finger into place. 'Just look away – look at Julia,' the doctor recommended. Then he popped the dislocated finger back where it belonged. 'We'll take an X ray tomorrow,' Dr Daruwalla said. 'Maybe we'll splint it, but not until it's stopped swelling. For now, keep putting it in ice.'

At the table in the Ladies' Garden, John D. responded to this advice by submersing his pinky in his water glass; most of the ice in the glass had melted, so Dr Daruwalla summoned Mr Sethna for more. Because the old Parsi seemed deeply disappointed that no one had congratulated him on his performance, Dhar said, 'Mr Sethna, that was really brilliant – how you fell over your own tray, for example. The distracting sound of the tray itself, your particularly purposeful but grace-ful awkwardness . . . truly brilliant.'

'Thank you,' Mr Sethna replied. 'I wasn't sure what to do with the menus.'

'That was brilliant, too – the menus in her lap. Per-fect!' said Inspector Dhar.

'Thank you,' the steward repeated; he went away – he was so pleased with himself that he forgot to bring the ice.

No one had eaten any lunch. Dr Daruwalla was the first to confess to a great hunger; Julia was so relieved that Mrs Dogar was gone, she admitted to having a considerable appetite herself. John D. ate with them, although he seemed indifferent to the food.

Farrokh reminded Mr Sethna that he'd forgotten to bring the ice, which the steward finally delivered to the table in a silver bowl; it was a bowl that was normally reserved for chilling tiger prawns, and the movie star stuck his swollen pinky finger in it with a vaguely mortified expression. Although the finger was still swelling, especially at the joint of the big knuckle, Dhar's pinky was not nearly as discolored as his lip.

The actor drank more beer than he usually permitted himself at midday, and his conversation was entirely concerned with when he would leave India. Certainly before the end of the month, he thought. He questioned whether or not he'd bother to do his fair share of pub-licity for *Inspector Dhar and the Towers of Silence;* now that the real-life version of the cage-girl killer was captured, Dhar commented that there might (for once) be some *favorable* publicity attached to his brief presence in Bombay. The more he mused out loud about it, the closer Dhar came to deciding that there was really nothing keeping him in India; from John D.'s point of view, the sooner he went back to Switzerland, the better.

The doctor remarked that he thought he and Julia would return to Canada earlier than they'd planned; Dr Daruwalla also asserted that he couldn't imagine coming back to Bombay in the near future, and the longer one stayed away . . . well, the harder it would be to *ever* come back. Julia let them talk. She knew how men hated to feel overwhelmed; they were really such babies whenever they weren't in control of their surroundings – whenever they felt that they didn't belong where they were. Also, Julia had often heard Farrokh say that he was never coming back to India; she knew he always came back.

The late-afternoon sun was slanting sideways through the trellis in the Ladies' Garden; the light fell in long slashes across the tablecloth, where the most famous male movie star in Bombay entertained himself by flicking stray crumbs with his fork. The ice in the prawn bowl had melted. It was time for Dr and Mrs Daruwalla to make an appearance at the celebration at St Ignatius; Julia had to remind the doctor that she'd promised Martin Mills an early arrival. Understandably, the scholastic wanted to wear clean bandages to the high-tea jubilee, his introduction to the Catholic community.

'Why does he need bandages?' John D. asked. 'What's the matter with him now?'

'Your twin was bitten by a chimpanzee,' Farrokh informed the actor. 'Probably rabid.'

There was certainly a lot of biting going around, Dhar thought, but the events of the day had sharply curtailed his inclination toward sarcasm. His finger throbbed and he knew his lip was ugly. Inspector Dhar didn't say a word.

When the Daruwallas left him sitting in the Ladies' Garden, the movie star closed his eyes; he looked asleep. Too much beer, the ever-watchful Mr Sethna surmised; then the steward reminded himself of his conviction that Dhar was stricken with a sexually transmitted disease. The old Parsi revised his opinion – he determined that Dhar was suffering from both the beer *and* the disease – and he ordered the busboys to leave the actor undisturbed at his table in the Ladies' Garden. Mr Sethna's disapproval of Dhar had softened considerably; the steward felt bloated with pride – to have had his small supporting role called 'brilliant' and 'perfect' by such a celebrity of the Hindi cinema!

But John D. wasn't asleep; he was trying to compose himself, which is an actor's nonstop job. He was thinking that it had been years since he'd felt the slightest sexual attraction to any woman; but Nancy had aroused him – it seemed to him that it was her anger he'd found so appealing – and for the second Mrs Dogar John D. had felt an even more disturbing desire. With his eyes still closed, the actor tried to imagine his own face with an ironic expression – not quite a sneer. He was 39, an age when it was unseemly to have one's sexual identity shaken. He concluded that it hadn't been Mrs Dogar who'd stimulated him; rather, he'd been reliving his attraction to the old Rahul – back in those Goa days when Rahul was still a sort of man. This thought comforted John D. Watching him, Mr Sethna saw what he thought was a sneer on the sleeping movie star's face; then something soothing must have crossed the actor's mind, for the sneer softened to a smile. He's thinking of the old days, the steward imagined . . . before he contracted the presumed dread disease. But Inspector Dhar had amused himself with a radical idea.

Shit, I hope I'm not about to become interested in *women*! the actor thought. What a mess that would make of things.

At this same moment, Dr Daruwalla was experiencing another kind of irony. His arrival at the mission of St Ignatius marked his first occasion in Christian company since the doctor had discovered who'd bitten his big toe. Dr Daruwalla's awareness that the source of his conversion to Christianity was the love bite of a transsexual serial killer had further diminished the doctor's already declining religious zeal; that the toe-biter had *not* been the ghost of the pilgrim who dismembered St Francis Xavier was more than a little disappointing. It was also a vulnerable time for Father Julian to have greeted Farrokh as the Father Rector did. 'Ah, Dr Daruwalla, our esteemed alumnus! Have you had any miracles happen to you lately?'

Thus baited, the doctor couldn't resist rebandaging Martin in an eccentric fashion. Dr Daruwalla padded the puncture wound in the scholastic's neck so that the bandage looked as if it were meant to conceal an enormous goiter. He then rebound the Jesuit's slashed hand in such a way that Martin had only partial use of his fingers. As for the half-eaten earlobe, the doctor was expansive with gauze and tape; he wrapped up the whole ear. The zealot could hear out of only one side of his head.

But the clean, bright bandages only served to heighten the new missionary's heroic appearance. Even Julia was impressed. And quickly the story circulated through the courtyard at dusk: the American missionary had just rescued two urchins from the streets of Bombay; he'd brought them to the relative safety of a circus, where a wild animal had attacked him. At the fringes of the high tea, where Dr Daruwalla stood sulking, he overheard the story that Martin Mills had been mauled by a *lion;* it was only the scholastic's self-deprecating nature that made him say the biting had been done by a monkey.

It further depressed the doctor to see that the source of this fantasy was the piano-playing Miss Tanuja; she'd traded her wing-tipped eye-glasses for what appeared to be rose-tinted contact lenses, which lent to her eyes the glowing red bedazzlement of a laboratory rat. She still spilled recklessly beyond the confines of her Western clothes, a schoolgirl voluptuary wearing her elderly aunt's dress. And she still sported the spear-headed bra, which uplifted and thrust forth her breasts like the sharp spires of a fallen church. As before, the crucifix that dangled between Miss Tanuja's highly armed bosoms seemed to subject the dying Christ to a new agony – or such was Dr Daruwalla's disillusionment with the religion he'd adopted when Rahul bit him.

Jubilee Day was definitely not the doctor's sort of celebration. He felt a vague loathing for such a hearty gathering of Christians in a non-Christian country; the atmosphere of religious complicity was uncomfortably claustrophobic. Julia found him engaged in stand-offish if not openly antisocial behavior; he'd been reading the examination scrolls in the entrance hall and had wandered to that spot, at the foot of the court-yard stairs, where the statue of Christ with the sick child was mounted on the wall alongside the fire extinguisher. Julia knew why Farrokh was loitering there; he was hoping that someone would speak to him and he could then comment on the irony of juxta-posing Jesus with a fire-fighting tool.

'I'm going to take you home,' Julia warned him. Then she noticed how tired he looked, and how utterly out of place – how lost. Christianity had tricked him; India was no longer his country. When Julia kissed his cheek, she realized he'd been crying.

'Please *do* take me home,' Farrokh told her.

26. GOOD-BYE, BOMBAY

Well, Then

Danny Mills died following a New Year's Eve party in New York. It was Tuesday, January 2, before Martin Mills and Dr Daruwalla were notified. The delay was attributed to the time difference – New York is 10½ hours behind Bombay – but the real reason was that Vera hadn't spent New Year's Eve with Danny. Danny, who was almost 75, died alone. Vera, who was 65, didn't discover Danny's body until the evening of New Year's Day.

When Vera returned to their hotel, she wasn't fully recovered from a tryst with a rising star of a light-beer commercial – an unbefitting fling for a woman her age. She doubtless failed to note the irony that Danny had died with the DO NOT DISTURB sign hanging optimistically from their hotel-room door. The medical examiner concluded that Danny had choked on his own vomit, which was (like his blood) nearly 20 percent alcohol.

In her two telegrams, Vera cited no clinical evidence; yet she managed to convey Danny's inebriation to Martin in pejorative terms.

YOUR FATHER DIED DRUNK IN A NEW YORK HOTEL

This also communicated to her son the sordidness, not to mention the inconvenience; Vera was going to have to spend nearly all of that Tuesday shopping. Coming from California – their visit was intended to be short – neither Danny nor Vera had packed for an extended stay in the January climate.

Vera's telegram to Martin continued in a bitter vein.

BEING CATHOLIC, ALTHOUGH HARDLY A MODEL OF
THE SPECIES, I'M SURE DANNY WOULD HAVE WANTED
YOU TO ARRANGE SOME SUITABLE SERVICE OR LAST
BIT OR WHATEVER IT'S CALLED

'Hardly a model of the species' was the sort of
language Vera had learned from the moisturizer commercial of her son's long-ago and damaged youth.

The last dig was pure Vera – even in what passed for
grief, she took a swipe at her son.

WILL OF COURSE UNDERSTAND COMPLETELY IF YOUR
VOW OF POVERTY MAKES IT IMPOSSIBLE FOR YOU TO
ASSIST ME IN THIS MATTER / MOM

There followed only the name of the hotel in New
York. Martin's 'vow of poverty' notwithstanding, Vera
wasn't offering to pay for his trip with *her* money.

Her telegram to Dr Daruwalla was also pure Vera.

I FAIL TO IMAGINE HOW DANNY'S DEATH SHOULD
ALTER YOUR DECISION TO KEEP MARTIN FROM ANY
KNOWLEDGE OF HIS TWIN

So suddenly it's *my* decision, Dr Daruwalla thought.

PLEASE DON'T UPSET POOR MARTIN WITH MORE BAD
NEWS

So now it's 'poor Martin' who would be upset! Farrokh
observed.

SINCE MARTIN HAS CHOSEN POVERTY FOR A PRO-
FESSION, AND DANNY HAS LEFT ME A WOMAN OF
INSUFFICIENT MEANS, PERHAPS YOU'LL BE SO KIND
AS TO AID MARTIN WITH THE AIRFARE / OF COURSE
IT'S DANNY WHO WOULD HAVE WANTED HIM HERE /
VERA

The only good news, which Dr Daruwalla didn't know at the time, was that Danny Mills had left Vera a woman of even less means than she supposed. Danny had bequeathed what little he had to the Catholic Church – secure in the knowledge that if he'd given anything to Martin, that's what Martin would have done with the money. In the end, not even Vera would consider the amount worth fighting for.

In Bombay, the day after Jubilee Day was a big one for news. Danny's death and Vera's manipulations overlapped with Mr Das's announcement that Madhu had left the Great Blue Nile with her new husband; both Martin Mills and Dr Daruwalla had little doubt that Madhu's new husband was Mr Garg. Farrokh was so sure of this that his brief telegram to the Bengali ringmaster was a statement, not a question.

YOU SAID THAT THE MAN WHO MARRIED MADHU HAD A SCAR / ACID, I PRESUME

Both the doctor and the missionary were outraged that Mr and Mrs Das had virtually sold Madhu to a man like Garg, but Martin urged Farrokh not to take the ringmaster to task. In the spirit of encouraging the Great Blue Nile to support the efforts of the elephant-footed cripple, Dr Daruwalla concluded his telegram to Mr Das in Junagadh on a tactful note.

I TRUST THAT THE BOY GANESH WILL BE WELL LOOKED AFTER

He didn't 'trust'; he *hoped*.

In the light of Ranjit's message from Mr Subhash (that Tata Two had given Dr Daruwalla the HIV test results for the wrong Madhu), the doctor had sizably less hope for Madhu than for Ganesh. Ranjit's account of Mr Subhash's offhand manner – the ancient secretary's virtual dismissal of the error – was infuriating, but even a proper apology from Dr Tata wouldn't have lessened the fact that Madhu was HIV-positive. She didn't have AIDS yet; she was merely carrying the virus.

'How can you even think "merely"?' cried Martin Mills, who seemed to be more devastated by Madhu's medical destiny than by the news of Danny's death; after all, Danny had been dying for years.

It was only midmorning; Martin had to interrupt their phone conversation in order to teach a class. Farrokh agreed to keep the missionary informed of the day's developments. The upper-school boys at St Ignatius were about to receive a Catholic interpretation of Graham Greene's *The Heart of the Matter*, while Dr Daruwalla attempted to find Madhu. But the doctor discovered that Garg's phone number was no longer in service; Mr Garg was lying low. Vinod told Dr Daruwalla that Deepa had already talked to Garg; according to the dwarf's wife, the owner of the Wetness Cabaret had complained about the doctor.

'Garg is thinking you are being too moral with him,' the dwarf explained.

It was not morality that the doctor wanted to discuss with Madhu, or with Garg. The doctor's disapproval of Garg notwithstanding, Dr Daruwalla wanted the opportunity to tell Madhu what it *meant* to be HIV-positive. Vinod implied that any opportunity for direct communication with Madhu was unpromising.

'It is working better another way,' the dwarf suggested. 'You are telling me. I am telling Deepa. She is telling Garg. Garg is telling the girl.'

It was hard for Dr Daruwalla to accept this as a 'better' way, but the doctor was beginning to understand the essence of the dwarf's Good Samaritanism. Rescuing children from the brothels was simply what Vinod and Deepa did with their spare time; they would just keep doing it – needing to succeed at it might have diminished their efforts.

'Tell Garg he was misinformed,' Dr Daruwalla told Vinod. 'Tell him Madhu is HIV-positive.'

Interestingly, if Garg was uninfected, his odds were good; he probably wouldn't contract HIV from Madhu. (The nature of HIV transmission is such that it's not easy for a woman to give it to a man.) Depressingly, if Garg *was* infected, Madhu had probably contracted it from him.

The dwarf must have sensed the doctor's depression; Vinod knew that a functioning Good Samaritan can't dwell on every little failure. 'We are only showing them the net,' Vinod tried to explain. 'We are not being their wings.'

'Their wings? *What* wings?' Farrokh asked.

'Not every girl is being able to fly,' the dwarf said. 'They are not all falling in the net.'

It occurred to Dr Daruwalla that he should impart this lesson to Martin Mills, but the scholastic was still in the process of watering down Graham Greene for the upper-school boys. Instead, the doctor called the deputy commissioner.

'Patel here,' said the cold voice. The clatter of typewriters resounded in the background; rising, and then falling out of hearing, was the mindless revving of a motorcycle. Like punctuation to their phone conversation, there came and went the sharp barking of the Dobermans, complaining in the courtyard kennel. Dr Daruwalla imagined that just out of his hearing a prisoner was professing his innocence, or else declaring that he'd spoken the truth. The doctor wondered if Rahul was there. What would she be wearing?

'I know this isn't exactly a crime-branch matter,' Farrokh apologized in advance; then he told the deputy commissioner everything he knew about Madhu and Mr Garg.

'Lots of pimps marry their best girls,' Detective Patel informed the doctor. 'Garg runs the Wetness Cabaret, but he's a pimp on the side.'

'I just want a chance to tell her what to expect,' said Dr Daruwalla.

'She's another man's wife,' Patel replied. 'You want

me to tell another man's wife that she has to talk to you?'

'Can't you *ask* her?' Farrokh asked.

'I can't believe I'm speaking to the creator of Inspector Dhar,' the deputy commissioner said. 'How does it go? It's one of my all-time favorites: "The police don't *ask* – the police arrest, or the police harass." Isn't that the line?'

'Yes, that's how it goes,' Dr Daruwalla confessed.

'So do you want me to harass her – and Garg, too?' the policeman asked. When the doctor didn't answer him, the deputy commissioner continued. 'When Garg throws her out on the street, or when she runs away, then I can bring her in for questioning. *Then* you can talk to her. The problem is, if he throws her out or she runs away, I won't be able to find her. From what you say, she's too pretty and smart to be a street prostitute. She'll go to a brothel, and once she's in the brothel, she won't be out on the street. Someone will bring her food; the madam will buy her clothes.'

'And when she gets sick?' the doctor asked.

'There are doctors who go to the brothels,' Patel replied. 'When she gets so sick she can't be a prostitute, most madams would put her out on the street. But by then she'll be immune.'

'What do you mean, "immune"?' Dr Daruwalla asked.

'When you're on the street and very sick, everyone leaves you alone. When nobody comes near you, you're immune,' the policeman said.

'And then you could find her,' Farrokh remarked.

'Then we *might* find her,' Patel corrected him. 'But by then it would hardly be necessary for you to tell her what to expect.'

'So you're saying, "Forget her." Is that it?' the doctor asked.

'In your profession, you treat crippled children – isn't that right?' the deputy commissioner inquired.

'That's right,' Dr Daruwalla replied.

'Well, I don't know anything about your field,' said Detective Patel, 'but I would guess that your odds of success are slightly higher than in the red-light district.'

'I get your point,' Farrokh said. 'And what are the odds that Rahul will hang?'

For a while, the policeman was silent. Only the typewriters responded to the question; they were the constant, occasionally interrupted by the revving motorcycle or the cacophony of Dobermans. 'Do you hear the typewriters?' the deputy commissioner finally asked.

'Of course,' Dr Daruwalla answered.

'The report on Rahul will be very lengthy,' Patel promised him. 'But not even the sensational number of murders will impress the judge. I mean, just look at who most of the victims were – they weren't important.'

'You mean they were prostitutes,' said Dr Daruwalla.

'Precisely,' Patel replied. 'We will need to develop another argument – namely, that Rahul must be confined with other women. Anatomically, she *is* a woman . . .'

'So the operation was complete,' the doctor interrupted.

'So I'm told. Naturally, I didn't examine her myself,' the deputy commissioner added.

'No, of course not . . .' Dr Daruwalla said.

'What I mean is, Rahul cannot be imprisoned with men – Rahul is a woman,' the detective said. 'And solitary confinement is too expensive – impossible in cases of life imprisonment. And yet, if Rahul is confined with women prisoners, there's a problem. She's as strong as a man, and she has a history of killing women – you see my point?'

'So you're saying that she might receive the death penalty only because of how awkward it will be to imprison her with other women?' Farrokh asked.

'Precisely,' Patel said. 'That's our best argument. But I still don't believe she'll be hanged.'

'Why not?' the doctor asked.

'Almost no one is hanged,' the deputy commissioner replied. 'With Rahul, they'll probably try hard labor and life imprisonment; then something will happen. Maybe she'll kill another prisoner.'

'Or bite her,' Dr Daruwalla said.

'They won't hang her for biting,' the policeman said. 'But something will happen. Then they'll *have* to hang her.'

'Naturally, this will take a long time,' Farrokh guessed.

'Precisely,' Patel said. 'And it won't be very satisfying,' the detective added.

That was a theme with the deputy commissioner, Dr Daruwalla knew. It led the doctor to ask a different sort of question. 'And what will *you* do – you and your wife?' Farrokh inquired.

'What do you mean?' said Detective Patel; for the first time, he sounded surprised.

'I mean, will you stay here – in Bombay, in India?' the doctor asked.

'Are you offering me a job?' the policeman replied.

Farrokh laughed. 'Well, no,' he admitted. 'I was just curious if you were *staying*.'

'But this is my country,' the deputy commissioner told him. '*You're* the one who's not at home here.'

This was awkward; first from Vinod and now from Detective Patel, the doctor had learned something. In both cases, the subject of the lesson was the acceptance of something unsatisfying.

'If you ever come to Canada,' Farrokh blurted out, 'I would be happy to be your host – to show you around.'

It was the deputy commissioner's turn to laugh. 'It's much more likely that I'll see you when you're back in Bombay,' Patel said.

'I'm not coming back to Bombay,' Dr Daruwalla insisted. It wasn't the first time he'd spoken his thoughts so unequivocally on this subject.

Although Detective Patel politely accepted the statement, Dr Daruwalla could tell that the deputy commissioner didn't believe him. 'Well, then,' Patel said. It was all there was to say. Not 'Good-bye'; just 'Well, then.'

Not a Word

Martin Mills again confessed to Father Cecil, who this time managed to stay awake. The scholastic was guilty of jumping to conclusions; Martin interpreted Danny's death and his mother's request that he come to her assistance in New York as a sign. After all, Jesuits are relentless in seeking God's will, and Martin was an especially zealous example; the scholastic not only sought God's will, but he too often believed that he'd spontaneously intuited what it was. In this case, Martin confessed, his mother was still capable of making him feel guilty, for he was inclined to go to New York at her bidding; Martin also confessed that he didn't want to go. The conclusion Martin then jumped to was that this weakness – his inability to stand up to Vera – was an indication that he lacked the faith to become ordained. Worse, the child prostitute had not only forsaken the circus and returned to her life of sin, but she would almost certainly die of AIDS; what had befallen Madhu was an even darker sign, which Martin interpreted as a warning that he would be ineffectual as a priest.

'This is clearly meant to show me that I shall be unable to renew the grace received from God in ordination,' Martin confessed to old Father Cecil, who wished that the Father Rector were hearing this; Father Julian would have put the presumptuous fool in his place. How impertinent – how utterly immodest – to be analyzing every moment of self-doubt as a sign from God! Whatever God's will was, Father Cecil was sure that Martin Mills had *not* been singled out to receive as much of it as he'd imagined.

Since he'd always been Martin's defender, Father Cecil surprised himself by saying, 'If you doubt yourself so much, Martin, maybe you *shouldn't* be a priest.'

'Oh, thank you, Father!' Martin said. It astonished Father Cecil to hear the now-*former* scholastic sound so relieved.

At the news of Martin's shocking decision – to leave the 'Life,' as it is called; not to be 'One of Ours,' as the Jesuits call themselves – the Father Rector was nonplussed but philosophic.

'India isn't for everybody,' Father Julian remarked, preferring to give Martin's abrupt choice a secular interpretation. Blame it on Bombay, so to speak. Father Julian, after all, was English, and he credited himself with doubting the fitness of *American* missionaries; even on the slim evidence of Martin Mills's dossier, the Father Rector had expressed his reservations. Father Cecil, who was Indian, said he'd be sorry to see young Martin leave; the scholastic's energy as a teacher had been a welcome addition to St Ignatius School.

Brother Gabriel, who quite liked and admired Martin, nevertheless remembered the bloody socks that the scholastic had been wringing in his hands – not to mention the 'I'll take the turkey' prayer. The elderly Spaniard retreated, as he often did, to his icon-collection room; these countless images of suffering, which the Russian and Byzantine icons afforded Brother Gabriel, were at least traditional – thus reassuring. The Decapitation of John the Baptist, the Last Supper, the Deposition, which was the taking of Christ's body from the cross – even these terrible moments were preferable to that image of Martin Mills which poor old Brother Gabriel was doomed to remember: the crazed Californian with his bloody bandages awry, looking like the composite image of many murdered missionaries past. Perhaps it *was* God's will that Martin Mills should be summoned to New York.

'You're going to do *what*?' Dr Daruwalla cried, for in

the time it had taken the doctor to talk to Vinod and Detective Patel, Martin had not only given the St Ignatius upper-school boys a Catholic interpretation of *The Heart of the Matter*; he had also 'interpreted' God's will. According to Martin, God didn't want him to be a priest – God wanted him to go to New York!

'Let me see if I follow you,' Farrokh said. 'You've decided that Madhu's tragedy is your own personal failure. I know the feeling – we're both fools. And, in addition, you doubt the strength of your conviction to be ordained because you can still be manipulated by your mother, who's made a career out of manipulating everybody. So you're going to New York – just to prove her power over you – and also for Danny's sake, although Danny won't know if you go to New York or not. Or do you believe Danny will know?'

'That's a simplistic way to put it,' Martin said. 'I may lack the necessary will to be a priest, but I haven't entirely lost my faith.'

'Your mother's a bitch,' Dr Daruwalla told him.

'That's a simplistic way to put it,' Martin repeated. 'Besides, I already know what she is.'

How the doctor was tempted. *Tell* him – tell him *now*! Dr Daruwalla thought.

'Naturally, I'll pay you back – I won't take the plane ticket as a gift,' Martin Mills explained. 'After all, my vow of poverty no longer applies. I do have the academic credentials to teach. I won't make a lot of money teaching, but certainly enough to pay you back – if you'll just give me a little time.'

'It's not the money! I can afford to buy you a plane ticket – I can afford to buy you *twenty* plane tickets!' Farrokh cried. 'But you're giving up your goal – that's what's so crazy about you. You're giving up, and for such stupid reasons!'

'It's not the reasons – it's my doubt,' Martin said. 'Just look at me. I'm thirty-nine. If I were going to be a priest, I should have already become one. No one

763

who's still trying to "find himself" at thirty-nine is very reliable.'

You took the words right out of my mouth! Dr Daruwalla thought, but all the doctor said was, 'Don't worry about the ticket – I'll get you a ticket.' He hated to see the fool look so defeated; Martin *was* a fool, but he was an idealistic fool. The idiot's idealism had grown on Dr Daruwalla. And Martin was candid – unlike his twin! Ironically, the doctor felt he'd learned more about John D. from Martin Mills – in less than a week – than he'd learned from John D. in 39 years.

Dr Daruwalla wondered if John D.'s remoteness, his not-thereness – his iconlike and opaque character – wasn't that part of him which was created *not* upon his birth but upon his becoming Inspector Dhar. Then the doctor reminded himself that John D. had been an actor before he became Inspector Dhar. If the identical twin of a gay male had a 52 percent chance of being gay, in what other ways did John D. and Martin Mills have a 52 percent chance of being alike? It occurred to Dr Daruwalla that the twins had a 48 percent chance of being *un*alike, too; nevertheless, the doctor doubted that Danny Mills could be the twins' father. Moreover, Farrokh had grown too fond of Martin to continue to deceive him.

Tell him – tell him *now*! Farrokh told himself, but the words wouldn't come. Dr Daruwalla could say only to himself what he wanted to say to Martin.

You *don't* have to deal with Danny's remains. Probably Neville Eden is your father, and Neville's remains were settled many years ago. You *don't* have to assist your mother, who's worse than a bitch. You *don't* know what she is, or all that she is. And there's someone you might like to know; you might even be of mutual assistance to each other. He could teach you how to relax – maybe even how to have some fun. You might teach him a little candor – maybe even how *not* to be an actor, at least not all the time.

But the doctor didn't say it. Not a word.

'So ... he's a quitter,' said Inspector Dhar, of his twin.

'He's confused, anyway,' Dr Daruwalla replied.

'A thirty-nine-year-old man shouldn't still be finding himself,' John D. declared. The actor delivered the line with almost perfect indignation, never hinting that the matter of 'finding himself' was at all familiar to him.

'I think you'd like him,' Farrokh said cautiously.

'Well, you're the *writer*,' Dhar remarked with almost perfect ambiguity. Dr Daruwalla wondered: Does he mean that the matter of whether or not they meet is in *my* hands? Or does he mean that only a writer would waste his time fantasizing that the twins *should* meet?

They were standing on the Daruwallas' balcony at sunset. The Arabian Sea was the faded purple of John D.'s slowly healing lower lip. The splint on his broken pinky finger provided the actor with an instrument for pointing; Dhar liked to point.

'Remember how Nancy responded to this view?' the actor asked, pointing west.

'All the way to Iowa,' the doctor remarked.

'If you're never coming back to Bombay, Farrokh, you might give the deputy commissioner and Mrs Patel this apartment.' The line was delivered with almost perfect indifference. The screenwriter had to marvel at the hidden character he'd created; Dhar was almost perfectly mysterious. 'I don't mean actually *give* it to them – the good detective would doubtless construe that as a bribe,' Dhar went on. 'But perhaps you could sell it to them for a ridiculous sum – a hundred rupees, for example. Of course you could stipulate that the Patels would have to maintain the servants – for as long as Nalin and Roopa are alive. I know you wouldn't want to turn them out on the street. As for the Residents' Society, I'm sure they wouldn't object to the Patels – every apartment dweller wants to have a policeman in the building.' Dhar pointed his splint west again. 'I believe this view would do Nancy some good,' the actor added.

'I can see you've been thinking about this,' Farrokh said.

'It's just an idea – *if* you're never coming back to Bombay,' John D. replied. 'I mean *really* never.'

'Are *you* ever coming back?' Dr Daruwalla asked him.

'Not in a million years,' said Inspector Dhar.

'*That* old line!' Farrokh said fondly.

'You wrote it,' John D. reminded him.

'You keep reminding me,' the doctor said.

They stayed on the balcony until the Arabian Sea was the color of an overripe cherry, almost black. Julia had to clear the contents of John D.'s pockets off the glass-topped table in order for them to have their dinner. It was a habit that John D. had maintained from childhood. He would come into the house or the apartment, take off his coat and his shoes or sandals, and empty the contents of his pockets on the nearest table; this was more than a gesture to make himself feel at home, for the source lay with the Daruwallas' daughters. When they'd lived at home, they liked nothing better than wrestling with John D. He would lie on his back on the rug or the floor, or sometimes on the couch, and the younger girls would pounce on him; he never hurt them, just fended them off. And so Farrokh and Julia never chastised him for the contents of his pockets, which were messily in evidence on the tabletop of every house or apartment they'd ever lived in, although there were no children for John D. to wrestle with anymore. Keys, a wallet, sometimes a passport ... and this evening, on the glass-topped table of the Daruwallas' Marine Drive apartment, a plane ticket.

'You're leaving Thursday?' Julia asked him.

'Thursday!' Dr Daruwalla exclaimed. 'That's the day after tomorrow!'

'Actually, I have to go to the airport Wednesday night – it's such an early-morning flight, you know,' John D. said.

'That's tomorrow night!' Farrokh cried. The doctor took Dhar's wallet, keys and plane ticket from Julia and put them on the sideboard.

'Not there,' Julia told him; she was serving one of their dinner dishes from the sideboard. Therefore, Dr Daruwalla carried the contents of John D.'s pockets into the foyer and placed them on a low table by the door – that way, the doctor thought, John D. would be sure to see his things and not forget them when he left.

'Why should I stay longer?' John D. was asking Julia. 'You're not staying much longer, are you?'

But Dr Daruwalla lingered in the foyer; he had a look at Dhar's plane ticket. Swissair, nonstop to Zürich. Flight 197, departing Thursday at 1:45 A.M. It was first class, seat 4B. Dhar always chose an aisle seat. This was because he was a beer drinker; on a nine-hour flight, he got up to pee a lot – he didn't want to keep climbing over someone else.

That quickly – by the time Dr Daruwalla had rejoined John D. and Julia, and even before he sat down to dinner – the doctor had made his decision; after all, as Dhar had told him, he was the writer. A writer could make things happen. They were twins; they didn't have to like each other, but they didn't have to be lonely.

Farrokh sat happily at his supper (as he insisted on calling it), smiling lovingly at John D. I'll teach you to be ambiguous with me! the doctor thought, but what Dr Daruwalla said was, 'Why *should* you stay any longer, indeed! Now's as good a time to go as any.'

Both Julia and John D. looked at him as if he were having a seizure. 'Well, I mean I'll miss you, of course – but I'll see you soon, one place or another. Canada or Switzerland . . . I'm looking forward to spending more time in the mountains.'

'You *are?*' Julia asked him. Farrokh hated mountains. Inspector Dhar just stared.

'Yes, it's very healthy,' the doctor replied. 'All that Swiss . . . air,' he remarked absently; he was thinking of the airline of that name, and how he would buy a first-class ticket to Zürich for Martin Mills on Swissair 197, departing early Thursday morning. Seat 4A. Farrokh hoped that the ex-missionary would appreciate the window seat, *and* his interesting traveling companion.

They had a wonderful dinner, a lively time. Normally, when Dr Daruwalla knew he was parting from John D., he was morose. But tonight the doctor felt euphoric.

'John D. has a terrific idea – about this apartment,' Farrokh told his wife. Julia liked the idea very much; the three of them talked about it at length. Detective Patel was proud; so was Nancy. They would be sensitive if they felt the apartment was offered to them as charity; the trick would be to make them think they were doing the Daruwallas a favor by looking after and 'maintaining' the old servants. The diners spoke admiringly of the deputy commissioner; they could have talked for hours about Nancy – she was certainly complex.

It was always easier, with John D., when the subject of conversation was someone else; it was himself, as a subject, that the actor avoided. And the diners were animated in their discussion of what the deputy commissioner had confided to the doctor about Rahul . . . the unlikelihood of her hanging.

Julia and John D. had rarely seen Farrokh so relaxed. The doctor spoke of his great desire to see more of his daughters and grandchildren, and he kept repeating that he wanted to see more of John D. – 'in your Swiss life.' The two men drank a lot of beer and sat up late on the balcony; they outlasted the traffic on Marine Drive. Julia sat up with them.

'You know, Farrokh, I *do* appreciate everything you've done for me,' the actor said.

'It's been fun,' the screenwriter replied. Farrokh fought back his tears – he was a sentimental man. He managed to feel quite happy, sitting there in the darkness. The smell of the Arabian Sea, the fumes of the city – even the constantly clogged drains and the persistence of human shit – rose almost comfortingly around them. Dr Daruwalla insisted on drinking a toast to Danny Mills; Dhar politely drank to Danny's memory.

'He wasn't your father – I'm quite sure of that,' Farrokh told John D.

'I'm quite sure of that, too,' the actor replied.

'Why are you so happy, *Liebchen*?' Julia asked Farrokh.

'He's happy because he's leaving India and he's never coming back,' Inspector Dhar answered; the line was delivered with almost perfect authority. This was mildly irritating to Farrokh, who suspected that leaving India and never coming back was an act of cowardice on his part. John D. was thinking of him, as he thought of his twin, as a quitter – *if* John D. truly believed that the doctor was never coming back.

'You'll see why I'm happy,' Dr Daruwalla told them. When he fell asleep on the balcony, John D. carried him to his bed.

'Look at him,' Julia said. 'He's smiling in his sleep.'

There would be time to mourn Madhu another day. There would be time to worry about Ganesh, the elephant boy, too. And on his next birthday, the doctor would be 60. But right now Dr Daruwalla was imagining the twins together on Swissair 197. Nine hours in the air should be sufficient for starting a relationship, the doctor thought.

Julia tried to read in bed, but Farrokh distracted her; he laughed out loud in his sleep. He must be drunk, she thought. Then she saw a frown cross his face. What a shame it was, Dr Daruwalla was thinking; he wanted to be on the same plane with them – just to watch them, and to listen. Which seat is across the aisle from

4B? the doctor wondered. Seat 4J? Farrokh had taken that flight to Zürich many times. It was a 747; the seat across the aisle from 4B was 4J, he hoped.

'Four J,' he told the flight attendant. Julia put down her book and stared at him.

'*Liebchen*,' she whispered, 'either wake up or go to sleep.' But her husband was once again smiling serenely. Dr Daruwalla was where he wanted to be. It was early Thursday morning − 1:45 A.M., to be exact − and Swissair 197 was taking off from Sahar. Across the aisle, the twins were staring at each other; neither of them could talk. It would take a little time for one of them to break the ice, but the doctor felt confident that they couldn't maintain their silence for the full nine hours. Although the actor had more interesting information, Farrokh bet that the ex-missionary would be the one to start blabbing. Martin Mills would blab all night, if John D. didn't start talking in self-defense.

Julia watched her sleeping husband touch his belly with his hands. Dr Daruwalla was checking to be sure that his seat belt was correctly fastened; then he settled back, ready to enjoy the long flight.

Just Close Your Eyes

The next day was Wednesday. Dr Daruwalla was watching the sunset from his balcony, this time with Dhar's twin. Martin was full of questions about his plane tickets. The screenwriter evaded these questions with the skill of someone who'd already imagined the possible dialogue.

'I fly to Zürich? That's strange − that's not the way I came,' the ex-missionary remarked.

'I have connections with Swissair,' Farrokh told him. 'I'm a frequent flyer, so I get a special deal.'

'Oh, I see. Well, I'm very grateful. I hear it's a marvelous airline,' the former scholastic said. 'These are first-class tickets!' Martin suddenly cried. 'I can't repay you for first class!'

'I won't allow you to repay me,' the doctor said. 'I said I have connections – I get a special deal for first class. I won't let you repay me because the plane tickets cost me practically nothing.'

'Oh, I see. I've never flown first class,' the recent zealot said. Farrokh could tell that Martin was puzzling over the ticket for the connecting flight, from Zürich to New York. He would arrive in Zürich at 6:00 in the morning; his plane to New York didn't leave Zürich until 1:00 in the afternoon – a long layover, the onetime Jesuit was thinking . . . and there was something different about the New York ticket.

'That's an open ticket to New York,' Farrokh said in an offhand manner. 'It's a daily nonstop flight. You don't have to fly to New York on the day you arrive in Switzerland. You have a valid ticket for any day when there's an available seat in first class. I thought you might like to spend a day or two in Zürich – maybe the weekend. You'd be better rested when you got to New York.'

'Well, that's awfully kind of you. But I'm not sure what I'd do in Zürich . . .' Martin was saying. Then he found the hotel voucher; it was with his plane tickets.

'Three nights at the Hotel zum Storchen – a decent hotel,' Farrokh explained. 'Your room overlooks the Limmat. You can walk in the old town, or to the lake. Have you ever been in Europe?'

'No, I haven't,' said Martin Mills. He kept staring at the hotel voucher; it included his meals.

'Well, then,' Dr Daruwalla replied. Since the deputy commissioner had found this phrase so meaningful, the doctor thought he'd give it a try; it appeared to work on Martin Mills. Throughout dinner, the re-formed Jesuit wasn't at all argumentative; he seemed subdued. Julia worried that it might have been the food, or that Dhar's unfortunate twin was ill, but Dr

Daruwalla had experienced failure before; the doctor knew what was bothering the ex-missionary.

John D. was wrong; his twin wasn't a quitter. Martin Mills had abandoned a quest, but he'd given up the priesthood when the priesthood was in sight – when it was easily obtainable. He'd not failed to be ordained; he'd been afraid of the kind of priest he might become. His decision to retreat, which had appeared to be so whimsical and sudden, had not come out of the blue; to Martin, his retreat must have seemed lifelong.

Because the security checks were so extensive, Martin Mills was required to be at Sahar two or three hours before his scheduled departure. Farrokh felt it would be unsafe to let him take a taxi with anyone but Vinod, and Vinod was unavailable; the dwarf was driving Dhar to the airport. Dr Daruwalla hired an alleged luxury taxi from the fleet of Vinod's Blue Nile, Ltd. They were en route to Sahar when the doctor first realized how much he would miss the ex-missionary.

'I'm getting used to this,' Martin said. They were passing a dead dog in the road, and Farrokh thought that Martin was commenting on his growing familiarity with slain animals. Martin explained that he meant he was getting used to leaving places in mild disgrace. 'Oh, there's never anything scandalous – I'm never run out of town on a rail,' he went on. 'It's a sort of slinking away. I don't suppose I'm anything more than a passing embarrassment to those people who put their faith in me. I feel the same way about myself, really. There's never a crushing sense of disappointment, or of loss – it's more like a fleeting dishonor.'

I'm going to miss this moron, Dr Daruwalla thought, but what the doctor said was, 'Do me a favor – just close your eyes.'

'Is there something dead in the road?' Martin asked.

'Probably,' the doctor replied. 'But that's not the reason. Just close your eyes. Are they closed?'

'Yes, my eyes are closed,' the former scholastic said. 'What are you going to do?' he asked nervously.

772

'Just relax,' Farrokh told him. 'We're going to play a game.'

'I don't like games!' Martin cried. He opened his eyes and looked wildly around.

'Close your eyes!' Dr Daruwalla shouted. Although his vow of obedience was behind him, Martin obeyed. 'I want you to imagine that parking lot with the Jesus statue,' the doctor told him. 'Can you see it?'

'Yes, of course,' Martin Mills replied.

'Is Christ still there, in the parking lot?' Farrokh asked him. The fool opened his eyes.

'Well, I don't know about that – they were always expanding the capacity of the parking lot,' Martin said. 'There was always a lot of construction equipment around. They may have torn up that section of the lot – they might have had to move the statue . . .'

'That's not what I mean! Close your eyes!' Dr Daruwalla cried. 'What I mean is, in your *mind*, can you still see the damn statue? Jesus Christ in the dark parking lot – can you still *see* him?'

'Well, naturally – yes,' Martin Mills admitted. He kept his eyes tightly closed, as if in pain; his mouth was shut, too, and his nose was wrinkled. They were passing a slum encampment lit only by rubbish fires, but the stench of human feces overpowered what they could smell of the burning trash. 'Is that all?' Martin asked, eyes closed.

'Isn't that enough?' the doctor asked him. 'For God's sake, open your eyes!'

Martin opened them. 'Was that the game – the whole game?' he inquired.

'You saw Jesus Christ, didn't you? What more do you want?' Farrokh asked. 'You must realize that it's possible to be a good Christian, as Christians are always saying, and at the same time *not* be a Catholic priest.'

'Oh, is *that* what you mean?' said Martin Mills. 'Well, certainly – I realize that!'

'I can't believe I'm going to miss you, but I really am,' Dr Daruwalla told him.

'I shall miss you, too, of course,' Dhar's twin replied. 'In particular, our little talks.'

At the airport, there was the usual lineup for the security checks. After they'd said their good-byes (they actually embraced), Dr Daruwalla continued to observe Martin from a distance. The doctor crossed a police barrier in order to keep watching him. It was hard to tell if his bandages drew everyone's attention or if it was his resemblance to Dhar, which leaped out at some observers and was utterly missed by others. The doctor had once again changed Martin's bandages; the neck wound was minimally covered with a gauze patch, and the mangled earlobe was left uncovered – it was ugly but largely healed. The hand was still mittened in gauze. To everyone who gawked at him, the chimpanzee's victim winked and smiled; it was a genuine smile, not Dhar's sneer, yet Farrokh felt that the ex-missionary had never looked like such a dead ringer for Dhar. At the end of every Inspector Dhar movie, Dhar is walking away from the camera; in this case, Dr Daruwalla was the camera. Farrokh felt greatly moved; he wondered if it was because Martin more and more reminded him of John D., or if it was because Martin himself had touched him.

John D. was nowhere to be seen. Dr Daruwalla knew that the actor was always the first to board a plane – *any* plane – but the doctor kept looking for him. Aesthetically, Farrokh would have been disappointed if Inspector Dhar and Martin Mills met in the security lineup; the screenwriter wanted the twins to meet on the plane. Ideally, they should be sitting down, Dr Daruwalla thought.

As he waited in line and then shuffled forward, and then waited again, Martin looked almost normal. There was something pathetic about his wearing the tropical-weight black suit over the Hawaiian shirt; he'd surely have to buy something warmer in Zürich, the expense of which had prompted Dr Daruwalla to hand him several hundred Swiss francs – at the last minute, so that Martin had no time to refuse the money. And there was something barely noticeable but odd about his habit of closing his eyes while he waited in line. When the line stopped moving, Martin closed his eyes and smiled; then the line would inch forward, Martin with it, looking like a man refreshed. Farrokh knew what the fool was doing. Martin Mills was making sure that Jesus Christ was still in the parking lot.

Not even a mob of Indian workers returning from the Gulf could distract the former Jesuit from the latest of his spiritual exercises. The workers were what Farrokh's mother, Meher, used to call the Persia-returned crowd, but these workers weren't coming from Iran; they were returning from Kuwait – their two-in-ones or their three-in-ones were blasting. In addition to their boom boxes, they carried their foam mattresses; their plastic shoulder bags were bursting with whiskey bottles and wristwatches and assorted aftershaves and pocket calculators – some had even stolen the cutlery from the plane. Sometimes the workers went to Oman – or Qatar or Dubai. In Meher's day, the so-called Persia-returned crowd had brought back gold ingots in their hands – at least a sovereign or two. Nowadays, Farrokh guessed, they weren't bringing home much gold. Nevertheless, they got drunk on the plane. But even as he was jostled by the most unruly of these Persia-returned people, Martin Mills kept closing his eyes and smiling; as long as Jesus was still in that parking lot, all was right with Martin's world.

For his remaining days in Bombay, Dr Daruwalla would regret that, when he closed *his* eyes, he saw no such reassuring vision; no Christ – not even a parking lot. He told Julia that he was suffering the sort of recurring dream that he hadn't had since he'd first left India for Austria; it was a common dream among adolescents, old Lowji had told him – for one reason or another, you find yourself naked in a public place. Long ago, Farrokh's opinionated father had offered an unlikely interpretation. 'It's a new immigrant's dream,' Lowji had declared. Maybe it was, Farrokh now believed. He'd left India many times before, but this was the first time he would leave his birthplace with the *certain* knowledge that he wasn't coming back; he'd never felt so sure.

For most of his adult life, he'd lived with the discomfort (especially in India) of feeling that he wasn't really Indian. Now how would he feel, living in Toronto with the discomfort of knowing that he'd never truly been assimilated there? Although he was a citizen of Canada, Dr Daruwalla knew he was no Canadian; he would never feel 'assimilated.' Old Lowji's nasty remark would haunt Farrokh forever: 'Immigrants are immigrants all their lives.' Once someone makes such a negative pronouncement, you might refute it but you never forget it; some ideas are so vividly planted, they become visible objects, actual things.

For example, a racial insult – not forgetting the accompanying loss of self-esteem. Or one of those more subtle Anglo-Saxon nuances, which frequently assailed Farrokh in Canada and made him feel that he was always standing at the periphery; this could be simply a sour glance – that familiar dour expression which attended the most commonplace exchange. The way they examined the signature on your credit card, as if it couldn't possibly comply with *your* signature; or when they gave you back your change, how their looks always lingered on the color of your upturned palm – it was a different color from the back of your hand. The difference was somehow greater than that difference which they took for granted – namely, between *their* palms and the backs of *their* hands. ('Immigrants are immigrants all their lives!')

The first time he saw Suman perform the Skywalk at the Great Royal Circus, Farrokh didn't believe she could fall; she looked perfect – she was so beautiful and her steps were so precise. Then, one time, he saw her standing in the wing of the main tent before her performance. He was surprised that she wasn't stretching her muscles. She wasn't even moving her feet; she stood completely still. Maybe she was concentrating, Dr Daruwalla thought; he didn't want her to notice him looking at her – he didn't want to distract her.

When Suman turned to him, Farrokh realized that she really must have been concentrating because she didn't acknowledge him and she was always very polite; she looked right past him, or through him. The fresh puja mark on her forehead was smudged. It was the slightest flaw, but when Dr Daruwalla saw the smudge, he instantly knew that Suman was mortal. From that moment, Farrokh believed she could fall. After that, he could never relax when he saw her skywalking – she seemed unbearably vulnerable. If someone ever were to tell him that Suman had fallen and died, Dr Daruwalla would see her lying in the dirt with her puja mark smeared. ('Immigrants are immigrants all their lives' was this kind of smudge.)

It might have helped Dr Daruwalla if he could have left Bombay as quickly as the twins had left. But retiring movie stars and ex-missionaries can leave town faster than doctors; surgeons have their operating schedules and their recovering patients. As for screenwriters, like other writers, they have their messy little details to attend to, too.

Farrokh knew he would never talk to Madhu; at best, he might communicate with her, or learn of her condition, through Vinod or Deepa. The doctor wished the child might have had the good luck to die in the circus; the death he'd created for his Pinky character – killed by a lion who mistakes her for a peacock – was a lot quicker than the one he imagined for Madhu.

Similarly, the screenwriter entertained little hope that the real Ganesh would succeed at the circus, at least not to the degree that the fictional Ganesh succeeds. There would be no skywalking for the elephant boy, which was a pity – it was such a perfect ending. If the real cripple became a successful cook's helper, that would be ample satisfaction for Farrokh. To this end, he wrote a friendly letter to Mr and Mrs Das at the Great Blue Nile; although the elephant-footed boy could never be trained as an acrobat, the doctor wanted the ringmaster and his wife to encourage Ganesh to be a good cook's helper. Dr Daruwalla also wrote to Mr and Mrs Bhagwan – the knife thrower and his wife-assistant, the skywalker. Perhaps the sky-walker would be so kind as to *gently* disabuse the elephant boy of his silly idea that he could perform the Skywalk. Possibly Mrs Bhagwan could *show* Ganesh how hard it was to skywalk. She might let the cripple try it, using the model of that ladderlike device which hung from the roof of her own troupe tent; that would show him how impossible skywalking was – it would also be a safe exercise.

As for his screenplay, Farrokh had again titled it *Limo Roulette*; he came back to this title because *Escaping Maharashtra* struck him as overoptimistic, if not wholly improbable. The screenplay had suffered from even the briefest passage of time. The horror of Acid Man, the sensationalism of the lion striking down the star of the circus (that innocent little girl) ... Farrokh feared that these elements echoed a Grand Guignol drama, which he recognized as the essence of an Inspector Dhar story. Maybe the screenwriter hadn't ventured as far from his old genre as he'd first imagined.

Yet Farrokh disputed that opinion of himself which he'd read in so many reviews – namely, that he was a deus-ex-machina writer, always calling on the avail-able gods (and other artificial devices) to bail himself out of his plot. Real life itself was a deus-ex-machina *mess*! Dr Daruwalla thought. Look at how he'd put Dhar and his twin together – *somebody* had to do it! And hadn't he remembered that shiny something which the shitting crow had held in its beak and then lost? It was a deus-ex-machina *world*!

Still, the screenwriter was insecure. Before he left Bombay, Farrokh thought he'd like to talk to Balraj Gupta, the director. *Limo Roulette* might be only a small departure for the screenwriter, but Dr Daruwalla wanted Gupta's advice. Although Farrokh was certain that this wasn't a Hindi cinema sort of film – a small circus was definitely not a likely venue for Balraj Gupta – Gupta was the only director the screenwriter knew.

Dr Daruwalla should have known better than to talk to Balraj Gupta about art – even flawed art. It didn't take long for Gupta to smell out the 'art' in the story; Farrokh never finished with his synopsis. 'Did you say a child *dies*?' Gupta interrupted him. 'Do you bring it back to life?'

'No,' Farrokh admitted.

'Can't a god save the child, or something?' Balraj Gupta asked.

'It's not that kind of film – that's what I'm trying to tell you,' Farrokh explained.

'Better give it to the Bengalis,' Gupta advised. 'If it's arty realism that you're up to, better make it in Calcutta.' When the screenwriter didn't respond, Balraj Gupta said, 'Maybe it's a *foreign* film. *Limo Roulette* – it sounds French!'

Farrokh thought of saying that the part of the missionary would be a wonderful role for John D. And the screenwriter might have added that Inspector Dhar, the actual star of the Hindi cinema, could have a dual role; the mistaken-identity theme could be amusing. John D. could play the missionary *and* he could make a cameo appearance as Dhar! But Dr Daruwalla knew what Balraj Gupta would say to *that* idea: 'Let the critics mock him – he's a movie star. But movie stars shouldn't mock themselves.' Farrokh had heard the director say it. Besides, if the Europeans or the Americans made *Limo Roulette*, they would never cast John D. as the missionary. Inspector Dhar meant nothing to Europeans or Americans; they would insist on casting one of *their* stars in that role.

Dr Daruwalla was silent. He presumed that Balraj Gupta was angry with him for putting an end to the Inspector Dhar series; he already knew Gupta was angry with John D. because John D. had left town without doing much to promote *Inspector Dhar and the Towers of Silence*.

'I think you're angry with me,' Farrokh began cautiously.

'Oh, no – not for a minute!' Gupta cried. 'I never get angry with people who decide they're tired of making money. Such people are veritable emblems of humanity – don't you agree?'

'I *knew* you were angry with me,' Dr Daruwalla replied.

'Tell me about the love interest in your art film,' Gupta demanded. 'That will make you or break you, despite all this other foolishness. Dead children . . . why not show it to the South Indian socialists? *They* might like it!'

Dr Daruwalla tried to talk about the love interest in the screenplay as if he believed in it. There was the American missionary, the would-be priest who falls in love with a beautiful circus acrobat; Suman was an actual acrobat, not an actress, the screenwriter explained.

'An acrobat!' cried Balraj Gupta. 'Are you crazy? Have you seen their thighs? Women acrobats have terrifying thighs! And their thighs are magnified on film.'

'I'm talking to the wrong person – I *must* be crazy,' Farrokh replied. 'Anyone who'd discuss a serious film with you is truly certifiable.'

'The telltale word is "serious,"' Balraj Gupta said. 'I can see you've learned nothing from your success. Have you lost your bananas? Are you marbles?' the director shouted.

The screenwriter tried to correct the director's difficulties with English. 'The phrases are, "Have you lost your marbles?" and "Are you bananas?" – I believe,' Dr Daruwalla told him.

'That's what I said!' Gupta shouted; like most directors, Balraj Gupta was always right. The doctor hung up the phone and packed his screenplay. *Limo Roulette* was the first thing Farrokh put in his suitcase; then he covered it with his Toronto clothes.

Just India

Vinod drove Dr and Mrs Daruwalla to the airport; the dwarf wept the whole way to Sahar, and Farrokh was afraid they'd have an accident. The thug driver had lost Inspector Dhar as a client; now, in addition to this tragedy, Vinod was losing his personal physician. It was shortly before midnight on a Monday evening; as if symbolic of Dhar's last film, the poster-wallas were already covering over some of the advertisements for *Inspector Dhar and the Towers of Silence*. The new posters weren't advertising a movie; they were proclamations of a different kind – celebratory announcements of Anti-Leprosy Day. That would be tomorrow, Tuesday, January 30. Julia and Farrokh would be leaving India on Anti-Leprosy Day at 2:50 A.M. on Air India 185. Bombay to Delhi, Delhi to London, London to Toronto (but you don't have to change planes). The Daruwallas would break up the long flight by staying a few nights in London.

In the intervening time since Dhar and his twin had departed for Switzerland, Dr Daruwalla was disappointed to have heard so little from them. At first, Farrokh had worried that they were angry with him, or that their meeting had not gone well. Then a post-card came from the Upper Engadine: a cross-country skier, a *Langläufer*, is crossing a frozen white lake; the lake is rimmed with mountains, the sky cloudless and blue. The message, in John D.'s handwriting, was familiar to Farrokh because it was another of Inspector

Dhar's repeated lines. In the movies, after the cool detective has slept with a new woman, something always interrupts them; they never have time to talk. Perhaps a gunfight breaks out, possibly a villain sets fire to their hotel (or their bed). In the ensuing and breathless action, Inspector Dhar and his lover have scarcely a moment to exchange pleasantries; they're usually fighting for their lives. But then there comes the inevitable break in the action – a brief pause before the grenade assault. The audience, already loathing him, is anticipating Dhar's signature remark to his lover. 'By the way,' he tells her, 'thanks.' That was John D.'s message on the postcard from the Upper Engadine.

By the way, thanks

Julia told Farrokh it was a touching message, because both twins had signed the postcard. She said it was what newlyweds did with Christmas cards and birthday greetings, but Dr Daruwalla said (in his experience) it was what people did in doctors' offices when there was a group gift; the receptionist signed it, the secretaries signed it, the nurses signed it, the other surgeons signed it. What was so special or 'touching' about that? John D. always signed his name as just plain 'D.' In unfamiliar handwriting, on the same postcard, was the name 'Martin.' So they were somewhere in the mountains. Farrokh hoped that John D. wasn't trying to teach his fool twin how to ski!

'At least they're together, and they appreciate it,' Julia told him, but Farrokh wanted more. It almost killed him not to know every line of the dialogue between them.

When the Daruwallas arrived at the airport, Vinod weepingly handed the doctor a present. 'Maybe you are never seeing me again,' the dwarf said. As for the present, it was heavy and hard and rectangular; Vinod had wrapped it in newspapers. Through his sniffles, the dwarf managed to say that Farrokh was not to open the present until he was on the plane.

Later, the doctor would think that this was probably what terrorists said to unsuspecting passengers to whom they'd handed a bomb; just then the metal detector sounded, and Dr Daruwalla was quickly surrounded by frightened men with guns. They asked him what was wrapped up in the newspapers. What could he tell them? A present from a dwarf? They made the doctor unwrap the newspapers while they stood at some distance; they looked less ready to shoot than to flee – to 'abscond,' as *The Times of India* would report the incident. But there was no incident.

Inside the newspapers was a brass plaque, a big brass sign; Dr Daruwalla recognized it immediately. Vinod had removed the offensive message from the elevator of Farrokh's apartment building on Marine Drive.

SERVANTS ARE NOT ALLOWED
TO USE THE LIFT
UNLESS ACCOMPANIED BY CHILDREN

Julia told Farrokh that Vinod's gift was 'touching,' but although the security officers were relieved, they questioned the doctor about the source of the sign. They wanted to be sure that it hadn't been stolen from an historically protected building – that it was stolen from somewhere else didn't trouble them. Perhaps they didn't like the message any better than Farrokh and Vinod had liked it.

'A souvenir,' Dr Daruwalla assured them. To the doctor's surprise, the security officers let him keep the sign. It was cumbersome to carry it on board the plane, and even in first class the flight attendants were bitchy about stowing it out of everyone's way. First they made him unwrap it (again); then he was left with the unwanted newspapers.

'Remind me never to fly Air India,' the doctor

complained to his wife; he announced this loudly enough for the nearest flight attendant to hear him.

'I remind you every time,' Julia replied, also loudly enough. To any fellow first-class passenger overhearing them, they might have seemed the epitome of a wealthy couple who commonly abuse those lesser people whose chore it is to wait on them. But this impression of the Daruwallas would be false; they were simply of a generation that reacted strongly to rudeness from anyone – they were well enough educated and old enough to be intolerant of intolerance. But what hadn't occurred to Farrokh or Julia was that perhaps the flight attendants were ill mannered about stowing the elevator sign *not* because of the inconvenience but because of the message; possibly the flight attendants were also incensed that servants weren't allowed to use the lift unless accompanied by children.

It was one of those little misunderstandings that no one would ever solve; it was a suitably sour note on which to leave one's country for the last time, Farrokh thought. Nor was he pleased by *The Times of India*, with which Vinod had wrapped the stolen sign. Of great prominence in the news lately was the report of food poisoning in East Delhi. Two children had died and eight others were hospitalized after they'd consumed some 'stale' food from a garbage dump in the Shakurpur area. Dr Daruwalla had been following this report with the keenest attention; he knew that the children hadn't died from eating 'stale' food – the stupid newspaper meant 'rotten' or 'contaminated.'

As far as Farrokh was concerned, the airplane couldn't take off fast enough. Like Dhar, the doctor preferred the aisle seat because he planned to drink beer and he would need to pee; Julia would sit by the window. It would be almost 10·00 in the morning, London time, before they landed in England. It would be dark all the way to Delhi. Literally, before he even left, the doctor thought he'd already seen the last of India.

Although Martin Mills might be tempted to say that it was God's will (that Dr Daruwalla was saying good-bye to Bombay), the doctor wouldn't have agreed. It wasn't God's will; it was India, which wasn't for every-body – as Father Julian, unbeknownst to Dr Daruwalla, had said. It was *not* God's will, Farrokh felt certain; it was just India, which was more than enough.

When Air India 185 lifted off the runway in Sahar, Dhar's thug taxi driver was again cruising the streets of Bombay; the dwarf was still crying – he was too upset to sleep. Vinod had returned to town too late to catch the last show at the Wetness Cabaret, where he'd been hoping to get a glimpse of Madhu; he'd have to look for her another night. It depressed the dwarf to keep cruising the red-light district, although it was a night like any night – Vinod might have found and saved a stray. At 3:00 A.M., the dwarf felt that the brothels resembled a failed circus. The ex-clown imagined the cages of lifeless animals – the rows of tents, full of exhausted and injured acrobats. He drove on.

It was almost 4:00 in the morning when Vinod parked the Ambassador in the alley alongside the Daruwallas' apartment building on Marine Drive. No one saw him slip into the building, but the dwarf roamed around the lobby, breathing heavily, until he had all the first-floor dogs barking. Then Vinod swaggered back to his taxi; he felt only mildly uplifted by the insults of the screaming residents, who'd earlier been disturbed by the report that their all-important elevator sign had been stolen.

Wherever the sad dwarf drove, the life of the city seemed to be eluding him; still, he wouldn't go home. In the predawn light, Vinod stopped the Ambassador to joke with a traffic policeman in Mazagaon.

'Where is the traffic being?' Vinod asked the con-stable. The policeman had his baton out, as if there were a crowd or a riot to direct. No one was anywhere around: not another car, not a single bicycle, not one pedestrian. Of the sidewalk sleepers, the few who were awake hadn't risen beyond a sitting position or from their knees. The constable recognized Dhar's thug driver – every policeman knew Vinod. The constable said there'd been a disturbance – a religious procession streaming out of Sophia Zuber Road – but Vinod had missed it. The abandoned traffic policeman said he'd be obliged to the dwarf if Vinod would drive him the length of Sophia Zuber Road, just to prove that there was no more trouble. And so, with the lonely constable in the car, Vinod cautiously proceeded through one of Bombay's better slums.

There wasn't much to see; more sidewalk sleepers were waking up, but the slum dwellers were still sleeping. At that part of Sophia Zuber Road where Martin Mills, almost a month ago, had encountered the mortally wounded cow, Vinod and the traffic policeman saw the tail end of a procession – a few sadhus chanting, the usual flower flingers. There was a huge clotted bloodstain in the gutter of the road, where the cow had finally died; the earlier disturbance, the religious procession, had been merely the removal of the dead cow's body. Some zealots had managed to keep the cow alive all this time.

This zeal was also not God's will, Dr Daruwalla would have said; this doomed effort was also 'just India,' which was more than enough.

786

27. EPILOGUE

The Volunteer

On a Friday in May, more than two years after the Daruwallas had returned to Toronto from Bombay, Farrokh felt an urge to show Little India to his friend Macfarlane. They took Mac's car. It was their lunch hour, but the traffic on Gerrard was so congested, they soon realized they wouldn't have much time for lunch; they might barely have time to get to Little India and back to the hospital.

They'd been spending their lunch hour together for the past 18 months, ever since Macfarlane had tested HIV-positive; Mac's boyfriend – Dr Duncan Frasier, the gay geneticist – had died of AIDS over a year ago. As for debating the merits of his dwarf-blood project, Farrokh had found no one to replace Frasier, and Mac hadn't found a new boyfriend.

The shorthand nature of the conversation between Dr Daruwalla and Dr Macfarlane, in regard to Mac's living with the AIDS virus, was a model of emotional restraint.

'How have you been doing?' Dr Daruwalla would ask.

'Good,' Dr Macfarlane would reply. 'I'm off AZT – switched to DDI. Didn't I tell you?'

'No – but why? Were your T cells dropping?'

'Kind of,' Mac would say. 'They dropped below two hundred. I was feeling like shit on AZT, so Schwartz decided to switch me to DDI. I feel better – I'm more energetic now. And I'm taking Bactrim prophylactically . . . to prevent PCP pneumonia.'

'Oh,' Farrokh would say.

'It isn't as bad as it sounds. I feel great,' Mac would

say. 'If the DDI stops working, there's DDC and many more – I hope.'

'I'm glad you feel that way,' Farrokh would find himself saying.

'Meanwhile,' Macfarlane would say, 'I've got this little game going. I sit and visualize my healthy T cells – I picture them resisting the virus. I see my T cells shooting bullets at the virus, and the virus being cut down in a hail of gunfire – that's the idea, anyway.'

'Is that Schwartz's idea?' Dr Daruwalla would ask.

'No, it's *my* idea!'

'It sounds like Schwartz.'

'And I go to my support group,' Mac would add. 'Support groups seem to be one of the things that correlate with long-term survival.'

'Really,' Farrokh would say.

'Really,' Macfarlane would repeat. 'And of course what they call taking charge of your illness – not being passive, and not necessarily accepting everything your doctor tells you.'

'Poor Schwartz,' Dr Daruwalla would reply. 'I'm glad *I'm* not your doctor.'

'That makes two of us,' Mac would say.

This was their two-minute drill; usually, they could cover the subject that quickly – at least they tried to. They liked to let their lunch hour be about other things: for example, Dr Daruwalla's sudden desire to take Dr Macfarlane to Little India.

It had been in May when the ractist goons had driven Farrokh to Little India against his will; that had also been a Friday, a day when much of Little India had appeared to be closed – or were only the butcher shops closed? Dr Daruwalla wondered if this was because the Friday prayers were faithfully attended by the local Muslims; it was one of those things he didn't know. Farrokh knew only that he wanted Macfarlane to see Little India, and he had this sudden feeling that he wanted all the conditions to be the same – the same weather, the same shops, the same mannequins (if not the same saris).

Doubtless, Dr Daruwalla had been inspired by something he'd read in the newspapers, probably something about the Heritage Front. It greatly upset him to read about the Heritage Front – those neo-Nazi louts, that white supremacist scum. Since there were antihate laws in Canada, Dr Daruwalla wondered why groups like the Heritage Front were allowed to foment so much racist hatred.

Macfarlane had no difficulty finding a place to park; as before, Little India was fairly deserted – in this respect, it wasn't like India at all. Farrokh stopped walking in front of the Ahmad Grocers on Gerrard, at Coxwell; he pointed diagonally across the street to the boarded-up offices of the Canadian Ethnic Immigration Services – it looked closed for good, not just because it was Friday.

'This is where I was dragged out of the car,' Dr Daruwalla explained. They continued walking on Gerrard. Pindi Embroidery was gone, but a clothes rack of kaftans stood lifelessly on the sidewalk. 'There was more wind the day I was here,' Farrokh told Mac. 'The kaftans were dancing in the wind.'

At the corner of Rhodes and Gerrard, Nirma Fashions was still in business. They noted the Singh Farm, advertising fresh fruits and vegetables. They viewed the façade of the United Church, which also served as the Shri Ram Hindu Temple; the Reverend Lawrence Pushee, minister of the former, had chosen an interesting theme for the coming Sunday service. A Gandhi quotation forewarned the congregation: 'There is enough for everyone's need but not enough for everyone's greed.'

Not only the Canadian Ethnic Immigration Services, but also the Chinese were experiencing hard times; the Luck City Poultry Company was closed down. At the corner of Craven and Gerrard, the 'Indian Cuisine Specialists,' formerly the Nirala restaurant, were now calling themselves Hira Moti, and the familiar advertisement for Kingfisher lager promised that the beer was (as always) INSTILLED WITH INNER STRENGTH. A MEGASTARS poster advertised the arrival of Jeetendra and Bali of Patel Rap; Sapna Mukerjee was also performing.

'I walked along here, bleeding,' Farrokh said to Mac. In the window of either Kala Kendar or Sonali's, the same blond mannequin was wearing a sari; she still looked out of place among the other mannequins. Dr Daruwalla thought of Nancy.

They passed Satyam, 'the store for the whole family'; they read an old announcement for the Miss Diwali competition. They walked up and down and across Gerrard, with no purpose. Farrokh kept repeating the names of the places. The Kohinoor supermarket, the Madras Durbar, the Apollo Video (promising ASIAN MOVIES), the India Theater — NOW PLAYING, TAMIL MOVIES! At the Chaat Hut, Farrokh explained to Mac what was meant by 'all kinds of chaats.' At the Bombay Bhel, they barely had time to eat their aloo tikki and drink their Thunderbolt beer.

Before they went back to the hospital, the doctors stopped at J. S. Addison Plumbing, at the corner of Woodfield. Dr Daruwalla was looking for that splendid copper bathtub with the ornate faucets; the handles were tiger heads, the tigers roaring — it was exactly like the tub he'd bathed in as a boy on old Ridge Road, Malabar Hill. He'd had that bathtub on his mind ever since his last, unplanned visit to Little India. But the tub had been sold. What Farrokh found, instead, was another marvel of Victorian ornamentation. It was that same sink spout, with tusks for faucets, which had captured Rahul's imagination in the ladies' room of the Duckworth Club; it was that elephant-headed spigot, with the water spraying from the elephant's trunk. Farrokh touched the two tusks, one for hot water and the other for cold. Macfarlane thought it was ghastly, but Dr Daruwalla didn't hesitate to buy it; it was the product of a recognizably British imagination, but it was made in India.

'Does it have a sentimental value?' Mac asked.

'Not exactly,' Farrokh replied. Dr Daruwalla wondered what he'd do with the ugly thing; he knew Julia would absolutely hate it.

'Those men who drove you here, and left you . . .' Mac suddenly said.

'What about them?'

'Do you imagine that they bring other people here – like they brought you?'

'All the time,' Farrokh said. 'I imagine that they're bringing people here all the time.'

Mac thought Farrokh looked mortally depressed and told him so.

How can I ever feel assimilated? Dr Daruwalla wondered. 'How am I supposed to feel like a Canadian?' Farrokh asked Mac.

Indeed, if one could believe the newspapers, there was a growing resistance to immigration; demographers were predicting a 'racist backlash.' The resistance to immigration *was* racist, Dr Daruwalla believed; the doctor had become very sensitive to the phrase 'visible minorities.' He knew this didn't mean the Italians or the Germans or the Portuguese; they'd come to Canada in the 1950's. Until the last decade, by far the greatest proportion of immigrants came from Britain.

But not now; the new immigrants came from Hong Kong and China and India – half the immigrants who'd come to Canada in this decade were Asians. In Toronto, almost 40 percent of the population was immigrant – more than a million people.

Macfarlane suffered to see Farrokh so despondent. 'Believe me, Farrokh,' Mac said. 'I know it's no circus to be an immigrant in this country, and although I trust that those thugs who dumped you in Little India have assaulted other immigrants in the city, I *don't* believe that they're transporting people all over town "all the time," as you say.'

'Don't you mean it's *no picnic*? You said "no circus,"' Farrokh told Mac.

'It's the same expression,' Macfarlane replied.

'Do you know what my father said to me?' Dr Daruwalla asked.

'Could it be, "Immigrants are immigrants all their lives"?' Macfarlane inquired.

'Oh – I've already told you,' Farrokh said.

'Too many times to count,' Mac replied. 'But I suppose you go around thinking of it all the time.'

'All the time,' Farrokh repeated. He felt grateful for what a good friend Mac was.

It had been Dr Macfarlane who'd persuaded Dr Daruwalla to volunteer his time at the AIDS hospice in Toronto; Duncan Frasier had died there. Farrokh had worked at the hospice for over a year. At first, he suspected his own motives, which he'd confessed to Mac; on Mac's advice, Farrokh had also discussed his special interest in the hospice with the director of nursing.

It had been awkward for Farrokh to tell a stranger the story of his relationship with John D. – how this young man, who was like an adopted son to Dr Daruwalla, had always been a homosexual, but the doctor hadn't known it until John D. was almost 40; how, even now, when John D.'s sexual orientation was plainly clear, Farrokh and the not-so-young 'young' man still didn't speak of the matter (at least not in depth). Dr Daruwalla told Dr Macfarlane *and* the hospice's director of nursing that he wanted to be involved with AIDS patients because he wanted to know more about the elusive John D. Farrokh admitted that he was terrified for John D.; that his beloved almost-like-a-son might die of AIDS was Farrokh's greatest fear. (Yes, he was afraid for Martin, too.)

Emotional restraint, which was repeatedly demonstrated in Dr Daruwalla's friendship with Dr Macfarlane – their understated conversation regarding the status of Macfarlane's HIV-positive condition was but one example – prevented Farrokh from admitting to his friend that he was also afraid of watching Mac die of AIDS. But it was perfectly well understood, by both doctors *and* by the hospice's director of nursing, that this was another motive underlying Farrokh's desire to familiarize himself with the functions of an AIDS hospice.

Dr Daruwalla believed that the more naturally he could learn to behave in the presence of AIDS patients, not to mention gay men, the closer his relationship with John D. might become. They'd already grown closer together, ever since John D. had told Farrokh that he'd always been gay. Doubtless, Dr Daruwalla's friendship with Dr Macfarlane had helped. But what 'father' can ever feel close enough to his 'son' – that was the issue, wasn't it? Farrokh had asked Mac.

'Don't try to get *too* close to John D.,' Macfarlane had advised. 'Remember, you're not his father – and you're not gay.'

It had been awkward – how Dr Daruwalla had first tried to fit in at the hospice. As Mac had warned him, he had to learn that he wasn't *their* doctor – he was just a volunteer. He asked lots of doctor-type questions and generally drove the nurses crazy; taking orders from nurses was something Dr Daruwalla had to get used to. It was an effort for him to limit his expertise to the issue of bed sores; he still couldn't be stopped from prescribing little exercises to combat the muscular wasting of the patients. He so freely dispensed tennis balls for squeezing that one of the nurses nicknamed him 'Dr Balls.' After a while, the name pleased him.

He was good at taking care of the catheters, and he was capable of giving morphine injections when one of the hospice doctors or nurses asked him to. He grew familiar with the feeding tubes; he hated seeing the seizures. He hoped that he would never watch John D. die with fulminant diarrhea . . . with an uncontrolled infection . . . with a spiking fever.

'I hope not, too,' Mac told him. 'But if you're not

prepared to watch *me* die, you'll be worthless to me when the time comes.'

Dr Daruwalla wanted to be prepared. Usually, his voluntary time was spent in ordinary chores. One night, he did the laundry, just as Macfarlane had proudly bragged about doing it years earlier – all the bed linens and the towels. He also read aloud to patients who couldn't read. He wrote letters for them, too.

One night, when Farrokh was working the switchboard, an angry woman called; she was indignant because she'd just learned that her only son was dying in the hospice and no one had officially informed her – not even her son. She was outraged, she said. She wanted to speak to someone in charge; she didn't ask to speak to her son.

Dr Daruwalla supposed that, although he wasn't 'in charge,' the woman might as well speak to him; he knew the hospice and its rules well enough to advise her how to visit – when to come, how to show respect for privacy and so forth. But the woman wouldn't hear of it.

'*You're* not in charge!' she kept shouting. 'I want to speak to a *doctor*!' she cried. 'I want to talk to the *head* of the place!'

Dr Daruwalla was about to tell her his full name, his profession, his age – even the number of his children and his grandchildren, if she liked. But before he could speak, she screamed at him. 'Who *are* you, anyway? *What* are you?'

Dr Daruwalla answered her with such conviction and pride that he surprised himself. 'I'm a volunteer,' the doctor said. The concept pleased him. Farrokh wondered if it felt as good to be assimilated as it did to be a volunteer.

The Bottommost Drawer

After Dr Daruwalla left Bombay, there were other departures; in one case, there was a departure and a return. Suman, the skywalker par excellence, left the Great Royal Circus. She married a man in the milk business. Then, after various discussions with Pratap Walawalkar, the owner, Suman came back to the Great Royal, bringing her milk-business husband with her. Only recently, the doctor had heard that Suman's husband had become one of the managers of the Great Royal Circus, and that Suman was once again walking on the sky; she was still very much the star.

Farrokh also learned that Pratap Singh had quit the Great Royal; the ringmaster and wild-animal trainer had left with his wife, Sumi, and their troupe of child acrobats – the real Pinky among them – to join the New Grand Circus. Unlike the Pinky character in *Limo Roulette*, the real Pinky wasn't killed by a lion who mistook her for a peacock; the real Pinky was still performing, in one town after another. She would be 11 or 12, Farrokh guessed.

Dr Daruwalla had heard that a girl named Ratna was performing the Skywalk at the New Grand; remarkably, Ratna could skywalk *backward*! The doctor was further informed that, by the time the New Grand Circus performed in Changanacheri, Pinky's name had been changed to Choti Rani, which means Little Queen. Possibly Pratap had chosen the new name not only because Choti Rani was suitably theatrical, but also because Pinky was so special to him; Pratap always said she was absolutely the best. Just plain Pinky was a little queen now.

As for Deepa and Shivaji, the dwarf's dwarf son, they had escaped the Great Blue Nile. Shivaji was very much Vinod's son, in respect to the dwarf's determination; as for Shivaji's talent, the young man was a better acrobat than his father – and, at worst, Vinod's equal as a clown. On the strength of Shivaji's abilities, he and his mother had moved to the Great Royal Circus, which was unquestionably a move up from the Great Blue Nile – and one that Deepa never could have made on the strength of her own *or* Vinod's talents. Farrokh had heard that the subtleties of Shivaji's Farting Clown act – not to mention the dwarf's signature item, which was called Elephant Dodging – put India's other farting clowns to shame.

The fate of those lesser performers who toiled for the Great Blue Nile was altogether less kind; there would be no escape for them. The elephant-footed boy had never been content to be a cook's helper; a higher aspiration afflicted him. The knife thrower's wife, Mrs Bhagwan – the most mechanical of skywalkers – had failed to dissuade Ganesh from his delusions of athleticism. Despite falling many times from that model of the ladderlike device which hung from the roof of the Bhagwan's troupe tent, the cripple would never let go of the idea that he could learn to skywalk.

The perfect ending to Farrokh's screenplay is that the cripple learns to walk without a limp by walking on the sky; such an ending would *not* conclude the real Ganesh's story. The *real* Ganesh wouldn't rest until he'd tried the real thing. It was almost as Dr Daruwalla had imagined it, almost as it was written. But it's unlikely that the real Ganesh was as eloquent; there would have been no voice-over. The elephant boy must have looked down at least once – enough to know that he shouldn't look down again. From the apex of the main tent, the ground was 80 feet below him. With his feet in the loops, it's doubtful that he even *thought* as poetically as Farrokh's fictional character.

('There is a moment when you must let go with your hands. At that moment, you are in no one's hands. At that moment, everyone walks on the sky.') Not likely – not a sentiment that would spontaneously leap to the mind of a cook's helper. The elephant-footed boy would probably have made the mistake of counting the loops, too. Whether counting or not counting, it's far-fetched to imagine him coaching himself across the ladder.

('What I tell myself is, I am walking without a limp.') That would be the day! Dr Daruwalla thought. Judging from where they found the cripple's body, the real Ganesh fell when he was less than halfway across the top of the tent. There were 18 loops in the ladder; the Skywalk was 16 steps. It was Mrs Bhagwan's expert opinion that the elephant boy had fallen after only four or five steps; he'd never managed more than four or five steps across the roof of *her* tent, the skywalker said.

This news came slowly to Toronto. Mr and Mrs Das conveyed their regrets, by letter, to Dr Daruwalla; the letter was late – it was misaddressed. The ringmaster and his wife added that Mrs Bhagwan blamed herself for the accident, but she also felt certain that the cripple could never have been taught to skywalk. Doubtless her distress distracted her. The next news from Mr and Mrs Das was that Mrs Bhagwan had been cut by her knife-throwing husband as she lay spread-eagled on the revolving bull's-eye; it wasn't a serious wound, but she gave herself no time to heal. The following night, she fell from the Skywalk. She was only as far across the top of the tent as Ganesh had been, and she fell without a cry. Her husband said that she'd been having trouble with the fourth and fifth steps ever since the elephant boy had fallen.

Mr Bhagwan wouldn't throw another knife, not even when they offered him a choice of targets, all of whom were small girls. The widower went into semi-retirement, performing only the Elephant Passing item. There seemed to be some self-punishment about this elephant act – or so the ringmaster confided to Dr Daruwalla. Mr Bhagwan would lie down under the elephant – at first with fewer and fewer mattresses between his body and the elephant-walking plank, and between his body and the ground. Then he did it

797

with no mattresses at all. There were internal injuries, the ringmaster and his wife implied. Mr Bhagwan became ill; he was sent home. Later, Mr and Mrs Das heard that Mr Bhagwan had died.

Then Dr Daruwalla heard that they'd *all* become ill. There were no more letters from Mr and Mrs Das. The Great Blue Nile Circus had vanished. Their last place of performance was Poona, where the prevailing story about the Blue Nile was that they were brought down by a flood; it was a small flood, not a major disaster, except that the hygiene at the circus became lax. An unidentified disease killed several of the big cats, and bouts of diarrhea and gastroenteritis were rampant among the acrobats. Just that quickly, the Great Blue Nile was gone.

Had Gautam's death been a harbinger? The old chimpanzee had died of rabies not two weeks after he'd bitten Martin Mills; Kunal's efforts to discipline the ape by beating him had been wasted. But, among them all, Dr Daruwalla mainly remembered Mrs Bhagwan – her tough feet and her long black shiny hair.

The death of the elephant boy (a cripple no more) destroyed a small but imporant part of Farrokh. What happened to the real Ganesh had an immediate and diminishing effect on the screenwriter's already waning confidence in his powers of creation. The screenplay of *Limo Roulette* had suffered from comparisons to real life. In the end, the real Ganesh's remark rang truest. 'You can't fix what elephants do,' the cripple had said.

Like Mr Bhagwan, who had retreated into Elephant Passing, which led to his death, the screenplay of *Limo Roulette* went into radical retirement. It occupied the bottommost drawer in Dr Daruwalla's desk at home; he wouldn't keep a copy in his office at the hospital. If he were to die suddenly, he wouldn't have wanted anyone but Julia to discover the unproduced screenplay. The single copy was in a folder marked for it was Farrokh's conviction that only John D. would one day know what to do with it.

Doubtless there would be compromises required in order for *Limo Roulette* to be produced; there were always compromises in the movie business. Someone would say that the voice-over was 'emotionally distancing' – that was the fashionable opinion of voice-over. Someone would complain about the little girl being killed by the lion. (Couldn't Pinky be confined to a wheelchair, but happy, for the rest of the movie?) And despite what had happened to the real Ganesh, the screenwriter loved the ending as it was written; someone would want to tamper with that ending, which Dr Daruwalla could never allow. The doctor knew that *Limo Roulette* would never be as perfect as it was in those days when he was writing it and he imagined that he was a better writer than he was.

It was a deep drawer for a mere 118 pages. As if to keep the abandoned screenplay company, Farrokh filled the drawer with photographs of chromosomes; ever since Duncan Frasier had died, Dr Daruwalla's dwarf-blood project had passed beyond languishing – the doctor's enthusiasm for drawing blood from dwarfs was as dead as the gay geneticist. If anything or anyone were to tempt Dr Daruwalla to return to India, this time the doctor couldn't claim that the dwarfs were bringing him back.

From time to time, Dr Daruwalla would read that perfect ending to *Limo Roulette* – when the cripple walks on the sky – for only by this artificial means could the doctor keep the *real* Ganesh alive. The screenwriter loved that moment after the Skywalk when the boy is descending on the dental trapeze, spinning in the spotlight as the gleaming sequins on his singlet throw back the light. Farrokh loved how the cripple never touches the ground; how he descends into Pratap's waiting arms, and how Pratap holds the boy up to the cheering crowd. Then Pratap runs out of the ring with Ganesh in his arms, because after a cripple has walked on the sky, no one should see him limp. It could have worked, the screenwriter thought; it *should* have worked.

Dr Daruwalla was 62; he was reasonably healthy. His weight was a small problem and he'd done little to rid his diet of admitted excesses, but the doctor nevertheless expected to live for another decade or two. John D. might well be in *his* sixties by the time *Limo Roulette* was put into the actor's hands. The former Inspector Dhar would know for whom the part of the missionary had been intended; the actor would also be relatively free of any personal attachments to the story or its characters. If certain compromises were necessary in order to produce *Limo Roulette*, John D. would be able to look at the screenplay objectively. Dr Daruwalla had no doubt that the ex-Inspector Dhar would know what to do with the material.

But for now – for the rest of his life, Farrokh knew – the story belonged in the bottommost drawer.

Sort of Fading Now

Almost three years after he left Bombay, the retired screenwriter read about the destruction of the Mosque of Babar; the unending hostilities he'd once mocked in *Inspector Dhar and the Hanging Mali* had turned uglier still. Fanatical Hindus had destroyed the 16th-century Babri mosque; rioting had left more than 400 dead – Prime Minister Rao called for shooting rioters on sight, both in Bhopal and in Bombay. Hindu fundamentalists weren't pleased by Mr Rao's promise to rebuild the mosque; these fanatics continued to claim that the mosque had been built on the birthplace of the Hindu god Rama – they'd already begun building a temple to Rama at the site of the destroyed mosque. The hostilities would go on and on, Dr Daruwalla knew. The violence would endure; it was always what lasted longest.

And although Madhu would never be found, Detective Patel would keep inquiring for the girl; the child prostitute would be a woman now – if she was still managing to live with the AIDS virus, which was unlikely.

'If we crash, do we burn or fly apart in little pieces?' Madhu had asked Dr Daruwalla. 'Something will get me,' she'd told the doctor. Farrokh couldn't stop imagining her. He was always envisioning Madhu with Mr Garg; they were traveling together from Junagadh to Bombay, escaping the Great Blue Nile. Although it would have been considered highly disgraceful, they would probably have been touching each other, not even secretly – secure in the misinformation that all that was wrong with them was a case of chlamydia.

And almost as the deputy commissioner had predicted, the second Mrs Dogar would be unable to resist the terrible temptations that presented themselves to her in her confinement with women. She bit off a fellow prisoner's nose. In the course of the subsequent and extremely hard labor to which Rahul was then subjected, she would rebel; it would be unnecessry to hang her, for she was beaten to death by her guards.

In another of life's little passages, Ranjit would both retire and remarry. Dr Daruwalla had never met the woman whose matrimonial advertisement in *The Times of India* finally snared his faithful medical secretary; however, the doctor had read the ad – Ranjit sent it to him. 'An attractive woman of indeterminate age – innocently divorced, without issue – seeks a mature man, preferably a widower. Neatness and civility still count.' Indeed, they do, the doctor thought. Julia joked that Ranjit had probably been attracted to the woman's punctuation.

Other couples came and went, but the nature of couples, like violence, would endure. Even little Amy

Sorabjee had married. (God help her husband.) And although Mrs Bannerjee had died, Mr Bannerjee wasn't a widower for long; he married the widow Lal. Of these unsavory couplings, of course, the unchanging Mr Sethna steadfastly disapproved.

However set in his ways, the old steward still ruled the Duckworth Club dining room and the Ladies' Garden with a possessiveness that was said to be enhanced by his newly acquired sense of himself as a promising actor. Dr Sorabjee wrote to Dr Daruwalla that Mr Sethna had been seen addressing himself in the men's-room mirror – long monologues of a thespian nature. And the old steward was observed to be slavishly devoted to Deputy Commissioner Patel, if not to the big blond wife who went everywhere with the esteemed detective. Apparently, the famous tea-pouring Parsi also fancied himself a promising policeman. Crime-branch investigation was no doubt perceived by Mr Sethna as a heightened form of eavesdropping.

Astonishingly, the old steward appeared to approve of something! The unorthodoxy of the deputy commissioner and his American wife becoming members of the Duckworth Club didn't bother Mr Sethna; it bothered many an orthodox Duckworthian. Clearly, the deputy commisioner hadn't waited 22 years for his membership; although Detective Patel satisfied the requirement for 'community leadership,' his instant acceptance at the club suggested that someone had bent the rules – someone had been looking for (and had found) a loophole. To many Duckworthians, the policeman's membership amounted to a miracle; it was also considered a scandal.

It was a *minor* miracle, in Detective Patel's opinion, that no one was ever bitten by the escaped cobras in Mahalaxmi, for (according to the deputy commissioner) those cobras had been 'assimilated' into the life of Bombay without a single reported bite.

It wasn't even a minor miracle that the phone calls

from the woman who tried to sound like a man continued – not only after Rahul's imprisonment, but also after her death. It strangely comforted Dr Daruwalla to know that the caller had never been Rahul. Every time, as if reading from a script, the caller would leave nothing out. 'Your father's head was off, completely *off*! I saw it sitting on the passenger seat before flames engulfed the car.'

Farrokh had learned how to interrupt the unslackening voice. 'I know – I know already,' Dr Daruwalla would say. 'And his hands couldn't let go of the steering wheel, even though his fingers were on fire – is that what you're going to tell me? I've already heard it.'

But the voice never relented. 'I did it. I blew his head off. I watched him burn,' said the woman who tried to sound like a man. 'And I'm telling you, he deserved it. Your whole family deserves it.'

'Oh, fuck you,' Farrokh had learned to say, although he generally disliked such language.

Sometimes he would watch the video of *Inspector Dhar and the Cage-Girl Killer* (that was Farrokh's favorite) or *Inspector Dhar and the Towers of Silence*, which the former screenwriter believed was the most underrated of the Dhar films. But to his best friend, Mac, Farrokh would never confide that he'd written anything – not a word. Inspector Dhar was part of the doctor's past. John D. had almost completely let Dhar go. Dr Daruwalla had to keep trying.

For three years, the twins had teased him; neither John D. nor Martin Mills would tell Dr Daruwalla what had passed between them on their flight to Switzerland. While the doctor sought clarification, the twins deliberately confused him; they must have done it to exasperate him – Farrokh was such a lot of fun when he was exasperated. The former Inspector Dhar's most irritating (and least believable) response was, 'I don't remember.' Martin Mills claimed to remember everything. But Martin never told the same story twice, and when John D. *did* admit to remembering something,

803

the actor's version unfailingly contradicted the ex-missionary's.

'Let's try to begin at the beginning,' Dr Daruwalla would say. 'I'm interested in that moment of recognition, the realization that you were face-to-face with your second self – so to speak.'

'*I* boarded the plane first,' both twins would tell him.

'I always do the same thing whenever I leave India,' the retired Inspector Dhar insisted. 'I find my seat and get my little complementary toilet kit from the flight attendant. Then I go to the lavatory and shave off my mustache, while they're still boarding the plane.'

This much was true. It was what John D. did to un-Dhar himself. This was an established fact, one of the few that Farrokh could cling to: both twins were mustacheless when they met.

'I was sitting in my seat when this man came out of the lavatory, and I thought I recognized him,' Martin said.

'You were looking out the window,' John D. declared. 'You didn't turn to look at me until I'd sat down beside you and had spoken your name.'

'You spoke his name?' Dr Daruwalla always asked.

'Of course. I knew who he was instantly,' the ex-Inspector Dhar would reply. 'I thought to myself: Farrokh must imagine he's awfully clever – writing a script for everyone.'

'He never spoke my name,' Martin told the doctor. 'I remember thinking that he was Satan, and that Satan had chosen to look like me, to take my own form – what a horror! I thought you were my dark side, my evil half.'

'Your *smarter* half, you mean,' John D. would invariably reply.

'He was just like the Devil. He was frighteningly arrogant,' Martin told Farrokh.

'I simply told him that I knew who he was,' John D. argued.

'You said nothing of the kind,' Martin interjected.

'You said, "Fasten your fucking seat belt, pal, because are *you* ever in for a surprise!"'

'That sounds like what you'd say,' Farrokh told the former Dhar.

'I couldn't get a word in edgewise,' John D. complained. 'Here I knew all about him, but *he* was the one who wouldn't stop talking. All the way to Zürich, he never shut up.'

Dr Daruwalla had to admit that this sounded like what Martin Mills would do.

'I kept thinking: This is Satan. I give up the idea of the priesthood and I meet the Devil – in first class! He had this constant sneer,' Martin said. 'It was a *Satanic* sneer – or so I thought.'

'He started right out about Vera, our sainted mother,' John D. related. 'We were still crossing the Arabian Sea – utter darkness above and below us – when he got to the part about the roommate's suicide. I hadn't said a word!'

'That's not true – he kept interrupting me,' Martin told Farrokh. 'He kept asking me, "Are you gay, or do you just not know it yet?" Honestly, I thought he was the rudest man I'd ever met!'

'Listen to me,' the actor said. 'You meet your twin brother on an airplane and you start right out with a list of everyone your mother's slept with. And you think *I'm* rude.'

'You called me a "quitter" before we'd even reached our cruising altitude,' Martin said.

'But you must have started by telling him that you were his twin,' Farrokh said to John D.

'He did nothing of the kind,' said Martin Mills. 'He said, "You already know the bad news: your father died. Now here's the good news: he wasn't your father."'

'You *didn't*!' Dr Daruwalla said to John D.

'I can't remember,' the actor would say.

'The word "twin" – just tell me, who said it first?' the doctor asked.

'I asked the flight attendant if she saw any resemblance between us – *she* was the first to say the word "twin,"' John D. replied.

'That's not exactly how it happened,' Martin argued. 'What he said to the flight attendant was, "We were separated at birth. Try to guess which one of us has had the better time."'

'He simply exhibited all the common symptoms of denial,' John D. would respond. 'He kept asking me if I had *proof* that we were related.'

'He was utterly shameless,' Martin told Farrokh. 'He said, "You can't deny that you've had at least one homosexual infatuation – there's your proof."'

'That was bold of you,' the doctor told John D. 'Actually, there's only a fifty-two percent chance . . .'

'I knew he was gay the second I saw him,' the retired movie star said.

'But when did you realize how much . . . else you had in common?' Dr Daruwalla asked. 'When did you begin to recognize the traits you shared? When did your obvious similarities emerge?'

'Oh, long before we got to Zürich,' Martin answered quickly.

'*What* similarities?' John D. asked.

'That's what I mean by arrogant – he's arrogant *and* rude,' Martin told Farrokh.

'And when did you decide *not* to go to New York?' the doctor asked the ex-missionary. Dr Daruwalla was especially interested in the part of the story where the twins told Vera off.

'We were working on our telegram to the bitch before we landed,' John D. replied.

'But what did the telegram say?' Farrokh asked.

'I don't remember,' John D. would always answer

'Of *course* you remember!' cried Martin Mills. 'You wrote it! He wouldn't let me write a word of the telegram,' Martin told Dr Daruwalla. 'He said he was in the business of one-liners – he insisted on doing it himself.'

'What *you* wanted to say to her wouldn't have fit in a telegram,' John D. reminded his twin.

'What he said to her was unspeakably cruel. I couldn't believe how cruel he could be. And he didn't even know her!' Martin Mills told the doctor.

'He asked me to send the telegram. He had no second thoughts,' John D. told Farrokh.

'But what was it that you said? What did the damn telegram *say*?' Dr Daruwalla cried.

'It was unspeakably cruel,' Martin repeated.

'She had it coming, and you know it,' said the ex-Inspector Dhar.

Whatever the telegram said, Dr Daruwalla knew that Vera didn't live very long after she received it. There was only her hysterical phone call to Farrokh, who was still in Bombay; Vera called the doctor's office and left a message with Ranjit.

'This is Veronica Rose – the actress,' she told Dr Daruwalla's secretary. Ranjit knew who she was; he would never forget typing the report on the problem Vera had with her knees, which turned out to be gynecological – 'vaginal itching,' Dr Lowji Daruwalla had said.

'Tell the fucking doctor I know that he betrayed me!' Vera said to Ranjit.

'Is it your . . . knees again?' the old secretary had asked her.

Dr Daruwalla never returned her call. Vera never made it back to California before she died; her death was related to the sleeping pills she regularly took, which she'd irregularly mixed with vodka.

Martin would stay in Europe. Switzerland suited him, he said. And the outings in the Alps – although the former scholastic had never been athletically inclined, these outings with John D. were wonderful for Martin Mills. He couldn't be taught to downhill-ski (he was too uncoordinated), but he liked cross-country skiing and hiking; he loved being with his brother. Even John D. admitted, albeit belatedly, that they loved being with each other.

The ex-missionary kept himself busy; he taught at City University (in the general-studies program) and at the American International School of Zürich – he was active at the Swiss Jesuit Centre, too. Occasionally, he would travel to other Jesuit institutions; there were youth centers and students' homes in Basel and Bern, and adult-education centers in Fribourg and Bad Schönbrunn – Martin Mills was doubtless effective as an inspirational speaker. Farrokh could only imagine that this meant more Christ-in-the-parking-lot sermonizing; the former zealot hadn't lost his energy for improving the attitudes of others.

As for John D., he continued in his craft; the journeyman actor was content with his roles at the Schauspielhaus Zürich. His friends were in the theater, or affiliated with the university, or with a publishing firm of excellent reputation – and of course he saw a great deal of Farrokh's brother, Jamshed, and Jamshed's wife (and Julia's sister), Josefine.

It was to this social circle that John D. would introduce his twin. An oddity at first – everyone is interested in a twins-separated-at-birth story – Martin made many friends in this community; in three years, the ex-missionary probably had more friends than the actor. In fact, Martin's first lover was an ex-boyfriend of John D.'s, which Dr Daruwalla found strange; the twins made a joke of it – probably to exasperate him, the doctor thought.

As for lovers, Matthias Frei died; the onetime terror of the Zürich avant-garde had been John D.'s long-standing partner. It was Julia who informed Farrokh of this; she'd known for quite some time that John D. and Frei were a couple. 'Frei didn't die of AIDS, did he?' the doctor asked his wife. She gave him the same sort of look that John D. would have given him; it was that smile from movie posters of faded memory, recalling the cutting sneer of Inspector Dhar.

'No, Frei didn't die of AIDS – he had a heart attack,' Julia told her husband.

No one ever tells me anything! the doctor thought. It was just like that twinly conversation on Swissair 197, Bombay to Zürich, which would occupy a sizable part of Farrokh's imagination, largely because John D. and Martin Mills were so secretive about it.

'Now, listen to me, both of you,' Dr Daruwalla would tell the twins. 'I'm *not* prying, I *do* respect your privacy – it's just that you know how much dialogue interests me. This feeling of closeness between you, for it's obvious to me that the two of you *are* close . . . did it come from your very first meeting? It must have happened on the plane! There's surely something more between you than your mutual hatred of your late mother – or did the telegram to Vera really bring you together?'

'The telegram wasn't dialogue – I thought you were interested only in our *dialogue*,' John D. replied.

'Such a telegram would never have occured to *me*!' said Martin Mills.

'I couldn't get a word in edgewise,' John D. repeated. 'We didn't have any dialogue. Martin had one monologue after another.'

'He's an actor, all right,' Martin told Farrokh. 'I know he can *create* a character, as they say, but I'm telling you I was convinced he was Satan – I mean the real thing.'

'Nine hours is a long time to talk with anyone,' John D. was fond of saying.

'The flight was nearly nine hours and fifteen minutes, to be more exact,' Martin corrected him.

'The point is, I was dying to get off the plane,' John D. told Dr Daruwalla. 'He kept telling me it was God's will that we met. I thought I was going to go mad. The only time I could get away from him was when I went to the lavatory.'

'You practically *lived* in the lavatory! You drank so much beer. And it *was* God's will – you see that now, don't you?' Martin asked John D.

'It was *Farrokh's* will,' John D. replied.

'You really *are* the Devil!' Martin told his twin.

'No, *both* of you are the Devil!' Dr Daruwalla told them, although he would discover that he loved them – if never quite equally. He looked forward to seeing them, and to their letters or their calls. Martin wrote lengthy letters; John D. seldom wrote letters, but he called frequently. Sometimes, when he called, it was hard to know what he wanted. Occasionally, not often, it was hard to know *who* was calling – John D. or the old Inspector Dhar.

'Hi, it's *me*,' he said to Farrokh one morning; he sounded smashed. It would have been early afternoon in Zürich. John D. said he'd just had a foolish lunch; when the actor called his lunch or dinner 'foolish,' it usually meant that he'd had something stronger to drink than beer. Only two glasses of wine made him drunk.

'I hope you're not performing tonight!' Dr Daruwalla said, regretting that he sounded like an overcritical father.

'It's my understudy's night to perform,' the actor told him. Farrokh knew very little about the theater; he hadn't known that there were understudies at the Schauspielhaus – also, he was sure that John D. was currently playing a small supporting role.

'It's impressive that you have an understudy for such a little part,' the doctor said cautiously.

'My "understudy" is Martin,' the twin confessed. 'We thought we'd try it – just to see if anyone noticed.'

Once again Farrokh sounded like an overcritical father. 'You should be more protective of your career than that,' Dr Daruwalla chided John D. 'Martin can be a clod! What if he can't act at all? He could completely embarrass you!'

'We've been practising,' said the old Inspector Dhar.

'And I suppose you've been posing as *him*,' Farrokh remarked. 'Lectures on Graham Greene, no doubt – Martin's favorite "Catholic interpretation." And a few inspirational speeches at those Jesuit centers – a Jesus in every parking lot, more than enough Christs to go around . . . that kind of thing.'

'Yes,' John D. admitted. 'It's been fun.'

'You should be ashamed – *both* of you!' Dr Daruwalla cried.

'You put us together,' John D. replied.

Nowadays, Farrokh knew, the twins were much more alike in their appearance. John D. had lost a little weight; Martin had put the pounds on – incredibly, the former Jesuit was going to a gym. They also cut their hair the same way. Having been separated for 39 years, the twins took being identical somewhat seriously.

Then there was that particularly transatlantic silence, with a rhythmic bleeping – a sound that seemed to count the time. And John D. remarked, 'So . . . it's probably sunset there.' When John D. said 'there,' he meant Bombay. Counting 10½ hours, Dr Daruwalla figured that it would be more or less sunset. 'I'll bet she's on the balcony, just watching,' John D. went on. 'What do you bet?' Dr Daruwalla knew that the ex-Inspector Dhar was thinking of Nancy and her view to the west.

'I guess it's about that time,' the doctor answered carefully.

'It's probably too early for the good policeman to be home,' John D. continued. 'She's all alone, but I'll bet she's on the balcony – just watching.'

'Yes – probably,' Dr Daruwalla said.

'Want to bet?' John D. asked. 'Why don't you call her and see if she's there? You can tell by how long it takes her to get to the phone.'

'Why don't *you* call her?' Farrokh asked.

'I never call Nancy,' John D. told him.

'She'd probably enjoy hearing from you,' Farrokh lied.

'No, she wouldn't,' John D. said. 'But I'll bet you anything she's on the balcony. Go on and call her.'

'*I* don't want to call her!' Dr Daruwalla cried. 'But I

811

agree with you – she's probably on the balcony. So . . . you win the bet, or there's no bet. She's on the balcony. Just leave it at that.' Where *else* would Nancy be? the doctor wondered; he was quite sure John D. was drunk.

'Please call her. Please do it for me, Farrokh,' John D. said to him.

There wasn't much to it. Dr Daruwalla called his former Marine Drive apartment. The phone rang and rang; it rang so long, the doctor almost hung up. Then Nancy picked up the phone. There was her defeated voice, expecting nothing. The doctor chatted aimlessly for a while; he pretended that the call was of no importance – just a whim. Vijay wasn't yet back from Crime Branch Headquarters, Nancy informed him. They would have dinner at the Duckworth Club, but a bit later than usual. She knew there'd been another bombing, but she didn't know the details.

'Is there a nice sunset?' Farrokh asked.

'Oh, yes . . . sort of fading now,' Nancy told him.

'Well, I'll let you get back to it!' he told her a little too heartily. Then he called John D. and told him that she'd definitely been on the balcony; Farrokh repeated Nancy's remark about the sunset – 'sort of fading now.' The retired Inspector Dhar kept saying the line; he wouldn't stop practicing the phrase until Dr Daruwalla assured him that he had it right – that he was saying it precisely as Nancy had said it. He really *is* a good actor, the former screenwriter thought; it was impressive how closely John D. could imitate the exact degree of deadness in Nancy's voice.

'Sort of fading now,' John D. kept saying. 'How's that?'

'That's it – you've got it,' Farrokh told him.

'Sort of fading now,' John D. repeated. 'Is that better?'

'Yes, that's perfect,' Dr Daruwalla said.

'Sort of fading now,' said the actor.

'Stop it,' the ex-screenwriter said.

As a former guest chairman of the Membership Committee, Dr Daruwalla knew the rules of the Duckworth Club; the 22-year waiting list for applicants was inviolable. The death of a Duckworthian – for example, Mr Dogar's fatal stroke, which followed fast upon the news that the second Mrs Dogar had been beaten to death by her guards – did not necessarily speed up the process of membership. The Membership Committee never crassly viewed a fellow Duckworthian's death as a matter of making room. Not even the death of Mr Dua would 'make room' for a new member. And Mr Dua was sorely missed; his deafness in one ear was legendary – the never-to-be-forgotten tennis injury; the senseless blow from the flung racket of his doubles partner (who'd double-faulted). Dead at last, poor Mr Dua was deaf in both ears now; yet not one new membership came of it.

However, Farrokh knew that not even the rules of the Duckworth Club were safe from a single most interesting loophole. It was stated that upon the formal resignation of a Duckworthian, as distinct from a Duckworthian's demise, a new member could be spontaneously appointed to take the resigning member's place; such an appointment circumvented the normal process of nomination and election and the 22-year waiting list. Had this exception to the rules been overused, it doubtless would have been criticized and eliminated, but Duckworthians didn't resign. Even when they moved away from Bombay, they paid their dues and retained their membership; Duckworthians were Duckworthians forever.

Three years after he left India – 'for good,' or so he'd said – Dr Daruwalla still faithfully paid his dues to the Duckworth Club; even in Toronto, the doctor read the club's monthly newsletter. But John D. did the unexpected, unheard-of, un-Duckworthian thing: he resigned his membership. Deputy Commissioner Patel was 'spontaneously appointed' in the retired Inspector Dhar's stead. The former movie star was replaced by the real policeman, who (all agreed) had distinguished himself in 'community leadership.' If there were objections to the big blond wife who went everywhere with the esteemed detective, these objections were never too openly expressed, although Mr Sethna was committed to remembering Nancy's furry navel and the day she'd stood on a chair and reached into the mechanism of the ceiling fan – not to mention the night she'd danced with Dhar and left the club in tears, or the day after, when she'd left the club in anger (with Dhar's dwarf).

Dr Daruwalla would learn that Detective Patel and Nancy were controversial additions to the Duckworth Club. But the old club, the doctor knew, was just one more oasis – a place where Nancy might hope to contain herself, and where the deputy commissioner could indulge in a brief respite from the labors of his profession. This was how Farrokh preferred to think of the Patels – relaxing in the Ladies' Garden, watching a slower life go by than the life they'd lived. They deserved a break, didn't they? And although it had taken three years, the swimming pool was finally finished; in the hottest months, before the monsoon, the pool would be nice for Nancy.

It was never acknowledged that John D. had played the role of the Patels' benefactor or the part of Nancy's guardian angel. But not only had John D.'s resignation from the Duckworth Club provided a membership for the Patels; it had been John D.'s idea that the view from the Daruwallas' balcony would do Nancy some good. Without questioning the doctor's motives, the Patels had moved into the Marine Drive apartment – ostensibly to look after the aged servants.

In one of several flawlessly typed letters, Deputy Commissioner Patel wrote to Dr Daruwalla that although the offensive elevator sign had not been replaced – that is, after it was stolen a *second* time – the

814

Daruwallas' ancient servants nevertheless continued to struggle up and down the stairs. The old rules had penetrated Nalin and Roopa; the rules were permanently in place – they would outlive any sign. The servants themselves refused to ride in the lift; their tragic preconditioning couldn't be helped. The policeman expressed a deeper sympathy for the thief. The Residents' Society had assigned the task of catching the culprit to Detective Patel. The deputy commissioner confided to Dr Daruwalla that he wasn't making much progress in solving the case, but that he suspected the *second* thief was Nancy – not Vinod.

As for the continued disruption to the building that was caused by the first-floor dogs, this always happened at an ungodly hour of the early morning. The first-floor residents claimed that the dogs were deliberately incited to bark by a familiar, violent-looking dwarf taxi driver – formerly a 'chauffeur' for Dr Daruwalla and the retired Inspector Dhar – but Detective Patel was inclined to lay the blame on various stray beggars off Chowpatty Beach. Even after a lock was fashioned for the lobby door, the dogs were occasionally driven insane, and the first-floor residents insisted that the dwarf had managed to gain unlawful entrance to the lobby; several of them said they'd seen an off-white Ambassador driving away. But these allegations were discounted by the deputy commissioner, for the first-floor dogs were barking in May of 1993 – more than a month after those Bombay bombings that killed more than 200 people, Vinod among them.

The dogs were still barking, Detective Patel wrote to Dr Daruwalla. It was Vinod's ghost who was disturbing them, Farrokh felt certain.

On the door of the downstairs bathroom in the Daruwallas' house on Russell Hill Road, there hung the sign that the dwarf had stolen for them. It was a big hit with their friends in Toronto.

SERVANTS ARE NOT ALLOWED
TO USE THE LIFT
UNLESS ACCOMPANIED BY CHILDREN

In retrospect, it seemed cruel that the ex-clown had survived the terrible teeterboard accident at the Great Blue Nile. It appeared that the gods had toyed with Vinod's fate – that he'd been launched by an elephant into the bleachers and had risen to a kind of local stardom in the private-taxi business seemed trivial. And that the dwarf had come to the rescue of Martin Mills, who'd fallen among those unusually violent prostitutes, seemed merely mock-heroic now. It struck Dr Daruwalla as completely unfair that Vinod had been blown up in the bombing of the Air India building.

On the afternoon of March 12, 1993, a car bomb exploded on the exit ramp of the driveway, not far from the offices of the Bank of Oman. People were killed on the street; others were killed in the bank, which occupied that part of the Air India building nearest the site of the explosion. The Bank of Oman was demolished. Probably Vinod was waiting for a passenger who was doing business in the bank. The dwarf had been sitting at the wheel of his taxi, which was unfortunately parked next to the vehicle containing the car bomb. Only Deputy Commissoner Patel was capable of explaining why so many squash-racquet handles and old tennis balls were scattered all over the street.

There was a clock on the Air India hoarding, the billboard above the building; for two or three days after the bombing, the time was stuck at 2:48 – strangely, Dr Daruwalla would wonder if Vinod had noticed the time. The deputy commissioner implied that the dwarf had died instantly.

Patel reported that the pitiful assets of Vinod's Blue Nile, Ltd., would scarcely provide for the dwarf's wife and son; but Shivaji's success at the Great Royal Circus

816

would take care of the young dwarf and his mother, and Deepa had earlier been left a sizable inheritance. To her surprise, she'd been more than mentioned in Mr Garg's will. (Acid Man had died of AIDS within a year of the Daruwallas' departure from Bombay.) The holdings of the Wetness Cabaret had been huge in comparison to those of Vinod's Blue Nile, Ltd. The size of Deepa's share of the strip joint had been sufficient to close the cabaret down.

Exotic dancing had never meant actual stripping – real strip joints weren't allowed in Bombay. What passed for exotic dancing at the Wetness Cabaret had never amounted to more than strip*teasing*. The clientele, as Muriel had once observed, was truly vile, but the reason someone had thrown an orange at her was that the exotic dancer wouldn't take off her clothes. Muriel was a stripper who wouldn't strip, just as Garg had been a Good Samaritan who *wasn't* a Good Samaritan – or so Dr Daruwalla supposed.

There was a photograph of Vinod that John D. had framed; the actor kept it on his desk in his Zürich apartment. It wasn't a picture of the dwarf in his car-driving days, when the former Inspector Dhar had known Vinod best; it was an old circus photo. It had always been John D.'s favorite photograph of Vinod. In the picture, the dwarf is wearing his clown costume; the baggy polka-dotted pants are so short, Vinod appears to be standing on his knees. He's wearing a tank top, a muscle shirt – with spiraling stripes, like the stripes on a barber's pole – and he's grinning at the camera, his smile enhanced by the larger smile that's painted on his face; the edges of his painted smile extend to the corners of the dwarf's bright eyes.

Standing directly beside Vinod, in profile to the camera, is an open-mouthed hippopotamus. What's shocking about the photograph is that the whole dwarf, standing up straight, would easily fit in the hippo's yawning mouth. The oddly opposed lower

817

teeth are within Vinod's reach; the hippo's teeth are as long as the dwarf's arms. At the time, the little clown must have felt the heat from the hippo's mouth – the breath of rotting vegetables, the result of the lettuce that Vinod recalled feeding to the hippo, who swallowed the heads whole. 'Like grapes,' the dwarf had said.

Not even Deepa could remember how long ago the Great Blue Nile had had a hippo; by the time the dwarf's wife joined the circus, the hippopotamus had died. After the dwarf's death, John D. typed an epitaph for Vinod on the bottom of the hippo picture. Clearly, the epitaph was composed in memory of the forbidden elevator – that elite lift which the dwarf had never officially been allowed to use. *Presently accompanied by children*, the commemoration read.

It wasn't a bad epitaph, the retired screenwriter thought. Farrokh had acquired quite a collection of photographs of Vinod, most of which the dwarf had given him over the years. When Dr Daruwalla wrote his condolences to Deepa, the doctor wanted to include a photo that he hoped the dwarf's wife and son would like. It was hard to select only one; the doctor had so many pictures of Vinod – many more were in his mind, of course.

While Farrokh was trying to find the perfect picture of Vinod to send to Deepa, the dwarf's wife wrote to him. It was just a postcard from Ahmedabad, where the Great Royal was performing, but the thought was what mattered to Dr Daruwalla. Deepa had wanted the doctor to know that she and Shivaji were all right. 'Still falling in the net,' the dwarf's wife wrote.

That helped Farrokh find the photo he was looking for; it was a picture of Vinod in the dwarf's ward at the Hospital for Crippled Children. The dwarf is recovering from surgery, following the results of the Elephant on a Teeterboard item. This time, there's no clownish smile painted over Vinod's grin; the dwarf's natural smile is sufficient. In his stubby-fingered, trident hand, Vinod is clutching that list of his talents which featured car driving; the dwarf is holding his future in one hand. Dr Daruwalla only vaguely remembered taking the picture.

Under the circumstances, Farrokh felt it was necessary for him to inscribe some endearment on the back of the photograph; Deepa wouldn't need to be reminded of the occasion of the photo – at the time, she'd been occupying a bed in the women's ward of the same hospital, recovering from the doctor's surgery on her hip. Inspired by John D.'s epitaph for Vinod, the doctor continued with the forbidden-elevator theme. *Allowed to use the lift at last*, the former screenwriter wrote, for although Vinod had missed the net, the dwarf had finally escaped the rules of the Residents' Society.

Not the Dwarfs

One day, how would Dr Daruwalla be remembered? As a good doctor, of course; as a good husband, a good father – a good man, by all counts, though not a great writer. But whether he was walking on Bloor Street or stepping into a taxi on Avenue Road, almost no one seeing him would have thought twice about him; he was so seemingly assimilated. A well-dressed immigrant, perhaps; a nice, naturalized Canadian – maybe a well-to-do tourist. Although he was small, one could quibble about his weight; for a man in the late afternoon of his life, he would be wise to be thinner. Nevertheless, he was distinguished-looking.

Sometimes he seemed a little tired – chiefly in the area of his eyes – or else there was something faraway about his thoughts, which, for the most part, he kept to himself. No one could have fathomed what a life he'd led, for it was chiefly a life lived in his mind. Possibly what passed for his tiredness was nothing more than the cost of his considerable imagination, which had never found the outlet that it sought.

At the AIDS hospice, Farrokh would forever be

remembered as Dr Balls, but this was largely out of fondness. The one patient who'd *bounced* his tennis ball instead of squeezing it hadn't irritated the nurses or the other staff for very long. When a patient died, that patient's tennis ball would be returned to Dr Daruwalla. The doctor had been only briefly bitten by religion; he wasn't religious anymore. Yet these tennis balls of former patients were almost holy objects to Farrokh.

At first, he would be at a loss with what to do with the old balls; he could never bring himself to throw them away, nor did he approve of giving them to new patients. Eventually, he disposed of them – but in an oddly ritualistic fashion. He buried them in Julia's herb garden, where dogs would occasionally dig them up. Dr Daruwalla didn't mind that the dogs got to play with the tennis balls; the doctor found this a suitable conclusion to the life of these old balls – a pleasing cycle.

As for the damage to the herb garden, Julia put up with it; after all, it wasn't her husband's only eccentricity. She respected his rich and hidden interior life, which she thoroughly expected to yield a puzzling exterior; she knew Farrokh was an interior man. He had always been a daydreamer; now that he didn't write, he seemed to daydream a little more.

Once, Farrokh told Julia that he wondered if he was an avatar. In Hindu mythology, an avatar is a deity, descended to earth in an incarnate form or some manifest shape. Did Dr Daruwalla really believe he was the incarnation of a god?

'*Which* god?' Julia asked him.

'I don't know,' Farrokh humbly told her. Certainly he was no Lord Krishna, 'the dark one' – an avatar of Vishnu. Just whom did he imagine he was an avatar *of*? The doctor was no more the incarnation of a god than he was a writer; he was, like most men, principally a dreamer.

It's best to picture him on a snowy evening, when

darkness has fallen early in Toronto. Snow always made him melancholic, for it snowed all night the night his mother died. On snowy mornings, Farrokh would go sit in the guest bedroom where Meher had drifted away; some of her clothes were in the closet – something of her scent, which was the scent of a foreign country and its cooking, still lingered in her hanging saris.

But picture Dr Daruwalla in the streetlight, standing directly under a lamppost in the falling snow. Picture him at the northeast corner of Lonsdale and Russell Hill Road; this Forest Hill intersection was familiar and comforting to Farrokh, not only because it was within a block of where he lived, but because, from this junction, he could view the route he'd taken those many days when he'd walked his children to school. In the opposite direction, there was Grace Church on-the-Hill . . . where he'd passed a few reflective hours in the safety of his former faith. From this street corner, Dr Daruwalla could also see the chapel and the Bishop Strachan School, where the doctor's daughters had ably demonstrated their intelligence; and Farrokh wasn't far from Upper Canada College, where his sons might have gone to school – if he'd had sons. But, the doctor reconsidered, he'd had *two* sons – counting John D. *and* the retired Inspector Dhar.

Farrokh tipped his face up to the falling snow; he felt the snow wet his eyelashes. Although Christmas was long past, Dr Daruwalla was pleased to see that some of his neighbors' houses still displayed their yuletide ornamentation, which gave them unusual color and cheer. The snow falling in the streetlight gave the doctor such a pure-white, lonely feeling, Farrokh almost forgot why he was standing on this street corner on a winter evening. But he was waiting for his wife; the former Julia Zilk was due to pick him up. Julia was driving from one of her women's groups; she'd phoned and told Farrokh to wait at the corner. The Daruwallas were dining at a new restaurant not far from Harbourfront; Farrokh and Julia were a faithful audience for the authors' readings at Harbourfront.

As for the restaurant, Dr Daruwalla would find it ordinary; also, they were eating too early for the doctor's taste. As for the authors' readings, Farrokh detested readings; so few writers knew how to read aloud. When you were reading a book to yourself, you could close the cover without shame and try something else, or watch a video, which the ex-screenwriter was more and more apt to do. His usual beer – and he often had wine with his dinner – made him too sleepy to read. At Harbourfront, he feared he'd start snoring in the audience and embarrass Julia; she loved the readings, which the doctor increasingly viewed as an endurance sport. Often, too many writers read in a single night, as if to make a public demonstration of Canada's esteemed subsidy of the arts; usually, there was an intermission, which was Dr Daruwalla's principal reason for loathing the theater. And at the Harbourfront intermission, they'd be surrounded by Julia's well-read friends; her friends were more literary than Farrokh, and they knew it.

On this particular evening (Julia had warned him), there was an Indian author reading from his or her work; that always presented problems for Dr Daruwalla. There was the palpable expectation that the doctor should 'relate' to this author in some meaningful way, as if there were that recognizable 'it' which the author would either get right or get wrong. In the case of an Indian writer, even Julia and her literary friends would defer to Farrokh's opinion; therefore, he would be pressed to *have* an opinion, *and* to state his views. Often, he had no views and would hide during the intermission; on occasion, to his shame, the retired screenwriter had hidden in the men's room.

Recently, quite a celebrated Parsi writer had read at Harbourfront; Dr Daruwalla had the feeling that Julia and her friends expected the doctor to be aggressive enough to speak to the author, for Farrokh had read the justly acclaimed novel – he'd much admired it. The story concerned a small but sturdy pillar of a Parsi community in Bombay – a decent, compassionate family man was severely tested by the political corruption and deceit of that time when India and Pakistan were at war.

How could Julia and her friends imagine that Farrokh could talk with this author? What did Dr Daruwalla know of a *real* Parsi community – either in Bombay or in Toronto? What 'community' could the doctor presume to talk about?

Farrokh could only tell tales of the Duckworth Club – Lady Duckworth exposing herself, flashing her famous breasts. One didn't have to be a Duckworthian to have already heard that story, but what other stories did Dr Daruwalla know? Only the doctor's own story, which was decidedly unsuitable for first acquaintances. Sex change and serial slaying; a conversion by love bite; the lost children who were *not* saved by the circus; Farrokh's father, blown to smithereens . . . and how could he talk about the twins to a total stranger?

It seemed to Dr Daruwalla that his story was the opposite of universal; his story was simply strange – the doctor himself was singularly foreign. What Farrokh came in contact with, everywhere he went, was a perpetual foreignness – a reflection of that foreignness he carried with him, in the peculiarities of his heart. And so, in the falling snow, in Forest Hill, a Bombayite stood waiting for his Viennese wife to take him into downtown Toronto, where they would listen to an unknown Indian reader – perhaps a Sikh, possibly a Hindu, maybe a Muslim, or even another Parsi. It was likely that there would be other readers, too.

Across Russell Hill Road, the wet snow clung to the shoulders and hair of a mother and her small son; like Dr Daruwalla, they stood under a lamppost, where the radiant streetlight brightened the snow and sharpened the features of their watchful faces – they appeared to be waiting for someone, too. The young boy seemed far less impatient than his mother. The child had his head tilted back, with his tongue stuck out to catch the falling snow, and he swung himself dreamily from his mother's arm – whereas she kept clutching at his hand, as if he were slipping from her grasp. She would occasionally jerk his arm to make him stop swinging, but this never worked for long, and nothing could compel the boy to withdraw his tongue; it remained sticking out, catching the snow.

As an orthopedist, Dr Daruwalla disapproved of the way the mother jerked on her son's arm, which was totally relaxed – the boy was almost limp. The doctor feared for the child's elbow or his shoulder. But the mother had no intention of hurting her son; she was just impatient, and it was tedious for her – how the boy hung on her arm.

For a moment, Dr Daruwalla smiled openly at this Madonna and Child; they were so clearly illuminated under their lamppost, the doctor should have known that they could see him standing under *his* lamppost – just as clearly. But Farrokh had forgotten where he was – not in India – and he'd overlooked the racial wariness he might provoke in the woman, who now regarded his unfamiliar face in the streetlight (and in the whiteness of the falling snow) as she might have regarded the sudden appearance of a large, unleashed dog. Why was this foreigner smiling at her?

The woman's obvious fear both offended and shamed Dr Daruwalla; he quickly stopped smiling and looked away. Then the doctor realized that he was standing on the wrong corner of the intersection. Julia had plainly instructed him to stand on the north*west* corner of Lonsdale and Russell Hill Road, which was exactly where the mother and her son were standing. Farrokh knew that by crossing the street and standing beside them, he would probably create mayhem in the woman's mind – at best, extreme apprehension. At worst, she might scream for help; there would be accusations that could rouse the neighbors – conceivably, summon the police!

Therefore, Dr Daruwalla crossed Russell Hill Road awkwardly, sidling head-down and furtively, which doubtless gave the woman all the more cause to suspect him of criminal behavior. Slinking across the street, Farrokh looked full of felonious intentions. He passed the woman and child quickly, scuttling by without a greeting – for a greeting, the doctor was sure, would startle the woman to such a degree that she might bolt into the traffic. (There *was* no traffic.) Dr Daruwalla took up a position that was 10 yards away from where Julia was expecting to spot him. There the doctor stood, like a pervert getting up his nerve for a cowardly assault; he was aware that the streetlight barely reached to the curb where he waited.

The mother, who was of medium height and figure – and now thoroughly frightened – began to pace, dragging her small son with her. She was a well-dressed young woman in her twenties, but neither her attire nor her youth could conceal her struggle to combat her rising terror. From her expression, it was clear to Dr Daruwalla that she believed she understood his heinous intentions. Under his seemingly tasteful topcoat, which was black wool with a black velvet collar and black velvet lapels, there surely lurked a naked man who was dying to expose himself to her and her child. The mother turned her trembling back on the doctor's reprehensible figure, but her small son had also noticed the stranger. The boy was unafraid – just curious. He kept tugging on his distraught mother's arm; with his little tongue still sticking straight out into the snow, the child couldn't take his eyes off the exotic foreigner.

Dr Daruwalla tried to concentrate on the snow. Impulsively, the doctor stuck out his tongue; it was a reflex imitation of what he'd seen the small boy do – it hadn't occurred to Dr Daruwalla to stick out his tongue for years. But now, in the falling snow, the young mother could see that the foreigner was radically deranged; his mouth lolled open, with his tongue sticking out, and his eyes blinked as the snowflakes fell on his lashes.

As for his eyelids, Farrokh felt they were heavy; to the casual observer, his eyelids were puffy – his age, his tiredness, the years of beer and wine. But to this young mother, in her growing panic, they must have struck her as the eyelids of the demonic East; slightly beyond illumination in the streetlight, Dr Daruwalla's eyes appeared to be hooded – like a serpent's.

However, her son had no fear of the foreigner; their tongues in the snow seemed to connect them. The kinship of their extended tongues took immediate effect on the small boy. Farrokh's childish, unconscious gesture must have overridden the boy's natural reluctance to speak to strangers, for he suddenly broke free of his mother's grasp and ran with outstretched arms toward the astonished Indian.

The mother was too terrified to give clear utterance to her son's name. She managed only a gargling sound, a strangled gasp. She hesitated before stumbling after her son, as if her legs had turned to ice or stone. She was resigned to her fate; how well she knew what would happen next! The black topcoat would open as she approached the stranger, and she would be confronted with the male genitalia of the *truly* inscrutable East.

In order not to frighten her further, Dr Daruwalla pretended not to notice that the child was running to him. He could imagine the mother thinking, Oh – these perverts are sly! Particularly those of us who are 'of color,' the doctor thought bitterly. This was precisely the situation that foreigners (especially those 'of color') are taught to dread. Absolutely nothing was happening; yet the young woman was sure that she and her son teetered on the brink of a shocking, possibly even a scarring, episode.

Farrokh nearly cried out: Excuse me, pretty lady, but

there is no episode here! He would have run away from the child, except that he suspected the boy could run faster; also, Julia was coming to pick him up, and there he would be – running away from a mother and her small son. That would be too absurd.

That was when the small boy touched him; it was a firm but gentle tug on his sleeve – then the miniature mittened hand grasped the doctor's gloved index finger and pulled. Dr Daruwalla had no choice but to look down into the wide-eyed face that was peering up at him; the whiteness of the boy's cheeks was rose-tinted against the purer whiteness of the snow.

'Excuse me,' the little gentleman said. 'Where are you from?'

Well, that's the question, isn't it? thought Dr Daruwalla. It was always the question. For his whole adult life, it was the question he usually answered with the literal truth, which in his heart felt like a lie.

'I'm from India,' the doctor would say, but he didn't feel it; it didn't ring true. 'I'm from Toronto,' he sometimes said, but with more mischief than authority. Or else he would be clever. 'I'm from Toronto, via Bombay,' he would say. If he really wanted to be cute, he would answer, 'I'm from Toronto, via Vienna and Bombay.' He could go on, elaborating the lie – namely, that he was from *anywhere*.

He could always enhance the European qualities of his education, if he chose; he could create a spicy masala mixture for his childhood in Bombay, giving his accent that Hindi flavor; he could also kill the conversation with his merciless, deadpan Torontonian reserve. ('As you may know, there are many Indians in Toronto,' he could say, when he felt like it.) Dr Daruwalla could *seem* as comfortable with the places he'd lived as he was, truly, *un*comfortable.

But suddenly the boy's innocence demanded of the doctor a different kind of truth; in the child's face, Dr Daruwalla could discern only frank curiosity – only the most genuine desire to know. It also moved the doctor that the boy had not let go of his index finger. Farrokh was aware that he had no time in which to formulate a witty answer or an ambiguous remark; the terrified mother would any second interrupt the moment, which would never return.

'Where are you from?' the child had asked him.

Dr Daruwalla wished he knew; never had he so much wanted to tell the truth, and (more important) to feel that his response was as pure and natural as the currently falling snow. Bending close to the boy, so that the child could not mistake a word of his answer, and giving the boy's trusting hand a reflexive squeeze, the doctor spoke clearly in the sharp winter air.

'I'm from the circus,' Farrokh said, without thinking – it was utterly spontaneous – but by the instant delight that was apparent in the child's broad smile and in his bright, admiring eyes, Dr Daruwalla could tell that he'd answered the question correctly. What he saw in the boy's happy face was something he'd never felt before in his cold, adopted country. Such uncritical acceptance was the most satisfying pleasure that Dr Daruwalla (or any immigrant of color) would ever know.

Then a car horn was blowing and the woman pulled her son away; the boy's father, the woman's husband – whoever he was – was helping them into his car. If Farrokh heard nothing of what the mother said, he would remember what the child told the man. 'The circus is in town!' the boy said. Then they drove away, leaving Dr Daruwalla there; the doctor had the street corner to himself.

Julia was late. Farrokh fretted that they wouldn't have time to eat before the interminable Harbourfront readings. Then he needn't worry that he'd fall asleep and snore; instead, the audience and the unfortunate authors would be treated to his growling stomach.

The snow kept falling. No cars passed. In a distant window, the lights on a Christmas tree were blinking; Dr Daruwalla tried to count the colors. The colored lights through the window glass were reminiscent of that light which is reflected in sequins – that glitter which is sewn into the singlets of the circus acrobats. Was there anything as wonderful as that reflected light? Farrokh wondered.

A car was passing; it threatened to break the spell that the doctor was under, for Dr Daruwalla was half-way around the world from the corner of Lonsdale and Russell Hill Road. 'Go home!' someone shouted to him from the window of the passing car.

It was an irony that the doctor didn't hear this, for he was in a position to inform the person that going home was easier said than done. More sounds, torn from the window of the moving car, were muffled by the snow – receding laughter, possibly a racial slur. But Dr Daruwalla heard none of it. His eyes had risen from the Christmas tree in the window; at first he'd blinked at the falling snow, but then he allowed his eyes to close – the snow coolly covered his eyelids.

Farrokh saw the elephant-footed boy in his singlet with the blue-green sequins – as the little beggar was never dressed in real life. Farrokh saw Ganesh descending in the spotlight, twirling down – the cripple's teeth clamped tightly on the dental trapeze. This was the completion of another succesful Skywalk, which in reality had never happened and never would. The *real* cripple was dead; it was only in the retired screenwriter's mind that Ganesh was a skywalker. Probably the movie would never be made. Yet, in his mind's eye, Farrokh saw the elephant boy walk without a limp across the sky. To Dr Daruwalla, this existed; it was as real as the India the doctor thought he'd left behind. Now he saw that he was destined to see Bombay again. Farrokh knew there was no escaping Maharashtra, which was no circus.

That was when he knew he was going back – again and again, he would keep returning. It was India that kept bringing him back; this time, the dwarfs would have nothing to do with it. Farrokh knew this as distinctly as he could hear the applause for the sky-walker. Dr Daruwalla heard them clapping as the elephant boy descended on the dental trapeze; the doctor could hear them cheering for the cripple.

Julia, who'd stopped the car and was waiting for her distracted husband, honked the horn. But Dr Daruwalla didn't hear her. Farrokh was listening to the applause – he was still at the circus.

THE END

A SELECTED LIST OF FINE WRITING
AVAILABLE FROM BLACK SWAN

THE PRICES SHOWN BELOW WERE CORRECT AT THE TIME OF GOING TO PRESS. HOWEVER TRANSWORLD PUBLISHERS RESERVE THE RIGHT TO SHOW NEW RETAIL PRICES ON COVERS WHICH MAY DIFFER FROM THOSE PREVIOUSLY ADVERTISED IN THE TEXT OR ELSEWHERE.

☐	99531 2	**AFTER THE HOLE**	*Guy Burt*	£5.99
☐	99348 4	**SUCKING SHERBET LEMONS**	*Michael Carson*	£5.99
☐	99599 1	**SEPARATION**	*Dan Franck*	£5.99
☐	99616 5	**SIMPLE PRAYERS**	*Michael Golding*	£5.99
☐	99466 9	**A SMOKING DOT IN THE DISTANCE**	*Ivor Gould*	£6.99
☐	99609 2	**FORREST GUMP**	*Winston Groom*	£5.99
☐	99169 4	**GOD KNOWS**	*Joseph Heller*	£7.99
☐	99538 X	**GOOD AS GOLD**	*Joseph Heller*	£6.99
☐	99208 9	**THE 158LB MARRIAGE**	*John Irving*	£5.99
☐	99204 6	**THE CIDER HOUSE RULES**	*John Irving*	£6.99
☐	99209 7	**THE HOTEL NEW HAMPSHIRE**	*John Irving*	£6.99
☐	99369 7	**A PRAYER FOR OWEN MEANY**	*John Irving*	£7.99
☐	99206 2	**SETTING FREE THE BEARS**	*John Irving*	£5.99
☐	99207 0	**THE WATER-METHOD MAN**	*John Irving*	£6.99
☐	99205 4	**THE WORLD ACCORDING TO GARP**	*John Irving*	£6.99
☐	99573 8	**TRYING TO SAVE PIGGY SNEED**	*John Irving*	£6.99
☐	99567 3	**SAILOR SONG**	*Ken Kesey*	£6.99
☐	99542 8	**SWEET THAMES**	*Matthew Kneale*	£6.99
☐	99037 X	**BEING THERE**	*Jerzy Kosinski*	£3.99
☐	99595 9	**LITTLE FOLLIES**	*Eric Kraft*	£5.99
☐	99569 X	**MAYBE THE MOON**	*Armistead Maupin*	£5.99
☐	99603 3	**ADAM'S WISH**	*Paul Micou*	£5.99
☐	99597 5	**COYOTE BLUE**	*Christopher Moore*	£5.99
☐	99536 3	**IN THE PLACE OF FALLEN LEAVES**	*Tim Pears*	£5.99
☐	99547 9	**CRIMINAL CONVERSATIONS**	*Freddie Stockdale*	£5.99
☐	99500 2	**THE RUINS OF TIME**	*Ben Woolfenden*	£4.99